TOEFL
iBT READING &
LISTENING

不是權威不出書！練托福，
當然就讓最專業的托福總監帶你練！

捷徑文化
Royal Road Publishing Group

托福總監說在前頭

▶托福總監告訴你！ 百分百真正的托福考點攻略在這裡！

　　在閱讀本書時，你可能會發現許多特別的語言學習方式，這些都是托福總監秦蘇珊老師精心研發的「有機英語學習法」！透過此學習法讓大家能在時間內有效學習托福必考的考點全攻略。

考點攻略 1. 透過「詞彙語塊」的形式記憶，自然形成大腦資料庫。

　　什麼是「語塊」？語塊是指經常在一起使用的一組詞，類似片語或搭配詞。語塊既有可能是習慣搭配，如：sedimentary rock（沉積岩），也有可能是片語動詞，如follow up on an issue（追蹤一個問題）。

　　語言學家和神經學家發現，比起孤立地記單字，人們對語塊的記憶會更加準確牢固。且當學習者從其大腦的「資料庫」裡「調出」語塊時，因為不是用母語詞對詞地做翻譯，所以語言使用者的犯錯機率減少，反應速度也同時提高了。因此，本書每一章都收錄了精心挑選的、涉及重要情境的學習語塊。

例 genetic composition 基因組成　　　　aquatic animal 水棲動物
respiratory surface 呼吸面　　　　　　larval stage 幼蟲期
protective envelope 保護性的外殼

考點攻略 2. 無論聽說讀寫，都要會換句話說。

　　換句話說的能力是通往考高分最重要的技能！原因有：

❶ **因為 100% 會考**！沒錯，新托福考試的閱讀部分會直接考你會不會換句話說，而聽力、口語和寫作部分也會間接考查這一能力。閱讀和聽力題中很多選擇題的選項都是對原文語句的改述；而在閱讀部分，有一類難度較高的題型：句子簡化題，其實就是在考你怎麼換句話說。

❷ 因為在訓練換句話說的能力時，考生將被迫用英語思考，這會使考生在考試中更加有自信，並提高做題速度。

❸ 考托福的你，想必是想出國唸書的，要是什麼句子都只會一種說法，在國外會很辛苦，所以除了為了考試做練習，更要**為了你的未來生活做練習**，換句話說的能力是不可或缺的！

　　把學術性語言換句話說，對於詞彙量不足或對相關主題缺少瞭解的考生會非常難，因此本書從第 1 章開始，就會引導考生熟悉各種類型的情境，幫助考生擴大詞彙量，累積實用句型，提高閱讀速度、聽力能力和用英語思考的能力。

考點攻略 3. ── 訓練用關鍵字記筆記。

　　有些考試是不允許記筆記的，因此在準備時，大家常會忽略這一項。但**托福可以記筆記，所以考生應儘早開始訓練，嘗試用各種不同方式記筆記**。本書會提供大量有針對性的記筆記策略，例如：

例 筆記範例說明

1. 在 Sun 上畫圈是因為它是中心論點。
2. S 是 Sun 的縮寫形式。
3. 符號→表示「引起」、「影響」。Sun → ALL weather 表示太陽影響所有天氣情況。
4. 符號 > 表示大於，因為教授說太陽的質量比地球的大。

考點攻略 4. ── 培養預測下文的能力。

　　預測下文的能力對於任何希望取得新托福考試高分的考生都非常重要。在聽學術類講座時，**如果能預知下文將要呈現的資訊，那作答速度就會快上許多。而且還能更快地抓住要點、更準確地記下關鍵資訊**。在聽講座或對話時，考生如果能預測到教授接下來很可能會講什麼，那麼即使沒聽出一兩個單字，也不必過於擔心。

考點攻略 5. ─ 培養略讀能力、建立掃讀能力

　　由於新托福考試的閱讀文章都有 650～750 個詞，包括 4～7 個段落，很多考生都覺得要想按時讀完每一篇文章並做完所有題目是很困難的。當然，大部分新托福考試的閱讀題目都會指明在文章中的哪一段落尋找答案，以便考生快速閱讀該段。但是，很多推論題和篇章結構題都沒有答案所在段落的提示，這就意味著考生需要快速略讀全文。此外，在內容總結題中，考生需要分辨真假論述、區別主次論點。如果考生掌握了略讀技巧，這類題目就會更容易做。另外，考生必須能夠在很短的時間內找出關鍵字或關鍵資訊。考生需要知道如何略過不重要的內容，這些都是需要經過訓練的技巧。

考點攻略 6. ─ 掌握篇章中的大特點（如：開頭語、主題擴展、例證、結論等）。

　　篇章中的「大」特點有很多，例如文章的組織結構，或例如作者開始談論某個歷史事件的方式。另外，理解教授在講座中提供範例的能力也是一種重要的技巧。**當考生抓住了篇章的整體，就能進行更細的資訊處理。這樣即使不認識文章裡的某些單字，也能基本理解文章的主要意思**！

> **例** 掌握教授學術講座的思路
> 以本章下文聽力為例：教授談到了壁畫。考生需要仔細聽有關壁畫的各種細節資訊。以下是對教授講座思路的分析：
> 1. 開場白：This course will introduce you to some of the methods... But before we start our studio project...
> 2. 主要觀點（第一次提出）：I thought it might be helpful to go over some of the concepts and history related to murals.

考點攻略 7. ─ 掌握篇章中的小特點（如：詞性、單字、修辭等）。

　　這種技能一般是指對一篇閱讀文章或聽力文本的語言特徵的掌握能力。**這些特徵既包括單字的發音方式，也包括在學術類閱讀文章、講座和對話中使用的字彙、片語。**考生一定都希望記住經常出現在新托福考試中的單字和片語，因此本書列出了大量這類單字和片語。

例 有關情感和態度的表達
積極的：
to like...   to approve of...   to enjoy...   to be content with...
消極的：
to dislike...   to disapprove of...   to condemn...
to be troubled by...

考點攻略 8. — 搭配題材記憶、聚焦學習記得牢。

　　本書的分類方式以「題材」為依據，而非將同個題型中各種可能碰到的情境與話題都混合在一起考。將一個一個題材區分開來，這種學習是最為科學的。**研究人類記憶的專家發現，人們在記憶事實或學習技能時，若能將其呈現在一個具體的「情境」或「題材」中，人們就會記得更深、學得更好**。因此這本書為考生們在記單字和掌握詞彙、片語的過程中，搭配題材學習能使考生記得更牢、更好。

▶托福總監告訴你！這本書的結構與重點

★本書內容

- ·新托福題目類型分析
- ·各題型的解題策略與模擬試題
- ·精闢完整的試題解答
- ·聽力文本、解析與詞彙表

★本書結構

　　本書包括新托福題目類型分析、解題策略和類比試題等內容，書後還提供了完整的試題答案、聽力文本、解析以及詞彙表。本書致力於幫助新托福考生快速提高應試技能。為了增強考生解答學術類問題的能力，相同題材（如天文學）下的閱讀文章和學術講座（以及一整套試題）都歸在一個章節裡。這種編排結構可以使考生更好地學習和掌握與常考主題相關的基礎知識和詞彙（這些詞彙會在閱讀和聽力部分反覆出現）。把對話單獨放在一個部分也是出於類似原因，這些經常考到的校園生活場景全部都經過了精心挑選。

　　第一部分整體介紹新托福考試，並詳細描述閱讀和聽力部分的結構和題目類型。

　　第二部分「學術類閱讀和聽力」共 20 章，分別介紹四大學術領域的不同主題。這四大學術領域分別是：物理科學、人文藝術、生命科學和社會科學。每一章都包括閱讀試題和聽力試題，這些精選的閱讀和聽力材料所呈現的全部是最常考的題材。考生熟悉了這些題材的閱讀和聽力試題後，就可以自信地參加考試了。

　　第三部分「對話類聽力」分為 8 章，所述內容均為常考校園生活場景，如學生住宿問題等。每一章都包含校園生活類聽力題和服務諮詢類聽力題。聽力材料經過精心挑選，結構設計科學合理，可以確保學習效果事半功倍。本部分還為考生提供了與場景有關的文化背景知識，可以說，文化背景知識是做校園生活場景試題不可或缺的基礎。

　　特別收錄介紹了新托福考試評分標準，相信也會對你大有幫助。

▶托福總監告訴你！
這本書適合誰用？該怎麼用？

★本書適用對象

本書專為希望提高寫作能力的新托福考生編寫。通過運用「有機英語學習法」，指導考生進行有重點、有系統的學習，從而在短時間內提高英語技能並順利通過新托福考試。英語自學者以及新托福考試輔導教師均可從本書中獲益。

★自學的我，該怎麼運用這本書？

首先，可以制定一個學習計畫，列出時間和學習安排。如果自學者認為自己的閱讀能力相對薄弱，那麼就應該在閱讀方面適當增加學習時間。如果聽力理解方面薄弱，那麼就應該在聽力上多花些時間。

無論是在課堂上學習還是自學，學習者每天都應該記錄下本書中的語塊以及換句話說的方式。這很重要，因為新托福考試經常會考到常用單字和片語的換句話說。例如，自學者可以把 theoretical perspective 當作一個語塊來記，並且記得這個語塊換句話說就是 theoretical point of view。或者也可以把 give a recap of something 與意近的 run through something again 一起記。自學者一定要把重要的語塊都背下來，因為它們經常會出現在新托福考試中！

每篇文章和講座之後都設有練習題，書後對所有練習題都提供了答案。建議學習者可以找朋友們一起練習，互相鼓勵、共同提高語言能力！

★我是老師，該怎麼運用這本書？

建議使用本書的教師可以在課堂上使用「有機英語學習方法」。例如，教師可以幫助學生理解什麼是題材、場景。要想瞭解可以利用的資源和更多關於「有機英語學習方法」的建議，可以登錄 http://blog.sina.com.cn/susanchyn，留言給我。你的任何問題我都會悉心回答喔！

Preface 作者序

托福命題總監想對你說

從很久以前開始，我的朋友和學生們就都常跑來求我寫一套新托福考試的備考輔導書。這都是因為我曾在美國教育考試服務中心（ETS）工作過很多年，在那裡取得了終身職位，所以對托福的考試方式、出題方式都非常熟悉。我曾在 ETS 的多個崗位任職過，從最初的單個項目作者，一直到負責多種英語考試研發工作的主管，其中也包括了托福和多益考試的研發工作。因此，我對研發考試方式和英語考試標準化的專業方法都十分熟悉。

在 ETS 時，我很幸運有機會向專家們學習，而且隨著職位的上升，還有幸參與制定並調整新的考試評估體系。大家現在所看到的托福 iBT，就是我與團隊成員努力的成果！

在本系列書中，我依自己從 ETS 獲得的多年經驗，制定出一套全新的準備考試大綱，以期幫助考生順利通過新托福考試，並為他們以後的語言學習奠定基礎。本系列圖書是專門為以中文為母語的你們量身編寫的。與很多其他西方教育者不同，我因為個人生活和工作的緣故，對華人文化和你們的學習方式都比較瞭解，非常清楚你們在學習英語過程中的優勢和劣勢。所以在本系列圖書的編寫過程中，我結合你們的優勢，幫助你們在最短的時間內取得最顯著的進步；同時也指出你們常見的不足之處，以便於你們有重點地去彌補和提高學習效率。我把這種學習方法稱為「有機英語學習方法」，也就是把大家熟悉的學習方式（如背誦和模擬考）與科學的學習策略（如語言學）結合在一起，可以說是中西合璧的一種學習方法吧！

對於考生來說，時間很緊迫，而且壓力很大，高分似乎永遠遙不可及。不過現在你們可以放下心來，因為在本系列圖書中，我所選取的學習材料和提供的學習策略都能確保你快速提升學習能力，並在新托福考試中考取高分。如果認真讀完了本系列圖書，我保證你們的時間不會白費。當你們坐在考場中時，就會知道自己已經做了最充足的準備！

祝大家好運！

托福考試命題總監

Susan Chyn 秦蘇珊

Contents 目錄

第1部分 An Overview of the TOEFL ® iBT
新托福考試怎麼命題

第2部分 How to Prepare for Academic Reading and Listening
學術類閱讀和聽力怎麼考

第3部分

How to Prepare for Conversational Listening
對話類聽力怎麼考

特別收錄

Section ❶

An Overview of the TOEFL ® iBT

第❶部分
新托福考試怎麼命題

What the TOEFL ® iBT Measures
新托福考試考什麼？

　　進考場前，多少要知道一下新托福考試的實際情況。新托福考試的時間長度大約為四小時，分為四個部分。我們這裡要學習的閱讀與聽力部分在前面，之後有一次短暫的休息，才進入之後的口語與寫作部分。

新托福考試測驗題目與時間表
（上色的字為不計分的實驗性題目）

	題目類別	題數	時間長度
閱讀	3 篇閱讀文章 +2 篇實驗性閱讀文章	每篇 12 ～ 14 道題目	60 分 + 40 分鐘
聽力	2 段對話、4 段講座 或 +1 段考前講座和 1 段考前對話	對話：每篇 5 道題目 講座：每篇 6 道題目	60 分鐘 + 30 分鐘
中間休息			10 分鐘
口語	2 小段閱讀文章、 2 小段對話、 2 小段講座	6 道題目	20 分鐘
寫作	1 小段閱讀文章、 1 小段講座	2 道題目	50 分鐘

★口語和寫作部分沒有不計分的實驗性試題。

★新托福考試的四類考題都允許考生記筆記。考試結束後，所有筆記會被統一收集起來並銷毀。

A Comprehensive Look at the Reading and Listening Sections
新托福考試怎麼命題：
閱讀和聽力命題全解

　　本章將逐一介紹新托福考試閱讀和聽力部分的題型，並提供大致的解題方向。更具體的準備方式和解題策略與技巧將在接下來的 Section 2（第 2 部分）與 Section 3（第 3 部分）分別加以介紹。本章所選閱讀文章、講座、對話和題目都是新托福考試中最常見的類型喔！

▶簡單介紹閱讀測驗

　　閱讀是新托福考試的第一個部分。考生將在電腦顯示器的一角上看到一個鐘錶，該鐘錶顯示的是每一部分所剩餘的考試時間。閱讀文章顯示在電腦螢幕的右側，其內容無法全部顯示在一個頁面上，所以考生必須使用滑鼠上下拉動。閱讀文章中的粗體詞或專業性術語都有注釋，考生點擊這些詞就可以看到其簡短定義。

　　閱讀題只考查閱讀理解能力，並不考查綜合性技能。現行的沒有實驗性試題（此部分試題不計分）的閱讀部分考試時間為 60 分鐘，考生需閱讀三篇學術類文章，每篇文章長度為 650 ～ 750 個詞，這大約是筆考新託福閱讀文章平均長度的兩倍。

　　閱讀文章選自四大學術領域：物理科學、人文藝術、社會科學和生命科學。新托福考試的每一篇閱讀文章後都有 12 ～ 14 道題目，大部分為選擇題，整個閱讀部分共有 36 ～ 42 道題目。有些考生可能會遇到兩篇不計分數的實驗性閱讀文章，但是考生無法判斷哪兩篇閱讀文章是實驗性的，所以必須盡全力答好每一道題。有一點需要搞清楚的是，如果考生在閱讀部分遇到了實驗性文章，那麼在聽力部分就不會遇到了。

　　下面來具體舉例一下你可能會遇到的情形：

新托福考試閱讀部分：模擬案例

	文章	題目數量	時間
有效測試部分 （3 篇文章）	社會科學	12 ～ 14	20 分鐘
	物理科學	12 ～ 14	20 分鐘
	生命科學	12 ～ 14	20 分鐘
實驗性測試部分 （2 篇文章）	人文藝術	12 ～ 14	20 分鐘
	社會科學	12 ～ 14	20 分鐘

▶閱讀文章類型

新托福考試的閱讀部分會包括各種體裁的文章，如說明文（描述或解釋一個話題）、議論文（提供論點和論據）以及記敘文（敘述事件）。本書將在後面章節中提供每種文章的範例和解題策略。

▶電腦螢幕上怎麼做閱讀題

閱讀部分的不同題型要用不同方式使用滑鼠作答。大部分試題為「選擇題」，考生只需從四個選項中選出正確的一項，用滑鼠點擊其前面的橢圓形符號。而對於「插入句子題」，考生則需用滑鼠點擊段落中的數個黑色方塊之一，用以表明句子應該插入的位置。對於其他題型，如「內容總結題」和「資訊歸類題」，考生需要用滑鼠把所選答案「拖」到螢幕上的正確位置。

▶閱讀試題的考查內容

閱讀試題要求考生回答三類語言問題：

基礎題：考查對字面意思和具體細節的理解能力。此類題目包括語境詞彙題、細節資訊題以及其他考查考生對具體片語和句子理解能力的題目。

推論題：考查考生依據閱讀文章中的事實和陳述進行概括和推斷的能力。推論題種類繁多，例如推斷作者的隱含目的。

篇章結構題：即 ETS 所稱的「閱讀學習」題，考查考生對文章組織結構的識別能力，或者考查考生對文章主要觀點和次要觀點的辨別能力。

對於基礎題，考生需要強化基礎技能，如對詞彙片語和文法的掌握。而對於推論題和篇章結構題，除了基礎技能外，考生還需要掌握好進行邏輯推理和識別文章組織結構的能力。總體來說，閱讀試題會按照相關資訊在閱讀文章中的出現順序排列，但有一道題目例外，即最後一道：內容總結題（佔 2 分）或者資訊歸類題（佔 4 分）。

考生在做閱讀題時，可以利用螢幕上的回查鍵快速瀏覽已做完的題目並檢查答案，同時也可以查看哪些題目還沒有完成。

▶ 10 大閱讀題型

閱讀部分共有 10 種題型，分別代表 10 種「關鍵技能」。

1 語境詞彙題

語境詞彙題要求考生先看一個句子中的某個詞或片語，然後從選項中選出具有相同意思的詞或片語。每篇閱讀文章後會有 3 ～ 5 道語境詞彙題。文中考查的詞或片語會在電腦螢幕上突出顯示，以方便考生找到。

- **Reading Tips**

語境詞彙題的提幹形式通常如下：

The word "invisible" in Paragraph 1 is closest in meaning to...

The phrase "let down" in the second paragraph is closest in meaning to...

- **Reading Sample**

(1) In the earliest photographs, action was not recorded. The immediate and widespread acclaim for Daguerre's positive prints was due in no small part to the unprecedented level of detail of the work; it was as if one were looking through a magnifying glass. Yet this praise was tempered with the criticism that, in depicting motion, Daguerre was far less successful than in photographing architecture. One critic went so far as to state that a moving object could never be rendered without the aid of memory.

The word "tempered" in Paragraph 1 is closest in meaning to _____ .

A. angered　　　　B. overlooked　　　　C. joined　　　　D. dampened

托福總監評析

因為文中說 Daguerre 不僅受到讚揚，同時也遭到批評，以致讚揚之聲受到削弱，只有 D 最符合上下文的意思。干擾項 A 中的 angered 與名詞 temper 在意思上有些關聯，容易使人想到 bad temper（壞脾氣），因此有些考生可能會被誤導。

2 指代關係題

指代關係題考查文章中某個代名詞的具體所指，常考代名詞有 one、it、they 和 which 等。每套閱讀題中通常有一道指代關係題（有時則沒有，極少情況下會出現兩道）。由於指代關係詞在學術篇章中具有重要作用，因此這類指代關係題也是很重要的。與語境詞彙題類似，指代關係題考查的代名詞在閱讀文章中也是突出顯示的，考生很容易就可找到。

- **Reading Sample**

(2) Eadweard Muybridge was one of the early experimenters with the photography of moving objects. He devised a way for making stop-action photographs that demonstrated the gap between what the mind thinks it sees and what the eye actually perceives. The businessman and former California governor Leland Stanford was a passionate race-horse raiser who was very interested in how horses move. Specifically, he was curious about whether, when a horse was at full gallop, all four hooves were off the ground. To resolve the question, he sought out Muybridge, who used fifty cameras

to photograph a horse galloping in fast motion. The cameras' shutters were controlled by wires **which** were triggered by the horse's hooves...

The word "which" in Paragraph 2 refers to_____.
A. wires   B. cameras   C. shutters   D. hooves

托福總監評析

　　此題要求考生確定關係代名詞 which 指代什麼。因為 which 緊跟在名詞 wires 之後，且子句 which were triggered by the horse's hooves 也提示馬蹄觸碰的就是 wires，所以選 A。

3 細節資訊題

　　因為新托福考試的閱讀文章都比較長，所以閱讀部分通常沒有「中心思想」題，而細節和事實性資訊的題目較多。每篇閱讀文章後通常會有 3 ～ 6 道細節資訊題。要做好此類題目，考生需要多種閱讀「武器」，包括略讀和掃讀技能。

• Reading Sample

(1) In the earliest photographs, action was not recorded. The immediate and widespread acclaim for Daguerre's positive prints was due in no small part to the unprecedented level of detail of the work; it was as if one were looking through a magnifying glass. Yet this praise was tempered with the criticism that, in depicting motion, Daguerre was far less successful than in photographing architecture. One critic went so far as to state that a moving object could never be rendered without the aid of memory. Some of the first photographs in which action appeared were the so-called stereoscopic views of city streets, images peopled with minute figures of pedestrians. Later, when extremely detailed glass transparencies were exhibited in 1860 in Paris, they too met with enthusiastic response. Viewers were captivated by the fact that the images of pedestrians showed very little sign of movement or blurriness.

　　According to Paragraph 1, what did critics feel about Daguerre's treatment of architecture?

    A. It was rather unsuccessful.
    B. It exhibited an excess of detail.
    C. It looked better with the use of a magnifying glass.
    D. It was superior to his handling of motion.

托福總監評析

　　要解答這道題目，考生必須快速掃讀文章第一段，找到有關 Daguerre 在建築方面嘗試的資訊。第三句提到：Yet this praise was tempered with the criticism that, in depicting motion, Daguerre was far less successful than in photographing architecture.（然而這些讚揚受到了削弱，因為也有人批評說，在展現運動方面，Daguerre 遠不如他在建築物攝影方面成功。）由此可知，D 為正確答案。

4 句子簡化（換句話說）題

　　新托福考試的四個部分都會直接或間接地考查換句話說的能力。在閱讀部分，換句話說的能力直接通過句子簡化題型來考查。雖然並不是三篇閱讀文章後都會有句子簡化題，但至少有兩篇會有。

　　句子簡化題的考查形式通常是：考生先看文章中一個突出顯示的句子，然後從題目所給的四個選項中選出意思最接近的一個。該突出顯示的句子通常是一個複雜的句子，可能包含子句、被動結構或者關係子句。

• Reading Tips

　　句子簡化題的題幹形式通常為：

Which of the following best expresses the essential information in the highlighted sentence? Incorrect choices change the meaning in major ways or leave out important information.

• Reading Sample

(2) Eadweard Muybridge was one of the early experimenters with the photography of moving objects. He devised a way for making stop-action photographs that demonstrated the gap between what the mind thinks it sees and what the eye actually perceives. The businessman and former California governor Leland Stanford was a passionate race-horse raiser who was very interested in how horses move. Specifically, he was curious about whether, when a horse was at full gallop, all four hooves were off the ground. To resolve the question, he sought out Muybridge, who used fifty cameras to photograph a horse galloping in fast motion. The cameras' shutters were controlled by wires which were triggered by the horse's hooves...

A. Between the black and white areas in the photographs, there was a space revealing subtle traces of movement.

B. By making stop-action pictures, he was able to show how emotional people's attitudes had been.

C. The photographic method he invented yielded photos illustrating the difference between perception and reality.

D. In the stop-action device that he created, there were gaps in the technical performance, especially in the clarity of the pictures.

托福總監評析

這一段的關鍵資訊是相片顯示出大腦所「見到」的事物與眼睛實際所看到的事物的區別，illustrate 是 demonstrate 的同義換句話說。

很多干擾項通常都與所考的句子意思相反，但有時錯誤的選項之所以錯，是因為漏掉了重要資訊。考生需要弄清楚句子的文法結構以及 since 和 as 等連接詞的意思。

5 否定事實題

否定事實題其實也算是一種細節資訊題，只是這類題目的題幹總包含某個否定詞或排他性詞，如 not 或 except。否定詞全用大寫字母顯示，如：

Which of the following is NOT true about Daguerre?

解答否定事實題時，考生必須先閱讀四個選項，然後閱讀文章段落，找出哪三個選項陳述的內容與文章內容相符，哪一個選項與文章內容不相符。有時，考生需要略讀整篇文章才能作出正確的判斷。每篇閱讀文章後有 0 ～ 2 道否定事實題。

• **Reading Sample**

According to the passage, Muybridge did all of the following EXCEPT _____ .

A. conceive of the zoopraxiscope

B. draw cartoons of objects in motion

C. investigate the placement of horse's hooves

D. experiment with stop-action photography

托福總監評析

考生快速閱讀完整篇文章後，即可確定哪個選項文中沒有提及。此題正確答案為 B，因為文中沒有提到過卡通。

6 推論題

推論題考查考生能否根據文章內容得出結論。一般來說，考生回答問題時需要進行歸納推理，換言之，他們需要利用具體的資訊、事實進行總結或者預測。在有些情況下，考生還需要進行演繹推理，即從一般規則推出具體情況。

　　有些推論題只需從一個段落即可得出答案，而有些推論題則需要結合文章的多處資訊才能作答。如果閱讀部分共有 12 ～ 14 道題目，那麼推論題最多可能有兩道，也可能一道都沒有。

• **Reading Tips**

推論題的形式：

1. 推論題的題幹通常是就某一具體話題直接詢問「可以推導出什麼」（what can be inferred），如：

   What can we infer about the photographers at the end of the 19th century?

2. 有時推論題的題幹是由 why 引導的疑問句，如：

   Why was Muybridge's work probably used later in studies of the mechanics of athletics?

• **Reading Sample**

(4) Muybridge's early studies were taken with wet plates; however with the development of gelatin plates, he was able to improve his technique greatly. In 1884–85, Muybridge produced 781 sequence photographs of many kinds of animals, as well as men and women. His subjects were often photographed in little or no clothing and were engaged in a variety of activities, from boxing, to walking down stairs and even small children walking to their mother. In this respect, Muybridge's work was a point of departure for the study of biomechanics and the mechanics of athletics. Moreover, his major work, "Animal Locomotion" (1887), remains to this day an instructive source for cartoonists and scientists alike.

　　Why was Muybridge's work probably used later in studies of the mechanics of athletics?

　　A. To prove people could run faster than horses.
　　B. To improve athletes' performance.
　　C. To promote his zoopraxiscope device.
　　D. To allow athletes to express themselves more freely.

托福總監評析

　　根據第 4 段內容，特別是 Muybridge's work was a point of departure for the study of biomechanics and the mechanics of athletics 一句，可以推斷出 Muybridge 的運動照片可以使運動員明白如何更有效地運動。因此，B 是正確答案。

7 插入句子題

要想正確回答插入句子題，考生必須明白特定段落中各個句子之間的文法關係和邏輯關係。此類題型最常考的兩個重點就是銜接性和連貫性。

此類題型考查考生在段落層次上的篇章結構把握能力，有時也會考全文的篇章結構把握能力（理解主要大意）。換言之，考生需要判斷部分（句子）和整體（文章）的位置關係。在閱讀部分，插入句子題有一道或兩道，但最多不會超過兩道，也就是說，三篇閱讀文章中至少有一篇後面不會有插入句子題。

• Reading Tips

插入句子題的形式：要求考生把一個單獨給出的句子插入到文章中合適的位置，使所在段落邏輯通順、文法正確。文章中會用黑色方塊標記出四個位置，多數情況下是在同一段落內，但有時也會分佈在前後兩個段落的末尾和開始部分。在實際考試時，考生選出的句子要插入哪個位置，必須點擊該位置上的黑色方塊。

• Reading Sample

Look at the four squares [■] that indicate where the following sentence could be added to the passage.

Specifically, he was curious about whether, when a horse was at full gallop, all four hooves were off the ground.

(2) Eadweard Muybridge was one of the early experimenters with the photography of moving objects. He devised a way for making stop-action photographs that demonstrated the gap between what the mind thinks it sees and what the eye actually perceives. ■ 1The businessman and former California governor Leland Stanford was a passionate race-horse raiser who was very interested in how horses move. ■ 2 To resolve the question, he sought out Muybridge, who used fifty cameras to photograph a horse galloping in fast motion. The cameras' shutters were controlled by wires which were triggered by the horse's hooves. This series of photos, called "The Horse in Motion" (1882), showed that indeed the hooves all left the ground, although not at the point of full extension forward and back, as the illustrators of the 19th century had presumed. ■ 3 Rather, at the moment when all the hooves are tucked under the horse's body, it switches from "pulling" from the front legs to "pushing" from the back legs. ■ 4

托福總監評析

該段中只有兩個人物，從上下文意思可知，所給句子中的 he 指代的應是 Leland Stanford，而且他感興趣的是馬如何能夠運動。該句具體說明了 Stanford 對馬的某種運動方式（全速奔跑）感到好奇。

8 修辭目的題

　　什麼是「修辭」？修辭是指利用語言說服人的藝術手法。作者寫作時，會借助修辭手段來說服讀者。因為每一個寫作者都有其潛在的寫作目的，所以作者所用的語言也都有特定目的。修辭目的題正是考你看不看得出這些特定目的。

　　具體來說，考生可能需要回答作者為何使用某些例子或措詞，或作者為何以某種方式組織文章內容。閱讀部分會出現 0 ～ 2 道修辭目的題。

• Reading Sample

(1) In the earliest photographs, action was not recorded. The immediate and widespread acclaim for Daguerre's positive prints was due in no small part to the unprecedented level of detail of the work; it was as if one were looking through **a magnifying glass**. Yet this praise was tempered with the criticism that, in depicting motion, Daguerre was far less successful than in photographing architecture. One critic went so far as to state that a moving object could never be rendered without the aid of memory. Some of the first photographs in which action appeared were the so-called stereoscopic views of city streets, images peopled with minute figures of pedestrians. Later, when extremely detailed glass transparencies were exhibited in 1860 in Paris, they too met with enthusiastic response. Viewers were captivated by the fact that the images of pedestrians showed very little sign of movement or blurriness.

In Paragraph 1, why does the author mention "a magnifying glass"?
A. To stress that Daguerre's prints showed minute details.
B. To promote the scientific approach to photography.
C. To show how much attention critics paid to Daguerre's prints.
D. To illustrate the popularity of motion picture movies.

托福總監評析

　　在第一段中，as if one were looking through a magnifying glass 說明的是人們觀看 Daguerre 的照片時的感覺：其作品展現的細節達到了前所未有的程度。

9 內容總結題

　　內容總結題通常會有六個選項，考生需要從中選擇三項，正確答案連在一起就是文章的中心大意，有些選項是對資訊的綜合。內容總結題的題目要求相對固定，每篇閱讀文章後通常會有一道內容總結題，但偶爾也有可能沒有。內容總結題總是最後一題，每題占 2 分。考生選對全部三個選項就得 2 分；選對其中兩個得 1 分；如果只選對其中一個或全部沒有選對，則不得分。

• Reading Sample

(1) In the earliest photographs, action was not recorded. The immediate and widespread acclaim for Daguerre's positive prints was due in no small part to the unprecedented level of detail of the work; it was as if one were looking through a magnifying glass. Yet this praise was tempered with the criticism that, in depicting motion, Daguerre was far less successful than in photographing architecture. One critic went so far as to state that a moving object could never be rendered without the aid of memory. Some of the first photographs in which action appeared were the so-called stereoscopic views of city streets, images peopled with minute figures of pedestrians. Later, when extremely detailed glass transparencies were exhibited in 1860 in Paris, they too met with enthusiastic response. Viewers were captivated by the fact that the images of pedestrians showed very little sign of movement or blurriness.

(2) Eadweard Muybridge was one of the early experimenters with the photography of moving objects. He devised a way for making stop-action photographs that demonstrated the gap between what the mind thinks it sees and what the eye actually perceives. The businessman and former California governor Leland Stanford was a passionate race-horse raiser who was very interested in how horses move. To resolve the question, he sought out Muybridge, who used fifty cameras to photograph a horse galloping in fast motion. The cameras' shutters were controlled by wires which were triggered by the horse's hooves. This series of photos, called "The Horse in Motion" (1882), showed that indeed the hooves all left the ground, although not at the point of full extension forward and back, as the illustrators of the 19th century had presumed. Rather, at the moment when all the hooves are tucked under the horse's body, it switches from "pulling" from the front legs to "pushing" from the back legs.

(3) Muybridge's work in stop-action series photography soon led to his invention of the zoopraxiscope, in 1879. This machine, designed to accommodate the growing interest of amateur photographers, projected images that could be perceived as realistic motion. The zoopraxiscope constituted an advancement over the zoetrope—a topless drum on which various pictures could be pasted and then twirled around. Both the zoetrope and the zoopraxiscope are considered to be precursors of the motion picture.

(4) Muybridge's early studies were taken with wet plates; however with the development of gelatin plates, he was able to improve his technique greatly. In 1884–85, Muybridge produced 781 sequence photographs of many kinds of animals, as well as men and women. His subjects were often photographed in little or no clothing and were engaged in a variety of activities, from boxing, to walking down stairs and even small children walking to their mother. In this respect, Muybridge's work was a point of departure for the study of biomechanics and the mechanics of athletics. Moreover, his major work, "Animal Locomotion" (1887), remains to this day an instructive source for cartoonists and scientists alike.

(5) Many of Muybridge's contemporaries, however, rejected the new technology, saying that photographs of objects in motion actually made it seem that all feeling of motion was lost. Art critics suggested the brush strokes in painting better conveyed a feeling of movement—unlike the "frozen" images in the photographs. Even many photographers rejected the aesthetics of motion, instead exploring avenues other than the photo-mechanical representation of reality. Members of the pictorialist movement, for example, believed that art photography needed to emulate painting and etching. Consequently, many of these pictorialist photographs were black and white or sepia. Among the methods used were soft focus, special filters and lens coatings, and exotic printing processes. From 1898 rough-surface printing papers were added to the repertoire, to further break up a picture's sharpness. The aim of such techniques was not realism but rather "personal artistic expression."

Directions: An introductory sentence for a brief summary of the passage is provided below. Complete the summary by selecting the THREE answer choices that express the most important ideas in the passage. Some answer choices do not belong in the summary because they express ideas that are not presented in the passage or are minor ideas in the passage. **This question is worth 2 points.**

This passage traces the development of how motion was captured by photography in the 19th century.

-
-
-

Answer Choices

1. Daguerre is generally regarded as the first person to shoot movies of everyday people.

2. Muybridge's photos of horses in motion showed that artists had been drawing horses accurately.

3. Stop-action pictures became important tools for people who wanted to understand the mechanics of moving bodies.

4. Wet plates were considered a major advancement over gelatin plates.

5. Muybridge invented a series of photographic devices that allowed viewers to perceive motion.

6. Not all photographers responded positively to Muybridge because they felt his pictures were not artistic.

托福總監評析

選項 3、5 和 6 都是文章強調的主要論點。而選項 1、2 和 4 的說法都不準確。

10 資訊歸類題

資訊歸類題又稱填表題，考查考生能否通過通讀一篇學術性英語文章的諸多段落，將文中的主要觀點進行邏輯分類。考生需要具備分類、歸類和匹配的能力。閱讀部分的資訊歸類題與聽力部分的關聯內容題有很多相似之處。在這兩種題型中，考生都必須從文章中提煉觀點、分出類別，並建立關聯，從而在大腦中形成對文章框架的整體認識。

在做資訊歸類題時，考生需要點擊選項，並將其拖到圖表中正確的類別欄裡。每篇閱讀文章後最多有一道資訊歸類題，而且如果有內容總結題，就不會出現資訊歸類題；反之亦然。

資訊歸類題的分值為 3 分或 4 分。

• Reading Tips

資訊歸類題中的表格有兩或三欄（列），答案選項為 5 個 7 個，可能的組合形式如下：

1. 兩欄（列），5 個正確選項（3 分）
2. 三欄（列），5 個正確選項（3 分）
3. 兩欄（列），7 個正確選項（4 分）
4. 三欄（列），7 個正確選項（4 分）

在前兩種情況下，如果考生做對的答案不超過 2 個，則不得分；如果考生做對了 3 道題目，得 1 分；如果考生做對了 4 道題目，得 2 分；如果全對，則得滿分 3 分。

在後兩種情況下，如果考生做對的答案不超過 3 個，則不得分；如果考生做對了 4 道題目，得 1 分；如果考生做對了 5 道題目，得 2 分；如果做對了 6 道題目，得 3 分；如果全對，則得滿分 4 分。

• Reading Sample

下面再以前文有關照片的那篇閱讀文章為材料，看一道資訊歸類題。

Directions: Complete the table below by indicating which answer choice characterizes the photography of Daguerre and which characterizes the photography of Muybridge. **This question is worth 3 points.**

Daguerre	• •
Muybridge	• • •

Answer Choices

1. Resource for biomechanics research

2. Motion not well represented

3. Experimentation with stop-action photography

4. Detailed pictures of building styles

5. Famous for the soft focus method

6. Skill in the use of gelatin plates

托福總監評析

Daguerre	• 2. Motion not well represented • 4. Detailed pictures of building styles
Muybridge	• 1. Resource for biomechanics research • 3. Experimentation with stop-action photography • 6. Skill in the use of gelatin plates

　　文章最後一段指出，有些 Muybridge 的批評者更喜歡柔焦、特殊濾光器和鏡頭塗層等攝影方法。所以 Famous for the soft focus method 一項既不是 Daguerre 攝影術的特點，也不是 Muybridge 攝影術的特點。

通用閱讀策略

　　在規定的時間內做完閱讀題，這一點很關鍵！答題時，如果能夠跟隨作者的思路，並能夠追溯事實層面和詞彙層面的資訊，那麼閱讀部分就不成問題。為此考生要努力擴大詞彙量，記住詞語在情境中的用法。最後，考生還必須以各種形式勤加練習換句話說。

閱讀題答題步驟

1. 快速略讀文章。
2. 快速閱讀每道題的題幹及其選項。
3. 排除明顯錯誤的選項。
4. 回到文章中，快速尋找答案所在的位置。
5. 按下正確答案，繼續做下一題。

▶簡單介紹聽力測驗

　　聽力部分的時間長度大約為一小時，考生需要聽兩段對話和四段學術講座的錄音。如果考生在聽力部分遇到實驗性試題，則時間會增加 30 分鐘。

每段對話的時間為 2～3 分鐘，有 5 道題目。每段學術講座的時間為 4～6 分鐘，包括 700～800 個單字，每段講座後有 6 道題目。電腦螢幕下方會顯示一個時鐘，告訴考生每段對話或講座的剩餘時間。

在對話或講座的播放過程中，考生的電腦螢幕上會顯示教授或學生的圖片，讓考生能理解情境。有時，螢幕上還會顯示重要的片語和圖表，就像課堂上的板書一樣。

對話有兩種類型：辦公時間對話和服務諮詢對話。其中「辦公時間」（Office hours）指教授每週用來會見學生討論課業問題的時間。辦公時間對話的話題有可能是學生就其學習中遇到的困難求教教授，也可能是教授對學生未能完成作業進行詢問。服務諮詢對話是發生在非學術性場景中的交流，如開立銀行帳戶、去學生中心洗衣服或去圖書館等。

與閱讀文章相同，講座內容也選自四大學術領域：物理科學、人文藝術、社會科學和生命科學。例如，在一段講座中，考生有可能會聽到一名科學老師在向全班學生講解雲的形成。很多講座中都會有學生向教師提問和交流的環節。

下面是考生很可能會遇到的具體情形：

新托福考試聽力部分：模擬案例
含 3 個實驗性試題（套色部分）

聽力內容	類型	題目數量	時間
對話	辦公時間對話	5	
講座	物理科學	6	30 分鐘
講座	社會科學	6	
對話	服務諮詢對話	5	
講座	生命科學	6	30 分鐘
講座	人文藝術	6	
對話	辦公時間對話或服務諮詢對話	5	
講座	四大學術領域中選兩類	6	30 分鐘
講座		6	

▶聽學術講座的語言特點

在學術講座中，如果遇到很多聽不懂的單字和語句，也不用驚慌！這不表示你準備不夠，其實有些單字是某個學術領域內的專業術語，就算是土生土長的美國人也沒聽過。只要記錄下反覆聽到、或者對教授的主要觀點很重要的關鍵字就好了！記住，試題只有 6 道，而講座時間長度大約會有五、六分鐘，這表示考生將聽到大量詞語，而其中大部分詞語和觀點都不會考到，因此漏聽一兩個詞並不會有太大關係。

在新托福考試中，講座和對話中有時會使用專業術語、專有名詞和縮寫詞。這些詞大多會顯示在電腦螢幕上。在本書中，重要詞彙和專有名詞等會作為關鍵字放在方框中，作為學習指導，你可以在聽講座前複習這些關鍵字，或者在需要時查閱。

▶對話的語言特點

對話使用的是日常會話語言，大多是兩個人之間的對話。通常，每段對話中都會含有某個需要處理的問題或情況，對話中的兩個人會協商解決問題。

▶口語

口語是新托福考試聽力部分的一個重要特點。口語是指英語母語人士實際交談時所用的語言形式，例如，教授和學生在説話時都會經常使用縮略形式，如 gonna 和 would've。口語中還包括禮貌地打岔或搶話、語塞（一句話只説了開頭部分，然後變換措詞重新説）、説錯話或口誤（單字或片語發錯音）之後糾正、填充詞、停頓或結巴、誤解、離題、省略、不合文法以及句子不完整等情況。在口語中，説話者有時會通過語音語調來表達情感，考試中考生也會遇到詢問説話者感情或語氣的題目。

▶聽力題的考法

在聽力部分，大部分試題都是有四個選項的選擇題，有些題只有一個正確答案，有些則會有兩個。考生作答時需要點擊正確選項旁邊的橢圓形按鈕。對於另外一些題型，如要求考生對事件或過程步驟進行排序的試題，或者資訊歸類題，考生則需要使用電腦滑鼠將答案選項「拖」到螢幕上的正確位置。聽力題的順序通常與相關資訊在聽力錄音中出現的順序一致。

一段對話或講座播放完畢後，在答案選項出現在電腦螢幕上之前，考生會看到或聽到每一道試題。大部分聽力題的錄音只播放一遍。但有一類聽力題會重放一部分對話，然後要求考生選出某個句子或片語在對話或講座中的意思。有時，片語會朗讀兩遍，在此過程中考生會在螢幕上看到一個耳機圖示。在聽力部分，一旦考生選定了某道題的答案，就不能再回到那道題。

▶八大聽力題型

1 主旨大意題

每個學術講座後的六道題中都會有一道主旨題。主旨題有兩種：主旨大意題和主要目的題。不過，學術講座後以主旨大意題居多。

• Listening Tips

主旨大意題的題幹形式通常如下：

What is the main idea?
What is the professor mainly discussing?
What aspect of (the theory) is the professor mainly describing?
What does the lecture mainly discuss?
What is the talk mainly about?

在回答主旨大意題時考生一定要警惕。有時候教授可能在對話開頭提及一個話題，但接著會轉移到另一話題上進行論述。考生千萬不要以為在對話中聽到的第一個話題就是主旨大意題的正確答案。

不過，講座的開頭部分可能會提供答題線索，考生必須從講座一開始就集中注意力，找出主要話題或中心思想。在記筆記的過程中，考生需要注意判斷講座的主要觀點及其論據。

• Listening Sample

Narrator

Listen to part of a lecture about films and filmmaking.

Professor

Good afternoon, everyone. Last week we watched a Russian film and talked about the technique of montage in early Russian cinema. Today we move on to the concept of realism—what it means for a movie to be "realistic"—and how a cinematographer achieves the feeling of realism. The name of today's film—*Citizen Kane* is undoubtedly well known to you—this film is the "darling" of the film studies crowd. [laughs and pauses] Year after year, *Citizen Kane* tops polls for the greatest motion picture of all times.

Before we watch this two-hour film, I want to talk about why this film—which by the way was produced in 1941—is so unique in the history of film. There are so many ways in which the twenty-six-year old Orson Welles—who directed, acted and co-authored the screenplay—changed the landscape of moviemaking. This afternoon I'll be concentrating on three of Welles' most notable achievements.

First and foremost, through expert cinematography, *Citizen Kane* made unprecedented use of deep-focus photography. Let's stop and talk a little bit about what deep-focus photography is—it's when the camera simultaneously keeps the background, middle ground and foreground all in sharp focus. This approach brought the audience in closer contact than they would be even in real life. [pause] How is this possible, you may ask? As you watch the various objects on the screen, your eyes are not drawn to one particular thing—that means you are free to gaze about—one moment looking at the great Charles Kane—the next moment at his wife. What is their relationship? You may even focus on a physical object which has some symbolic value to one of the characters. The point is, the filmmaker has chosen consciously not to guide your focus, which means you the viewer are less passive—and must spend more energy evaluating what is important, what is not.

And while I'm on the topic of cinematic focus, I should mention Welles' use of scale. In film, the term "scale" refers to the relative size of objects appearing in the cinematic frame. And in *Citizen Kane*, Welles' characters are often framed in the right or left foreground, while in the background an action is taking place—an action which disturbs them, or which they are somehow controlling. So, for example, the political poster of Kane that hangs behind the podium seems very large when Kane is speaking, but suddenly appears tiny when viewed from the balcony of Kane's rival, who is an even more powerful man.

OK, then—to come back to the second pioneering technique in *Citizen Kane*—that of experimental lighting. Welles used backlighting to light his interior scenes. Because his movie sets were lit from below rather than from above, and filmed from low angles. As a result, we often find ourselves looking at ceilings and shadows—a technique Welles borrowed from British films. And, well—to skip ahead a bit in our syllabus—when we get to *The Big Sleep* later on and the study of film noir, you will see how the "look and feel" of these crime stories resembles Welles' expressionistic lighting. Indeed, *Citizen Kane* is considered by many to be an early manifestation of the film noir tradition.

I bring this point up now, so that, in a little bit, when we watch the film, you can pay attention to how the lighting has been designed. And—uh well, I can share with you—it wouldn't hurt for you to take a few notes, as lighting will be covered on the midterm exam.

Finally, I would like to draw your attention to Welles' use of overlapping dialogue. Welles was a total newcomer to the world of filmmaking prior to shooting *Citizen Kane*, so he spent hours viewing great films. One thing he noticed in other films—and found totally ridiculous—quite understandably, I might add—was the convention of one actor speaking at a time. Welles was striving for some level of realism—and he realized he didn't know a single soul who spoke in such an ordered, regular fashion. He pointed out the obvious—that people in real life constantly interrupt each other, even speak at the same time. In *Citizen Kane*, the actors were urged to adopt natural speaking behavior—to cut into one another's lines. The resulting dialogue, as you will see in a moment, was highly naturalistic and constituted a major change in the way films were made.

There are many other novel techniques in this movie that I could mention, but we need to begin the film now if we are to finish by the end of class. Again, take good notes. And now, if we could dim the lights, the 1941 movie classic, Orson Welles' *Citizen Kane*.

What aspect of film studies does the professor largely discuss?

A. The biography of filmmaker Orson Welles.
B. Cinematographers of the 20th century.
C. Innovations in the movie *Citizen Kane*.
D. The impact of Russian filmmakers.

托福總監評析

教授在講座中從幾個方面談論了電影《大國民》的創新，所以 C 是正確答案。

2 主要目的題（主旨目的題）

主要目的題通常考查考生是否理解講座或對話中的說話者為何說這些話。考生需要聽懂說話者的目的或動機，並識別出隱含資訊。

每篇聽力材料後通常只有一道主要目的題，也可能沒有。一般來說，主要目的題都出現在對話部分，而學術講座部分一般以主旨大意題開始。當然，也會有例外情況。

• Listening Tips

主要目的題通常都是以 why 開始的問句：
Why does the professor want to see the student?
Why does the student have to go to the library?

3 細節資訊題

在形式和考查目的上，聽力部分的細節資訊題與閱讀部分的細節資訊題十分相似，都詢問具體事實或資訊，其題幹形式通常為：According to the lecture, what is...? 或 According to the professor, when was...? 每個學術講座後有 1 ～ 2 道細節資訊題，每段對話後有 2 ～ 3 道細節資訊題。

新托福考試聽力部分有兩類細節資訊題，一類只有一個正確答案，另一類有兩個正確答案。兩種類型的試題都佔 1 分。後者的題目要求中都會有「Choose 2 answers」的提示資訊，考生很容易識別。參考上篇聽力材料，看看下面的題目：

• Listening Sample

What does the professor say about Orson Welles?
Choose 2 answers.
A. He liked viewers to focus on one subject.
B. He was critical of Russian films.

C. He had never made a film before he produced *Citizen Kane*.

D. He watched many movies by famous directors.

托福總監評析

　　如果考生認真聽了錄音並好好地記了筆記，就不難判斷出選項 C 和 D 為正確答案，因為教授說 Welles 是電影製作行業的新手，他看過很多優秀的影片。

According to the professor, what was the effect of deep-focus photography?

A. It focused on the most profound emotional moments of a film.

B. It put the background in the sharpest focus.

C. It allowed viewers to become actively engaged in all parts of the scene.

D. It caused the audience to tune out distractions.

托福總監評析

　　此題考查考生是否理解了深焦攝影技術這一概念。教授在講座中花了很長時間解釋說明深焦攝影技術，所以考生應有充分心理準備回答有關此話題的題目。

4 語用功能題（或修辭功能題）

　　語用功能題通常詢問說話者具體某句話的目的或隱含意義。通常情況下，每篇學術講座和對話後都會有一道此類題目。

• Listening Tips

　　語用功能題的題幹形式通常如下：

What did the speaker mean when she said...?

Why does the speaker...?

Why does the man say this: ...

• Listening Sample

Why does the professor say this:

　　*And—uh well, I can share with you—it wouldn't hurt for you to take a few notes, as lighting will be covered on the midterm exam. And—uh well, I can share with you—it wouldn't hurt for you to take a few notes, as lighting will be covered on the midterm exam.

（＊在實際考試中，此段僅為錄音內容，不會顯示在電腦螢幕上。）

A. She is telling the students not to be so lazy.

B. She wants to warn the class what will be on a test.

C. She is emphasizing that lighting is not the only aspect of film.

D. She wants to teach the class how to install film lighting.

托福總監評析

　　考生會再次聽到這一部分的錄音：教授正在提醒學生注意聽有關電影燈光的內容，因為期中考試會考。因此 B 為正確答案。

5 立場觀點題（或態度題）

　　立場觀點題或態度題考的是考生是否理解說話者的隱含觀點或情感。這種題型在對話和講座題中都會出現。

• Listening Tips

　　立場觀點題的題幹形式通常如下：

What is the professor's **attitude toward**...?

What is the professor's **view on**...?

What is the professor's **position on**...?

What is the professor's **opinion about**...?

What does the lecturer probably **think about**...?

How does the woman (seem to) **feel about**...?

Which of the following sentences best **expresses how the student feels**?

　　立場觀點題的選項中可能會包含表示情感的詞，如 happy、bored 等，也可能包含表示判斷的動詞，如 thinks... is good 或 doubts... is true。再以上篇聽力材料為例：

• Listening Sample

What is the professor's opinion of Welles' use of overlapping dialogue?

A. She thinks it was long overdue.

B. She thinks it was artificial.

C. She feels it could have been more realistic.

D. She feels it was reminiscent of film noir.

托福總監評析

　　教授在講座中提到，她認為重疊式對話本應更早就應用於電影中。她說：「他（Welles）注意到一個問題，並且發現這個問題十分可笑——我認為這是可以理解的——那就是一段時間內只能有一位演員獨白。」根據教授的語氣可知 A 項正確。

6 組織結構題

　　組織結構題（或理解結構題）考的是考生是否明白說話者組織其想法的方式以及採用該方式的原因，比如會問考生教授為何以某種方式組織其觀點內容，或者問是否明白教授在哪裡突然偏離主題。

　　考生需要清楚聽力內容的整體組織架構，並明白整篇的組織順序：是按從過去到現在的時間順序，還是按論點的重要程度順序？還是先從人們最熟知的某個事實或人物開始，逐步過渡到鮮為人知的事實？再以上篇聽力材料為例：

• Listening Sample

Why does the professor introduce the topic of "scale", or relative size?

A. To relate the use of scale to the use of deep focus.
B. To compare Kane's size to his wife's size.
C. To illustrate how disturbing small screens can be.
D. To demonstrate the fame of Orson Welles.

托福總監評析

　　教授解釋完深焦攝影技術（使背景、中景和近景全部聚焦）的概念後，接著又談到了「比例」這一相關概念。這是因為用深焦技術拍攝的物體可能會顯得過小或過大。因此正確答案為 A。

7 關聯內容題

　　關聯內容題只出現在講座部分。與閱讀部分的資訊歸類題相似，關聯內容題也包含表格。考生需要從全部講座內容中提取相關資訊填入表格，主要考查考生的推理、推測和舉一反三的能力。同時，考生還需具有按一定的時間或先後順序將事件進行排序的能力。

　　此類題型最簡單的一種出題形式是給出一個簡單的表格，要求考生就某一事實作出二選一的回答，如問：某種植物是否是一種基因改良植物？考生只需判斷 Yes 或 No。又如：所談論的動物是哺乳動物還是兩棲動物？其他出題形式則要求考生根據講座中介紹的特點將事物或觀點進行分類。以上篇聽力材料為例：

• Listening Sample

The professor talks about various innovations in Citizen Kane. Indicate whether each of the following is a one of those innovations. Place a ✓ mark in the correct box.

Feature	Yes	No
Color filter		
Deep-focus shots		
Animation		
Backlighting		

托福總監評析

考生如果認真聽完錄音並做了筆記，就會知道教授沒有提及彩色過濾和動畫這兩項內容。因此正確答案是：

Feature	Yes	No
Color filter		✓
Deep-focus shots	✓	
Animation		✓
Backlighting	✓	

8 推論題

在聽力部分中，推論題通常有三道或者更多。因果關係和時間先後關係常為推論題考查的重點。

• Listening Tips

有些推論題和語用功能題類似，也需要考生重複聽一段錄音內容：

What does the professor imply when he says this: (replay)...

還有些推論題的題幹形式如下：

What can we **infer about**...?

What does the professor **imply about**...?

What can we **conclude about**...?

What will the man **probably do next**?

• Listening Sample

What does the professor imply about Welles when she says this:

Welles was a total newcomer to the world of filmmaking prior to shooting *Citizen Kane*, so he spent hours viewing great films.

A. He wasted precious time watching experimental films.
B. He learned to make movies by watching other films.
C. His earliest movies were not very professional.
D. He invested numerous hours in the filming of *Citizen Kane*.

托福總監評析

　　從文中可知 Welles 在電影製作行業是個新手，也就是說，他還在學習過程中。正因如此，他花很多時間觀看其他人的影片。因此可以推斷「他通過觀看其他影來學習電影製作」，答案為 B。

▶聽力題答題步驟

做好聽力題的關鍵是集中精神和記筆記。答題步驟為：

1. 從一開始聽錄音就預測其主題。
2. 盡力做好筆記，記下關鍵字和重要舉例。
3. 利用自己的知識先排除錯誤選項。
4. 選出答案後，深呼吸一下，然後準備好聽下一道題。
5. 即使感覺沒有答對某道題也不要驚慌；保持注意力集中，保持積極的心態。

Section ②

How to Prepare for Academic Reading and Listening

第❷部分
學術類閱讀和聽力怎麼考

① Physical Sciences, Topic 1: Astronomy
物理科學常考主題 1：天文學

　　本章內容以物理科學範疇的天文學為知識背景。天文學是研究空間的科學，其研究對象包括行星、恆星、星系、彗星和星雲等，所以常用詞彙有 Mars（火星）、Venus（金星）、meteorite（隕石）以及物理學相關片語如 speed of light（光速）和 zero gravity（零重力，失重狀態）等。請注意本章中出現的片語，並記住它們。

⋯⋯⋯⋯⋯⋯⋯⋯⋯⋯⋯ 天文學：閱讀 ⋯⋯⋯⋯⋯⋯⋯⋯⋯⋯⋯

▶句子簡化題型答題策略 1

　　換句話說的能力和識別換句話說後資訊的能力對解答所有新托福考試題都很重要，而其重要性在解答「句子簡化題」時尤為突出。此類試題的應對策略有很多，不過首要的一步是一定要弄清楚句子的文法結構和加粗部分的意思，特別是要準確找出句子的主詞。

　　瞭解標點符號和修飾性片語與子句的用法會大有幫助，因為複合句中常含有各種子句和分詞片語結構，而這些都是句子簡化題考查的內容。如果這方面的知識不夠的話，就有可能會把一個作修飾性成分的名詞片語誤以為是句子的主詞，以致作出錯誤選擇並丟分。

　　下面舉一個例子，這題也會在接下來的擬真試題中出現：

• Reading Sample

　　Which of the sentences below best expresses the essential information in the highlighted sentence in the passage? Incorrect choices change the meaning in major ways or leave out important information.

　　Subsequent to Leavitt's discovery of what are now referred to as the Cepheid-variables of the Small Magellanic Cloud, researchers could use variable stars as a cosmic yardstick.

A. After researchers started using standard measurements, Leavitt could identify the variables now called Cepheid variables.

B. In their work to measure the universe, scientists were able to make use of the variable stars found by Leavitt.

C. Scientists could have made use of the Cepheid variable stars if only Leavitt had access to more precise tools.

D. Previous to Leavitt, some researchers had detected what appeared to be variable stars, but their measurements of the cosmos turned out to be inaccurate.

托福總監評析

　　要先弄清楚試卷中加粗句子的結構，所以先找到句子裡的逗號，逗號前面是 subsequent to（在……之後）引導的很長的介系詞片語，而逗號後面則是一個獨立的主句，主詞為 researchers。分清這一點很重要，因為現在就可以把關注重點放在主詞的訊息上，即研究者們能夠把變星（variable stars）用作宇宙衡量的一種標準。根據這一資訊便可排除 C 項和 D 項。A 項是干擾項，因為本句的主詞並不是 Leavitt。

　　當然，單憑對標點和文法規則的瞭解是不夠的，還必須能夠理解句子中的詞彙片語及其他同義表達方式。下面來看一些原句中的片語及其同義表達方式：

Researchers → scientists
Leavitt's discovery of [stars] → [stars] found by Leavitt
could use... → were able to make use of...
cosmic yardstick → something that can measure the universe

　　關於句子簡化題的更多解題策略和練習將在後文提供。目前階段，你應該大量學習詞彙及其用法，訓練自己的換句話說能力。這種技能比其他任何技能都重要，可以幫助你在新托福考試中取得高分。

　　從今天起就開始提高換句話說能力吧，你一定能夠成功！下面開始練習吧。

▶ **模擬試題**（解答請見 P. 300）

Henrietta Leavitt and the Stars

(1) At the end of the 19th century, Harvard University purchased 12 acres of land called Summer House Hill on which to build a large telescope. Harvard hoped eventually to establish the largest observatory in the world. Today the telescope is no longer in operational use, but Harvard's "Great Refractor" was for many years state-of-the-art technology. An advanced 15-inch-diameter lens was ordered from Munich, Germany, and installed, and on an afternoon in June, 1847, the first observation took place, of the Moon. During the early decades, the observatory was largely engaged in determining stellar positions as well as the observation of planets, variable stars, comets, and nebulae.

(2) Then, in 1877, a physicist named Edward Pickering took over the laboratory and began to oversee the work of cataloging the brightness of stars. It is important to note that astronomical studies of the time focused largely on two details: a star's position and a star's motion in space. Pickering, however, realized that there was little data on a star's true brightness, or luminosity, and its color, a characteristic that could indicate the chemical composition of the star.

(3) Henrietta Leavitt arrived at the observatory in 1893, where she would work for seven hours a day, six days a week, for 25 cents an hour. In the days when women were often barred from scientific careers, Leavitt was known as a "computer" or a "counter," hired to calculate the positions and brightness of stars in astronomical photographs. Few men were interested in such tedious work, so the jobs usually went to women. Looking at tiny dots on photographic plates, Leavitt compared each pinpoint against stars whose brightness was already known. During a time exposure, the brighter stars leave larger spots on a photographic plate, chemically darkening more grains. Size is therefore an indicator of brightness. Early on Pickering had asked Leavitt to look for "variable stars," stars that waxed and waned with regularity. Some of these variable stars completed a cycle every few days; other cycles took weeks, even months. The rhythms were slow and subtle. Only by measuring stars at various intervals through the year could one detect the variations in luminosity.

(4) Over the many years Leavitt spent poring over photographic plates containing thousands of stars, she was able to observe certain relationships between the average apparent brightness, in other words the magnitude of luminosity as observed from the Earth, and the period, or cycle length, of certain stars. Leavitt looked at the vast stellar mass in the two Magellan Clouds and analyzed the variable stars. She plotted 25 of these on a graph, with brightness on one axis and period on the other. It dawned on her that the longer the period of a variable star, the greater its natural brightness, a relation which we now know is based on the fact that brightness is proportional to surface area. This is because large, bright variable stars pulsate over a relatively long period just as large bells resonate at a lower frequency (or longer period) than smaller bells.

(5) Subsequent to Leavitt's discovery of what are now referred to as the Cepheid-variables of the Small Magellanic Cloud, researchers could use variable stars as a cosmic yardstick. They were eager to answer such questions "How big is the universe?" Drawing on Leavitt's work, the legendary astronomer Edwin Hubble compared the apparent brightness of the Cepheid variable stars with their "absolute brightness"—a measure equal to the apparent brightness a star would have if it were located exactly 32.6 light-years away from the Earth. In this way, Hubble was able to determine a Cepheid's distance from our planet. Hubble's method worked because Cepheids with the same periods have about the same absolute brightness.

(6) As a result in 1919 Edwin Hubble definitively showed that stars existed beyond the Milky Way. Most scientists at that time held that the universe was only as large as the Milky Way and that it was a constant size, and Hubble's idea that the Milky Way was just one of many changed forever the way we view our place in the universe.

• Reading Questions

1. According to Paragraph 2, what attribute of a star provides information about its

chemical makeup?
   A. Its luminosity.
   B. Its color.
   C. Its location.
   D. Its pulsing.

2. According to Paragraph 3, what task was Henrietta Leavitt employed to do at the observatory?
   A. Measure variations in stars' gravity.
   B. Create a catalog of black holes.
   C. Make photographs of heavenly bodies.
   D. Evaluate the brightness of stars.

3. The word "subtle" in Paragraph 3 is closest in meaning to_____ .
   A. unobvious
   B. unimportant
   C. demanding
   D. repetitive

4. The phrase "poring over" in Paragraph 4 is closest in meaning to _____.
   A. processing
   B. mapping
   C. modifying
   D. examining

5. The word "other" in Paragraph 4 refers to _____.
   A. graph
   B. brightness
   C. axis
   D. period

6. In Paragraph 4, why does the author mention "bells"?
   A. To illustrate how size relates to luminosity.
   B. To show what happens to sound in a vacuum.
   C. To make a point about the speed of light.
   D. To indicate the curved shape of variable stars.

7. What can be inferred about the Great Refractor in the 1890s?
   A. It was no longer considered advanced technology.
   B. It was not able to see the Magellanic Clouds.
   C. It was often borrowed by foreign countries.
   D. It was used to take photographs of stellar matter.

8. Which of the sentences below best expresses the essential information in the highlighted sentence in the passage? Incorrect choices change the meaning in major ways or leave out important information.

Subsequent to Leavitt's discovery of what are now referred to as the Cepheid-variables of the Small Magellanic Cloud, researchers could use variable stars as a cosmic yardstick.

A. After researchers started using standard measurements, Leavitt could identify the variables now called Cepheid variables.

B. In their work to measure the universe, scientists were able to make use of the variable stars found by Leavitt.

C. Scientists could have made use of the Cepheid variable stars if only Leavitt had access to more precise tools.

D. Previous to Leavitt, some researchers had detected what appeared to be variable stars, but their measurements of the cosmos turned out to be inaccurate.

9. According to Paragraph 5, what data about Cepheids did Edwin Hubble NOT make use of to calculate their distance from the Earth?
   A. Their periods.
   B. Their constellations.
   C. Their absolute brightness.
   D. Their apparent brightness.

10. The phrase "drawing on" in Paragraph 5 is closest in meaning to _____ .
   A. illustrating
   B. revising
   C. utilizing
   D. approaching

11. According to Paragraph 6, in the beginning of the 1900s, what did scientists generally believe to be true about the universe?
   A. The universe was expanding.
   B. The universe included several galaxies.
   C. The Milky Way was constantly gaining new stars.
   D. The Milky Way housed all heavenly bodies.

12. The word "definitively" in Paragraph 6 is closest in meaning to _____.
   A. of course
   B. against all odds
   C. conclusively
   D. brightly

13. **Directions**: An introductory sentence for a brief summary of the passage is provided below. Complete the summary by selecting the THREE answer choices that express

the most important ideas in the passage. Some answer choices do not belong in the summary because they express ideas that are not presented in the passage or are minor ideas in the passage.

This question is worth 2 points.
This passage discusses how activities at the Harvard observatory in the late 19th century changed the way in which astronomers looked at the universe.

-
-
-

Answer Choices

1. Although a star's coordinates can be found on a star chart, they are not always accurate.

2. 19th-century scientists knew that the Magellanic Clouds contained millions of stars that were located just outside our galaxy.

3. Henrietta Leavitt was able to calculate the distance between the Cepheid variable stars and the Earth.

4. By comparing a Cepheid's apparent brightness to its absolute brightness, astronomers were able to determine a celestial body's distance from the Earth.

5. The luminosity of bright Cepheid stars was found to fluctuate over relatively long intervals.

6. Based on data regarding the distances of variable stars, astronomers reevaluated their assumptions about the Milky Way.

關鍵語塊

- **Great Refractor** 大折射望遠鏡
  （特指 19 世紀哈佛大學購買的望遠鏡）
- **period** 週期
- **state-of-the-art technology**
  最先進的技術
- **stellar mass** 星群
- **comet** 彗星
- **the Magellanic Clouds** 大麥哲倫星系
- **nebula (pl. nebulae)** 星雲
- **the longer the…, the greater
  the...** ……越長，……越大
- **take over** 接收，接管
- **... is proportional to...**
  ……與……成正比

- **there was little data on...**
  關於……的資料很少
- **resonate at a... frequency**
  以……頻率共振
- **luminosity** （恆星等的）光度，亮度
- **the Cepheid variable star** 造父變星
- **be barred from** 禁止，不准
- **absolute brightness** 絕對亮度
- **wax and wane** （月的）盈虧，圓缺
- **the Milky Way** 銀河
- **apparent brightness** 視亮度
  （指地球上肉眼所見的某個星體的亮度）

• **Exercise 1**　（解答請見 P. 301）

Write a correct paraphrase for each of the following sentences.

ⓐ Today the telescope is no longer in operational use, but Harvard's "Great Refractor" was for many years state-of-the-art technology.

_____

_____

ⓑ Looking at tiny dots on photographic plates, Leavitt compared each pinpoint against stars whose brightness was already known.

_____

_____

ⓒ Only by measuring stars at various intervals through the year could one detect the variations in luminosity.

_____

_____

⋯⋯⋯⋯⋯⋯ 天文學：聽力 ⋯⋯⋯⋯⋯⋯

▶如何做好筆記

　　學術講座的時間長度為 4 ～ 5 分鐘，這表示考生聽到的資訊量非常大。有時，教授會開門見山、直接切入主題，但有時，教授在開頭會先講某項該交的作業或上週講授的課程內容。要想確保跟上教授的思路，唯一的辦法就是多記筆記，記下講座的重點大意、重要的細節資訊和例證。

　　然而，快速記筆記是有難度的，尤其是用英語記，而且結構混亂的筆記也不易閱讀，因此最好的策略是記「結構性筆記」。其目的是使考生在以一定的格式記錄單字和片語的同時，也能掌握講座的組織結構。這樣記筆記就能輕鬆把握教授的思路，並更好地預測後面將會談論的內容。

　　記筆記的方法有很多，考生需要多加練習，找到最適合自己的方法。有些考生以提綱形式記筆記，如下所示：

Intro（開頭）

Main idea（中心大意）

　Key concept（主要觀點）

　　Example（例證）

　　Example（例證）

　Contrasting concept（反方觀點）

　　Example（例證）

St Q（學生問題）

Prof Ans（教授回答）

有些考生喜歡用表格形式記錄要點，如下所示：

Topic（主題）	Features（內容）
Prof （教授） 1	Concept（觀點） Example（例證）
2	Concept（觀點） Example（例證）
St Q（學生問題）	Prof Ans（教授回答）

　　如果你覺得使用提綱或表格形式很難，也可以在紙上畫一個大方框，在裡面寫下關鍵字，並在關鍵字周圍留出足夠的空間。然後，隨著你對聽力內容的理解不斷加深，關鍵字與觀點之間的關係逐漸清晰，就可以使用連線、小方框或者各種記號來表明聽力內容的組織結構。

　　這種自由式的記筆記方法如下圖所示：

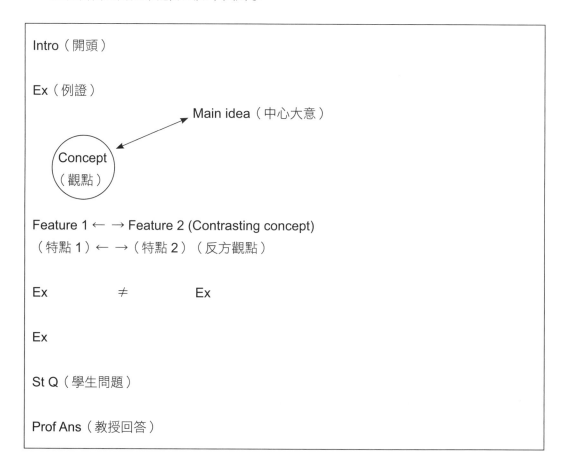

可以使用「＝、≠、＜、＞、＋、－」以及其他任何你可以看懂的符號；也可以只寫出一個單字的開頭部分，如用 intr 代替 introduced 或用 trad 代替 traditional；甚至可以用中文。只要能抓住聽力內容的關鍵字、思路以及觀點之間的關係，就可以從容應對後面的考題。

▶聽天文學講座時如何記結構性筆記

聽力要想取得高分，最佳策略就是預測考的內容。當考生開始總結講座的中心大意或主要觀點時就可以預測。本章下文的天文學講座中，當聽到教授說：We'll be talking about solar activity later in the course, getting into things like solar winds. But right now it's important for us to understand more about the Sun itself. 就可以確定該講座的主題是太陽，於是在草稿紙上快速寫上 Sun，畫個圓圈圈住它，然後認真聽教授接下來講的具體內容。

當聽到教授把一個事物與另一個事物進行對比時，這是另一個重要資訊，此時也需要記筆記。如果講座中出現對比內容，無論是相似之處的對比還是不同之處的對比，幾乎可以肯定後面會有關於這些內容的考題。例如，本章下文的天文學講座中會比較太陽內部和太陽表面的能量變化過程，此時，我們就應該記下 core 和 surface 各自的特點。

• Listening Tip

使用本書練習聽力時，如果聽第一遍錄音時不看聽力文本，你的聽力會提高得更快。

▶模擬試題（解答請見 P. 301）

Now listen to a lecture about ASTRONOMY.　　　*Track 001*

★ Keywords

core （天體的）核，中心	proton 質子	hydrogen（化學元素）氫
photon 光子	helium（化學元素）氦	

• Listening Questions　　　*Track 002*

1. What is the talk mainly about?
   A. The Sun's effect on space weather.
   B. Electrical charges in nuclear reactions.
   C. How the Sun creates energy.
   D. How gravity influences radiation.

2. Listen again to part of the lecture. Then answer the question.

 *Please listen to Track 002 for this part of the question.*

Why does the professor say this:

Please listen to Track 002 for this part of the question.

  A. To tell the students the correct answer on the test.
  B. To provide a brief explanation at this time.
  C. To indicate the drawbacks of the proposed solution.
  D. To apologize for failing to explain better last week.

3. In his talk, what does the professor say about gravity and the Sun?
  A. Gravity on the Sun is greater than gravity on the Earth.
  B. Gravity on the Sun is greater than gravity on other stars.
  C. The gravitational pull from the Sun seldom affects gravity at the surface of the Earth.
  D. It is very difficult to measure surface gravity on the Sun because of the extreme heat.

4. According to the professor, what is true about the Sun's core?
  Choose 2 answers.
  A. Collisions in the core release light in the form of gamma rays.
  B. Nuclear fusion of hydrogen takes place just outside the core.
  C. High-energy visible light is sent directly from the core to the Earth.
  D. The core contains protons that are hitting against one another.

5. Why does the professor mention water boiling in a pot?
  A. To show how hydrogen and oxygen come together.
  B. To assign a physics lab experiment to the students.
  C. To compare the cohesion of liquids to that of plasma.
  D. To illustrate the conditions causing atoms to move.

6. The professor talks about the activities occurring in two portions of the Sun—the core and the surface. Indicate for each example below what activity occurs in each area. Place a ✓ in the correct box.

	Core	Surface
Protons colliding		
Visible light quickly emitted		
Nuclear reatction		

• Exercise 2 　（解答請見 P. 304）

  Play the audio again and try taking structured notes using some of the approaches discussed in this chapter.

② Humanities and the Arts, Topic 1: Crafts and Folk Arts
人文藝術常考主題 1：民俗藝術

　　本章以人文藝術範疇的民俗藝術為知識背景，這也是新托福考試中經常考查的一個主題。有關藝術的詞彙通常都是描述性的，如形容詞 ornamental（裝飾的）和 delicate（精美的）。然而，有關藝術和藝術品的文章卻經常包含對生產工藝的描述，比如 wood carving（木雕）和 quilting（縫棉被）。請注意本章中出現的片語，並記住它們。

·············· 民俗藝術：閱讀 ··············

▶ 練習略讀的技巧

　　由於閱讀文章的長度有 650 ～ 750 詞，包含 4 ～ 7 個段落，所以很多考生擔心自己在 20 分鐘內做不完閱讀題。為了解決這個難題，考生需要做兩件事情。第一，學習如何略讀文章，在回答具體問題前能夠通過略讀得知文章大意和段落大意。第二，提高自己的總體閱讀能力（理解力和速度）。

　　略讀時，重點應該是關注重要資訊和作者的思路；不要擔心第一遍閱讀時抓不住細節內容。考試題目的順序通常與文章內容的呈現順序一致，瞭解這一點很關鍵（違反此規則的試題一般為否定事實題、插入句子題、部分推論題、內容總結題和資訊歸類題）。

　　有時，考生只需閱讀每段的第一句就可獲取足夠的答題資訊。不過，大多數時候，考生需要閱讀到每段的中部。例如，本章下文關於依努特人的文章裡，第一段的中心句為第二句：According to the still-debated New World migration model, a small group of Paleo-Americans migrated eastwards from the Eurasian landmass to North America. 這個重要句子的主要含義是：很久以前有一批人從歐亞大陸遷移到了北美洲。通過略讀第一段，考生就可以回答第一道題：In the first paragraph, what does the author say about the New World migration model? 當然，要想排除三個錯誤選項並確定正確選項，還需要再次閱讀文章內容，通過略讀獲取問題中涉及的細節資訊。

　　要想提高整體閱讀速度，考生要做大量的練習。如果方法得當，那麼讀得越多，速度就會越快。在閱讀時要嘗試一次看幾個單字、一個片語或者一整個句子，不要逐字地閱讀。不要在心裡把每個詞都讀出來，也不要翻譯。下面來看本章下文一個簡單的例子（第六段開頭）。

托福總監帶你練習

The Inuit sculptures	embody	a variety of styles.
第一個語塊	第二個語塊	第三個語塊

要想讀得快，閱讀時眼睛應該能夠迅速抓到上面的三個語塊內容。如果做得到，你的閱讀速度就會至少提高一倍喔！

下面再來看一個長句子（為文章最後一句），把它劃分成一個一個的語塊試試看：

The **final stage of carving** is **the polishing,** which **is done** with **several grades of waterproof sandpaper** and **hours** of **rubbing**.

練習通過一個個較大的語塊進行略讀時，要跳過不重要的詞，如功能詞（the、of、is 等）。也要跳過不熟悉的單字，如果答題時需要用到這些不熟悉的詞，那麼就自己猜猜它們的意思吧！一直執著在上面也不會幫助答題的。

▶語義詞彙題答題策略

在新托福考試中，每篇閱讀文章後通常至少會有三道詞彙題，有時可多達五道題。任何詞性都可能會考，尤以動詞居多，其中可能還會包括一道考片語的題目。雖然大部分考的單字都相對容易，但也不排除某些單字相對難一些。不管怎樣，可以放心的是，新托福考試中不會考超生僻的低頻詞。

● 無法確定某個單字的意思時，可使用下列策略：

策略 1 仔細分析整個單字的結構，利用字首字尾、字根或其他線索進行猜測。

以本章下文中的題目為例：

• **Reading Sample 1**

2. The word "appease" in Paragraph 3 is closest in meaning to _____.
   A. attract　　B. transform　　C. calm　　D. worship

托福總監評析

　　單字 appease 源自意為「和平」的拉丁文單字，據此可以猜測 calm 可能與其同義。

策略 2 不要在心裡把單字翻譯成你的母語。要善於利用自己已有的知識來猜測文中的生字。

• READING SAMPLE 2

4. The word "barter" in Paragraph 4 is closest in meaning to _____.
   A. exchanges   B. encounters   C. work   D. alliance

托福總監評析

barter 所在句為：In their barter with whalers and missionaries, the 19th-century Inuit supplied carvings of animals, as well as replicas of western-style objects fashioned from walrus ivory, such as letter openers. 該句意為：在與捕鯨人和傳教士的 barter 中，19 世紀的依努特人提供動物雕像以及海象牙製成的西方風格物品的複製品，如開信刀。

根據對工業社會的瞭解，我們可以猜測那時依努特人還沒有貨幣，因而不能用貨幣從捕鯨人和傳教士那裡購買貨物。但是，他們也需要進行 barter，即「交換商品」。運用邏輯推理和已有知識可知，選項 A 為正確答案。

策略 3 通過把握作者的整體思路來判斷具體單字和片語的意思。尋找上下文線索，排除明顯錯誤的選項進行猜測。

當你準備新托福時，如果訓練了換句話說的能力，就能提高做對詞彙題的機率。準備一個記錄英語語塊的日記本，記下單字在句子中的實際用法，用這種方法背單字非常有效，最終會幫助你提高做對題的機率！

• Exercise 1　（解答請見 P. 306）

For each of the underlined words in the first column, use the "clue words" to help guess the correct synonym in the third column.

Vocabulary in context	Clue words	Synonym
1. <u>festive</u> occasion	festival	a. precise
2. <u>time-honored</u> practice	honor, time	b. joyful
3. <u>ingenious</u> design	genius	c. careful
4. <u>painstaking</u> process	take, pains	d. respected
5. <u>refined</u> carvings	fine	e. clever

▶模擬試題（解答請見 P. 306）

Inuit Carvings

★ **Keyword**

> Paleo-American 原始美洲人

(1) There are many expressions of indigenous art in North America, ranging from works that predate European colonization to contemporary pieces reflecting the old traditions. According to the still-debated New World migration model, a small group of Paleo-Americans migrated eastwards from the Eurasian landmass to North America. Some speculate that people traveled over Beringia, a land bridge which formerly connected the two continents and the present location of the Bering Strait. The minimum time depth that this migration occurred is 12,000 years ago, but the first wave may well have occurred much earlier. Over time, these people spread throughout North and South America, diversifying into many hundreds of culturally distinct nations and tribes. Inuit people and their art emerged as part of this movement.

(2) The descendants of Paleo-Inuit people journeyed to the regions of what is now Arctic Canada and Greenland, terrain often covered in ice or snow. These Inuit-speaking peoples ultimately evolved into the Dorset culture, producing vast quantities of figurative art between 600 B.C. and 1000 A.D. The Dorsets took ivory, bone, antler, and occasionally stone and carved small birds, bears, walruses, and seals, often with skeleton markings. They also carved human figures and masks. Many of these objects had religious or magical purposes, and were, for example, worn as amulets to ward off evil spirits or used in shamanic rituals.

(3) Around the first millennium A.D., the people of the Thule culture migrated from northern Alaska and replaced the Dorset culture. Thule art differed from the Dorset art in that it had a distinctive Alaskan style and included utilitarian objects such as combs, buttons, needle cases, cooking pots, ornate spears and harpoons. The graphic decorations carved on them were ornamental, bearing no religious significance. It appears the main purpose of this art was not to appease spirits or the forces of nature.

(4) The Thule culture ended during the 16th century and transitioned to Inuit culture some time between 1600 and 1850, at the same time European explorers were entering the northern region. In their barter with whalers and missionaries, the 19th-century Inuit supplied carvings of animals, as well as replicas of western-style objects fashioned from walrus ivory, such as letter openers. Most Inuit still lived in small family camps, used dogsleds for travel, lived in igloos during the winter and divided their time between trapping white fox and hunting. Utensils, tools and weapons were still made by hand from natural materials: stone, bone, ivory, antler, and animal hides. A nomadic people

could take very little else but necessities with them; nevertheless, a few miniature, non-utilitarian objects were carved and carried around. These included earrings, dance masks, and intricate combs and figures that represented their legends.

(5) In the mid-1940s Inuit conditions began to deteriorate, caused to a great extent by the plummeting prices of white fox on the world market. ■ 1 In light of this development, the Canadian government decided to take steps to facilitate an alternative revenue source for the Inuit trappers. ■ 2 Once the previously nomadic Inuits settled into communities, their carved pieces became appreciably larger. ■ 3 The quality of the carvings was high, with the result that artists began to receive commissions to produce specific works of art. Sculpture, prints and other art forms gradually replaced pelts as the major source of livelihood. ■ 4 By the 1960s, active co-operatives existed in most settlements and the Inuit art market was flourishing. At that point, the Inuit artisans became entrepreneurs, effectively quarrying their own stones, fashioning their own carving tools, creating objects of beauty and showing their work in urban galleries.

(6) The Inuit sculptures embody a variety of styles. Some are rooted in naturalism and an interest in both wildlife and the spirit world, such as dancing bears that balance delicately on one leg, caught in movement. Some styles are abstract; others are decorative. The stone used ranges from many stunning shades of green to white dolomite and varicolored marble. Various greenstones, especially the apple-green and cream-colored shades, are highly prized. Although power tools are certainly available to them, most Inuit artists today prefer to use just axes and files as this affords more control. Using these simple tools, the artist frees the animal spirit contained within the mass of stone. The final stage of carving is the polishing, which is done with several grades of waterproof sandpaper and hours of rubbing.

• Reading Questions

1. In the first paragraph, what does the author say about the New World migration model?
   A. The model hypothesizes that migration began with hundreds of tribes traveling to North America.
   B. The theory presumes that Inuit people descended from the first wave of New World migrants.
   C. The theory argues that ancient tribes sailed southwards from Eurasia across a channel.
   D. Although there was originally some disagreement, the migration model is now well established.

2. The word "appease" in Paragraph 3 is closest in meaning to _____.
   A. attract　　B. transform　　C. calm　　　　D. worship

3. All of the following statements about Thule carvings are correct EXCEPT _____.
   A. their designs depict the magic of shamans
   B. some of them were created 1,000 years ago
   C. they include decorative spears and harpoons
   D. they show a unique Alaskan influence

4. The word "barter" in Paragraph 4 is closest in meaning to _____.
   A. exchanges
   B. encounters
   C. work
   D. alliance

5. Which of the sentences below best expresses the essential information in the highlighted sentence in the passage? Incorrect choices change the meaning in major ways or leave out important information.
   A nomadic people could take very little else but necessities with them; nevertheless, a few miniature, non-utilitarian objects were carved and carried around.
   A. Because the lifestyles of nomads allowed them to carry very few things along with them, they were not able to carry about art objects.
   B. Despite the difficulties that nomadic peoples had in transporting their belongings, they were able to bring small, practical objects vital to their needs.
   C. Everything but carved decorative objects was carried about by the nomads, who considered things such as tools and weapons necessities.
   D. The nomads brought along some carved objects that were not essential, even though the priority was functional objects.

6. The word "effectively" in Paragraph 5 is closest in meaning to _____.
   A. industrially
   B. intentionally
   C. for all practical purposes
   D. for the most part

7. How did the Inuit primarily support themselves before the 1940s?
   A. Selling miniatures.
   B. Trapping animals.
   C. Fishing.
   D. Tourism.

8. What does the author say about how the Inuits produce art today?
   A. They have modernized their sculptural tools.
   B. They are limited by the lack of quality stone in quarries.
   C. They give only a few quality pieces to art galleries in cities.
   D. They treat stone carving as a business venture.

9. The word "them" in Paragraph 6 refers to _____.
   A. greenstones
   B. tools
   C. artists
   D. axes

10. In Paragraph 6, why does the author mention "dancing bears"?
    A. To demonstrate the life force in sculpture.
    B. To illustrate the power of abstract sculpture.
    C. To show how greenstone was the stone of preference.
    D. To exemplify the Inuit's love of natural music.

11. It can be inferred from the passage that Inuit artists receive the most commissions for sculptures made of which of the following materials?
    A. Sandstone.
    B. White dolomite.
    C. Varicolored marble.
    D. Cream-colored greenstone.

12. Look at the four squares [■] that indicate where the following sentence could be added to the passage.

    The Canadian Handicraft Guild in Montreal introduced Inuit carvings to the world in 1949.

    Where would the sentence best fit?

    ■ 1
    ■ 2
    ■ 3
    ■ 4

13. **Directions:** An introductory sentence for a brief summary of the passage is provided below. Complete the summary by selecting the THREE answer choices that express the most important ideas in the passage. Some answer choices do not belong in the summary because they express ideas that are not presented in the passage or are minor ideas in the passage. **This question is worth 2 points.**
    This passage explores the various historical factors shaping the development of Inuit carvings today.

    -
    -
    -

Answer Choices

1. Over one thousand years ago, Inuit ancestors created many small sculptures depicting animals.

2. Initially, the Dorset people were afraid to carve masks because they feared evil spirits.

3. Seeking shelter, Inuits lived in igloos during the harsh winter months.

4. Thule carvings were often very practical; for example, the carvers engraved designs on utensils and hunting tools.

5. Inuit sculptures currently are often produced by entrepreneurial artists participating in cooperatives.

6. Early European explorers and whalers caused the Inuit population to dwindle.

關鍵語塊

- **expression of art** 藝術表現形式
- **graphic decoration** 圖形裝飾
- **indigenous** 本土的；當地的
- **bearing no (religious) significance** 沒有（宗教）意義
- **predate** 早於，先於
- **barter** 以物換物；交換
- **still-debated** 仍有爭議的
- **replica** 複製品，仿製品
- **migration** 遷移
- **letter opener** 開信刀
- **minimum time depth** 距今最近的發生時間
- **divide one's time between... and...** 將某人的時間分配在……和……上
- **spread throughout** 遍佈
- **nomadic people** 遊牧民族
- **culturally distinct** 文化上非常獨特的
- **deteriorate** 惡化
- **emerge** 出現
- **plummeting** 驟然下跌的；（從高處）快速落下的
- **Inuit** 依努特人
- **appreciably** 明顯地，顯著地
- **figurative art** 寫實藝術；形象藝術
- **receive commissions to** 接到……任務
- **amulet** 護身符
- **effectively** 實際上，事實上
- **ward off** 趕走
- **fashion** 製造
- **shamanic** 薩滿教巫師的
- **urban gallery** 城市藝術畫廊
- **millennium** 一千年；千年期
- **stunning** 非常美的
- **utilitarian object** 日常用品，實用的物品
- **be highly prized** 受到高度評價
- **harpoon** 魚叉
- **power tool** 電動工具

民俗藝術：聽力

▶連貫學術講座的用語

儘管每套新托福考試題中學術講座的內容各有不同，但還是有一定規律可循的。這是因為講座反映的都是教授在實際課堂上的講話內容。例如，教授可能一會談論主題內容，一會又改變話題談論下個星期的作業內容。考生在聽錄音時，需要做好各種準備。

平時學術講座的聽力練習練得越多，考場上就會越放鬆。前文已經說過，認真記筆記是一個重要方法，在此不再贅述。另一個應對學術講座題的好辦法是透過開頭用語、過渡用詞、例子等把整篇有效地連貫起來。

下面來仔細分析一下本章下文關於棉被縫紉藝術的講座，看看教授如何進入話題，如何過渡到主要內容並給出例證，最後是如何以點評學生作業和介紹下次講座主題來結束講座。注意教授在講座的每部分開頭都是怎麼說的？我們可以透過這些開頭知道接下來會聽到什麼內容。這些開頭用語實質上都表示教授在說：And now I'm going to talk about...

教授的講座思路	
開頭用語	Throughout this course, we'll... Today, we'll start with... Our major focus will be... Later on this semester, we'll look at... But right now, I want you to immerse yourselves in...
主要觀點（首次提出）	It's [Art is] a product of a certain time and a certain environment.
給出兩個古代的例子	Egypt, China
回到主要話題	OK then, back to our topic.
給出美洲殖民時期的例子	Coastal vs. Inland, Northeastern (New England) vs. Southern
主要觀點（再次提出）	...we can get a sense of the social and historical conditions of the time.
例子	Story of Massachusetts quilt, ending with "... an accurate indication of when the quilt was created."
講座結論	All right, then.
話題轉移到作業	As a reminder, for today you should have already read the first two chapters...
轉移到下次講課	In my next lecture, I'll turn to... As we move through the history of quilts, you'll see first-hand...

通過瞭解一篇學術講座的思路以及各種能幫助猜測下文的詞語，考生就可以更加放鬆，更好地記筆記，可以更加全面地理解講座的中心大意和例證。

• Exercise 2 （解答請見 P. 307）

Write a correct paraphrase for each of the following signal words and phrases.

ⓐ All during this course, we'll...

_____

ⓑ Our major focus will be...

_____

ⓒ As we move through the history of...

_____

▶ **模擬試題**（解答請見 P. 307）

Now listen to a lecture about FOLK ARTS.

 Track 003

★ **Keywords**

patchwork 拼布	quilting 縫被子

• Listening Questions

 Track 004

1. What is the main topic of the talk?
    A. Quilting techniques in ancient times.
    B. Diverse methods for mending quilts.
    C. The effect of war on women's handicrafts.
    D. Traditional quilts in colonial America.

2. Why does the professor mention an Egyptian pharaoh?
    A. To illustrate how ancient rulers influenced textile practices.
    B. To contrast the garment styles of royalty and commoners.
    C. To cite early evidence of a person wearing quilted cloth.
    D. To show how quality quilting was valued as much as ivory.

3. Listen again to part of the lecture. Then answer the question.

 Please listen to Track 004 for this part of the question.

Why does the professor say this:

 Please listen to Track 004 for this part of the question.

    A. To indicate that all artwork is grounded in a specific context.
    B. To show the contrast between New England quilts and art quilts.
    C. To encourage students to read novels set in colonial times.
    D. To remind us that the creators of quilts often kept diaries.

4. According to the professor, how do quilting practices in New England and the South compare?

   Choose 2 answers.
   A. Unlike southern quilters, New England quilters made designs involving political events.
   B. In contrast with New England, quilts in the South contained more refined patterns in stitching.
   C. Quilters in the South did not use paper patterns to create their pieces.
   D. Both New England and southern quilters eventually created Crazy Quilts.

5. How were historians able to determine the date of the quilt in Massachusetts?
   A. They discovered an advertisement for quilts in an old newspaper.
   B. They found a publication date on a piece of newspaper embedded in the quilt.
   C. They confirmed the quilt's woolen fabric was the same as fabric from Europe.
   D. They compared the quilt's pattern to old patterns on a computer database.

6. How does the professor organize the material she presents?
   A. In chronological order.
   B. In ascending importance.
   C. By types of textile.
   D. By monetary value.

3 Life Sciences, Topic 1: Zoology
生命科學常考主題 1：動物學

本章內容以生命科學範疇的動物學為知識背景。動物學詞彙中很多是描述動物身體的，如 muscle（肌肉）和 bone（骨骼）。有關動物的文章常包含對動物生理過程的說明，其中可能含有諸如 respiratory system（呼吸系統）stimulate the nerves（刺激神經）等片語。請注意本章中出現的語塊，並記住它們。

·············· 動物學：閱讀 ··············

▶ 熟悉分類型文章的目的和結構

在很多新托福考試閱讀文章和聽力講座中，寫文章的人和說話者會將具體內容或觀點進行分類，這類文章叫做分類型文章。分類在學術性文章中很常見，在生命科學領域的文章中尤其普遍。本章下文的閱讀文章（關於群居昆蟲的智慧）和學術講座（關於海洋生命）中都對不同種類的動物進行了分類。考生如果能夠熟悉分類型文章的寫作目的和結構，那麼在理解文章內容和答題目時一定會感到輕鬆很多。

在分類型篇章的寫作中，作者會集中討論一個主要話題，如一種生物物種，並給出諸多例子。有時文章也會對動物身體器官和生理過程進行描述。在這類篇章後，很多題目都會以該種動物所具有的特點為考查內容。

另一種情況是，作者會通過將一種動物與另一種相似物種進行比較來劃分其種類。這類篇章後的考題通常會詢問不同動物之間的相似或不同之處。

下面來看看本章下文這篇關於群居昆蟲的智慧的文章，作者是如果利用舉例來說明分類體系的。

所在段落	動物	特徵
1	many animals in general →	cannot solve problems
2	honey bees (many social insects), certain vertebrates (some fish, some birds, one aquatic mammal) →	can solve problems
3	**main example of passage:** termites (social insects) → (like human miners)	can make complicated structures

所在段落	動物	特徵
4	some termites (e.g., compass termites of Australia) →	can make complicated structures aboveground
5	some termites in ground → some termites in trees → some termites with giant nests →	can build tunnels eat the trees they live in can make complicated air management systems
6	African termite species →	example of termites who make complicated air management systems
7	African termite species →	continuation of example; they each make pillars that curve and connect in an arch

　　我們可以看到，作者在文中例舉了一些群居昆蟲，先是蜜蜂，而後是各種白蟻，用來說明它們解決問題的能力和智慧。作者劃分的兩大類別（第一段）是沒有解決問題能力的動物和具有解決問題能力的動物。後面的段落則包含更加精確的分類以及對各種具有解決問題能力的群居昆蟲（白蟻）的具體說明。

● 遇到分類型篇章時，可使用下列策略：

策略 1 遇到不認識的名詞或術語時不要驚慌。

　　如 the African species *Macrotermes bellicosus*，這種學名沒人要你背，這些詞多半只是為説明某一概念或類別所舉的例子，而概念或類別在文中都會有明確説明。

策略 2 在文章中尋找表示舉例的句型。

　　如：With animals such as honeybees... 和 Consider, for example, the African species... 這些句型能幫助你在文中快速定位，找到文章的主要論點和重要例證。

• Exercise 1 （解答請見 P. 311）

Write a correct paraphrase for each of the following sentences taken from zoology classification texts.

ⓐ In his classification system, Linnaeus grouped plants and animals based on their structural likeness.

_____

_____

ⓑ The discovery that crows could create primitive tools astounded scientists, who had thought that the ability to fashion tools was unique to primates.

_____

_____

ⓒ Gray squirrels and the larger fox squirrels rarely occur together in large numbers because one species usually dominates to the apparent exclusion of the other.

_____

_____

▶ 模擬試題（解答請見 P. 311）

Intelligence of Social Insects

★ **Keywords**

termite 白蟻	buttress 扶壁；支撐物

(1) Even among vertebrates, animals reared without the opportunity to learn about their natural homes are able to select appropriate material and build a species-specific structure. Yet much of the construction conducted by animals is organized as a strict series of task-oriented steps; the animals stop one task and begin another. There is little to suggest much in the way of cognitive powers.

(2) With animals such as honey bees, however, we see a genuine flexibility, an apparent ability to modify or choose from innate behaviors to solve problems. This problem-solving ability seems to require an animal to understand the goal of an undertaking; only then can the animal determine what must be done; for example, to complete or modify its home. Goal-oriented flexibility is probably what allows bees to plan routes or design ad hoc solutions to novel challenges. Indeed it seems to inform the nest-building behavior of many social insects, as well as certain vertebrates, ranging from a few remarkable species of fish to a number of birds and at least one aquatic mammal.

(3) The nests of certain termites are so massive that elaborate provisions must be made for ventilation, cooling and defense against predators. Termite colonies comprise hundreds of thousands or tens of millions of individuals who remove so much earth that, like human miners, they must reinforce the walls of the tunnels. Instead of timber, these insects use mud mixed with their own secretions, a compound that dries to the consistency of cement.

(4) Some termite species construct enormous aboveground structures. The air-cooling chimneys of certain rainforest species look like multi-roofed pagodas, the layering providing protection from tropical rains. The mounds of the compass termites of Australia, up to five meters high, are oriented toward the sun: facing east and west, the broad sides catch the early and late warmth and avoid the heat of the noonday sun. No matter what their configuration is above ground, all termite nests begin underground, with an initial excavation for the chamber for the king and queen. These are quickly followed by increasing numbers of underground breeding chambers for the eggs and still other chambers for storing food.

(5) When termite nests are built in the ground, the worker termites must tunnel up 50 meters to forage for vegetation and seeds. Some termite species build their nests in trees, which they then slowly consume. As the termite nest grows in size, so do the problems of ventilation and cooling. The carbon dioxide and heat generated by the larvae and adults must be dissipated if the colony is not to suffocate. The insects' solutions to such air-management problems suggest a sophisticated degree of planning.

(6) Consider, for example, the African species *Macrotermes bellicosus*, whose nests in the Ivory Coast were studied in detail by Martin Luescher. The nests are built so that air may circulate: ■ 1 Cool air is drawn up from a cellar into an attic by the heat produced by the biological processes of the termites and by the fungi that they grow. ■ 2 The air is then directed to the ten or so buttresses that project from the base to near the top of the above-ground portion of the nest. ■ 3 Through holes in these interconnecting buttresses, warm carbon dioxide-rich air from the attic is exchanged with the cooler, oxygen-rich air outside. ■ 4

(7) The coordinated building of these elaborate structures by millions of blind insects exceeds the limits of the usual behavioral programming. No two nests are ever alike. It is possible that the individual termites have some functional picture of the end result and, from a menu of inborn behavioral programs, choose the most appropriate one to bring the work closer to the goal. The same mechanism probably controls the construction of the many nest support structures. In total darkness, individuals begin the two pillars of an arch at the appropriate distance. Then, by moving back and forth from each of the growing pillars to the other, the two termites each start the curves at the same height, in the correct direction and at the appropriate angle.

• Reading Questions

1. The word "reared" in the first paragraph is closest in meaning to _____.
   A. observed
   B. assembled
   C. brought up
   D. held back

2. According to the first paragraph, how do most animals know how to build their homes?
   A. Their parents teach them the techniques.
   B. They repetitively practice each task.
   C. The young imitate the motions of their peers.
   D. They instinctively know the specific steps.

3. The word "innate" in Paragraph 2 is closest in meaning to _____.
   A. intersecting
   B. inborn
   C. appropriate
   D. complex

4. In Paragraph 3, why does the author mention "human miners" ?
   A. To show that termite and human excavations involve similar efforts.
   B. To emphasize that more termite workers are required than human workers.
   C. To compare the type of soil being dug out by termites and humans.
   D. To explain that individual termites must work harder than humans.

5. The word "they" in Paragraph 3 refers to _____.
   A. colonies
   B. millions
   C. individuals
   D. miners

6. According to Paragraph 4, what architectural design feature does a termite colony use to shield against rain?
   A. Thatched roofs.
   B. Staggered chimneys.
   C. East-side exposure.
   D. Sculpted mounds.

7. Each of the following statements about termite nests is true EXCEPT _____.
   A. the original portion of the nest is situated under the Earth
   B. the nest is initially occupied by the king and queen termites
   C. termites often build nests a great distance away from their food supply
   D. termites instinctively know not to eat the tree where their nest is housed

8. The word "dissipated" in Paragraph 5 is closest in meaning to _____.
   A. inhaled
   B. wasted
   C. driven away
   D. cooled down

9. What can we infer about the African species of termites mentioned in Paragraph 6?
   A. They are larger than species on other continents.
   B. They prefer terrains with high altitudes for their habitats.
   C. They often die when the temperature outside changes.
   D. They constitute a relatively intelligent species of termites.

10. According to Paragraph 7, what is the most likely reason that the nests of the African termites are unlike one another?

A. The blind termites have trouble with unexpected events.

B. The king and queen communicate unique orders.

C. The termites adjust the structure to an individual goal.

D. The support structures are not always coordinated.

11. Look at the four squares [■] that indicate where the following sentence could be added to the passage.

This cooler air descends through the buttresses, until the air enters the cellar, where it is cooled even further by contact with the subsoil.

Where would the sentence best fit?

■ 1

■ 2

■ 3

■ 4

12. Complete the chart below about two types of animal cognition mentioned in the passage. Choose five of the seven answer choices and match these behaviors to the type of animal cognition with which they are associated. **This question is worth 3 points.**

Types of animal cognition	Behaviors
Able to solve problems when building a shelter	• • •
Not able to solve problems when building a shelter	• •

Answer Choices

1. Carries out a sequence of task-oriented steps

2. Revises actions in the middle of a plan

3. Trains workers to perform tasks

4. Ends one innate task and begins the next

5. Evaluates progress toward goal

6. Visualizes an end target

7. Plans architecture based on queen's instructions

關鍵語塊

- **rear** 撫養；養育
- **cognitive** 認知的
- **ad hoc** 臨時的，無準備的
- **novel** 新奇的
- **inform the behavior of...** 形成……的行為
- **social insect** 群居昆蟲
- **ventilation** 通風，換氣
- **defense against** 抵禦
- **human miner** 人類的礦工
- **secretion** 分泌物
- **consistency** 濃度，密度
- **cement** 水泥
- **mound** 土墩
- **compass termite** 指南針白蟻
- **excavation** 挖掘
- **chamber** 室，房間
- **breeding chamber** 孵化室
- **forage for** （動物）覓食
- **larva (pl . larvae)** 幼蟲
- **suffocate** 使窒息
- **sophisticated** 複雜的
- **suggest a sophisticated degree of planning** 展現出規劃的複雜程度
- **cellar** 地下室
- **attic** 閣樓
- **a menu of** 一批，一堆
- **arch** 拱
- **pillar** 柱子；支柱

·········· **動物學：聽力** ··········

▶主旨大意題的選項陷阱和答題策略

學術講座題目中幾乎都會有一道主旨大意題，考查考生能否識別講座的重點。這類題目有一定難度。首先，有些考生簡單地以為講座中涉及的第一個話題就是主旨內容，但實際並非如此。講座開始時教授有可能會先談論上週講座的主題或是某項需完成的課外作業。

主旨大意題的另一陷阱在於選項的措詞，有可能過於寬泛或者過於具體。在很多情況下，主旨大意題的干擾項概括得過於籠統；而有時干擾項只概括了某個用作例子或比較方法的觀點或內容，以偏概全。以下文的模擬試題為例：

• LISTENING SAMPLE 1

1. What is the lecture mainly about?

A. The anatomy of animals without backbones.

B. The unique behavior of squids.

C. The wide range of octopus habitats.

D. The biological functioning of the octopus.

托福總監評析

　　仔細觀察四個選項，看哪些陳述是概括性的，哪些是具體的。將主要觀點與例證進行比較。這些都是聽教授的講座時需要注意的內容。當然，在新托福考試中，聽講座之前考生是看不到試題的，因此考生必須訓練自己在聽講座時能夠做到注意力高度集中，並有策略地去猜測講座的主要內容。

● 判斷學術類講座的主旨大意時，可使用以下策略：

策略 1 注意聽導言。

　　每個講座一開始，「講解員」會介紹講座涉及的領域，例如：Now listen to part of a lecture in a zoology class. 這是預測講座主題的第一條線索。聽到這樣的介紹後，就要想像自己是在上一堂動物學課。

策略 2 利用自己對該主題的認識以及從本書中學到的學術領域知識，逐步縮小講座主題的預測範圍。

策略 3 特別注意聽教授的開場白。

　　在教授講座的開始部分，認真聽關於 today's lecture 的明確預告，注意聽有沒有下面的語句：

Today we're going to look **at**...
Last week we did... I want to **focus now on a particular**...
I want to **take a minute** to talk about...
OK, **in this class** I want to talk about...
What we're going to focus on **this morning** is...

　　當聽到上面的某個語句或類似表述（特別是含有 today 或 in this class 等表示時間的表達）時，記錄下該主題，這很可能就是後面主旨大意題的答案。要注意，教授在講座後面可能會說 Now I want to mention...，不要被迷惑，教授這樣說只是為了提出一個次要觀點。

策略 4 要做好應對變化的心理準備。

　　並非所有的教授都用同樣的方式呈現講座內容。有些教授呈現資訊時採用直線式，步驟分明；有些教授可能會以奇聞軼事作為開場白；還有些教授會不斷從一個主題跳到另一主題，通篇對比分析。另外，喜歡使用歸納法教學的教授絕不會直接預告所要講到的事實、理論或因果關係，他們甚至會以提問的形式開始講座。

• LISTENING SAMPLE 2

Professor: We've been talking for a while about amphibians such as frogs and their dependence on water throughout their lives. Today we're going to look at how reptiles such as turtles and snakes. How do the reptiles reproduce in environments with very little moisture? What are the differences between the eggs of amphibians and reptiles? Many of you may have seen frog eggs floating in a pond. But have you ever seen snake eggs out in nature; for example, lying in the sand, unprotected?

從以上開場白中，你能猜出教授的講座主題是什麼嗎？

北美的教授（尤其是科學相關科系的教授）經常使用歸納法。為了引出某個自然現象的發生規律，他們會先讓學生們觀察自然。如果你對教授使用歸納法教學這種方式不習慣的話，就要多練習聽這類講座。瞭解了教授呈現講座內容的各種方式，你才能更有效地預測題目，從而提高得分。

策略 5 在聽取主旨大意時，不要過於注意錄音中學生的提問。

很多時候，學生的提問只是要求教授澄清某個細節問題，而非講座的主旨。

策略 6 注意聽總結歸納性的資訊。

雖然考試中的講座內容只是一個節選的片段，但其中也會包含某些總結性的內容。例如，注意教授是否使用了如下說法：

And that **in a nutshell** is...
In conclusion,...
To recap,...
Summing up, ...
As we have seen,...

以上這些句型後面的內容常常就是講座的主旨大意。

策略 7 多練習記筆記。

多練習記筆記，並要養成一邊聽錄音，一邊積極思考講座主題的習慣。要不停地問自己這樣一個問題：中心思想是什麼？要區分主要觀點和次要觀點。要記錄細節，就算不完全明白某些句子的意思也要記。記得要使用符號來標明各觀點之間的關係，例如：主要觀點→次要觀點；原理／論點→論據。聽錄音時記的筆記，無論多麼支離破碎，都會在答題時變得無比寶貴。這是因為當你看到題目時，其中的措詞會幫助你回想你記下的隻言片語與題目之間的聯繫。此外，當你快速回顧所做的詳細記錄時，或許還能通過資訊綜合出主旨大意。

請記住，為了做對主旨大意題，你需要做好筆記，並努力把握主題大意，切勿「只見樹木不見林」。

► **模擬試題**（解答請見 P. 312）

Now listen to a lecture about ZOOLOGY. **Track 005**

★ **Keywords**

| squid 烏賊 | octopus 章魚 | tentacle （章魚等的）觸鬚，觸角 |

• **Listening Questions** **Track 006**

1. What is the lecture mainly about?
   A. The anatomy of animals without backbones.
   B. The unique behavior of squids.
   C. The wide range of octopus habitats.
   D. The biological functioning of the octopus.

2. What does the professor say about the word "tentacle"?
   A. He advises students to avoid using the term altogether.
   B. He thinks that "tentacle" is more accurate than "foot".
   C. It is not technically correct to use it to describe squids.
   D. It is often misused by people in everyday speech.

3. According to the professor, how are octopuses able to move quickly through the water?
   A. They ride underwater currents at great speeds.
   B. They shoot water out of an opening in their bodies.
   C. They make use of the small fins next to their mouths.
   D. They position their arms in a parallel arrangement.

4. Listen again to part of the talk. Then answer the question.

   Please listen to Track 006 for this part of the question.

   What is the professor's attitude toward the actions of the octopus described by the woman?
   A. He believes the actions are a matter of life and death.
   B. He agrees that the actions are quite humorous.
   C. He thinks scientists don't know enough about octopuses.
   D. He doubts that octopuses really lean on two arms.

5. The professor mentions various aspects of squids and octopuses. For each item below, indicate which characteristic is associated with which animal.

Place a ✓ mark in the correct box. **This question is worth 2 points.**

Characteristic	Squids	Octopuses	Both squids and octopuses
Retains a trace of hard shell or bone			
Use jet propulsion			
More developed than most animals without backbones			
Has multiple arms			

• Exercise 2　（解答請見 P. 315）

　　Play the audio again and take structured notes, making note of the key points and the examples. Draw lines linking related concepts. Circle the main idea. When you are finished, compare your notes to the sample notes. How could your notes have been arranged differently?

Social Sciences, Topic 1: Psychology
社會科學常考主題 1：心理學

　　本章內容以社會科學範疇的心理學為知識背景。心理學有很多子領域，如實驗心理學、社會心理學、發展心理學等。心理學領域中的單字和片語多與心理功能有關，如 cognition（認知）和 brain functioning（大腦機能）。與心理學有關的語塊常表示諸如 stereotype（刻板印象）、prejudice（偏見）以及 positive reinforcement（正面幫助）等社會行為。請注意本章中出現的語塊，並記住它們。

······心理學：閱讀······

▶細節資訊題的考查範圍和答題策略

　　每篇新托福閱讀文章後通常會有三道細節資訊題，有時多達六道。由於一篇閱讀文章最多會有七個段落，所以有些段落的內容不會用作細節資訊題的出題點。多數情況下，出題者為減輕考生負擔，會在考題中說明相關資訊所在的段落，如：According to Paragraph 3... 此外，在電腦螢幕上，考生還會在相關段落的旁邊看到一個箭頭（⇨）。然而，並非所有考題中都會明確指出段落，考生有時需要在文中尋找線索進行資訊定位，或者需要快速略讀全文。

　　細節資訊題涉及文章裡的任何資訊，包括人物、事物、地點和時間等。細節資訊題通常都可以在文中直接找出答案。

　　以本章模擬試題為例：

• READING SAMPLE 1

4. D.W. Fiske is important because he was able to do which of the following?

　　A. Identify 22 trait variables affecting personality.

　　B. Suggest a relatively simple factor structure.

　　C. Show that many more personality types existed.

　　D. Create a unique process for conducting self-ratings.

托福總監評析

　　題幹中沒有指明具體段落，所以必須從整篇文章中尋找答案。題幹中有人名，所以只需在文中尋找該人名即可。快速瀏覽文章，發現第四段提到了 Fiske 這個人物。先排除選項 A，因為文中提到 Fiske 的貢獻只是提出了五大分類，而不是發現了 22 個變數。選項 C 和 D 都不正確，可排除。B 項 Suggest a relatively simple factor structure 是對原文 constructed simplified descriptions from them 的換句話說，因此正確。

● **READING SAMPLE 2**

10. According to Paragraph 7, the author is in agreement with which of the following statements about the Big Five?

A. They do not provide a complete theory.

B. They do not describe regular behavior.

C. They focus too much on individual people.

D. They are not valuable for scientists.

托福總監評析

　　根據題幹直接找到第七段。根據第二、三句：More than one critic has argued that it does not provide a complete theory of personality. I don't disagree. 可知，選項 A 為正確答案。注意體會「雙重否定」的用法。I don't disagree 與 I agree 意思是一樣的喔！不過，最好也瀏覽一下其他選項，再重新讀該段內容，確定其他選項都不正確。

● **現在我們一起回顧一下解答細節資訊題時使用的策略：**

策略 1 多花些時間看題目，確保完全理解了題目的含義。

策略 2 利用題目中的段落提示或其他線索定位。

策略 3 快速掃讀定位到的段落。

策略 4 先排除明顯錯誤的選項。

策略 5 在文章中尋找其餘選項的同義說法。

策略 6 選出與文章內容最符合的選項。

▶重點技能：掃讀

掃讀的目的是快速尋找具體線索或資訊。在掃讀時，需要跳過不重要的語塊內容。

有些考生可能會問：怎樣才能做到最有效的掃讀？好的閱讀技巧需要多方面的技能，詞彙和文法上也要有一定的基礎。不過，像略讀和掃讀這樣的技能，也可以通過集中訓練得以提高。

● 提高掃讀技能的策略：

策略 1 快速從上至下瀏覽頁面，尋找單字和語塊（在電腦上，可以利用下頁鍵）。

策略 2 尋找結構性線索，如一系列數位或字母。

策略 3 尋找幫助判斷項目數的信號詞，如 first、second 或 next。

策略 4 尋找帶有大寫字母的首字母縮寫以及人名、地名和其他事物名稱等。

策略 5 尋找加粗、突出顯示、斜體或用不同字體顯示的單字。

策略 6 要大膽地跳過某些詞語，甚至整個句子。

策略 7 不要害怕從下到上地「倒著讀」。

▶模擬試題（解答請見 P. 316）

Dimensions in Personality

★ Keywords

> trait 品質；特徵

(1) The concept of personality has over the years been scrutinized from a variety of theoretical perspectives, and at various levels of abstraction or breadth. Each of these approaches has contributed to our understanding of individual differences in behavior and experience. Psychologists created new scales with overlapping terminology for personality traits; for instance, "active", "aggressive" and "extroverted". Consequently, the number of traits, as well as the number of measurement scales designed to assess these traits, increased to such an extent that confusion resulted. Clinical psychologists and other practitioners were faced with a bewildering array of personality scales from which to choose. What made matters worse was that scales with the same name often measured concepts that were not the same, and scales with different names often measured concepts that were quite similar. ■ 1

(2) What personality psychologists needed was an overarching descriptive model, or taxonomy, of its subject matter. ■ 2 It was hoped that such a framework would permit researchers to work with a few specified domains of personality characteristics, rather

than examining separately the thousands of particular traits that make human beings individual and unique. ■ 3 On a practical level, a generally accepted taxonomy could greatly facilitate the professional communication of empirical findings by offering a standard vocabulary, or nomenclature. ■ 4

(3) Some pioneering studies and a relatively short list of personality trait variables stimulated a new wave of researchers to carry out factor analyses, in which they explored factor structure in personality. These social scientists wanted to understand how individual variables fit into cohesive groupings; each grouping of trait variables would then constitute a personality "factor", and "dimension". The resulting factor structure would presumably be robust enough to encompass the universe of all personality types. Thus several investigators went on to create what are now known as the "Big Five" dimensions of personality.

(4) Most notably, D.W. Fiske took 22 trait variables that were part of an individual's personality and constructed simplified descriptions from them. The key factor structures that Fiske derived from self-ratings and ratings by peers and working psychologists led to the formation of the "Big Five". To refine these factor structures, other scientists subsequently analyzed data in eight diverse samples of people, ranging from air force personnel with no more than a high-school education to first-year graduate students, all of whom had been rated by supervisors, teachers or experienced clinicians in settings as diverse as military training courses and university housing. In their analyses, the scientists found five relatively strong and recurrent component factors. The factors were initially labeled:

(5) (I) Extroversion (talkative, assertive, energetic)
(II) Agreeableness (good-natured, cooperative, trustful)
(III) Conscientiousness (orderly, responsible, dependable)
(IV) Emotional Stability (calm, not neurotic or easily upset)
(V) Culture (intellectual, independent-minded)

(6) These component factors underwent some changes in labeling, but eventually became known as the "Big Five"—a title chosen not to reflect the intrinsic greatness of the factors but to emphasize that each of these factor categories is extremely broad. Moreover, the structure does not imply that personality differences can be reduced to a mere five traits. Rather, it tells us that each of these five dimensions represents the broadest level of abstraction, covering a large number of distinct, more specific personality characteristics.

(7) Like any scientific model, the Big Five taxonomy has its limitations. More than one critic has argued that it does not provide a complete theory of personality. I don't disagree. The Big Five was never intended as a comprehensive personality theory; it was developed to account for the structural relations among personality traits. Thus, like most structural models it is more descriptive than explanatory. In other words, the taxonomy gives us insights into regularities in behavior, rather than a clear understanding of

underlying developmental processes that can only be inferred. It focuses on personality trait variables rather than on individual human beings, or even types of human beings. Nonetheless, the Big Five taxonomy of trait terms provides a conceptual foundation that helps researchers and practitioners delve into these theoretical issues.

• Reading Questions

1. The word "scrutinized" in Paragraph 1 is closest in meaning to _____.
   A. criticized
   B. manipulated
   C. challenged
   D. examined

2. In Paragraph 1, why does the author mention the words "active", "aggressive" and "extroverted"?
   A. To cite several terms that are similar in meaning.
   B. To demonstrate how personality is dynamic in nature.
   C. To clarify why psychologists felt the need to create new traits.
   D. To illustrate the terminology that should be used in the taxonomy.

3. All of the following are mentioned as problems with personality scales EXCEPT _____.
   A. researchers felt that some personality traits were left out of the scales
   B. descriptive terms referring to personality traits were often used inconsistently
   C. scales with similar names were used to assess diverse psychological concepts
   D. an extremely large number of personality traits were in existence

4. D.W. Fiske is important because he was able to do which of the following?
   A. Identify 22 trait variables affecting personality.
   B. Suggest a relatively simple factor structure.
   C. Show that many more personality types existed.
   D. Create a unique process for conducting self-ratings.

5. The word "peers" in Paragraph 4 is closest in meaning to _____.
   A. experts
   B. volunteers
   C. colleagues
   D. students

6. According to Paragraph 4, what did scientists discover when they looked at data from eight samples of people?
   A. They found the military had diverse personalities.
   B. They could build on the results of earlier findings.

C. They noticed that the traits were more refined.

D. They realized education was a critical factor in personality.

7. The phrase "account for" in Paragraph 7 is closest in meaning to _____.

A. calculate

B. balance

C. explain

D. combine

8. The phrase "delve into" in Paragraph 7 is closest in meaning to _____.

A. order

B. investigate

C. add onto

D. care about

9. Which of the sentences below best expresses the essential information in the highlighted sentence in the passage? Incorrect choices change the meaning in major ways or leave out important information.

Moreover, the structure does not imply that personality differences can be reduced to a mere five traits.

A. It is further possible that no more than five traits underlie the many different types of personality.

B. The lack of structure in the diverse personalities is not an indication that the sample size should be increased.

C. Personality differences are even greater than we originally thought, because the five trait structures are rather inaccurate.

D. One should not assume from the structure that there are only five personality traits.

10. According to Paragraph 7, the author is in agreement with which of the following statements about the Big Five?

A. They do not provide a complete theory.

B. They do not describe regular behavior.

C. They focus too much on individual people.

D. They are not valuable for scientists.

11. How does the author organize the ideas in the passage?

A. By defining a technical term, then giving examples of usage.

B. By introducing an abstract model, then showing how it has failed.

C. By outlining a problem, then giving a theoretical solution.

D. By describing a state-of-the-art technique, then tracing its history.

12. Look at the four squares [■] that indicate where the following sentence could be added to the passage.

   This proliferation of different measurement approaches and descriptive terminology also made it extremely difficult for researchers to interpret all the findings and to communicate clearly with one another.
   Where would the sentence best fit?
   ■ 1
   ■ 2
   ■ 3
   ■ 4

13. **Directions:** An introductory sentence for a brief summary of the passage is provided below. Complete the summary by selecting the THREE answer choices that express the most important ideas in the passage. Some answer choices do not belong in the summary because they express ideas that are not presented in the passage or are minor ideas in the passage.
   This question is worth 2 points.
   This passage traces the attempts of psychologists to better understand the major dimensions of human personality.

•
•
•

Answer Choices

1. Many professional terms describing personality are incorrect and thus need to be replaced.

2. Social scientists engaged in personality research were able to identify five separate factors.

3. The large number of personality scales has puzzled many practicing psychologists, who are not sure how each relates to the other.

4. Researchers in the field of personality have not been able to come to agreement on what extraversion is.

5. According to some personality psychologists, there are five types of human beings.

6. By creating a classification system with broad categories, researchers allowed practitioners a way to better communicate with one another.

• Exercise 1　（解答請見 P. 317）

Write a correct paraphrase for each of the following sentences.

ⓐ Each of these approaches has contributed to our understanding of individual differences in behavior and experience.

_____

_____

ⓑ The resulting factor structure would presumably be robust enough to encompass the universe of all personality types.

_____

_____

ⓒ Like any scientific model, the Big Five taxonomy has its limitations.

_____

_____

關鍵語塊

- **scrutinized** 仔細檢查；仔細觀察
- **theoretical perspective** 理論角度
- **level of abstraction** 抽象程度
- **breadth** 廣度，廣泛性
- **scale** 標準；等級
- **overlapping terminology** 含義相近的術語
- **personality trait** 性格特徵
- **measurement scale** 衡量標準
- **to such an extent that... resulted...** 如此……以致……
- **confusion** 混亂；混淆
- **clinical psychologist** 臨床心理學家
- **practitioner** 從業者，執業者
- **be faced with** 面對，面臨
- **bewildering array of** 紛亂排列，複雜排列
- **what made matters worse** 使問題更糟的是
- **overarching** 包羅萬象的
- **descriptive model** （理論）描述的模型
- **taxonomy** 分類體系
- **subject matter** 主題，主旨
- **on a practical level** 從實踐的角度
- **empirical finding** 實驗發現
- **nomenclature** 術語
- **pioneering study** 開拓性研究
- **variable** 可變因素；變數
- **factor** 因素；要素
- **factor analysis** 因素分析
- **factor structure** 因素結構
- **dimension** 因素；維度
- **robust** 穩固的，強大的
- **go on to do sth.** 繼續做某事
- **notably** 顯著地；特別地
- **derive from** 從……得出
- **self-rating** 自我衡量
- **peer** 同輩
- **working psychologist** 職業心理學家
- **refine** 改善，改良，完善
- **recurrent** 反覆出現的
- **component factor** 構成因素
- **extroversion** 外向
- **agreeableness** 隨和
- **intrinsic** 內在的，本質的
- **be developed to account for...** 為……做出解釋
- **underlying developmental process** 內在發展過程
- **...that can only be inferred** 只能被推斷出……
- **nonetheless** 然而，不過
- **conceptual foundation** 理論基礎
- **delve into** 鑽研，深入研究

·················· 心理學：聽力 ··················

▶重複聽力題的考點和答題策略

每 5～6 道新托福考試聽力考題中就會包含一道重複聽力題。學術講座中通常至少有一道此類題型，而對話題中有可能有兩道。

在重複聽力題中，對話的某個片段會為考生至少重放一遍。此類題型出現時，考生會在螢幕上看到一個耳機的圖示，不過錄音內容不會顯示在螢幕上。有時候，所選取的對話片段會重複播放兩次。

重複聽力題考查多種重要技能，包括推理能力和說話者的態度、立場等。有時 ETS 的出題者會用此類考題考查考生是否理解講話者的隱含意思或目的，而不只是語言的表面意思。

• LISTENING TIPS

重複聽力題有以下兩種出題形式：

Example 1:

N: Why does the professor say this:
[Replay]

Example 2:

N: Listen again to part of the lecture. Then answer the question.
[Replay]

N: What does the professor imply when she says this:
[Replay]

在第二個例子中，所要考的部分實際共重複播放了三次！這讓考生有充分的時間聽清楚錄音的內容和意思。

第一遍重播時，節選的句子一般不會超過六句。而第二遍重播時，節選的是第一遍重播裡的某句話。

以本章模擬試題為例：

• LISTENING SAMPLE

3. Listen again to part of the conversation. Then answer the question.

P: Now what do you think would be the most dominant need in humans? [pause] Yes?

S: Professor Smith, I think that we all need friendships—or, I guess one could call it "human love."

P: Well, Maslow would tell you that if you say what you need most is love, that means you're getting plenty to eat at the student cafeteria. Let me explain in another way. Another word for the "dominant" need is the most "basic" need.

What can be inferred about the professor when she says this:

P: Well, Maslow would tell you that if you say what you need most is love, that means you're getting plenty to eat at the student cafeteria.

A. She's teasing the student about the error he made.
B. She's disappointed in the student's lack of preparation.
C. She's implying the student needs to lose a few pounds.
D. She's telling the student to go back and read the text.

托福總監評析

　　第一次聽錄音片段時，要儘量聽懂大意並把握講話者的語氣。考題很有可能考查教授的態度，所以需要注意對方的語氣。在這個例子中，可以聽到教授笑了，這表示她的心情不錯，或是可能在開玩笑。如果認真聽，會注意到她接著說道：Let me explain in another way. 即使不能完全確定她談論的是什麼，至少應該能從這句話判斷她仍在做解釋，在耐心地為學生澄清一個問題。

　　接下來，當聽更短的錄音片段時，就要注意聽具體的措詞和準確的意思了。當聽到：Well, Maslow would tell you that if you say what you need most is love, that means... 時，就可以猜出教授是在用開玩笑的口吻來說明食物是比愛情更基本的一種需要。

　　根據第一遍聽錄音時對大意和語氣的把握，應先排除選項 B 和 D，因為教授的語氣是肯定的。如果第二遍聽錄音時注意到了具體詞的意思，那麼就會知道選項 C 是錯誤的，因為教授說過 Maslow would tell you... 而 Maslow 最不可能談到學生的體重，所以根據教授的語氣和話語，可以信心十足地選擇 A。

　　很多新托福考試的重複聽力題是以教授和學生之間的交流為出題點的，瞭解這一點很重要，所以當聽到學生提問時一定要做好筆記，更要留意對話雙方的語氣。

● **重複聽力題的答題策略：**

　　策略 1　一邊注意聽錄音內容，一般盡可能多地做筆記。

策略 2 注意講話者的情緒和態度。

重複聽力題多半會考你對講話者的感情和觀點的理解。注意非語言線索：錄音中有笑聲嗎？有尷尬的停頓嗎？

策略 3 注意描述性語言，如比喻和成語的運用。

托福常考到此類修辭手段，因為出題者會要求你能藉由上下文理解它們。此類考題的題幹通常為：What does the professor mean when he says...

策略 4 如果錄音中有學生的對話，要注意學生與教授的對話內容。

問自己：教授有耐心還是沒耐心？學生高興還是沮喪？如果理解了學生與教授對話時的情緒，就能更準確地猜出重複聽力題的答案。

策略 5 如果題目中錄音片段播放兩遍，聽第一遍時要注意把握大意和語氣，聽第二遍時則注意具體詞語的意思。

▶模擬試題（解答請見 P. 318）

Now listen to a lecture about PSYCHOLOGY.　　🎧 *Track 007*

★ **Keywords**

hierarchy 體制；體系	self-actualization 自我實現

• Listening Questions　　🎧 *Track 008*

1. What is the main topic of the lecture?
   A. What Maslow discovered about employee motivation.
   B. Why hierarchy is important in social groups.
   C. How human needs are acted upon in society.
   D. Why human beings need recognition for their work.

2. Why does the professor mention wild animals?
   A. To give one example of a threat to security.
   B. To show that predators also need to seek shelter.
   C. To dispute the hypothesis about violent societies.
   D. To persuade us to give up our fear of the unknown.

3. Listen again to part of the talk. Then answer the question.

 Please listen to Track 008 for this part of the question.

What can be inferred about the professor when she says this:

 Please listen to Track 008 for this part of the question.

A. She's teasing the student about the error he made.
B. She's disappointed in the student's lack of preparation.
C. She's implying the student needs to lose a few pounds.
D. She's telling the student to go back and read the text.

4. Listen again to part of the talk. Then answer the question.

 Please listen to Track 008 for this part of the question.

Why does the professor say this:

 Please listen to Track 008 for this part of the question.

A. To contrast the motivation in selling with buying.
B. To probe psychological urges in younger people.
C. To hypothesize about the impact of instant rewards.
D. To illustrate how a need for self-esteem was filled.

5. The professor mentions various examples of Maslow's needs. For each item below, indicate which example is associated with which type of need.
   Place a ✓ mark in the correct box. **This question is worth 2 points.**

	Type of Need		
	Security	Love	Esteem
Insurance			
Strength			
Spouse			
Familiar things			

• Exercise 2 （解答請見 P. 320）

Write down at least one answer for the following repeated listening question based on the psychology lecture.

N: Listen again to part of the conversation. Then answer the question.

P: One way of classifying human motivation is to talk about motivation in the context of needs. Now, let me ask all of you: Do you think that human beings need the same things that other animals need?

N: Why does the professor say this:

P: Do you think that human beings need the same things that other animals need?

_____

_____

⑤ Physical Sciences, Topic 2: Geology and Seismology
物理科學常考主題 2：地質學和地震學

　　本章內容以物理科學範疇的地質學和地震學為知識背景。這兩類學科相比較而言，地質學在新托福考試中出現的機率高一些。地質學領域的單字和片語大致分為兩大類：物理地質學詞彙，如 sedimentary rock（沉積岩）和 clay mineral（黏土礦物）；歷史地質學詞彙，如 fossil record（化石記錄）和 Big Bang Theory（大爆炸理論）。請注意本章中出現的語塊類型，並盡可能記住它們。

··········地質學和地震學：閱讀··········

▶重點技能：熟悉表示對比關係的「信號詞」

　　由於新托福考試學術類閱讀文章一般篇幅較長，包含大量資訊，要想快速讀完是頗具挑戰性的。更糟糕的是，有些考生在答題時，對某些部分的意思並不理解，最後只能胡亂猜測一個答案。

　　解決這個問題的一種途徑是熟悉某些影響意思的重要詞語如何使用，如 moreover 和 however 等。如同路標能幫助旅行者在陌生的地方找到路徑一樣，這種「信號詞」可以讓讀者（或聽者）理解文章（或所聽內容）的意思。通過掌握這些「信號詞」的意思和用法，考生可以加快閱讀速度，更能理解作者的意思，並提高答題的正確率。

　　考生應多記一記這一類的「信號詞」。不同類型的信號詞在使用時形式各異，其功能、文法和用法都各不相同。

　　本章將帶你掌握表示對比關係的信號詞。為什麼呢？因為新托福考試閱讀文章大多為「比較對比型」，即説明某些事物或觀點的相同之處和不同之處。通常題目中，只會拿出兩種事物或觀點來進行比較和對比。

　　下面來看看模擬試題的文章中表示對比關係的信號詞：

Although _____, there is no _____.（第一段）
Yet until we can _____, we will be helpless to _____.（第一段）
The first approach is more _____, but it _____.（第六段）
If a network of stations is used with _____, the benefit is _____. However, _____（第七段）
Conversely, _____ provides more rapid data, but in doing so _____.（第七段）

　　在上述每一個例子中，作者都是在將兩種概念進行對比。下面是一些表示對比關係的信號詞，應盡可能地記住。

表示對比關係的信號詞

But...	Compared to	Then again
However	Compared with	Until now
And yet...	Although / Though...	Regardless of the fact that...
Yet...	Even	Regardless
Instead	Conversely	Meanwhile
By way of contrast	On the other hand	At the same time
In contrast to	Alternatively	As opposed to
In marked contrast to	Although this may be true	Unlike...
Whereas...	Still	Neither... nor
Nevertheless	Despite	This is distinguished from
On the contrary	In spite of the fact that...	This is a departure from
By comparison	Despite the fact that...	One way is...; another way is...

• **Exercise 1** （解答請見 P. 321）

Write a correct paraphrase for each of the following contrastive sentences:

ⓐ The on-site warning approach is less reliable, but it is very fast.

_____

_____

ⓑ Unlike the Mercalli intensity scale, the Richter measurement scale has no defined "highest reading" for the magnitude of earthquake.

_____

_____

ⓒ When molten rock moves slowly up to the surface of the Earth, it cools slowly and forms minerals with large crystals. Volcanic rock, by contrast, cools quickly and thus has smaller crystals.

_____

_____

▶ 模擬試題（解答請見 P. 321）

Early Warning Systems

★ **Keywords**

telemetry 遙感勘測

(1) Although most earthquakes occur at the tectonic plate boundaries of the Earth's crust, there is no reliable method of accurately predicting the time, place and magnitude of

a quake. Most current research is thus concerned with minimizing the risk associated with earthquakes through assessing the seismic hazard and the vulnerability of an area. Seismology can provide key information on the structure of Earth, as well as the physics of earthquakes. Yet until we understand nucleation—the earliest phase of an earthquake— and the complex rupture process that follows, we will be helpless to accurately predict earthquakes.

(2) ■ 1 Seismometers have been in existence for more than1,800 years; a seismograph that represents earthquake ground motion as a continuous function of time was invented in the 19th century. ■ 2 More recently, geophysicists have exploited new technologies to lessen earthquake damage by using "real-time" seismology, in which seismic data are collected and analyzed very quickly after a seismic event.

(3) ■ 3 Scientists are handicapped by the fact that in most cases the timescale involved in realtime seismology runs from minutes to hours. ■ 4 By the time the data is released, the earthquake is over, and the information can be used only for post-earthquake emergency responses, field work planning, and public information. However, if information about an earthquake were accessible in a matter of seconds to minutes, it could inform the early warning process, and the severity of the shake could be communicated before the tremors began at the site. This is a theoretical possibility because of the difference between the speed of the seismic waves (3-7 kilometers per second) and the fast speed of radio waves (close to the speed of light).

(4) Although technologies which enable very rapid processing of seismic data have proved far more difficult to build than those designed for post-earthquake information systems, some progress has been made. Monitoring systems were built in California in the 1960s, allowing limited transmission of data to regional sites. By the late 80s, the basic technology was fully developed for remote transmission and rapid processing of seismic data. These systems allow earthquake parameters to be broadcast to users only a few minutes after an earthquake occurs. Concurrent with the evolution of seismic instruments, telemetry, computers and data storage technologies, seismic networks have been constructed in many countries. Most of these networks have some type of rapid notification system. In the context of rapid post-earthquake notification, it is fair to say that a global infrastructure for "real-time" seismology is already in place.

(5) Two approaches to earthquake early warnings are possible: (a) regional warnings and (b) onsite warnings. In the regional warning approach, traditional seismological methods are used to locate an earthquake's epicenter, determine its magnitude and estimate the ground motion at other sites. In an on-site warning approach, the beginning of the ground motion (mainly P waves) observed at a site is used to predict the ensuing ground motion (mainly S and surface waves, which are the most destructive) at the same site. No attempt is made to locate the epicenter of the quake and estimate the magnitude.

(6) The first approach is more reliable, but it takes a longer time and cannot be used for sites at short distances. In contrast, the second approach is less reliable, but it is very fast and can provide early warning to short-distance sites, where warning is most needed. This latter approach requires that the geophysicist quickly measure the nature of the progressing earthquake or the ground motions at an early stage of the ground rupture.

(7) If a network of stations is used with the regional warning method, the benefit is relatively detailed and reliable information about impending ground motion, such as waveform and quake duration. However, the regional warning approach takes additional time to process the data and encompasses a fairly large "blind zone" an area for which a warning cannot be received in time. Conversely, the on-site method provides more rapid data, but in doing so reduces the radius of the blind zone, despite the fact that data are limited to relatively simple parameters. At present, then, it appears that a hybrid use of both regional and on-site warning approaches may be the best way to build an early warning system.

• Reading Questions

1. In Paragraph 1, what does the author say about the nucleation of an earthquake?
   A. It occurs directly after the ground ruptures.
   B. It is the initiating process of an earthquake.
   C. It determines the ultimate size of an earthquake.
   D. It is a result of magnetic waves penetrating the crust.

2. According to Paragraph 2, what was the importance of the seismograph created during the 1800s?
   A. It was not really a significant advancement beyond earlier seismometers.
   B. It allowed scientists to watch the ongoing process of seismic waves.
   C. It was able to measure the permanent ruptures created by seismic waves.
   D. It provided immediate data about vibrations to residents after an earthquake.

3. The word "exploited" in Paragraph 2 is closest in meaning to _____.
   A. pioneered
   B. misunderstood
   C. sought out
   D. took advantage of

4. The word "it" in Paragraph 3 refers to _____.
   A. information
   B. earthquake
   C. matter
   D. process

5. In Paragraph 3, why does the author mention "the speed of light"?
    A. To show how quickly earthquake vibrations can move.
    B. To explain that radio waves travel more rapidly than light does.
    C. To emphasize that seismic theory is still in an early stage.
    D. To demonstrate that radio waves are powerful tools.

6. Which of the sentences below best expresses the essential information in the highlighted sentence in the passage? Incorrect choices change the meaning in major ways or leave out important information.
    Although technologies which enable very rapid processing of seismic data have proved far more difficult to build than those designed for post-earthquake information systems, some progress has been made.
    A. Unfortunately, the hardware infrastructure for high-speed computer systems has been impossible to develop in seismic applications.
    B. Even if we could quickly process the real-time data coming from earthquakes, we still would have trouble predicting their occurrence.
    C. Scientists have made a few breakthroughs in real-time seismic data processing in spite of some unexpected challenges.
    D. Systems created to analyze the results of earthquake tremors are not as easy to implement as originally expected; moreover, some researchers are not up-to-date.

7. The phrase "concurrent with" in Paragraph 4 is closest in meaning to _____.
    A. simultaneous to
    B. similar to
    C. following after
    D. depending upon

8. According to Paragraph 5, in what way are P waves detected?
    A. By checking the source of surface waves.
    B. By monitoring the earliest ground motion.
    C. Through regional warning systems.
    D. Through conventional seismic analyses.

9. The word "duration" in Paragraph 7 is closest in meaning to _____.
    A. probability
    B. direction
    C. length
    D. intensity

10. It can be inferred from the passage that the author believes which of the following about the earthquake infrastructure?
    A. It can quickly determine precise quake movement, but only in remote areas.
    B. It does not have stations for transmitting data in some parts of California.

C. It is in relatively good shape, but many building structures cannot stand up to a large earthquake.

D. It is lacking in its ability to make advanced notification of earthquake time and locations.

11. Look at the four squares [■] that indicate where the following sentence could be added to the passage.

Nevertheless, instrumentation does enable us to track earthquakes once they begin.

Where would the sentence best fit?

■ 1

■ 2

■ 3

■ 4

12. **Directions:** Complete the chart below by matching five of the seven answer choices with the type of warning system that they exemplify. **This question is worth 3 points.**

Type of early warning system	Characteristics of system
Regional	• • •
On-site	• •

Answer Choices

1. Transmission range contains a big section that gets no signal

2. Better choice for site areas that are not too far away

3. Measures ground motions at the beginning of the rupture

4. Superior system for forecasting aftershocks at other locations

5. Provides more accurate information on distant ground motion

6. More accurate for calculating the probability of seismic hazard

7. Preferable for tracking the earthquake epicenter

關鍵語塊

- earthquake 地震
- plate boundary 板塊邊界
- seismology 地震學
- magnitude 地震規模
- minimize the risk 將風險降到最低
- seismic hazard 地震災害
- vulnerability 弱點；脆弱性
- nucleation 成核；核化
- rupture 斷裂，破裂
- seismometer 地震檢波器
- seismograph 地震儀；測震儀
- function of time
  隨著時間的變化而變化
- real-time 即時
- timescale 時間表；時段；時標
- emergency response
  緊急回應，應急處理
- accessible 易得到的

- early warning 早期預警
- a matter of (seconds) 大約（幾秒鐘）
- inform 對……有影響
- severity 強度；嚴重性
- tremor 震動
- earthquake parameter 地震參數
- broadcast 廣播；使廣為人知
- concurrent with 與……同時
- in place 到位
- epicenter 震央
- network of (seismic) station
  （地震）網路
- impending 即將來臨的
- waveform 波形
- radius 半徑
- blind zone 盲點
- hybrid 混合物

················· 地質學和地震學：聽力 ·················

▶關聯內容題的考點和答題策略

新托福考試聽力部分也有表格題，其中大多為關聯內容題。該類題目不僅僅只要求考生關注一個觀點，而且要把講座中各部分的觀點聯繫起來。完成表格時考生需要將資訊和觀點進行綜合分析，運用各種推理能力，如推測、舉一反三的能力等。有些題目會給出一些歷史事件或科學步驟，要求將它們按時間順序歸類或排序。

此類題型最簡單的考查方式是二選一，如詢問：Is rock... an example of a sedimentary rock? 考生只需在 Yes 或 No 欄下打勾即可。如下所示：

N: What sex is each of these individuals? Place a ✓ mark in the correct box.

	Male	Female
Abraham Lincoln	✓	
Diana, Princess of Wales		✓
Yao Ming	✓	

　　也有較為複雜的表格題，要求考生對聽力內容進行更深入的「挖掘」和思考。例如，考生可能需要識別引起某一歷史問題或科學發現的原因。這類較複雜的表格題分值為 2 分。整個聽力部分中一般有一道關聯內容題，且通常為最後一題。

　　這類題目看起來很難，但實際並非如此。由於此類題目總是以表格形式出現，就有了一個相對系統性的答題框架。考生不必組織語言填寫，只需識別觀點之間的關係。當然，有時需要把事件或觀點進行分類，也可能需要給它們排序，有時也可能需要根據講座中提出的原則就事件或觀點做出推測。

　　對於大多數考生來說，這個考題的難度在於如何準確地收集填表所需的資訊。要想破解一個棋局，沒有掌握全部或大部分「棋子」是不行的。收集事實和各種細節資訊時，需要好好記筆記，並保持積極思考的狀態。再次重申，考生只有聽完全部錄音之後才能看到實際考題，因此無法事先知道需要哪些「棋子」，這表示考生必須記錄下所有自己感覺重要的資訊，以備使用。

● 關聯內容題的答題策略：

策略 1 記筆記時預測哪些內容有可能成為關聯內容題的出題點。

策略 2 注意聽與「種類」有關的信號詞。

有不少信號詞表示分類或比較。本章前面已經列出一部分，下面再列出一些。
表示特徵的信號詞

One instance of this is...	A typical characteristic of... is...
One special role that... plays is...	What is noteworthy about... is...
One defining feature of... is...	What is unusual here is...
One aspect of... is...	Particularly interesting is...
One characteristic of... is...	Especially important is..., which...
One quality of... is...	Notably,
One issue related to this is...	Remarkably,
One function of this is...	We see this in... with...
One attribute related to this...	These features help to...

策略 3 利用做其他題目時獲得的資訊解答關聯內容題。

　　考生很可能會在筆記中發現幾個之前沒有聽明白的詞彙語塊，冷靜地思考一下，這些資訊也許在做關聯內容題時用得上。

▶**模擬試題**（解答請見 P. 322）

Now listen to a lecture about GEOLOGY.   *Track 009*

★ **Keywords**

the Earth's plate 地球板塊	plate boundaries 板塊邊界（即板塊交界地方）
ridge 山脊	

• **Listening Questions**   *Track 010*

1. What is the main topic of the lecture?
   A. Several unusual land features in ocean basins.
   B. Why a mountain chain wraps around the Earth.
   C. How the Earth's plates join together.
   D. Ocean plates that collide with continents.

2. The professor describes an underwater mountain ridge in the Atlantic Ocean. Why does the professor mention this ridge?
   A. To demonstrate the frequent volcanic activity under the ocean.
   B. To contrast the features of this ridge to features of ridges elsewhere in the world.
   C. To explain how divergent plate boundaries function.
   D. To emphasize that this land feature is part of a larger system.

3. Listen again to part of the lecture. Then answer the question.

    Please listen to Track 010 for this part of the question.

   What can be inferred about the professor when she says this:

    Please listen to Track 010 for this part of the question.

   A. She wants students to be attentive to the detailed appearance of landforms.
   B. She hopes the class can develop a strong sense of scientific inquiry.
   C. She's providing hints about the questions that will be on the test.
   D. She doubts there is anyone who doesn't know the Earth has multiple layers.

4. What does the professor say about the Earth's plates?
   A. They are stiff and rigid.
   B. They have several layers at their edges.
   C. Ocean plates are thicker than continental ones.
   D. Scientists now agree the Earth has seven plates.

5. The professor gives examples of converging plate boundaries on the Earth's surface. Indicate for each example below what type of boundary is represented.

Place a ✓ mark in the correct box. **This question is worth 2 points.**

	Converging Boundary Types		
	Continent-Continent	Ocean-Continent	Ocean-Ocean
Forms deep trenches and island chains			
Forms high mountains such as the Himalayas			
Forms explosive volcanoes when plate partly melts			

• **Exercise 2** （解答請見 P. 325）

Below is another connecting content chart, based on the lecture on Geology. Listen to the lecture one more time and fill in the chart.

The professor describes the characteristics of two plate boundary types, converging and diverging. Indicate for each example below what type of boundary is represented.

Place a ✓ mark in the correct box.

	Converging	Diverging
New crust is formed from melted rock		
Plates bump into one another		
Ocean plate may slip under land plate		

6 Humanities and the Arts, Topic 2: Literature
人文藝術常考主題 2：文學

　　本章內容以人文藝術範疇的文學為知識背景。文學包括創造性寫作，即詩歌、短篇故事、小說、戲劇，甚至散文等。文學領域中用到的一些詞和片語可能與文學作品有關，例如 heroic character（主角性格）和 satirical comedy（諷刺喜劇）。也可能會描述作者的獨特寫作方式，如 earthy style（樸實的風格）和 narrator's point of view（敘述者的觀點）。請注意本章中出現的語塊，並記住它們。

············· 文學：閱讀 ·············

▶推論題的特點和答題策略

　　推論題是新托福閱讀部分較難的題型。略讀、掃讀和換句話說等技能可能還不夠，還必須利用邏輯推理的能力。

　　有時考生要確定一些事實，並根據這些事實得出一個合理的結論；有時可能需要考生評論文章的作者，並描述其觀點；另外，還可能需要考生根據文中介紹的規則或原則推斷發生了什麼事情。

　　儘管並非每一篇文章都有一道推論題，但在閱讀部分，考生可能至少會碰到兩道推論題。最簡單的推論題會引用某個段落的某個具體概念或片語，如：Which of the following can be inferred from Paragraph 4 about Liberia?

• READING TIPS

　　推論題還會以很多其他方式出現：

The author of the passage **implies** that...

Langston Hughes **probably** wrote "The Negro[1] Speaks of Rivers" in which of the following places?

When was "The Negro Speaks of Rivers" was **most likely** written?

1 注：negro 這個詞含有貶義，「黑人」一般用 African American。

• READING SAMPLE

　　為了更好地掌握做推論題的技巧，右頁來看看本章 Langston Hughes and Africa 文章後面的推論題：

11. What can we infer about Countee Cullen from the passage?

A. He wrote in a more refined literary style than Hughes did.

B. He never had an opportunity to visit the African continent.

C. He shared Hughes's need to reconcile himself with Africa.

D. He was often engaged in heated literary debates with Hughes.

托福總監評析

　　要選出正確答案，必須合乎邏輯地剔除其他三個不正確的選項。例如，選項 A 中的 more refined literary style 會迷惑一部分考生，這些考生沒有意識到 Cullen 在詩中提出了一個雄辯的問題。文中沒有提到 Cullen 的旅行，因此無法推斷選項 B 正確。選項 D 是錯誤的，但是可能會騙到誤認為 Cullen 是「被迫對抗」Hughes 的考生。選項 C 正確，因為 Cullen 和 Hughes 都有矛盾心理，必須調整自己，融入非洲。

● **推論題的答題策略：**

策略 1 如果題目涉及具體段落，略讀該段落，看看能得出什麼合理結論。

策略 2 如果題目沒有涉及具體段落，掃讀全文，直到找到需要的詞或資訊。

策略 3 對於因果關係的推論題（如：**What probably caused Hughes to write "African Morning"**），掃讀全文，尋找有用的因素或事件。

策略 4 對於時序關係的推論題（如：**When did Hughes most likely write " African Morning"**），掃讀全文，尋找日期（月、年）和 **before**、**during** 和 **after** 之類的時間片語。

策略 5 如果題幹中有不明白的詞、名稱或概念，掃讀全文，找到不明白的詞、名稱或概念，利用上下文推測。

策略 6 多數推論題的錯誤選項在邏輯上是不通的；而有些錯誤選項說法正確，但文章中沒有論及。

● **Exercise 1**　（解答請見 P. 326）

Write a correct paraphrase for each of the following sentences.

ⓐ By saying that Elizabeth Bishop was a "poet's poet", the author of the passage implies that her poetry was appreciated only by poets.

_____

_____

ⓑ What can we infer about the lives of prosperous 19th-century women from the novel *Daisy Miller*?

_____

_____

ⓒ Because John Updike was able to write poems on technical subjects such as neutrinos and planets, it can be concluded that he was scientifically literate.

_____

_____

▶ **模擬試題**（解答請見 P. 326）

Langston Hughes and Africa

(1) In 1923, the twenty-one-year-old African-American poet Langston Hughes set sail for Africa. Several years before, Hughes had penned the poem "The Negro Speaks of Rivers", in which he traced the continuous river of black history beginning with the Euphrates, moving on to the Congo and the Nile and ending with the "muddy bosom" of the Mississippi River. The poem utilized the rivers as a metaphor to present a view, almost a timeline in miniature, of the African-American experience. Determined to see the source of these rivers firsthand, he signed on as a steward on a steamer bound from New York to West Africa. As the ship was about to clear land, he went below deck and collected the crate of his most-prized books he had brought along. Then, alone on the stern, he tossed the books into the sea one by one, symbolically discarding his book-bound Western identity.

(2) One would be hard-pressed to find any individual whose work better captured the spirit of the 1920s: the yearning for authentic experience; the contempt for civilized hypocrisy; the value of the African-American soul. Hughes fully partook of the growing fascination with Africa. In an era in which people with black skin were viewed as containing a depth and vitality lacking in whites, it was inevitable that Africa would exert a pull on many people. Africa was the taproot, the primal source of this energy. Evidence of this enthusiasm was everywhere, from the mounting of major exhibitions of African art in European and American museums, to the beats of West African drums, to the career of Josephine Baker, whose bare-breasted dance made her the toast of Paris.

(3) In many ways Hughes's voyage, indeed his entire career, demonstrates Africa's persistent hold on the African-American imagination at the time. But what ultimately distinguished Hughes from most of his contemporaries was not his ideas about Africa but the fact that he actually went there. In years to come, Hughes would offer diverse accounts of his African journey, at times rendering the continent in glowing, romantic terms; at others, conveying disillusionment. One short story in particular, "African Morning", expressed Hughes's conflicted thoughts about how an individual could search for a sense of identity and home. For Hughes, traveling to Africa was supposed to resolve this problem. Hughes had crossed

the ocean, thrown his books overboard and written poems about palm trees and the bright sun; yet in spite of all of these experiences, he remained a stranger, unable to bridge the great historical chasm that separated him from Africa. It was an unsettling predicament.

(4) Since the late 18th century, successive waves of African Americans have traveled to Africa, retracing the passage of millions of African captives. Over the years, travelers have ranged from freed slaves and missionaries to poets and Peace Corps volunteers. Some settled permanently in Africa, while others, like Hughes, passed through only fleetingly. In the 19th century the most common destination was Liberia, an African-American colony established on the Windward Coast of West Africa in 1820, but over the years travelers have found their way to every corner of the African continent. Hundreds of memoirs have been published, reflecting upon these passages.

(5) ■ 1 The travels illuminate the chronicles of African-American history in seemingly contradictory ways; they highlight Africa's abiding presence in Black American political, intellectual and imaginative life. ■ 2 By the time of the Civil War, only about one percent of the black population in the United States was African-born, and direct memories of the continent were fading; yet African Americans continued to look to Africa, seeking clues to the meaning of their own identity and history. ■ 3 Langston Hughes imagined an idyllic homeland, whereas supporters of Marcus Garvey's back-to-Africa movement saw the continent as the future seat of a great black empire. ■ 4 Whatever the individual motives and aspirations, African Americans were compelled to confront the question that Hughes's contemporary Countee Cullen posed so eloquently in his poem "Heritage", where he asks: "What is Africa to me?"

• **Reading Questions**

1. The passage says that the poem "The Negro Speaks of Rivers" was important for what reason?
   A. It conveyed how river culture led to fertile economies.
   B. It showed how much time Hughes spent traveling.
   C. It talked about the spiritual experiences influencing jazz.
   D. It captured the cultural history of the black race.

2. According to Paragraph 1, why did Hughes toss books into the ocean?
   A. He no longer wished to be a celebrated author.
   B. He was angry at the way the ship staff was treated.
   C. He wanted to show he was cutting off his past.
   D. He had decided to read African-language publications.

3. The phrase "yearning for" in Paragraph 2 is closest in meaning to _____.
   A. snapshots of
   B. acquisition of

C. admiration for

D. longing for

4. In Paragraph 3, the author mentions the short story "African Morning" in order to illustrate what concept?

A. A quest for self-understanding.

B. An artist's feeling of growing optimism.

C. Sunrise on an African journey.

D. Social development in Africa.

5. The words "an unsettling" in Paragraph 3 are closest in meaning to _____.

A. a novel

B. a troubling

C. a cruel

D. a valuable

6. The passage mentions all of the following as evidence of wide public interest in Africa EXCEPT _____.

A. gallery exhibits

B. exotic dancing

C. jungle wildlife

D. beating of drums

7. According to the passage, what is true about most African Americans who went to Africa in the 1800s?

A. They were driven by political ideals.

B. They sought to publish their journals.

C. They stayed a very short time.

D. They chose to travel to Liberia.

8. The word "they" in Paragraph 5 refers to _____.

A. travels

B. chronicles

C. ways

D. African Americans

9. The word "fading" in Paragraph 5 is closest in meaning to _____.

A. being recorded

B. becoming fainter

C. altering

D. resurfacing

10. The word "compelled" in Paragraph 5 is closest in meaning to _____.

    A. obliged

    B. invited

    C. planning

    D. reluctant

11. What can we infer about Countee Cullen from the passage?

    A. He wrote in a more refined literary style than Hughes did.

    B. He never had an opportunity to visit the African continent.

    C. He shared Hughes's need to reconcile himself with Africa.

    D. He was often engaged in heated literary debates with Hughes.

12. Look at the four squares [■] that indicate where the following sentence could be added to the passage.

Still others, traveling at different times, cast Africa as a "Dark Continent" crying out for Christian civilization, a headquarters for global anti-colonial revolution, or a field of opportunity for entrepreneurs.

Where would the sentence best fit?

    ■ 1

    ■ 2

    ■ 3

    ■ 4

13. **Directions:** An introductory sentence for a brief summary of the passage is provided below. Complete the summary by selecting the THREE answer choices that express the most important ideas in the passage. Some answer choices do not belong in the summary because they express ideas that are not presented in the passage or are minor ideas in the passage.

This question is worth 2 points.

This passage discusses poet Langston Hughes's complex relationship with the continent of Africa.

-
-
-

Answer Choices

1　In his poetry, Hughes wrote harshly of the Mississippi River because it reminded him of bitter experiences.

2　Like many people in the 1920s, Hughes collected African sculpture and other art objects.

3 Hughes was absorbed by the origins of African American history and sought to trace his roots.

4 Despite his desire to feel at home in Africa, Hughes found it difficult to assimilate.

5 Many liberated slaves decided to sail from the United States to Africa, where they created a new life.

6 Many African Americans, including poets and memoirs writers, wrote about Africa in an effort to better understand their cultural identity.

關鍵語塊

- **pen** 寫下
- **muddy bosom** 渾濁的胸膛
- **steward** （船上的）服務員
- **steamer** 汽船
- **bound from... to...** 行程從……到……
- **about to clear land** 即將登陸
- **below deck** 甲板下面
- **stern** 船尾
- **book-bound** 侷限於書本的
- **be hard-pressed to do sth.** 難以做某事
- **civilized hypocrisy** 文明社會中的虛偽
- **fully partook of** 完全沉浸於
- **exert a pull on sb** 對某人有吸引力
- **taproot** （植物的）主根；根基
- **primal source** 最初源頭
- **toast of Paris** 巴黎炙手可熱的人
- **rendering sth. in glowing terms** 積極地描述某物
- **conflicted thought** 矛盾的想法

- **sense of identity** 身份認同感
- **throw sth. overboard** 將某物扔向船外
- **bridge the chasm** 跨越鴻溝
- **unsettling predicament** 令人困擾的問題
- **successive waves of...** ……的連續發生
- **retrace** 追溯
- **have ranged from... to...** 範圍從……到……
- **fleetingly** 短暫地
- **reflect upon sth.** 仔細想某物
- **illuminate** 闡明
- **chronicle** 編年史，大事年表
- **abiding presence** 永久存在
- **idyllic** 田園詩般的
- **Garvey's "back to Africa" movement** 加維的「回到非洲」運動
- **pose** 提出

文學：聽力

▶聽力推論題的答題策略

　　新托福考試的聽力部分至少有三道推論題。值得慶幸的是，聽力中的推論題通常比閱讀中的推論題要容易些，因為出題者知道考生不能返回去仔細核對細節資訊。然而，即使簡單一些，考生仍然需要做好有關主旨和例證的筆記，因為推論題肯定會涉及簡單的推理。

• LISTENING TIPS

聽力部分的推論題題幹形式有：

What can we **infer about** crime fiction?

What does the professor **imply about** Edgar Allen Poe?

What can we **conclude about** the police forces in the 19th century?

What will the man **probably** do next?（一般出現在對話題中）

What does the professor **imply when he says this:** (replay...)

• LISTENING SAMPLE

以本章模擬試題中的題為例：

4. Listen again to part of the lecture. Then answer the question.

P: In literature, the classic detective is often a talented amateur, a man who is perhaps rather eccentric in his personality, and who has unusual hobbies, such as growing roses or playing the violin. When I say "he," by the way, I should add that in the 19th century, virtually all fictional detectives were men, and this was the case up until the 1970s, when women detectives became popular.

What does the professor mean when he says this:

P: When I say "he", by the way, I should add that in the 19th century, virtually all fictional detectives were men, and this was the case up until the 1970s, when women detectives became popular.

A. He doesn't want the class to think he is using the pronoun "he" to stand for both men and women.

B. He is indicating that most women would have had difficulties solving crimes in the 19th century.

C. He thinks that the women detectives portrayed in stories written before 1970 were not very credible.

D. He is implying that in the beginning years there were fewer amateur men detectives than amateur women detectives.

托福總監評析

　　從教授說 by the way 可知後面是附帶提到的內容，他在提供補充性見解，從而增強對講座主旨的論證，選項中只有 A 的說法和錄音內容相符。

　　這種推論題考的是說話者的言外之意。這類題目不僅考查考生是否理解詞語表面的意思，更考查考生是否理解說話者的言外之意或潛在動機。

　　你可能已經注意到，回答聽力的推論題所需的策略與回答關聯內容題所用的策略類似。主要區別在於關聯內容題需要從講座中多處資訊源中得出答案，而且涉及範圍更廣的觀點。

● 聽力推論題的答題策略：

策略 1 聽講座時，當聽到有因果關係、時序關係（某個特定事件前後的事件）的事情，或教授（或學生）覺得某人做某事的原因時，要特別留心，盡可能做好筆記。

策略 2 絕大多數正確答案都會含有試題甚至錄音材料中所用詞的換句話說。

策略 3 在重聽推論題時，要注意說話者話語的表層含義和潛在含義。利用說話者的語氣尋找線索。

策略 4 如果一時理解不了遇到的推論題，不要慌張，利用常識推理做出最佳猜測。一定要冷靜，以便應對下一道題。

▶ **模擬試題**（解答請見 P. 327）

Now listen to a lecture about LITERATURE.　　 *Track 011*

★ **Keywords**

> detective fiction 偵探小說
> *The Moonstone* 《月光石》（被譽為「第一部英國偵探小說」）

• **Listening Questions**　　 *Track 012*

1. What aspect of fiction does the professor mainly discuss?
   A. The role of the scientific method.
   B. The origin of the detective genre.
   C. Edgar Allen Poe's use of suspense.
   D. Narrative techniques in short stories.

2. What does the professor say about the development of science in the 19th century? **Choose 2 answers.**

   A. It influenced how the author handled the character of the detective.

   B. It caused readers to become less tolerant of eccentric personalities.

   C. It was responsible for reducing the number of crimes in society.

   D. It brought with it new technologies for crime-solving.

3. According to the professor, what is the purpose of the police officer character in classical detective conventions?

   A. To demonstrate his superior deductive powers.

   B. To draw a contrast with eccentric detective.

   C. To highlight the official's range of crime-solving tools.

   D. To create suspense in the unfolding of the plot.

4. Listen again to part of the lecture. Then answer the question.

 Please listen to Track 012 for this part of the question.

What does the professor mean when he says this:

 Please listen to Track 012 for this part of the question.

   A. He doesn't want the class to think he is using the pronoun "he" to stand for both men and women.

   B. He is indicating that most women would have had difficulties solving crimes in the 19th century.

   C. He thinks that the women detectives portrayed in stories written before 1970 were not very credible.

   D. He is implying that in the beginning years there were fewer amateur men detectives than amateur women detectives.

5. Why does the professor mention *The Moonstone*?

   A. To exemplify an outstanding detective short story.

   B. To demonstrate an example of an amateur detective.

   C. To introduce the first novel in detective fiction.

   D. To illustrate the realism used in detective plots.

6. Listen again to part of the lecture. Then answer the question.

 Please listen to Track 012 for this part of the question.

What does the professor mean when he says this:

 Please listen to Track 012 for this part of the question.

A. He wants to spend some time on this issue now.

B. He wants him to know that he covered that topic already.

C. He is telling the student not to interrupt his lecture.

D. He is proposing that they revisit the issue at a later time.

• Exercise 2 　（解答請見 P. 330）

For each of the inference statements in the box below, find the supporting fact in the lecture about detective fiction. The first one is done for you.

Inference	Supporting Fact
1. In the 19th century, urban areas probably had more crime than rural areas did.	The professor says that in the early 19th century, police forces became more systematic, partly to handle an increase in crime in cities.
2. It can be assumed that, among *The Moonstone* characters, there is an ineffective police officer who has trouble solving crimes.	
3. Based on the professor's remarks, we can infer he thinks the Sherlock Holmes stories show innovation, and aren't just "copies."	

7 Life Sciences, Topic 2: Ecology
生命科學常考主題 2：生態學

　　本章內容以生命科學範疇的生態學為知識背景。生態學是生物學的一個分支，關注生物與其環境之間的關係。生態學中用到的一些單字或片語常涉及動物之間的相互關係，如 carnivore（肉食性動物）和 prey（被獵者）。其他與生態學相關的語塊可能會涉及植物，如 pollination（授粉）和 symbiosis（共棲）。也有一些詞彙會涉及廣泛的生態系統，如 natural habitat（自然棲息處），population density（種群密度）和 biodiversity（生物多樣性）。請注意本章中出現的語塊，並記住它們。

⋯⋯⋯⋯⋯生態學：閱讀⋯⋯⋯⋯⋯

▶重點技能：如何處理陌生的專業術語

　　新托福考試閱讀部分有四篇文章，每篇考查一個不同的學術領域。對於絕大多數考生來說，這表示至少有一或兩篇文章的相關主題不在考生熟悉的知識範圍之內。例如，如果考生的專業是人文科學，就可能不熟悉生命科學和物理科學領域的知識。廣泛地閱讀各種學術主題的書籍肯定會大有幫助，尤其是用英語閱讀，這可以作為一條備考策略。但是，無論你的閱讀量有多大，到了真正考試的那一刻，必然還是會遇到你不認識的專業詞彙、片語和概念。這表示你需要有很好的策略來處理考試中碰到的陌生詞彙和片語。

● 碰到陌生的專業術語時，可以採用以下策略：

策略 1 從上下文尋找有關情景或學術主題的線索。

策略 2 利用已知詞彙推測陌生詞彙的意思。

　　比如，如果看到 host plant 這一片語，因為你認識單字 host（主人）和 plant（植物），所以應該能夠猜出 host plant 在生態學語境中大概是指「寄主植物」。那麼當看到這樣的句子：The host plant provides a habitat to the parasite and is the source of all required nutrients. 即使你不知道單字 parasite 的意思，也可以猜出其意思。在植物生態學中，寄主植物肯定是為「寄生物」或「寄生植物」提供 habitat，是其營養的來源。

策略 3 當一個概念介紹完後，尋找分句中的注釋，以及「隱藏」在文章中的定義。

以本章下文的《動物環境》為例：

Sponges and other non-mobile marine animals have a larval stage, a developmental stage which makes movement possible. 分句 a developmental stage which makes movement possible 是術語 larval stage 的注釋。那麼，即使我們對 larval 的詞意還不是很清楚，但知道它大概指海洋動物的某個成長階段。除此之外，作者在另一句（Carried by tidal and other currents, the larvae carry out the business of dispersing the species.）中提到了 larvae，從句中可以看出，larvae 似乎是一種能游動的小生物，是名詞。而 larval 修飾 stage，是形容詞！這樣，根據這些上下文的線索可以確定 larval 和 larvae 的意思。確定這兩個詞的意思非常重要，因為作者頻繁提到 larvae（幼蟲）和 larval stages（幼蟲階段）。凡是反覆出現的詞，考到的可能性就高一些。

策略 4 尋找段落中的「重複資訊」，注意作者使用了哪些其他詞來表示相同的事物。

尋找重複資訊與上面提到的尋找「注釋」的策略非常類似。在學術文章中，作者會頻繁地「插入」重複資訊，或「重述」，以幫助讀者瞭解新的事實和概念。考生可以利用這些重複資訊來猜測生詞的意思。以本章下文的《動物環境》為例：

• READING SMAPLE

The buoyancy of sea water reduces the animals' need for a skeleton. It is therefore not surprising that the largest animals without backbones—for example, giant squids—are marine. Additionally, the body tissue of marine invertebrates typically has an osmotic pressure that is equal to sea water.

托福總監評析

在這段摘錄中，有幾個詞我們可能不認識，如 buoyancy（浮力），squids（魷魚）和 invertebrates（無脊椎動物）。通讀這些句子可知，作者在談論能在海水中生存的大型無脊椎動物。第二句提到無脊椎動物，破折號之後舉例說明，squids 是一種無脊椎動物，marine invertebrates 是沒有脊椎的海洋生物。看完這些句子，我們可能仍然不太確定 buoyancy 的意思，但是有望根據其他知識（在海水中漂浮比在淡水中漂浮要容易些）來進行猜測。假設 buoyancy（浮力）與漂浮有關，在下段中便能得到證實。切記，獲得高分的考生是那些能夠利用這種重複資訊的人。

策略 5 文章中最專業的詞可能不會考。

例如：Wastes are commonly excreted as urea or uric acid, which are less toxic and require less water for removal than ammonia does. 這個句子中的專業詞彙 urea、uric acid 和 ammonia 較為生僻。除非是生物學家，否則母語國家的人也可能不熟悉這些詞。其實，出題者知道這一點，他們很可能不會直接考這些詞意。我們的任務就是大致理解這些詞，清楚文章的主題。如果我們保持冷靜，重點關注文章中的要點和示例，這些生僻的專業詞彙不會影響我們的發揮。

策略 6 充分利用電腦螢幕上出現的示意圖和圖表。

有了這些示意圖輔助，你應該能夠猜出很多專業詞彙和概念的意思。

• Exercise 1 （解答請見 P. 331）

Read the following short passage containing several technical terms. Then use the above strategies to guess the meaning of the three underlined words. Write down your answers.

When tree branches are continually bent in one direction by prevailing winds, they become "wind trained" and hold their position permanently. Moreover, new growth can be so desiccated on the side of a tree facing the wind that it is killed before it can develop. The threat of desiccation is present for the two main types of trees, conifer and broad-leafed, because wind removes moisture from leaf surfaces whether they are needle-shaped or wide and flat.

ⓐ _____

ⓑ _____

ⓒ _____

▶ 模擬試題（解答請見 P. 331）

Animal Environments

★ **Keyword**

osmotic pressure 滲透壓

(1) All animals must solve the same problems of existence—procurement of food and oxygen, maintenance of water and salt balance, removal of wastes and perpetuation of the species. The design of an animal's body is related to four factors: (a) the type of environment—marine, fresh water or terrestrial (land-living)—in which the animal lives; (b) the size of the animal; (c) how the animal lives; and (d) the limitations of the animal's genetic composition.

(2) The three major types of environment—salt water, fresh water, and land—are markedly different in the way they influence an animal's biological functioning.

(3) The marine environment is generally the most stable. Wave action, tides and ocean currents produce a continual mixing of sea water, ensuring an environment in which the concentration of dissolved gases and salts fluctuates relatively little. The buoyancy of sea water reduces the animals' need for a skeleton. It is therefore not surprising that the largest animals without backbones—for example, giant squids—are marine. Additionally, the body tissue of marine invertebrates typically has an osmotic pressure that is equal to sea water. That means it is relatively simple for these animals to maintain a balance between water and salt.

(4) Moreover, the buoyancy and uniformity of sea water provide an ideal medium for animal reproduction. Eggs in sea water can be shed and fertilized, enabling marine species to develop as floating embryos with little danger of becoming dried out, having salt imbalance or of being swept away by rapid currents into less favorable environments. Sponges and other non-mobile marine animals have a larval stage, a developmental stage which makes movement possible. Carried by tidal and other currents, the larvae carry out the business of dispersing the species.

(5) Fresh water is a much less constant environment than sea water. ■ 1 Streams vary greatly in cloudiness, velocity and volume, not only along their course but also as a result of droughts or heavy rains. ■ 2 In large lakes, the environment changes radically with increasing depth. ■ 3 Like salt water, fresh water allows organisms to float and aids in support. ■ 4 The low salt concentration of fresh water, however, makes it difficult to maintain a water and salt balance. Because the body of the animal contains a higher osmotic concentration than that of the external environment, water has a tendency to diffuse inward. The animal thus has the problem of getting rid of excess water. As a consequence, freshwater animals usually have some mechanism for pumping water out of their bodies while holding onto the salt.

(6) In general, the eggs of fresh water animals are either retained by the parent or attached to the bottom of the stream or lake, rather than being free floating, as is often the case with marine animals. In addition, larval stages are usually absent, because floating eggs and free-swimming larvae would be too easily swept away by seasonal currents. Because freshwater eggs develop directly into adults without an intermediate larval stage that feeds, the eggs typically contain considerable amounts of yolk for nourishment. Wastes of aquatic animals, both marine and freshwater, are usually excreted as ammonia. Ammonia is very soluble and toxic and requires considerable water for its removal; however, because there is no danger of water loss in aquatic animals, the excretion of ammonia presents no difficulty.

(7) Land animals live in the harshest environment. The supporting buoyancy of water is absent. Most critical, however, is the problem of water loss by evaporation, a primary factor in the evolution of many adaptations for life on land. The outer covering of land animals presents a better barrier between the internal and the external environments than that of aquatic animals. Nonetheless, respiratory surfaces must be moist and are usually located in the interior of the body, thereby reducing the possibility of them drying out. Wastes are commonly excreted as urea or uric acid, which are less toxic and require less water for removal than ammonia does. Fertilization must be internal; the eggs are usually enclosed in a protective envelope or deposited in a moist environment. Development in land animals is direct, except in insects, which have multiple stages of development. The eggs of most land animals are endowed with large amounts of yolk. Species that are not well adapted to dry conditions are either nocturnal or restricted to moist habitats.

• **Reading Questions**

1. The word "perpetuation" in Paragraph 1 is closest in meaning to _____.
   A. adaptation
   B. continuation
   C. supremacy
   D. enhancement

2. The word "markedly" in Paragraph 2 is closest in meaning to _____.
   A. physically
   B. strangely
   C. distinctly
   D. functionally

3. According to Paragraph 3, animals can be supported in marine environments because of _____.
   A. ocean buoyancy
   B. wave action
   C. mixed gases
   D. osmotic pressure

4. The word "shed" in Paragraph 4 is closest in meaning to _____.
   A. hatched
   B. seen
   C. looked after
   D. cast off

5. In Paragraph 4, the author mentions sponges to illustrate which of the following points?
   A. Stationary species run less of a risk of being damaged by violent currents.
   B. Species that normally cannot swim are able to move when in a larval form.
   C. Marine species that automatically take in water can regulate salt balance.
   D. Species which are not able to move bear more eggs than mobile species.

6. The word "that" in Paragraph 5 refers to _____.
   A. body
   B. animal
   C. concentration
   D. environment

7. According to Paragraph 5, what must a fresh water animal do to deal with the flow of water from the external environment?
   A. Find a way to periodically recycle the water and the salt.
   B. Dilute the salt concentration by flushing water through the body.

C. Limit the intake of water by controlling the internal levels of salt.

D. Retain the salt and expel the surplus quantities of water.

8. In Paragraph 6, the author says that which of the following has caused larvae to be relatively uncommon in fresh water animals?

A. Species with free-floating larvae tend to be consumed by free-swimming animals.

B. Unattached larvae risk being washed away by sudden changes in water flow.

C. The abundance of yolk in freshwater eggs has caused larval species to die off.

D. Larval-stage freshwater animals are less able to process waste toxins such as ammonia.

9. The word "soluble" in Paragraph 6 is closest in meaning to _____.

A. dissolvable

B. transferable

C. concentrated

D. widespread

10. Which of the sentences below best expresses the essential information in the highlighted sentence in the passage? Incorrect choices change the meaning in major ways or leave out important information.

Nonetheless, respiratory surfaces must be moist and are usually located in the interior of the body, thereby reducing the possibility of them drying out.

A. In spite of moist respiratory surfaces and their internal position, the body can sometimes become dry.

B. None of the respiratory surfaces have to be moist because of their interior location, which can help regulate dryness.

C. A few of the respiratory surfaces must be somewhat moist; these are typically internal structures, which seldom become too dry.

D. Even still, the extent of drying is limited by virtue of moist respiratory surfaces that are tucked inside the body.

11. Look at the four squares [■] that indicate where the following sentence could be added to the passage.

Similarly, small ponds fluctuate in cloudiness and water volume, but they also fluctuate in oxygen content.

Where would the sentence best fit?

■ 1

■ 2

■ 3

■ 4

12. Directions: Complete the chart below about animal environments. Choose five of the seven answer choices and match them to the type of environment with which they are associated.

This question is worth 3 points.

Marine environment	• •
Fresh water environment	• •
Land environment	•

Answer Choices

1. Best conditions for separating the animal's insides from the outside environment

2. Ideal surroundings for organisms with complex genetic make-up

3. Eggs of the organism are often anchored to something

4. Cloudiness favorable for reproduction when predators are present

5. Living conditions are most favorable for large animals without spines

6. Surrounding conditions are relatively consistent from day to day

7. Salt and water balance of the organism is challenging

關鍵語塊

- **procurement of sth.** 獲得某物
- **marine** 海洋的
- **genetic composition** 遺傳組成
- **concentration** 濃度
- **buoyancy** 浮力
- **body tissue** 機體組織
- **invertebrate** 無脊椎動物
- **uniformity** 一致（性）；均衡
- **medium** 介質，周邊環境
- **fertilize** 使受精
- **embryo** 胚胎
- **sponge** 海綿（一種海洋動物）
- **larval stage** 幼蟲期
- **disperse** 分散
- **velocity** 速度
- **volume** 量
- **drought** 乾旱
- **osmotic concentration** 滲透濃度
- **diffuse inward** 向內擴散，向內滲透
- **hold onto** 保持住
- **free floating** 自由浮動
- **intermediate** 中間的
- **yolk** 蛋黃
- **aquatic animal** 水棲動物
- **excrete** 排泄
- **ammonia** 氨；氨水
- **toxic** 有毒的
- **evaporation** 蒸發
- **respiratory surface** 呼吸面
- **urea** 尿素
- **uric acid** 尿酸
- **protective envelope** 保護外殼
- **be endowed with...** 天生具有⋯⋯
- **nocturnal** 夜間活動的

·················生態學：聽力·················

▶語用功能題的考試重點和答題策略

所謂的「語用功能題」問的是說話者提到某件事的含義或目的。在語用功能題中，出題者有時會根據上下文考查某個習語或片語，有時會詢問說話者是否在請求、建議、道歉、澄清或者糾正自己或他人。

在六道聽力題目中至少有一道語用功能題。講座和對話都是考查考生對某種情境中語言表達的含義或目的的領悟能力。從形式上來看，語用功能題通常都會重複播放題目，這表示我們在做這類題之前可以至少聽到兩遍考查內容。

• LISTENING TIPS

語用功能題往往以下面的形式出現：

What did the speaker mean when he said:

Why does the speaker explain the concept of crossbreeding?

Why does the man say this:

• LISTENING SAMPLE

下面是本章模擬試題中的語用功能題：

6. Listen again to part of the lecture. Then answer the question.

P: Unfortunately, though, we think only a portion of these inoculated trees will show enough resistance to survive. Over the long term, then, crossbreeding may prove the more effective solution. Of course, tree scientists are using both approaches now, just in case.

What does the professor mean when he says this:

P: Of course, tree scientists are using both approaches now, just in case.

A. He is worried about the fact that more chestnut trees haven't been immunized.

B. He believes it is probably wise for scientists to experiment with a variety of methods.

C. He thinks that the two scientific approaches were equally successful in this study.

D. He has scientific proof that hybridization is the way to move forward.

托福總監評析

　　本題的關鍵是理解片語 just in case 的意思，其意思是「以防萬一」（to provide for all possible situations）。但是即使不確定該片語的意思，也能利用情境來確定教授的意思。教授說為了預防疾病，給栗樹注射了疫苗，但這不一定能完全扼制住栗樹的死亡，而雜交繁殖經證明可能是更有效的解決方案。為了以防萬一，科學家們採用了以上這種方案。言下之意，就是他贊同用多種方法來解決這個問題。

▶「自上而下」和「自下而上」：兩種聽力認知過程

　　要做好語用功能題和其他聽力題，需要掌握好我們大腦的運作方式。在聆聽的時候，我們會用兩種不同的方式來處理聽到的資訊。一方面，我們會進行「自上而下處理」，即以線性方式逐步解讀口語文本，試圖抓住聽到的單字和片語的意思。另一方面，也可以進行「自下而上處理」，即根據自己對外部世界的瞭解來獲取或猜測句子的意思。

　　下面來看一個自下而上處理聽力資訊的實例：教授正在課堂上講授沙漠生態學。如果我們發現自己不熟悉她所用的一些單字，可以想想自己已經瞭解的沙漠知識。例如，我們知道沙漠中有一些植物，如沙漠野花和仙人掌。我們知道沙漠中降雨極少，可能一年中只有春天才降一次雨。只要我們能聽懂教授說的一些詞彙，就能利用外部已有的知識來猜出生字的意思，並將意思拼湊出來。我們可能會突然明白 cactus（仙人掌）原來是指某種沙漠植物！這些自下而上的處理方法用得越多，聽力理解能力就進步越大。

● 語用功能題的答題策略：

策略 1 遵循講座的一般思路。

　　從講話者開始講話的時刻起，問自己：說話者的觀點是什麼？他或她為什麼會提出這個觀點？他或她的語氣是怎樣的？

策略 2 熟悉自然語言。

　　自然語言指的就是一般母語人士隨口會說出的語言，像「口語」和「間接表達」都算在內，非母語者需要聽很多自然語言，才能熟悉它、抓到「潛在意思」，即說話者隱含的意思和目的。

策略 3

　　熟悉與談論、授課、學習相關的動詞和動詞片語，如 to explain、to remind 和 to ask about。語用功能題的選項通常用不定詞片語表示，如 to suggest something to the professor 或 to verify that her answer was correct。

策略 4 採用「自上而下」和「自下而上」的聽力資訊處理方式，試著理解說話者的意思。不要害怕進行大膽猜測。

策略 5 對教授從一個話題跳到另一個話題要有所準備。

講話者常常會提到自己先前說的事，或突然插入一句解釋、說明。當聽到這些「附帶說明」時要做筆記，因為這是語用功能題的考試重點。

• Exercise 2 （解答請見 P. 332）

Write down at least one answer for the following pragmatic function question related to ecology.

N: Listen again to part of the talk. Then answer the question.

P: We can also categorize animals on the basis of the specific type of food they eat. You've all heard of carnivores—meat-eaters and herbivores—plant-eaters. But how about "frugivores"? Can you take a shot at that one?

N: What does the professor mean when she says this:

P: Can you take a shot at that one?

_____

_____

▶ 模擬試題（解答請見 P. 332）

Now listen to part of a lecture in a FOREST ECOLOGY class. Track 013

• Listening Questions Track 014

1. What is the professor mainly discussing?
   A. What happens to the ecosystem when one species becomes extinct.
   B. A study about how trees grow more quickly in certain environments.
   C. The scientific techniques used to create hybrid trees in forests.
   D. How the overcrowding of forests can lead to fungus disease.

2. What does the professor imply when he says this:

   Please listen to Track 014 for this part of the question.

   A. The students should carefully guard against inbreeding of tree species.
   B. It would be preferable for the students to work in public forest reserves.
   C. Many species of forest trees will become extinct in future generations.
   D. The quality of lumber will be superior if the students manage forests well.

3. According to the professor, why was American chestnut wood valued for construction?
   A. It was less expensive than other hardwoods.
   B. The wood fibers were denser and heavier.

C. There were many varieties to choose from.

D. The trees grew to maturity relatively quickly.

4. According to the professor, how were the trees harmed?

A. They became sick after being bred together with Asian varieties.

B. Their bark was attacked by fungus spores which grew inside them.

C. Their branches died when wood-boring insects burrowed into them.

D. They were crowded out of forests by an invasive chestnut species.

5. Based on the information in the lecture, indicate whether the statements below represent the benefits of viral inoculations. Place a ✓ mark in the correct box.

	Yes	No
They take effect very rapidly.		
They are saving the majority of the trees.		
They will get rid of fungus disease in the future.		

6. Listen again to part of the lecture. Then answer the question.

 Please listen to Track 014 for this part of the question.

What does the professor mean when he says this:

 Please listen to Track 014 for this part of the question.

A. He is worried about the fact that more chestnut trees haven't been immunized.

B. He believes it is probably wise for scientists to experiment with a variety of methods.

C. He thinks that the two scientific approaches were equally successful in this study.

D. He has scientific proof that hybridization is the way to move forward.

Social Sciences, Topic 2: Anthropology
社會科學常考主題 2：人類學

本章內容以社會科學範疇的人類學為知識背景。在人類學中，有許多專業化的分支，包括文化人類學和生物人類學。人類學領域用到的詞彙和片語有 caste system（種姓制度），kinship relationship（親屬關係）和 patriarchy（父權制）等。請注意本章中出現的語塊，並記住它們。

·························· 人類學：閱讀··························

▶指代關係題的重點和答題策略

新托福考試中的指代關係題考的是考生是否清楚某個指代名詞的具體所指物件。在形式上，指代題與情境詞彙題類似，考查的詞在文章中都是用灰底突出顯示出來。在新托福考試中，每篇閱讀文章後通常至少會有一道指代關係題。

• READING SAMPLE 1

以下文關於特林基特人文章中的指代關係題為例：

Raven's most compelling feature is his dual or multiple personality, which has intrigued listeners from the earliest time to the present day.

8. The word "which" in Paragraph 5 refers to .

A. Raven's   B. feature   C. dual   D. personality

> **托福總監評析**
>
> 關係代名詞 which 指代的是與其最鄰近的名詞 personality。dual 和 multiple 都是 personality 的修飾語。在這道題中，指代對象為先行詞。

從上例可以看出，使用代名詞是為了避免相同詞語的重複。但是有時候，代名詞所指代的可能並不是其鄰近的名詞，而是前面（也可能是後面）的某個名詞、名詞片語，甚至是整句話。有時代名詞與其指代的物件之間甚至會相隔好幾個分句，或者一兩個句子。因此要想做對指代關係題，必須弄清楚以下問題：先行詞是單數還是複數？是第一人稱嗎？是指女性嗎？是無生命的嗎？

• READING SAMPLE 2

舉一個代名詞的指代物件位於其後面的例子：

Moving away from their early hypotheses, scientists now believe Canada's First Nations people came to North America at the end of the last ice age.

A. away　　　　B. hypotheses　　　　C. scientists　　　　D. people

托福總監評析

> 本句主詞是 scientists，their 指代主詞。

一般情況下，代名詞在句子結構中多位於所指代的名詞之後，但有時候代名詞也會出現在名詞之前。

如果你對代名詞的各種形式都瞭若指掌，那麼指代關係題就可以勝券在握了。

● 指代關係題的答題策略有：

策略 1 答題前，要思考代名詞所在段落和所在句的意思。如果看到代名詞就快速尋找與其鄰近的詞而不考慮上下文意思，那麼就很容易犯錯。

策略 2 先排除與該代名詞在性、數、格上不一致的選項。

策略 3 做出選擇後，將所選答案放到句子中檢查文法是否正確。

策略 4 如果不明白某些詞或文法結構的意思，不要驚慌。可以利用你對全文的理解以及文章主題進行推測。

• Exercise 1 　（解答請見 P. 336）

Read the following passage about Anthropology and fill in each blank with an appropriate referent.

In the 18th and 19th centuries, as Europeans penetrated further and further into some of the world's most inaccessible parts, _____ encountered peoples _____ seemed to turn everything _____ thought they knew about human behavior upside down. From attempts to make sense of what they had seen, and to help them understand the nature of what it means to be human, the idea of anthropology was born. The "science of man", as anthropology was dubbed, experienced _____ prime in the early 20th century.

▶ **模擬試題**（解答請見 P. 336）

Stories of the Tlingit People

★ **Keyword**

> Tlingit 特林吉特人

(1) Origin stories are by nature theoretical; they constitute our opinions about the origins and meaning of the world and life as we know it. In origin stories, we deal with human attempts to codify and transmit a cultural message orally and in writing. Sometimes the versions themselves, as well as the opinions about the versions, conflict. It should thus not surprise us to find more than one version of the origin story among the Tlingit people of southeast Alaska, and to find these versions evolving. The creation of the world remains an especially sensitive and hotly debated topic.

(2) Anyone interested in Tlingit origin stories will eventually encounter two formats. The first is the written record, now over 200 years old, containing analysis by outside observers. The second consists of the oral explanations that one hears by asking the Tlingit man or woman on the street what he or she thinks about this story or that. The nature and personality of the mythological Raven is never far from the center of the debate. In the history of publications about Tlingit Raven, we find both Native Tlingits and non-natives arguing that Raven is God and that Raven is not God.

(3) Tlingit origin stories may be grouped into four broad categories, based on the style, content, and time relationship of the narratives: a) early myth time; b) Raven myth time (Raven as "culture hero" and Raven as "trickster"); c) legendary time; and d) historical time. The historical consciousness shaping Tlingit oral literature seems to involve flow among the four categories. For example, over time, a personal history or a family's collection of stories might attain the status of a community or national legend. Over an even longer period, the historical context might change again, and a legend could acquire the status of a distant myth. In conventional folklore terminology, a myth refers to that which is sacred and true, usually in the remote past, with divinities, superhumans or nonhumans as characters. A legend, in contrast, is an account which is historical and true, with only human characters.

(4) The term "early myth time" is a convenient rubric for grouping what are essentially the odds and ends of the Tlingit creation accounts dealing with cosmic phenomena—for example, Sun, Moon, thunder, earthquakes, and winds, all of which existed before the birth of Raven. The most interesting and typical stories within this group are about the origins of the Sun and Moon, and Thunder and Earthquake. Thunder is created by the wings of the Thunderbird, and earthquakes are caused by Old Woman Below, who shakes the column supporting Earth whenever Raven tries to pull her away. Thunder and Earthquake are brother and sister who had to separate forever for unspecified reasons.

(5) The largest and most popular group of Tlingit origin stories involves Raven. Raven's most compelling feature is his dual or multiple personality, which has intrigued listeners from the earliest time to the present day. Raven myths can be classified into two categories, "culture hero" and "trickster". The stories themselves are often mixed, but it is convenient to separate the personality traits for purposes of discussion. The most famous stories tell about Raven as "culture hero"—his theft and distribution of the Sun, Moon, stars and daylight; how he courageously brings fresh water to the people; and how he creates salmon runs so that salmons can swim upstream and lay eggs. In many of these situations, the natural phenomena already exist, but are being hoarded by one individual. Raven manages to steal the items and redistribute them to the people.

(6) In other Raven myths, the bird acts as a trickster, driven entirely by ego and greed, with no evident altruistic motives. These stories often demonstrate how such-and-such animal acquired some physical feature following an encounter with Raven, such as Killer Whale's blowhole, or how a particular feature of landscape reflects an event in the Raven Cycle. Humans are usually not involved at all. Rarely do the animals that Raven encounters benefit from the experience: The Small Birds are lucky to go away hungry but alive after Raven cheats them out of their share of the King Salmon; Bear loses the fat from his thighs.

• Reading Questions

1. What does the author say about the written documents containing Tlingit origin stories?
   A. The written versions contain more authentic stories than oral versions do.
   B. The oldest ones were created by people outside the Tlingit tribe.
   C. They capture the various views of everyday people walking on the street.
   D. They are criticized passionately by the Native Tlingit people.

2. Which of the sentences below best expresses the essential information in the highlighted sentence in the passage? Incorrect choices change the meaning in major ways or leave out important information.
   Sometimes the versions themselves, as well as the opinions about the versions, conflict.
   A. The stories being told are often inconsistent, but people usually agree that the stories are good.
   B. The original story has continued up until this time, but some critics argue about the possible meanings.
   C. In some instances, the storytellers borrow from one another and then fight; but in the end they try to get along.
   D. Not only do people disagree about whether the stories are true; there are different forms of the story.

3. According to Paragraph 3, which of the following oral narratives would most likely reflect the oldest story?
   A. A national legend.
   B. A Raven myth.
   C. A family history.
   D. A distant myth.

4. The phrase "odds and ends" in Paragraph 4 is closest in meaning to _____.
   A. diverse items
   B. strange findings
   C. final elements
   D. unclear parts

5. According to Tlingit mythology, what is true about Thunder and Earthquake?
   A. They belong to the same family.
   B. They are produced by Sun and Moon.
   C. They appear on Earth for no obvious reason.
   D. They get into quarrels with the Old Woman.

6. According to the author, all of the following characters are contained in stories about the creation of the universe EXCEPT _____.
   A. Earthquake
   B. Old Woman Below
   C. Blue Heron
   D. Thunderbird

7. The word "hoarded" in Paragraph 5 is closest in meaning to _____.
   A. transformed
   B. polluted
   C. kept
   D. used

8. The word "which" in Paragraph 5 refers to _____.
   A. Raven's
   B. feature
   C. dual
   D. personality

9. The word "altruistic" in Paragraph 6 is closest in meaning to _____.
   A. satisfying
   B. generous
   C. realistic
   D. spiritual

10. In Tlingit mythology, Raven enabled salmons to reproduce in which of the following ways?
    A. By carrying them fresh water.
    B. By tricking the supernatural powers.
    C. By inventing salmon runs.
    D. By keeping the Small Birds away.

11. In Paragraph 6, why does the author introduce the statement "Bear loses the fat from his thighs"?
    A. To show that Bear was mystically linked to human beings.
    B. To illustrate how animals suffered at Raven's expense.
    C. To show that King Salmon ranked higher than Bear in the hierarchy.
    D. To symbolize that everyday people did not have enough to eat.

12. Directions: Complete the chart below about Raven myths. Choose five of the seven answer choices and match them to the type of Raven myth with which they are associated. **This question is worth 3 points.**

Types of Raven myth	Story Examples
Trickster	• • •
Culture hero	• •

Answer Choices

1. Clever animals scheme to outwit Raven

2. Fresh water is given to the people

3. The Old Woman is harmed in an earthquake

4. The Sun is stolen away

5. Bear's body is injured

6. The whale gets a hole on top of its head

7. Small Birds fail to get their portion of salmon

關鍵語塊

- **by nature** 本質上
- **constitute** 構成
- **life as we know it** 我們所理解的生命
- **codify** 編纂
- **versions themselves** 版本本身；說法本身
- **origin story** 起源故事
- **hotly debated topic** 引起激烈討論的話題
- **culture hero** 文化上的英雄人物
- **trickster** 騙子，無賴
- **historical consciousness** 歷史意識
- **legend** 傳說
- **historical context** 歷史背景
- **attain the status of sth.** 得到了某身分、地位
- **folklore** 民間風俗，民間傳說
- **sacred** 神聖的
- **remote past** 遙遠的過去
- **divinity** 神

- **format** 形式
- **outside observer** 外部的觀察者；局外人
- **consist of** 包括
- **this story or that** 各種故事
- **never far from the center of...** 對……起著至關重要的作用
- **grouped into... categories** 被分成……類
- **myth** 神話
- **superhuman** 超人
- **rubric** 標題，類目
- **cosmic** 宇宙的
- **unspecified reason** 不明原因
- **compelling** 引人入勝的
- **intrigue** 使……好奇，使……著迷
- **swim upstream** 逆流而上
- **such-and-such** 這樣那樣的
- **blowhole** （鯨等的）呼吸孔
- **cheat sb. out of** 騙取某人的……

······················· 人類學：聽力 ·······················

▶重點技能：理解講座的開場白

　　雖然新托福考試中的學術類講座篇幅相當長，時間長度達 5 分鐘之久，但它們並不會像完整的講座那樣冗長、複雜。

　　講座有時選自長篇講座。但大多數情況下，學術講座都會被編排成一個完整的小型講座的形式，具有開場白、正文和結語。這就表示教授的開頭幾句話一般會很簡短。

　　此外，由於考生剛開始聽聽力時一般都會比較緊張，所以經常會聽不出開頭幾句話的用詞和含義。儘管引導句（Now listen to part of a lecture in an Anthropology class.）可以幫助考生做好聽開場白的準備，但是很多考生還是摸不清教授要談論的內容。他是會先談論考試還是作業？他會開門見山地直接講座主題嗎？

• LISTENING TIPS

　　一般來說，教授會採用以下幾種方式作開場白：

　　1. 向學生說明講座主題為何重要，進而引出講座主題。例如，要談論考古挖掘重要性的人類學教授的開場白可能會這樣：As you may know, only this week in southern Mexico,

specialists discovered tools that confirm that in the 15th century the people there spun cotton, used to create warrior garments.

　　2. 給講座中的重要概念或術語下定義。例如，人類學教授的開場白可能會這樣：Today we will talk about kinship. Kinship can be seen as a basic unit of human social relations. It is structured in many different ways to define groups and the differences between them; for example, blood relationships and relationships by marriage.

　　3. 告訴學生接下來的講座會涵蓋哪些要點。例如，教授可能會說：Today I want to initiate you into the secret lore of anthropology: What makes us distinctive as a discipline. You will not learn about this in Geography, Sociology, Prehistory or History. Today I will also explain the terminology used to describe kinship structures.

　　在本章的講座中，教授的開場白是：As we trace the history of human evolution, it's important to remember that... 這是什麼類型的開場白？請注意聽，看看上面說的新知識對你理解講座的開場白有沒有幫助吧！

• Exercise 2　（解答請見 P. 337）

Write a correct paraphrase for each of the following opening sentences.

ⓐ Today, my major objective is to introduce you the basic concepts of cultural anthropology, one of the important disciplines of social science.

_____

_____

ⓑ It may sound difficult, but anthropologists are always attempting to see the culture from inside it. In other words, cultural anthropologists want to discover how people see their world.

_____

_____

▶ 模擬試題（解答請見 P. 337）

Now listen to a lecture about ANTHROPOLOGY.　　🎧 *Track 015*

★ Keywords

primates 靈長目動物	the Pliocene Epoch 上新世
savanna 稀樹大草原	*Australopithecus* 南方古猿

• Listening Questions　　🎧 *Track 016*

1. What aspect of evolutionary anthropology does the professor talk mainly about?
    A. What area of primate research requires more evidence.
    B. Where higher primates are distributed in Africa.
    C. How brains in primates have changed over the years.
    D. How our human ancestors adapted to climate change.

2. Listen again to part of the lecture. Then answer the question.

 Please listen to Track 016 for this part of the question.

What does the professor mean when she says this:

 Please listen to Track 016 for this part of the question.

    A. The students can definitely locate the most valuable fossil sites.
    B. The students will find the time spent very rewarding.
    C. The students should work together to do record-keeping well.
    D. The students who have trouble finding good data should contact her.

3. Listen again to part of the lecture. Then answer the question.

 Please listen to Track 016 for this part of the question.

What does the professor indicate about the Pliocene Epoch when she says this:

 Please listen to Track 016 for this part of the question.

    A. She thinks it displayed classic evolutionary adaptation.
    B. She thinks it showed extraordinarily rich diversity of life forms.
    C. She questions whether the popular theory about it can be accurate.
    D. She believes the soil conditions during this time were ideal for change.

4. What does the professor say about savannas?
    Choose 2 answers.
    A. They require a climate with very warm temperatures.
    B. Their specialized vegetation requires steady monthly rain.
    C. They occupied many parts of the world in the Pliocene.
    D. The grasses must compete for water with fruit trees and shrubs.

5. The professor mentions two different types of *Australopithecus* species. For each item below, indicate which characteristic is associated with which species.
Place a ✓ mark in the correct box. **This question is worth 2 points.**

Characteristic	Large species	Small species	Neither species
Sharp incisors			
Grinding molars			
Lived mainly in forest areas			
Disappeared a million years ago			

⑨ Physical Sciences, Topic 3: Acoustics and Dynamics
物理科學常考主題 3：聲學和力學

本章內容以物理科學範疇的聲學和力學為知識背景。聲學是指聲音科學；力學是指涉及物體運動的機械學的一個分支學科。關於物理學這些分支的學術文章可能會對原理和過程進行簡單介紹，或者對闡釋這些物理原理的物體或機械進行介紹。聲學領域中用到的詞彙和片語如 sound transmission（聲音傳遞）和 microphone（麥克風）等。與力學相關的語塊有 airplane wing（飛機機翼）和 force of gravity（重力）等。請注意本章中出現的語塊，並記住它們。

聲學和力學：閱讀

▶資訊歸類題的考試重點和答題策略

資訊歸類題（或稱填表題）考查考生能否通過通讀一篇學術性文章，將文中的觀點進行適當的邏輯分類。

每篇閱讀文章後最多只有一道資訊歸類題，而且如果有內容總結題時，就不會再有資訊歸類題；反之亦然。與內容總結題一樣，資訊歸類題一般出現在文章後面的最後一道題。資訊歸類題的分值為 3 分或 4 分，視正確答案選項的數目而定。

以本章下文的《音樂合成器》的題目為例：

• READING SAMPLE

12. **Directions:** Complete the following chart below by matching five of the seven answer choices with the synthesizer that they exemplify. **This question is worth 3 points.**

Type of Synthesizer	Associated Characteristics
Performance	• • •
Modular	• •

Answer Choices

1. Requires more effort to prepare it for use

2. Adjustments are possible during real-time sound generation

3. Preferred synthesizer type for copying digital audio signals

4. Often purchased for university use

5. Lacks an abstracted control interface

6. Signal follows an established conduit

7. Connections between units are permanent

Type of Synthesizer	Associated Characteristics
Performance	• 2. Adjustments are possible during real-time sound generation • 6. Signal follows an established conduit • 7. Connections between units are permanent
Modular	• 1. Requires more effort to prepare it for use • 4. Often purchased for university use

托福總監評析

　　回答本題的最快方法是掃讀全文尋找 performance 和 modular 合成器。第五段首次提到了這些合成器，出現在字母 a) 和 b) 後面。接著，在第六段，可以找到這兩類合成器的詳細說明。

　　在做這類題時，考生要快速通讀七個選項，然後將每個選項逐一正確歸類。為了快速將這些答案選項分類，可以將答案選項拖入相應的表格位置中。記住，七個選項中，有兩個是與文章內容不符或者文中沒有提到。在實際考試中，你要將答案拖到正確的位置。

● 資訊歸類題的答題策略：

策略 1 做好結構性筆記，記錄下主要觀點和例證。

策略 2 尋找表示不同類型的事物和觀點的字母或數字。

策略 3 仔細留意概念的分類方式。資訊歸類題中的事物或觀點通常有兩或三種類型。

策略 4 仔細留意概念組織框架。

　　注意該框架包含正反觀點，還是比較和對比內容？如果是與歷史有關的，是按時間順序敘述事件嗎？

策略 5 尋找關鍵概念和事物的定義，尤其是有兩個或三個相關項時。

這些定義可能含有選項中提到的特性和特徵。

策略 6 仔細留意列舉的實例。

是否有兩個或三個闡述重要原理或類型的不同實例？這些實例可能會作為關鍵「類型」或類型的關鍵「實例」出現在圖表中。

策略 7 考試前，練習換句話說。考試時，掃讀每個選項的換句話說用詞。這有助於你提高填表的速度。

▶ **模擬試題**（解答請見 P. 341）

Music Synthesizers

★ **Keyword**

> music synthesizer 音樂合成器

(1) There are many types of synthesizers—video synthesizers, color synthesizers and sound synthesizers, to name a few. They are all similar in concept, the major differences being in their output formats and the way they produce that output. Synthesizers have two basic functional components: a control interface, which is how the parameters defining the end product are set and a synthesis "engine," which interprets these parameter values and produces the actual sound output. In most cases the control interface is a simplified abstraction of the synthesis engine itself. This is because the synthesis process is extremely complex, and it is necessary to give the end user a simpler model in the control panel.

(2) Sound synthesis is the process of producing sound. The synthesizer can reuse existing sounds by processing them, or it can generate sound electronically or mechanically. It may use mathematics, physics or even biology; moreover, it brings together art and science in a mix of musical skill and technical expertise. Used carefully, synthesizers can produce emotional performances which paint sonic landscapes with a rich and huge set of timbres, limited only by the imagination of the creator. Yet sound synthesis is not solely concerned with sophisticated computer-generated timbres. The wide availability of high quality recording technology has made acoustic sounds much easier for musicians and technicians to mix, but the technology is nothing more than a set of tools. Without the creative skills of the performer, musician or technician, the music would become mundane.

(3) The first synthesizer might have been an early ancestor of Homo sapiens hitting a hollow log or perhaps learning to whistle. ■ 1 All musical instruments can be thought of as being "synthesizers," although few people would think of them in this way. ■ 2 A clarinet is viewed as being "natural," whereas a synthesizer is seen as "artificial." In recent years the word "synthesizer" has come to mean only an electronic instrument capable of producing

a wide range of different sounds. The actual categories of sounds that qualify for the label of synthesizer are also very specific. Purely imitative sounds are frequently regarded as nothing other than recordings of the actual instrument; the synthesizer is seen as little more than a replay device. In other words, the general public seems to expect synthesizers to produce "synthetic" sounds. ■ 3 This can be readily seen in many low-cost keyboard instruments intended for home use, which typically have a number of familiar sounds with names like "piano" and "guitar." But they also have sounds labeled "synth" for sounds which do not fit into the "naturalistic" scheme. As synthesizers become better at fusing elements of real and synthetic sounds, the boundaries are becoming increasingly fuzzy. ■ 4

(4) This blurring has resulted in broad public acceptance of a number of "hyper-real" instrument sounds, where the distinctive characteristics of an instrument are exaggerated. For example, drum sounds are frequently enhanced; and yet, unless they cross the boundary line of what sounds "real," their generation is not questioned. This can cause difficulties for drummers, who are expected to reproduce the same sound as the compact disk (CD) in a live environment.

(5) Synthesizers come in several different varieties, although many of the constituent parts are common to all of the types. Most synthesizers have one or more audio outputs; one or more control inputs; some sort of display; and buttons to control the operation of the unit. The major split is into a) performance synthesizers and b) modular synthesizers.

(6) In performance synthesizers, connections among individual internal synthesis modules are already built in. It is usually not possible to change these, and so the signal flow always follows a set path through the synthesizer. This enables the rapid patching of commonly used configurations, but limits flexibility. Performance synthesizers form the vast majority of commercial synthesizer products. Conversely, modular synthesizers have no fixed connections among the synthesis modules, and they can be connected in any way. Changes can be made to the connections whilst the synthesizer is making a sound. Because relatively more connections need to be made, modular synthesizers are more time-consuming to set up, but they do have greater flexibility. Modular synthesizers are much rarer than performance synthesizers, and are often used for academic or research purposes.

• **Reading Questions**

1. According to the first paragraph, what do synthesizers have in common?
   A. The sound generation of the device.
   B. The format of the output information.
   C. The parameter values of the engine.
   D. The concept of an interface management.

2. The word "which" in Paragraph 2 refers to _____.
   A. synthesizers
   B. performances
   C. landscapes
   D. timbres

3. The word "mundane" in Paragraph 2 is closest in meaning to _____.
   A. commercial
   B. academic
   C. routine
   D. imprecise

4. In Paragraph 2, the author says that the advanced recording technology available today has led to which of the following consequences?
   A. Performers have begun to secretly patch digital files into "live" performances.
   B. Professional musicians have found it more convenient to edit sounds.
   C. Mathematicians and physicists with no musical background have made recordings.
   D. Technicians have begun to play too large a role in the music industry.

5. In Paragraph 3, why does the author mention the "clarinet"?
   A. To make the point that instruments are in fact a kind of synthesizer.
   B. To contrast the sound of real clarinets with the sound of a machine imitation of a clarinet.
   C. To illustrate the wide range of sound waves that a clarinet could produce.
   D. To demonstrate how much the sound of the clarinet differs from the sound of the human voice.

6. The phrase "qualify for" Paragraph 3 is closest in meaning to _____.
   A. are displayed on
   B. are eligible for
   C. compete for
   D. excel within

7. The word "fusing" in Paragraph 3 is closest in meaning to _____.
   A. valuing
   B. confounding
   C. harmonizing
   D. blending

8. According to Paragraph 3, everyday users of inexpensive synthesizers think that these synthesizers should _____.
   A. produce unmistakably artificial sounds
   B. have a keyboard with a large menu

C. contain several types of piano and guitar sounds

D. accurately imitate orchestra instruments

9. Which of the sentences below best expresses the essential information in the highlighted sentence in the passage? Incorrect choices change the meaning in major ways or leave out important information.

This can cause difficulties for drummers, who are expected to reproduce the same sound as the compact disk (CD) in a live environment.

A. People who play drums make problems for other musicians when they record compact disks.

B. The drummers who do not make the same sounds as the electronic drummers are not encouraged to make recordings.

C. Drummers are impacted by this phenomenon because a live audience will notice a difference in the sounds.

D. People attending a real concert do not like the drum sounds produced by this type of synthesizer.

10. We can infer from the passage that the author has which of the following opinions about synthesizers?

A. They should be used to mix sounds, but not to create real music.

B. They are especially good tools for improvising at live performances.

C. They should be used thoughtfully, just like any other instrument.

D. They are used too much in the production of commercial music.

11. Look at the four squares [■] that indicate where the following sentence could be added to the passage.

Singing uses a sophisticated synthesizer whose capabilities are often forgotten—the human vocal tract.

Where would the sentence best fit?

■ 1

■ 2

■ 3

■ 4

12. Directions: Complete the following chart below by matching five of the seven answer choices with the synthesizer that they exemplify. **This question is worth 3 points.**

Type of Synthesizer	Associated Characteristics
Performance	• • •
Modular	• •

Answer Choices

1. Requires more effort to prepare it for use

2. Adjustments are possible during real-time sound generation

3. Preferred synthesizer type for copying digital audio signals

4. Often purchased for university use

5. Lacks an abstracted control interface

6. Signal follows an established conduit

7. Connections between units are permanent

關鍵語塊

- **similar in concept**　在概念上類似
- **output**　輸出；作品
- **output format**　輸出格式
- **functional component**　功能元件
- **interface**　介面
- **parameter**　參數
- **synthesis "engine"**　合成「引擎」
- **abstraction**　抽象化
- **end user**　終端使用者，終端客戶
- **control panel**　控制台
- **sonic**　聲音的
- **paint sonic landscape**　用聲音來描繪的景觀
- **timbre**　音質
- **recording technology**　燒錄技術
- **acoustic sound**　樂器原聲
- **hollow log**　空心圓木
- **whistle**　吹口哨
- **blurring**　模糊
- **hyper-real**　超真實的；過度真實的
- **exaggerated**　誇張的
- **cross the boundary line**　跨越了邊界線
- **compact disk**　光碟
- **live environment**　現場環境
- **constituent part**　構成部件
- **display**　（電腦螢幕上的）顯示，顯像
- **button**　按鈕
- **major split**　主要分類
- **performance synthesizer**　音效合成器
- **modular synthesizer**　模組化合成器
- **signal flow**　信號流
- **follow a set path**　流向固定的導管
- **patch**　修補
- **time-consuming**　耗時的

• Exercise 1 （解答請見 P. 342）

Practice looking for categories by scanning through the passage and answering each question below.

ⓐ What are the three types of synthesizers mentioned by the author in Paragraph 1?

_____

ⓑ What are some different methods of producing sound as mentioned in Paragraph 2?

_____

_____

ⓒ What are the different "synthesizers" (and "instruments") mentioned by the author in Paragraphs 3 and 4?

_____

·····················**聲學和力學：聽力**·····················

▶**重點技能：換句話說**

換句話說，即用不同的詞來表達一個片語或句子的相同意思，是應對新托福考試的關鍵技能之一。如前所述，新托福考試的四個部分都會直接或間接考查換句話說的技能。

練習改述不僅僅能擴充單字量，更重要的是能訓練自己在聽、說、讀、寫過程中用英語來思考。此外，練習改述還可以訓練自己應對任何情景，並做到輕鬆自如地接受語言輸入，進而轉化為語言輸出。

在新托福考試的聽力部分，考生從四個選項中選擇正確答案時，換句話說的能力能派上用場。考生閱讀每個選項時，如果能快速識別與你在講座或對話中聽到的意思相同的選項，那麼就可以滿懷信心地做好這道題目。

以本章模擬試題中的講座為例：

• LISTENING SAMPLE

原文表達	同義表達
covered (the Physics of Motion)	talked about (the Physics of Motion)
grappled with (the physical properties of...)	struggled with (the physical properties of...)
(wing shape) was perfect for flight	(wing shape) was ideally suited for flying
as opposed to (the pulley and cables)	in contrast to (the pulley and cables)
both of these methods achieve roll control	both methods suffice to control roll

比較上面表格中表達相同概念的兩種方式。注意詞彙和文法方面的差異。

另外，要記得：最好是在情境中記憶語塊，而不是記憶單個孤立的詞彙。例如，應該記 was perfect for sth.，而不要只記 perfect。那樣的話，當你讀到或聽到這個語塊時，就能容易理解整個句子。

▶模擬試題（解答請見 P. 342）

Now listen to a lecture about PHYSICS. *Track 017*

★ Keywords

Wright brothers 萊特兄弟	pitch （飛機的）俯仰	yaw 偏航
roll （飛機）橫滾，側滾	aileron 副翼	

• Listening Questions　*Track 018*

1. What is the lecture mainly about?
   A. The controls used in flight.
   B. The way to turn an aircraft.
   C. How the Wrights powered their aircraft.
   D. How soaring birds stay airborne.

2. Why does the professor say this:

 Please listen to Track 018 for this part of the question.

   A. To teach the students to construct a working airplane.
   B. To encourage the students to keep on studying.
   C. To compare building an aircraft to building a road.
   D. To show that the Wrights did not bother with theoretical physics.

3. In order to balance the aircraft, the Wright brothers discovered that they would need to change _____.
   A. the height of the tail
   B. the direction of the nose
   C. the contour of the wing
   D. the weight of the lateral axis

4. What were the characteristics of the motions discussed by the professor?
   Place a ✓ mark in the correct box. **This question is worth 2 points.**

Attributes	Motions		
	Pitch	Yaw	Roll
Motion causing the nose to go left or right			
Upwards or downwards motion of one wing or the other			
Motion that makes the aircraft nose move up or down			
Motion that is acted upon by aircraft rudders			

5. What does the professor say about modern airlines?

    A. Their reliance on computers has made pilots more aware of physical forces.

    B. Their component parts no longer include an elevator at the aircraft's aft.

    C. They are programmed to focus on roll and pitch, but less so on yaw.

    D. They tackle the same needs for control that the Wrights did.

• Exercise 2　（解答請見 P. 345）

Write a correct paraphrase for each of the following sentences.

ⓐ The Wrights watched hawks maneuver with their wings.

_____

ⓑ Lateral control is necessary for turning the aircraft.

_____

ⓒ They caused one of the wings to roll to the left, in preparation for a turn.

_____

Humanities and the Arts, Topic 3: Music and Music History
人文藝術常考主題 3：音樂和音樂史

　　本章內容以人文藝術範疇的音樂和音樂史為知識背景。新托福考試中有關音樂的閱讀文章和講座一般涉及音樂理論或音樂風格，而關於音樂史的文章則可能會與特定歷史時期的音樂或作曲家的生活有關。音樂領域用到的語塊有 rhythm（節奏，韻律）和 melodic line（旋律）等。與音樂史有關的語塊有 Baroque period（巴羅克時期），chamber music（室內樂）和 orchestra（管弦樂團）等。請注意本章中出現的語塊，並記住它們。

···········音樂和音樂史：閱讀···········

▶插入句子題的考點和答題策略

　　新托福考試的插入句子題會為考生提供一個閱讀文章中未曾出現的句子。考生必須瀏覽不同位置（大多數在一個段落中）的四個黑色方塊，然後確定這一句話擺在哪個位置最適合。在考場中，考生需要用滑鼠點擊正確的黑色方塊，表明這就是正確答案。在閱讀部分，最多會有兩道插入句子題。

　　插入句子題考查考生銜接性和連貫性方面的能力。通讀全文時，一個插入正確位置的句子在邏輯上和文法上都必須通順、無誤。

　　下面來看看本章下文關於爵士樂文章中的插入句子題：

• READING SAMPLE

12. Look at the four squares [■] that indicate where the following sentence could be added to the passage.

   Despite that type of criticism—and in part perhaps because of it, ragtime had indeed come to stay.

   Where would the sentence best fit?
   ■ 1
   ■ 2
   ■ 3
   ■ 4

　　By the mid-1890s, three new kinds of music had begun to filter into New Orleans, three strains without which there would have been no jazz. The first was ragtime, the outgrowth of the decades-old African-American improvisational practice of "ragging" tunes—rearranging them to provide livelier, more danceable versions. Created by black musicians in the urban Midwest who had found a way to recreate the percussive sound of the banjo on the piano, ragtime drew upon everything that had gone before—spiritual songs and minstrel tunes, European folk melodies, operatic arias and military marches—all filled with broken chords and set to fresh rhythms. Spread first by traveling pianists and then through the sale of sheet music, ragtime music caught the fancy of young dancers all over the country who loved it all the more because it encouraged young men and women to dance close together as couples rather than in groups. Their parents were less than enthusiastic. ■ 1 "Ragtime is syncopation gone mad," wrote one critic. "Whether it is a passing phase in our decadent art culture or an infectious disease which has come to stay, only time will tell."

　　■ 2 Self-assured, dynamic, irresistible, it would be America's best-loved music for a quarter of a century. ■ 3 Nowhere was ragtime more popular or more ubiquitous than in the city of New Orleans. ■ 4 By the turn of the century, New Orleans musicians, in dance halls as well as street parades, were routinely giving every kind of music the ragtime treatment.

托福總監評析

　　所給的句子中有兩個信號詞：Despite 和 that criticism。這是重要的線索！根據 Despite 可知該句與前句的觀點形成對比。而 that criticism 表明前句可能提到了某類批評。於是當進一步讀這個句子時，我們看到主句的主詞 ragtime（拉格泰姆音樂）。因此就有了「搜索條件」：需要尋找的位置須位於批評拉格泰姆音樂的句子之後、正面介紹拉格泰姆音樂的句子之前。

　　第一個黑色方塊處之前的句子對拉格泰姆音樂持否定觀點的句子（parents were less than enthusiastic），但該處後面緊接的兩個句子都是對其持負面觀點的句子（Ragtime is syncopation gone mad），因此，第一個黑色方塊處不正確。

　　第二個黑色方塊位於下一段的開頭，因此必須回頭看看第一段最後一句。第一段最後一句也是對拉格泰姆音樂的否定陳述。到目前為止還好吧！接下來再看看第二個黑色方塊後面的句子，是有關拉格泰姆音樂的好評（Self-assured, dynamic, irresistible, it would be America's best-loved music for a quarter of a century）。這符合分析出來的兩個「搜索條件」，可能這裡就是正確答案。

　　但是，我們還需要確認待插入的句子是否適合最後兩個位置。第三個黑色方塊後的句子是對拉格泰姆音樂的好評，只符合一個「搜索條件」，因此不能插入第三個黑色方塊之前。第四個黑色方塊處的句子和它前面的句子銜接得很好，顯然是上下句關系。事實上，這一整段的主題是對拉格泰姆音樂的積極肯定。因此可以確定帶有轉折詞 Despite 的插入句的唯一位置是這一段的開頭，即第二個黑色方塊處正確。

　　由此可知，考生在開始看文章之前，就一定要仔細分析要插入的句子。這種方法不僅節省時間，還可避免因為粗心而犯的錯誤。

● 插入句子題的答題策略：

策略 1 仔細閱讀要插入的句子並分析其結構。留意任何可以提供銜接線索的特徵和信號詞。

例如，注意代名詞、重複的詞和其他指代前一個句子或指代後一個句子的指代關係詞。

注意邏輯信號詞，如 therefore，Unlike [his father, Mozart] 和 as a result 等。

注意時序關聯詞， 如 not long after that，in the 20th century 和 [simple folk songs], which were followed by... 等。

策略 2 確定要插入的句子是否是提供一個基本原則的實例或陳述的實例。如果是，則要緊跟在基本原則或陳述的後面。

策略 3 從第一個黑色方塊選項開始，試著將句子放入每個方塊位置，看看是否符合要求。每個位置前後句意是否連貫，即句子中的觀點和示例是否在邏輯上說得通；前後句子的銜接是否自然，即句子中的連接詞、名詞和指代關係詞在文法上是否能組合在一起。

策略 4 初步確定答案後，將句子放到其他三個方塊的位置，再次確認所選的答案是否正確。

• Exercise 1 　（解答請見 P. 346）

The following five sentences come from a paragraph about popular music. Using your skills in COHESION and COHERENCE, arrange them into the correct sequence.

1. The first of these is that studies of youth subcultures are a useful way to understand popular music audiences.
2. However, in my view, this assumption is misguided.
3. The popular music experiences of older people should also be taken into consideration.
4. Two fallacies underlie most discussions of popular music audiences.
5. Undeniably, more than a few teachers and students believe the study of popular music is the study of music made by and for young people.

▶ **模擬試題**（解答請見 P. 346）

Early History of Jazz

★ **Keywords**

syncopation （音樂的）切分	bent notes 壓音

(1) By the mid-1890s, three new kinds of music had begun to filter into New Orleans, three strains without which there would have been no jazz. The first was ragtime, the outgrowth of the decades-old African-American improvisational practice of "ragging" tunes—rearranging them to provide livelier, more danceable versions. Created by black musicians

in the urban Midwest who had found a way to recreate the percussive sound of the banjo on the piano, ragtime drew upon everything that had gone before—spiritual songs and minstrel tunes, European folk melodies, operatic arias and military marches—all filled with broken chords and set to fresh rhythms. Spread first by traveling pianists and then through the sale of sheet music, ragtime music caught the fancy of young dancers all over the country who loved it all the more because it encouraged young men and women to dance close together as couples rather than in groups. Their parents were less than enthusiastic. ■ 1 "Ragtime is syncopation gone mad," wrote one critic. "Whether it is a passing phase in our decadent art culture or an infectious disease which has come to stay, only time will tell."

(2) ■ 2 Self-assured, dynamic, irresistible, it would be America's best-loved music for a quarter of a century. ■ 3 Nowhere was ragtime more popular or more ubiquitous than in the city of New Orleans. ■ 4 By the turn of the century, New Orleans musicians, in dance halls as well as street parades, were routinely giving every kind of music the ragtime treatment.

(3) Meanwhile, a steady stream of African Americans from the Mississippi Delta was pouring into New Orleans, people for whom even the hard labor on the levee promised a better life than any they could hope to have back home, chopping cotton or cutting sugar cane. They brought with them two interrelated forms essential to the development of jazz—the sacred music of the Baptist church and that music's profane twin, the blues.

(4) No one knows where or when the blues was born. Blues lyrics could be about anything—empty pockets, a mean boss, the devil himself—but most were about the relationship between men and women. Each performer was expected to tell a story and to make the listener feel better, not worse. The earliest blues singers—wandering guitarists who played for pennies along southern roads—followed no strict musical form. But as first New Orleans musicians and then others around the country began to play the blues on their instruments and songwriters started to see commercial possibilities in them, an agreed-upon form was developed: Stripped to the essentials, the blues came to be built on just three chords most often arranged in twelvebar sequences that somehow allowed for an infinite number of variations and were capable of expressing an infinite number of emotions.

(5) The blues were good-time music, which was why, to many churchgoers, they were considered the work of the devil. But musically, the blues and the hymns black Baptists sang and played in church had always been virtually interchangeable—filled with identical bent notes, moans and cries. And in the 1890s, the distinction would blur still further as the new Holiness churches that had begun to spring up nationwide in the black neighborhoods of big cities started employing tambourines, drums, pianos cornets, even trombones in order to make their noise still more joyful to the Lord. "Those Baptist rhythms were similar to the jazz rhythms," said the New Orleans banjoist John St. Cyr, "and the singing was very much on the blues side."

(6) Both spirituals and blues were a form of prayer. One way was praying to God and the other was praying to what's human. Jazz music would eventually embody both kinds of invocation, the sacred and the secular, and New Orleans musicians would be the first to deepen the infinitely expressive sound of the blues by bringing it to their horns, the first to echo the collective "moan" of the congregation, the first to reproduce the call-and-response patterns of the religious leader and his or her flock.

• **Reading Questions**

1. The phrase "outgrowth of" in Paragraph 1 is closest in meaning to _____.
   A. exception to
   B. solution to
   C. development of
   D. embellishment of

2. In Paragraph 1, all of the following types of music are mentioned as contributing to ragtime EXCEPT _____.
   A. opera solos
   B. religious songs
   C. martial music
   D. dance music

3. In the first paragraph, why does the author include this quotation: "**Whether it is a passing phase in our decadent art culture or an infectious disease which has come to stay, only time will tell.**"
   A. To demonstrate the hostility of older people to ragtime.
   B. To show that some listeners were relatively tolerant of ragtime.
   C. To question the claim that many citizens had become ill in recent years.
   D. To argue that some artistic traditions should be continued forever.

4. The word "irresistible" in Paragraph 2 is closest in meaning to _____.
   A. reckless
   B. underappreciated
   C. extremely intense
   D. very appealing

5. According to the author, what was true about ragtime in New Orleans in the early 20th century?
   A. It had lost much of the syncopation.
   B. It was less fashionable there than in other cities.
   C. It was influencing most musical genres.
   D. It could be heard more in dance clubs than in parades.

6. The word "**them**" in Paragraph 4 refers to _____.
   A. musicians
   B. blues
   C. instruments
   D. songwriters

7. Who was responsible for introducing the blues genre to the New Orleans music scene?
   A. Traveling pastors.
   B. European folk artists.
   C. Professional piano players.
   D. Farm workers.

8. The phrase "**stripped to**" in Paragraph 4 is closest in meaning to _____.
   A. transformed to
   B. reduced to
   C. associated with
   D. trimmed with

9. In Paragraph 3, what does the author say about the use of three chords in blues music?
   A. Different three-chord sets chords were used in different regions of the country.
   B. The use of just three chords allowed people with limited musical training to express themselves.
   C. Musicians were able to express diverse emotions despite the small number of chords.
   D. By using a small, finite number of chords, the performers were forced to become more creative than they would have been otherwise.

10. We can infer from Paragraph 5 that a number of people who regularly attended church felt uncomfortable about the blues due to _____.
    A. the blues kept people from working as hard as they should
    B. blues music was associated with the crowded urban lifestyle
    C. the emotion conveyed in blues music was often sorrowful
    D. the musical form of the blues did not follow that of Baptist hymns

11. What does the author say about early horn players and their approach toward jazz?
    A. They interacted musically based on practices of church congregations.
    B. They frequently gave jazz concerts in churches throughout New Orleans.
    C. They began to perform jazz music before other instrumentalists did.
    D. They were denounced by the Holiness churches for being too worldly in their playing.

12. Look at the four squares [■] that indicate where the following sentence could be added to the passage.

   Despite that type of criticism—and in part perhaps because of it, ragtime had indeed come to stay.

   Where would the sentence best fit?

   ■ 1

   ■ 2

   ■ 3

   ■ 4

13. **Directions:** An introductory sentence for a brief summary of the passage is provided below. Complete the summary by selecting the THREE answer choices that express the most important ideas in the passage. Some answer choices do not belong in the summary because they express ideas that are not presented in the passage or are minor ideas in the passage. **This question is worth 2 points.**

   The history of jazz in New Orleans can be traced back to several musical traditions which converged in the late 19th century.

   -
   -
   -

Answer Choices

1. The soulful three-chord sequences of ragtime captivated dance audiences of the time.

2. Marching bands were especially important because the first jazz musicians learned how to play instruments and read music in these bands.

3. The syncopated rhythms characteristic of ragtime influenced the full spectrum of music in New Orleans and paved the way for the development of jazz.

4. Fostered by the singers and guitar players coming from Mississippi farms, improvisation and the emotional telling of stories became a fundamental expression of jazz.

5. The blues were viewed with suspicion by many religious believers, and in fact, Baptist church singing and blues singing had little in common.

6. In New Orleans in the 1890s, both sacred and secular influences came to shape the form and content of jazz expression, in the form of spirituals and the blues.

7. At first young people preferred to listen to lively jazz music to dancing to it, but after many years, it became acceptable to dance to jazz.

關鍵語塊

- filter into 滲入
- strain 類型，風格
- improvisational practice 即興練習
- urban Midwest （美國）中西部城市
- percussive sound 敲打聲
- had gone before 以前存在過的
- spiritual song 聖歌，靈歌
- minstrel tune 吟遊曲調
- broken chord 分解和絃
- less than enthusiastic 缺乏熱情
- sth. gone mad 瘋狂的某事物
- ubiquitous 普遍存在的
- a steady stream of... ……源源不斷地湧入
- the Mississippi Delta 密西西比河三角洲
- levee 堤壩
- Baptist church 浸禮教會
- profane twin 世俗孿生子
- twelve-bar sequence 連續十二小節
- Holiness church 聖教會
- invocation 祈禱
- congregation 教堂會眾
- flock 教會內的全體教徒

音樂和音樂史：聽力

▶重點技能：聽表示時間順序的過渡詞

　　教授講授的歷史講座往往會以時間順序來敘述事實。在課堂上，他們可能會比較發生在不同地點不同時期的歷史事件；甚至還會將過去的歷史事件或人物與現在的事件或人物進行比較。教授做這些講解時需要穿插使用簡單易懂的銜接過渡詞（從事件到事件、從觀點到觀點），才能把問題説清楚。

　　按時間順序組織的講座，教授往往會從最早的時間點開始講起，可能是某年或某個歷史時期。例如，在本章下文的音樂史講座中，教授開場白時説學生已經 finished the Classical epoch（學完了古典音樂時期的音樂），現在要 turn to Romanticism（轉向浪漫主義）。由此可推斷，接下來的講座內容將與浪漫主義音樂和那個時期有關，浪漫主義音樂時期是緊接著古典主義音樂時期的一段時期。考生應及時為講座內容的展開做好準備，並注意時間片語和其他時間線索。

　　但是，教授不會只談論日期。要讓學生明白一個歷史事件如何引發另一個歷史事件，講授者必須闡明這些事件中的關聯；例如，德國浪漫主義文學對浪漫主義音樂有何影響？鋼琴在浪漫主義時期為什麼大受歡迎？要解釋特定歷史時期或歷史運動的社會和經濟背景，教授還會用其他的信號詞和連接詞。這類信號詞會讓你的思路跟上一系列事件的發展，因為它們讓前後句子有了連貫性與銜接性。

　　下面來看看教授在接下來的講座中用到的一些過渡策略。每段摘錄的內容後面都有換句話説。

1. Similarly, before I begin in earnest, I want to clear up another potentially confusing semantic issue...

   (→ Before I talk about a lot of historical dates, let me explain a confusing term.)

2. What about Romanticism in music, then?

   (→ I've talked about Romanticism in other contexts, and now I'm about to tell you about Romanticism in music.)

3. But we can point to definite changes occurring around 1800. It's helpful to look at the transition from Classicism to Romanticism by looking at the works of Beethoven,...

   (→ The year 1800 is important in history, because we can see real changes that reflect the move from Classicism to Romanticism. We can see evidence of these changes in the various compositions written by Beethoven.)

4. What were the social and economic factors shaping this artistic movement?

   (→ I've already told you about this artistic movement. And now I'm going to tell you about how the social and economic conditions of that time influenced the movement.)

5. Also, as the middle class became educated about music, audiences became increasingly sophisticated.

   (→ And another thing I want to tell you is a cause-effect phenomenon: Because the growing middle class became better educated, they started to like a different type of music— sophisticated music.)

6. Of course, when we think of Romantic piano music, we think of Chopin.

   (→ While I'm on the topic of piano music in the Romantic period, I have to mention a famous example, the composer and pianist Chopin.)

托福總監評析

　　談論歷史事件時，該教授用了什麼策略？第一個範例中，教授表示在她解釋專業術語之前，不會談歷史時間框架。在範例 2 和範例 4 中，她以提問的方式過渡到下一個要點。在範例 3 和範例 6 中，她通過列舉音樂時代有代表性的作曲家來進行過渡。在範例 5 中，她通過闡述因果關係（受過教育的中產階級更欣賞 19 世紀的這類音樂表演）進一步展開講座。

　　所以說，考生熟悉文章中的時序信號詞至關重要。因此，考生務必要記住表示事件順序的時序信號詞。

時序信號詞

First..., second..., third...	Previously,...	In the interim,...
Next	Before this,...	Since that time,...
Then / later / later on	Prior to this time,...	Following that,...
Initially..., secondly...	Preceding this,...	Soon thereafter,...
To start with,...	At the same time,...	Not long after that,...

To begin with,...	Simultaneously,...	After that,...
First of all,...	Concurrently,...	And then...
For starters,...	In conjunction with...	Subsequently,...
In the first place,...	During this period,...	Consequently,...
Formerly,...	Meanwhile,...	Finally,...
Originally,...	Concurrent with this,...	Eventually,...
At the outset,...	Contemporaneous with...	Afterward,...

• Exercise 2 （解答請見 P. 347）

Read the following lecture on music history. From the list provided, fill in the blanks with the correct time word or phrase.

after   by   during   earliest   following that   later on   now   ever since then   ultimately

Professor: _____ I want to talk about a remarkable example of a musician who transitioned from Classical music to jazz. This is the story of violinist Regina Carter, who was born in 1966 in Detroit, the home of the Motown Sound and R&B. Her _____ musical training was completely classical; she started piano lessons at age two. But _____ age four, she'd switched to the violin. _____, _____ high school, she fell in love with jazz _____ hearing a French violinist play that kind of music. _____, Carter attended the New England Conservatory, and joined a jazz band, performing and recording records. _____, Regina Carter launched a solo career, creating an album for Atlantic Records. _____, she's proved that the violin has a home in the realm of jazz.

▶ **模擬試題**（解答請見 P. 348）

Now listen to a lecture in a music history class.　　　🔊 *Track 019*

★ **Keywords**

Romantic 浪漫主義的	Beethoven 貝多芬
Eroica Symphony（貝多芬的）《英雄交響曲》	Chopin 蕭邦

• Listening Questions　　　🔊 *Track 020*

1. What is the main topic of the lecture?
    A. How literature influenced music in the 19th century.
    B. Significant developments in the piano in the 19th century.
    C. The differences between Classical and Romantic symphonies.
    D. The history and style of romanticism in music.

2. What does the professor mean when she says this:

Please listen to Track 020 for this part of the question.

   A. Romanticism goes well with certain types of music.
   B. Romantic art is not limited to works about love.
   C. Love is a universal theme running though all of the arts.
   D. Love songs are part of both popular and classical music.

3. What does the professor say about Beethoven's Third Symphony?
   Choose 2 answers.
   A. It is a typical example of the Neo-Classical style of music.
   B. It was inspired by a non-musical theme involving heroism.
   C. It conveyed an emotional energy not previous heard in symphonies.
   D. It was a turning point in the composer's life, before he became deaf.

4. In the lecture, the professor talks about the social and economic conditions of the 19th century. Indicate whether each of the following was mentioned as a factor. Place a ✓ mark in the YES or NO column. **This question is worth 2 points.**

	YES	NO
The middle class preferred popular music to romantic music.		
Following the Industrial Revolution, more people acquired the pianos.		
Audiences began to ask for musical compositions about love.		
With stronger steel, the pianos produced louder acoustical sounds.		

5. Listen again to part of the lecture. Then answer the question.

Please listen to Track 020 for this part of the question.

What does the professor mean when she says this:

Please listen to Track 020 for this part of the question.

   A. She finds most stars nowadays are only popular for a short period of time.
   B. She wishes that modern musicians would find ways to perform better.
   C. She thinks the audience cultures of the two eras are comparable.
   D. She thinks the performers today are technically superior.

6. Why does the professor mention nocturnes?
   A. To illustrate one of the forms of short character pieces for the piano.
   B. To support the claim that Beethoven was a revolutionary force.
   C. To demonstrate how tone color in piano music differs from that in vocal music.
   D. To give an example of the kind of music frequently played in evening concerts.

Life Sciences, Topic 3: Cell Biology
生命科學常考主題 3：細胞生物學

　　本章內容以生命科學範疇的細胞生物學為知識背景。細胞生物學是研究細胞活動、功能和結構的生物學分支。該領域中常用的一些詞彙和片語有 chromosome（染色體），organic molecule（有機分子），mitosis（有絲分裂）和 cloning（無性繁殖）等。請注意本章中出現的語塊，並記住它們。

····················· 細胞生物學：閱讀 ·····················

▶把握科學史文章的篇章技巧

　　由於新托福考試是一項為諸多不同背景的人設計的英語語言測試，對科學主題的討論不可能太深入，也不可能太過理論化或者太過專業化，所以，科學文章（尤其是物理科學文章）都只含有對科學史的簡要敘述。這些論述的範圍都限定在非專業人員容易理解的基本概念上。

　　科學史研究人類從古代到現代對自然界的認知發展過程。它有可能涵蓋任何科學研究，但其重點往往在生命科學（如醫學）和物理科學（如技術）。科學史的文章通常涉及科學家及其科學貢獻的故事。在各個國家，歷代科學家都提出過新的理論，檢驗過新的假設（其中有些被證明是正確的）。新一代科學家進而會提出更新的觀點、發明更新的儀器，進行新的研究，並推翻一些舊觀點。科學史也會討論社會、文化和經濟狀況。

　　新托福考試閱讀文章中可能會包含以下內容的科學史文章（有時聽力講座中也會有）：

- astronomy, mathematics and medicine in Ancient Egypt（古埃及的天文學、數學和醫學）
- discussions of natural philosophy by Plato and Aristotle（柏拉圖和亞里斯多德的有關自然哲學的討論）
- inventions of the compass, paper, gunpowder and printing in China（中國指南針、造紙術、火藥和印刷術的發明）
- astronomy and mathematics in India（印度的天文學和數學）
- chemistry and experimental methods in Islam（伊斯蘭教國家的化學和實驗方法）
- 17th century — Scientific Revolution (for example, Isaac Newton)（17 世紀的科學革命，如牛頓）
- 18th century — Enlightenment (for example, Halley's Comet)（18 世紀啟蒙運動時期的科學，如哈雷彗星）

- 19th century — Industrial Revolution (for example, Darwin and evolution)（19 世紀工業革命時期的科學，如達爾文和進化論）
- 20th century — Einstein and physics（20 世紀的愛因斯坦和物理學）

　　如何應對這類文章呢？多閱讀介紹著名科學家的生活經歷和思想觀點的資料，會很有幫助。另一種很好的應對策略是熟悉這類文章使用的語言。下面來看看摘自本章下文關於細胞生物學文章中的典型語言用法：

1. 使用被動語態的句子

   This theory **was proposed for plants** in 1837 by the German botanist Mathias Schleiden and **was extended to animals** by his friend, the physiologist Theodor Schwann.

2. 使用過去完成時的句子（通常是被動語態）

   By the turn of the century, a number of important cell parts **had been described and named**.

3. 使用虛擬語氣的句子（多種過去式形式）

   Just think of **what we would miss** in our own world **if no detail smaller than inches could be distinguished**, and **what classical microscopists would have seen had they been able to magnify the living cell** a millionfold.

托福總監評析

　　科技寫作中多使用被動語態。

　　關於科學史的文章中作者也常用被動語態，並用過去時態來表達，如上面第一句所示。

　　同樣，在有關科學成就的文章裡，作者也常用過去完成時來描述在某個日期或重要轉捩點之前發生的活動，如上面的第二個範例。

　　在有關科學理論和假說的文章中，作者會常用虛擬語氣，因為他們在探討理論，而且是推測過去發生的事件。

• **Exercise 1**　（解答請見 P. 352）

　　Write a correct paraphrase for each of the following sentences.

ⓐ Through three pairs of matched lenses, the sharpness of the images was dramatically increased.

_____

_____

ⓑ Even before the 1700s, scientists had fashioned primitive microscopes to better view natural phenomena.

_____

_____

ⓒ Had William Harvey been aware of the invention of microscopes, he could have used that scientific tool to study the heart and blood circulation.

_____

_____

▼模擬試題（解答請見 P. 352）

Looking at Living Cells

(1) Although the fossil record holds few clues to the evolution of cells, recent advances in biochemistry and molecular biology have provided powerful new means of reconstructing the past by probing the present. Hardly 300 years have elapsed since the day when a living cell was first glimpsed by the human eye. Throughout that period, every milestone about cell discovery bears the name of a new tool or instrument.

(2) The world of cells remained entirely unknown and unexplored until the middle of the 17th century, when individuals of prying minds served by skilled hands started grinding lenses and using them to extend their power of vision. One of the first designers of microscopes was the English scientist Robert Hooke—physicist, meteorologist, biologist, engineer, architect—a most remarkable product of his time. In 1665, he published a popular collection called Micrographia; among the beautiful drawings of his observations was one of a thin slice of cork showing a honeycomb structure, an array of what he called "microscopic pores" or "cells." In his description of it, Hooke used the word "cell" in its original meaning of small chamber, as in the cell of a prisoner or a monk. The word has remained, not to describe the little holes that Hooke saw in dead bark, but rather to designate the little blobs of matter that are the inmates of the holes in the living tree.

(3) One of Hooke's most gifted contemporaries was the Netherlander Antonie van Leeuwenhoek, who made almost three hundred microscopes of a very distinct design—a small bead of glass inserted in a copper plate. By holding this contraption close to his eye and peering through the glass bead at an object held on a needle he manipulated with a screw, Leeuwenhoek succeeded in obtaining magnification 270 times that of the naked eye. He was able to see for the first time what he called "animalcules" in blood, sperm and the water of marshes and ponds. Amazingly, he even saw bacteria, which he drew so accurately that specialists can identify them today.

(4) Not all early users of microscopes were as perceptive. The images they were able to observe with their simple instruments—especially when it came to objects as small as living cells—were so blurred that most details had to be filled in by the imagination. Many showed admirable restraint in the use of this faculty. Others took full advantage of it, as did the French scientist Gautier D'Agoty, who believed that a fully formed baby existed within a sperm cell.

(5) For a long time, microscopy did little more than hover around the world of cells until, in 1827, the Italian physicist Giovanni Battista Amici succeeded in correcting the major optical aberrations Section 2 How to Prepare for Academic Reading and Listening of lenses. Through three pairs of matched lenses that could deflect light without separating it into colors, the sharpness of the images was dramatically increased; so much so that only a few years later the generalized theory was formulated that plants and animals are made of one or more similar units—cells. This theory was proposed for plants in 1837 by the German botanist Mathias Schleiden and was extended to animals by his friend, the physiologist Theodor Schwann. The theory was subsequently completed by the pathologist Rudolf Virchow, when he proclaimed in 1855: "Every cell arises from a cell," an altered version of "Every living being arises from an egg." The latter was an assertion made by William Harvey, the English physician who discovered blood circulation and who had died shortly before Robert Hooke's discovery. By the turn of the century, a number of important cell parts had been described and named.

(6) Later investigators found themselves confronting a new obstacle, seemingly insurmountable, as it was set by the very laws of physics. Even with a perfect instrument, no detail smaller than about half the wavelength of the light used can be perceived, which puts the absolute limit of resolution of a microscope utilizing visible light at .25 millionth of a meter. In the world of cells, such a dimension is quite large, relatively speaking. Just think of what we would miss in our own world if no detail smaller than inches could be distinguished, and what classical microscopists would have seen had they been able to magnify the living cell a millionfold.

• Reading Questions

1. In the first paragraph, the author says that our present understanding of cells is largely due to _____.
   A. the accumulation of fossil evidence
   B. the discovery of the molecule
   C. an innovation in instrumentation
   D. a development in the science of light

2. The word "prying" in Paragraph 2 is closest in meaning to _____.
   A. inquisitive
   B. unusual
   C. persevering
   D. precise

3. The word "them" in Paragraph 2 refers to _____.
   A. individuals
   B. minds

C. hands

D. lenses

4. In order to describe Robert Hooke, the author mentions all of the following EXCEPT _____.

　A. he was skillful at sketching life forms

　B. he published a microscope catalog

　C. he was an early manufacturer

　D. he coined the term "cell"

5. In Paragraph 3, the author says that "animalcule" was most likely a name for which of the following?

　A. A microscope designed to look at molecules.

　B. A variety of cells and microorganisms.

　C. A parasite residing in the human bloodstream.

　D. An animal found in swamps and other freshwater bodies.

6. The word "manipulated" in Paragraph 3 is closest in meaning to _____.

　A. fastened

　B. tightened

　C. guided

　D. thread

7. In Paragraph 4, why does the author introduce the statement "Many showed admirable restraint in the use of this faculty"?

　A. To ridicule the absurd theories made by "imaginative" scientists.

　B. To emphasize how limited the early microscope models were.

　C. To point out the wisdom of consulting with other scholars.

　D. To criticize the investigators for not being more imaginative.

8. The word "aberrations" in Paragraph 5 is closest in meaning to _____.

　A. cracks

　B. reflections

　C. magnifications

　D. deviations

9. In Paragraph 5, the author says that what was learned about plant and animal cells during the 1830s?

　A. They are composed of the same core elements.

　B. They both contain more than one cell systems.

　C. Scientists understood animal cells before they did plant cells.

　D. The reproductive functions in animal cells are unlike those in plant cells.

10. Which of the sentences below best expresses the essential information in the highlighted sentence in the passage? Incorrect choices change the meaning in major ways or leave out important information.

Later investigators found themselves confronting a new obstacle, seemingly insurmountable, as it was set by the very laws of physics.

    A. After a while, the scientists unexpectedly discovered a new principle in physics, even though it was difficult.

    B. Subsequent studies were deterred by unforeseen physical constraints that appeared to be unsolvable.

    C. Some of the scientists were convinced that they could find even more cell parts because they were working a novel branch of physics.

    D. Although it was too late for scientists with traditional backgrounds to tackle the problem, they were optimistic that the scientific barrier would be overcome.

11. In Paragraph 5, what does the author imply about William Harvey?

    A. He was not very competent at setting up experimental controls.

    B. He should not have borrowed descriptive language from a fellow scientist.

    C. He probably would have revised his theory had he lived a little longer.

    D. He lacked the tools to determine that blood circulates in the human body.

12. **Directions:** Complete the chart below about two of the microscope makers mentioned in the passage. Choose five of the seven answer choices and match them to the microscope with which they are associated. **This question is worth 3 points.**

Microscope	Features
Leeuwenhoek	• • •
Amici	• •

Answer Choices

1. A glass droplet causes the specimen to be enlarged almost 300 times

2. The instrument represented the earliest microscope used to view cell walls in cork tissue

3. The enhanced image resolution led to the theory that plants contain similar cells

4. The specimen to be viewed is manipulated by the means of screws

5. Drawings of microorganisms led to the popularization of the microscope in many circles

6. The microscopes allowed the viewer to see microorganisms, including bacteria

7. The design made use of multiple pairs of matched lenses processed light without color separation

關鍵語塊

- **cell** 細胞
- **biochemistry** 生物化學
- **molecular biology** 分子生物學
- **reconstruct the past** 重現過去
- **probe** 探索
- **elapse** 消逝
- **glimpse** 瞥見
- **by the human eye** 憑肉眼
- **milestone** 劃時代的事件
- **bear the name of...** 被稱為⋯⋯
- **grind lenses** 磨鏡片
- **product of his time** 時代的產物
- **Micrographia** 《顯微圖譜》
- **cork** 表皮
- **honeycomb** 蜂巢
- **an array of** 一排，一群，一批
- **pore** 小孔
- **blobs of matter** 黏糊糊的一團膠狀物
- **inmates of ...** （監獄裡的）犯人（此 處為雙關語，指「細胞質」）
- **Netherlander** 荷蘭人

- **bead of glass** 玻璃珠
- **magnification** 放大
- **naked eye** 肉眼
- **animalcule** 微生物
- **sperm** 精液
- **marsh** 沼澤
- **pond** 池塘
- **blurred** 模糊不清的
- **admirable restraint** 值得稱讚的自制力
- **faculty** 能力
- **microscopy** 顯微鏡學
- **hover around** 徘徊於
- **deflect light** 使光線偏斜、折射
- **sharpness** 清晰度
- **physiologist** 生理學家
- **pathologist** 病理學家
- **blood circulation** 血液循環
- **insurmountable** 不能克服的
- **resolution** 解析度
- **magnify** 放大
- **millionfold** 百萬倍的

細胞生物學：聽力

▶細節資訊題的聽力技巧和做題策略

聽力部分的講座和對話後的細節資訊題通常詢問說話者直接傳達的一些具體事實。每篇學術講座後的六道試題中一般含有一至兩道細節資訊題；每則對話後的五道試題中會有兩至三道細節資訊題。

聽力部分的細節資訊題有兩種類型。第一種題型與閱讀部分的細節資訊題類似，要求考生從四個選項中選出一個正確答案。第二種題型要求考生從四個選項中選出兩個正確答案，問題後面會有 Choose 2 answers 的提示資訊。兩種類型的細節資訊題的分數都是 1 分。

• LISTENING TIP

學術講座後的細節資訊題通常以下面的形式出現：

According to the lecture, how were cells first discovered?

According to the professor, when did bacteria appear on the Earth?

What does the professor say about the function of the nucleus? Choose 2 answers.

表面上，聽力部分的細節資訊題與閱讀部分的細節資訊題非常相似，但是，二者所採用的應試策略是不同的。原因如下：講座和對話部分的螢幕圖像和錄音只出現一次，所以考生必須要專注於細節。而在閱讀部分，考生隨時都可以往回略讀和掃讀以找出細節資訊題的答案。此外，播放錄音之前，考生看不到試題。這樣就不可能知道錄音中將會出現的具體詞彙，也不可能提前略讀選項以排除錯誤選項。而且，一旦確認了聽力題的答案，便不能再返回。

幸運的是，考生可以通過記筆記來抓住需要的細節。記筆記絕對是做對大多數聽力細節資訊題所必需的，我認為這是重中之重。

同時，還需要多聽多練。每天花 20 分鐘聽難度適中的材料，堅持 6 個月，聽力能力一定會提高。

除了上述準備外，如果想捕捉住細節，還需要在基礎技能上下功夫：

1）聽不同領域的詞彙語塊（包括意思、用法以及它們在情境中的發音方式）

2）注意教授和學生頻繁用到的文法結構類型，以鞏固聽力文法技能。

一般來說，新托福聽力題不會問一些次要細節，但可能會詢問論據（supporting ideas）。如果考生沒有聽清一兩個句子，或者不確定某個片語的意思，就會很容易漏掉主要觀點。處理這種情形的唯一方法是多做筆記，做題目時也許這些筆記就能派上用場。

● 聽力細節資訊題的答題策略：

策略 1 對於講座，要注意聽引導句。

因為引導句可能會提到將要涉及的情境。聽的時候要記住，教授的主題和詞語一定與該情境有關。

策略 2 認真記下主題。

如果講座是關於某個人的，那麼題目可能就會出現一道關於這個人的主要貢獻的問題。你可以利用自己在該主題範圍內已有知識來幫助理解說話者說了哪些細節資訊。

策略 3 快速記下一切能記下的詞語。

跟上說話者的思路，並儘量記下概念之間的關係，如 Rigid wall → no movement。

策略 4 注意電腦螢幕上出現的詞彙和圖表。

出題者讓你看到這些，是為了讓你聽到這些專業術語或概念時不會感到困惑。當然，出題者很可能會就其中一個概念出一道考題，因此，當你看到詞彙或圖表時，要準備好回答與此相關的細節資訊題。

策略 5 要記住或寫下所給的例子。

新托福聽力考試中常常會考講座中講到的例子，有時以細節資訊題的形式出現，有時以其他題型出現，如語用功能題和組織結構題（見第 14 章）。

策略 6 聽力細節資訊題通常是以 who、what、where、when 和 why 引導的問句。聽講座時，要試著思考這 5 個 W 的問題。

注意，細節資訊題有時會以 According to the professor 開頭。這類題目的選項往往是對教授原話的換句話説。

策略 7 如果無法記住細節，就猜測答案，然後深呼吸，為下一道聽力題做好準備。在做剩下的題目時，不要因為漏掉一個細節就失去冷靜。

現在請聽有關細胞生物學的講座，試著做好詳細的筆記，並運用你所學到的策略。

▶ **模擬試題**（解答請見 P. 353）

Now listen to a lecture about CELL BIOLOGY.　 *Track 021*

Cell Biology

★ **Keywords**

cell wall 細胞壁	cell membrane 細胞膜	vacuole 液泡

• **Listening Questions**　 *Track 022*

1. What does the professor mainly discuss?
   A. How bacteria evolved into complex organisms.
   B. How plant cells are able to reproduce.
   C. A comparison of plant and animal cells.
   D. The functions of plant cell structures.

2. Listen again to part of the lecture. Then answer the question.

    Please listen to Track 022 for this part of the question.

   What does the professor mean when he says this:

    Please listen to Track 022 for this part of the question.

   A. The exteriors of plants and animals do not look similar at all.
   B. The cells of these living organisms have things in common.
   C. Apple trees will often vary with age and growth conditions.
   D. Small living things do not behave the way large ones do.

3. What does the professor say about the size of living cells?
   Choose 2 answers.
   A. The cell size of life forms does not differ in a major way.
   B. Ancient cells were smaller than cells in modern organisms.

C. The larger the organism is, the larger the cell size will be.

D. Plant cells tend to be somewhat larger than animal cells.

4. Why does the professor mention lettuce?

　A. To illustrate how nutrients are taken up into plants.

　B. To demonstrate the effect of fluids on vacuoles.

　C. To instruct the students how to set up for the lab on cells.

　D. To contrast lettuce cells with the cells of other plants.

5. The professor mentions various features of plant and animal cells. For each item below, indicate which feature is associated with which cell type.

　Place a ✓ mark in the correct box. **This question is worth 2 points.**

Feature	Plants	Animals	Both plants and animals
Have cell membranes			
Have relatively large surface-to-volume ratio			
Have a long shape			
Have the ability to move			

• Exercise 2 　（解答請見 P. 356）

　　Detailed information questions often ask "W" questions such as "what" and "where." To practice listening for detail, listen to the lecture on cells once again and write down the answers as you go.

1. earliest cells — When? _____

2. bacteria — Where? _____

3. cell membrane — What organism? _____

4. animal cells are round — Why? _____

5. vacuole — What function? _____

12 Social Sciences, Topic 3: Law
社會科學常考主題 3：法學

　　本章內容以社會科學範疇的法學為知識背景。法學有多種類型，例如民法、刑法、國際法、合同法和憲法。法學領域常見的語塊有 defense attorney（辯護律師），legally binding（法律約束力）和 preliminary hearing（預審）等。請注意本章中出現的語塊，並記住它們。

·······················法學：閱讀·······················

▶內容總結題的考試重點和答題策略

　　內容總結題有六個選項，需要從中選擇三個。將三個正確答案連在一起就是文章的主要大意。

　　每篇閱讀文章後有時有一道內容總結題，有時沒有。因為內容總結題本來就具有綜合性，而且是考題中最難的一道，所以通常是最後一題。內容總結題的配分為 2 分。考生選對全部三個選項，得 2 分；選對其中兩個得 1 分；如果只選對其中一個或全部沒有選對，則不得分。

　　內容總結題的題目要求相對固定，基本上已標準化，內容如下：

Directions: An introductory sentence for a brief summary of the passage is provided below. Complete the summary by selecting the THREE answer choices that express the most important ideas in the passage. Some answer choices do not belong in the summary because they express ideas that are not presented in the passage or are minor ideas in the passage. **This question is worth 2 points.**

　　題目意思是： 下面給出了本文文章大意的開頭句子。選擇最能表達本文重要觀點的三個選項。有些選項不正確是因為它們表達的觀點在文章中沒有提到或者不是文章的主要觀點。本題 2 分。

• READING TIPS

　　內容總結題的正確選項通常會有以下特徵：
• 它們是文章中重複的主題。
• 它們通常是一般原則或現象。
• 它們是主要觀點的改述。
• 幾個句子合在一起，就基本組成了文章的中心大意。
• 幾個句子合在一起，可以綜合概括文章的主題。

• READING SAMPLE

下面以本章模擬試題中的第 13 題為例：

This passage discusses the doctrine of coverture and the impact this law had on family life.

-
-
-

Answer Choices

1. In the US, a feme covert was not permitted to obtain an education against her husband's wishes.
2. Stemming from English common law, the doctrine of coverture limited women's rights up until the 1900s.
3. The coverture model consists of property ownership exclusively by husbands, and a system wherein women own their output is a self-ownership model.
4. Under coverture, married women worked at home to perform tasks such as sewing, which they sold on the market as piece goods.
5. A woman who signed a special contract could act as a legal principal and represent her husband's interests.
6. Economic interests frequently determine how a married couple spend their time, whether on market activities or in the home.

托福總監評析

　　主題句已說出：This passage discusses the doctrine of coverture and the impact this law had on family life. 這個主題句是第一個句子，後面須添加三個總結文章大意的句子。考生可以用電腦滑鼠將三個主要觀點拖入總結表格裡。正確選項為第二、第三和第六個選項。第二個選項概述了女性在法律上受丈夫監護的歷史。第三個選項綜合介紹了女性受丈夫監護的經濟模式和自己擁有勞動收入的經濟模式。這是對文章關鍵內容的總結，因為它體現了受丈夫監護模式和不受丈夫監護模式的經濟意義。第六個選項綜合了第六段和第七段的要點。其他選項文章中沒有提到或者與文章內容矛盾。

● 內容總結題的做題策略：

策略 1 閱讀文章時，要仔細看文章的構架。

例如，有關下文女性由丈夫監護文章的框架是：a) 女子由丈夫監護的歷史；b) 轉變為自我擁有法律；c) 受丈夫監護和自我擁有財產的經濟狀況（時間的分配 v.s. 對財產的擁有權）；d) 這兩種法律模式與家庭經濟狀況之間的相互影響。

策略 2 閱讀文章時，儘量抓住要點。會區分主要觀點和次要觀點。

策略 3 仔細留意那些反覆出現的觀點，特別是有定義或者舉例說明的觀點。

策略 4 閱讀六個選項時，先找出那些出現次數最多的觀點和句子。

策略 5 多注意包含概括性表述而非細節性表述的選項。

策略 6 選出三個句子，將這三個句子連在一起看是否能構成文章的大意。

策略 7 要記住，錯誤的選項可能是：a) 次要觀點，b) 文章中沒有提到的觀點和 c) 與文章內容不符的主要觀點或次要觀點。

• **Exercise 1** （解答請見 P. 357）

Read the following passage about law. Then write down what you think the three main ideas are. Condense and synthesize whenever possible.

Contract Law

A contract is an exchange of promises associated with a specific action (for example, compensation), should those promises be broken. In an agreement where promises have been broken, there is said to be a breach of contract. English contract law comes from the Latin principle "pacta sunt servanda" ("pacts must be kept") and dates back to the earliest trade in ancient times. As contract law developed, breach of contract has come to be recognized in formal terms by the common law legal system. As a result, obligations have been established between legal parties (individuals, corporations, countries). Legal parties can enter freely into these agreements. If one party makes an offer for an arrangement in a contract and the other accepts, this is called a "concurrence of wills." The offer-and-acceptance agreement does not always need to be expressed in writing, or even orally. Moreover, not all contracts are two-sided. There are also unilateral contracts, where only one party makes an express promise. The case of Carlill v. Carbolic Smoke Ball Co. is a classic example of a unilateral contract.

(a) _____

_____

(b) _____

_____

(c) _____

_____

▶ **模擬試題**（解答請見 P. 357）

The Doctrine of Coverture

(1) In law, coverture refers to the inclusion of a woman in the "legal person" of her husband after marriage. Under traditional English common law, an adult unmarried woman was a considered to have the legal status of feme sole (the medieval French term that was used in British law for a single woman), while a married woman had the status of feme covert (or "covered" woman). In coverture, married women lacked the legal capacity to hold their own property or to contract on their own behalf; similarly, a husband's tax payments or jury duty "covered" his wife as well.

(2) Until the beginning of the twentieth century in England and even in the US, the doctrine of coverture restricted women's choices in virtually every aspect of their lives. Up to that time, a married woman—a feme covert—could not make contracts or sign legal documents, buy and sell property, sue or be sued, obtain an education against her husband's wishes or draft wills. Not only would the husband control any property she brought to the marriage, he would own any wages she earned.

(3) The legal doctrine of coverture is no longer used in most countries, and so women now control rights themselves and own the products of their labor. The shift in property rights from coverture is a constructive example of how family economics have shaped property rights, and visa-a-versa. In economic terms, coverture is a system in which men control married women and own their output, whereas self-ownership can be said to be a system in which married women own themselves and their output.

(4) Using this economic model, it is interesting to look at how the coverture and self-ownership systems differ from one another in terms of how husbands and wives allocate their time, i.e., whether their time is spent in the household or spent on market activities. We find that the nature of the property rights held by the husband and the wife determine the behavior of each person and ultimately the total economic value of the marriage.

(5) Under coverture, the husband determined his own allocation of time, and he also guided the allocation of his wife's time. Because the husband owned the wife's earnings, the coverture model of the family took on a specific form. First, the husband was treated as a legal "principal," meaning he was legally responsible for his wife and "owned" all of the household output. Second, because labor and goods markets were closed to married women, a wife had no individual rights to market goods and thus was merely an "agent" for her husband, who was the principal. Third, whereas married woman were restricted from working outside the home in the market, it was sometimes possible for them to spend their days in leisure because their husbands could not always monitor their household efforts.

(6) Under self-ownership, however, women are free to allocate their time across both market and household activities. This leads to a different economic model of the family. First, the husband and wife jointly own their final market goods. ■ 1 Second, within a marriage, husband and wife each own one-half of the household products and one-half of the property income. ■ 2 Finally, because the wife has access to labor markets, she is not as likely to be tempted into leisure at home. ■ 3 This model means that each partner in the marriage can choose his or her optimal allocation of time between market and household work, based on the nature of the marriage contract and the behavior of the other partner. ■ 4

(7) The doctrine of coverture granted most rights to men, but the laws were sometimes flexible. For example, some doctrines allowed women to become exempt from coverture or to have options for contracting out of coverture. Deviation from coverture law usually indicated that husbands themselves would also be better off if their wives were to acquire additional property rights. Examples of such additional rights included the access to labor and commercial markets, ownership of market earnings, ownership of separate property and greater control of household output. Historical evidence shows us that legal departures from coverture rules were most prevalent in marriages with greater wealth and in marriages where the wives were performing tasks that were difficult to track.

• **Reading Questions**

1. According to Paragraph 1, what is true about a woman's rights under the English law of coverture?
   A. Widowed women had more rights than single women.
   B. Unmarried women were not allowed to get married without consent.
   C. Women were permitted to pay a lower tax rate than men were.
   D. After marrying, women had no individual legal status.

2. In Paragraph 1, the author explains the concept of coverture by _____.
   A. clarifying the origin of the expression
   B. comparing common law to statutory law
   C. citing the case law of the United Kingdom
   D. highlighting its strengths and weaknesses

3. Which of the sentences below best expresses the essential information in the highlighted sentence in the passage? Incorrect choices change the meaning in major ways or leave out important information.
   Not only would the husband control any property she brought to the marriage, he would own any wages she earned.
   A. Although the husband had control over his wife's wages, he was not responsible for her assets.

B. A husband had authority over the property a wife owned before marriage and her future salary as well.

C. Only the husband controlled the finances; the wife took charge of the household.

D. Even if the husband was not able to manage the property that the wife possessed, he could take control of his wife's income.

4. The word "shift" in Paragraph 3 is closest in meaning to _____.

　A. phase

　B. improvement

　C. division

　D. change

5. In Paragraph 3, the author says that which of the following factors led to changes in property rights?

　A. International trends.

　B. A legal decision.

　C. Family finances.

　D. Labor activism.

6. The word "monitor" in Paragraph 5 is closest in meaning to _____.

　A. check on

　B. build up

　C. influence

　D. trust

7. According to the passage, why would women under coverture be motivated to choose to spend time relaxing?

　A. They felt their hard work wasn't appreciated.

　B. They were tired from doing so much housework.

　C. Their husbands did not know what they were doing.

　D. Their husbands encouraged them to take it easy.

8. The phrase "exempt from" in Paragraph 7 is closest in meaning to _____.

　A. impoverished from

　B. free from

　C. beneficiaries of

　D. models of

9. The word "prevalent" in Paragraph 7 is closest in meaning to _____.

　A. satisfactory

　B. commonplace

　C. challenged

　D. documented

10. Each of the following illustrates the extra rights for women mentioned by the author in Paragraph 7 EXCEPT _____.
   A. having a separate bank account
   B. personally owning a summer cottage
   C. filing a law suit
   D. working as a teacher

11. Which of the following statements most accurately reflects the author's opinion about coverture?
   A. Coverture was a reasonable law for women from wealthy families.
   B. Coverture was essentially a very efficient social and economic system.
   C. Women were the only ones who wanted to make changes to coverture laws.
   D. It is fortunate that economic incentives helped eliminate coverture.

12. Look at the four squares [■] that indicate where the following sentence could be added to the passage.
   Rather, she is more likely to work more in the market and purchase market goods.
   Where would the sentence best fit?
   ■ 1
   ■ 2
   ■ 3
   ■ 4

13. **Directions:** An introductory sentence for a brief summary of the passage is provided below.
   Complete the summary by selecting the THREE answer choices that express the most important ideas in the passage. Some answer choices do not belong in the summary because they express ideas that are not presented in the passage or are minor ideas in the passage. **This question is worth 2 points.**
   This passage discusses the doctrine of coverture and the impact this law had on family life.

•   •   •

Answer Choices

1. In the US, a feme covert was not permitted to obtain an education against her husband's wishes.

2. Stemming from English common law, the doctrine of coverture limited women's rights up until the 1900s.

3. The coverture model consists of property ownership exclusively by husbands, and a system wherein women own their output is a self-ownership model.

4. Under coverture, married women worked at home to perform tasks such as sewing, which they sold on the market as piece goods.

5. A woman who signed a special contract could act as a legal principal and represent her husband's interests.

6. Economic interests frequently determine how a married couple spend their time, whether on market activities or in the home.

關鍵語塊

- **coverture** （受丈夫保護的）已婚婦女的法律身份
- **legal person** 法人
- **English common law** 英國普通法，英國習慣法
- **legal status** 法律地位
- **feme sole** 單身女子
- **feme covert** 已婚女子
- **jury duty** 陪審員的義務
- **doctrine** 原則
- **sue sb** 控告某人
- **draft will** 草擬遺囑
- **constructive example** 有建設性的實例
- **property rights** 財產權
- **visa-a-versa** 反之亦然
- **allocation of time** 時間分配
- **principal** 〔法〕委託人
- **market goods** 交易商品
- **agent** 代理人
- **optimal allocation** 最優配置
- **marriage contract** 婚姻契約
- **grant rights to sb.** 授予某人以權利
- **contract out of** 終止協議（或合同等）
- **household output** 家庭的生產量
- **track** 觀察

法學：聽力

▶重點技能：掌握表示舉例的信號詞

　　在講座中，優秀的老師能夠把複雜難懂的概念解釋地非常清楚。講述時，他們會使用一些技巧，包括對術語的簡單解釋以及對學術材料進行合乎邏輯和有趣的介紹。有經驗的老師也會為事實和概念列舉一些具體的實例。考生需要學會如何聽這些例子並利用它們，以便更好地領會講座的意思並正確地回答關於這些例子的問題。

　　有時候，教授會用某些信號詞來讓我們知道即將會列舉實例。最典型的有 for example 和 for instance。下面的圖表是常用的表示舉例的信號詞，考生需要熟練掌握。

講座中表示舉例的信號詞

For instance, ...	Let's take... as an example.
For example, ... is...	There are many examples, for instance...
By way of example, we see...	There are many examples, such as...
One instance of this is....	There are many examples, like...
Consider..., which...	In our example of..., we saw that...
We see this in... with....	An example of... would be that...
This is illustrated by...	An instance of... is....
As an illustration, let me tell you about...	There are other types of..., such as...
Take..., which is...	One type of... is...
Take the case of...	..., for example, may involve...

　　顯然，教授在列舉實例時，不可能總說 for example，或使用上面的詞語。他們也可能會先引用一個基本原理，然後直接給出詳細實例。在這種情況下，考生需要積極地思考講座的內容和思路。這裡再重申一次，把實例記下來是新托福考試聽力部分拿高分的關鍵。

▶ **模擬試題**（解答請見 P. 358）

Now listen to a lecture about LAW. *Track 023*

• **Listening Questions**  *Track 024*

1. What does the professor mainly talk about?
   A. Appropriate punishments.
   B. Types of social control.
   C. Values in non-industrial societies.
   D. The history of economic incentives.

2. Why does the professor say this:

 Please listen to Track 024 for this part of the question.

   A. To illustrate that rules need not be official in order to be effective.
   B. To say we should pass only those laws which are socially appropriate.
   C. To complain that many laws are written in vague official language.
   D. To emphasize that law and order is the highest need of society.

3. Why does the professor mention the example of throwing litter on the ground?
   A. To give a reason why strict laws are needed.
   B. To profile a person who deviates from the norm.
   C. To illustrate an informal social mechanism.
   D. To provide an example of an explicit social rule.

4. What does the professor say about homogeneous societies?
   Choose 2 answers.
   A. Laws are frequently aimed at foreigners or other outsiders.
   B. Rules are handed down to each generation by word of mouth.
   C. There are fewer known criminals and it is easier to target them.
   D. There is a high degree of consistency in what rules are accepted.

5. The professor talks about social sanctions. Indicate whether each of the ideas below was presented as part of the lecture.
   Place a ✓ mark in the YES or NO column. **This question is worth 2 points.**

	YES	NO
Positive sanctions have been proven to be impractical.		
Societies count on individuals to self-sanction.		
Disgracing a person who deviates from the norm is an external sanction.		

6. What does the professor imply about the legal system when he says this:

 Please listen to Track 024 for this part of the question.

   A. It needs to be expanded to absorb the heavy case load.
   B. It is a fine system but can be unfair if one party cannot afford a lawyer.
   C. It wastes a lot of time on complaints that do not really merit attention.
   D. It is not particularly effective in shaping people's attitudes.

Physical Sciences, Topic 4: Chemistry and Biochemistry
物理科學常考主題 4：化學和生物化學

本章內容以物理科學範疇的化學和生物化學為知識背景。化學是對物質的組成、作用和變化的研究。化學的常見分支有物理化學、無機化學和有機化學。生物化學是對有機生物體的化學作用的研究。化學中用到的語塊有 ion（離子），periodic table（週期表）和 chemical bond（化學鍵）等。生物化學相關的語塊有 immune system（免疫系統），enzyme（酶）和 dilution（稀釋）等。請注意本章中出現的語塊，並記住它們。

····················化學和生物化學：閱讀····················

▶修辭目的題的考試重點和答題策略

修辭目的題要求考生回答作者語言組織的用意。有些題目詢問一個詞或一個片語的用意，有些題目直接問作者為什麼以某種方式組織文章內容。

在整個閱讀部分，最多會有兩道修辭目的題，也可能一道也沒有。

• READING TIPS

修辭目的題的題幹有多種形式：

Why does the author mention...?

Why does the author give details about...?

Why does the author mention that... is...?

Why does the author introduce the statement that...?

Why does the author talk about...?

Why does the author organize the material (in a certain way)?

The author cites... as an example of...

The author mentions... in order to...

這種題型的大多數選項都是由「To + Verb」構成，因為問題是問目的：目的是什麼？下面圖表中列出了新托福考試修辭目的題最常用的動詞和動詞語塊。

修辭目的題選項中最常用的語塊

Verb（動詞）	Verb CHUNKS（動詞語塊）
to argue	to provide an argument
to compare	to make a comparison
to contrast	to provide a contrast
to criticize	to provide a criticism
to define	to provide a definition
to demonstrate	to provide a demonstration
to describe	to provide a description
to emphasize	to give emphasis to
to exemplify	to provide an example
to explain	to give an explanation
to illustrate	to provide an illustration
to indicate	to point out
to predict	to make a prediction
to prove	to provide proof
to question	to pose a question
to refute	to provide a rebuttal to
to ridicule	to make fun of
to show	to provide evidence
to suggest	to make a suggestion

• READING SAMPLE

下面來看本章模擬試題中的一道修辭目的題：

8. In Paragraph 6, why does the author introduce this statement **However, the spontaneous formation of complex, long-chain polymers from small, chemically generated monomers is not at all a straightforward process.**
   A. To indicate the length of time that Miller's experiment would have taken.
   B. To criticize the method that Miller and Urey used in simulating atmospheric conditions.
   C. To show future researchers the correct process for creating complex polymers.
   D. To imply that complex molecules may not have resulted spontaneously.

托福總監評析

　　略讀第六段可知，該段講述 Stanley Miller 如何嘗試研究化學進化周圍的條件。作者先介紹 Miller 的初次實驗，然後提到了幾次後續實驗，在後續實驗中，科學家們獲得了一定的成功。本題加粗的句子是本段的最後一句，它之前的句子是：These molecules may have accumulated and provided a rich environment for chemical evolution. 從句首 however 可知，該句應該是對前面的觀點提出質疑；本句還提到，從單分子到聚合物並非一個直接的過程。聚合物可能不是自然形成的，因為原始環境相對複雜。因此選項 D 為正確答案。

　　要做好這種題型，應該弄清楚修辭目的題的意思。修辭是指說服的藝術或技巧，往往通過語言的運用技巧來達到目的。每一個作者在選用特定的詞彙和片語時都有其潛在的寫作目的。修辭目的題正是要求讀者準確推斷其目的。

● 修辭目的題的答題策略：

　　策略 1 熟悉各類修辭功能和目的。

　　策略 2 閱讀文章時，思考作者的意圖和作者的寫作技巧，並住作者如何使用語言或某種行文組織結構來陳述觀點。試著弄清作者的立場。增強對修辭結構的瞭解，例如 on the other hand。

　　策略 3 讀一篇文章時，多留意作者用來說明觀點的隱喻、舉例和例證，預測可能會問哪些問題。

　　策略 4 當碰到一道關於片語或句子的修辭目的題時，要仔細閱讀上下文，理清觀點間的邏輯思路。猜出作者的觀點後，運用邏輯來確定語言的目的和功能。

▶ 模擬試題（解答請見 P. 362）

Chemical Origins of Life

★ **Keywords**

peptides 肽	reflux apparatus 回流裝置

(1) The conditions that existed on Earth in its first billion years are still a matter of dispute. Was the surface initially molten? Did the atmosphere contain ammonia? Or methane? Everyone seems to agree that the Earth was a violent place with volcanic eruptions, lightning and torrential rains. There was little if any free oxygen and no layer of ozone to absorb the ultraviolet radiation from the Sun. By its photochemical action, the radiation may have helped to keep the atmosphere rich in reactive molecules and far from chemical

equilibrium. Certainly, the first living systems were much simpler than any cells alive today. The transition from nonliving to living was gradual, and no single event led to life in all its modern complexity.

(2) Typically, scientific attempts to define life have included the following criteria: An aggregate of cells is considered "alive" if it 1) can use chemical energy or electromagnetic energy for chemical reactions; 2) can increase its mass through controlled chemical synthesis; and 3) possesses an information coding system as well as a system for translating coded information into molecules which can allow for maintenance and reproduction.

(3) The best estimate for the age of the Earth is about 4.54 billion years, and the oldest microfossils superficially resembling bacteria have been dated at 3.5 billion years. Thus, chemical evolution, defined as the synthesis of amino acids and their combination into peptides, during the first 1.0 to 1.5 billion years of Earth history probably preceded the appearance of cellular life and its subsequent biological evolution.

(4) The major opinion is that Earth's atmosphere was nearly neutral, was non-oxidizing and contained primarily nitrogen, carbon dioxide, hydrogen sulfide and water. Microfossils resembling modern blue-green bacteria have been found in limestone rocks called stromatolites 3.5 billion years old. Presumably these ancient photosynthetic bacteria produced oxygen by splitting water molecules into hydrogen and oxygen, just as blue-green bacteria do today. Over more than another billion years, oxygen slowly began to accumulate, eventually causing the primitive atmosphere to become oxidizing.

(5) There are two major scientific theories regarding how life came to be on Earth. It either evolved on Earth from nonliving chemicals, or it evolved elsewhere in the universe and was brought to Earth by comets or meteorites (the panspermia theory). Amino acids and other precursors of modern macromolecules have been found in meteorites, and so chemical evolution of these molecules might have been—and still may be—widespread in the cosmos.

(6) In May 1953 the graduate student Stanley Miller, at the suggestion of his mentor Harold Urey, used a reflux apparatus to reproduce ancient atmospheric conditions that existed prior to the chemical evolution of biological molecules. ■ 1 To do this, Miller recirculated water, vapor and other gases (CH_4, NH_3 and H_2) through a chamber where they were exposed to a continuous highvoltage electrical discharge that simulated natural lightning. ■ 2 After a few days, the mixture was analyzed and found to contain sugars, lipids and some of the building blocks for life, nucleic acids. ■ 3 However, nucleic acids (DNA, RNA) themselves were not formed! ■ 4 The experiment also produced compounds which would be toxic to most life forms. But these compounds, which include formaldehyde and cyanide, are necessary for creating important biochemical compounds, including amino acids. Subsequent experiments by Miller and other researchers using different molecule mixtures and energy sources produced a variety of other building blocks of more complex molecules.

These molecules may have accumulated and provided a rich environment for chemical evolution. However, the spontaneous formation of complex, long-chain polymers from small, chemically generated monomers is not at all a straightforward process.

(7) Proteinlike peptides can also be synthesized from amino acids on clay mineral surfaces. Clay consists of alternating layers of inorganic ions and water molecules. The highly ordered structure of clay strongly attracts organic molecules and promotes chemical reactions between them. Polypeptides, which are molecules of many joined amino acids, have been detected in laboratory simulations of these reactions. Interestingly, when solutions of these peptides are heated in water and then allowed to cool, small, spherical particles called microspheres are formed. The microspheres are about the same size and shape as spherical bacteria. Some are able to add mass through proteinlike peptides and lipids and subsequently proliferate.

• Reading Questions

1. According to Paragraph 1, what role might ultraviolet radiation have played in shaping conditions on the Earth?
   A. It destroyed the ozone layer.
   B. It facilitated chemical reactions.
   C. It contributed to incidents of lightning.
   D. It delayed the origin of simple cells.

2. The word "its" in Paragraph 1 refers to _____.
   A. ozone
   B. the Sun
   C. action
   D. radiation

3. All of the following are mentioned in Paragraph 2 as preconditions for living cells EXCEPT .
   A. ability for one cell to create different kinds of cells
   B. ability to decode information
   C. capacity to use energy
   D. capacity to grow

4. The word "presumably" in Paragraph 4 is closest in meaning to _____.
   A. inevitably
   B. gradually
   C. apparently
   D. systematically

5. In Paragraph 4, what does the author say about oxygen and the Earth's atmosphere?
   A. Oxygen was released into the Earth's atmosphere through the interaction of limestone with ocean water.
   B. Photosynthesis did not take place in the atmosphere for billions of years because of carbon dioxide and nitrogen gases.
   C. Oxygen molecules found in stromatolite rocks indicate that there was an oxidizing atmosphere billions of years ago.
   D. Blue-green bacteria may have, over time, extracted large quantities of oxygen from water.

6. The word "precursors" Paragraph 5 is closest in meaning to _____.
   A. forerunners
   B. relatives
   C. duplicates
   D. products

7. According to Paragraph 6, how did Stanley Miller reproduce the climate of early Earth?
   A. By putting amino acids in a heated chamber with gases.
   B. By sending a charge of electricity into a chamber with gases.
   C. By mixing poisonous materials with oxidizing gases.
   D. By recycling building block molecules through water and gases.

8. In Paragraph 6, why does the author introduce this statement **However, the spontaneous formation of complex, long-chain polymers from small, chemically generated monomers is not at all a straightforward process.**
   A. To indicate the length of time that Miller's experiment would have taken.
   B. To criticize the method that Miller and Urey used in simulating atmospheric conditions.
   C. To show future researchers the correct process for creating complex polymers.
   D. To imply that complex molecules may not have resulted spontaneously.

9. The word "proliferate" in Paragraph 7 is closest in meaning to _____.
   A. combine
   B. develop
   C. multiply
   D. mature

10. In Paragraph 7, what does the author imply about the microspheres which are formed in scientific simulations?
    A. The microspheres probably house a sort of parasitic bacteria.
    B. The microspheres contained pieces of clay inside them.
    C. There may be an evolutionary link between microspheres and the ancient bacteria.
    D. There is a more rapid rate of growth in microspheres than in spherical bacteria.

11. Look at the four squares [■] that indicate where the following sentence could be added to the passage.

Specifically, he hoped to create certain small molecules of life (monomers), such as amino acids.

Where would the sentence best fit?

■ 1

■ 2

■ 3

■ 4

12. The author talks about areas of knowledge on which scientists agree and disagree. Complete the chart below about the status of the theories on early chemical evolution. Choose five of the seven answer choices that are specifically mentioned in the passage. **This question is worth 3 points.**

	Scientific Theories
Areas on which scientists agree	• • •
Areas on which scientists disagree	• •

Answer Choices

1. Life came into existence from nonliving chemicals

2. Blue-green bacteria were damaged by ultraviolet radiation

3. The Earth's climate was very destructive

4. There is evidence of amino acids in meteorites

5. The earliest instance of fossilized life dates back 3.5 billion years

6. The Earth's atmosphere included methane gas

7. Molecules were chemically synthesized in hot deep-ocean vents

關鍵語塊

- **a matter of dispute** 爭議的問題
- **molten** 熔化的，熾熱的
- **methane** 甲烷
- **volcanic eruption** 火山噴發
- **torrential rain** 暴雨
- **little if any…** 即使有……，也沒多少
- **free oxygen** 游離氧
- **ultraviolet radiation** 紫外線輻射
- **photochemical action** 光化作用
- **chemical equilibrium** 化學平衡
- **aggregate of…** ……的聚集
- **chemical synthesis** 化學合成
- **microfossil** 微化石
- **amino acid** 氨基酸

- **stromatolite** 疊層（石）
- **meteorite** 隕石
- **panspermia theory** 胚種論
- **precursor of…** ……的前身
- **macromolecule** 大分子
- **cosmos** 宇宙
- **lipid** 脂類
- **nucleic acid** 核酸
- **formaldehyde** 甲醛
- **cyanide** 氰化物
- **polymer** 聚合物
- **monomer** 單分子
- **clay** 黏土
- **microsphere** 微球體

• Exercise 1　（解答請見 P. 363）

Write an answer to each of the following author's rhetorical purpose questions, based on the passage about chemical evolution.

ⓐ Why does the author mention lightning in Paragraph 1?

_____

ⓑ Why does the author give details about the panspermia theory in Paragraph 5?

_____

ⓒ In Paragraph 7, why does the author introduce the statement **Some are able to add mass through protein-like peptides and lipids and subsequently proliferate?**

_____

_____

·············· 化學和生物化學：聽力 ··············

▶重點技能：熟悉表示因果關係的信號詞

　　在學術講座中，尤其是在關於生物和物理原理的講座中，教授通常會談到促使事情發生變化的條件和因素。在諸如物理、化學和生物化學等科學中，對因果關係的解釋並不總是直截了當，因為現象可能不是直接發生或可觀察到的東西，例如一些分子的反應。

　　幸運的是，新托福考試中設計的講座目的是能讓那些非專業的人也聽得懂。此外，如果考生熟悉談論因果關係時最常用的語塊和信號詞，那麼就能輕鬆地跟上教授的講解。

以本章下文聽力為例：

• LISTENING SAMPLE

Many of the properties of _____ are due to _____.
Each _____ has _____, allowing the _____ to _____.
That means that _____ can force _____ into a _____ state.
The assumption is that _____ creates _____.
We also think that the principle of _____ may help explain how _____.
在上面的每個句子中，教授用不同的方式將科學方面的原因與結果關聯起來。

說話者會使用很多信號詞來連接原因和結果。最典型的有 for example 和 for instance。下面的表格中列出了更多其他的信號詞：

講座中表示原因和結果的信號詞
X = 原因　　Y = 結果

Due to x, y...	Y is a result of x
Because of x, y...	Y is caused by x
X leads to y	Y is an outcome of x
X gives rise to y	Y happens because of x
X brings about y	X allows y to...
X creates y	X triggers y
X is responsible for y	X initiates y
X causes y	As a result, y...
X makes y VERB	Consequently, y...
Y results from x	The reason that y can VERB is X.

• Exercise 2　（解答請見 P. 364）

Read the short mini-lecture related to the cooling effect of expanding gas. Then write a correct paraphrase for each of the underlined sentences.

Professor: Spacecraft designers need to be able to cool infrared cameras to very cold temperatures. a. <u>The reason why the cameras need to be cool is that "warm" cameras cannot detect the warmth—or infared radiation—of other objects.</u> There are not very many cooling options that work well in zero gravity. Consequently, space scientists often use expanding gas to cool their infared cameras. b. <u>When gas expands, the decrease in pressure causes the molecules to slow down.</u> c. <u>This makes the gas cold.</u>

a. _____

_____

b. _____

_____

c. _____

_____

▶ **模擬試題**（解答請見 P. 364）

Now listen to a lecture about CHEMISTRY.　　🎧 *Track 025*

★ **Keywords**

states of matter 物質的狀態　　hydrogen bonding 氫鍵結合

• **Listening Questions**　　🎧 *Track 026*

1. What does the professor mainly discuss?
   A. The properties of liquid water.
   B. The structure of hydrogen atoms.
   C. How pressure affects glacier ice.
   D. Why ice becomes slippery.

2. Listen again to part of the lecture. Then answer the question.

   🎧 *Please listen to Track 026 for this part of the question.*

   What does the professor imply when she says this:

   🎧 *Please listen to Track 026 for this part of the question.*

   A. Students who haven't studied enough risk failure.
   B. The students have made a false assumption.
   C. Testing a hypothesis is central to the scientific method.
   D. Future chemists must acquire strong reasoning skills.

3. In the lecture, what does the professor say is unusual about water?
   Choose 2 answers.
   A. Unlike other substances, water can absorb heat with no significant increase in temperature.
   B. Unlike most other substances, water has a high surface tension that enables a razor blade to float on the surface.
   C. Unlike other substances, water becomes less dense when the temperature reaches freezing.
   D. Unlike other substances, ice's melting point decreases when pressure is applied.

4. Listen again to part of the lecture. Then answer the question.

 Please listen to Track 026 for this part of the question.

What does the professor mean when she says this:

 Please listen to Track 026 for this part of the question.

    A. She is making a little joke about temperature.
    B. She doesn't intend to get involved in the dispute.
    C. She hopes the students will continue to follow this debate.
    D. She does not want the students to be misled by the media.

5. Why does the professor mention molecule chains?
    A. To confess we do not know why ice's surface vibrates.
    B. To explain the theory of a slippery layer in ice.
    C. To demonstrate how very tightly the molecules are bonded.
    D. To refute the theory that ice crystals are structurally different.

6. The professor talks about ice skating in the lecture. Indicate for each of the following scientific hypotheses whether the professor agrees or not.
Place a ✓ mark in the YES or NO column.

	YES	NO
has a natural, very thin layer of liquid on it.		
Friction on ice causes some melting.		
Pressure from skates is what allows skaters to glide on ice.		

⑭ Humanities and the Arts, Topic 4: History
人文藝術常考主題 4：歷史

　　本章內容以人文藝術範疇的歷史為知識背景。歷史是對過去事件的研究。在學術研究中，有很多研究歷史的方式，如按時期或地理位置。涉及的語塊會有：world history（世界史），Renaissance（文藝復興）和 peace agreement（和平公約）等。其他與歷史相關的語塊可能涉及經濟現象，如 working class（工人階級），money-lending practices（貸款業務）和 incentive policies（激勵政策）等。請注意本章中出現的語塊，並記住它們。

...................................歷史：閱讀...................................

▶重點技能：掌握敘事文的文體特點

　　敘事文敘述發生在一定時間內的某個事件。作者挑選一些特定的事件，以特定的順序來組織這些事件，並從某個角度和某個時間點來描述這些事件。從時間上來看，作者有可能是從過去的某個時間點回顧更早的過去，也可能會來回穿越時空地談論事件。儘管許多敘事文是小說作品，但新托福考試閱讀文章中的敘事文為非小說類作品。這些文章可能摘自傳記、自傳和通史等文體的作品。

　　在大多數歷史文章中，事件進展是按時間順序來安排的。作者通常會使用各種動詞時態（一般過去時、現在完成時和過去完成時）來闡明事情發生的先後順序。如果作者在時間上來回穿越的話，那麼這些動詞時態尤其會讓英語為非母語的考生感到困惑。例如，將一個歷史事件與另一個歷史事件進行對比，或者將過去的情景與現在的情景進行對比。

　　在本章下文的關於哈萊姆黑人居住區的文章中，作者先介紹了哈萊姆的地理位置，並預示該區域將成為黑人社區。作者追溯了該區域從 17 世紀到 18、19 和 20 世紀的歷史，然後評論哈萊姆於 20 世紀 20 年代全盛期如何成為成功的和有才能的非裔美國人的聚集地。通過敘述歷史事件，作者談到了影響哈萊姆歷史的社會和經濟因素，例如，地鐵延伸至曼哈頓上城促使開發商在第 130 大街上建造新式的房屋，並形成了影響每次移民浪潮的各種力量。

• READING SAMPLE

　　下面來看看這篇敘事文中的句子用到的一些關鍵動詞。每個粗體動詞或動詞片語都提供了改述。

1. Harlem **would become** the biggest and one of the most important African American communities.

   would become → ultimately became

2. The area **remained** an agricultural community until after the Civil War.

remained → continued to be

3. Thus, by the late 19th century Harlem **had again emerged** as an elite enclave, boasting some of the most beautiful architecture and most interesting topography in New York City.

had again emerged as → once again became

要想快速輕鬆地理解敘事文，考生需要熟悉含有日期和其他時間片語的複雜句子。密切關注各種動詞時態和時間片語，如 until after the Civil War。要盡可能記住這些句子，那樣當你在新托福考試中碰到敘事文時，就可以輕鬆地閱讀類似的語句了。

• **Exercise 1** （解答請見 P. 367）

Write a correct paraphrase for the following sentences taken from a text about the history of blue jeans.

ⓐ The history of blue jeans goes back to 16th-century Europe.

_____

ⓑ The word "jean" is derived from "Genoa," the Italian city where the coarse cloth jean was made and worn by the sailors there.

_____

_____

ⓒ By the end of the 16th century, jean was already being produced in Lancaster, England.

_____

_____

▶ **模擬試題**（解答請見 P. 367）

Harlem, New York City

(1) ■ 1 Bounded by the Harlem River to the northeast and Washington Heights to the north; by 110th Street to the south and Morningside Heights to the southwest—Harlem would become the biggest and one of the most important African American communities. But in 1658 this land was still a rolling pastoral landscape, reminding the newly arrived Dutch farmers of the Holland town of Haarlem. ■ 2 Their new settlement, christened "Nieuw Haarlem," was a distant nine miles away from New York City, whose population was still clustered around the southern tip of Manhattan Island. ■ 3

(2) During the 18th century, elite New Yorkers came to Harlem to establish working farms and country estates. The area remained an agricultural community until after the Civil War. ■ 4 The gentlemen farmers had overworked the land, depleting the soil, so that by the Antebellum Period Harlem was home to mostly poor farmers and Irish squatters. However, urban growth began to push New Yorkers uptown. By 1880, elevated trains ran

as far north as 129th Street, and the neighborhood was attracting tens of thousands of upper-class whites, with poorer Italians and Jews settling to the east and south.

(3) Thus, by the late 19th century Harlem had again emerged as an elite enclave, boasting some of the most beautiful architecture and most interesting topography in New York City. Charming brownstones were constructed. Harlem had become a genteel suburb, a haven from the overcrowded city. The extension of the subway line up Lenox Avenue in 1904 encouraged another wave of speculative building, especially above 130th Street. But white middle-class tenants failed to materialize. The depressed real estate market coincided with a major influx of African Americans to New York City. Southern blacks, fleeing racial violence and seeking economic opportunity, began migrating en masse. During the 1920s, roughly 120,000 blacks, mostly new arrivals from the Caribbean and the South, traveled to Harlem. An equal number of whites moved out.

(4) The black elite chose to live in privately owned brownstones or in exclusive apartment buildings. The heaviest concentrations were to be found on what had come to be known as Strivers Row and Sugar Hill. Strivers Row was the name that poorer Harlemites gave to the tree-lined blocks of 138th and 139th Streets between Seventh and Eighth Avenues. On those blocks were some of the finest town houses in Harlem. Designed by Stanford White, among other architects, for the developer David H. King, Jr., they had been built in 1891 as homes for Harlem's white well-to-do. In 1918 the houses were taken over by the Equitable Life Insurance Company, but by 1919, African Americans started buying or renting the buildings. They were subsequently called the "Kingscourt Houses", a name so indicative of exclusiveness that the new black residents made every effort to live up to it.

(5) If Strivers Row was for individuals who were working hard to make it, Sugar Hill was for those who had succeeded. Sugar Hill—"sugar" being slang for money—sloped north from 145th Street to 155th Street and lay roughly between Amsterdam Avenue, to the west, and Edgecombe Avenue, to the east. From the top of the Hill, at 155th Street and Edgecombe, one looked down—literally and socially—on most of the Valley, as central Harlem was called. Nearly all the poorer Harlemites lived in the Valley.

(6) The Hill was special. The people up there lived in splendid brownstones and high-rent apartment houses. Sugar Hill became a black neighborhood some years after Strivers Row did. When blacks first began settling there during the late nineteen-twenties, the area was occupied chiefly by upper-middleclass Jewish, German and Irish families. As the blacks moved in, these families moved away, either to the suburbs or to the great apartment buildings along West End Avenue and Riverside Drive. African American celebrities of all sorts—the moneyed, the talented, the socially prominent, the intellectually distinguished, the fast crowd—lived along the streets and avenues of Sugar Hill.

(7) By the 1920s, Harlem, especially above 125th Street, had become the undisputed capital of Afro-America, home to its political institutions and cultural life. During that decade,

Harlem's nightlife became legendary, as did a tremendous outpouring of African American arts and letters, which would become known as the Harlem Renaissance.

• Reading Questions

1. The phrase "bounded by" in Paragraph 1 is closest in meaning to _____.
   A. headed for
   B. known for
   C. passing by
   D. defined by

2. According to the passage, in the 17th century what was true of the region presently known as Harlem?
   A. It had the largest population of African American settlers.
   B. Its economy depended on the lower portion of Manhattan.
   C. It had vast spaces of gently sloping terrain.
   D. Its border was delineated by several main roads.

3. The word "speculative" in Paragraph 3 is closest in meaning to _____.
   A. risky
   B. inexpensive
   C. residential
   D. inspired

4. The phrase "fleeing" in Paragraph 3 is closest in meaning to _____.
   A. passing
   B. escaping
   C. combating
   D. enduring

5. In Paragraph 3, the author says that the new construction in the upper part of Harlem was motivated by _____.
   A. immigrant farmers
   B. European investors
   C. the underground transit
   D. a thriving nightlife

6. Which of the sentences below best expresses the essential information in the highlighted sentence in the passage? Incorrect choices change the meaning in major ways or leave out important information.
   They were subsequently called the "Kingscourt Houses", a name so indicative of exclusiveness that the new black residents made every effort to live up to it.

A. Although the new name of the buildings projected an image of a very upper-class neighborhood, many residents could not afford the rent at Kingscourt Houses.

B. The new occupants thought that the "Kingscourt Houses" were quite prestigious and tried to act as if they too were very elite.

C. After first calling the apartment "Kingscourt Houses", they changed the name to attract a wealthier clientele.

D. The name "Kingscourt Houses" was so snobbish that many of the new inhabitants felt a little uncomfortable about living up there.

7. In Paragraph 5, why does the author introduce the statement **From the top of the Hill, at 155th Street and Edgecombe, one looked down—literally and socially—on most of the Valley, as central Harlem was called.**

A. To provide detailed directions for people seeking to travel to the valley.

B. To paint a scenic picture of the panorama of the Harlem River.

C. To demonstrate that Harlem was a large, sprawling metropolitan area.

D. To emphasize both the geography and the status of a neighborhood.

8. According to the author, the name "Sugar Hill" was given to the area because of its _____.

A. landscape

B. wealth

C. architecture

D. shops

9. According to the passage, each of the following statements about Strivers Row is true EXCEPT _____.

A. it contained stylish brownstone structures

B. it housed many socially mobile people

C. it became all black after Sugar Row did

D. it featured homes on 138th and 139th Streets

10. The word "its" in Paragraph 7 refers to _____.

A. Harlem

B. 125th Street

C. capital

D. Afro-America

11. What does the author say about Harlem during the "Harlem Renaissance"?

A. It was a magnet for many gifted African Americans.

B. It received many visitors from the continent of Africa.

C. It became an administrative capital of a New York district.

D. It altered the boundaries of the neighborhood known as Harlem.

12. Look at the four squares [■] that indicate where the following sentence could be added to the passage.

    Only when Dutch rule ceded to British in 1664, was the name Anglicized to the present spelling.

    Where would the sentence best fit?

    ■ 1

    ■ 2

    ■ 3

    ■ 4

13. **Directions:** An introductory sentence for a brief summary of the passage is provided below. Complete the summary by selecting the THREE answer choices that express the most important ideas in the passage. Some answer choices do not belong in the summary because they express ideas that are not presented in the passage or are minor ideas in the passage. **This question is worth 2 points.**

    Diverse historical forces shaped Harlem, ultimately transforming it into a vibrant African American cultural center.

    -
    -
    -

Answer Choices

1. The first European settlement in what is now Harlem started out as a Dutch farming community and remained a rural area for almost a hundred years.

2. Underground mass transit began to travel up to 129th Street around 1880, allowing many middle class Irish residents access to the northern part of Manhattan.

3. The town houses on Strivers Row were built on 138th and 139th Streets to accommodate the need for housing by the many African American professionals.

4. Over the years, Harlem attracted residents from many different backgrounds, including prosperous people who moved into stylish neighborhoods.

5. In the period just before the Civil War, the rich farmers tried hard to push the poorer farmers and squatters out of their Harlem farmland.

6. By the 1920s, Harlem had become an African American community, which hosted rich cultural offerings and produced the Harlem Renaissance.

關鍵語塊

- **bounded by...** 以⋯⋯為分界
- **the Harlem River** 哈萊姆河
- **Washington Heights** 華盛頓高地
- **Morningside Heights** 晨邊高地
- **pastoral landscape** 田園景觀
- **Haarlem** 哈勒姆（荷蘭西部一城市）
- **christen** （施洗禮時）為⋯⋯命名
- **Nieuw Haarlem**
  〔荷蘭語〕新哈萊姆區
- **cluster around...** 環繞著
- **elite** 菁英
- **country estate** 莊園
- **gentleman farmer** 以農耕為消遣的富裕農場主
- **overwork the land** 過度耕種土地
- **deplete the soil** 使土壤貧瘠
- **Antebellum Period** 美國南北戰爭以前
- **squatter** 擅自佔用房屋或土地的人
- **uptown** 向城外（本文指城市的北部）
- **elevated train** 高架鐵路
- **enclave** 被包圍的領土
- **topography** 地貌
- **brownstone** 赤褐色砂石建築
- **haven from...** ⋯⋯的庇護所
- **tenant** 租戶
- **fail to do** 未能做
- **coincide with...** 與⋯⋯同時發生
- **influx** 湧進；流入
- **racial violence** 種族暴力
- **en masse** 全體，一起
- **Strivers Row** 西哈萊姆區的三排聯排別墅
- **well-to-do** 富裕的
- **indicative of...** 顯示出⋯⋯
- **sloped** 傾斜的
- **look down on** 從高處往下看（此處為雙關語，指「看不起」）
- **fast crowd** 經常出去喝酒和跳舞的人群
- **arts and letters** 藝術和文學
- **Harlem Renaissance** 哈萊姆文藝復興

歷史：聽力

▶組織結構題的考點和做題策略

　　新托福考試聽力部分的組織結構題通常詢問考生是否明白說話者說其中一句話或一件事的原因。如教授為什麼要以某種方式組織其講座內容？當教授偏離主題談論其他話題時，考生能辨別嗎？說話者是如何闡述其論點的？

　　就這方面而言，聽力部分的組織結構題有點類似於閱讀部分的修辭目的題。還有些組織結構題看起來非常類似於聽力部分的語用功能題。聽力部分可能會有三或四道組織結構題，絕大多數出現在學術講座後面，而對話後面通常沒有。

• LISTENING TIPS

以下是組織結構題常見的題幹：
How does the professor **organize the information** about railroads?
How does the professor **clarify the points** she makes about canals?
How is the lecture **organized**?

Why does the professor **mention wheat**?

How does the professor **illustrate her point** about private investment?

What point does the professor make when she refers to foreign technology?

• LISTENING SAMPLE

以本章模擬試題中的組織結構題為例：

6. Why does the professor talk about the stops made by trains in early journeys?

A. To show the relatively undependable nature of the technology.

B. To demonstrate how the stopovers contributed to town growth.

C. To give an example of how towns worked together to build lines.

D. To explain why western trains had to halt more often than eastern ones.

托福總監評析

從選項推測，教授似乎在談論火車站點來說明某個歷史因果關係。聽這個講座時，考生要注意教授是如何闡述自己的觀點、如何例證的，然後將這些觀點和例證用筆記下來。

並非所有的組織結構題都會考觀點或實例，有些也會考查講座的整體組織結構。例如，講話內容是按什麼順序呈現？最常見的選項有1）時間順序；2）按重要性的順序；3）某個人或事件的知名程度（從最有名的到最不知名的展開）；以及4）以複雜程度為序（從最簡單的到最複雜的）。

記住，要注意聽諸如 First, we will talk about... 之類的語塊，這是尋找組織結構的相關線索。

組織結構題的解題線索

組織結構	典型句子
介紹或提供背景知識	Before I begin our discussion of the US Civil War, I want to set the stage by talking a little bit about slavery.
改變話題	Now I'd like to talk about how historians approach their craft.
轉移話題	Now let me show you just how anti-trust laws came to be passed.
舉例	Let me give you an example of the leadership structure in the Roman Republic.
插入話題	On another topic, I forgot to mention that your quiz this week will be on the Russian Revolution. We'll take it the first half hour of next class.
題外話	By the way, you should go to the city museum if you have a spare moment.

● 組織結構題的做題策略：

策略 1 通過講座或對話中的引導句來確定聽力材料的主題和情境。

策略 2 判斷說話者的講述方式。

是概述？詳述？還是兩者兼有？說話者下一步要說什麼？文章結構的組織原則是什麼？

策略 3 注意聽可以提供線索的信號詞。

例如，在後面關於歷史的講座中，教授提到跨洲鐵路時說：We'll talk about that milestone later on in the lecture, but now I'd like to provide an overview of the economic growth that accompanied the rollout of the railroad system. 這是一個很典型的例子：教授在表示自己將提供某個話題的背景資訊。這樣的信號詞和句子有助於解答組織結構題。

策略 4 注意聽例子和故事，並做好筆記。

說話者通常會使用有趣的例子和個人軼事來闡述複雜的原理。新托福聽力考試的組織結構題經常考到這些例子。

策略 5 注意聽類比和比喻。

例如，說話者可能會說某個歷史現象就像「無本之木」。如果聽到這樣的比喻性語言，要做筆記，因為可能會考查到。

▶模擬試題（解答請見 P. 368）

Now listen to a lecture about HISTORY.　　　　　🎧 *Track 027*

★ **Keywords**

Baltimore 巴爾的摩（美國城市）	the Hudson River 哈德遜河（紐約州東部）

• **Listening Questions**　　　　　🎧 *Track 028*

1. What aspect of railroads does the professor mainly discuss?
   A. The technological challenges.
   B. The reliance on government support.
   C. The major investors.
   D. The economic benefits.

2. Listen again to part of the lecture. Then answer the question.

 Please listen to Track 028 for this part of the question.

What does the professor mean when she says this:

Please listen to Track 028 for this part of the question.

    A. To point out a link between two events in railroad history.

    B. To indicate how fortunate the timing of the event was.

    C. To ask the class to talk more about Baltimore's population.

    D. To show how close New York came to being the first US railroad.

3. According to the lecture, what was Alexander Hamilton's position on US railways?

    A. He thought they should be overseen by individual states.

    B. He wanted to transfer more technology from Great Britain.

    C. He believed they should be paid for by the government.

    D. He thought private railway investors were taking harmful risks.

4. According to the lecture, what were two characteristics of the railway business owners?
   Choose 2 answers.

    A. They were willing to accept money from foreign investors.

    B. They sought control of both the railways and the trains.

    C. They continued to build canals in case the rail technology failed.

    D. They were careful to keep expenditures on steel to a minimum.

5. What can we infer about eastern farmers after the construction of the railroads?

    A. They were eager to travel by rail to western cities.

    B. They began to import livestock from Europe.

    C. They built small hotels on their properties.

    D. They planted crops other than wheat.

6. Why does the professor talk about the stops made by trains in early journeys?

    A. To show the relatively undependable nature of the technology.

    B. To demonstrate how the stopovers contributed to town growth.

    C. To give an example of how towns worked together to build lines.

    D. To explain why western trains had to halt more often than eastern ones.

• Exercise 2 　（解答請見 P. 371）

    These CHUNKS are taken from the lecture on history. For each item in the first column, write a paraphrase.

CHUNK	Paraphrase
1. pinnacle achievement	
2. ownership stake	
3. favorite means of...	
4. closely tied to...	
5. lightning speed	

Life Sciences, Topic 4: Anatomy and Physiology
⑮ 生命科學常考主題 4：解剖學與生理學

本章內容以生命科學範疇的解剖學與生理學為知識背景。解剖學中的語塊會涉及最常見的人體結構，如 lung（肺）和 bone tissue（骨組織）。與生理學有關的語塊會涉及人體功能，如 heart beat（心跳）和 sweating（流汗）。這些都是一般意義上的詞彙。作為一項英語語言測試，新托福考試不會出現專業性很強或敏感話題的文章，如威脅生命的疾病。請注意本章中出現的語塊，並盡可能記住。

·····················解剖學與生理學：閱讀·····················

▶重點技能：預測下文

新托福考試每篇閱讀文章及其考題的完成時間只有 20 分鐘，如果考生想順利答完所有題目，則需要快速而有策略地進行閱讀。這裡要介紹的一種策略是提早把握「知識框架」，以便在閱讀時能預測文章將要講述的內容。

例如，在本章下文的閱讀文章中，考生可以根據標題 Rods and Cones 快速確定 rods 和 cones（視杆細胞和視錐細胞）就是主題。但是 rods 和 cones 是指什麼？考生可能知道 rod 和 cone 的普通含義，如 curtain rod（窗簾杆），ice cream cone（冰淇淋甜筒）。但是如果之前沒有讀過關於眼睛部位的英語文章，沒有學過 rods 和 cones 在生理學題材中的意思，此時可能就會感到困惑。在這種情況下，利用有效的閱讀策略就顯得至關重要，考生可以通過閱讀策略快速猜出意思，並預測文章的內容。

在第一段，作者介紹了 rods 和 cones，並將它們定義為能分別在黑暗和明亮的條件下產生視覺的細胞。

在實際考試中，如果讀到這一段，我們會問自己：What will the author talk about next? Will there be more specific information about rods and cones?

第二段第一句是：These two types of cells differ in much the same way that color film differs from black-and-white. 從這裡可以預測該段將會進行詳細的對比。結果，作者也真的將人眼的視杆細胞和視錐細胞與攝影師的黑白彩色膠捲進行了對比。

我們快速轉入第三段，這一段開頭在談論視網膜。retina（視網膜）這個詞很明顯是指眼睛部位，作者甚至還費心地下了定義。那麼就可以猜測第三段是講述視杆細胞和視錐細胞是如何分佈在視網膜上的。也許作者還會介紹感光細胞的結構，包括在眼睛的什麼部位會發生什麼事。事實上作者也真的告訴我們視杆細胞如何分佈以及怎樣影響夜視。

因為第三段集中討論視杆細胞，所以可推測第四段討論的主題將是另一種光感受器：視錐細胞。略讀該段的開頭兩句時，可以發現之前的預測得到了證實，作者說了：The color of an object is also received differently by the two types of cells. In the human eye, cones...

最後一段會講什麼呢？如果快速略讀開頭兩句，就會發現：Another factor influencing night vision is that, before anything at all can be seen in the dark, the eyes must have time to adjust. 過渡句 Another factor influencing night vision 給出了答案：這一段將提供關於夜視的其他資訊。當快速閱讀接下來的幾句時，我們應該密切關注重複、重述和銜接手段，並找出更多線索：This adjustment... 從這裡，我們可以確定最後一段的重點是介紹眼睛在黑暗中為了看得更清楚必須進行的調整。

綜上所述，我們需要利用各種信號詞、線索和策略來預測整篇文章以及每個段落的中心大意。這種方法能幫助我們快速而自信地閱讀文章。

● 可採用以下策略預測閱讀文章中的觀點：

策略 1 閱讀時確定要點，如果有時間的話，用縮寫將要點記下。

策略 2 找出這些要點的定義、例子和例證。

策略 3 利用上下文的情境來「破譯」或猜測不認識的片語。

策略 4 利用自己對相關主題已有的知識來推測文章內容，並預測將會出現哪些觀點。

策略 5 預測後，繼續閱讀並尋找重複的詞和重述資訊，幫助自己理解文意。

策略 6 利用邏輯推理和線索信號詞尋找句子或觀點之間的關係。

如果利用以上這些策略來練習閱讀 600 個字長度的文章，你的閱讀速度、流利度和理解力都會大大提升。

• **Exercise 1** （解答請見 P. 372）

Quickly skim the first couple of sentences of the following passage. Underline the sentences and predict what the paragraph will be about. Then read the entire text and see if your guess was correct.

Blushing

When we become embarrassed, we blush and our faces become red. We can feel this happening because our faces feel hot, and other people notice the difference in our skin coloring. This coloring is initiated when the body releases a spurt of adrenaline. The heart rate increases and breathing becomes more rapid. The blood vessels that deliver blood to the face open or relax. As a result, more blood than usual flows to the skin, and the face darkens or turns red.

This physical response is governed by what is known as a sympathetic nervous system, the same type of system that controls the "fight-or-flight" response when a person feels threatened. These particular sympathetic nerves are located near the center of the spinal cord. They generate signals unconsciously when our thoughts and emotions trigger them.

Interestingly, the area of our face that blushes is anatomically different in structure from other areas. Facial skin, for example, has more tiny blood vessels per unit volume than other skin areas. In addition, the blood vessels in the cheek are relatively wide in diameter and nearer the surface.

Paragraph 1

_____

_____

Paragraph 2

_____

_____

Paragraph 3

_____

_____

▶ **模擬試題**（解答請見 P. 372）

Rods and Cones

(1) The light-sensitive cells in the human eye are called photoreceptors, and there are two kinds: rods and cones. Rods, which constitute two-thirds of the photoreceptors, are straight and thin. Cones make up the other third and are more bulbous in shape. These two types of cells lie tightly packed together on the back of the retina, the thin layer of neural cells lining the back of the eyeball. Here, within an area the size of a postage stamp, are almost 130 million photoreceptors. Humans have these two kinds because, like many other animals, they live in two kinds of visual worlds: day and night. The plump cones, some seven million of them, are used for detailed examination in bright light; the rods, almost 18 times as numerous, for dim light.

(2) These two types of cells differ in much the same way that color film differs from black-andwhite. In the daytime a photographer can capture all the color in a scene with color film. But in extremely dim light, color film will not work well; it is simply not sensitive enough for the job. To record the scene, the photographer must give up the idea of getting a color picture and settle for one in black-and-white. Black-and-white film is much more sensitive and will respond in dimmer light. ■ 1 In a sense, the human eye viewing an object is like a camera with two kinds of film in it at all times. ■ 2 The cones come into play when the light is strong and give humans color vision. ■ 3 But at night, only the rods will work, and they give only black-and-white responses. ■ 4

(3) In the retina, the rods and cones are mixed together, which allows the eye to switch from one type of photoreceptor to the other with relative ease. However, the distribution of rods and cones is not even, and this produces some interesting results in the way humans see. In the center of the retina, for example, is a little dimple called the fovea. The fovea contains only cones, and this concentration makes it the most accurate place for

vision in bright light. The fovea is small and therefore allows only a limited field of view—about four-square inches at eight feet. To compensate for this constraint, the eyeball must move almost continuously to keep the image on the concentration of cones. There are, of course, cones on the periphery of the retina, but there are not enough of them to give humans sharp vision. The periphery serves primarily as a warning system. When people see something in their peripheral vision, they must shift their eyeballs so that the image will fall on the fovea, the location of maximum acuity. However, because the fovea contains only cones, it is useless in dim light. To see an object in semidarkness, a person must look not directly at it, but just to one side, so that the light entering the eye will fall not on the fovea but on the periphery of the retina, where there is a concentration of rods.

(4) The color of an object is also received differently by the two types of cells. In the human eye, cones are most responsive to the yellowish-green part of the color spectrum, whereas rods, although still giving only black-and-white vision, respond best to blue-green wavelengths. As a result, a red flower and a blue one may appear equally bright in daylight but not at night. The blue one, to which the dim-light rods respond, will seem much brighter than the red one, which will look almost black. That is because the cones, which normally respond to red, are not functioning properly in the dark, and the rods are relatively insensitive to red.

(5) Another factor influencing night vision is that, before anything at all can be seen in the dark, the eyes must have time to adjust. This adjustment to changing light conditions, known as dark and light adaptation, is a far more intricate process than it might seem. The study of this process has related much about the mechanism by which the pigment in each photoreceptor converts light into signals for the brain.

• Reading Questions

1. According to the passage, why do humans have two kinds of photoreceptors?
   A. To shield against damage from brightness.
   B. To deal with different light environments.
   C. To identify and store varied visual memories.
   D. To be able to fit into the cramped retinal space.

2. The word "lining" in Paragraph 1 is closest in meaning to _____.
   A. connecting
   B. following
   C. covering
   D. approaching

3. The word "plump" in Paragraph 1 is closest in meaning to _____.
   A. roundish
   B. sensitive

C. intense

D. short

4. Why does the author mention a photographer and film in Paragraph 2?

   A. To accentuate the importance of color in human vision.

   B. To illustrate how human vision evolved from black and white.

   C. To contrast them to the storage mechanisms for brain images.

   D. To equate them to human eyes and sensory processes.

5. The word "it" in Paragraph 2 refers to _____.

   A. eye

   B. object

   C. camera

   D. film

6. According to Paragraph 3, each of the following descriptions about the fovea is true EXCEPT _____.

   A. it is part of the retina of the eye

   B. it adjusts its cones in dim conditions

   C. it provides good vision in bright light

   D. it is used for a narrow area of visibility

7. Which of the sentences below best expresses the essential information in the highlighted sentence in the passage? Incorrect choices change the meaning in major ways or leave out important information.

   To compensate for this constraint, the eyeball must move almost continuously to keep the image on the concentration of cones.

   A. In order to see all the cones, the eyeball frequently shifts to one side to keep the image symmetrical.

   B. Unfortunately, humans are often unable to view groups of cones at one time due to the constant motion of the eyeball.

   C. Most of the object is visible if the human eye works hard, but there are limitations, especially during continual motion.

   D. The eyeball has to keep moving to focus on the cones because of inherent limitations in human vision.

8. In Paragraph 4, the author says that a red flower may appear black at nighttime due to which of the following reasons?

   A. The cones do not work very well without sufficient light.

   B. The rods interfere with the proper functioning of the cones.

   C. The physical properties of the light spectrum are different after dark.

   D. If the eye is focusing on a blue object, it mistakenly perceives red as black.

9. The author says that which of the following is critical for seeing well in darkness?
   A. The ability to see the color red.
   B. Appropriate placement of cones.
   C. Time to fine-tune one's eyes.
   D. Superior peripheral vision.

10. The word "pigment" in Paragraph 5 is closest in meaning to _____.
   A. coloring
   B. membrane
   C. chemical
   D. tissue

11. Look at the four squares [■] that indicate where the following sentence could be added to the passage.

   This explains why colors disappear at night and all things appear to be different shades of gray.

   Where would the sentence best fit?
   ■ 1
   ■ 2
   ■ 3
   ■ 4

12. Directions: The author talks about types of photoreceptors in the eye. Complete the chart below by indicating which characteristics describe rods and which describe cones. Choose five of the seven answer choices that are specifically mentioned in the passage. **This question is worth 3 points.**

Type of Photoreceptor	Associated Characteristics
Rods	• •
Cones	• •
Both rods and cones	•

Answer Choices

1. Are used to see up close

2. Are located behind the retina

3. Make the inner eye have a dark color

4. Allows humans to see the color red

5. Have a slender profile

6. Are used in dark conditions

7. Are clustered on the fovea

關鍵語塊

- **photoreceptor** 光感受器；對光敏感的神經感受器
- **rod** 視杆細胞
- **cone** 視錐細胞
- **constitute** 構成
- **bulbous** 球莖狀的
- **tightly packed** 密集的
- **retina** 視網膜
- **neural cell** 神經細胞
- **postage stamp** 郵票
- **dim light** 弱光
- **give up the idea of...** 放棄……的念頭

- **come into play** 開始起作用
- **switch from... to...** 從……切換到……
- **fovea** 小凹（尤指視網膜的中央凹）
- **concentration** 集中
- **field of view** 視野
- **periphery of...** ……的週邊
- **serve as...** 用作……；充當……
- **acuity** 敏銳
- **semidarkness** 半暗
- **adjustment to** 調整
- **intricate process** 錯綜複雜的過程

⋯⋯⋯⋯⋯⋯⋯⋯⋯⋯⋯⋯解剖學與生理學：聽力⋯⋯⋯⋯⋯⋯⋯⋯⋯⋯

▶立場觀點題（或態度題）的考點和做題策略

聽力部分經常會考查說話者的「立場」或「態度」。立場觀點題出現得不是很多，整個聽力部分可能只有兩三道。

• LISTENING TIPS

立場觀點題的題幹形式通常如下：
What is the professor's **attitude toward**...?
What is the professor's **view on**...?
What is the professor's **opinion about**...?
How does the woman seem to **feel about**...?
Which of the following sentences **best expresses how the student feels**?

立場觀點題的選項常含有使役動詞：
"... made... (feel) angry / tired."
"... caused... to feel proud."
還有一些較為複雜的立場觀點題中，選項會描述隨時間而變化的情感，例如：
The professor felt confused at first, but more relaxed later on.

• LISTENING SAMPLE

以本章下文模擬試題為例：

5. What does the professor think about the people in Los Angeles who are going to bed later than other people?

A. He assumes that they sleep roughly the same hours, just at different times.

B. He worries that they may be at significant risk of becoming physically ill.

C. He believes they compensate for any sleep loss by exposing themselves to quantities of sunlight.

D. He thinks their sleep patterns may be similar to people who live in Arctic latitudes.

托福總監評析

　　每個選項都含有一個描述教授想法或態度的片語。有時，選項中只含有表示情感的詞，如：The professor is happy / bored... 但有時候，正如此例，選項中會含有表示判斷的動詞，如：The professor thinks... is good. 或 The professor doubts... is true. 教授說由於睡眠不足人們會疲勞，這種長期的慢性疲勞（chronic fatigue）實在是對人不健康，因此選項 B 正確。

英語中有很多表達觀點、態度和情緒狀態的不同方式。最常用的片語如下：

有關情感和態度的表達

積極的	消極的
to like...	to dislike...
to approve of...	to disapprove of...
to enjoy...	to condemn...
to be content with...	to be troubled by...
to feel positively toward...	to feel negatively toward...
to be sympathetic toward...	to be hostile toward...
to think... is good / better than... / the best	to think... is bad / worse than... / the worst
to think... is amusing / funny / comical	to think... is sad / tragic / disappointing
to be amused by... / at...	to be annoyed at... / over...
to be cheerful about...	to be depressed about...
to be optimistic about...	to be pessimistic about...
to be pleased about... / with...	to be frustrated at... / with...
to feel happy about...	to feel unhappy about...
to feel confident about...	to be worried about...
to be delighted about...	to be angry about... / over...
to be hopeful that + clause	to feel anxious about... / over...

to find... exciting	to become enraged at... / over...
to be excited about...	to be shocked at... / by...
To be satisfied about... / with...	to be dissatisfied about... / with...
to be impressed by... / with...	to be unimpressed by... / with...
to find... boring	to find... interesting
to feel afraid of...	to feel calm about...
to be / feel certain (about...)	to feel unsure / doubtful about...
to feel resigned	toward... to feel bitter about...
to feel relieved about...	to feel resentful about...
to be willing to do...	to be unwilling to do...
to feel sure about...	to feel confused about...
to feel grateful for...	to feel apologetic about...
to be curious about...	to feel sorry about...

● 立場觀點題的答題策略：

策略 1 注意捕捉說話者的觀點。

認真聽，邊聽邊思考：說話者為什麼那麼說？他或她的潛在目的是什麼？接下來可能會說什麼？

策略 2 注意聽語調。

說話聲是響亮還是柔和？聽起來是高興還是生氣？聽力錄音通常會給出一般情緒狀態的一些提示，即使說話者是平靜和放鬆的。

策略 3 注意聽猶豫和停頓之處。

當一個人說 Hmmmm，Mmmmmm 和 Uhhhh 時，就表示他或她在停頓。當說話者在講座期間停頓時，有時表示話題轉換，但停頓也有可能表示一種感情狀態：不確定、不願直言或者畏懼！仔細聽這些停頓之處，它們是瞭解說話者立場的線索。

策略 4 注意聽感嘆詞。

感嘆詞是用來表達情感的簡短話語。如：Wow / Great / Good / Excellent / Oh no / That's too bad / Cool! 在書面語中，感嘆詞後面往往會跟一個感嘆號。而口語中，音調往往是開始時高、結尾處降低。這些傳達情感的詞語都是有用的信號，能傳達說話者的想法或感受。

策略 5 注意聽評價性語言。

一個人的語言往往含有反映其判斷或傾向的詞，尤其是說話者使用的副詞。

如：Unfortunately, the lights in Los Angeles are affecting sleep habits. 這句話的另一種說法就是：I think it is bad that the lights are on in Los Angeles.

策略 6 注意聽說服性語言。

說話者常用更直接的方式來表達他們的傾向，例如通過情態動詞：The city of Los Angeles should have implemented eco-friendly policies to control light usage.

• Exercise 2 （解答請見 P. 373）

Write a correct paraphrase for each of the following stance-related answer choices.

ⓐ The professor questioned the theory that the main purpose of sweating is to get rid of salt.

_____

ⓑ She believed that human eyes benefited from exposure to sunlight.

_____

ⓒ The professor praised Harvey's discovery of the circulation of blood.

_____

▶ **模擬試題**（解答請見 P. 373）

Now listen to a lecture about human PHYSIOLOGY and sleep. 🎧 *Track 029*

★ **Keywords**

REM sleep 快速動眼睡眠	non-REM sleep 非快速動眼睡眠
procedural memory 程式性記憶　trampoline 跳床	segmented sleep 分段睡眠

• Listening Questions *Track 030*

1. What aspect of sleep is the lecture mainly about?
   A. The stages of sleep.
   B. Cultural variation in sleep patterns.
   C. How learning can be improved.
   D. How REM sleep affects us.

2. According to the professor, the brain consolidates learning during sleep by doing which of the following?
   A. Strengthening neural connections.
   B. Resting in non-REM sleep stages.
   C. Reviewing the new memories many times.
   D. Putting all the memories in working memory.

3. What examples of procedural memory does the professor give in the lecture?
   Choose 2 answers.
   A. Memorizing the stages of sleep.
   B. Remembering a computer password.
   C. Playing the piano.
   D. Jumping on a trampoline.

4. Listen again to part of the lecture. Then answer the question.

 Please listen to Track 030 for this part of the question.

What does the woman mean when she says this:

 Please listen to Track 030 for this part of the question.

   A. She started to reflect on even more areas of difference.
   B. She thinks her grandmother probably sleeps too little.
   C. She wonders if there is something wrong with her body.
   D. She has changed her mind about the need to get more sleep.

5. What does the professor think about the people in Los Angeles who are going to bed later than other people?
   A. He assumes that they sleep roughly the same hours, just at different times.
   B. He worries that they may be at significant risk of becoming physically ill.
   C. He believes they compensate for any sleep loss by exposing themselves to quantities of sunlight.
   D. He thinks their sleep patterns may be similar to people who live in Arctic latitudes.

6. What point does the professor make when he refers to Africa and Latin America?
   A. People tend to sleep longer hours in relatively hot climates.
   B. Segmented sleep behavior exists where there is no artificial light.
   C. Sleep disorders can occur in any culture, in any part of the world.
   D. People have sleeping-waking cycles corresponding to the 24-hour cycle of the Sun.

Social Sciences, Topic 4: Mass Communication
16 社會科學常考主題 4：大眾傳播學

本章內容以社會科學範疇的大眾傳播學為知識背景。大眾傳播學領域的語塊會涉及媒體機構及其運作程序，如 digital age（數位化時代），radio broadcast（無線電廣播）和 media channel（媒體頻道），也可能涉及對公眾輿論的引導，如 public relations（公共關係）和 image building（形象塑造）。請注意本章中出現的語塊，並記住它們。

·················· 大眾傳播學：閱讀 ··················

▶否定事實題的出題方式和答題策略

否定事實題是一種細節資訊題，不過在邏輯上正好相反，因為否定事實題的題幹中總是含有某個否定詞或排除性詞語，如 not、all but、everything except 和 except。在這類題型中，否定性詞語都用大寫字母顯示。

否定事實題的出題方式多種多樣。有時，考生必須閱讀選項中的四個觀點，然後閱讀文章判斷其中哪三個句子是正確的，哪個是錯誤的。有時，考生則必須掃讀文章，判斷文章中是否包含選項中的說法。因此這些題目的題幹往往是：What isn't true / What wasn't mentioned? 無論是哪種情況，四個選項中總會有三個正確，有一個錯誤或文章中沒有提到過。

• READING TIPS

否定事實題可能會使用以下題幹形式：

All of the following are **true EXCEPT**...

All of the following are **mentioned EXCEPT**...

Which of the following is **NOT true**?

Which of the following is **NOT mentioned**?

Which of the following is **NOT an example of** a media campaign?

Which of the following is **NOT** an accurate characterization of blogs?

The author's definition of public relations includes all of the following **EXCEPT**...

• READING SAMPLE

以本章的模擬試題為例：

4. All of the following factors were driving forces behind the introduction of Sesame Street EXCEPT _____.

A. the nation felt that there were not enough channels for education

B. ample financial support was available for development and production

C. test results showed that children's basic skills were weak overall

D. people were worried about the education of poor city children

托福總監評析

　　這道題要求考生找出三個正確選項和一個錯誤選項。要回答此題，最好先逐個閱讀選項，然後從文章中為各選項找到對應資訊。乍一看，選項 A 的說法似乎錯誤，因為在第一段中，作者說 Federal Communications Commission reserved 242 channels for education。但在確定答案應選 A 之前，應該再看看其他選項。選項 B 的說法正確，因為作者說兒童電視工作室得到了慷慨資助（lavishly funded）。選項 C 的說法正確，因為文中說目標兒童有 low attainment in basic skills。選項 D 也正確，因為文中指出，人們在關注城市中在多元文化環境中成長的貧窮兒童。因此，可以確定選項 A 是唯一沒有說明《芝麻街》推廣背後的驅動力的句子。

● 否定事實題的做題策略：

策略 1 認真研究題幹，確認理解題幹意思。

　　題目是要求從四個選項中找出一個說法錯誤的句子還是要求找出一個文中沒有提及的句子？

策略 2 看看題幹是否明確針對第幾段的內容提問。

策略 3 看完每個選項的意思，快速掃讀文章中的相關內容，尋找相符的說法。

策略 4 不要擔心選項的順序與文中資訊的順序不一樣，冷靜下來仔細尋找相關資訊在文章中的位置。

策略 5 如果某個選項的說法錯誤，那麼該選項就是正確答案。或者，如果不能在文章中為某個選項找到對應的說法，那麼該選項就是正確答案。

策略 6 要拓寬思路，有邏輯地思考。不要被否定性副詞和介系詞所迷惑。

• Exercise 1　（解答請見 P. 376）

Write a paraphrase of each of the following negatively expressed sentences.

ⓐ News in developed countries does not give a great deal of space to foreign news, except in specialist or elite publications.

_____

_____

ⓑ In the early medieval period, the book was not regarded primarily as a means of communication, but rather as a repository of wisdom.

_____

_____

ⓒ If a person is not dependent on the media, media will not be of great importance to that individual.

_____

_____

▶ 模擬試題（解答請見 P. 376）

Children's Educational Television

★ Keyword

vacuum tube boxes 真空管電視機

(1) In the United States, television in the service of children's education developed when the 1952 Federal Communications Commission reserved 242 channels for education. Financial support from the Ford Foundation later established National Educational Television to procure and distribute programs and to encourage production. Not until the late 1960s did school teachers see television as a significant educational force; however, children showed little interest in educational television. Educational programming output for children lacked an organizing framework, and the production quality was low.

(2) The creation of the Corporation for Public Broadcasting led directly to the formation of Children's Television Workshop in 1968 (later renamed Sesame Street Workshop), and the launch of the program Sesame Street a year later. The move was in response to a perceived national need. Continued concern about low attainment in basic skills was allied to concern about the disenfranchisement of poor, urban multicultural youth. Lavishly funded, supported from the first by high-quality research to shape and reshape its output and sustained by strong educational and political support, Children's Television Workshop proved, first, that educational broadcasts could compete with commercially produced television for children's attention and, second, they could teach.

(3) Unlike most educational programs, Sesame Street was designed to speak directly to the child, acting as the teacher. Its running time of 60 minutes was three or four times the length of the typical educational television program, intended to introduce or illustrate a teacher's work with a class. Through a combination of puppets, animation and live actors, Sesame Street taught such skills as letter and word recognition, as well as numbers, addition and subtraction. The program's success demonstrated that educational television could compete head on with popular children's output and that research had a practical value in making educational television more competitive. The heavy investment in research would be a key element in the success the program would steadily garner in enhancing basic literacy and numeracy, as well as civics. At a critical time in the history of urban America, teams of researchers were hired to test scripts and to conduct field research on experimental segments and pilot programs. The influence of this formative research on the morale of professionals using television worldwide, even in university settings, and on the design of distance-learning projects and outreach adult-learning schemes, is hard to overstate.

(4) Researchers demonstrated children could benefit academically from television productions designed to be both entertaining and instructional. Television proved to be effective for disadvantaged children and for pre-school children as young as three. Learning was further enhanced when supplementary materials and a supportive adult were present.

(5) In the 1970s, public demand for more and better children's television led to the creation of the Public Broadcasting Service (PBS), which continued to oversee public television licensees and to create and distribute a wide range of television materials. Political attitudes toward PBS blew hot and cold over time, forcing cable stations to seek increased proportions of their revenue from sponsorship and donations. From the 1990s onward, all but the largest organizations led a precarious existence. As national excitement over the educational potential of computers and online resources grew, observers noted that the strengths of educational television were being forgotten; it was as if it had gone out of vogue.

(6) Of course, that is not to deny the role that technology has played in the history of teaching. At the outset of its emergence in schools in the 1950s and 1960s, television was only available in monochrome; recording was expensive and complex and external scenes were shot on 16mm film. Receivers were clumsy, unreliable vacuum tube boxes, delivering images and sound of quality that no 21st-century child would accept. By the late 1970s, with color television receivers universally available in homes in the developed world and educational programs being produced to high standards at high cost, teachers and children took for granted the idea that television played an educative role. Finally, as technical performance of video recorders (VCRs) rose and prices fell, schools and parents found educational ways to leverage that device. In most parts of the developed world it was not until the 1980s that educational television reached its full educational potential.

• Reading Questions

1. The word "procure" in the first paragraph is closest in meaning to _____.
   A. investigate
   B. broadcast
   C. design
   D. obtain

2. According to the first paragraph, why were children not eager to watch educational television in the 1960s?
   A. Their teachers compelled them to watch tedious productions.
   B. Program content was not arranged in any systematic order.
   C. There were not very many children's channels to watch.
   D. Most monitors could display only black and white pictures.

3. The word "lavishly" in Paragraph 2 is closest in meaning to _____.
   A. creatively
   B. strategically
   C. generously
   D. anonymously

4. All of the following factors were driving forces behind the introduction of Sesame Street EXCEPT _____.
   A. the nation felt that there were not enough channels for education
   B. ample financial support was available for development and production
   C. test results showed that children's basic skills were weak overall
   D. people were worried about the education of poor city children

5. According to Paragraph 3, Sesame Street differed from the conventional educational program in that the new program _____.
   A. was considerably shorter in length
   B. showed teachers interacting with children
   C. communicated to child viewers directly
   D. recorded the activities in live productions

6. Which of the sentences below best expresses the essential information in the highlighted sentence in the passage? Incorrect choices change the meaning in major ways or leave out important information.
   The heavy investment in research would be a key element in the success the program would steadily garner in enhancing basic literacy and numeracy, as well as civics.

A. It was hoped that research in literacy, numeracy and civics could ultimately yield positive results.

B. By gradually investing in research, the program was able to learn as much about literacy and numeracy as it had learned about civics.

C. If the program wanted more money for research, it would have to demonstrate concrete success in literacy, numeracy and civics.

D. The reason for the program's ultimate effectiveness in literacy, numeracy and civics was a large focus on research.

7. In Paragraph 3, what does the author say about the impact of Sesame Street Workshop on children's programming overseas in the 1970s?

A. The ripple effects on other countries were highly exaggerated by the media.

B. International educators were greatly encouraged by the research results.

C. Many distance-learning initiatives began to use live actors and puppets.

D. The program content was considered too US-centric to be applied in other countries.

8. The word "precarious" in Paragraph 5 is closest in meaning to _____.

A. tentative

B. short-lived

C. valiant

D. fateful

9. According to the author, why was the Public Broadcasting Service established?

A. Government officials decided it would be a politically savvy move.

B. The public became critical of the fees charged by television cable stations.

C. There was a general consensus that not enough programs were available.

D. Children had begun to watch too many programs with adult content.

10. The word "its" in Paragraph 6 refers to _____.

A. technology

B. history

C. teaching

D. television

11. In Paragraph 6, why does the author mention VCRs?

A. To show how economics facilitated the integration of educational television.

B. To emphasize the fact that most machines were prone to malfunction.

C. To lament that the applied technology had arrived in public schools so late.

D. To illustrate how many families could still not afford this equipment.

12. We can infer from the passage that the author holds which of the following views toward educational children's television programming?

    A. The use of animation was not properly researched at the very outset.

    B. It was unwisely neglected in the 1990s in favor of computer education.

    C. It was a fad briefly but teachers decided there were better ways to teach.

    D. Over the past 20 years, government has played a vital role in funding programs.

13. **Directions:** An introductory sentence for a brief summary of the passage is provided below. Complete the summary by selecting the THREE answer choices that express the most important ideas in the passage. Some answer choices do not belong in the summary because they express ideas that are not presented in the passage or are minor ideas in the passage. **This question is worth 2 points.**

This passage discusses an important part of the history of children's educational television programming.

> -
> -
> -

Answer Choices

1. Although the government provided significant funding for educational television early on, educators waited for over fifteen years to take action.

2. By the 1970s, many commercial television programs were considered to have educational value, especially for pre-school children.

3. Despite the large amount of money invested in television research, it was difficult to come up with a design that satisfied all people.

4. The impetus for quality children's television programming was the recognition that many children needed education in literacy, numeracy and other skills.

5. Color monitors and quality content persuaded child viewers and school teachers that television could be put to good use in teaching.

6. Computers were introduced to school systems in the 1990s, effectively replacing the need for educational television.

關鍵語塊

- in the service of…
  為……服務；造福於……
- Federal Communications
  Commission 聯邦通訊委員會
- channel 頻道
- Ford Foundation 福特基金會
- National Education Television
  （美國）全國教育電視網
- output 廣播電視作品
- organizing framework 組織框架
- Corporation for Public
  Broadcasting 公共廣播公司
- Children's Television Workshop
  兒童電視工作室
- Sesame Street
  芝麻街（幼稚教育電視節目）
- perceived national need
  全國普遍反映的需求
- allied to 聯合
- disenfranchisement 剝奪……的權利
- multicultural youth
  多元文化背景下成長的青年
- broadcast 廣播
- running time 播放時間

- compete head on
  正面競爭；正面交鋒
- garner 累積
- literacy 讀寫能力
- numeracy 計算能力
- civics 公民學
- segment 片段，模組
- pilot program 試點節目
- formative research 發展性研究
- distance-learning 遠端學習的
- outreach 擴大服務範圍
- hard to overstate 怎麼說都不為過
- further enhanced sth.
  進一步加強了某事物
- Public Broadcasting Service
  公共廣播服務
- blew hot and cold （態度）搖擺不定
- cable station 有線電視臺
- gone out of vogue 已不流行
- monochrome 黑白的
- clumsy 笨拙的
- took for granted the idea that…
  理所當然地認為……
- video recorder 錄影機
- leverage 利用

大眾傳播學：聽力

▶重點技能：利用圖形預測下文

為了讓考生理解，新托福考試四個部分的電腦螢幕上都會出現圖片或其他圖形。在聽力部分，用來表現對話或講座中的教授和學生的人物圖片很常見。這些圖片往往反映對話或講座的場景，例如教室或圖書館。

學術講座可能會配有圖解。例如，動物學講座中可能會有動物身體部位的圖解；而在氣象學講座中，可能會配有說明氣候形成過程的線條圖。這些簡單的圖類似教授上課時在白板上畫的圖形或者做演示時顯示在螢幕上的示意圖。新托福試題不會直接考查這些圖解，它們只是用於補充文章的內容，尤其是涉及專業術語、理論模型或空間關係時。

無論是圖片還是圖解，它們都很重要，因為它們能夠傳達意思。對考生來說，這些圖可以讓他們更理解文章大意和詞彙，所以和閱讀和聽力內容一樣有價值。沒有圖形，有些詞彙和句子會令人費解。

下面來看看本章有關大眾傳播學的講座所附帶的圖形。

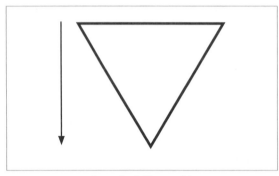

Inverted Pyramid
倒金字塔

inverted 和 pyramid 這兩個詞雖然並不常用，但是其概念很簡單。考生可以用 upside-down triangle 來改述 Inverted Pyramid。在聽講座的過程中，考生應該在聽解釋和定義時看著這個圖形。這個圖形應能使考生更容易理解講座內容。例如，當教授說：You will find that in a hard news story the important information and any background material often form the shape of an inverted pyramid. The small part of the pyramid is at the very top, and the widest part is at the bottom. In this approach, some of the most newsworthy information comes at the beginning, or top, and then the remaining information follows in order of importance, with the least important details at the bottom. 此時，考生就應該注意觀察這個圖形。

● 當看到電腦螢幕上出現圖解或其他圖形時，可採用以下策略：

策略 1 熟悉常見題型，尤其在聽力中，以便瞭解試題中一般會用到什麼圖形。

策略 2 熟悉不同題型的圖片類型。

聽力講座中通常會出現一張照片，顯示一位教授和一些學生在一個教室或會議室裡。而辦公時間對話，螢幕上也會出現一張照片，上面為一名學生和一位教授。在學生交流對話中，看到的照片是一名學生和大學裡的非教師職員。

策略 3 聽力講座中如果有圖解，一定要在聽的時候仔細看圖。

電腦螢幕上出現圖片是一種資訊提示，幫你更理解文章。也許是有一些低頻詞彙或對某一過程的說明。

策略 4 不要擔心圖片中用來標注細小部位或細節的低頻詞彙。要把關注的重點放在文章表達的主旨和重要例子上。

• Exercise 2　（解答請見 P. 377）

Write a description of the communication cycle represented in the following diagram.

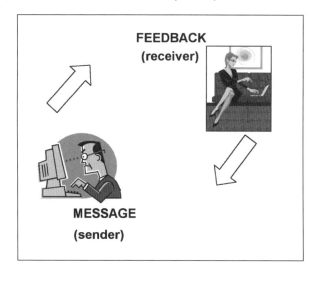

_____

_____

_____

_____

▶模擬試題（解答請見 P. 377）

Now listen to a lecture about MASS COMMUNICATION.　 *Track 031*

★ Keywords

inverted pyramid format 倒金字塔形式	lead （新聞）導語

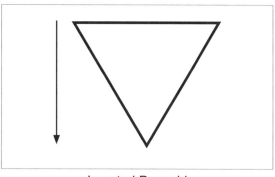

Inverted Pyramid
倒金字塔

• Listening Questions *Track 032*

1. What is the talk mainly about?
    A. The different categories of news media.
    B. The content of hard and soft news articles.
    C. How to tailor a news piece to online audiences.
    D. How to organize ideas in a hard news story.

2. In his talk, what does the professor say about the inverted pyramid format?
    Choose 2 answers.
    A. It starts out with an indirect quote.
    B. It is often used in hard news.
    C. It contains two main components.
    D. It typically ends with a factual summary.

3. Why does the professor say this:

 Please listen to Track 032 for this part of the question.

    A. To give an example of what a lead should be.
    B. To inform the students he has taken a new position.
    C. To alert the students that there is a good job opening.
    D. To pay tribute to a former student who has done well.

4. Why does the professor mention "string"?
    A. To compare weaving string fibers to communicating ideas.
    B. To explain how writers can determine an article's length.
    C. To stress that there will always be deadlines for writers.
    D. To teach writers to write comprehensible conclusions.

5. The professor talks about various aspects of hard news and soft news. For each item below, indicate which type of news it is associated with.
    Place a ✓ mark in the correct box. **This question is worth 2 points.**

Characteristic or example	Hard news	Soft news	Both hard and soft news
Features			
Leads			
Inverted pyramid			
String			

Physical Sciences, Topic 5: Computers and Software Engineering
物理科學常考主題 5：電腦和軟體工程

　　本章內容以物理科學範疇的電腦和軟體工程為知識背景。電腦涉及計算和電腦科技、硬體和軟體。與電腦有關的語塊有 mouse（滑鼠），data processing（資料處理）和 hard drive（硬碟驅動器）等。軟體工程指軟體系統的設計和製作過程。與軟體工程有關的語塊有 version（版本）和 user interface（使用者介面）等。請注意本章中出現的語塊，並記住它們。

⋯⋯⋯⋯⋯⋯⋯⋯⋯電腦和軟體工程：閱讀⋯⋯⋯⋯⋯⋯⋯⋯⋯

▶情境詞彙題的做題技巧和策略

　　做詞彙題的最好方法是根據上下文猜測詞意。另外，還有一種很有用的方法是根據詞形知識來猜測詞意。字首、字根、字尾有時可以幫助考生對詞的意思做出正確推測。

　　來看看本章下文這篇關於軟體安全的文章中考查的一些詞彙。

• READING SAMPLE 1

1. The word "advent" in Paragraph 1 is closest in meaning to _____.
   A. dominance   B. arrival   C. revolution   D. scope

> **托福總監評析**
>
> 　　字首 ad- 的含義是「朝向」或者「接近」。那麼，即使考生不知道 vent 來源於拉丁語 to come，也可以猜出選項 B 為正確答案。

• READING SAMPLE 2

6. The word "prohibitive" in Paragraph 3 is closest in meaning to _____.
   A. illegitimate   B. complicated   C. foolhardy   D. unaffordable

托福總監評析

　　字首 pro- 有多種含義，如：「代替，支持；在……之前，早於」等，因而此處很難根據字首猜測其含義。hibit 來源於拉丁語 to hold。該詞實際上是取 in front of + holding 的意思，表示阻止某人向前移動，但絕大多數人都不懂拉丁文。

　　不過，可以採用另一種策略。動詞 prohibit 的意思是 to forbid or prevent；而 -ive 是常用的形容詞尾碼。由此推測 prohibitive 的意思大概是 preventing。

　　快速瀏覽選項，看看是否有意思與 preventing 或 forbidding 相同的詞。D 項 unaffordable 在上下文中與 preventing 或 forbidding 的意思相近。在此處關於設計軟體系統的情境中，prohibitive 的意思是在購買想要的東西時因負擔過重而受到阻止（prevented），即無法承擔的（unaffordable）。

　　下表中列出了考生必須記住的常見字首和字尾：

常見字首

表示「肯定」或「中性」的字首	含義	例子
auto-	self	sign an autograph（簽名）
re-	again, back	reproduced photograph（複製的照片）
chrono-	time	historical chronology（歷史事件發生的順序）
pre-	before	legal precedent（法律先例）
pro-	for, before	promote your software（推廣軟體）
homo-	same	homogenous group（相同類型的一組）
hyper-	over, excessive	hyperactive child（過動兒）
ethno-	people, race	ethnocentric views（種族中心主義觀點）
super-	above, superior	supernatural powers（超自然力量）
geo-	Earth, geography	geopolitical border（地緣政治的邊界）

表示「否定」的字首	含義	例子
a-	not, without	atypical case（非典型病例）
anti-	against	anti-aging cream（抗衰老面霜）
dis-	not	dishonest person（不誠實的人）

表示「否定」的字首	含義	例子
il-	not	illegitimate reason（不符合邏輯的原因）
im-	not	imbalanced nutrition（不均衡的營養）
in-	not	incorrect answer（不正確的答案）
ir-	not	irresponsible behavior（不負責任的行為）
mal-	bad	program malfunction（程式故障）
pseudo-	false	popular pseudoscience（流行的偽科學）
un-	not, reverse	unable to back up my file（不能備份我的檔案）

常見字尾

名詞字尾	含義	例子
-acy	state of being	nutritional adequacy（營養充足）
-al	relating to	emotional condition（情緒狀態）
-ance, -ence	state of being	show dominance（顯示優勢）
-dom	quality	gain freedom（獲得自由）
-er, -or	person who	computer programmer（電腦程式設計師）
-ism	belief	growing nationalism（日益增長的民族主義）
-ity, -ty	state of being	data integrity（資料完整）
-ment	result of	city government（市政府）
-ness	state of being	act of carelessness（粗心大意的行為）
-sion, -tion	state of being	transition phase（過渡階段）

動詞字尾	含義	例子
-ate	to make	pollinate flowers（給花授粉）
-en	made of	frozen vegetables（冷藏蔬菜）
-ify, -fy	to make	falsify documents（偽造文件）
-ize, -ise	to make	sanitize the hard disk（幫硬碟消毒）

形容詞字尾	含義	例子
-able	capable of	copyable files（可複製的檔）
-al	related to	optional download（選擇性的下載）
-ful	full of	delightful music（令人愉快的音樂）
-ic, -ical	nature of	technical support（技術性支持）
-ine	nature of	feminine culture（女性文化）
-ious, -ous	full of	spacious digital memory（空間很大的數位記憶體）
-ish	like	stylish clothes（時尚的衣服）
-ive	related to	permissive parents（寬容的父母）
-less	without	wireless communication（無線通訊）
-oid	resembling	speeding asteroid（快速行進的小行星）

● **詞彙題的答題策略：**

策略 1 遇到生字，最好的方法是根據上下文來猜測。如果這種方法沒有作用，就觀察單字的詞性。

策略 2 如果知道某個詞的字首、字根或其他部分的含義，就根據這些含義來猜測其意思。即使得不到準確的意思，至少可以知道該單字的含義是肯定的還是否定的。

策略 3 推測單字的含義後，排除錯誤選項，找出同義詞（正確答案）。

策略 4 最後，將選中的選項放在句子中檢查，看看是否說得通。

▶**模擬試題**（解答請見 P. 380）

Software Security

★ **Keyword**

> HTTP 超文字傳輸協定

(1) Virtually every software system deployed in the 21st century must defend itself from malicious adversaries. Both the personal and professional realms of modern society are critically dependent on a wide range of software systems. Threats from a software security breach can range from the relatively benign, such as the defeat of copy protection in a video game, to the disastrous, such as intrusion into a nuclear power plant control system. With the advent of the Internet and increasing reliance on public networks such as

applications for e-commerce and telecommuting, the risks for banks and other companies are proliferating. Software system designers in this era must think not only of how to serve end users, but also of how to deter hackers from accessing customer databases or infecting websites with malware. Security concerns must inform every phase of software development, from the engineering of requirements to design, implementation, testing and deployment.

(2) Changes in software development practices and software architectures have opened up opportunities for applying security engineering. Techniques such as cryptography and tamperresistant hardware can be used to safeguard software tools and processes. ■ 1 Opportunities for enhanced security arise in part because software systems are no longer monolithic, single-vendor creations. ■ 2 Off-the-shelf software offers significant savings over custom-written software, though this advantage is somewhat offset by the fact that vendors, seeking to protect intellectual property, routinely sell components without source code or design documentation. ■ 3 Faced with the risks of constructing systems out of unknown, black-box components, developers must spend more time on due diligence analyses. ■ 4 In this context, there is even more of a need to become versant with the ever-expanding array of defensive technologies. Tamper-resistant microprocessors, for example, can be used to store and process sensitive information as in electronic transfers using credit or debit cards. The microchips in these cards are designed so that information is accessed through embedded encryption software.

(3) Security requirements have traditionally not been the beneficiary of the type of rigorous analysis so often carried out for other functional requirements. In mature markets, non-security software engineers have strategically chosen features from a variety of possibilities, deploying those most in demand by customers and most likely to maximize revenue. Designing a truly secure system, to the extent that it defended against all credible threats, would prove prohibitive. In practice, limited resources force compromises upon the security software designer, compromises made on an ad-hoc basis, mostly as an afterthought. Systems engineering must be merged with security engineering. Just as systems engineers are tasked with analyzing and selecting market-critical features, security engineers must develop viable threat models. As new applications are introduced, engineers should think not only of how they can be used, but how they can be abused. From this planning, a robust menu of the security measures can be generated and strategically deployed, so that the integrated system contains an appropriate balance of attractive customer features and selected security measures.

(4) Software designers involved in reengineering projects have long recognized the need to incorporate considerations such as performance and reliability into software design processes. It is well understood that adding performance and reliability requirements into software architectures after the fact can be problematic—or even impossible. All the same, to the detriment of all concerned, security-oriented requirements for performance

and reliability are regularly built in last. This typically means that policy enforcement mechanisms have to be "shoehorned" into a preexisting design, leading to costly and sometimes impossible design challenges for the rest of the system. The only solution to this problem is for software engineers to hone the requirements process such that security issues receive priority from the outset.

(5) Apart from poor planning, there are other reasons that security fails to be considered in the initial systems design. When older legacy systems—which have been operating for some time within secure intranets—need to be reengineered for network applications, including those on the open Internet, there is no choice but to add security after the fact. Several technical problems result from architectural mismatch; for example, data incompatibilities may render it difficult for an engineer to make a system's services available via standard protocols, such as HTTP.

• **Reading Questions**

1. The word "advent" in Paragraph 1 is closest in meaning to _____.
   A. dominance
   B. arrival
   C. revolution
   D. scope

2. In Paragraph 1, the author mentions all of the following as being software threats EXCEPT _____.
   A. breaching a utility plant
   B. making illegal reproductions
   C. penetrating customer records
   D. infiltrating e-mail accounts

3. According to Paragraph 2, what is true about off-the-shelf software?
   A. It is inexpensive, but often offers security features that are not really needed.
   B. It does not guard against threats as well as custom-built software does.
   C. It can help build in security, but frequently does not provide written manuals.
   D. It is testable for various security features, but requires special tools to do so.

4. Which of the sentences below best expresses the essential information in the highlighted sentence in the passage? Incorrect choices change the meaning in major ways or leave out important information.
   Security requirements have traditionally not been the beneficiary of the type of rigorous analysis so often carried out for other functional requirements.
   A. Less attention has been paid to security requirements than to most other functional requirements.

B. The engineers responsible for creating security requirements were not willing to do frequent analysis work for the other functional requirements.

C. Because security requirements were not usually beneficial to the company, other functional requirements were often done instead.

D. In the past, more effort was given to security requirements than to the numerous other functional requirements.

5. The word "those" in Paragraph 3 refers to _____.
   A. markets
   B. engineers
   C. features
   D. customers

6. The word "prohibitive" in Paragraph 3 is closest in meaning to _____.
   A. illegitimate
   B. complicated
   C. foolhardy
   D. unaffordable

7. According to Paragraph 3, why do software engineers often encounter problems with their final product?
   A. They write general programs to deal with every possible threat.
   B. They make poor choices on the list of security features to be added.
   C. They care more about technical issues than about customer needs.
   D. They spend too much time developing abstract models for threats.

8. According to Paragraph 4, what happens when requirements are built in at the end?
   A. Development expenses go up.
   B. Confidential data are compromised.
   C. Software reliability is enhanced.
   D. New manuals are created.

9. The word "hone" in Paragraph 4 is closest in meaning to _____.
   A. substitute
   B. refine
   C. select
   D. audit

10. Why does the author talk about legacy systems in Paragraph 5?
   A. To illustrate how planning efforts have traditionally been very ineffective in systems design.
   B. To emphasize how much the field of network technology has progressed over the years.

C. To point out that network specialists are not the best people to write security programs.

D. To explain that older systems may have constraints preventing security changes.

11. It can be inferred from the passage that the author most likely believes which of the following about current practices in security software development?

A. Overall, software engineers lack the technical tools to adequately address security problems.

B. At present the individuals administering company networks would benefit from training in software security.

C. In product development, market and customer input has overshadowed security concerns.

D. Former computer hackers should probably not be employed as designers of security software.

12. Look at the four squares [■] that indicate where the following sentence could be added to the passage.

Instead, systems are becoming ever complex configurations pieced together with commercial off-the-shelf elements.

Where would the sentence best fit?

■ 1

■ 2

■ 3

■ 4

13. **Directions:** An introductory sentence for a brief summary of the passage is provided below. Complete the summary by selecting the THREE answer choices that express the most important ideas in the passage. Some answer choices do not belong in the summary because they express ideas that are not presented in the passage or are minor ideas in the passage. **This question is worth 2 points.**

This passage discusses the efforts that computer scientists have made to address software security issues.

-
-
-

Answer Choices

1. Many end users are ill-informed about the risks of malicious software on the Internet.

2. Software developers have traditionally not taken into account security considerations in the early design stages.

3. When computers are provided with tamper-resistant locks, hardware becomes much easier to safeguard.

4. The current level of threat from cybercriminals necessitates that engineers take active steps to prevent breaches.

5. In addition to analyzing customer preferences, software designers should identify defensive features as part of product development.

6. In spite of relatively weak planning efforts, software practitioners have been able to effectively cope with network security applications.

關鍵語塊

- **deploy** 部署；散佈
- **malicious adversary** 惡意的對手
- **realm** 領域
- **security breach** 安全性漏洞
- **benign** 無危險的
- **copy protection** 複製保護
- **intrusion into** 入侵
- **public network** 公共網路
- **application** 應用程式；應用軟體
- **e-commerce** 電子商務
- **telecommuting** 遠端辦公
- **proliferating** 激增的
- **deter** 阻止
- **hacker** 電腦駭客
- **infecting website** 感染病毒的網站
- **malware** 惡意軟體
- **software architecture** 軟體架構
- **open opportunities for...**
  為……創造了新契機
- **cryptography** 密碼學
- **tamper-resistant hardware**
  防篡改硬體
- **monolithic** 完全統一的
- **single-vendor creation**
  單一供應商的產品
- **off-the-shelf elements** 現成的元件，
  買來就可用的元件
- **custom-written software** 訂製的軟體

- **offset by the fact that...** 被……抵消
- **preexisting design** 已有的設計
- **from the outset** 從一開始
- **legacy system** 遺留系統，舊系統
- **vendor** 供應商
- **intellectual property** 智慧財產權
- **source code** 原始程式碼
- **design documentation** 設計資料
- **black-box component** 黑盒子元件
- **due diligence analysis** 盡職調查分析
- **versant** 精通的，熟悉的
- **microprocessor** 微處理器
- **microchip** 微晶片
- **embedded** 嵌入式的
- **encryption software** 加密軟體
- **beneficiary of...** ……的受惠者
- **force compromises on...**
  迫使在……上妥協
- **make on an ad-hoc basis** 臨時做出
- **as an afterthought** 事後產生的想法；
  後來添加的東西
- **market-critical feature** 決定產品暢銷
  市場的特點
- **abuse** 濫用
- **robust menu** 強大的功能選擇單
- **reengineering project**
  流程重設計專案
- **after the fact** 事後

> **關鍵語塊** ▲ （續前頁）
>
> * **all the same** 儘管如此
> * **to the detriment of all concerned**
>   對所有涉及的人不利
> * **performance** 性能
> * **reliability** 可靠性
> * ... **"shoehorned" into**...
>   將……「硬塞」進……
>
> * **architectural mismatch**
>   架構搭配不起來
> * **data incompatibility** 資料不相容
> * **standard protocol** 標準協定

• Exercise 1 （解答請見 P. 382）

Use your knowledge of prefix meanings to guess the meanings of these words from the reading passage on computer security:

1. malware (mal + ware) _____

2. cryptography (crypt + ography) _____

3. monolithic (mono + lith + ic) _____

4. vendor (vend + or) _____

5. encryption (en + crypt + ion) _____

·······························**電腦和軟體工程：聽力**·······························

▶重點技能：講座中有師生互動環節時怎麼辦

　　新托福聽力考試中的學術講座有兩種形式：1）不含學生互動環節的講座 和 2）含有學生提問、回答問題和發表評論環節的講座。這兩種講座的數量通常是一樣的。

　　在沒有學生互動環節的講座中，就只有教授不停地談論主題。教授可能會逐步展開講座內容。教授的語言往往是學術性的。相對而言，有學生互動的講座往往含有簡短和自發的自然對話。學生常常會聽不懂教授的觀點而需要教授進一步說明，因而會與教授有交流互動。這種語言可能非常隨意，結構鬆散，但是這些對話通常對教授的教學工作極為重要。這就是為什麼新托福講座中會有師生對話。

　　以下文模擬試題為例：

• LISTENING SAMPLE 1

P: ... This was centralized computing, in that all computing was performed by one big brain—a central processing unit in the mainframe. It was not the most efficient arrangement.

S: [interrupting] Sorry to interrupt, but I would think one centralized "brain" would be super efficient, 'cause you'd have one decision-making center that would be reliable.

托福總監評析

　　在上面的範例中，教授講課時有個學生突然打斷並提出問題。學生使用的表達是：Sorry to interrupt, but... 這是常用說法。學生的問題提得很好，正中要害。

• **LISTENING SAMPLE 2**

　　講座中，另一種類型的學生參與是教授提問，學生回答。

P: Let me ask you all, can anyone give me some examples of popular applications in cloud computing?

S: Uh, maybe e-mail?

P: That's certainly one. Any others?

托福總監評析

　　上面的範例是學生直接回答教授所提問題的情況，這在新托福學術講座中也經常出現。可以看到，學生的答案是試探性的，而且非常簡短。這意味著如果我們要理解其含義，必須注意對話情境。

　　雖然題目並不總是詢問學生說話的內容，不過在語用功能題、推論題和立場題中，有時會直接考教授和學生之間的對話。此外，師生對話有時會暗示講座要點，所以，最好將學生所說的要點以及學生提到的原因記下來。

● 在講座中聽到學生說話時，可採用以下策略：

　　策略 1 大概有一半的學術講座中會有學生互動。遇到學生突然「插話」或教授講話節奏改變時，請注意聽。

　　策略 2 當教授和學生互動時，要特別注意他們對話的目的。

　　策略 3 利用螢幕上的圖片來設想教授和學生之間的互動場景。這有助於預測並跟上對話的思路。

　　策略 4 想像自己就是對話中的學生，讓自己處在相同的情境。

　　學生是在努力思考答案嗎？還是在就一個較難的主題提出問題？通過設身處地思考，就能更理解對話的含義。

● **Exercise 2** （解答請見 P. 382）

Each of the following is a short dialog between a professor and a student. Write a sentence in the blank that demonstrates meaningful, natural communication.

Professor: Today I'm going to talk about speech recognition technology. But first, I want to ask you all a question: When you call a company's customer service phone number, how do you feel when you have to talk to a computer?

Student: _____

ⓑ

Student: I am having trouble understanding exactly how to create the database. I thought I did, but...

Professor: _____

ⓒ

Professor: Nowadays, I know all of you take your laptops with you everywhere. But can anyone tell me when the first computer was invented?

Student: _____

▶ 模擬試題（解答請見 P. 382）

Now listen to a lecture about COMPUTER ENGINEERING.   🎧 *Track 033*

★ **Keywords**

cloud computing 雲端計算   web-based application 網頁應用程式
browser 瀏覽器

Cloud Symbol

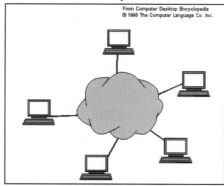

Computing in the Cloud

• **Listening Questions** *Track 034*

1. What aspect of cloud computing does the professor mainly discuss?
   A. Its role in business.
   B. Its impact on manufacturing.
   C. Its weak points.
   D. Its processing model.

2. According to the professor, what does a cloud represent in a computer diagram?
   A. An unspecified network.
   B. An undefined error.
   C. A remote control device.
   D. A remote browser.

3. Listen again to part of the lecture. Then answer the question.

    Please listen to Track 034 for this part of the question.

   What does the professor mean when he says this:

    Please listen to Track 034 for this part of the question.

   A. To talk about a visit he made to a company.
   B. To ask permission to wander back in time.
   C. To tell the students to go to the technology lab.
   D. To encourage the students to use their imaginations.

4. According to the professor, what are the advantages of centralization to a computer user?
   Choose 2 answers.
   A. Better control of data.
   B. Greater number of options.
   C. Lower cost rate.
   D. Less maintenance.

5. Why does the professor mention brains?
   A. To make the point that the new browsers are better.
   B. To demonstrate how artificial intelligence is used in laptops.
   C. To illustrate where computer processing takes place.
   D. To show that human brains function in distributed mode.

6. What is the professor's opinion about cloud computing?
   A. He thinks it is a passing fad in computer networking.
   B. He thinks the applications have yet to be perfected.
   C. He thinks web browsers are not centralized enough.
   D. He thinks fewer social networking platforms should use it.

18 Humanities and the Arts, Topic 5: Art and Art History
人文藝術常考主題 5：藝術和藝術史

　　本章內容以人文藝術範疇的藝術和藝術史為知識背景。藝術領域中用到的語塊可能與表現形式有關，如 watercolor（水彩畫），artist's perspective（藝術家的視角）和 printmaking（版畫複製）。與藝術史相關的語塊可能會涉及藝術風格和藝術運動，如 abstract expressionism（抽象表現主義）和 contemporary art（當代藝術）。請注意本章中出現的語塊，並記住它們。

·················· 藝術和藝術史：閱讀 ··················

▶修辭目的題的解題策略

　　第 13 章介紹過修辭目的題的考試重點，並對這種題型的最佳解題策略進行了概括，其中最重要的一點是要掌握邏輯思路，判斷考查內容與上下文之間的關係。

　　下面以本章下文題目為例，具體介紹一下這類題型的解題策略。

• READING SAMPLE I

8. In Paragraph 6, the author mentions the actor Marilyn Monroe in order to illustrate what concept?

　　A. To lament that the art collection was overly commercial.

　　B. To suggest the celebrity artist was beginning to overshadow the art itself.

　　C. To provide a celebrated example of modernist portrait painting.

　　D. To illustrate the growing importance of the media in the art world.

托福總監評析

　　這道題目問作者為何提到了某個人。回答這類題，考生應該先快速從文章裡找到題目提到的這個人（此處為 Marilyn Monroe）的句子。第六段：Picasso was the dazzling Marilyn Monroe of modern painting. 作者將這位著名的藝術家比作電影明星瑪麗蓮·夢露。作者為什麼要作此類比呢？

最佳策略是看上下文，該句前一句：Initially, he was seen as but one innovator among many modernists, yet by the 1960s he had become a virtual icon representing the glory days of modern art. 這句話很重要，因為它提供了瑪麗蓮·夢露重要性的兩個原因線索。首先，我們知道畢卡索成了 virtual icon（偶像），是個偉大的象徵。其次，這種象徵代表了 glory days（輝煌歲月）。glory 有 magnificence 和 splendor 的意思。因此 glory days 是指一個人或一個時代的偉大成就。因此，作者似乎是說畢卡索就像一位電影明星。

作者之前沒有談商業化問題，只談明星效應現象，所以 A 項不正確。電影雖然也可以說是一種媒體，但作者的敘述重點並不是媒體，所以 D 項也不正確。從上下文可知，作者例舉瑪麗蓮·夢露是為了說明名人藝術家的光芒蓋過了藝術本身，所以 B 項正確。

• READING SAMPLE 2

11. In the passage, the author uses which of the following organizational structures to present the subject material?
A. Chronologically by artist, then by date of art work with discussion.
B. Thesis statement first, followed by examples of American artists.
C. One American style briefly shown, followed by contrasting American styles.
D. Geographically by region, then analysis of each artist within region.

托福總監評析

做這類考題，考生必須通篇考慮全文。也許考生已經知道文章的組織框架了，但如果不清楚也不要擔心。

單就這道組織結構題來說，排除錯誤的選項並不容易，因為該題的每個選項都有兩個必須核對的部分。選項 A「作者按照藝術家生活年代的順序依次提到每個藝術家，每位藝術家的作品也是按照創作時間的先後順序依次列出，每個作品後都附有論述」，該說法不正確，因為作者在文章開頭談到了畢卡索（在時間上他並非最早的藝術家），也沒有逐一列舉或介紹畢卡索的藝術作品。

選項 B 可能正確，因為文章第一句是中心思想句，指出畢卡索幾乎影響了 20 世紀上半葉的每一位美國藝術家。但為了保險起見，還應該快速看看選項 C 和 D 並將其排除。

選項 C「作者在文章開頭簡單介紹了一種美國藝術風格，然後將這種風格與其他風格進行比較」，這顯然不正確，因為作者開頭介紹的是西班牙藝術家畢卡索。

選項 D 不正確，因為地域並非作者的敘述重點，文章的內容並非按照地域來組織的。那麼，選項 B 肯定就是正確答案了。

這道題目，我們通過閱讀前兩段就能排除掉錯誤選項。但有些閱讀文章中，考生必須略讀幾段內容才能判斷選項是否正確。顯然，需要讀的段落越少，解題速度就越快。因此，建議一開始就仔細閱讀第一段，看看能否從四個選項中初步確定正確答案或排除一些選項。

▶**模擬試題**（解答請見 P. 385）

Picasso and American Artists

(1) Almost every American artist of the first half of the 20th century was influenced by the Spanish artist Pablo Picasso. For at least 50 years, Picasso was the one to watch. He was also the one to beat.

(2) The Armenian-born Abstract Expressionist painter Arshile Gorky said it most succinctly: "If Picasso drips," he said, "I drip." That was in the late 1930s, a time when deciphering Picasso's intentions, from Cubism to Neoclassicism, from Surrealism to the antiwar mural "Guernica," was an all-important matter to the small but elite group of American artists who did not embrace the style of "American Scene realism." Jackson Pollock, another abstract painter, tried to blot out the Spaniard's influence—figuratively, but also literally. In at least one painting, Pollock began a "drip" canvas highly reminiscent of the Picasso style, only to paint over what he had done. Picasso had already done everything, he complained, and his view was shared by many others. One American artist after another discovered the foreign genius, then came to grips with what Picasso's peculiar art meant, struggling to crawl out from under its shadow.

(3) Had Picasso's art never crossed the Atlantic, the entire history of 20th-century American art would have been different. The artist himself never made the trip to American soil. It was the painter Max Weber, a Russian Jewish emigre, who brought the first Picasso canvas to New York in 1909. At a time when Picasso was already deep into his experimentations with modernist Cubism, the most advanced American painting meant the Ashcan School of Realism or the pleasant brushwork of Childe Hassam, who continued to paint landscapes. Not even Paul Cezanne had entered much into American sensibilities, much less Cubism.

(4) The first Picasso show was held in 1911 at the pioneering 291 Gallery in New York City. That exhibition included at least some of his newest Cubist images. For budding American modernists, it was a first glimpse of work that would transform their own. All through the 1920s more of Picasso's work found its way into the US, through occasional, short-lived exhibitions or black-and-white reproductions. Then, when the Museum of Modern Art opened in Manhattan in 1929, it allowed for the first permanent display of a few real Picassos in the city where most alert American artists were gathered.

(5) In the Depression years of the thirties, the obscure painters who would one day revolutionize American art, many recent immigrants, talked well into the night in shabby

New York cafeterias over nickel cups of coffee. ■ 1They spoke passionately about the painters of the past, including Michelangelo; they debated about the innovative pioneers, especially Cezanne. ■ 2 They held forth on their near contemporaries, including Miro, Matisse and Mondrian. But the artist they talked about the most was Picasso. ■ 3 Not because he was the biggest or best; others were arguably as important. But the other painters kept to their games, working within boundaries. ■ 4

(6) From the 1910 to time of Picasso's death in 1973, American artists had diverse images of the artist to contend with. Initially, he was seen as but one innovator among many modernists, yet by the 1960s he had become a virtual icon representing the glory days of modern art. Picasso was the dazzling Marilyn Monroe of modern painting.

(7) The brightness of the American paintings throughout the decades of Picasso's extended influence suggests the painters were universally energized by his works. But this was not always the case. In 1939, when New York's Museum of Modern Art mounted the first Picasso retrospective, many artists attended. Painter Louise Bourgeois, who was 28 at the time, recorded her visit to this exhibit, where four hundred Picasso paintings were been displayed. "Forty years' work," she wrote. "It was so beautiful, and it revealed such genius and such a collection of treasures that I did not pick up a paintbrush for a month."

• Reading Questions

1. In the first paragraph, the attitude of US artists toward Picasso during the first part of the 20th century is described as which of the following?
   A. Embarrassment.
   B. Competition.
   C. Patience.
   D. Detachment.

2. The word "deciphering" in Paragraph 2 is closest in meaning to _____.
   A. imitating
   B. verifying
   C. defending
   D. decoding

3. The phrase "came to grips with" in Paragraph 2 is closest in meaning to _____.
   A. felt resentful about
   B. observed firsthand
   C. absorbed
   D. questioned

4. According to Paragraph 2, Jackson Pollock did which of the following with his canvas?
   A. Covered up drops of paint that made him think of Picasso.

B. Revised his work to be more like the original drip technique.

C. Created a colorful design that resembled the Guernica mural.

D. Repeatedly satirized the Picasso style in his own paintings.

5. Which of the sentences below best expresses the essential information in the highlighted sentence in the passage? Incorrect choices change the meaning in major ways or leave out important information.

Not even Paul Cezanne had entered much into American sensibilities, much less Cubism.

A. In spite of the many paintings by Cezanne, there was still very little evidence of Cubism in America.

B. Cezanne was not yet influencing American artists, and so of course Cubism was not either.

C. There tended to be fewer Cubism admirers in the United States because Cezanne had not arrived there yet.

D. Not many foreign paintings were coming into United States galleries, and there were fewer Cezanne works than Cubist works.

6. According to Paragraph 3, which of the following demonstrated the most interest in Picasso's modernist experiment?

A. Max Weber

B. Ashcan School

C. Childe Hassam

D. Paul Cezanne

7. The word "shabby" in Paragraph 5 is closest in meaning to _____.

A. cozy

B. unknown

C. rundown

D. smoky

8. In Paragraph 6, the author mentions the actor Marilyn Monroe in order to illustrate what concept?

A. To lament that the art collection was overly commercial.

B. To suggest the celebrity artist was beginning to overshadow the art itself.

C. To provide a celebrated example of modernist portrait painting.

D. To illustrate the growing importance of the media in the art world.

9. The phrase "virtual icon" in Paragraph 6 is closest in meaning to _____.

A. near idol

B. elusive force

C. inspiring genius

D. commanding godfather

10. According to Paragraph 7, all of the following statements about Louise Bourgeois are true EXCEPT _____.

    A. she felt intimated by the scope of Picasso's works

    B. she found the modern paintings to be a stunning collection

    C. she was reluctant at first to visit the retrospective

    D. she kept a diary of her response to Picasso paintings

11. In the passage, the author uses which of the following organizational structures to present the subject material?

    A. Chronologically by artist, then by date of art work with discussion.

    B. Thesis statement first, followed by examples of American artists.

    C. One American style briefly shown, followed by contrasting American styles.

    D. Geographically by region, then analysis of each artist within region.

12. Look at the four squares [■] that indicate where the following sentence could be added to the passage.

    They did not possess modernity itself.

    Where would the sentence best fit?

    ■ 1

    ■ 2

    ■ 3

    ■ 4

13. Directions: An introductory sentence for a brief summary of the passage is provided below. Complete the summary by selecting the THREE answer choices that express the most important ideas in the passage. Some answer choices do not belong in the summary because they express ideas that are not presented in the passage or are minor ideas in the passage. **This question is worth 2 points.**

    This passage discusses how the artist Pablo Picasso influenced artists in the United States during the first half of the 20th century.

    -
    -
    -

Answer Choices

1. Although the American art scene was late to receive the influence of Picasso, the impact when it did come was immense.

2. Initially, unconventional painting techniques such as the drip technique were not accepted by American artists.

3. Picasso's exhibits in Spain influenced the art community there, attracting many American painters to travel to Europe to see his experimental works.

4. An elite group based in New York was captivated with the multifaceted aspects of Picasso's modernism and went on to forge new American art styles.

5. Just as American artists were inspired by Picasso's genius, they were at the same time also crippled by it.

6. By the time of the Depression, American critics considered Picasso the most important artist in the world.

關鍵語塊

- **one to beat**
  一位待擊敗的人或待超越的人
- **succinctly** 簡潔地；簡要地
- **drip** 滴下
- **Cubism** 立體主義；立體畫派
- **Neoclassicism** 新古典主義
- **Surrealism** 超現實主義
- **antiwar** 反戰的
- **mural** 壁畫
- **Guernica**
  《格爾尼卡》（畢卡索的名畫之一）
- **all-important matter** 非常重要的事
- **blot out** 排除，清除
- **figuratively** 象徵性地
- **literally** 不加誇張地；確實地
- **canvas** 油畫布
- **reminiscent of…**
  令人回憶起……；使人想起……
- **paint over** 用塗料遮蓋
- **crawl out from under its shadow**
  從它的影響中走出來
- **émigré** 移居外國的人；移民
- **deep into** 深入進行

- **Ashcan School of Realism** 用現實主義手法描繪城市生活的垃圾箱畫派
- **landscape** 風景畫；山水畫
- **Cézanne** 塞尚（印象畫派的代表人物）
- **budding** 新興的；初露頭角的
- **a first glimpse of** 初步的認識
- **alert** 思維敏捷的
- **Depression years**
  （美國）大蕭條年代
- **cafeteria** 自助餐廳
- **nickel** 五分鎳幣
- **hold forth on** 滔滔不絕地談論
- **arguably** 可辯論地
- **keep to their games** 堅持自己的方式
- **working within boundaries**
  循規蹈矩地做事
- **contend with** 處理；應付
- **glory days** 輝煌歲月
- **dazzling** 耀眼的
- **universally** 無例外地
- **mount the first Picasso retrospective**
  舉辦第一場畢卡索回顧展

• Exercise 1　（解答請見 P. 386）

Write an answer to each of the following author's rhetorical purpose questions, based on the passage about Picasso.

ⓐ In Paragraph 2, why does the author give details about dripping paint?

_____

_____

ⓑ In Paragraph 5, why does the author introduce the statement **But the other painters kept to their games, working within boundaries?**

_____

_____

ⓒ Why does the author mention Louise Bourgeois in Paragraph 7?

_____

_____

藝術和藝術史：聽力

▶重點技巧：掌握教授學術講座的思路

以本章下文聽力為例：教授談到了壁畫。考生需要仔細聽有關壁畫的各種細節資訊。一條線索是教授提到學生將要做一個「工作室專案」（studio project），這提示我們這門美術課是在工作室裡上的，學生在隨後的課程中要自己創作壁畫。

根據第一句可以斷定這是第一堂美術課。考生應該想像自己正坐在美術課的教室裡，這樣可以更好地跟上教授的思路，跟隨她從一個話題轉入另一個話題。

以下是對教授講座思路的分析：

教授講話的思路

開場白	"This course will introduce you to some of the methods..." "But before we start out studio project..."
主要觀點（第一次提出）	"... I thought it might be helpful to go over some of the concepts and history related to murals. Hopefully you'll walk away with ideas for your own work."
基本背景資訊	Where and why people paint on walls "People have always painted on walls."
說明類別	Two types of murals: "True fresco" and "dry fresco" defined
舉例	Egypt, Ancient Greece, Ancient Rome
主要觀點（第二次提出）	"As artists, we can get a lot of ideas from these old fresco designs..."

舉例	Geese on a fragment from an Egyptian tomb Simple design features Professor cites these features and gives advice: "Murals that are overcrowded and overworked are rarely successful."
古埃及藝術的背景知識	"Their art served a sacred purpose..."
古埃及、古希臘和古羅馬壁畫的比較	"The Romans were capable of creating perspective and multidimensional depth..."
故事例證	"Two famous Greek fresco painters wanted to see who was best and had a contest."

　　聽講座時，要將最有可能考查的內容用筆記錄下來。例如，我們可以猜測至少會有一道題目考查事物之間的對比，尤其是當教授講解不同類型的事物時，如壁畫法的類型。在這個講座中，教授介紹了兩種壁畫法中用到的材料和方法。一聽到這種分類，就要明白後面肯定有相關考題！

　　可能會有兩個答案的細節資訊題，也有可能會出現組織結構題。此外，教授講的奇聞軼事很有可能是考試重點，這時也應該做好筆記。

▶ 模擬試題（解答請見 P. 386）

Now listen to a lecture about ART.　　　　　 *Track 035*

★ **Keywords**

fresco 壁畫技法　　sekh（古埃及文字）寫、畫和塗

• **Listening Questions**　　　　　 *Track 036*

1. What is the main purpose of the lecture?
   A. To teach the students about the chemistry of pigments.
   B. To give the students some ideas for their mural projects.
   C. To compare several ancient Greek and Roman frescoes.
   D. To show how cave painting designs influenced murals.

2. According to the professor, what are the unique features of a true fresco?
   Choose 2 answers.
   A. A permanent chemical reaction occurs in the plaster.
   B. Colors go into a binding material before painting begins.
   C. The painting is the least durable of all fresco methods.
   D. Pigment colors are absorbed into the wet plaster.

3. Listen again to part of the lecture. Then answer the question.

 Please listen to Track 036 for this part of the question.

Why does the professor say this:

 Please listen to Track 036 for this part of the question.

    A. To highlight the pictorial nature of ancient Egyptian writing.

    B. To show that Egyptian painting was more important than writing.

    C. To teach the class how to write one Egyptian hieroglyphic symbol.

    D. To affirm that ancient Egyptian painting is not easy to understand.

4. Why does the professor tell the story about two famous Greek painters?

    A. To stress that risk-taking is important when creating great art.

    B. To provide background on the social status of Greek painters.

    C. To give some examples of the fool-the-eye style of fresco.

    D. To illustrate how wealthy families competed for talented artists.

5. The professor mentions several various aspects of frescoes from different places. For each item below, indicate which characteristic is associated with which fresco.
Place a ✓ mark in the correct box. **This question is worth 2 points.**

Characteristic	Ancient Egypt	Ancient Greece and Rome
Impression of light and shadows		
Flat, two-dimensional surface		
Images that play tricks on the eye		
Patterns served a decorative function		

• Exercise 2　（解答請見 P. 389）

    Write a correct paraphrase for each of the following sentences.

ⓐ But the earliest images on cave walls were not painted for decoration.

_____

ⓑ As artists, we can get a lot of ideas from these old fresco designs, because we are facing the same design challenges as they were.

_____

ⓒ No doubt, you'll find the Egyptian style of murals simple to imitate.

_____

Life Sciences, Topic 5: Evolution and Genetics

⑲ 生命科學常考主題 5：進化學和遺傳學

本章內容以生命科學範疇的進化學和遺傳學為知識背景。進化學研究生物起源、進化和演變的進程。該領域中用到的語塊有 origin of the species（物種起源）和 offspring（後代）等。遺傳學是生物學的分支，研究生物的基因和基因結構、功能與演變。遺傳學相關的語塊有 recessive gene（隱性基因）和 cell mutation（細胞突變）等。請注意本章中出現的語塊，並記住它們。

·····························進化學和遺傳學：閱讀·····························

▶插入句子題的做題步驟

插入句子題考查考生對文章的銜接性與連貫性的把握。要做好這類題目，考生必須採取兩個做題步驟：

步驟一：仔細分析插入句，分析句子時要考慮詞彙和文法結構，尋找「話語特徵」和「信號詞」，從而歸納出做題線索。

步驟二：分析文章的意思和邏輯思路，看看上下文是否銜接、連貫。

以本章下文的第 11 題為例：

• READING SAMPLE

插入句：A well-known example is the jack pine, which sheds seeds for germination only after being subjected to the high temperatures of a forest fire.

原文：

■ 1 It is commonly assumed that plant and animal communities are delicate—intricately balanced yet vulnerable networks of dependencies and interactions. ■ 2 Each species has a place and a role in its ecological community, earned through millions of years of adaptation and coordinated with the evolution of other species. Each community is even thought by some to evolve and adapt as if it were an organism itself. Remove one piece of this complex network and other pieces will be lost, perhaps the whole thing. ■ 3 Yet this view of nature, deeply ingrained, is exaggerated. Although the thousands of interdependencies are important, plant and animal communities are more resilient than the stereotypical view might suggest. ■ 4

托福總監評析

利用以上做題步驟，可找到以下線索：1）該句是一個「例子」（話語特徵）和2）這個例子說明對高溫的生物反應（話語特徵）。從這些線索推測，要插入的句子前面的句子可能是一個概括性的陳述句，解釋某個與高溫反應相關的生物原理。

下一步是將這個句子插入每個黑色方塊位置，檢查上下文是否銜接和連貫。第一個黑色方塊位置說不通，因為這例子似乎是突然冒出來的。第二個黑色方塊前面的句子是談論一般性假設（general assumptions），後面的句子是談論每個物種都有其作用，關於短葉松（Jack pine）的例子不適合放在這個位置。第三個黑色方塊位置不正確，因為前一個句子說如果去除一個物種，生態系統就會遭到破壞，而要插入的句子是談論自然災害後的復原。第四個黑色方塊前面的句子是說植物和動物群落 are more resilient than the stereotypical view might suggest。插入句說的是短葉松在經受森林火災的高溫後是如何繁殖的，該例子證實了動植物群落對環境驚人的適應性，所以最後一個黑色方塊位置是正確答案。

從這個例題可知，最重要的線索是：這個插入句中，有一個「例子」。作者通常會使用具體的例子來闡釋一般原理。雖然例子有時也可以位於一個段落的開頭，但是在本文中，所給段落是文章的第一段，所以就不可能位於段落開頭了。而當找到了文章中需要舉例說明的概述句（"... plant and animal communities are more resilient than the stereotypical view might suggest"），也就找到了答案！

• **Exercise 1** （解答請見 P. 390）

The following five sentences come from a paragraph about how cats adapted in evolution. Using your skills in COHESION and COHERENCE, arrange them into the correct sequence.

1. It is likely that the cat domestication process began almost 10,000 years ago, when wildcats crept into villages where people were just beginning to plant wheat and barley.

2. Rodents living in the villagers' homes and granaries attracted the wildcats, and they were also eager to escape forest predators such as hyenas.

3. In contrast, cattle, sheep, goats, horses and dogs were intentionally domesticated by people for milk, meat, wool or labor.

4. The fact that the wildcats freely chose to come to human habitats might account for the relative independent attitude of cats today.

5. Of all the animals to have become adapted to human environments, cats are the only ones which "domesticated" themselves.

▶**模擬試題**（解答請見 P. 390）

Extinction of Species

(1) ■ 1 It is commonly assumed that plant and animal communities are delicate—intricately balanced yet vulnerable networks of dependencies and interactions. ■ 2 Each species has a place and a role in its ecological community, earned through millions of years of adaptation and coordinated with the evolution of other species. Each community is even thought by some to evolve and adapt as if it were an organism itself. Remove one piece of this complex network and other pieces will be lost, perhaps the whole thing. ■ 3 Yet this view of nature, deeply ingrained, is exaggerated. Although the thousands of interdependencies are important, plant and animal communities are more resilient than the stereotypical view might suggest. ■ 4

(2) The community-as-organism model, championed by those ecologists who presume considerable dependencies among species, is important to explore more fully. That is because a related question—concerning the extent to which species are fragile—is germane to the issue of extinction. If species are vulnerable to extinction, the stresses that cause extinction may be relatively mild. But if species are inherently resilient, conditions must be relatively severe to cause extinction. Similarly, if natural communities are delicate networks of interdependencies, the loss of one species may cause the loss of others. But if communities are not highly integrated, species extinctions may occur independently of on another.

(3) Almost any stress, physical or biological, can lead to extinction. The extermination of the heath hen by over-hunting is a classic example, one of the best-documented in modern times. Human activities played the principal role, but several complexities of the case make it useful as an introduction to biological causes of extinction. In colonial America, the heath hen was highly edible, easy to kill and abundant throughout much of the eastern seaboard, from Maine to Virginia. Its preferred habitat was scrubby grassland and low shrubs and meadows, where it built its nests. Intensive hunting, coupled with habitat destruction by an expanding human population, gradually reduced the heath hens' geographic range. By 1840 they were limited to Long Island, parts of Pennsylvania and a few other places. From 1870 on they existed only on the island of Martha's Vineyard, off the coast of Massachusetts. The heath hen population there continued to decline until 1908, when a reserve was established to protect the remaining fifty birds. The population grew steadily.

(4) Then in 1916 a series of unanticipated and mostly natural events led to the final extinction. These were 1) a natural fire, spread by a strong gale, that destroyed much of the grass; 2) a hard winter immediately following the fire and accompanied by an unusual influx of predatory hawks; 3) inbreeding caused by the reduced population size and the accident of distorted sex ratio (during the fire the females refused to leave their nests); and 4)

the introduction of a poultry disease introduced from domestic turkeys, which infected a substantial number of remaining birds. The last heath hen was seen in 1932.

(5) What is important about the heath hen extinction is that it developed in two distinct stages. The first involved the devastation of habitat and the drop in population due to a new and sudden stress—human hunting. These factors led to a drastic reduction in geographic range. The next stage involved a series of accidents—some physical and some biological—that led to the final extinction. Yet none of these would have been significant had the range of the species not been limited to Martha's Vineyard.

(6) In its former range, the heath hen could have survived any of these stresses, even all of them at the same time. However, island species are at special risk because of the limited range and because they tend to have low population numbers. A species with a small population can easily be drawn into what is known as an "extinction vortex," in which interacting factors work progressively to make small populations smaller and smaller, drawing them into extinction like a whirlpool. Thus, whereas factors such as habitat certainly affect the community and ecosystem, it is the population's smallness itself that finally drives it to extinction. This happens because the impact of random variation in reproductive and mortality rates is much greater on small populations than on large ones.

• Reading Questions

1. In the first paragraph, what does the author say about the resilience of ecological communities?
   A. Although networks seem to be quite delicate, ecologists have not been able to determine why.
   B. Communities are surprisingly able to survive challenging environmental conditions.
   C. Community species are so interdependent that a stress on one will in turn harm the others.
   D. Individual species are unable to adapt quickly enough to withstand unexpected stresses.

2. The phrase "deeply ingrained" in the first paragraph is closest in meaning to _____.
   A. highly suspect
   B. intuitively obvious
   C. long accepted
   D. much discussed

3. The word "championed" in Paragraph 2 is closest in meaning to _____.
   A. advocated
   B. achieved
   C. required
   D. probed

4. The phrase "**germane to**" in Paragraph 2 is closest in meaning to _____.
   A. obscuring
   B. changing
   C. applied to
   D. pertinent to

5. According to Paragraph 3, all of the following were true about the heath hen EXCEPT _____.
   A. they were unhappy on island terrain
   B. they could be easily found in their habitat
   C. they were considered very tasty
   D. they once occupied a wide territory

6. The word "**first**" in Paragraph 5 refers to _____.
   A. heath hen
   B. extinction
   C. stage
   D. habitat

7. According to Paragraph 5, why was geographic range critical in the case of the heath hen?
   A. Hunters could more easily shoot down the heath hens within a restricted area.
   B. The habitat in the geographic range could not adequately support a heath hen population.
   C. The island was the only place heath hens were found, putting the species at particular risk.
   D. Because more than one species of hen lived together on Martha's Vineyard, there were problems.

8. Which of the sentences below best expresses the essential information in the highlighted sentence in the passage? Incorrect choices change the meaning in major ways or leave out important information.
   Thus, whereas factors such as habitat certainly affect the community and eco-system, it is the population's smallness itself that finally drives it to extinction.
   A. Consequently, in places where habitat was critical to the community and ecosystem, the species numbers became very small, causing extinction.
   B. The small size of the species population was the key factor causing extinction, even though harm to the overall environment was also important.
   C. Even though many events were damaging to the heath hen community and ecosystem, the few remaining hens should have been safe in that habitat.
   D. Because of environmental factors, the community and ecosystem were unable to support a large population, and so the heath hens became extinct.

9. According to Paragraph 6, which of the following best describes how an extinction vortex works?

   A. A species with a small population is suddenly threatened by a strong external force.

   B. An ecological community is confronted with a more competitive species and driven to extinction.

   C. A series of events acts on a small population step by step, causing it to be exterminated.

   D. A species is forced into an area with limited range of habitat and starves to death.

10. The author implies that in 1916 the heath hens' low rate of reproduction was mainly due to which of the following?

    A. Unusual climate conditions.

    B. Human intervention.

    C. Over-abundance of males.

    D. Lack of nesting habitat.

11. Look at the four squares [■] that indicate where the following sentence could be added to the passage.

    A well-known example is the jack pine, which sheds seeds for germination only after being subjected to the high temperatures of a forest fire.

    Where would the sentence best fit?

    ■ 1

    ■ 2

    ■ 3

    ■ 4

12. Directions: Complete the chart below about the factors that made up the two phases in heath hen extinction. Choose five of the seven answer choices and match them to the phase with which they are associated. **This question is worth 3 points.**

Extinction Process	Factors
Phase 1	• •
Phase 2	• • •

Answer Choices

1. Targeting of heath hens for food

2. Bitterly cold winter season

3. Large number of females refused to mate

4. Burning of grassland nesting area

5. Commercial land development

6. Bringing domestic fowl into the habitat

7. Competition for habitat with hardier species

關鍵語塊

- **delicate** 脆弱的
- **intricately** 複雜地；雜亂地
- **vulnerable** 易受傷害的；脆弱的
- **species** 物種
- **ecological community** 生態群落
- **adaptation** （動植物在構造、機能等方面對環境的）適應
- **evolve** 進化
- **organism** 有機體；生物體
- **resilient** 適應性強的；有抗性的
- **stereotypical view** 老套的觀點；傳統觀點
- **extinction** 滅絕
- **stress** 壓力
- **extermination of...** ……的滅絕
- **heath hen** 琴雞
- **over-hunting** 過度狩獵
- **classic example** 典型例子

- **abundant** 豐富的；充裕的
- **eastern seaboard** （美國）東海岸
- **habitat** （動植物的）棲生地
- **geographic range** 地理分佈區
- **population** 種群
- **reserve** 自然保護區
- **natural event** 自然事件
- **gale** 大風；狂風
- **inbreeding** 近親交配；同系繁殖
- **distorted sex ratio** 不均衡的性別比例
- **infect** 使……受感染
- **devastation** 破壞
- **extinction vortex** 滅絕漩渦
- **whirlpool** 漩渦
- **ecosystem** 生態系統
- **drive it to...** 迫使它至……的境地
- **reproductive rate** 繁殖率
- **mortality rate** 死亡率

進化學和遺傳學：聽力

▶重點技能：掌握複雜的聽力文法

　　由於種種原因，聽外語的學術講座是非常有挑戰性的。講座主題陌生，講座使用的語言又很正式，或者過於理論化。當然，教授會力圖使抽象和難懂的概念更加具體，並更容易理解。但是，由於說話是自發的，且課堂是動態變化的，教授對難懂概念和術語的解釋可能會比較鬆散，使英語為非母語的人難以理解。

　　雖然新托福學術講座是非專業人士也能聽懂的，但考生仍然可能會感到有一定難度。這可能是由於考生缺乏對主題的瞭解或學術詞彙（概念詞彙、相對低頻和專業的詞彙）匱乏。講座之所以會較難的另一個原因則是學術語言有專門的文法和用法。考生掌握的文法規則在閱讀文章中很容易理解，但以口語形式出現時，就難以辨別。的確，如果考生不熟

悉學術講座的話語特徵和語言特徵，聽力文法結構的識別可能會是一項令人望而生畏的艱鉅任務。

　　因此，要提高理解講座的能力，熟悉和牢記一些最常見的聽力文法結構是很重要的。這樣我們就更有可能在考試時明白它們的含義。

　　以本章下文聽力文本為例：

• LISTENING SAMPLE

1. You'll remember, it's non-sexual division that produces most of our cells, cells that allow us to grow from infancy and to replace the older cells.

   文法結構：It's NOUN x that produces NOUN y, NOUN y that z...

   這個句子含有兩種重要的聽力句式：

   強調句：It's... that...

   強調句由 there is 或 it is（或其他形式的 be 動詞）構成。在口語中，我們最常聽到的是這些句式的縮略形式，there's 和 it's。如：

   There's clearly a hereditary link to spatial ability.

   It's a good summary of the research on cloning.

   使役句：NOUN that allow us to VERB

   使役動詞表示使某事或導致某事發生的動詞形式。在口語中，使役動詞往往用在子句中。如：

   After four hours of sitting, our bodies start to send signals that cause the genes regulating glucose and fat to shut down.

   The reproduction and development of organisms follow patterns that allow adaptation to changing environments.

2. The membrane of the nucleus dissolves, which allows the DNA strands to separate.

   文法結構：The NOUN x dissolves（動詞）, which allows NOUN y to（動詞）...

   學術對話中常會使用各種子句來解釋含有多個步驟的過程。在該句中，前面的主句說明了過程，後面的子句說明了結果。

   關係子句：分句，which（或其他關係代詞）+ 謂語動詞 ...

   這個句子也用了使役動詞：to allow。這個使役動詞用在 which 引導的子句中，致使考生聽的時候難以理解。下面再來看看這種 which 引導的關係子句的例子：

   The microbodies in our experiment are then manipulated, which as you will see permits the DNA to penetrate to the cells.

   Now, a change in gene pool leads to better fitness, which leads to adaptation, which in turn leads to reproductive success.

3. But other cells are rarely duplicated—the cells in our brains and hearts, for example.

   文法結構：名詞或名詞性子句 + 破折號 + 起擴展、加強或闡釋作用的名詞或名詞性子從句

   在口語中，尤其是當解釋概念時，說話者往往會加一些語言來表達自己的觀點。這種添加的語言往往用破折號來表示，破折號後面緊跟起擴展、加強或闡釋作用的片語或分句。

破折號擴展句型：—the cells in our brains and hearts（名詞性子句）

這種句型為什麼在新托福講座中很重要？邊講邊思考的教授常常會使用破折號擴展句型。他們在説一句話時會突然中斷，加入評論或補充內容，如笑話或觀點。如：

And the publication of *On the Origin of Species* caused a real furor—every copy of the book was sold the day that it came out; all the more remarkable because the book was over 500 pages.

In the mid-1980's, the scientific community began debating what was at that time a pretty radical idea—the sequencing of the human genome.

• Exercise 2　（解答請見 P. 393）

Below are more sentences containing complex grammar patterns from academic lectures. Write a correct paraphrase for each. You will probably need to write two sentences to capture the full meaning.

ⓐ I'm going to switch to another widely used genetic model, which is the fruit fly, which you see in the summer around rotting fruit.

_____

_____

ⓑ It's the position of the larynx—the "voice box" that regulates air going into the lungs—that allows humans to make more sounds than Neanderthals.

_____

_____

ⓒ Unlike his father, Charles Darwin didn't want to be a doctor, and in college he studied theology—a high-status career track Darwin's father chose for him.

_____

_____

▶ 模擬試題（解答請見 P. 392）

Now listen to a lecture about GENETICS.　　*Track 037*

★ Keywords

| chromosome 染色體　　telomere 端粒（在染色體端位上的著絲點） |

• Listening Questions　　*Track 038*

1. What is the lecture mainly about?
   A. How human genes are vertically arranged in cell tissue.
   B. How DNA can be damaged in cell duplication and division.
   C. Differences between sexual and non-sexual cell division.
   D. Biological mechanisms that control body cell division.

2. Listen again to part of the lecture. Then answer the question.

Please listen to Track 038 for this part of the question.

What does the professor mean when he says this:

Please listen to Track 038 for this part of the question.

    A. Scientists have been using diverse research approaches.
    B. Animal telomeres tend to be slightly shorter in length.
    C. The student's question should have been better framed.
    D. The scientific findings have been somewhat ambiguous.

3. In the professor's explanation of a telomere, he compares it to which of the following?
    A. Shoestring.
    B. Piece of plastic.
    C. Daughter.
    D. Wizard.

4. According to the professor, DNA in telomeres is interesting to scientists for which of the following reasons?
    Choose 2 answers.
    A. It becomes shorter during cell division.
    B. It is an essential part of the genetic code.
    C. It guards against the loss of necessary genes.
    D. It prevents against certain types of cancer.

5. What does the professor think about the clock theory of telomeres?
    A. He agrees telomeres affect cells but believes aging cannot be slowed.
    B. He doubts the clock theory is responsible for aging in the heart and brain.
    C. He thinks telomeres affect a person's life span but cannot give reasons why.
    D. He fears there are risks for scientists who tinker with genetic biotechnology.

6. The professor talks about a research study involving a sample of twins. For each of the following, indicate whether the study supported this finding.
    Place ✓ mark in the YES or NO column.

	YES	NO
More white blood cells were found in people who exercised more.		
Telomere length was shorter in people who exercised less.		
Exercisers tend to have children with relatively long telomeres.		

Social Sciences, Topic 5: Marketing and Business
社會科學常考主題 5：市場行銷學與商學

本章內容以社會科學範疇的市場行銷學和商學為知識背景。市場行銷學研究組織機構如何滿足客戶的需求，如何迎合客戶以及如何通過行銷獲得利潤。商學的研究有多個分支，包括會計、財務和管理等。市場行銷學也可視為商學的一部分。市場行銷學領域用到的語塊有 generic brand（通用品牌），focus group（目標群體）和 product life cycle（產品生命周期）等。商學相關的語塊有 venture capital（風險資本），e-commerce（電子商務）和 financial statement（財務報表）等。請注意本章中出現的語塊，並記住它們。

······················市場行銷學與商學：閱讀······················

▶句子簡化題的做題策略 2

從前面的學習中我們已經認識到換句話說的重要性，換句話說能力強，可以大幅提高考生的成績，尤其是在做句子簡化題時。通過學習同義詞和在多種情境中擴大詞彙量，我們可以加強語言的熟練程度，儲備好表達相同意思的各種方法。此外，解答句子簡化題的另一種策略是瞭解最常用的文法結構、功能詞和邏輯體系。

新托福考試出題者有時會在句子簡化題中利用某個詞的多重含義來設考點。例如，考生可能會碰到涉及以下方面的錯誤選項：

介系詞和連接詞：因為很多介系詞和連接詞都有多重含義，所以有些考生經常會混淆。例如：for 的意思有：1）代表；2）因為；3）在（某一特定時間），如 for many years 中的 for；for 也可以作為片語動詞的一部分，如 look for 或 ask for。since 的意思有：1）因為；2）自某時以來，如 ever since the time of。as 的意思有：1）因為；2）作為；3）當……時；和 4）像……一樣。while 的意思有：1) 當……的時候和 2）然而。

情態助動詞：句子簡化題中常常會出現 may、can、might、would、could、must 的情態助動詞和其否定形式。如：

Sourcing plans for international business must take into account organizational resources, strengths and weaknesses, factor costs, transportation costs and realistic assessments of political risk, as well as the security of one's investment position in the target market.

這種題型大多考句子的文法結構知識。下面是另外一些可能會遇到的句型：

比較句：這種句型中會包含比較級或最高級形式，包括 more than 和 less than 以及表示比較的其他方式，如：The investor preferred securities to stocks.（prefer... to... 更喜歡……）

另外，有些連接詞也可用來表示比較，如：

Whereas some management candidates may have no previous supervisory experience and be naturally gifted managers, other candidates may have supervisory experience but achieve a low score on the supervisory capability test.

條件句和虛擬語氣：If the investment is sufficient... 和 Had the firm conducted an audit... 的結構常常出現在換句話說題中，考查考生是否理解句子的邏輯含義。如：

If cash outflow exceeds the inflow, a company has a negative cash flow, perhaps due to obsolete inventory or the inability to collect past-due accounts.

主動句和被動句：當用外語讀一篇文章時，我們往往難以確定「誰對誰做了什麼」。新托福出題者知道這一點，所以在句子簡化題中常以施事者為考查內容。干擾項可能利用主動語態和被動語態迷惑考生，如：

Inflation was compounded by the exchange rate of the Japanese yen and a series of storms.

其他考查行為動作的句子則可能利用既可作及物動詞也可作不及物的動詞設置干擾項。如：

The unsympathetic attitudes of the new managers, as reflected in the questionnaire survey, worried both the researchers and the executives.

因果關係句：因果關係是句子簡化題中經常考的一個點。這些句子中可能含有使役動詞，如 affect（影響），promote（促進）和 make（使），或者可能含有類似 a result of good management 的片語。如：

The competency model for human resources was not chosen because the compensation plan was too cumbersome.

以本章模擬試題中的題目為例：

• READING SAMPLE

8. Which of the sentences below best expresses the essential information in the highlighted sentence in the passage? Incorrect choices change the meaning in major ways or leave out important information.

   True, much market research tends to validate hypotheses for issues that are already known; but when structured well, it can identify new opportunities, market niches or ways to improve sales and marketing activities.

   A. It is well established that much market research is wasted because it tells us the obvious, at the expense of many new opportunities in sales and marketing.

   B. Too much market research fails to present an accurate picture of the real world and focuses instead on new ways to do sales and marketing.

   C. Although a considerable amount of market research is confirmatory in nature, there is no reason why it cannot inform sales and marketing projects as well.

   D. It must be acknowledged that a lot of market research consists of pure guesswork, yet we still need to work hard to market and sell our products.

托福總監評析

　　在這道題目中，找到正確換句話說方式的最佳策略是分析文法結構。考查的句子比較長，結構有點複雜。事實上，這個句子含有兩個由分號隔開的句子。第一個句子的句型為：主詞（market research）＋謂語動詞（tends to validate）＋受詞（hypotheses for issues...）。第二個句子的句型為：子句（when structured well）＋主句（it can identify new opportunities...）。

　　還有兩個信號詞：第一個句子之前的副詞 true 和連接兩個句子的連接詞 but。從意思上看，這個句子可以換句話說為：Marketing research is not perfect, but it can still help. 那麼，選項 A 和 B 都不正確，因為這兩個選項都說市場調查被浪費掉了，不起作用。選項 C 和 D 似乎都合理。選項 D 不正確，因為考查的句子裡沒有 we still need to work hard to... 的意思。

● 句子簡化題的答題策略：

策略 1 仔細分析考查句，弄懂句意，掌握其文法結構和內在的邏輯。

策略 2 看看考查句前面的情境。有必要閱讀一下該句前面的一行或兩行。

策略 3 考查句中的準確表述和邏輯性對於尋找換句話說的句子十分重要。不要選擇展開邏輯推理的選項。注意，這種題型與推論題是不同的！

如：The managers tended to have high salaries. 與 Managers earn a lot of money. 不同。換句話說的句子應為：In general, managers earned a lot of money.

策略 4 選項中的句子往往比考查的句子短，而且簡潔。而且在四個選項中，一般會有一個選項包含的資訊比其他三個選項都要多。

策略 5 做完了題目要檢查。

　　因為這種題型常設干擾項，這些干擾項的內容可能部分正確。一定要找到最全面的改述！

• Exercise 1 （解答請見 P. 395）

Write a correct paraphrase for each of the following sentences.

ⓐ If an insurance policy is issued to an individual, as opposed to an organization, the individual applies for the policy and pays the fees directly.

_____

_____

ⓑ Entrepreneurs who do not have responsible recordkeeping practices may be unaware of ways to minimize risk and maximize profits.

_____

_____

ⓒ Strong brands which are well established will need less advertising to maintain their value than brands of new products.

_____

_____

▶ 模擬試題（解答請見 P. 395）

Market Research in Publishing

(1) The strategic purpose of a publisher's long-term business planning is to make the ultimate dayto-day running of the business less volatile and more apt to produce the desired results. For many organizations, a key aspect of the thinking that goes into planning is research. This is less common in publishing, though there are exceptions. Yet systematic fact-finding and analysis can enrich decision-making and make results more likely. Research can be used, for instance, to clarify the choice of marketing strategy, identify areas of future potential and help fix on the actions that will bolster progress.

(2) Although market research can be expensive, the expenditure is minimal when compared to the cost of failure. A defining characteristic of the book trade is that most books are sold on consignment. ■ 1 In this model, wholesalers and bookstores, as well as most other retail outlets, are generally allowed to return unsold copies of books to the publisher for credit, resulting in significant risk for publishers.　■ 2 The successful selection of titles will fuel strong direction and growth, and a research agenda can certainly help guide acquisitions. And a formal research agenda isn't enough in itself; a publishing house should be just as concerned with having a research-oriented business approach. Too many companies do too much on the basis of hunch. Intuition should not be decried in principle, but rather used in harness with sound information. ■ 3 Research at its simplest level is a genuinely objective view of the marketplace. ■ 4 In some instances this can be achieved without great cost, even by the smallest firm.

(3) Take the case of a boutique publishing house that features business books and publications: This firm does some research before any new project, involving postal and telephone contact with selected people in the chosen market sector. Much of this activity is ongoing; for example, a regular panel meeting where opinions and guidance are offered on current issues or potential projects. Though somewhat time-consuming, the effort is undertaken by internal staff and costs are thus relatively low. The overall effect is to allow key executives to get their fingers on the pulse of the market.

(4) There is a parallel between research in book publishing and the story of Columbus and the "New World." When Columbus reached Cuba, he took for granted that it belonged to the mainland of Asia. So strong was his assumption that he prescribed punishment for anyone who alleged that it was not. Columbus went to his grave convinced that he had changed world history by establishing a passage to the East Indies. Before market research was adopted in earnest by the book publishing sector, it was apparent that management often behaved like Columbus. They were making decisions regarding sales targeting based only on assumptions. That situation is changing for increasing numbers of publishing houses. Nevertheless, some managing editors still rely on internal market information which fails to reflect how the imprints, titles and new multimedia products will be received in the real marketplace.

(5) Solid market research can serve publishers in many ways. It can identify the size, shape and nature of a market, so as to truly understand that marketplace; it can investigate the strengths and weaknesses of competitive titles; it can test out strategic ideas; and it can define when marketing expenditure, promotions and sales targeting need to be adjusted. True, much market research tends to validate hypotheses for issues that are already known; but when structured well, it can identify new opportunities, market niches or ways to improve sales and marketing activities.

(6) The variety of purpose here makes it clear that market research is not simply an initial appraisal of what new directions publishing executives should embrace; it also provides a means of checking and refining as operations proceed. Again, specific examples abound. Focus groups help editors understand the performance of imprints in the marketplace. Strategic research can help marketing professionals make prudent decisions about advertising formats, the content for press releases and the product mix, so that titles can be bundled optimally to enable distributors to maximize their merchandising efforts.

• Reading Questions

1. In Paragraph 1, what does the author say about the publishing industry and research?
   A. Most publishers have utilized databases and fact-finding to make market decisions.
   B. Publishing houses tend to research business issues on a routine, day-to-day basis.
   C. Research has traditionally played a minor role in publishers' strategic planning.
   D. With the exception of editorial fact-checking, research in publishing has been a priority.

2. The word "hunch" in Paragraph 2 is closest in meaning to _____.
   A. gut feeling
   B. rote tradition
   C. blind luck
   D. practical efficiency

3. In Paragraph 3, the author says boutique publishers can gather market research by doing which of the following?
   A. Asking for data from local postal officials.
   B. Tracking how much they spend internally on books.
   C. Commissioning a small agency to conduct surveys.
   D. Convening a group of well-versed individuals.

4. The word "it" in Paragraph 4 refers to _____.
   A. New World
   B. Cuba
   C. mainland
   D. assumption

5. In the author's analogy in Paragraph 4, Cuba is said to be like which of the following?
   A. the publishing industry
   B. an executive
   C. a sales goal
   D. product research

6. The phrase "in earnest" in Paragraph 4 is closest in meaning to _____.
   A. cautiously
   B. expertly
   C. successfully
   D. seriously

7. In the passage, all of the following uses for market research are mentioned EXCEPT _____.
   A. choosing the advertising agency that is most appropriate
   B. appreciating the strong points of other publishers' books
   C. increasing the amount of money invested in advertising
   D. calculating the full scope of the publishing marketplace

8. Which of the sentences below best expresses the essential information in the highlighted sentence in the passage? Incorrect choices change the meaning in major ways or leave out important information.
   True, much market research tends to validate hypotheses for issues that are already known; but when structured well, it can identify new opportunities, market niches or ways to improve sales and marketing activities.
   A. It is well established that much market research is wasted because it tells us the obvious, at the expense of many new opportunities in sales and marketing.
   B. Too much market research fails to present an accurate picture of the real world and focuses instead on new ways to do sales and marketing.

C. Although a considerable amount of market research is confirmatory in nature, there is no reason why it cannot inform sales and marketing projects as well.

D. It must be acknowledged that a lot of market research consists of pure guesswork, yet we still need to work hard to market and sell our products.

9. According to Paragraph 6, book retailers will benefit directly when a publisher does which of the following?
   A. Select an assortment of suitable books.
   B. Deploy persuasive advertisements.
   C. Improve upon operational efficiency.
   D. Hold focus groups with reading clubs.

10. The word "optimally" in Paragraph 6 is closest in meaning to _____.
    A. most attractively
    B. in the best way
    C. conveniently
    D. logically

11. The author implies that he thinks Columbus should have done which of the following?
    A. Traveled further until he reached Asia.
    B. Penalized the people who had misled him.
    C. Organized a team of Cuban explorers.
    D. Listened to what people were telling him.

12. Look at the four squares [■] that indicate where the following sentence could be added to the passage.
    It is easy to assume that one knows the market; yet sooner or later market visions become dated or inaccurate—or at worst, wishful thinking.
    Where would the sentence best fit?
    ■ 1
    ■ 2
    ■ 3
    ■ 4

13. Directions: An introductory sentence for a brief summary of the passage is provided below. Complete the summary by selecting the THREE answer choices that express the most important ideas in the passage. Some answer choices do not belong in the summary because they express ideas that are not presented in the passage or are minor ideas in the passage. **This question is worth 2 points.**
    This passage discusses the past and present use of market research by publishing houses.

-
-
-

Answer Choices

1. For a publishing house, it is more important to carry out a detailed analysis of core markets than it is to analyze one's competitors.

2. In the past, rigorous market research did not constitute an integral part of the planning process in publishing companies.

3. The benefits of market research include not only formal studies, but also a data-driven business strategy.

4. Research can serve various purposes, including but not limited to decisions about new projects, tracking of ongoing operations and use of marketing dollars.

5. New types of marketing research are being created, including techniques designed to see how customers will communicate informally about a product.

6. Although small publishers will not be able to afford costly market research, they can learn about markets by viewing advertisements in trade journals.

關鍵語塊

- **running of...** ……的經營
- **volatile** 不穩定的
- **apt to...** 易於；有……傾向的
- **fix on** 確定
- **bolster** 促進
- **defining characteristic of...** ……的明確特徵
- **book trade** 書業
- **sell on consignment** 寄售，托銷
- **wholesaler** 批發商
- **retail outlet** 零售店
- **return... for credit** 退貨並取回貨款
- **parallel between... and...** ……和……之間的類似之處
- **Columbus** 哥倫布
- **New World** 新大陸

- **prescribed punishment** 規定處罰
- **allege that** 宣稱
- **went to his grave convinced that** 至死還深信
- **East Indies** 東印度群島
- **title** 書名；標題
- **fuel** 刺激；推動
- **research agenda** 研究議題
- **acquisition** 獲得
- **intuition** 直覺
- **decry** 指責；反對
- **in harness with** 結合
- **sound** 合理的；可靠的
- **boutique publishing house** 專攻某個出版領域的出版社，專業出版社
- **panel meeting** 專家小組會議；小組討論會

關鍵語塊

- get their fingers on the pulse of the market 把握市場動向
- sales targeting 銷售目標
- multimedia product 多媒體產品
- test out 檢驗

- market niche 某個範圍的市場需求
- examples abound 例子舉不勝舉
- focus groups 焦點人群（代表大眾，其觀點可用於市場調查）
- product mix 產品搭配組合

市場行銷學與商學：聽力

▶重點技能：遇到故事敘述和案例研究怎麼辦

　　教授通常會在課堂上講故事以激發學生的積極性並把問題講清楚。這些故事可以是個人軼事，也可以是案例研究。案例研究最早出現在歐洲，已經在北美使用了一百多年。如今，從社會學到商學，從法學到醫學，各種學科的教授都採用案例研究的方法。因此，新托福學術講座為了追求真實度，自然會納入一些簡短的軼事和案例研究。

　　考生該如何應對學術講座中的故事或案例研究？下面來預覽一下本章模擬試題中關於管理的講座：

　　教授說：One classic example of how this integration can be accomplished is the story of Lee Lacocca... 以此來引出故事，然後花了三分之一的講座時間來講這個故事。

　　故事敘述語言可能非常個人化，如：None of you will remember—since you weren't even born yet—when the US automobile industry first started to react to government regulations...。講故事時，教授常常會從一種枯燥的學術演講轉入一種平易近人的敘事風格。但是，不要被這一點迷惑，注意做好筆記，因為後面的六道題中至少有一道題是關於故事內容或故事目的的。

• LISTENING SAMPLE

　　下面是從本章下文的講座中摘取的一些故事敘述語言：

As Lacocca was working to prepare these quarterly reports for stockholders, **it occurred to him that…**

The idea was that each manager would...

The two of them would talk about…

● 在學術講座中聽到故事或案例研究時，可採用如下策略：

策略 1　注意聽導入故事的用語，看看這個故事的主題和目的是什麼。

策略 2　故事一定會傳達一個資訊，聽的同時要積極思考是什麼資訊。

策略 3 準備好對資訊進行概括，以便解答推論題、語用功能題和組織結構題等各種題型。

策略 4 注意教授在講故事時的態度，以便做好回答立場觀點題的準備。

• Exercise 2 　（解答請見 P. 397）

The following sentences are part of a case study about a company that produces and repairs photocopiers. Pretend you are a management professor and turn these into a story, using the past tense and a storytelling style.

ⓐ In the 1980s and early 90s, the Xerox Corporation invests a large amount of money in manuals documenting how to repair photocopiers, but the repair technicians don't like to read lengthy manuals.

ⓑ The company notices that repair technicians used lunch times and breaks to chat usefully about work. Later, technicians start communicating with each other by phone on jobs, further sharing ways to trouble-shoot and repair various machines.

ⓒ The social interaction between repair people improves efficiency; experts in knowledge management realize technical knowledge is a socially distributed resource disseminated orally.

_____
_____
_____
_____
_____
_____
_____
_____
_____
_____

▶ 模擬試題 （解答請見 P. 397）

Now listen to a lecture about MANAGEMENT. 　*Track 039*

★ Keywords

quarterly performance review 季度業績評價 interim financial statements 期中財務報表

• Listening Questions 　*Track 040*

1. What aspect of management does the professor mainly discuss?
   A. Financial journals.
   B. Information technology systems.

C. Strategic leadership.

D. Employee evaluations.

2. According to the professor, how did interim financial statements influence Lacocca's management?

A. They taught him the real value of periodic communication.

B. They indicated the operations that needed restructuring.

C. They made him realize some managers were weak in finance.

D. They showed more frequent financial reporting was necessary.

3. Why does the professor mention corporate stockholders?

A. To show how good management practices benefit stock earnings.

B. To illustrate how corporate stakeholders risk being harmed.

C. To demonstrate how shareholder voting can influence policy.

D. To relate an anecdote about an enhancement in corporate planning.

4. According to the professor, what are the disadvantages of the quarterly performance review?

Choose 2 answers.

A. More problems tend to be found.

B. Reviewers lose focus on core tasks.

C. Over-detailed documentation is done.

D. Bosses lack time to be well informed.

5. Listen again to part of the lecture. Then answer the question.

 Please listen to Track 040 for this part of the question.

What does the professor say about financial knowledge?

A. Managing growth requires more focus on people than on accounting.

B. People with MBA degrees need practical experience to truly grasp finance.

C. The students should not neglect using the appropriate tracking methods.

D. The students with no knowledge of capital markets will risk failing an MBA unit.

6. Listen again to part of the lecture. Then answer the question.

 Please listen to Track 040 for this part of the question.

Why does the professor say this:

 Please listen to Track 040 for this part of the question.

A. To show that most management systems have outdated information.

B. To emphasize the importance of the material on next week's exam.

C. To ask the students to do a case study involving a competitor analysis .

D. To make the students aware of the needs in business decision-making.

Section ❸

How to Prepare for Conversational Listening

第❸部分
對話類聽力怎麼考

21 Frequently Tested Campus Life Contexts 1
常考校園生活場景 1

　　新托福考試聽力部分共有六段錄音文本，其中有兩個是不計分的實驗性對話。每段對話時間為 3 分鐘左右，對話後有五道題目。與講座內容相比，對話語言的學術性和抽象性都有所降低。

▶如何利用情境來答對話題

辦公時間對話

　　聽某人談話時，如果事先知道情境就會有助於我們理解說話者的語言和意思。這一點對用來評估非母語使用者語言能力的聽力測試尤其適用。因此，要做好新托福考試的對話類聽力題，考生應該儘量瞭解兩類典型情境下的對話：辦公時間對話和服務諮詢對話。本章只介紹辦公時間情境，服務諮詢情境將在下一章介紹。

　　辦公時間對話是指在教授辦公室中，教授與學生之間的對話。

托福總監提醒你文化背景

　　在北美和世界上許多國家，根據大學規定，教授和講師都要在正常授課時間之外另外安排時間與學生會面。有時會面時間不需要提前約定。但有時，教授會要求學生提前確定具體會面時間。老師們通常會將他們的辦公時間表貼在辦公室的門上和大學網站上。大學生在辦公室與教師會面的時間一般不長，有時只有半個小時。而研究生與教授的會面時間通常會長一些，尤其是當該教授是畢業論文或課題指導者的時候。

　　學生與老師會面有以下幾種原因：學生不理解某個概念或在作業上遇到了困難；教授要求學生來辦公室討論專案進展情況，如學期論文、實驗室作業或畢業論文；學生希望得到一份教授的推薦信或想聽聽職業建議。

• LISTENING TIPS

　　根據以上的情境，辦公時間對話可以總結出以下幾點：

　　1. 通常會包含某個需要解決的問題，例如學生錯過了一次重要的考試。

　　2. 通常會包含關於某個問題的原因和解決方法的討論，例如，學生得了一場大病，希望教授能允許補考。

　　3. 有時候教授會很樂意提供幫助；但有時候，教授會比較苛刻。所以對話會有「愉快的結局」和「不愉快的結局」。

　　4. 辦公時間情境通常會涉及某個情況的重要細節，如學生的主修科系或個人處境方面的具體問題。例如，學生要參加祖父的生日聚會而不能參加考試。

　　本部分的每章中將會給出辦公時間對話的示例。

▶ 主要目的題的答題策略

　　聽力對話題通常以主要目的題（主旨目的題）開始，如：Why does the student go see the professor? 這與學術講座中的第一道題目大不相同，學術講座中的第一道題目通常以主旨大意題開始，如：What is the lecture mainly about?

　　主要目的題通常是由 why 引導的問句（如：Why does the man go see the professor?），並用不定式片語作選項，如：To borrow a book.

　　下面是主要目的題選項常用的典型不定式片語。

To ask her whether...	To inform her about...
To inquire about...	To complain about...
To report on...	To apply for...
To get help on...	To persuade her that...
To explain that...	To check whether...

　　考生應該記住上面方框中的語塊，以便能將注意力更好地集中到每段對話中發生的具體活動上。

▶ 主要目的題的解題策略：

　　策略 1 認真聽每段對話開始之前的引導句，設想對話發生時的情景。

　　出題者給出引導句是為了給考生設定一個框架，就像一塊跳板！引導句可讓考生立刻投入到對話情境，將注意力集中到對話內容上。例如，在本章下文的辦公時間對話題目中，引導句為：

Listen to part of a conversation between a graduate student and a professor.

　　此處最重要的線索是 graduate student，因為這個資訊讓我們知道該對話情境很可能與研究所有關，而不是與大學有關。

　　策略 2 仔細看電腦螢幕上出現的圖片、繪圖或黑板板書。

　　雖然並不能從中得到答案，但是肯定會得到有關對話情境的更多線索。

　　策略 3 對上下文的大意理解得越透澈，就越容易把握說話者的語言，並能推斷出生字和概念的意思。

• Exercise 1　（解答請見 P. 400）

We can often guess the major purpose of a conversation from a key sentence spoken early on. Match each of the key sentences to an answer choice.

Key Sentence		Main Purpose: Why does the student go see the professor?	
1.	[Student] Yes, well—I was hoping to sign up for it, but my advisor said I needed your consent.	a.	To discuss why she got a bad grade
2.	[Student] Professor Jones, I don't know how to say this, but my experiment is kind of—well, I'm not sure what to do. It's probably ruined.	b.	To get permission to take a seminar class
3.	[Professor] Carol, as I mentioned on the phone, I wanted to chat because I'm concerned about your absence from classes.	c.	To communicate an unexpected situation
4.	[Professor] Tina, in your email you said you were having trouble understanding the lab assignment.	d.	To discuss her attendance record
5.	[Student] Um, do you have some time to go over my history midterm with me?	e.	To ask for help on a difficult assignment.

▶模擬試題

CONVERSATION 1 辦公時間對話：寫推薦信（錄音文本與解答請見 P. 400）

Listen to part of a conversation between a graduate student and a professor.

 Track 041

Now get ready to answer the questions. You may use your notes. *Track 042*

1. Why does the man talk with the professor?
   A. To ask her for a letter of support.
   B. To inquire about a position in her lab.
   C. To report on the status of his thesis.
   D. To find out about jobs in neuroscience.

2. Why is the man ready for a change?
   A. He resents the fact he is being exploited.
   B. He feels the scope of his research is too narrow.
   C. He's interested in doing studies on children.
   D. His research funding is not going to be renewed.

3. Why does the man think the professor will be able to help him?
   A. She is an expert in neuroscience.

B. She has more tenure than Dr. Allen.

C. She sits on his thesis committee.

D. She has been able to get grant money.

4. What is the professor's attitude toward Dr. Allen?

    A. She disapproves of his hiring policies.

    B. She acknowledges that his lab is a bit old-fashioned.

    C. She agrees that he thinks highly of himself.

    D. She thinks he will probably be fair to the student.

5. Listen again to part of the conversation. Then answer the question.

 Please listen to Track 042 for this part of the question.

What does the man imply when he says this:

 Please listen to Track 042 for this part of the question.

    A. He was hoping she would ask.

    B. He wants her to talk about his strengths.

    C. He isn't qualified for that position.

    D. He appreciates her kind invitation.

CONVERSATION 2 服務諮詢對話：學生宿舍維修問題（錄音文本與解答請見 P. 402）

Listen to part of a conversation at the student housing office.

 Track 043

Now answer the questions. You may use your notes.　　　　*Track 044*

1. Why does the woman go to the housing office?

    A. To inform the university that she has changed rooms.

    B. To complain about the resident assistant in her dorm.

    C. To apply for new housing for the second semester.

    D. To check on the status of a maintenance request.

2. Listen again to part of the conversation. Then answer the question.

 Please listen to Track 044 for this part of the question.

What does the woman mean when she says this:

 Please listen to Track 044 for this part of the question.

    A. She lacks experience in working on building repairs.

    B. She is reluctant to spend time on minor details.

C. She can't be expected to do the impossible.

D. She assumes things will be resolved before long.

3. According to the woman, what is causing the delay?

A. The resident assistant.

B. The maintenance crew.

C. The roof of the building.

D. The electrical wiring.

4. Why does the woman say this:

 Please listen to Track 044 for this part of the question.

A. To persuade the housing employee to let her move.

B. To inform the university her roommate is leaving.

C. To report on her roommate's medical condition.

D. To serve notice that she will be taking legal action.

5. What does the housing employee say he will do right away?

Choose 2 answers.

A. Contact the roommate's father.

B. Conduct an inspection of the damage.

C. Call the resident assistant.

D. Have the phone connection fixed.

• Exercise 2　（解答請見 P. 404）

Write a correct paraphrase for each of the following idiomatic sentences, taken from Conversation 2.

ⓐ What's your resident assistant doing to get you through this?

_____

ⓑ Well, the phone problem should be easier to tackle.

_____

ⓒ I'll explore with her the possibility of finding some temporary living space for the most critical cases.

_____

22 Frequently Tested Campus Life Contexts 2
常考校園生活場景 2

▶如何利用情境來答對話題

服務諮詢對話

　　辦公時間對話發生在校園內教授的辦公室裡，那麼服務諮詢對話的場景是什麼樣的呢？服務諮詢對話在校園的任何角落都有可能發生！這些對話都圍繞實際問題展開，可能發生在圖書館、學生中心、住宿辦公室、大學或院系的行政部門、餐廳、入學和註冊處、財務處、校園書店、校園停車場等地方。無論對話發生在哪裡，總有某個問題要解決。

　　服務諮詢對話的形式及其後面的考題與辦公時間對話部分都十分類似。通常有五個問題，以主要目的題開始，大多數情況下都會包括一道語用功能題。

• LISTENING TIPS

　　關於服務諮詢對話，要瞭解如下幾點：

　　1. 通常圍繞某個待解決的問題展開，例如，學生丟了錢包、沒有學生證而必須更換證件。

　　2. 對話雙方通常會反覆討論某個問題的原因及其解決辦法，例如，學生不能與其室友和睦相處，要求住宿管理處人員或宿舍管理員安排新的房間。

　　3. 有時候服務提供者肯通融，但更多的時候，會要學生服從命令。服務提供者會詢問很多問題，涉及與解決問題相關的諸多細節和其他措施。

　　4. 儘管服務諮詢對話有時含有一些學術詞語（例如：在學生與大學圖書管理員的對話中），但更多的時候，服務諮詢對話只含各種場合下日常討論用到的實用詞彙。

　　5. 辦公時間和服務諮詢對話都含有自然語言和習慣用語。

　　本部分的各章將提供服務諮詢對話的示例。此外，還會介紹四種常見的服務諮詢情境：1）註冊處和財務處；2）校園保全中心；3）學生事務處；和 4）學生住宿管理處。

▶慣用語對做語用功能題的重要性

　　前面已經介紹過，語用功能題考的是講話者使用某些用詞的目的。對話中會大量用到慣用語。考生需要掌握這些慣用語以及溝通中的間接表達方式或省略的用法，即考生需要掌握說話者在什麼時候省略某些慣用語。

下面是本章下文出現的一道語用功能題：

• LISTENING SAMPLE

2. Listen again to part of the conversation. Then answer the question.

S: Do you remember how, the evening before the midterm exam, there was a big ice storm? Well, I slipped on the steps to the library and broke my wrist.

P: Ouch. That can't have been pleasant.

Why does the professor say this:

P: Ouch.

A. He's embarrassed by that disclosure.

B. He thinks she may be mistaken.

C. He's teasing her about the event.

D. He empathizes with her situation.

托福總監評析

考生可能已經很熟悉感歎詞 Ouch。當人們突然感到疼痛時，有時就會說 Ouch（哎喲）。另外，當我們被告知犯了錯誤或被批評時，也可能會說 Ouch。在此例中，雖然是教授說的 Ouch，但卻是學生受了傷，因此題目問教授為什麼要說 Ouch。

找到正確答案的最簡單方法是利用情境，尤其要仔細聽上下文。可以從 That can't have been pleasant 這句話推斷出教授在談論發生在別人（學生）身上的事情。

在其他情境中，選項 A 可能正確，但在這裡不正確，因為教授聽到學生受傷後並不是感到尷尬。但是，根據情境和後面緊接的句子 That can't have been pleasant，可知教授在表示他能想像她的痛。換而言之，他對這位學生表示同情。因此選項 D 正確。

▶ 對話中的語用功能題的最佳解題策略：

策略 1 考試前多記些慣用語用法。

策略 2 在聽對話時，儘量理解說話者的處境，思考他們可能會有的想法和感受。

策略 3 密切關注重複問題的所有音檔部分，並做好筆記。

策略 4 如果不確定所考的慣用語的意思，可利用情境和上下文猜測答案。

• **Exercise 1**　（解答請見 P. 405）

Write a correct paraphrase for each of the following idiomatic sentences taken from Conversation 1.

ⓐ Yeah, just borderline passing.

_____

ⓑ But I'm rather curious as to why you didn't go to your Section TA with this problem earlier.

_____

ⓒ But now I'm afraid I'm going to mess up on the final exam.

_____

• **Exercise 2**　（解答請見 P. 405）

Each of the following is a short dialog between a university employment office employee and a student. Write a sentence in the blank that demonstrates meaningful, natural communication.

1.
Employee: First things first: What year are you in?
Student: _____

2.
Student: In the future, I promise to live up to the expectations of my supervisor. I don't want to make the university look bad.
Employee: _____

3.
Student: _____
Employee: Put it this way, I really think you should take the part-time position posted by the admissions office.

▶ 模擬試題

CONVERSATION 1 辦公時間對話：考試問題（錄音文本與解答請見 P. 405）

Listen to part of a conversation between a student and a professor.

 Track 045

Now get ready to answer the questions. You may use your notes. *Track 046*

1. Why does the woman go see the professor?
   A. To ask if she may sit for a make-up test.
   B. To obtain permission to drop out of the class.

C. To figure out how to get a passing grade.

D. To arrange for individual tutoring sessions.

2. Listen again to part of the conversation. Then answer the question.

 Please listen to Track 046 for this part of the question.

Why does the professor say this:

 Please listen to Track 046 for this part of the question.

A. He's embarrassed by that disclosure.

B. He thinks she may be mistaken.

C. He's teasing her about the event.

D. He empathizes with her situation.

3. Why did the woman not communicate the situation to the professor sooner?

A. She didn't think her grade would change much.

B. She was not thinking clearly after her mishap.

C. She thought her score was higher than it really was.

D. She assumed the teaching assistant had told him.

4. What is the professor's attitude toward the woman's request?

A. He is impressed by her determination.

B. He is less than enthusiastic about it.

C. He's disappointed, but mostly blames the TA.

D. He thinks that she's making up excuses.

5. What advice does the professor give to the woman? For each sentence, put a ✓ mark in the YES or NO column.

	YES	NO
Talk with her TA		
Solve problems independently		
Study with her roommate		
Arrange for a make-up test		

CONVERSATION 2 服務諮詢對話：學生兼職問題（錄音文本與解答請見 P. 407）

Listen to part of a conversation at the student employment center.

 Track 047

Now answer the questions. You may use your notes.　 *Track 048*

1. Why does the man go to the student employment center?
   A. To lodge a complaint about his employer.
   B. To communicate that he was dismissed.
   C. To inquire about a higher-paying job.
   D. To receive an evaluation of his performance.

2. Why does the center employee feel embarrassed?
   A. The student's requests are not reasonable.
   B. The student did not follow proper procedure.
   C. She forgot to tell the manager about the student's new job.
   D. She thought the bank would be more flexible.

3. Listen again to part of the conversation. Then answer the question.

    Please listen to Track 048 for this part of the question.

   What does the employee mean when she says this:

   Please listen to Track 048 for this part of the question.

   A. The student should not question her authority.
   B. It's too late because she's already heard the news.
   C. These days she isn't be surprised by anything.
   D. She will certainly keep the information confidential.

4. What job does the student say he likes the best?
   A. Bank teller.
   B. Admissions clerk.
   C. Legal assistant.
   D. Parking attendant.

5. What does the employee imply when she says this:

    Please listen to Track 048 for this part of the question.

   A. The student shouldn't expect the position.
   B. It's not a very convenient location to work.
   C. Many people have objected to the job duties.
   D. The student probably meets the minimum criteria.

Frequently Tested Campus Life Contexts 3
常考校園生活場景 3

▶對話中涉及學術內容的應對策略

新托福考試中的絕大部分對話都不會像講座一樣探討學術問題，不過，確實會有一些對話含有學術討論。對於這些對話，考生應怎樣應對？做筆記，因為考題可能會涉及學術討論的要點。

▶片語動詞對立場觀點題的重要性

前面我們已經學習過，「立場觀點題」或「態度題」考查考生是否明白說話者的立場、傾向或思想。因為態度的傳達方式既可以直接也可以間接，所以在對話中傾聽雙方話語的細微之處至關重要。

以本章下文 Conversation 1 為背景出一道立場觀點題：

• LISTENING SAMPLE

How does the professor feel about the student's participation in her Astronomy class?
A. She is proud that he chose to take this particular course.
B. She would have preferred he take a general science course.
C. She is satisfied with the progress he has made so far.
D. She wishes he were more conscientious about his work.

托福總監評析

該題問教授的「感覺」怎麼樣。四個選項都含有一個描述教授態度的片語。如果想知道教授的感覺，應該怎樣聽對話才最好呢？有一些片語和語塊可以提供一些線索。如，在對話中，會聽到教授說：I really wonder what you want out of this class, whether you want to succeed. 和 You may not be putting in enough hours of study. 這不是書面英語，而是典型的口頭表達，表達非常自然也非常直接。如果我們邊聽錄音邊思考，並儘量認同教授的角度，那麼就能選擇對的答案。例如，I really wonder... 暗示教授感到失望。You may not be putting in enough hours of study 其實是在委婉地說：You aren't studying enough! 因此，選項 D 為正確答案。

　　考生如果不熟悉某些片語動詞或語塊，就難以準確理解說話者在說什麼。或者，考生可能明白詞語的部分意思，因為他們學過這些詞語在字典上的意思，但是他們無法確定說話者的態度，因為他們沒有練習過在情境中記憶詞彙。為了幫助考生解決這個問題，下面列出了口語中常見的片語動詞，這些語塊都可以為理解說話者的態度或觀點提供線索。

表示情感的片語動詞表

片語動詞	釋義	例句
blow up over something	為某事發怒	John blew up over the mess in the kitchen.
blow over	被忘掉	There was a short argument at the faculty meeting, but it blew over quickly.
bounce back	恢復	For a while Tim was feeling kind of blue about his grades, but he's bounced back.
cheer up someone	使某人振作起來	My roommate had a fight with her boyfriend; let's go cheer her up.
clam up	閉口不言	When Professor Stone asks me a question, I get nervous and clam up.
fall through	（計畫）未能實現	Too bad; my plans for travel in Italy this summer fell through!
feel down in the dumps	感到沮喪，情緒低落	Larry didn't get financial aid this semester and he's feeling down in the dumps.
figure something out	搞懂某事	Embarrassingly, I couldn't figure out the calculus problems, so I had to ask my TA for help.
goof off	遊手好閒；不盡職	You've been goofing off all weekend; when are you going to write that paper?
iron out	處理，解決	I wish I were done with my research, but there are a few details I need to iron out.
knock oneself out	讀書極為勤奮	Melanie is exhausted; she really knocked herself out studying for her History exam.
let someone down	使某人失望	Our study team met last night, but Sarah didn't show up. She really let us down.
look up to someone	崇拜某人	That little boy who lives next door really looks up to his father.

lose sleep over something	為某事擔憂	Don't lose any sleep over missing this party; you can come to the next one!
luck out	走運	I lucked out on the Spanish quiz—I got an 84, even though I didn't study.
put something off	拖延某事	Ken is putting off taking his geophysics course until his senior year.
slip up	搞錯、露餡	I had my teacher change my grade; he slipped up when he added the subtotals.
take someone / something for granted	認為某人（某事）理所當然	Fran takes it for granted that she'll be accepted into an Ivy League school.
tell someone off	責備某人	Jerry's roommate told him off because he was playing rap music too loudly.

要理解口語，多掌握片語動詞是十分必要的。不過要注意，新托福聽力考試中不會出現大量純俚語；例如，不太可能聽到學生談論 scarfing down a pizza（狼吞虎嚥地吃披薩）。另一方面，對話中確實會出現很多常用的慣用語用法，如上表中的片語動詞。這樣的語塊，掌握得越多，聽力部分的表現就會越好。

▶俚語和自然語言

新托福考試中的講座和對話貼近真實、自然的語言。在自然語言中，話語自發產生，不一定總是遵守文法次序。口語中的用詞通常是非正式的。在本章的兩段對話中，可以聽到一些口語慣用語以及俚語，如 for goodness sake（看在上帝的份上），so majorly fast（非常快），go right over my head（無法理解），monster paper（長篇學期論文）。

比選詞更為重要的還有說話風格。新托福考試聽力錄音中的人物都會採用相對自然的發音和說話風格，如使用簡化詞形（reduced forms）和輕讀功能詞。在英語口語中，簡化詞形包括縮略形式（如 would've）、母音省略（如 Whatsa time? = What's the time?）、輕讀功能詞（如 I hafta go now = I have to go now）。

考生一定都聽過電視上和英語歌曲及電影中自然語言的聲調和節奏，這類語言對於學習者來說並不陌生。儘管如此，在考試時要想領會快速傳入耳朵的一連串聲音的意思卻頗具挑戰性。如何攻克這個難關？如果你練習過簡化的說法，就可以大大提高聽對話的能力。下面是最常使用的一些簡化說法：

常用簡化詞形表

簡化的說法	完整的說法	例句
coulda	could have	I coulda sworn I left my keys on the table.
dunno	don't know	Is it gonna rain? I dunno.

em	them	Laura bought two theater tickets and gav'em to me.
gimme	give me	Gimme a minute and I'll make you some iced tea.
gonna	going to	He's not gonna be home till 5:00.
gotcha	got you	I'll bet Grandma gotcha a new sweater for your birthday.
gotta run	got to run (have to run)	I'd like to talk more, but I gotta run.
hafta go	have to go	Do you hafta go now? We could play cards.
hangin' out	hanging out	Jerry doesn't like hangin' out with Max.
insteada	instead of	I want rice insteada noodles tonight.
kinda	kind of	That action movie was kinda bad.
lemme	let me	Hey, lemme help you! You've got, what, three bags of groceries?
lotta	lot of	If you take Advanced Chem, you're gonna get a lotta homework.
mighta	might have	I mighta left my purse in the car.
musta	must have	Professor Weeks musta got sick or something; we had a substitute teacher.
'n	and	All she ever wants to eat is rice'n beans.
oughta	ought to	You oughta wear a helmet when you ride your bike to work.
shoulda	should have	Mary shoulda been home an hour ago; I wonder where she is.
sorta	sort of	Those jeans are sorta small on you; let's go shopping tomorrow.
th'new'n	the new one	I liked Sam's old car OK, but I vastly prefer th'new'n.
walkin' aroun'	walking around	I'm so tired; I've been walkin' aroun' town all day.
wanna	want to, want a	He doesn't wanna invest in the stock market, says it's too risky.
whaddaya / whatcha doin'?	What are you doing?	Whaddaya doin'? I've already put salt in the stew.
woulda	would have	My dad said he woulda helped me move my stuff if he had more time.

在正式的說話場合，都不應使用俚語和簡化的說法。同樣地，除了私人之間的交流，如簡訊或電子郵件外，這些俚語和簡化的說法也不能用於書面寫作中。

• Exercise 1 　（解答請見 P. 410）

The following idiomatic sentences contain an emotive phrasal verb. Write a correct paraphrase for each bolded expression.

ⓐ My Botany professor tells the dumbest jokes but we end up laughing anyway. **He cracks me up.**

_____

_____

ⓑ **You look really burned out.** When was the last time you took a vacation?

_____

_____

ⓒ I didn't know you weren't going to Vancouver this summer—what, **did the bank internship not pan out?**

_____

_____

• Exercise 2 　（解答請見 P. 410）

Each of the following is a short dialog between a library employee and a student. Write a sentence in the blank that demonstrates meaningful, natural communication.

ⓐ
Student:　I can't seem to find what I'm looking for. Do you know where the oversized books are housed?

Employee: _____

ⓑ
Employee: _____

Student:　This is perfect, thanks! Now I just need to find the digitized collection of slides called Masters of Modern Architecture.

ⓒ
Student: _____

Employee: Oops, you were looking on the wrong floor. All the Arabic-language materials are on Floor B.

▶ 模擬試題

CONVERSATION 1 辦公時間對話：主修與興趣問題（錄音文本與解答請見 P. 410）

Listen to part of a conversation between a student and a professor.

 Track 049

Now get ready to answer the questions. You may use your notes.   *Track 050*

1. Why does the man go see the professor?
   A. The man was seeking help on a difficult concept.
   B. The man hoped to change his quiz score.
   C. The professor told him to come see her.
   D. The professor wanted to assign extra-credit work.

2. What was the topic of the man's last quiz?
   A. Why the Earth orbits the Sun.
   B. Why summer months are hot.
   C. How to calculate the summer solstice.
   D. When the Sun changes its apparent position.

3. Why does the professor talk about philosophy?
   A. To persuade the man that he can succeed in this course.
   B. To illustrate the difference between two astronomy classes.
   C. To punish the man so he will start coming to class.
   D. To tell the story of how modern astronomy evolved.

4. Listen again to part of the conversation. Then answer the question.

 Please listen to Track 050 for this part of the question.

   Why does the man say this:

 Please listen to Track 050 for this part of the question.

   A. He thinks he will be able to learn that equation.
   B. He's excited about taking on a new assignment.
   C. He's certain he can do part of the work, but maybe not all.
   D. He realizes he will need to redouble his efforts.

5. Why does the professor ask the man to draw star charts?
   A. To better prepare for the upcoming quiz.
   B. To solve equations related to star coordinates.
   C. To give him a chance to gain bonus points.
   D. To help him consolidate new information.

CONVERSATION 2 服務諮詢對話：圖書館借書（錄音文本與解答請見 P. 412）

Listen to part of a conversation in a university library.

 Track 051

★ **Keyword**

Trebonianus Gallus 加盧斯（羅馬帝國皇帝）

Now answer the questions. You may use your notes. *Track 052*

1. Why does the woman come to talk with the library employee?
   A. To find out where the art collections are.
   B. To identify sources for a research paper.
   C. To learn how to check out special materials.
   D. To inquire about foreign-language resources.

2. What division of the university library is the woman most familiar with?
   A. The Main Library.
   B. The Fine Arts Library.
   C. The Ancient History Collection.
   D. The Photography Collection.

3. Listen again to part of the conversation. Then answer the question.

    Please listen to Track 052 for this part of the question.

   Why does the library employee say this:

   Please listen to Track 052 for this part of the question.

   A. He wants the student to pick up the pace.
   B. He's heard of that classical art movement.
   C. He's ready to see the resources on the upper floors.
   D. He presumes the sculpture styles changed over time.

4. Which of the following keywords did the library employee use in his search?
   Choose 2 answers.
   A. Third century.
   B. Emperor portraits.
   C. Roman sculpture.
   D. Oversized art books.

5. What does the woman mean when she says this:

    Please listen to Track 052 for this part of the question.

   A. She still has some misgivings about the quality of these sources.
   B. She's sure to get some sources, but maybe not the same ones.
   C. She's afraid the materials won't be where they are supposed to be.
   D. She is optimistic about the fruits of the employee's search.

**Frequently Tested Campus Life Contexts 4
常考校園生活場景 4**

▶主修課和選修課

　　新托福考試中的辦公時間對話是以師生交流為主，其中很多話題會涉及學生向教授諮詢與主修相關的問題和選課問題。如果考生想要把握好這類聽力內容，就必須非常熟悉相關的流程和英語術語。

托福總監提醒你文化背景

　　在北美，學院和大學對學位的要求會有非常大的不同。有的院系（例如「文理學院」、「工程學院」等等），學生自主選擇課程時可能受限制，而有的院系則非常靈活。與許多國家的大學課程相比，北美的學生能上很多選修課。

　　學生選主修科系時，也有各種要求。學生在申請大學、入校，甚至在校第二學期末時，都可以選科系，具體時間由各個院校決定。如今，很多大學院校都鼓勵低年級學生讀完大一後就確定主修科系。在絕大多數情況下，主修科系由院系管理，但也有跨學科的和跨院系的主修方式。有些大學允許學生選擇「主修課程」、「分軌制課程」或「證書課程」，這些都是具體的專業課程名稱。

　　學生也可以選擇一個輔修科系。主修科系所要求的課程數量往往是輔修科系課程數量的兩倍。有些學生會選「雙主修」。在這樣的情況下，學生可能需要花五年時間（而非正常的四年）或在暑期上課以達到兩個主修科系的要求。

　　許多大學允許平均分數比較高的大學二年級學生創設「個人化主修」，並自己設置課程。這些「個人化主修」必須經學科指導老師批准，且往往需要深入的研究和深難的畢業論文。在接下來的對話中，我們將聽到：主修科系和輔修科系的課程必須由所屬院系的指導老師批准。例如，一位準備主修歷史的學生要與歷史系聯繫，然後系裡安排一位指導老師幫助其制定課程。這些指導老師通常會在預先註冊（提前一個學期選修某些課程）之前會見新生，討論並確定課程。

　　記住，在英語中，科系名稱的首字母通常須大寫，如：I'm majoring in International Studies.

▶能找到核心問題就會做主要目的題

　　幫助考生解答主要目的題的一種策略是分析對話中的核心問題。主要目的題的正確答案通常是對問題的總結或綜述，所以，如果我們可以搞清楚問題在哪裡，就會做主要目的題。

• LISTENING TIPS

如何能快速確定對話中的核心問題？聽的過程中，我們應該自問如下幾個問題：

1. 在兩人中，誰遇到了比較大的問題？教授，還是大學職員？或學生？
2. 哪個人非常需要一樣東西？（通常是學生，但不一定）
3. 學生想要達成什麼目的呢？
4. 教授或學校職員想要達成什麼目的呢？
5. 對話中出現了什麼樣的新資訊使情況發生了轉變？
6. 每位説話者的感覺如何？（急躁、和藹、沮喪、憤怒？）
7. 情況得到解決了嗎？如果解決了，是如何解決的？

當然，考試中沒有時間做好所有這些問題的筆記。但我們可以訓練自己聽這些要點，以便在問題出現的時候做好準備。

• LISTENING SAMPLE

下面來看看本章 Conversation 2 的一道主要目的題，試試運用這種方法。

1. Why does the woman go to the technology center?
   A. She needs updated anti-virus software installed.
   B. She wants to work in their wireless "hotspot" area.
   C. Her computer suddenly stopped functioning.
   D. Someone mistakenly dropped her computer.

托福總監評析

瀏覽選項可知每個選項都與一種電腦問題相關。再看看學生的第一句話：
I've brought my laptop for a diagnosis. I can't get it to work.

一聽到這句話，就可以推斷這位女性的電腦故障了，並且可以推測出該主要目的題會與這位女性及她遇到的問題有關，於是就做好準備聽有關電腦故障的資訊。對於受損電腦的具體描述就是本題的正確答案。

▶ **主要目的題的做題策略：**

策略 1 主要目的題的答案可能是在開頭的幾句話中，也可能是在對話逐漸展開的過程中。要訓練自己盡可能地獲取細節資訊。

策略 2 儘管主要目的題不像立場觀點題那樣直接詢問説話者的態度和感覺，但是如果你明白説話者的心理活動，那麼答對主要目的題的機率就高。

策略 3 記住，並非每個問題都能得到滿意的解決。有些對話中的事情會有「愉快的結局」，但有些卻不一定。在很多時候，對話中根本就沒有達成解決方案。

• Exercise 1　（解答請見 P. 415）

We have seen how a succinct description of a problem is often the answer to a main purpose question. Match each of the problem statements to an answer choice.

	Problem Statement		Main Purpose: Why does the student go to see the university employee?
1.	[Student] The thing is—I don't know where the soccer field is, and I'm supposed to be covering the match to write a feature article for the university newspaper.	a.	To retrieve a lost item
2.	[Student] I'm having trouble getting my printer to connect with my laptop.	b.	To ask for a new dorm room
3.	[Employee] Yes, we have a black backpack here. Could you confirm it is yours by telling us what personal items are in it?	c.	To dispute a laboratory fee
4.	[Employee] Our policy is clear. When you dropped the class, you were supposed to return your lab equipment to the office. That's why we charged you.	d.	To troubleshoot a computer problem
5.	[Student] It's not that my roommate isn't a nice person; but she's always on the phone or listening to loud music. If I stay there, I can't study.	e.	To enquire about directions

• Exercise 2　（解答請見 P. 415）

Below is a short dialog from an advising session between a professor and a student. Choosing from the list of CHUNKS about academic majors, fill in the blanks. There are two extra choices.

declared a major track	requirement prerequisites for	electives waiver	register for place out of	enroll

Student: I tried to a. _____ Organic Chemistry yesterday and was refused. I'm really confused.

Professor: You're a sophomore, right? Have you already b. _____?

Student: Yes, I'm on a pre-med c. _____; I want to be a pediatrician some day.

Professor: And you've taken Chemistry 101 and 102 and the lab courses? They're d. _____ Organic Chemistry.

Student: No. But I had Chemistry in high school. Can't you give me an instructor e. _____?

Professor: Sorry, I can't do that. I suggest you rush down to the Chemistry Department and try to f. _____ those basic courses. If you do well enough, your Chemistry g. _____ will be met and you can sign up for Organic Chemistry tomorrow.

▶模擬試題

CONVERSATION 1 辦公時間對話：學生轉系（錄音文本與解答請見 P. 415）

Listen to part of a conversation between a student and a professor.

🎧 *Track 053*

★ Keyword

> Balkan States 巴爾幹半島諸國

Now get ready to answer the questions. You may use your notes. 🎧 *Track 054*

1. Why does the man go to see the professor?
    A. He is unhappy with the departmental requirements.
    B. He wants to apply for the summer overseas program.
    C. The professor invited him to talk about the honors program.
    D. The professor has received a complaint about his work.

2. What academic topic is the man particularly interested in?
    A. Global economic pressures.
    B. People traveling across borders.
    C. Linguistic diversity in Eastern Europe.
    D. Foundations of European civilization.

3. Listen again to part of the conversation. Then answer the question.

 Please listen to Track 054 for this part of the question.

   What does the man mean when he says this:

 Please listen to Track 054 for this part of the question.

    A. He isn't clear about the details.
    B. He will research those cities.
    C. He's in reluctant agreement.
    D. He's unable to commit right now.

4. What suggestions does the professor ultimately give the man? For each sentence, put a ✓ mark in the YES or NO column.

	YES	NO
Select special courses to create his own major		
Travel to Vienna this summer to learn German		
Join the Near Eastern Studies Department		
Enroll in the university's double major program		

5. What can we infer about the man when he says this:

 Please listen to Track 054 for this part of the question.

    A. He wants to think about the issue more.

B. He is unwilling to stay abroad for long.

C. He does not plan to study ancient cultures.

D. He will change academic departments.

CONVERSATION 2 服務諮詢對話：電腦維修（錄音文本與解答請見 P. 417）

Listen to part of a conversation at the university's technology center.

 Track 055

Now answer the questions. You may use your notes.   *Track 056*

1. Why does the woman go to the technology center?

    A. She needs updated anti-virus software installed.

    B. She wants to work in their wireless "hotspot" area.

    C. Her computer suddenly stopped functioning.

    D. Someone mistakenly dropped her computer.

2. Why does the employee ask where the laptop came from?

    A. He thinks it may have second-hand parts in it.

    B. He fears the software is incompatible with the network.

    C. He would like to understand the warranty conditions.

    D. He wonders if computer security had been breached.

3. What does the employee mean when he says this:

Please listen to Track 056 for this part of the question.

    A. The woman should really not take these risks.

    B. Unfortunately some of her data is already lost.

    C. He meets a lot of unpleasant people in his job.

    D. The woman should start using a protective case.

4. What does the employee think the problem might be?

    A. A computer virus.

    B. A faulty device driver.

    C. Damaged system memory.

    D. Loose circuitry.

5. Listen again to part of the conversation. Then answer the question.

 Please listen to Track 056 for this part of the question.

What does the woman mean when she says this:

 Please listen to Track 056 for this part of the question.

    A. She can finally relax after a big scare.

    B. She will text her friends the news.

    C. She's very grateful to him for his help.

    D. She's hoping that things will turn out well.

25 Frequently Tested Campus Life Contexts 5
常考校園生活場景 5

▶校園生活情境：教務處和財務處

很多服務諮詢對話是以教務處和財務處為場景的交流。儘管全球大學裡的機構都有行政辦事處，但在北美，教務處和財務部門的人員會採用一些不同的工作流程，其對話中涉及的英語術語就會不盡相同，這些都是新托福考生必須瞭解的。

托福總監提醒你文化背景

在北美，尤其是在美國，會有一個所謂的「registrar」，是指負責學生入學和在校學習的行政管理者，有點像是我們所說的教務處。「registrar」的具體功能和任務包括學生註冊、課程安排、保管班級名冊以及依照規定評選學業優良的學生。另外，還要負責保管學生的分數和保護學生的隱私，並按要求提供成績單。在某些情況下，也負責醫療保險和稅務等事務。儘管「registrar」和招生辦合作密切，但兩者是相互獨立的。在某些大學裡，「registrar」也被稱為「檔案處」。

大學財務部門的主管（bursar）是專業的財務管理者，類似於公司的財務主管或首席財務官。財務處負責日常的財務管理工作，如收取學費、發放工資和其他款項，如助學金。財務預算、清算帳目和電子付款等都是財務處工作的內容。學生通常只有在交學費和其他費用、要求退款、領取獎學金和助學貸款，或陷入經濟問題的時候才會與財務人員打交道。

因為許多新托福聽力材料的主題都是學生設法解決學習和生活中遇到的問題，所以我們要自問：學生在教務處和財務處經常會碰到什麼樣的問題？任何繁忙的行政機構都會出現工作上的失誤、疏漏或工作流程上的一些問題，大學也不例外。例如，教務處的電腦系統上記錄出錯；沒有正確填寫表格的學生不能及時收到申請工作用的成績單。與此類似，當出現錢款問題時，學生也需要與財務處人員進行交流。由於學生只有在財務帳戶結清之後才能註冊上課，所以那些沒能結清費用而試圖註冊的學生就得找財務人員澄清和解決問題。

▶捕捉到對話場景就不怕細節資訊題

我們已經學習過解答講座後的細節資訊題的策略，主要是：1）熟悉學術情境；2）認真做好結構性筆記，記錄主要觀點及其例證。

　　解答對話部分的細節資訊題時，也需要注意對話場景。事實上，由於對話的交流速度很快，因此情境變得更為重要。我們要訓練自己用稍微不同的方式來傾聽事實。

　　在聽對話時，你應該假裝自己是一名報紙記者，正在傾聽兩個人談話並做記錄，以便寫報導用。為什麼呢？因為如果你是一名記者，你就可以不用太擔心那些深入的理論性觀點，而是更關注對話情景中的人物、事件、地點、時間和原因。

　　理解並記住可以回答五個「W」疑問詞（who、what、where、when 和 why）的關鍵事實，將會決定你的新托福聽力考試成績。

▶ 對話部分細節資訊題的做題策略：

　　策略 1 利用對話中的一切線索，如引導句或開始幾句中出現的詞彙，儘快把握住對話的語境和場景。

　　策略 2 對話往往圍繞學生遇到的某個問題。細節資訊題會考查該問題的實質，因此要盡可能掌握與該問題有關的資訊。

　　策略 3 做好對話筆記。

使用簡潔明瞭的片語可幫你解決對話中最常問到的那些問題。

　　策略 4 聽對話時，要像記者一樣思考，尋找五個「W」疑問詞，並準備好回答相關問題。

　　策略 5 當聽到說話者針對應該做（或不應該做）某事給出了兩個或多個理由時，要準備好回答有兩個答案的細節資訊題。

　　策略 6 細節資訊題的選項是聽力材料中相關語句的換句話說，準備好尋找同義詞。

　　策略 7 如果不能確定答案，可以利用自己對情境的理解和常識來猜測答案。

• Exercise 1 　（解答請見 P. 420）

Below is a short dialog between a student and an employee in the Registrar's Office. Choosing from the list of CHUNKS, fill in the blanks. There are two extra choices.

an outstanding balance		paid up	documentation	registration
enroll in	standing	full-time	waiver	miss

Student: Hi, I'm Lynn Jones. Um, I just found out I don't have any health insurance, and I need some sort of university a. _____ to give the insurance company.

Employee: Sure, we can give you a certificate. What's your b. _____?

Student: I'm going to be a junior; oh, and I'm a c. _____ student.

Employee: For some reason, you don't seem to be on the Registrar's list of enrolled students. Do you know if you're all d. _____ on your tuition, fees and stuff?

Student: I'm not sure. There may be e. _____ for my insurance fee. But that was a long time ago. Last spring.

Employee: Yes, I've found your record. You owe two hundred dollars. And Lynn, a heads-up: You probably won't be able to f. _____ any classes until you get this fee taken care of.

• Exercise 2　（解答請見 P. 420）

Write a correct paraphrase for each of the following idiomatic sentences taken from Conversation 1.

ⓐ Your draft has a lot of bulk, but this is nowhere near ready for submission.

_____

ⓑ Remember, Mark, you can't just retell the plot.

_____

ⓒ You got it!

_____

▶模擬試題

CONVERSATION 1　辦公時間對話：論文書寫討論（錄音文本與解答請見 P. 420）

Listen to part of a conversation between a student and a professor.

 Track 057

Now get ready to answer the questions. You may use your notes.　 Track 058

1. Why does the professor want to talk with the man?
   A. To provide feedback on his paper.
   B. To critique his short documentary.
   C. To have him revise the film studies newsletter.
   D. To plan for the university's Asian film festival.

2. Why did the man want to include a discussion of Hollywood movies?
   A. To demonstrate that Hong Kong martial arts films were much superior.
   B. To illustrate why some films weren't box office successes in Hong Kong.
   C. To explain how the financing of action movies has become international.
   D. To show how Hong Kong film styles influenced mainstream movies.

3. What does the man think about Wong Kar-wai's films?
   A. He thinks they appeal to westerners more than to Chinese people.
   B. He wishes the plots were clearer, but he loves the characters.
   C. He enjoys the special moods that are created in the scenes.
   D. He believes they are artistically interesting, but too confusing.

4. What section of the thesis does the professor ask the man to remove?
   A. The opening sequence.
   B. The part on globalization.
   C. The biography of Wong Kar-wai.
   D. The section with an in-depth analysis.

5. Listen again to part of the conversation. Then answer the question.

 Please listen to Track 058 for this part of the question.

Why does the professor say this:

 Please listen to Track 058 for this part of the question.

   A. To tell him his style of writing shouldn't be quite so literary.
   B. To advise him not to take another English Department class.
   C. To explain that his main priority should be technical aspects.
   D. To emphasize that Asian movies are preferred for the event.

CONVERSATION 2 服務諮詢對話：開學註冊與付款問題（錄音文本與解答請見 P. 422）

Listen to part of a conversation between a student and an employee in the Office of the Registrar.

 Track 059

Now answer the questions. You may use your notes.　　 *Track 060*

1. Why did the woman go to the Registrar's Office?
   A. To pay her spring tuition fees.
   B. To report a erroneous bill.
   C. To check on her insurance status.
   D. To learn why she couldn't enroll.

2. Why does the woman owe the university money?
   Choose 2 answers.
   A. She never received a billing statement.
   B. She had the wrong idea about the university health policy.
   C. She was unwilling to pay for unnecessary services.
   D. She had unexpected expenses during the winter break.

3. After talking with the employee, what does the student decide to do?
   A. Dispute the late fee by writing a letter.
   B. Talk with the people at the lab.
   C. Make a full payment to the cashier.
   D. Request a temporary student loan.

4. Listen again to part of the conversation. Then answer the question.

 Please listen to Track 060 for this part of the question.

Why does the employee say this:

 Please listen to Track 060 for this part of the question.

    A. To apologize for the university's error.
    B. To express understanding of her problem.
    C. To soften the bad news he has to give her.
    D. To indicate he doesn't know what she wants.

5. What is the employee's attitude toward the people who share a house with the student?
    A. He is hopeful they will reimburse the student.
    B. He is sympathetic toward their situation.
    C. He feels the student is using them as an excuse.
    D. He believes they acted irresponsibly.

26 Frequently Tested Campus Life Contexts 6
常考校園生活場景 6

▶校園生活情境：校園安全

　　服務諮詢對話經常發生在「校園安全問題」的情境中。有關校園安全的對話涉及的都是相對常規的問題，諸如違規停車罰單和丟失宿舍鑰匙等，因為新托福考試中的對話不會涉及恐怖或會引起恐慌的場景。

托福總監提醒你文化背景

　　北美的學院和大學採用不同的管理方法來保障校園安全。不過，這些教育機構也有一些共同的安全保障措施。例如，絕大多數大型院校都有一支大學員警隊伍，有些員警會在校園裡巡邏以確保大學安全，還有些員警會在行政部門為教師和學生服務。較小的機構，如社區學院會設立一個安全部門，該部門的保安人員負責保護學院的財產安全，執行學院的規章制度，包括停車場管理和交通管制。如今，所有校園都在努力提高學生的安全意識，以避免不幸事件的發生。

　　新托福對話中，最常見的校園安全場景之一是「失物招領處」（Lost and Found Office），即學生尋找丟失物品的地方。另一個常見的情景是物品被盜，如筆記型電腦、iPod、錢包、DVD 播放機和房間鑰匙等。校園保衛人員可能會建議學生登記他們的個人筆記型電腦以及其他電子設備的序號，以便這些物品丟失或被盜時能易於找回。

　　還有一個典型的場景是學生丟失了身分證。一般來說，很多校園安全對話的內容都是學生以各種方式尋找丟失或被盜的物品，並解決由此引發的問題。例如，學生可能無法回宿舍而必須更換學生證；學生可能需要填寫表格，並出示其他身分證明以證明其身分。

　　此外，還有一種校園安全情景對話是涉及「交通和停車違規類」問題，如學生拖欠違規停車罰款，或者學生發現車窗被砸開，車上的筆電被盜。

　　有時候，消防安全情景也有可能出現在對話中，例如，在宿舍發現有人違規用電鍋煮飯造成走火，或化學實驗室發生一起小火災。在這些情景對話中，學生通常會與消防人員進行交流、填寫表格甚至付費。

▶對話中組織結構題的考查範圍

　　我們已經學習了不少解答組織結構題的策略，尤其是學術講座所附帶的組織結構題。這裡再概括一下：解答組織結構題的最佳策略包括 (1) 把握學術情境，(2) 確定說話者的方式，(3) 仔細聽取信號詞、例子、類比和隱喻。學術講座後常出現組織結構題，偶爾，組織結構題也會出現在對話後面。

那對話後的組織結構題考什麼呢？由於對話通常較短，所以題幹顯然不會出現：How is the information organized? 對話後的組織結構題往往是詢問說話者的隱含目的或措辭用法。有些辦公時間對話會深入討論學生的課程，這些對話與講座類似，可能會有話題轉換、解釋說明和偏離話題等情況。這些情況都是組織結構題的考點。不過，考對話中的這類語言現象時，語用功能題、推論題和立場觀點題更為常見。

以本章 Conversation 1 的組織結構題為例：

• LISTENING SAMPLE

3. Why does the professor mention "mass customization"?

    A. To question whether quality wallpaper can be produced en masse.

    B. To provide an example of another manufacturing technique.

    C. To label the economic model that was described by the student.

    D. To commend the technical expertise of the wallpaper makers.

托福總監評析

    瀏覽四個選項可知教授可能有四種目的。那麼，教授是在提問、解釋說明、歸類，還是稱讚？實際上，組織結構題考查考生能否理解說話者的措辭目的。這道題很難，但是如果考生做好了筆記，就會容易一點。在學生介紹了她最近發現的電腦桌布設計軟體後，教授說：It's a sort of "mass customization" approach, isn't it? Being applied to producing wallpaper designs for consumers. 選項 C 正確，因為教授是在告訴學生她所說的桌布生產模式已經存在。

• Exercise 1 （解答請見 P. 425）

Below is a short dialog between a student and an employee in the Office of Campus Security. Choosing from the list of CHUNKS, fill in the blanks. There are two extra choices.

deter theft	patrolling	filed a report	personal asset	insurance
retrieving	lost property	stolen	only gone	

Employee: Did you want to make a report about a. _____ ?

Student: I called earlier. My laptop was b. _____ some time this morning.

Employee: This was your c. _____. Right. Now, where was the laptop when it was taken?

Student: In my dorm. I dashed down the hall to buy a soda and was d. _____ a minute. I guess I should have locked the door.

Employee: A minute is all it takes. You'd be surprised how many laptops disappear every day. One way to e. _____ is to physically attach the laptop to your desk.

Student: I'll look into that. The next computer I get, I'm definitely going to register on your public safety website. That way I'll have a better chance of f. _____ it.

Employee: OK, If you'd fill out this "Stolen Electronic Media Form," and make sure you indicate whether you g. _____ with the city police.

• Exercise 2　（解答請見 P. 425）

Write a correct paraphrase for the following idiomatic sentences taken from Conversation 1.

ⓐ I had you down for ten o'clock.

_____

ⓑ I'd heard that this kind of manufacturing technique was in the works.

_____

ⓒ But the fact remains that I'll have to deduct points.

_____

▶模擬試題

CONVERSATION 1 辦公時間對話：論文提交問題（錄音文本與解答請見 P. 425）

Listen to part of a conversation between a student and a professor.

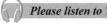 *Track 061*

Now get ready to answer the questions. You may use your notes. *Track 062*

1. Why does the woman go to see the professor?
   A. To discuss possible topics for her final paper.
   B. To get the professor's view on a new technology.
   C. To submit an outline for an important term paper.
   D. To explain why a written assignment was tardy.

2. Listen again to part of the conversation. Then answer the question.

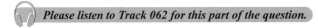 *Please listen to Track 062 for this part of the question.*

What dose the man mean when he says this:

Please listen to Track 062 for this part of the question.

   A. Please tell me.
   B. Do the paper soon.
   C. Continue the research.
   D. Include the new material.

3. Why does the professor mention "mass customization"?
   A. To question whether quality wallpaper can be produced en masse.
   B. To provide an example of another manufacturing technique.
   C. To label the economic model that was described by the student.
   D. To commend the technical expertise of the wallpaper makers.

4. What is the main focus of the student's paper?
   A. How manufacturing companies can profitably sell wallpaper.
   B. How technology influences the availability of design.
   C. How the price of wallpaper has influenced consumer preferences.
   D. How computers produce high-quality wallpaper designs.

5. What does the professor mean when he says this:

 Please listen to Track 062 for this part of the question.

   A. He won't be able to give her full credit.
   B. He will give her high marks in the future.
   C. He hopes she can include more supporting facts.
   D. He's afraid she needs some pointers on format.

CONVERSATION 2 服務諮詢對話：失物事件（錄音文本與解答請見 P. 427）

Listen to part of a conversation between a student and an officer at the Office of Campus Security.

 Track 063

Now answer the questions. You may use your notes.　　　 *Track 064*

1. Why does the man want to talk to the officer?
   A. To register a bicycle with campus police.
   B. To inquire about a missing bicycle.
   C. To inform her he has found a bicycle.
   D. To get the serial number of his cousin's bicycle.

2. Listen again to part of the conversation. Then answer the question.

 Please listen to Track 064 for this part of the question.

What does the man imply when he says this:

 Please listen to Track 064 for this part of the question.

   A. The bicycle was not properly locked.
   B. The racks were located too far away.

C. He thinks he saw a person ride off.

D. He took much longer than he expected.

3. To whom does the lost bicycle currently belong?

    A. The man.

    B. The man's cousin.

    C. The man's roommate.

    D. The Office of Campus Security.

4. Where does the officer tell the man to look for the serial number? For each item, put a ✓ mark in the YES or NO column.

	YES	NO
In the municipal police database		
In the old insurance records		
In the pawn shops		

5. According to the man, which task will he do first?

    A. Contact his cousin.

    B. Look for his roommate.

    C. Call the insurance company.

    D. Ride to where the stores are.

Frequently Tested Campus Life Contexts 7
常考校園生活場景 7

▶校園生活情境：學生事務

新托福聽力對話，尤其是服務諮詢對話，通常以學生事務為情境。這一點不足為奇，因為大學的日常生活就是各種學生事務，包括各種各樣的活動。

托福總監提醒你文化背景

因為每所大學都有其獨特之處，所以負責學生事務的部門所承擔的工作內容也各有不同。例如，在一些大學中，招生、學生衛生保健、學生住宿以及餐廳都被看做學生事務。但是一般來說，當絕大多數人談論「學生事務」時，是指學生組織和管理的工作，包括學生會、體育和娛樂活動、學生戲劇和音樂表演、學生報紙、學生社團等。另外，提供全職和兼職工作、社會服務、志工專案和出國留學專案的學生就業中心也可能歸學生事務部門管理。除此之外，由學生事務部門負責的其他活動還包括新生和轉學生的入學指導。所有這些活動都有可能出現在新托福聽力考試中。

校園生活情境一般不會涉及「返校慶祝」和「學生聯誼會」這樣的場景，因為那些活動只有一些學校有，甚至一些母語是英語的人都有可能不太瞭解。但相對常見的活動，如準備同學聚會則可能會出現在對話中。

在很多大學裡，「學生事務長」負責發展和督導學生活動。該職務的職責是平衡有益於學生的教育、文化和社會活動。因此，在服務諮詢對話中，學生可能會與學生事務長對話，不過更多時候是學生與上述學生活動有關的工作人員對話。例如，學生可能會與大學餐廳的管理人員對話，投訴食物的品質，或者學生可能要求校方正式認可一個新成立的社團。而在辦公時間對話中，學生可能會就暑期實習機會諮詢教授的意見。

▶關聯內容題考的範圍

我們已經學過許多解答關聯內容題的策略。這種題型並不只出現在學術講座題中，也會在對話題中出現。

在辦公時間對話中，關聯內容題的表格裡需要填入的內容通常是教授給學生的一系列建議或者大學工作人員所建議的「辦事步驟」（例如，工作人員告訴學生新學生證的辦理步驟）。考生需要仔細聽這些建議或步驟，並快速記下重要資訊。在對話中，判斷 YES / NO 的表格比相對複雜的分類圖表更為常見，而後者常用來考學術講座中較長的定義或描述。

▶ 對話中關聯內容題的做題策略：

策略 1 當教授或大學工作人員提出建議、任務或解決問題的步驟時，要仔細聽。

策略 2 當說話者描述一個物件或概括一個問題時，要仔細聽，這些描述中的特徵很可能會出現在關聯內容題的表格中。

策略 3 因為對話後的關聯內容題通常要求考生在表格中選 YES / NO，所以要做好準備去確認或否認你所看到的特徵或說法。可以把這些問題當做是非題來看。

策略 4 當說話者開始列舉時，認真做筆記。

• Exercise 1 （解答請見 P. 430）

Below is a short dialog between a student and an employee in the Office of Student Affairs. Choosing from the list of CHUNKS, fill in the blanks. There are two extra choices.

club	leadership	do the paperwork	make a good case
documentation	not formally	fill out	recognized by

Student: Are you the right person to talk to about a student activity? Someone told me we need to a. _____ a form.

Employee: Yeah, I work with student organizations. Is this about a b. _____?

Student: Not exactly. It's the college debate team. We've been debating for a year but have never had a coach. I mean, c. _____, at least.

Employee: It's true; legally, your coach needs to be d. _____ the college. Even though he or she may not get a salary.

Student: There's a graduate student in the School of Communications who's been working with us. But I'm the president of the debate team—can I e. _____ for him right now? We've got a tournament next week.

Employee: No, we need the coach to come in. But here, you can take these back to him. One of these forms lets you request financial support from our office, if you can f. _____.

▶**模擬試題**

CONVERSATION 1 辦公時間對話：職業選擇（錄音文本與解答請見 P. 430）

Listen to part of a conversation between a student and a professor.

Track 065

Now get ready to answer the questions. You may use your notes. *Track 066*

1. Why does the woman go see the professor?
   A. To inquire about an education class.
   B. To interview for a teaching position.
   C. To prepare for a professional teaching exam.
   D. To learn about how to become a teacher.

2. What can we infer about the professor when he says this:

   🎧 *Please listen to Track 066 for this part of the question.*

   A. He is confident she can get a high score on the exam.
   B. He is proud when his students go to "high-need" schools.
   C. He believes the private schools might not pay as well.
   D. He thinks she'll succeed no matter what path she chooses.

3. What does the woman say about teaching in Los Angeles?
   A. She hasn't had much chance to think about it yet.
   B. She would rather work in a place like New York.
   C. She isn't comfortable living in such a big city.
   D. She needs to discuss the issue with her family.

4. Listen again to part of the conversation. Then answer the question.

   🎧 *Please listen to Track 066 for this part of the question.*

   Why does the professor say this:

   🎧 *Please listen to Track 066 for this part of the question.*

   A. To request the woman to write a new draft.
   B. To change the woman's mind about teaching.
   C. To ask the woman to explain her motivations.
   D. To encourage the woman to study even harder.

5. What tasks does the professor assign to the woman? For each sentence, put a ✓ mark in the YES or NO column.

	YES	NO
Enroll in his spring course		
Modify her resume		
Register for the teaching test		
Tutor a high school student		

CONVERSATION 2 服務諮詢對話：組建大學社團（錄音文本與解答請見 P. 432）

Listen to part of a conversation between a student and an employee at the Office of Student Affairs.

 Track 067

Now answer the questions. You may use your notes.   *Track 068*

1. Why does the man talk to the employee?
   A. To petition for new facilities for club members.
   B. To request university credit for a student activity.
   C. To change the nature of an existing organization.
   D. To acquire additional funding for special training.

2. What does the man say he has been doing?
   Choose 2 answers.
   A. Scheduling more interesting competitions for the Aquatic Club.
   B. Identifying a swimming pool and a beach for future activities.
   C. Working closely with a Physical Education teacher.
   D. Planning opportunities for students who like to scuba dive.

3. Listen again to part of the conversation. Then answer the question.

 Please listen to Track 068 for this part of the question.

What can we infer about the employee when she says this:

 Please listen to Track 068 for this part of the question.

   A. She's trying to be very diplomatic.
   B. She'd like to hear the man's opinion.
   C. She isn't sure where that advisor is now.
   D. She's forgotten exactly what year that was.

4. What reason does the man give for proposing the university collaborate with Smith's Dive Shop?
   A. To provide both sides with enhanced public relations.
   B. To offer diving training to the townspeople.
   C. To ensure that diver certification will be reliable.
   D. To get free equipment for university students.

5. What is the employee's attitude about the student's request?
   A. She's persuaded that it is reasonable overall.
   B. She maintains serious reservations about it.
   C. She will do what the university lawyers advise.
   D. She's curious to learn which diving spots will be used.

• **Exercise 2** （解答請見 P. 435）

   Below is another connecting content chart, based on Conversation 2. Listen to the conversation again and fill in the chart.

   What suggestions does the employee make to the student? Place a ✓ mark in the correct column.

	YES	NO
Work with Dr. Morgan		
Sponsor ocean races		
Hold environmental awareness activities		
Practice diving in the university swimming pool		

28 Frequently Tested Campus Life Contexts 8
常考校園生活場景 8

▶校園生活情境：學生住宿

學生申請到大學院校或研究所唸書時總是要考慮住宿問題。住宿是一項基本需求，學生往往會面臨許多選擇以及許多令人頭痛之事。所以，學生住宿自然也是新托福的服務諮詢對話中的常見情境。

托福總監提醒你文化背景

北美大多數院校都會要求低年級的大學生住在校內的學生宿舍裡，而大三和大四的高年級學生通常可以根據自己的意願住在校外。新托福對話涉及的校園住宿問題比校外住宿問題要多，不過考試中兩種情景都會出現。考生需要熟悉這兩種情況和常用語言。

校內住宿生按規定會收到一份要簽字的合約或「住宿協議」。校方會發給所有學生一本《住宿手冊》，其中會列出各項事宜的具體規定，如怎樣退房、學生是否可獲得退款，以及在暑期如何訂宿舍等。

即使在同一所大學內，居住條件也會存在很大差異。有些宿舍有電話、有線電視和網路等設備，而有些宿舍可能只有簡單的家具。不過，學校對宿舍內的家具和其他財產的維護和修理都有嚴格的規定，一般也都有垃圾處理和回收方面的相關規定。不用說，宿舍管理規定還會涉及洗衣、腳踏車、吸菸、寵物和噪音限制等方面內容。

有些學生宿舍大樓內設有餐飲設施，有些則沒有。學生通常可以在眾多「用餐方案」中進行選擇，還可以用「飯卡」或「飯票」來代替現金。

由於學生不瞭解校內住宿的有些規定，所以會同校方有關人員進行交涉，所有這些與校內住宿有關的話題都有可能出現在新托福對話中。

儘管校外住宿的對話並不多，但考生仍然需要瞭解房東會與學生談論哪些問題，如租房合約、租金問題、損壞物品的維修等。還有些情境，如找不到停車位而遲到等，都與住在校外的學生有關。

無論是在校內還是校外住宿，很多對話都會涉及學生與室友的衝突。反映「室友關係問題」的說法有很多，考生需要掌握一些基本的句型，如 can't get along with sb.（與某人相處不好）、switch rooms（換房間）和 room swap（互換房間）。

此外，新托福對話中也會出現宿舍管理員（或宿舍指導員），他們與學生一起住在宿舍大樓裡，其職責是管理學生。在對話中，學生可能會向宿舍管理員抱怨室友過於吵鬧，或者向其詢問搬進或搬出宿舍的事宜。而涉及宿舍停車場、損壞物品、住宿合約以及其他管理方面問題的對話則一般發生在住宿管理辦公室裡，對話雙方是學生與大學工作人員。

▶對話中推論題的考點

在閱讀和聽力部分已經學過推論題的幾種答題策略，其中很多策略都能有效運用到對話中。前文說過，要特別注意聽因果關係和時序關係，因為推論題通常要求推斷接下來可能會發生什麼或者事情發生的原因。

對話中的推論題往往考的是說話者的隱含觀點，從這方面來看，推論題與立場觀點題相同。這樣的推論題通常也是要根據重新播放的某句對話內容來作答。

• LISTENING SAMPLE 1

一位女士正在看一間又小又暗的校外公寓。管理人員可能會問她：So, do you want to rent this room? It's very reasonable! 這位女士可能會回答：Um, I think I'll look around. Thanks, I'll be in touch.

關於這種場景的推論題可能會問：

What does the woman imply when she says this:

Um, I think I'll look around.

> **托福總監評析**
>
> 根據上下文以及這位女士的語調，可以推斷該女士已經下定決心，不租那間房子。

• LISTENING SAMPLE 2

再看 Conversation 2 上的一道推論題：

5. Listen again to part of the conversation. Then answer the question.

S: Yeah, that's not a bad idea. But I'm still going to try and find a way to get new roommates. I don't feel like paying for a second offense a few weeks from now.

What does the man imply when he says this:

S: I don't feel like paying for a second offense a few weeks from now.

   A. He thinks both policies are unreasonable.

   B. He hopes to know the official ruling before too long.

   C. The total amount is more than he can afford now.

   D. The roommates will keep on breaking rules.

托福總監評析

    先分析四個選項，瞭解推論題中考的句子類型。注意，沒有哪個選項是對這位男士所說話語的直接換句話說，所以必須運用推理技巧，弄清楚這位男士的想法和感受。他對什麼感到不高興呢？有人要他付錢嗎？對於推論題，考生必須從情景中尋找線索。在這種情況下，要尋找這位男士 doesn't feel like paying 的原因線索。

• **Exercise 1** （解答請見 P. 436）

    Below is a short dialog between a student and an employee in the Office of Student Housing. Choosing from the list of CHUNKS, fill in the blanks. There are two extra choices.

| a resume builder | conflict resolution | applications for | of advice |
| are assigned | physical layout | be interviewed | transcript |

Student: I'm thinking about becoming an RA. Are you still accepting a. _____ residence assistants?

Employee: The deadline is June 1. Here's the packet: You'll need a b. _____ and a letter of recommendation. And plan for two weeks of training in August.

Student: I've heard a few nightmare stories about RAs who've had trouble. Apparently their first-year students went wild. I don't know if I can handle that... But part of me thinks this would be valuable experience, c. _____.

Employee: The job is definitely demanding. One piece d. _____ that we always give new resident assistants is "Don't smile till Christmas." It's better to start off strict and then gradually loosen up.

Student: [laughing] That makes sense. [pause] So will all the applicants e. _____ in person?

Employee: Yes, we'll call to schedule. Oh, one more thing—you need to be aware that RAs can't choose their residence hall. If you want the job, you have to go where you f. _____.

▶ **模擬試題**

CONVERSATION 1 辦公時間對話：實驗結果討論（錄音文本與解答請見 P. 436）

Listen to a conversation between a student and a professor of Plant Genetics.

 Track 069

Now get ready to answer the questions. You may use your notes. *Track 070*

1. Why does the man go to see the professor?
   A. To submit his genetics lab notebook.
   B. To volunteer to participate in a study.
   C. To raise an issue about lab procedure.
   D. To complain about an outside service provider.

2. What does the man think has disturbed the mice?
   A. Unclean cages.
   B. Wood chips.
   C. Stressful handling.
   D. Paper bedding.

3. Listen again to part of the conversation. Then answer the question.

    Please listen to Track 070 for this part of the question.

   What does the professor say about the research findings?
   A. Unfortunately they won't be usable this time.
   B. Some scientists may very well question their validity.
   C. It's natural to have ambiguity with experiments.
   D. Lab conditions have been carefully controlled in the past.

4. Listen again to part of the conversation. Then answer the question.

    Please listen to Track 070 for this part of the question.

   What is the professor's attitude when she says this:

    Please listen to Track 070 for this part of the question.

   A. She feels somewhat unqualified.
   B. She is unhappy with the man's mistake.
   C. She is relieved no one noticed the problem.
   D. She finds the situation highly ironic.

5. What does the professor plan on doing about the situation?
   Choose 2 answers.
   A. Contacting her colleagues in research.
   B. Looking at the data in the lab book.
   C. Suspending the modified corn study.
   D. Cleaning and disinfecting the cages.

• **Exercise 2**   （解答請見 P. 438）

   Below are three inference questions based on Conversation 1. Listen to the conversation again and then write an answer for each question.

ⓐ What can we infer about the student when he says this:
No problem—I'll get the lab notebook in just a minute. Actually, I stopped by to ask about a concern I have with the lab environment for that study.
_____
_____

ⓑ What does the professor imply when she says this:
Sneezing, eh?
_____
_____

ⓒ What does the professor imply when she says this:
Write down everything in your lab book, and we'll make sense of it later.
_____
_____

CONVERSATION 2 服務諮詢對話：違反宿舍管理制度的問題
（錄音文本與解答請見 P. 438）

Listen to part of a conversation between a student and an employee in the housing office.

 Track 071

Now answer the questions. You may use your notes.   *Track 072*

1. Why does the man go to the housing office?
   A. To request a room change.
   B. To argue that he should not be fined.
   C. To report a fire on campus.
   D. To arrange a dorm meeting.

2. What does the employee say about the violation fine?
   Choose 2 answers.
   A. It is sometimes possible to appeal it.
   B. It is decided by the resident assistant.
   C. It must be paid by each resident.
   D. It is usually waived on the first offense.

3. Listen again to part of the conversation. Then answer the question.

 Please listen to Track 072 for this part of the question.

   What does the man mean when he says this:

 Please listen to Track 072 for this part of the question.

   A. He suspects chemicals must have caused the fire.
   B. He'd like to know more about what happened.
   C. He has no choice but to go to night classes.
   D. He's exceptionally annoyed that he was not present.

4. According to the employee, what will the man's resident assistant want to do?
   A. Talk to the safety inspector.
   B. Meet with the roommates.
   C. Reverse his decision.
   D. Find the man another room.

5. Listen again to part of the conversation. Then answer the question.

 Please listen to Track 072 for this part of the question.

   What does the man imply when he says this:

 Please listen to Track 072 for this part of the question.

   A. He thinks both policies are unreasonable.
   B. He hopes to know the official ruling before too long.
   C. The total amount is more than he can afford now.
   D. The roommates will keep on breaking rules.

Appendices

特別收錄

Appendix I — The Scoring of the TOEFL® iBT
特別收錄 ➊ 新托福考試的評分

★新托福考試成績概述

　　新托福考試為決策機構提供了兩套分數：總分和各部分得分。各部分的分數由「標準分」組成，標準分由原始分根據一個通用比例轉換而來。標準分很重要，因為它可讓決策者對學生進行更為公平的比較。

新托福考試成績的滿分如下：

閱讀： 30

聽力： 30

口語： 30

寫作： 30

總分： 120

　　考生會收到被稱為「成績回饋」的資訊。該資訊旨在 明考生該如何瞭解自己的整體表現。例如在閱讀和聽力部分，考生得分情況有 Low（0～13）、Intermediate（14～21）或 High（22～30）。口語部分， 考生得分情況有 Weak（0～9）、Limited（10～17）、Fair（18～25） 或 Good（26～30）。寫作部分，考生得分情況有 Limited（1～16）、Fair（17～23）或 Good（24～30）。

　　但是請注意，提交給大學的成績單中不會有該成績回饋資訊。只有考生個人會收到此資訊。

★新托福考試閱讀和聽力部分的評分

　　閱讀部分，每篇閱讀有 12～14 道題，閱讀部分的所有題目是 36～40 道。大多數題目分數為 1 分（原始分數）。內容總結題（2 分），資訊歸類題（3 或 4 分，視難度而定）的分數高一些。考生完成整個新托福考試後，電腦對每道閱讀試題進行評分，然後將原始分數轉換成 0 到 30 之間的標準分。

　　此外，可能還會考兩篇實驗性閱讀文章（總共 24～28 道題），但這些成績不會出現在成績單上。

　　聽力部分總共有 34 道題。大多數題目分數為 1 分（原始分數），但關聯內容題可得 1 分或 2 分（視難度而定）。和閱讀一樣，聽力題也是由電腦來評分，然後將原始分數轉換成 0 到 30 之間的標準分。

如果閱讀部分沒有實驗性題目，聽力部分就可能會有實驗性題目：兩個講座和一段對話（總共 17 道題）。同樣，這些成績也都不會出現在成績單上。

★其他重要資訊

1. 成績單

考生可在完成考試兩週後線上查看成績單，郵寄成績單的耗時則會更長一些（一週到一個月）。每位考生都會收到成績單，同時考試機構會將最多四份成績單的正本寄往考生所選定的教育機構。成績單上只顯示一次考試的成績，如果你以前參加過新托福考試，以前的成績將不會出現在最新的成績單上。新托福成績的有效期是參加考試後的兩年之內。

2. 所需的最低總分

許多考生問：「需要在新托福考試中得多少分才能被大學錄取？」答案是：「視大學而定；視級別（大學或研究生）而定；有時還會視大學裡的某個系而定」。目前，很多公認較有名的教育機構要求新托福總分最低為 80 分。頂尖學院，如哈佛大學、麻省理工學院和芝加哥大學，總分可能至少需要 100 分，尤其當該考生申請的是商業、法律或傳播學這類科系時更需要高分。相反地，理工科的學生可能只需要 80 分，甚至更低。也有院校總分只需 69 分便可入學。

3. 各部分所需的最低分數

有些大學對新托福考試各部分的最低分沒有要求，但有些大學會要求，也會規定最低總分。還有些大學雖然對各部分的最低分有要求，但沒有單獨列出最低總分。舉例來說，你可能會發現你要申請的學校要求你閱讀最低 21 分、聽力最低 18 分、口語最低 23 分、寫作最低 22 分。如果考生滿足上述最低要求，則考生的總分至少為 84 分。

4. 如何查詢你的目標大學對新托福成績的要求

如果你正在申請出國留學或獎學金，想瞭解你想去的學校對英文能力的要求，必須到目標大學的網站上查看是否規定了最低托福分數。查找此類資訊的最好方法是：先點擊 Admissions（招生），再點擊 International（國際），然後查找 English language proficiency（英語語言能力）或類似這樣的標題。

Appendix II ► Words, Answers, Explanations, and Listening Scripts

特別收錄 2 主題詞彙、答案、解析和錄音原文

① 物理科學常考主題 1 天文學詞彙、答案、解析和錄音原文

閱讀模擬試題答案詳解

1. **B** 細節資訊題
   〔**解析**〕作者指出，關於恆星亮度的資料很少，所以選項 A 不正確。雖然第二段提到了恆星的位置，但恆星的位置與其化學構成並無關係，所以選項 C 不正確。第二段沒有提及恆星的脈衝，所以排除選項 D。選項 B 正確，因為文中最後一句提到，顏色能夠顯示出恆星的化學成分。

2. **D** 細節資訊題
   〔**解析**〕Leavitt 的工作是在底片上比較恆星的大小，即將它們與已知的恆星進行比較，從而得出恆星的亮度，因此選項 D「確定恆星的亮度」正確。選項 A、B、C 的活動第三段中均未提及。

3. **A** 語境詞彙題
   〔**解析**〕從 slow and subtle 的句子結構可知 subtle 的語義與 slow 相近，四個選項中只有 A 項符合，「慢」與「細微的、不明顯的」語義相近。

4. **D** 語境詞彙題
   〔**解析**〕pore over sth. 意為「仔細檢查某物或認真查看某物」，因此選項 D「檢查」正確。選項 A、B、C 雖然都是 Leavitt 曾經從事過的活動，但都與 to pore over 意義不符。

5. **C** 指代關係題
   〔**解析**〕此題相對容易，考生只要知道 on the one hand 和 on the other 的用法，即可輕鬆作答。作者指出，圖中一個座標軸上顯示的是亮度，另一個（座標軸）顯示的是週期。on the other 後面承前省略了單字 axis。

6. **A** 修辭目的題
   〔**解析**〕本題有一定難度，要選對答案，需要幾個步驟才行。我們需要從第四段中找到 bells 這個詞。該詞位於第四段最後一句，作者將大恆星的「波動」與大鐘的「聲音」進行對比。我們從中可以推斷，作者的目的是為了說明：正如大鐘的聲音頻率低（即延續時間長），大恆星（因而也是亮星）的波動週期也長。

7. **D** 綜合推斷題
   〔**解析**〕快速閱讀文章可知，Great Refractor 和 the 1890s 在文中幾個地方都出現過。第一段講到 Great Refractor（大折射望遠鏡）在 19 世紀末時是當時最為先進的技術（state-of-the-art technology），因此選項 A 不正確。第四段中提到，Leavitt 觀察了麥哲倫雲中的恆星底片，因此選項 B 也不正確。大折射望遠鏡購自德國，但文中並沒有講到有哪個其他國家借用過它，所以選項 C 也不正確。排除了這三項，即可知 D 項正確。

8. **B** 句子簡化題
   〔**解析**〕見本章前文的「托福總監評析」。

9. **B** 否定事實題
〔**解析**〕回答此題最快的方法是先快速閱讀四個選項，然後從第五段中找到資訊的具體位置。第三句提到了 Hubble，而且 Hubble 利用了 Leavitt 對恆星週期的研究成果，因此選項 A 不正確。選項 C「絕對亮度」和選項 D「視亮度」都是 Hubble 的研究課題。第五段中沒有提及 constellations（星座），所以選項 B 正確。

10. **C** 語境詞彙題
〔**解析**〕illustrating 與 drawing 是同義詞，但與片語動詞 drawing on 並不同義，因此排除選項 A。to draw on 有時可意為 to approach（臨近），如：Night draws on.（夜幕降臨。）但從上下文來看，Hubble 是利用（utilizing）了 Leavitt 的研究成果，因此選項 C 正確。

11. **D** 細節資訊題
〔**解析**〕此題相對容易，考生只需認真閱讀第六段即可正確作答。選項 A、B、C 都不正確，因為大多數科學家認為宇宙的大小是個常量，而且宇宙僅與銀河一樣大。只有選項 D 正確。

12. **C** 語境詞彙題。
〔**解析**〕只有選項 C「conclusively」與 definitively 意思相同，意為「決定性地；毫無疑問地」。

13. **4** By comparing a Cepheid's apparent brightness to its absolute brightness, astronomers were able to determine a celestial body's distance from the Earth.
5 The luminosity of bright Cepheid stars was found to fluctuate over relatively long intervals.
6 Based on data regarding the distances of variable stars, astronomers reevaluated their assumptions about the Milky Way.
內容總結題
〔**解析**〕第一個選項不正確，因為文章的中心內容是恆星的亮度，而不是恆星的位置，而且作者也沒有講過其位置是不準確的。第二個選項也不正確，因為根據第四段的內容，Leavitt 只區分了麥哲倫星雲中的 25 個變星。第三個選項也不正確，因為根據第五段的內容，計算出變星與地球間距離的人是 Hubble，而不是 Leavitt。第四個選項是文章的一個主要觀點，是正確的。第五個選項說明了 Leavitt 的重要研究發現，從而使得後來的天文學家們對宇宙有了進一步的認識，是正確的。最後一個選項概括了全文的觀點，對文章最後一句話的意思進行了總結，也正確。

● **Answer Key to Exercise 1**

a. The "Great Refractor" was once considered cutting-edge technology, even though it is no longer in use.

b. Leavitt evaluated the relative size of the pinpoints by comparing them to known stars.

c. The only way to perceive the differences in star brightness was to measure them periodically during the year.

聽力模擬試題錄音文本　　*Track 001*
- -
N= Narrator　P=Professor　　S=Student　　下同。
N: Listen to part of a talk in an astronomy class.
P: Just before class, one of you asked me to talk a little bit about space weather, and if our weather on the Earth is influenced by space. Space weather is a big topic, so I don't have time to cover it in detail now. But the short answer is this: That the Sun—or should I say, the Sun's energy—influences space weather. The Sun influences weather patterns in all layers of the atmosphere, including the upper atmosphere of the Earth, where satellites are orbiting. We'll be talking about solar activity later in the course, getting into things like solar winds. But right now it's important for us to understand more about the Sun itself. The mass of the Sun

is greater than the mass of all of the other planets combined. Even though the Sun is huge, it is small when compared to other stars in the galaxy. Not surprisingly, given its mass, the Sun's surface gravity is almost 28 times that of the Earth. If you were able to stand on the surface of the Sun you would weigh about 28 times your weight on the Earth.

There is a core to the Sun, just as planets all have cores. But note that stars are different from planets in that most of that central mass is made of tons and tons of hydrogen and helium. And the Sun's core is a dense, hot region similar to what one would find in the middle of a nuclear explosion produced by a hydrogen bomb.

Now, how the Sun's energy is created in the Sun's core and then disseminated is a complex, but quite interesting, topic. In fact, scientists have yet to agree on the details of just how the reactions take place.

S: Are you saying we, uh, don't actually know what causes these solar nuclear reactions?

P: There are many aspects of the Sun that we still don't understand. But we do know that in the middle of our Sun, the "core" is composed of very hot gases. Because the temperatures are so high in this gas, the electrons in the atoms get separated from the protons. Protons, of course, are particles with a positive charge. These positively-charged protons slam together, and as they crash into one another, they're releasing energy.

So, to answer your question, as you know from your basic science classes, heat causes atoms to move. If you heat anything, it will move. For example, if you watch a pot of water just before it boils, you can see the ripples as the atoms move. In this case, deep in the Sun's core, these atoms are heated, packed closely together, and colliding. When they collide, they're producing heavier elements and releasing light in the form of gamma rays and x-rays. They're also producing extreme amounts of energy in the form of heat and radio waves.

S: Um, and is this where the light from the Sun comes from?

P: That's a good question. I guess the best way to explain is to say that the light comes from the merging of atoms at the core—but we on the Earth won't see that light until it goes through a lot of different processes. A complex interaction of radiation with matter creates photons, or light particles, which, over time, are finally able to move to the Sun's surface.

On average, the photon particles produced in the Sun's nuclear reactions take about a million years to move from the core to the surface. But by the time the particles finally reach the outer portion of the Sun, they have much lower energy. They have become "visible light" photons, and these are the light particles we end up seeing on the Earth.

And what's so amazing, you know—is the difference in the amount of time it takes for the photons to travel from the Sun's surface to the Earth. Basically, a photon may have to be around for millions of years before it gets to the surface of the Sun, but then after that it takes it only eight and a half minutes to reach the planet Earth! Remember, though, that visible light is not the only type of radiation coming from the Sun; there are many other types of waves. In fact, "visible light" constitutes only a small fraction of electromagnetic waves, but it is the only type of wave that can be detected by the human eye.

● **Transcripts for Question 2**

N: Listen again to part of the lecture. Then answer the question.

P: Space weather is a big topic, so I don't have time to cover it in detail now. But the short answer is this: That the Sun—or should I say, the Sun's energy—influences space weather.

N: Why does the professor say this:

P: But the short answer is this:

關鍵語塊

space weather 太空氣候	talk a little bit about 簡要談一下
is influenced by... 被……影響	short answer 簡短回答
principal driver 主要推動力	upper atmosphere 上層大氣，高層大氣
get into 開始談論	solar wind 太陽風
surface gravity 表面重力	nuclear explosion 核爆
disseminate （能量）擴散	have yet to agree on... 關於……尚無一致意見
electron 電子	atom 原子
positive charge 正電荷	slam together 撞在一起
crash into one another 互相撞擊	ripple 波動
collide 碰撞	heavier element 重元素
gamma ray 伽馬射線	visible light 可見光
electromagnetic wave 電磁波	

聽力模擬試題答案詳解

1. **C** 主旨大意題
   〔**解析**〕選項 A 是干擾項，因為教授只是在開頭部分提到有一個學生要求他談一談太空氣候。選項 B 不正確，因為教授只在講座結尾處才集中講到核反應。選項 D「重力對輻射的影響」講座中沒有提及。只有選項 C「太陽如何產生能量」全面、準確地概括了教授的講座。

2. **B** 語用功能題
   〔**解析**〕要想回答這道題目，考生必須瞭解：雖然教授沒有花很多時間詳談太空氣候這個話題，但是他確實想簡略回答一下。but the short answer is this 表明他會馬上提供一個簡略說明，所以選項 B 正確。

3. **A** 細節資訊題
   〔**解析**〕教授在談論重力和太陽時說道：Not surprisingly, given its mass, the Sun's surface gravity is almost 28 times that of the Earth. 因此選項 A 正確。選項 C 和選項 D 的說法講座中沒有提及。

4. **A、D** 細節資訊題
   〔**解析**〕選項 B 不正確，因為講座中說太陽的中心類似核爆的中心，氫原子的核聚變就發生在太陽中心。選項 C 不正確，因為講座中說 visible light 的光子是出現在太陽外部的低能量粒子，光子要經過很長時間才能從太陽中心運動到太陽表面，然後再輸送到地球。選項 A 正確，因為講座中說粒子相互撞擊時會釋放出伽馬射線和 X 射線形式的光。在同一段中，教授說到太陽中心包含互相撞擊的質子，因此 D 也正確。

5. **D** 組織結構題
   〔**解析**〕有學生問怎麼知道是什麼引起了太陽內部的核反應時，教授以水在鍋裡沸騰作類比，說明加熱會使原子發生運動。

6.

	Core	Surface
Protons colliding	✓	
Visible light quickly emitted		✓
Nuclear reactions	✓	

關聯內容題。

【解析】教授在講座中提到發生在太陽中心和表面的各種活動。這些資訊出現在講座的最後五段中,從教授說 There are many aspects of the Sun that we still dont understand 開始。在那一段中,教授說:These positively-charged protons slam together, and as they crash into one another, they're releasing energy. 由此可知質子是在太陽中心發生撞擊,因此第一個特點應在 core 下打勾。隨後,學生問太陽光來自何處,教授回答說光子或稱 light particles 能夠傳播到太陽表面,並強調說可見光八分半鐘就傳播到地球,因此第二個特點應在 Surface 下打勾。第三個特點 nuclear reactions 教授提到過多次,後來他說:On average, the photon particles produced in the Sun's nuclear reactions take about a million years to move from the core to the surface. 由此可知核反應是發生在太陽中心。

● **Answer Key to Exercise 2**

天文學講座「結構性筆記」範例

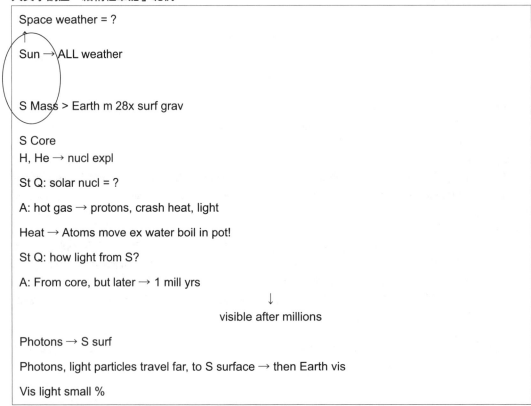

Space weather = ?

Sun → ALL weather

S Mass > Earth m 28x surf grav

S Core
H, He → nucl expl

St Q: solar nucl = ?

A: hot gas → protons, crash heat, light

Heat → Atoms move ex water boil in pot!

St Q: how light from S?

A: From core, but later → 1 mill yrs

↓
visible after millions

Photons → S surf

Photons, light particles travel far, to S surface → then Earth vis

Vis light small %

筆記範例說明

1. 在 Sun 上畫圈是因為它是中心論點。
2. S 是 Sun 的縮寫形式。
3. 符號 → 表示「引起」、「影響」。Sun → ALL weather 表示太陽影響所有天氣情況。
4. 符號 > 表示「大於」，因為教授說太陽的品質比地球的大。
5. 請注意縮寫詞，如 surf grav 代表 surface gravity。
6. 化學元素 hydrogen 和 helium 用 H 和 He 代表。
7. 縮寫形式 Ex 代表 example。

下面是一份真實的筆記。注意其中縮寫的使用和其他記錄重要詞彙和觀點的符號。

Astronomy-
Space weather = ?
(SUN) → all weather
S. mass > Earth m. 28X Surf. grav.
S. core
        H, He → nucl explos.

Stud solar nuc = ?
prof hot gas → protons, crash → heat
                                    Light
        heat atoms move
    Eg. water boiling
Stud how light
    from sun?
prof from core, but LATER → 1 mil yrs
                            ↓
                        visible aftr
                            millions
"photons" → S surface
core   ↓
        to Earth
Light particles travel far, to
                    Sun surf
visible later from
                Earth

Vis light small %

② 人文藝術常考主題 1 民俗藝術詞彙、答案、解析和錄音原文

● **Answer Key to Exercise 1**

1. b.　　2. d.　　3. e.　　4. c.　　5. a.

閱讀模擬試題答案詳解

1. **B 細節資訊題**

　　〔**解析**〕文中說，一小群人開始遷移，而不是 hundreds of tribes，所以選項 A 不正確。文中提到，依努特人的後代遷移時穿過了一座橋，而不是海峽，所以選項 C 不正確。選項 D 也不正確，因為從 still-debated（尚有爭論的）和 speculate（推測）推斷該遷移模式尚無定論。文中說，伴隨著第一波新大陸移民的浪潮，Inuit people and their art emerged，所以選項 B 正確。

2. **C 語境詞彙題**

　　〔**解析**〕通過上下文可知，物品上雕刻的圖像是裝飾性的，並沒有宗教含義。這種藝術的主要目的似乎不是精神或自然的力量。四個選項中，只有 calm（平息，安撫）符合語義，appease 有「安撫，撫慰」的意思。

3. **A 否定事實題**

　　〔**解析**〕第三段提到，西元 1000 年左右，圖勒文化取代了多塞特文化，所以選項 B 是正確陳述。第三段還提到，圖勒藝術注重實用的功能，包含了裝飾華麗的 spears and harpoons，所以選項 C 是正確陳述。選項 D 也是正確陳述，因為文中說圖勒文化 had a distinctive Alaskan style。本題應選 A，因為文中說圖勒文化在實用物品（utilitarian objects）上雕刻的圖案是裝飾性的，沒有宗教意義。

4. **A 語境詞彙題**

　　〔**解析**〕見本章前文的「托福總監評析」。

5. **D 句子簡化題**

　　〔**解析**〕粗體部分包括兩個並列分句，由副詞 nevertheless 分開，由此可以推測正確答案中可能會包含 nevertheless 的近義詞，如 but、yet、despite 或 even though 等，所以選項 A 和選項 C 可以先排除。選項 B 中的 practical objects（實用的物品）與原文矛盾。粗體部分所說少量 nonutilitarian objects 可換句話說為 carved objects that were not essential，所以選項 D 正確。

6. **C 語境詞彙題**

　　〔**解析**〕該題有一定難度，因為形容詞 effective 是個多義詞，useful、efficient 和 operative 都是其同義詞，所以很多考生會混淆。其實副詞 effectively 只有「實際上，事實上」的意思，相當於 in actuality、in reality 或 for all practical purposes，因此選項 C 正確。

7. **B 細節資訊題**

　　〔**解析**〕回答此題時需要掃讀全文找 1940s 這個關鍵字。第五段出現 1960s。第五句提到雕塑、印刷和其他的藝術形式逐漸取代了獸皮，成為他們主要的生活來源，由此可推知 20 世紀 40 年代之前，他們生活的主要來源是狩獵。

8. **D 細節資訊題**

　　〔**解析**〕在第五段作者說，到了 20 世紀 60 年代，一些依努特手工藝術家成了企業家，從事各種活動：開採石料、製造工具、製作石雕並在城市藝術館中展覽。由此可知依努特人將石雕看作一種商業活動，因此選項 D 正確。

9. **C 指代關係題**

　　〔**解析**〕在該詞的所在句中，人稱代名詞 them 並非用於前指，而是用作後指。語塊 available to them 通常用於表示 available to people，因此可以猜測答案可能是個表示人的名詞，或者是表示

有生命的事物。通過上下文（將電動工具與斧頭和銼刀進行對比）可以確定選項 C 正確。

10. **A** 修辭目的題

〔**解析**〕作者例舉舞蹈的熊來説明雕刻品栩栩如生、充滿動感的風格，該風格來源於自然主義和對自然生命和精神世界的共同關注，因此選項 A 正確。選項 B 不正確，因為舞蹈的熊是自然主義風格，而不是抽象風格。

11. **D** 推論題

〔**解析**〕此題相對容易。第六段提到 various greenstones, especially the apple-green and creamcolored shades, are highly prized，因此選項 D「Cream-colored greenstone」正確。

12. ■ **2** 插入句子題

In the mid-1940s Inuit conditions began to deteriorate, caused to a great extent by the plummeting prices of white fox on the world market. ■ 1 In light of this development, the Canadian government decided to take steps to facilitate an alternative revenue source for the Inuit trappers. **The Canadian Handicraft Guild in Montreal introduced Inuit carvings to the world in 1949.** ■ 2 Once the previously nomadic Inuits settled into communities, their carved pieces became appreciably larger. ■ 3 The quality of the carvings was high, with the result that artists began to receive commissions to produce specific works of art. Sculpture, prints and other art forms gradually replaced pelts as the major source of livelihood. ■ 4 By the 1960s, active co-operatives existed in most settlements and the Inuit art market was flourishing. At that point, the Inuit artisans became entrepreneurs, effectively quarrying their own stones, fashioning their own carving tools, creating objects of beauty and showing their work in urban galleries.

〔**解析**〕第一個標記處不正確，因為前一句沒有提及雕刻。最後兩個標記處也不正確，因為需要插入的句子中説雕刻品於 1949 年介紹給了世人，而最後兩個標記處前面的句子談論的都是雕刻品的發展。第二個標記處正確，因為需要插入的句子説明的正是前一句中提到的 alternative revenue source，並由此可以合理過渡到下一句，引出 their carved pieces became appreciably larger。

13. **1** Over one thousand years ago, Inuit ancestors created many small sculptures depicting animals.

4 Thule carvings were often very practical; for example, the carvers engraved designs on utensils and hunting tools.

5 Inuit sculptures currently are often produced by entrepreneurial artists participating in cooperatives.

內容總結題

〔**解析**〕第一個陳述正確，因為該項談論早期的雕刻品，文章後面的內容都是從該話題引申出來的。第二個陳述與文中事實（多塞特人雕刻出面具用以嚇跑鬼怪）不符。第三個陳述過於具體，缺乏與主題雕刻藝術發展的直接聯繫。第四個陳述準確説明了對當前雕刻藝術產生了巨大影響的圖勒藝術。第五個陳述總結了依努特人在現代與雕刻有關的活動，正確。最後一個陳述與文中事實不符，因為文中沒有提到歐洲人使依努特人的人口減少。

● **Answer Key to Exercise 2**

a. <u>Throughout this course, we'll...</u>

b. <u>Our primary subject of study will be...</u>

c. <u>As we gradually study the history of...</u>

聽力模擬試題錄音文本　 *Track 003*

N: Now listen to part of a lecture in a folk art class.

P: Many of the most widespread traditions in folk art involve the use of textiles—either fabric, or some other soft material. Throughout this course, we'll study a wide range of fibers and their use, including weaving. Today we'll start with traditional quilting. Our major focus will be the quilting traditions in North America, along with some social and historical background. Later on this semester, we'll look at contemporary quilts, or "art quilts." But right now, I want you to immerse yourselves in the traditional craft. And as you all know, art doesn't happen in a vacuum—it's a product of a certain time and a certain environment.

Now, for our purposes a quilt will be defined as a cover for a bed made of two layers of fabric that contains soft material sandwiched between those layers. There are patterns of stitching through the layers. Some quilts are made from patches of cloth that are pieced together, a process called "piecing" or "patchwork." Not all quilts have patchwork, however.

I'll bet most of you are unaware that quilting has existed for millennia. We know, for example, that almost 6,000 years ago ancient Egyptians were quilting. An ivory carving was found, a carving of a pharaoh wearing quilted clothing. And based on other archaeological records, we assume that quilts and quilting have an equally long history in China. So, for those of you who thought quilting was mainly a colonial American art form, you can see—quilting is actually quite universal.

OK then, back to our topic. When the colonists first arrived in North America, their quilts looked much like quilts from their native countries in Europe, but as time passed, they changed. We have many clues about these early American quilts that can help us determine their origin. From the style and material of the quilt, we not only can tell how wealthy the colonial family was, but also where the family lived. Families along the coast could obtain background fabrics more easily from Europe than the inland settlers could, due to the difficulty of transporting goods.

Inland families had to make their own cloth, and when the whole-cloth quilts and blankets they had brought from Europe began to wear out, they pieced together quilts made out of the saved pieces of old ones. Every scrap, no matter what size, shape and color, was used. This led to the birth of the so-called patchwork "Crazy Quilt," the oldest pattern in colonial America, and a pattern signifying a transition point in the quilting traditions.

The wealthy and socially prominent settlers, especially in the southern coastal states, based their patchwork quilts on English designs all the way up to the Revolutionary War. But after the War began, even the southern women began to use patchwork designs and patterns.

The traditional colonial quilts were usually made from patterns, and every pattern had a name. Patterns were designed to commemorate many aspects of life, including great events, political parties, and ethnic origins. New England women up in the Northeast favored pictorial patterns, whereas in the South, the quilts were characterized by elaborate needlework. So, once again, you can see that when we look at a quilt, we can get a sense of the social and historical conditions of the time. Every quilt tells a story.

I love to tell about the oldest surviving patchwork quilt from colonial times, a quilt in Massachusetts, dating from 1704. The story of how historians were able to identify the date is quite interesting. One common technique for quilting, even today, is to cut patterns out of paper and piece them together before starting to work on actual fabric. To make the Massachusetts quilt, the quilters cut patterns out of newspaper and the newspaper was then used as an inner lining for the quilt. As the outer fabric wore out, the date on the paper came into view, providing an accurate indication of when the quilt was created.

All right then. As a reminder, for today you should have already read the first two chapters on quilting in your textbook, taking note of the popular quilt patterns pictured in these chapters. Ill expect you to be able to identify all these early patterns and their names.

In my next lecture, I'll turn to the traditional quilts made in the 19th century—a time when quilt-making flourished. You'll see that the colors and designs become increasingly vibrant, and women begin to hang quilts on walls as works of art. As we move through the history of quilts, you'll see first-hand why many people refer to quilting as "soft painting."

● **Transcripts for Question 3**

N: Listen again to part of the lecture. Then answer the question.

P: New England women up in the Northeast favored pictorial patterns, whereas in the South, the quilts were characterized by elaborate needlework. So, once again, you can see that when we look at a quilt, we can get a sense of the social and historical conditions of the time. Every quilt tells a story.

N: Why does the professor say this:

P: Every quilt tells a story.

關鍵語塊

widespread tradition 廣為流傳的傳統	folk art 民間藝術
textile 布料；紡織品	soft material 柔軟的材料
contemporary quilts 當代棉被	immerse oneself in 沉浸於；專心於
happen in a vacuum 在封閉狀態中發生，脫離外界環境等因素而發生	for our purposes 為達到目的
cover 覆蓋物；床單	... the sandwiched between... 被夾在……中間
patches of cloth 一塊塊布料	piece together patches of 將……小塊連在一起
pharaoh 法老（古埃及國王）	universal 普遍的
have clues about 有關於……的線索	inland settler 內陸定居者
wear out 用壞	scrap 小片，廢料
lead to 導致	so-called 所謂的
Crazy Quilt 碎布縫成的被單	socially prominent 社會地位顯著的
be designed to 為……而設計	commemorate 紀念
pictorial pattern 繪畫圖案	elaborate needlework 精緻的刺繡
oldest surviving 現存最古老的	inner lining 內襯
a time when... flourished ……繁盛的時期	vibrant 充滿活力的；（色彩）鮮豔的
see first-hand 親眼目睹	

聽力模擬試題答案詳解

1. **D** 主旨大意題

【**解析**】選項 B 容易被誤選，教授並沒有談論修補棉被。開頭部分提到：Our major focus will be the quilting traditions in North America, along with some social and historical background. 講座的大部分內容都與殖民時期有關，因此選項 D 正確。

2. **C** 組織結構題

〔**解析**〕此題有一定難度。選項 A 不正確，因為教授沒有再繼續談論埃及的紡織實務。選項 B 不正確，因為教授沒有作任何對比。選項 C 正確，因為教授所講到的法老穿著一種早期的夾層棉服。

3. **A** 語用功能題

〔**解析**〕教授說：Every quilt tells a story. 這是為了說明每床棉被的用料和設計都反映出棉被製作者的背景，因此選項 A 正確。有些考生可能會把 story 和 novels 或 diaries 相聯繫而誤選 C 或 D。

4. **B**、**D** 細節資訊題

〔**解析**〕要想答對此題，考生在聽講座時必須記錄下重要的例證資訊。選項 A 不正確，因為教授沒有說過新英格蘭的棉被製作者用上了與政治有關的圖案設計而南方的棉被製作者沒有使用。教授說使用紙樣是一種「普遍的方法」，但沒有說過南方人不使用紙樣，因此選項 C 不正確。選項 B 和 D 正確，因為教授在講座中進行了這些方面的對比（in the South, the quilts were characterized by elaborate needlework 和 even the southern women began to use patchwork designs and patterns）。

5. **B** 細節資訊題

〔**解析**〕文中提及一份報紙，但 A 項不正確，因為講座中沒有提及給棉被做廣告的報紙。講座中沒有提到 woolen fabric 和 computer database，所以選項 C 和 D 都不正確。選項 B 正確，因為教授說，最初的棉被製作者用報紙做出圖形，並將其用作襯裡。

6. **A** 組織結構題

〔**解析**〕開頭語之後，教授從最早的棉被（埃及和中國）講起，一直談到美洲殖民時期的棉被，最後說下個星期的課上她會講 19 世紀的棉被。因此選項 A「In chronological order」（按時間順序）正確。

③ 生命科學常考主題 1 動物學詞彙、答案、解析和錄音原文

● **Answer Key to Exercise 1**

a. Linnaeus used the structural similarities of plants and animals to classify them.

b. Scientists were surprised to learn that crows could make basic tools because they thought that only primates could make tools.

c. Large populations of gray squirrels and fox squirrels are usually unable to co-exist as one of the species seems to drive the other away.

閱讀模擬試題答案詳解
- -

1. **C** 語境詞彙題

   〔**解析**〕有些考生可能會以為 rear 的意思是 back（後面），所以誤選 D。選項 C「brought up」與 rear 同義，為「撫養，養育」之意，為正確答案。

2. **D** 推論題

   〔**解析**〕本題難度較大，因為文中並未直接給出資訊。文中講到，即使是在遠離自然棲息地長大的動物也能夠搭建巢穴。從中可以推斷，這些動物沒有機會直接觀察如何搭建巢穴，所以選項 B 和 C 不正確。選項 A（父母所教）也不正確，因為第一段提到，動物不具有認知能力。由於動物們只是機械地完成一個任務後就開始下一個任務，所以推斷選項 D 正確。

3. **B** 語境詞彙題

   〔**解析**〕四個選項中只有 B「inborn」與 innate 意思相同，意為「天生的」。

4. **A** 修辭目的題

   〔**解析**〕從文中「像人類礦工一樣」可知，作者是在講述白蟻，因而選項 B 和 D（將白蟻與人類作比較）都不正確。選項 C 曲解了 remove so much earth 的意思。只有選項 A 正確，因為文中說，白蟻和人類都需要在移除土壤後構建地下結構。

5. **C** 指代關係題

   〔**解析**〕本題設計得比較巧妙，所有選項都是複數形式，且所考的代名詞前面有一個表示比較的片語（like human miners）。此處代名詞 they 指代前面的 individuals, who...，所以選項 C 正確。

6. **B** 細節資訊題

   〔**解析**〕文中並未提及茅草屋頂，所以選項 A 不正確。選項 C 也不正確，因為蟻穴朝向太陽並不能保護蟻穴免遭雨災。本段也未提及土墩，所以選項 D 不正確。第四段中說，煙囪看起來像是「多層的寶塔」，有防雨的效果，所以選項 B 正確。

7. **D** 否定事實題

   〔**解析**〕選項 A 正確，因為第四段中說：all termite nests begin underground，該段還說所有洞穴都有一間 chamber for the king and queen，所以選項 B 也正確。第五段說白蟻 must tunnel up 50 meters to forage for vegetation and seeds，所以選項 C 也正確。選項 D 不正確，因為第五段講到，有些種類的白蟻「慢慢地吃掉（slowly consume）」其洞穴周圍的樹木。

8. **C** 語境詞彙

   〔**解析**〕選項 A「inhale」意為「吸入」，選項 B「waste」是 dissipate 的一個釋義。與此類似，熱量散發後，溫度下降，所以選項 D 也很容易被誤選。考查詞所在的句子中，產生的熱量必須被「趕走」，這樣白蟻才不會死去。所以選項 C 正確。

9. **D** 推論題

   〔**解析**〕選項 A 不正確，因為文中沒有提到昆蟲的大小。選項 B 不正確，因為非洲白蟻洞穴外面

的空氣比地下洞穴中的空氣溫度高。選項 C 不正確，因為雖然溫度會升高或降低，但白蟻洞穴的空氣調節設施可以應對這一變化。選項 D 正確，因為非洲白蟻顯示出具有通過空氣流動體系控制溫度的能力，牠們是具有一定智慧的白蟻物種。

10. **C** 細節資訊題

【**解析**】第七段講到非洲白蟻時說，「沒有兩處洞穴是相似的（no two nests are ever alike）」，因為它們為達到某個具體的實際目標而「選擇最恰當的（choose the most appropriate）」方法，而方法是不太可能一樣的。

11. ■ **2** 句子插入題

Consider, for example, the African species *Macrotermes bellicosus*, whose nests in the Ivory Coast were studied in detail by Martin Luescher. The nests are built so that air may circulate: ■ 1 Cool air is drawn up from a cellar into an attic by the heat produced by the biological processes of the termites and by the fungi that they grow. ■ 2 This cooler air descends through the buttresses, until the air enters the cellar, where it is cooled even further by contact with the subsoil. The air is then directed to the ten or so buttresses that project from the base to near the top of the above-ground portion of the nest. ■ 3 Through holes in these interconnecting buttresses, warm carbon dioxiderich air from the attic is exchanged with the cooler, oxygen-rich air outside. ■ 4

【**解析**】此題比較容易。air 最先出現在第三句中的片語 cool air 裡，加粗的句子中說 this cooler air，從而不難判斷該句應插在第二個標記處。

12.

Types of animal cognition	Behaviors
Able to solve problems when building a shelter	• 2. Revises actions in the middle of a plan • 5. Evaluates progress toward goal • 6. Visualizes an end target
Not able to solve problems when building a shelter	• 1. Carries out a sequence of task-oriented steps • 4. Ends one innate task and begins the next

資訊歸類題

【**解析**】要想正確回答此題，考生必須先弄清楚動物認知的兩種類型：第一行空格處要求選擇表明動物具有解決問題能力的行為，第二行空格處則要求選擇表明動物不具有解決問題能力的行為。第一段末尾處提到的「執行一系列任務步驟（Carries out a sequence of task-oriented steps）」和「結束一項內在型任務後又開始下一個任務（Ends one innate task and begins the next）」不是用來表明動物具有「認知能力」的，而是表明動物不具有解決問題能力的例證。第三個選項和第七個選項所描述的內容在文中都沒有提及，所以不能選擇。

聽力模擬試題錄音文本 **Track 005**

N: Now listen to part of a lecture in a zoology class.

P: Today we'll continue to explore the sea animals who do not have backbones, moving from squids to octopuses. Last week we got to know squids, which, you'll remember, retain a slight trace of shell, or hard bone, from their evolutionary ancestors. Like squids, octopuses have evolved from hard-shelled ancestors. But unlike squids, the octopus has an entirely soft body—with no internal or external skeleton.

Octopuses are highly developed animals, more developed than most other animals without backbones. As we go through this unit, you'll want to pay close attention to the nervous system, especially that involving the brain and the nerve cells located on each of the eight arms.

Of course, the eight arms are the best known feature of octopuses. In everyday language, many people call these "legs," but the correct term, the term that I'd like for all of you to use, is "arms". Some people think the scientific term for octopus arms is "tentacle". A tentacle refers to a long structure with sucking organs, at the very tip, and as we saw last week, squids have two tentacles and many "arms." But octopuses do not have "tentacles" like squids do, in the strict scientific sense of the word.

OK, moving on to the rest of the octopus. All the body organs, including the breathing organs—the gills—are stored in a muscular bag. By expanding and contracting, this bag pumps water in and out, allowing oxygen to be absorbed. The exhaled water can provide a jet-like movement for the octopus by forcing water out. In other words, an octopus can move forwards or backwards very quickly—similar to the jet movement we saw in squids. Over the years, squids and octopuses have both evolved to propel themselves quickly—for reasons of efficiency and survival.

Now then, let's talk more about the bodily processes and behaviors of the octopus. We have said that octopuses are soft-bodied animals; they don't have an external shell or an internal skeleton. This means that they are able to squeeze through tiny holes into cracks in rocks, where they hide. But it also means that they are particularly vulnerable to attack by their predators, which include sharks, seals and eels. However, octopuses have developed even more ways to defend themselves.

The first—and most amazing—line of defense is its ability to hide in plain sight. Using a network of pigment cells and specialized muscles in its skin, the octopus can camouflage itself, matching the colors, patterns, and even textures of its surroundings. Predators swim by without even noticing it.

A second type of defense is ink. When the octopus is discovered by a shark, for example, it will often release a cloud of black ink to obscure the shark's view. This ink contains a substance that dulls the shark's sense of smell, making tracking more difficult. Additionally, as I have mentioned, octopuses are fast swimmers when they need to be. So a third type of defense is flight. Octopuses spend most of the time at rest, but they can quickly jet in any direction if a predator threatens.

And, as a last resort—if the octopus is not able to free itself from, say, a shark's jaws, it can sacrifice an arm in order to escape. Later, the octopus is able to grow it back, good as new.

S: I saw a video on the Internet of an octopus walking on two feet... I mean, two "arms." Was that for real?

P: [laughing] Yes. Very true.

S: You'd think that the other six arms would get in the way...

P: Yeah, you would. But scientists have observed that, when an octopus walks on two arms, the other six are pulled up under its body.

S: It's so comical to see them like that; they're like people, just taking a little stroll...

P: [interrupting, in a solemn tone] Yeah, what we've learned is that an octopus's very survival may sometimes depend on this "walking" behavior. When an octopus is camouflaged, it's standing still. But when a shark arrives out of the blue, if the octopus starts to swim away, it gives up that camouflage. On the other hand, if the octopus starts slowly "walking" away, it can maintain its camouflage, blending into the background until it is safely out of reach.

● **Transcripts for Question 4.**

N: Listen again to part of the talk. Then answer the question.

P: But scientists have observed that, when an octopus walks on two arms, the other six are pulled up under its body.

S: It's so comical to see them like that; they're like people, just taking a little stroll…

P: [interrupting, in a solemn tone] Yeah, what we've learned is that an octopus's very survival may sometimes depend on this "walking" behavior.

N: What is the professor's attitude toward the actions of the octopus described by the woman?

關鍵語塊

backbone 脊柱	trace of... ……的痕跡
evolutionary ancestor 進化的先祖	internal skeleton 內骨骼
external skeleton 外骨骼	pay close attention to 密切關注
nervous system 神經系統	nerve cell 神經元；神經細胞
scientific term 科學術語	sucking organ 吮吸器官
moving on to 話題轉移到；接著做	gill 腮
jet movement 噴氣式運動	squeeze through 擠過去，勉強通過
vulnerable to 易受……的攻擊	predator 食肉動物，掠食動物
seal 海豹	eel 泥鰍
defend oneself / defend oneself against 保護自己免受……的傷害	in plain sight 清晰可見
pigment 色素	camouflage 偽裝
texture 紋理	obscure 使模糊不清
tracking 追蹤	flight 逃跑
free oneself from 從……逃脫	jaw 下巴
sacrifice an arm 犧牲一個腕足	grow back 再生
good as new 像新的一樣	for real 真的
get in the way 阻礙，妨礙	(octopus's) very survival （章魚）得以倖存
out of the blue 突然	out of reach 夠不到

聽力模擬試題答案詳解

1. **D** 主旨大意題
   〔**解析**〕選項 A「無脊椎動物的結構」顯然偏離了主題。選項 B 不正確，因為講座圍繞章魚而不是魷魚展開的。選項 C 不正確，因為棲息地並不是講座的主題。選項 D「（章魚的）生物機能」是講座的中心內容，主要談了章魚如何呼吸並保護自己。

2. **D** 細節資訊題
   〔**解析**〕教授說科學術語 tentacle 用於指魷魚的觸鬚是準確的，但用於指章魚的「手臂」就不準確了，由此可知 tentacle 一詞常被誤用，所以選項 D 正確。

3. **B** 細節資訊題
   〔**解析**〕文中提到，噴氣式運動（jet movement）使章魚能在水裡快速運動，所以選項 B 正確。

4. **A** 立場觀點題

〔**解析**〕回答此題時，考生必須注意教授的語氣和用詞。當學生提到走路的章魚時，教授說「章魚的生死有時就取決於這一『行走』行為」。very survival 與 a matter of life and death 同義，所以選項 A 正確。

5.

Characteristic	Squids	Octopuses	Both squids and octopuses
Retains a trace of hard shell or bone	✓		
Use jet propulsion			✓
More developed than most animals without backbones		✓	
Has multiple arms			✓

關聯內容題

〔**解析**〕根據教授所說：Like squids, octopuses have evolved from hard-shelled ancestors. But unlike squids, the octopus has an entirely soft body... 第一個特點應在 Squids 欄打勾。根據教授所說：In other words, an octopus can move forwards or backwards very quickly—similar to the jet movement we saw in squids. 第二個特點應在 Both squids and octopuses 欄打勾。教授直接提到章魚比大多數其他無脊椎動物都進化得好，所以第三個特點應在 Octopuses 欄打勾。最後一個特點應在 Both squids and octopuses 欄打勾，因為教授說魷魚有兩條觸鬚，很多腕足，章魚有八條腕足。

● **Answer Key to Exercise 2**

下面是一份真實的筆記。注意記筆記者是如何使用縮寫以及其他記號來表示重要詞語和觀點的。

社會科學常考主題 1 心理學詞彙、答案、解析和錄音原文

閱讀模擬試題答案詳解

1. **D** 語境詞彙題
   〔**解析**〕選項中只有 examine 與 scrutinize 意思相同,意為「檢查,仔細察看」。

2. **A** 修辭目的題
   〔**解析**〕此題有一定難度,考生必須完全理解單字 scale(衡量標準)和語塊 overlapping terminology(意思相近的術語)的意思。幾個術語具有 overlapping meanings,是説它們的含義相近但又不完全相同,所以 A 為正確答案。如果考生誤以為作者是在介紹新衡量標準裡的術語,就有可能誤選 D。

3. **A** 否定事實題
   〔**解析**〕第一段作者講到,名稱相同的標準經常被用來衡量不同的概念,而名稱不同的標準反而經常被用來衡量相近的概念,由此可推斷,這些描述性的術語的用法經常不一致,B 的説法正確。作者在 overlapping terminology 中提到相似的名稱,所以選項 C 的説法正確。作者説 number of traits 大大增加了,所以選項 D 的説法也正確。只有選項 A 説有些特點被排除在衡量標準以外,與原文內容不相符,原文中作者是説對特點的描述過多了。所以選項 A 為正確答案。

4. **B** 細節資訊題
   〔**解析**〕見本章前文的「托福總監評析」。

5. **C** 語境詞彙題
   〔**解析**〕在上下文中,peer 和 colleague 是同義詞,意為「同事」,所以選項 C 正確。文中的 peers 是指建立理論模型的精神病學家,working psychologists 是指級別較低但從事臨床工作的專業心理學人員。選項 D 不正確,因為學生是創立不了 factor structures 的。

6. **B** 細節資訊題
   〔**解析**〕此題相對容易。選項 A 不正確,因為作者説採集多種樣本,而不是説軍人的人格具有多面性。選項 C 曲解了 refined 的意思,文中是説科學家們 refined(改進了)由 Fiske 提出的 22 個因素結構。通過對八個樣本的分析,科學家們在 Fiske 的研究成果基礎上提出了「人類性格特點的五大分類」,因此選項 B 正確。

7. **C** 語境詞彙題
   〔**解析**〕calculate 意為「計算」,balance 意為「平衡」,combine 意為「組合」,均與 to account for 的意思不符。動詞片語 to account for 的同義表達為 to explain,為「解釋」之意,因此選項 C 正確。

8. **B** 語境詞彙題
   〔**解析**〕選項中只有 investigate 與片語動詞 delve into 同義,意為「深入調查;鑽研」,所以選項 B 正確。

9. **D** 句子簡化題
   〔**解析**〕此題較難。所給句子是個否定句,而且包含一個受詞子句。選項 A 中的 It is further possible that... 與所給句開頭的 moreover 近義,容易被誤選,但是 A 並不正確,因為其中的否定詞修飾的只是 more than five traits。選項 B 也容易被誤選,因為 lack of structure 有可能被誤解為 reduced to a mere five traits,但是文中的原句並沒有關於 sample size(樣本大小)的資訊。選項 C 與所給句的意思相近,但有細微的差別:所給句中沒有説性格差異比我們想像的還要大。只有選項 D 與所給句的意思完全符合,one should not assume from the structure that 與 the structure does not imply that... 是同義説法。

10. **A** 細節資訊題

〔**解析**〕在第七段中作者寫道：More than one critic has argued that it does not provide a complete theory of personality. I don't disagree. 從第二句「我並沒有不同意」可知，選項 A 是正確答案。選項 B 不正確，因為作者說該模型提供了 insights into regularities in behavior。選項 C 不正確，因為作者說「五大分類體系」的研究物件是性格特點而非人類個體。選項 D 不正確，因為作者說「五大分類體系」對研究者有幫助。

11. **C** 修辭目的題

〔**解析**〕此題相對容易。選項 C 正確，因為作者先列舉了不同性格標準存在的各種問題，然後論述「五大分類」模式在很多方面使問題得以解決。有些考生可能會誤選 A，但實際上，文中並未給出 traits 和 scales 的定義。選項 B 不正確，因為文章開頭部分沒有介紹具體模式，而是講問題在於衡量標準過多，而且很多描述性術語具有重疊含義。選項 D 不正確，因為作者是在最後才說出最新的研究成果「五大分類」模式，而不是一開始就說。

12. **■ 1** 插入句子題

... What made matters worse was that scales with the same name often measured concepts that were not the same, and scales with different names often measured concepts that were quite similar. **■ 1** **This proliferation of different measurement approaches and descriptive terminology also made it extremely difficult for researchers to interpret all the findings and to communicate clearly with one another**.

What personality psychologists needed was an overarching descriptive model, or taxonomy, of its subject matter. **■ 2** It was hoped that such a framework would permit researchers to work with a few specified domains of personality characteristics, rather than examining separately the thousands of particular traits that make human beings individual and unique. **■ 3** On a practical level, a generally accepted taxonomy could greatly facilitate the professional communication of empirical findings by offering a standard vocabulary, or nomenclature. **■ 4**

〔**解析**〕第一個標記處正確，原因是：首先，粗體句子開頭的 this proliferation 指的是第一段描述的性格衡量標準存在的問題；其次，第二段開頭的句子：What personality psychologists needed was... 可以引出對問題解決方法的論述。因此，只有第一個標記處符合邏輯。

13. **2** Social scientists engaged in personality research were able to identify five separate factors.

3 The large number of personality scales has puzzled many practicing psychologists, who are not sure how each relates to the other.

6 By creating a classification system with broad categories, researchers allowed practitioners a way to better communicate with one another.

內容總結題

〔**解析**〕第一個選項不正確，因為作者並未說過那些術語是錯誤的，而是說具有相似含義的術語過多，結果導致混亂。第二個選項正確，因為 Fiske 和其他研究人員確定了具有五個因素的一種性格體系。第三個選項正確，因為作者在第一、二自然段用了大量篇幅論述由於衡量標準過多，以致人們難以理解每個標準衡量的是什麼。第四個選項很容易排除，因為儘管文中提到 extrovert 是具有重疊性含義的術語之一，但這並不是文章的主要觀點。第五個選項不正確，因為本文是針對人類性格而言，而非人的種類。最後一個選項是對文中 [The Big Five] provides a conceptual foundation that helps researchers and practitioners delve into these theoretical issues. 一句所表達觀點的擴展，是正確答案。

● **Answer Key to Exercise1**

a. We know more about individual personality differences from what these various methods have taught us.

b. The factor structure that was created could probably take in all the possible personality types in the world.

c. The Big Five classification system is not perfect; no theoretical model is.

聽力模擬試題錄音文本   **Track 007**

N: Now listen to part of a lecture in a psychology class.

P: So far, in our exploration of human behavior, we've seen how very complex human motivations can be, and how motivational urges are in constant flux. One way of classifying human motivation is to talk about motivation in the context of needs. Now, let me ask all of you: Do you think that human beings need the same things that other animals need? [pause] Human needs are tremendously broad in type and scope. In the 1940s, the psychologist Abraham Maslow proposed that the order—or sequence—in which we satisfy our needs is based on certain fixed principles. That is to say, the order in which we satisfy our needs forms a hierarchy—or framework—that affects our motivations.

How then did Maslow come up with this hierarchy? Early in his career, the psychologist worked with monkeys. He noticed that, for the monkeys, certain needs took precedence over others. For example, if a monkey was hungry and thirsty, it would try to take care of its thirst first. That's because a monkey can do without food for a week or so, but it can only live without water for a couple of days. Thirst is a "more powerful" or more dominant need than hunger. So, based on this observation, Maslow turned his focus to humans, and came up with five "levels" of need.

Now what do you think would be the most dominant need in humans? [pause] Yes?

S: Professor Smith, I think that we all need friendships—or, I guess we could call it "human love."

P: Well, Maslow would tell you that if you say what you need most is love, that means you're getting plenty to eat at the student cafeteria. Let me explain in another way. Another word for the "dominant" need is the most "basic" need.

And the most basic need has to be fulfilled first, as a precondition, before we can start thinking about the other needs. To be sure, humans have a definite need for receiving love and affection. But love is not the first level of need—in fact love comes at level three of Maslow's hierarchy. Our most basic human needs are physiological ones—our need for air, food, and water. And in that respect, we are not so different from the monkeys that Maslow observed.

So what is the second category of need? Maslow says that after our needs for basics like food and water are met, the new set of needs that emerges is called "security" needs. In prehistoric communities, an example of a security need would be humans wanting to live in an environment that is safe from wild animals. In modern societies, examples of security needs are things such as a preference to be around familiar things rather than unfamiliar things. We desire the security of a savings account and medical insurance.

The third level, um, comes when both physiological and security needs are well gratified, and this third level is when Maslow says the need for love emerges. A person who is at this level will feel the need for friends, a romantic counterpart, a spouse or children. An obvious example of the need for affection is the desire to get married. Another example is the desire to work in a company with a lot of co-workers.

Continuing up our need's pyramid. [pause] Most people need to think well of themselves; they need self-esteem. But people also want the respect of other people. How does a person get self-esteem? Through strength and achievement. How does a person get prestige? Through recognition by others. If my need for self-esteem is met, I'll have feelings of self-confidence and self-worth. But, if my need for self-esteem is not met, I'll feel inferior and helpless. Let's see now. A situation involving a satisfied need for achievement would be, say, if I were a young salesperson who'd just made her first big sale; whereas an instance of a person's need for recognition would be—well, say, a young man receiving a pat on the back from his boss at a meeting.

Finally, when these four needs are essentially satisfied, a new discontent may soon develop. This fifth need we call self-actualization, a person's desire for self-fulfillment. Every person wants to be able to develop his or her potential.

● **Transcripts for Question 3**

N: Listen again to part of the talk. Then answer the question.

P: Now what do you think would be the most dominant need in humans? [pause] Yes?

S: Professor Smith, I think that we all need friendships—or, I guess we could call it "human love."

P: Well, Maslow would tell you that if you say what you need most is love, that means you're getting plenty to eat at the student cafeteria. Let me explain in another way. Another word for the "dominant" need is the most "basic" need.

N: What can be inferred about the professor when she says this:

P: Well, Maslow would tell you that if you say what you need most is love, that means you're getting plenty to eat at the student cafeteria.

● **Transcripts for Question 4**

N: Listen again to part of the talk. Then answer the question.

P: Let's see now. A situation involving a satisfied need for achievement would be, say, if I were a young salesperson who'd just made her first big sale; whereas an instance of a person's need for recognition would be—well, say, a young man receiving a pat on the back from his boss at a meeting.

N: Why does the professor say this:

P: say, if I were a young salesperson who'd just made her first big sale

關鍵語塊

exploration of 對……的探索	complex 複雜的
human motivation 人類的動機	urge 強烈慾望
in constant flux 處於不斷變化中	in the context of 在……的背景下
Abraham Maslow 亞伯拉罕‧馬斯洛（提出人類動機學說的心理學家）	fixed principle 不變的原理
come up with 想出，提出	... takes precedence over... ……比……重要
take care of its thirst first 先解決口渴問題	can do without... 沒有……也行

dominant need 最主要的需求	precondition 前提
physiological 生理學的	prehistoric 史前的
be safe from... 不會受到……傷害的	preference to be... 偏愛……，優先選擇……
savings account 儲蓄帳戶	medical insurance 醫療保險
co-worker 同事	pyramid 金字塔
think well of someone 對某人有好感，重視某人	self-esteem 自尊
prestige 聲望，威望	feel inferior 自慚形穢
discontent 不滿；不滿意	develop one's potential 發展某人的潛力

聽力模擬試題答案詳解

1. **C** 主旨大意題

   〔解析〕選項 A 和 D 的論述過於片面。選項 B 不正確，因為 hierarchy in social groups 指的是社會等級，與主題不符。該講座闡釋了 Maslow 提出的「五大需要」的順序，因此選項 C 正確。

2. **A** 組織結構題

   〔解析〕此題相對簡單。教授在講到「安全需要」時，提到史前人類會選擇居住在沒有野生動物的環境中，也就是說野生動物會對他們的安全形成威脅，故答案為 A。

3. **A** 立場觀點題

   〔解析〕見本章前文的「托福總監評析」。

4. **D** 語用功能題

   〔解析〕選項 B 不正確，因為教授在講座中並未探討年輕人的心理。選項 C 不正確，因為教授不是在談論 instant rewards。教授說她想給出一個 satisfied need for achievement 的例子，而之前她所用的另一個同義說法就是 (need for) self-esteem，所以選項 D 正確。

5.

	Type of Need		
	Security	**Love**	**Esteem**
Insurance	✓		
Strength			✓
Spouse		✓	
Familiar things	✓		

   關聯內容題

   〔解析〕標題 Type of Need 是教授談論的五種需要中的後三種。教授在講座中把 savings account and medical insurance 用作安全需要的例子；她還說到一個人通過 strength and achievement 獲得自尊；當教授談論第四類需要（愛的需要）時，她給的例子是人會需要尋找配偶並希望結婚；最後一行的 familiar things 應屬於 Security 的範疇，因為教授說：… examples of security needs are things such as a preference to be around familiar things rather than unfamiliar things.

● **Answer Key to Exercise 2**

   <u>She wants to encourage student discussion about the different needs in humans and animals.</u>
   <u>/ She wants the students to contrast human needs with animal needs.</u>
   <u>/ She wants to show how the need for food and security are the same in humans and animals.</u>

⑤ 物理科學常考主題 2 地質學和地震學詞彙、答案、解析和錄音原文

● **Answer Key to Exercise1**

a. Although the on-site warning approach is extremely fast, it is not as reliable.

b. In contrast to the Mercalli intensity scale, the Richter measurement scale does not have a measurement "ceiling" for an earthquake's magnitude.

c. Because molten rock comes up to the Earth's surface relatively slowly, it cools slowly and thus turns into minerals with large-size crystals. This is in contrast to volcanic rock, which forms smaller crystals because it cools rapidly.

閱讀模擬試題答案詳解

1. **B** 細節資訊題

〔解析〕做對這道題目需要知道作者是如何定義 nucleation 的。快速瀏覽第一段不難找到 yet until we understand nucleation... 的說法，後面緊接著就是對 nucleation 所下的定義：the earliest phase of an earthquake。選項 B「the initiating process of an earthquake」是該定義的同義說法。

2. **B** 細節資訊題

〔解析〕選項 B 中的 the ongoing process of seismic waves 與文中 ground motion as a continuous function of time 是同義說法，因此選項 B 正確。文中並未提到 1800 年以前的地震儀，也沒有內容顯示 1800 年的地震儀比之前的不重要，故選項 A 的說法不正確。選項 C 看似正確，但實則不然，因為地震儀是用來測量地震的 ground motion 的，而不是測量地球內部的 permanent rupture 的。選項 D 不正確，因為其描述的是第二段段尾處提到的相對更先進的技術。

3 **D** 語境詞彙題

〔解析〕只有 take advantage of 是 exploit 的同義表達，意為「利用」，故 D 為正確答案。

4. **A** 指代關係題

〔解析〕此題不難。我們知道 information 與 inform 是同根詞，information 可用來表明某種決定或過程，因此選項 A 正確。選項 C「matter」位於表示時間的片語 in a matter of seconds to minutes 中，不符合上下文意思。

5. **D** 修辭目的題

〔解析〕第三段最後一句指出，fast speed of radio waves 接近光速，這兩種速度都比地震波速快。作者將無線電波與光波作比較的目的是為了說明無線電波的傳播速度非常快，可作為預報地震的重要工具。因此選項 D 正確。選項 A 不是作者的主要觀點；選項 B 說法不正確。

6. **C** 句子簡化題

〔解析〕選項 A 中的 impossible 與原文中 proved far more difficult 不符，並且漏掉了原句中的重要資訊：some progress has been made。選項 B 誤解了 although 引導的子句的意思。選項 D 中的第二個分句說法不準確。只有選項 C 與原句同義（a few breakthroughs = some progress; unexpected challenges = have proved far more difficult to build），為正確答案。

7. **A** 語境詞彙題

〔解析〕選項中只有 simultaneous to 與 concurrent with 同義，意為「與……同時」，故 A 為正確答案。

8. **B** 細節資訊題

〔解析〕選項 A 看似正確，但作者說的是 P 波先開始，而 S 波和表面波都是隨後產生的，因此 A

不正確。選項 C 和選項 D 都不正確，因為它們指的是區域性報警方法和傳統方法。選項 B 中的 monitoring the earliest ground motion 與 the beginning of the ground motion 同義，因此是正確答案。

9. **C** 語境詞彙題

〔**解析**〕選項中只有 length 與名詞 duration 同義，意為「持續長度」，故 C 為正確答案。

10. **D** 推論題

〔**解析**〕文章第六段指出，地震早期預警的兩種方法都有各自的缺陷，故 D 正確。選項 A 看似正確，實則不然，因為作者說第一種方法可靠，可用於傳遞長距離地震運動的資訊，但耗時長；第二種方法不可靠，但適用於短距離的地震。

11. ■ **1** 插入句子題

Nevertheless, instrumentation does enable us to track earthquakes once they begin. ■ 1 Seismometers have been in existence for more than 1,800 years, a seismograph that represents earthquake ground motion as a continuous function of time was invented in the 19th century. ■ 2 More recently, geophysicists have exploited new technologies to lessen earthquake damage by using "real-time" seismology, in which seismic data are collected and analyzed very quickly after a seismic event.

■ 3 Scientists are handicapped by the fact that in most cases the timescale involved in real-time seismology runs from minutes to hours. ■ 4 By the time the data is released, the earthquake is over, and the information can be used only for post-earthquake emergency responses, field work planning, and public information...

〔**解析**〕需要插入的句子以 nevertheless 開頭，表明該句會引入一個相反的觀點。第一段最後一句說，如果我們不能較好地瞭解地震的早期階段，就無法預測地震。在第二段中，第一個標記處後面講的都是地震發生後能夠測量地震的儀器。因此第一個標記處為正確答案。

12.

Type of early warning system	Characteristics of system
Regional	• 1. Transmission range contains a big section that gets no signal • 5. Provides more accurate information on distant ground motion • 7. Preferable for tracking the earthquake epicenter
On-site	• 2. Better choice for site areas that are not too far away • 3. Measures ground motions at the beginning of the rupture

資訊歸類題

〔**解析**〕作者從第五段開始到文末對兩種地震預警系統進行了比較。第一個選項是區域預警系統的特點之一，因為文中說該系統 encompasses a fairly large "blind zone"。第二個選項比較容易判斷，實地預警系統只能用於預測同一地點的運動。第三個選項為實地地震預警系統的特點，因為作者說：In an on-site warning approach, the beginning of the ground motion (mainly P waves)... 第五個選項是區域地震預警系統的特點，因為作者說區域地震預警系統能夠在其他地點預測地面運動。第七個選項應填在區域地震預警系統下，因為作者說該系統會使用傳統的方法來確定地震的震中。

文中並未提到這兩種系統可以預測別的地方的餘震，也未提到如何計算地震的危害程度，所以第四個和第六個選項描述的內容都不符合兩種系統的特點。

聽力模擬試題錄音文本 **Track 009**
- -

N: Now listen to part of a lecture in a Geology class.

P: OK, let's get going; we have a lot to cover. Today we'll talk about some of the physical processes governing the formation of the great basins on the Earth's surface. We learned last time that basins are deep depressions on the surface of the ocean floor. We looked at some land features in these ocean basins and saw some satellite images. Do you remember the photo of the underwater ocean ridge in the Atlantic Ocean? The reason I ask is that ridge is actually an underwater mountain and is part of a much longer mountain chain running down the middle of the ocean. In fact, the entire mid-ocean ridge system is extremely long, even longer than any single continent. So we've already observed many of the features at the bottom of the ocean. But today we're going to move beyond just observing landforms and start to answer some of the "why's". In particular, we're going to answer the question "Why do ocean and continental crusts on the Earth's surface behave the way they do?"

We can answer this question by using the theory of the Earth's plates, or plate tectonics.

We know, of course, that the hard outer layer of the Earth's crust covers the entire surface of the Earth. But this rocky, brittle outer layer is broken up into a lot of large plates. Some people say that there are about 14 plates; others say there are 10. No matter which, it's clear that seven of these plates occupy most of the Earth's surface area. Each plate is relatively thin and quite rigid—like a flat dinner plate. Not much happens at the inner part of the plates. Almost all changes to their form take place at the plate's edges. Not surprisingly, then, the edges are also where almost all earthquake activity takes place.

OK, so the Earth's crust is broken into many pieces, broken into plates which are large, movable segments. More importantly, these plates are all in motion relative to one another.

Which leads us to our discussion of plate boundaries? As I said, the Earth's plates are moving, are interacting with each other. So in total, there are three types of plate boundaries. Divergent boundaries, convergent boundaries and transform boundaries.

Let me define these three terms for you. Very briefly, divergent plate boundaries are when two plates are diverging; that is to say they are moving away from each other. In divergent boundaries, a new layer of crust gets created when melted rock is pushed up from the sea floor. In contrast, convergent boundaries are where two plates are converging, or coming together. When convergent plates bump into each other, old crust is destroyed. And then there is another type of boundary, called transform boundaries, where plates simply move past one another. I don't have time to go into this third type of boundary today.

Instead, what I'd like to really focus on today is convergent plate boundaries, the situations where plates are moving together.

There are three different types of convergent boundaries. These are easy to remember, because they cover all the logical possibilities for combining ocean plates and continental plates.

What are the three types? The first type of convergent boundary is the ocean-ocean boundary. In the ocean-ocean boundary, one of the two plates moves under the other one, forming a narrow and very deep depression, called an ocean trench. Ocean-ocean collisions lead to the formation of volcanic island chains, chains in the shape of a curved arc such as we see in Japan and New Zealand. Now the second type of convergent plate boundary is the ocean–continent boundary. When the colder, denser ocean plate comes together with land plate, or as it is better known, a "continental" plate, the ocean plate gets pushed underneath the continental plate. The sinking end of the ocean plate melts, and that creates pressure deep in the Earth. And because part of the ocean plate has melted, molten rock and gases rise to the surface. That action can cause violent volcanoes to form on the land, on the continental plate. We can find an example of this on the South American coast, along the Peru-Chile trench.

Last but not least, the third type of convergent boundary is obviously the continent-continent boundary. When two continental plates collide, these land plates may buckle and compress; or one plate may slide under the other one. Either of these actions will create long mountain ranges. The most famous example of a continent-continent boundary is the Himalayas. In those mountains, the continental Indian Plate has been pushed northwards under part of the central Asian plate, lifting up the central Asian plate and creating the Himalayan mountain range and the high plateaus in Tibet.

● **Transcripts for Question 3**

N: Listen again to part of the lecture. Then answer the question.

P: But today we're going to move beyond just observing landforms and start to answer some of the "why's". In particular, we're going to answer the question "Why do ocean and continental crusts on the Earth's surface behave the way they do?"

N: What can be inferred about the professor when she says this:

P: But today we're going to move beyond just observing landforms and start to answer some of the "why's".

關鍵語塊

Let's get going. 我們趕快開始吧。	ocean basin 洋盆
landform 地形，地貌	ocean ridge 洋脊，海嶺
mountain chain 山脈	continent 大陸；洲
plate tectonics 板塊構造論	continental crust 大陸地殼
brittle 脆的；易碎的	rigid 堅硬的
in motion relative to one another 在相對運動中	divergent boundary 擴張型邊界
convergent boundary 聚合型邊界	transform boundary 轉換型邊界
bump into each other 互相撞擊	go into (this) 詳細描述（這一點）
ocean-ocean boundary 海洋板塊與海洋板塊的邊界	trench 海溝
volcanic island chain 火山群島	arc 弧，拱形
molten rock 熔化的岩石	violent volcano 猛烈的火山
Peru-Chile trench 秘魯到智利的海溝	last but not least 最後但並非不重要的
buckle 使彎曲	compress 擠壓
plateau 高原	

聽力模擬試題答案詳解

1. **C** 主旨大意題

   〔解析〕選項 A 不正確，教授開場白時提到了該項內容，但這是對上一節課內容的回顧。選項 B 和 D 是講座中提到的次要話題。地球板塊的會合是教授講座的主要內容，並給出了很多例證，因此選項 C 是正確答案。

2. **D** 細節資訊題

〔**解析**〕教授在講座開頭就提到了大西洋海嶺，並清楚地告訴學生需要特別注意這一內容，因為大西洋海嶺實際上是一個更長的海嶺體系的一部分。因此選項 D 正確。

3. **B** 推論題

〔**解析**〕教授説不再討論對地貌的觀測，因此選項 A 不正確。教授鼓勵學生思考一些原因，包括物理作用怎樣改變了地貌。因此選項 B 正確。

4. **A** 細節資訊題

〔**解析**〕教授説板塊的變化大多發生在邊緣位置，但並未説邊緣位置有層次，因此選項 B 不正確。講座中未對海洋的深度和大陸板塊的厚度進行比較，因此選項 C 不正確。選項 D 也不正確，因為科學家對板塊的數量尚無一致意見，只是有些人估計有 14 個。教授只提到了板塊的不容易改變性，因此選項 A 正確。

5.

	Converging Boundary Types		
	Continent-Continent	Ocean-Continent	Ocean-Ocean
Forms deep trenches and island chains			✓
Forms high mountains such as Himalayas	✓		
Forms explosive volcanoes when plate partly melts		✓	

關聯內容題

〔**解析**〕此題並不難，但要想正確作答，考生需要記錄下教授對板塊邊界類型的定義和解釋。教授説：Ocean-ocean collisions lead to the formation of volcanic island chains... 教授以喜馬拉雅山脈為例説明了 continent-continent boundary；在解釋完海洋和大陸板塊的會合後，教授説此種運動 can cause violent volcanoes to form on the land。

● **Answer Key to Exercise 2**

	Converging	Diverging
New crust is formed from melted rock		✓
Plates bump into one another	✓	
Ocean plate may slip under land plate	✓	

⑥ 人文藝術常考主題 2 文學詞彙、答案、解析和錄音原文

● Answer Key to Exercise 1

a. In referring to Elizabeth Bishop as a "poet's poet", the author of the passage suggests that her poetry was respected only by other poets.

b. From our reading the novel *Daisy Miller*, what can be concluded about the everyday lives of wealthy women in the 19th century?

c. We can assume that John Updike was knowledgeable about science because he wrote poems on technical themes like neutrinos and planets.

閱讀模擬試題答案詳解

1. **D** 細節資訊題
   〔解析〕作者沒有提到經濟或爵士樂，因此選項 A 和選項 C 都不正確。選項 B 沒有把握原文的深層含義，所以不正確。選項 D 正確，因為作者說該詩 traced the continuous river of black history。

2. **C** 細節資訊題
   〔解析〕選項 D 是用來混淆視聽的，有些考生可能會貿然得出結論：Hughes 此時只想閱讀非洲出版物。正確答案應為 C，關鍵在於是否理解 symbolically discarding his book-bound Western identity 這一含義。休斯將書拋入水中的行為暗示他和過去說再見，重新開始生活。

3. **D** 語境詞彙題
   〔解析〕片語 yearning for 與 longing for 是同義表達，意為「渴望」，因此答案為 D。

4. **A** 修辭目的題
   〔解析〕選項 A 正確，因為文中說該短篇小說表達了個人對身分認同感和家園的追求。作者此處並沒有表現 Hughes 的樂觀主義，只是提到 Hughes 的情感很矛盾，兼具消極和積極的情感。

5. **B** 語境詞彙題
   〔解析〕unsettling 與 troubling 是同義詞，意為「未解決的，令人心煩的」，因此選項 B 正確。

6. **C** 否定事實題
   〔解析〕要回答這類題目，考生必須略讀全文，尋找與 wide public interest in Africa 相關的資訊。第二段提到：Evidence of this enthusiasm was everywhere, from the mounting of major exhibitions of African art in European and American museums, to the beats of West African drums, to the career of Josephine Baker, whose bare-breasted dance made her the toast of Paris. 只有野生動物沒有提到，因此選項 C 為正確答案。

7. **D** 細節資訊題
   〔解析〕選項 C 錯誤，因為第四段提到那些年（over the years）一些非洲裔美國人永久住下來了，而另一些人卻只是短時間停留。不過，文中說 In the 19th century the most common destination was Liberia，因此選項 D 正確。

8. **A** 指代關係題
   〔解析〕回答本題的關鍵是要知道該句含有兩個由分號隔開的獨立分句：The travels illuminate the chronicles of African-American history in seemingly contradictory ways; they highlight Africa's abiding presence in Black American political, intellectual and imaginative life. they 為第二個分句的主詞，指代前一個分句的主詞 travels。

9. **B** 語境詞彙題

〔**解析**〕描述回憶時常用 fading，fading 與 becoming fainter 是同義說法，意為「褪色的」。

10. **A** 語境詞彙題

　　〔**解析**〕compelled 與 obliged 是同義表達，意為「被迫的」，故 A 為正確答案。

11. **C** 推論題

　　〔**解析**〕見本章前文的「托福總監評析」。

12. ■ **4** 插入句子題

　　■ 1 The travels illuminate the chronicles of African-American history in seemingly contradictory ways; they highlight Africa's abiding presence in Black American political, intellectual and imaginative life. ■ 2 By the time of the Civil War, only about one percent of the black population in the United States was African-born, and direct memories of the continent were fading; yet African Americans continued to look to Africa, seeking clues to the meaning of their own identity and history. ■ 3 Langston Hughes imagined an idyllic homeland, whereas supporters of Garvey's back-to-Africa movement saw the continent as the future seat of a great black empire. ■ 4 **Still others, traveling at different times, cast Africa as a "Dark Continent" crying out for Christian civilization, a headquarters for global anti-colonial revolution, or a field of opportunity for entrepreneurs.** Whatever the individual motives and aspirations, African Americans were compelled to confront the question that Hughes's contemporary Countee Cullen posed so eloquently in his poem "Heritage," where he asks: "What is Africa to me?"

插入句子題

　　〔**解析**〕做對本題的關鍵是要理解句子中的 still others 是指人們，因為他們在 traveling。可以排除第一個黑色方塊處，因為前句是在談論 memoirs 而非人們。從邏輯上說，Still others 不會緊跟其後。同樣，第二個黑色方塊處也不可能，因為前句是在談論 Africa's abiding presence 而非人們。第三個黑色方塊處有混淆視聽的作用，因為此處提到了人們（關注非洲的「非裔美國人」）。將句子放在這個位置時，上下文缺乏銜接與連貫，因為 still others 是指其他非裔美國人，而在此之前文中尚未提到過非裔美國人。只有最後一個黑色方塊處合適，因為在此處之前文中已經提到過兩個非裔美國人的例子：Hughes 和 supporters of Garvey。在上下文中，still others 成為第三個例子，因此最後一個黑色方塊處正確。

13. **3** Hughes was absorbed by the origins of African American history and sought to trace his roots.

4 Despite his desire to feel at home in Africa, Hughes found it difficult to assimilate.

6 Many African Americans, including poets and memoirs writers, wrote about Africa in an effort to better understand their cultural identity.

內容總結題

　　〔**解析**〕第一個選項不正確，因為該句表述錯誤；Hughes 對密西西比河和 muddy bosom 懷著美好的感情。第二個選項也不正確，文中沒有提到 Hughes 收藏藝術品。第三個選項正確，因為總結了主題：Hughes 在非洲文化背景下尋找自己的人生定位。第四個選項正確，因為它抓住了一個要點：Hughes 對接受非洲身份的複雜情感：...in spite of all of these experiences, he remained a stranger, unable to bridge the great historical chasm that separated him from Africa. 第五個選項不是要點，本文的重點是 Hughes 的身份認同感。第六個選項正確，因為它綜述了非裔美國人（包括 Hughes、詩人 Countee Cullen 和寫回憶錄的其他遊歷者）的關鍵資訊。

聽力模擬試題錄音文本 *Track 011*
- -
N: Now listen to part of a lecture in a literature class.

P: In this lecture on crime fiction, we'll get a sense of how the genre of detective fiction evolved. You'll remember last week, how we said that every crime story really has two stories to it—

the story of the crime itself, and the story of its investigation? Well, for each story we examine, I'd like you to think separately about the crime and the investigation—because the unfolding of the narrative will relate to those two storylines.

Now the general consensus is that the detective story began with Edgar Allen Poe, in the form of a short story. Before I talk about Poe, though, let me give you a little social background. In the early nineteenth century, police forces were developing into systematic organizations, in part as a reaction to an increase in crime in the urban centers at that time. More and more, police work began to rely on methods grounded in science and reasoning. And the invention of photography in 1839 allowed law enforcement officials to record evidence of crimes in new ways, including identification of individuals through their fingerprints.

It was only natural for scientific procedures like these to be included in fictional works about crimes. And similarly, the first detective stories all featured a "detective" who was extremely analytical and rational; a person who could find a scientific solution to a crime that no one else could solve.

So, to get back to Edgar Allen Poe—this first detective story was a short story set in France and published in the year 1841. With this work, Poe established many of the conventions of the detective genre, essentially creating a template for crime fiction which continued for a century. In fact, many of these literary conventions are still in practice. Let's talk about some of these.

The most basic of these story-writing rules is, obviously, that a crime is committed by an unknown person. As the plot develops, both the detective and the reader need to try and answer the question, "Who committed the crime?" Clues will be provided along the way, but the story must maintain a level of suspense—suspense is core to all detective fiction.

OK. Another convention of classic detective fiction is the presence of a police officer who is clumsy and ineffective, especially in comparison to the analytical genius of the detective. This type of character is designed to create contrast—on the one hand you have an awkward policeman and on the other, a brilliant, if somewhat strange, detective.

Which leads me to the next convention, the nature of the detective himself. In literature, the classic detective is often a talented amateur, a man who is perhaps rather eccentric in his personality, and who has unusual hobbies, such as growing roses or playing the violin. When I say "he," by the way, I should add that in the 19th century, virtually all fictional detectives were men, and this was the case up until the 1970s, when women detectives became popular.

As I mentioned, Edgar Allen Poe's detective story was quite short. Still, even in its short form it contained many of the classic detective themes and conventions; for example, Poe's detective was a brilliant and eccentric man who used reasoning to identify the criminal. Both Poe's plot and characters provided a model for the author who wrote the first full-length detective novel. That man was Wilkie Collins, who wrote a book called *The Moonstone* some 20 years after Poe's detective short story.

The story of *The Moonstone* is set in England and tells of a young woman who inherits a large Indian diamond on her 18th birthday. I don't want to give the plot away, but I can tell you that a large diamond, called the "Moonstone", is stolen and there are some mysterious deaths.

When you read *The Moonstone* this week, you'll see the investigation is carried out by professionals and amateurs. Take careful note of the plot elements that are classic features of detective novels. See if there is a bungled investigation led by local police, only to be taken over by the more competent "detective", and if so, how the pattern evolves.

S: Um, I may be jumping ahead, but I have a question. Everyone knows about the Sherlock Holmes stories. Are you saying those books weren't very original—that the author just copied from other people?

P: Every author of detective fiction borrows some things and creates other things anew. But let's hold that question. I suspect you'll recognize the profile of the "analytical genius", but I'll let you form your own judgment about "copying" when we get to Sherlock Holmes next week.

● **Transcripts for Question 4**

N: Listen again to part of the lecture. Then answer the question.

P: **In literature, the classic detective is often a talented amateur, a man who is perhaps rather eccentric in his personality, and who has unusual hobbies, such as growing roses or playing the violin. When I say "he," by the way, I should add that in the 19th century, virtually all fictional detectives were men, and this was the case up until the 1970s, when women detectives became popular.**

N: What does the professor mean when he says this:

P: **When I say "he," by the way, I should add that in the 19th century, virtually all fictional detectives were men, and this was the case up until the 1970s, when women detectives became popular.**

● **Transcripts for Question 6**

N: Listen again to part of the lecture. Then answer the question.

S: **Everyone knows about the Sherlock Holmes stories. Are you saying those books weren't very original—that the author just copied from other people?**

P: **Every author of detective fiction borrows some things and creates other things anew. But let's hold that question. I suspect you'll recognize the profile of the "analytical genius", but I'll let you form your own judgment about "copying" when we get to Sherlock Holmes next week.**

N: What does the professor mean when he says this:

P: **But let's hold that question.**

關鍵語塊

crime fiction 犯罪小説	genre 體裁；類型
unfolding of the narrative 敘述的展開	storyline 故事情節
general consensus 大多數人的意見	social background 社會背景
police force 警力	systematic organization 系統性的組織
method grounded in... 利用……的方法	law enforcement official 執法人員
record evidence of sth. 記錄某事的證據	story set in... 以……為背景的故事
create a template 創建範例	convention （文藝的）傳統風格；慣例

clue will be provided 將會提供線索	... is core to... ……是……的核心
ineffective 無能的；效率低的	create contrast 形成對比
talented amateur 業餘高手	provide a model for 為……提供一個例子
inherit 繼承	I may be jumping ahead 我可能說得太早了
bungled investigation 搞砸的調查	

聽力模擬試題答案詳解

1. **B** 主旨大意題

〔解析〕選項 A 和 D 都不正確，因為這兩個選項過於寬泛。選項 C 有混淆視聽的作用，但不正確，因為其重點在 suspense（懸念），而沒有提到偵探小說本身。選項 B 為最佳答案，因為本文主要講偵探小說的起源和發展。

2. **A、D** 細節資訊題

〔解析〕教授說 19 世紀的許多偵探角色都很古怪，並沒有說讀者受不了這些角色，因此選項 B 不正確。教授提到 19 世紀早期犯罪率有所上升，所以選項 C 不正確。教授說最早虛構的偵探是那些 who could find a scientific solution to a crime 的人，而在 19 世紀時 police work began to rely on methods grounded in science and reasoning。因此，選項 A 和 D 都是正確答案。

3. **B** 細節資訊題

〔解析〕教授說設計警員這類角色是為了與古怪但聰明的偵探角色形成對比，所以選項 B 正確。

4. **A** 推論題

〔解析〕見本章前文的「托福總監評析」。

5. **C** 組織結構題

〔解析〕教授要求學生閱讀《月亮寶石》，並告訴學生這是第一本長篇偵探小說，因此選 C。

6. **D** 語用功能題

〔解析〕要正確回答本題，考生必須理解 let's hold that question，這個慣用語的意思是 let me answer that question at a later time。選項 D 正確。

● Answer Key to Exercise 2

Inference	Supporting Fact
1. In the 19th century, urban areas probably had more crime than rural areas did.	The professor says that in the early 19th century, police forces became more systematic, partly to handle an increase in crime in cities.
2. It can be assumed that, among *The Moonstone* characters, there is an ineffective police officer who has trouble solving crimes.	The professor tells the class to take note of the plot elements that are classic features of detective novels, to see whether there is a bungled investigation led by local police, and if so, how the pattern evolves.
3. Based on the professor's remarks, we can infer he thinks the Sherlock Holmes stories show innovation, and aren't just "copies."	Even though the professor says he wants to wait till later to answer the question about copying, he does say every author borrows some things and creates other new things.

生命科學常考主題 2 生態學詞彙、答案、解析和錄音原文

● **Answer Key to Exercise1**

a.　<u>customary; usual; typical</u>

b.　<u>to become dried out; to remove moisture from something</u>

c.　<u>trees that are typically needle-leaved; evergreen trees with needles</u>

閱讀模擬試題答案詳解

1.　**B** 語境詞彙題

〔**解析**〕四個選項中能與 species（物種）搭配又符合上下文的詞，只有 continuation，意為「持續，持久」。perpetuation of the species 意指「物種的延續」。

2.　**C** 語境詞彙題

〔**解析**〕選項 A 有混淆視聽的作用，因為作者是在比較外在環境，但是 physically 的意思不符合上下文。四個選項中能修飾 different 又符合上下文的副詞只有 distinctly，意為「明顯地」。

3.　**A** 細節資訊題

〔**解析**〕第三段提到海水浮力使得動物不再依賴骨架，因此大型無脊椎動物，如大烏賊，能夠在海洋裡生存。正確答案為選項 A。波浪作用只在水濃度的題材中提到，因此選項 B 不正確。osmotic pressure 被認為是保持鹽和水的平衡的一個因素，沒有支援作用，因此選項 D 也不正確。

4.　**D** 語境詞彙題

〔**解析**〕shed 所在句中有並列動詞 fertilize（使受精），據此推測 shed 在此處是「產卵，一連串地排出」的意思。四個選項中，cast off 有「排出」的含義。

5.　**B** 修辭目的題

〔**解析**〕選項 D 有混淆視聽的作用，因為作者說幼蟲能幫助分散物種，但作者沒有說不能動的物種能產更多的卵，所以不正確。作者舉出海綿動物作為定棲的海洋生物的一個實例，這種動物在其成蟲期不能移動，但其在幼蟲期可以移動。因此選項 B 正確。

6.　**C** 指代關係題

〔**解析**〕這道題目有點棘手，因為句中含有幾個帶 of 的名詞片語。有些考生可能沒有意識到是 animal 所在分句的受詞。作者是在將動物體內的濃度與海水（the animal's "external environment"）的濃度作比較。因此選項 C 正確。

7.　**D** 細節資訊題

〔**解析**〕要處理可能要流入體內的水，生活在淡水中的動物有一個 mechanism for pumping water out of their bodies while holding onto the salt，因此選項 D 正確。其他選項都與文中內容不符。

8.　**B** 細節資訊題

〔**解析**〕作者說由於季節性的水流變化，漂浮的卵和幼蟲容易被水流沖走，所以生活在淡水中的動物通常沒有幼蟲期。因此選項 B「孤立的幼蟲有被水沖走的危險」是正確答案。

9.　**A** 語境詞彙題。

〔**解析**〕dissolvable 與 soluble（可溶解的）是同義詞，意為「可溶解的」，故選項 A 為正確答案。

10.　**D** 句子簡化題

〔**解析**〕選項 A 不正確，因為 in spite of（儘管，不顧）使其與加粗句子的意思相反。選項 B 中的 None 是對 nonetheless 的誤解。要想選出正確答案，就要確定句子的主要結構：1) respiratory surfaces need to be moist；2) respiratory surfaces are usually inside the body 和

3) because of their inner location, the surfaces do not dry out as often。因此選項 D 為正確答案，thereby = by virtue of; reducing the possibility of them drying = the extent of drying is limited。

11. ■ **2** 插入句子題

Fresh water is a much less constant environment than sea water. ■ 1 Streams vary greatly in cloudiness, velocity and volume, not only along their course but also as a result of droughts or heavy rains.　■ 2 **Similarly, small ponds fluctuate in cloudiness and water volume, but they also fluctuate in oxygen content.** In large lakes, the environment changes radically with increasing depth. ■ 3 Like salt water, fresh water allows organisms to float and aids in support. ■ 4 The low salt concentration of fresh water, however, makes it difficult to maintain a water and salt balance. Because the body of the animal contains a higher osmotic concentration than that of the external environment, water has a tendency to diffuse inward. The animal thus has the problem of getting rid of excess water. As a consequence, freshwater animals usually have some mechanism for pumping water out of their bodies while holding onto the salt.

〔解析〕第一句談淡水環境變化比海洋環境變化要多一些。第二句談河流的變化因素，這是總分結構，不需要有粗體句的並列結構插入。插入第二個標記處會很自然地銜接前一個句子：Streams vary greatly in cloudiness, velocity and volume... 第二句談河流的變化因素，第三句談小池塘的變化因素，是並列關係。將句子放在第三個標記處沒有意義，因為前一個句子談到的是經歷了巨變的大湖泊，用 similarly 説不通。第四個標記處更不可能，因為前一個句子已經開始談到新主題：浮力。

12.

Marine environment	• 5. Living conditions are most favorable for large animals without spines • 6. Surrounding conditions are relatively consistent from day to day
Fresh water environment	• 3. Eggs of the organism are often anchored to something • 7. Salt and water balance of the organism is challenging
Land environment	• 1. Best conditions for separating the animal's insides from the outside environment

資訊歸類題

〔解析〕海洋環境特徵需要填入兩個選項（分別對應文中 generally the most stable 和 reduces the animals' need for a skeleton)。淡水環境特徵也需要填入兩個選項（分別對應文中 difficult to maintain a water and salt balance 和 attached to the bottom of the stream or lake）。陸地環境特徵只需填入一個選項（對應文中 better barrier between the internal and the external environments)。第二個選項 Ideal surroundings for organisms with complex genetic make-up 和第四個選項 Cloudiness favorable for reproduction when predators are present 的特徵與本文中的特定環境沒有關聯。

● **Answer Key to Exercise 2**

<u>She's requesting the students to guess what "frugivores" are / She's asking the class if they're willing to guess what "frugivores" are. / She wants the students to tell her what "frugivores" are.</u>
注：frugivore 食果動物

聽力模擬試題錄音文本　 *Track 013*

N: Now listen to part of a lecture in a forest ecology class.

P: We've looked at forests in tropical areas and talked about the ecologies there. In this lesson, we'll cover the material from Chapter Six—the issues related to forest management in temperate zones. By the time we finish this chapter, I hope you'll have a better understanding of forests in North America.

Before I get going on our case study for this week, I want to hammer home an important principle related to the conservation of species—not just in forests, but in any ecosystem. Whenever you have a greater variety of organisms within a certain species, it increases the chance of survival for that entire species. So, a word to the wise—in the future, whether you're managing a commercial forest for timber, or working in a national park, act with your fellow ecologists to maintain diverse gene pools.

All right. Let's look at the well-known case study involving the ecology of the American chestnut tree. As many of you know, the American chestnut tree once occupied a highly significant portion of forestland in North America. In the 19th century, American chestnut forests spanned huge areas, covering 200 million acres. Trees grew to over 100 feet tall. They were giants; you couldn't wrap your arms around many of them, because they'd get to be some 10 feet in diameter.

These forests were immensely valuable to farmers and lumber companies. In the fall, farmers sold sweet chestnuts to cities, and people would buy them roasted for snacks or use them in cooking. But by far the most valuable parts of the American chestnut tree were its timber and bark. Why? The wood was plentiful and versatile. It was strong, but still relatively light. American chestnut trees grew faster than many other hardwood trees. As a result, wood companies sought out chestnut for home and furniture building. The frames of houses were made from chestnut, as were hardwood floors.

But in the early 1900s, American chestnut trees started developing a fungus, and the ill trees would often die within several years. Tree experts believed this fungus disease came to North America on trees from Japan or China, where there were related species of chestnuts with the fungus, but they'd somehow developed resistance to it. The American chestnuts, however, were not resistant. Seed-like spores of the fungus penetrated the bark and grew in the part of the tree that carried nutrients up to the top. Eventually the tree died and the fungus on that tree created more spores, which spread whenever the wind blew. In two generations, the American chestnut was almost extinct.

Only when the science of genetics was understood did scientists have the tools to grapple with this ecological problem. Because the Chinese chestnut tree was fairly resistant to the fungus disease, scientists began experimenting with crossbreeding Chinese and American chestnut tree species. At first, these efforts were unsuccessful. The trees that resulted from this interbreeding were very small or lacked other traits that had been highly prized in the American species. Eventually, however, breeders learned that multiple crosses were required.

In order to create a hybrid species, a tree expert would first cut a twig off an American chestnut sprout and plant it in a tree farm, until it was large enough to be genetically crossed with the disease-resistant Chinese species. Then, the offspring of this hybrid were repeatedly crossed with a parent generation of American chestnut species. In this way, the fast-growth and other desirable characteristics of the American species could be recovered over time.

Crossbreeding is a labor-intensive process! It takes seven to nine years for an American chestnut to mature to flowering. So a horticulturalist sometimes has to wait 10 years to do the first cross. When scientists are able to successfully breed a vigorous species, we can let the trees reproduce naturally, and the goal is to reintroduce the tree to the eastern forests.

Now another way we've dealt with this fungus disease is to use a virus. This approach was first used by a French scientist, who isolated a weakened strain of the fungus disease in the lab. Then he successfully injected his French chestnuts with the virus, similar to the vaccine process for small pox. With viral inoculations, you can get results much faster than you can with crossbreeding. The disease never goes away, but its growth can be slowed so that the tree survives.

What we've seen is that the American chestnuts that have been injected with a virus grow pretty fast in controlled environments. Unfortunately, though, we think only a portion of these inoculated trees will show enough resistance to survive. Over the long term, then, crossbreeding may prove the more effective solution. Of course, tree scientists are using both approaches now, just in case.

● **Transcripts for Question 2**

N: What does the professor imply when he says this:

P: So, a word to the wise—in the future, whether you're managing a commercial forest for timber, or working in a national park, act with your fellow ecologists to maintain diverse gene pools.

● **Transcripts for Question 6.**

N: Listen again to part of the lecture. Then answer the question.

P: Unfortunately, though, we think only a portion of these inoculated trees will show enough resistance to survive. Over the long term, then, crossbreeding may prove the more effective solution. Of course, tree scientists are using both approaches now, just in case.

N: What does the professor mean when he says this:

P: Of course, tree scientists are using both approaches now, just in case.

關鍵語塊

forest ecology 森林生態學	tropical area 熱帶地區
temperate zone 溫帶	conservation 物種保護
get going on 開始進行	case study 案例研究
hammer home 再三強調	ecosystem 生態系統
organism 生物體	a word to the wise〔口語〕給聰明人的一個建議
commercial forest 經濟林	timber 木材
national park 國家公園	your fellow ecologist 你的生態學家夥伴
maintain diverse gene pools 維持基因庫的多樣性	American chestnut tree 美洲栗子樹
span 覆蓋，遍及	bark 樹皮
versatile 有多種用途的；多功能的	fungus disease 真菌病
develop resistance to 對……產生抗體	spore 孢子

penetrate 進入	carry nutrient 攜帶養分
extinct 滅絕的	genetics 遺傳學
crossbreeding 雜交育種	multiple crosses 多次雜交
twig 嫩枝	sprout 新芽；嫩枝
labor-intensive process 耗時的生產過程	horticulturalist 園藝學家
deal with 處理	virus 病毒
isolate 分離出	inject... with... 給……注射……
vaccine 疫苗	viral inoculation 病毒疫苗接種
just in case 以防萬一	

聽力模擬試題答案詳解

1. **C** 主旨大意題
   〔**解析**〕講座的重點是通過雜交育種努力挽救美國栗樹走向絕種，因此選項 C 為正確答案。

2. **A** 推論題
   〔**解析**〕在談論保護物種的原理時，教授告訴他的森林生態學班上的學生，未來他們應該維持基因庫的多樣性。結合聽力內容，教授一直在說美國栗樹的雜交使其生存了下來，現在說基因庫應多樣性，其隱含的意思是他們應該防止樹木的同系繁殖，所以選項 A 為正確答案。

3. **D** 細節資訊題
   〔**解析**〕教授說美國栗樹 was strong, but still relatively light，所以選項 B 不正確。教授說美國栗樹 grew faster than many other hardwood trees，因此選項 D 正確。選項 A 和 C 文中都沒提到。

4. **B** 細節資訊題
   〔**解析**〕教授說樹木受到來自日本或中國的真菌的侵襲。真菌孢子進入樹皮，然後在樹內生長，樹便死了，因此選項 B 為正確答案。侵襲樹木的是真菌，不是昆蟲，所以選項 C 不正確。

5.

	Yes	No
They take effect very rapidly.	✓	
They are saving the majority of the trees.		✓
They will get rid of fungus disease in the future.		✓

關聯內容題
   〔**解析**〕在最後兩段中，教授介紹了病毒疫苗接種的潛在優勢。他說，利用病毒疫苗接種得到的成果要比雜交育種快得多，因此第一句正確。他還說 only a portion of these inoculated trees will show enough resistance to survive，因此第二句錯誤。最後，他說 crossbreeding may prove the more effective solution，從這句可以推斷，未來的病毒疫苗接種可能無法根除真菌病。

6. **B** 語用功能題。
   〔**解析**〕見本章前文的「托福總監評析」。

⑧ 社會科學常考主題 2 人類學詞彙、答案、解析和錄音原文

● Answer Key to Exercise 1

In the 18th and 19th centuries, as Europeans penetrated further and further into some of the world's most inaccessible parts, they encountered peoples who seemed to turn everything they thought they knew about human behavior upside down. From their attempts to make sense of what they had seen, and to help them understand the nature of what it means to be human, the idea of anthropology was born. The "science of man," as anthropology was dubbed, experienced its prime in the early 20th century.

閱讀模擬試題答案詳解

1. **B** 細節資訊題
   〔解析〕第二段中作者提到特林吉特人的起源故事有兩個版本，其中一個版本是 analysis by outside observers，因此選項 B 正確。

2. **D** 句子簡化題
   〔解析〕加粗的句子雖然是個簡單句，但是由於句子中間有一個介系詞片語（as well as the opinions about the versions），所以這個句子就顯得有點複雜。不及物動詞 conflict 的意思是「矛盾，不一致」。本句話的意思是「有時，不同版本之間的說法不一致，而人們對這些版本的看法也不一致」。選項 D 的意思較為接近。

3. **D** 推論題
   〔解析〕第三段中的四種故事在一定程度上是以它們的形成年代來定義的。根據 a legend could acquire the status of a distant myth 的說法，可以推斷選項 D 是最古老的形式。

4. **A** 語境詞彙題
   〔解析〕選項 B 有混淆視聽的作用，因為 strange 有 odd（古怪的）的意思。然而，選項 A 為正確答案，因為片語 odds and ends 與 diverse items 是同義表達，意為「瑣碎物品，零星雜物」。

5. **A** 細節資訊題
   〔解析〕選項 C 中的 for no obvious reason 是對 Thunder 和 Earthquake 因 unspecified reasons（不明原因）而分離的誤解。第四段最後一句說 Thunder 和 Earthquake 是兄妹，因此選項 A 正確。

6. **C** 否定事實題
   〔解析〕這道題相對較簡單，但是考生必須掃讀全文，然後尋找每個人物的名稱。只有 Blue Heron 文中沒有提到，因此選項 C 為正確答案。

7. **C** 語境詞彙題
   〔解析〕只有 kept 與 hoarded 是同義詞，意為「保存；貯藏」。

8. **D** 指代關係題
   〔解析〕見本章前文的「托福總監評析」。

9. **B** 語境詞彙題
   〔解析〕文中提到 Raven 神話中，鳥類是騙子，自負又貪婪。從句型看，altruistic 是 ego 和 greed 的反義詞。四個選項中，只有 generous（慷慨的，無私心的）符合。

10. **C** 細節資訊題
    〔解析〕選項 A 有混淆視聽的作用，但不正確。在第五段中，作者告訴我們有些故事提到烏鴉 brings fresh water to the people，並且賦予鮭魚洄游（runs）的能力，鮭魚才能溯溪洄游和產卵，

因此選項 C 為正確答案。

11. **B** 修辭目的題

〔**解析**〕第六段提到在神話故事中，烏鴉遇到的動物很少能得好處的，要嘛是烏鴉獨自享用王鮭，讓小鳥們餓著肚子活著離開；要嘛是瘦到不成原形。舉這些例子是為了說明鳥兒給動物們帶來的不幸，因此，選項 B 正確。

12.

Types of Raven myth	Story Examples
Trickster	• 5. Bear's body is injured • 6. The whale gets a hole on top of its head • 7. Small Birds fail to get their portion of salmon
Culture hero	• 2. Fresh water is given to the people • 4. The Sun is stolen away

資訊歸類題

〔**解析**〕要正確選出答案，考生先必須識別出 trickster（騙子）故事和 culture hero（文化上的英雄人物）故事。第五段介紹了文化上的英雄人物故事。第六段中介紹了騙子故事。

第一個選項 Clever animals scheme to outwit Raven 和第三個選項 The Old Woman is harmed in an earthquake 文中都沒有提到。

● **Answer Key to Exercise 2**

a. What I hope to do in today's lecture is give you an introduction to some of the core ideas in an important social science, cultural anthropology.

b. Anthropologists seek to look at culture from the inside, even though it seems difficult to do so. And so we can say that the goal of cultural anthropologists is to understand how other people view their own world.

聽力模擬試題錄音文本　 *Track 015*

N: Now listen to part of a lecture in an Anthropology class.

P: As we trace the history of human evolution, it's important to remember that our understanding of early primates is in flux. For one thing, we continue to find new fossils every day, all over the world. Our theories about early primates will change based on whether the new evidence supports, or fails to support, a given theory. A new fossil find tomorrow could easily alter our understanding of early human ancestry. That means that a lot of what you'll be reading—whether it's your textbook, or information on the Internet—will be contradictory. Some of the information will be dated, and no longer valid. In other cases, you'll find that scientists have different points of views and different theories. So when you are reading or doing research in this field, make sure you check the data carefully. It can be painstaking work keeping track of all the various fossil sites and the periods of the fossil deposits. But in time you'll find it's well worth the effort.

Now I'd like to turn to the Pliocene Epoch, which began about five million years ago and ended less than two million years ago. As we look at changes in the early primates, we see that the environment, including the climate and physical terrain, influences how primates adapt over time. Environmental change sets the stage for all evolutionary change, and the Pliocene is no exception.

OK, during the middle of the Pliocene, around three million years ago, grasslands and savannas spread across most continents of the Earth. At that time, the tilt of the Earth changed, and so it pointed away from the Sun for longer periods. This caused an overall cooling of the Earth and led to the formation of these many grassland savannas. Now, savannas, by definition, are found in warm or hot climates where the annual rainfall is about 20 to 50 inches a year. But, for a savanna to exist, it is crucial that all the rain falls within a limited period, specifically within six to eight months of the year. After this rainy period, there must be a long period of drought—otherwise, the grasslands will turn into rainforests.

So why was this Pliocene climate change important in the evolution of our human ancestors? In Africa, temperatures dropped steeply and the air became stripped of moisture. Humid woodland shriveled away. Up to this point, many of the higher primates had been living in rain forests, where they had a diet of mostly fruit, supplemented by small insects. They got their food from the trees and slept in the branches, but spent part of the time on the ground. As the forests got smaller, there wasn't enough food for all the apes. The less aggressive species were driven out onto the open savanna.

Many of the humanlike primates that had relied on forests for food died out. Other species adapted in order to forage, searching for food in new ways and thus they expanded their diets. Some of these adaptations were successful; others were not. We know that the genus *Australopithecus* lived during the Pliocene Epoch. Remember, members of *Australopithecus* could walk on two feet. But contained within the genus *Australopithecus* were many different species. In Africa, one of these blood lines was a very large species that developed large molar teeth and a specialized jaw so that it could chew on the grass in the savannas. By becoming a highly specialized vegetarian, this species ensured a comfortable life for itself for the short term. But when the climate continued to cool, it became extinct. Thus this large species disappeared a million years ago. In contrast, there was a smaller species of *Australopithecus* that adapted to the climate change by evolving other body changes, changes including sharp teeth like fangs and sharp, pointed incisors—teeth similar to the ones humans have today. Consequently, it is believed that this "slender" form of *Australopithecus* was able to forage for more diverse foods, meaning it was also able to kill and eat meat. From the fossil evidence, we know that this small form gave rise to the humanlike primates of the genus "Homo." So they were the direct ancestors of *Homo sapiens*.

Of course, there is still a lot of controversy about what primate species was eating what foods at what time. But, carbon analyses show us that, after the climate change, meats and food from fresh-water or ocean shores became an increasing part of some primates' diet. In fact, it is believed that animal fat from this meat diet contributed to the spurt in brain growth in the line of primates leading directly to humans.

● **Transcripts for Question 2**

N: Listen again to part of the lecture. Then answer the question.

P: It can be painstaking work keeping track of all the various fossil sites and the periods of the fossil deposits. But in time you'll find it's well worth the effort.

N: What does the professor mean when she says this:

P: But in time you'll find it's well worth the effort.

● **Transcripts for Question 3**

N: Listen again to part of the lecture. Then answer the question.

P: As we look at changes in the early primates, we see that the environment, including the climate and physical terrain, influences how primates adapt over time. Environmental change sets the stage for all evolutionary change, and the Pliocene is no exception.

N: What does the professor indicate about the Pliocene Epoch when she says this:

P: Environmental change sets the stage for all evolutionary change, and the Pliocene is no exception.

關鍵語塊

trace the history of... 追溯……的歷史	evidence supports... theory 證據支持……理論
human ancestry 人類祖先	contradictory 矛盾的
painstaking work 仔細的工作	fossil deposit 化石沉積層
physical terrain 地形特徵	grassland 草原
tilt of the Earth 地軸傾斜	crucial 重要的
period of drought 乾旱時期	stripped of sth. 去除了某物
humid woodland 潮濕的林地	shrivel away 萎縮
higher primate 高級靈長類	supplemented by 外加
aggressive 有攻擊性的	forage 搜尋獵物
blood line 血統	molar teeth 臼齒
vegetarian 素食者	ensured sth. for itself 確保自身有某物
become extinct 滅絕	fang 尖牙
incisor 門牙	slender 細長的
fossil evidence 化石證據	Homo 人類（學名）
Homo sapiens 智人（現代人的學名）	controversy 爭論
spurt in growth 激增	

聽力模擬試題答案詳解

1. **D** 主旨大意題
〔**解析**〕選項 A 歸納錯誤，而選項 B 和選項 C 都太片面了。選項 D 正確，因為教授花了大量時間來闡述上新世的氣候變化是如何影響人類之前的靈長類動物的。

2. **B** 立場觀點題
〔**解析**〕上下文的情境是說記錄化石遺址、化石礦的時期要嚴謹，資料要準確。以後會發現所做的一切工作都是值得的。所以選 B。keep track of 有「記錄」的意思，選項 C 不正確，因為她沒有要求學生一起做記錄工作。

3. **A** 語用功能題
〔**解析**〕教授説上新世發生的氣候變化也不例外（no exception），她的意思是説氣候變化，導致了生物的進化。因此選項 A 為正確答案。選項 C 在邏輯上錯誤地理解了否定性片語 no exception。

4. **A**、**C** 細節資訊題

【**解析**】選項 B 不正確，因為雨絕不可能持續一整月。教授說 savannas, by definition, are found in warm or hot climates，而在上新世，grasslands and savannas spread across most continents of the Earth。因此選項 A 和選項 C 正確。

5.

Characteristic	Large species	Small species	Neither species
Sharp incisors		✓	
Grinding molars	✓		
Lived mainly in forest areas			✓
Disappeared a million years ago	✓		

關聯內容題

【**解析**】在講座中，教授提到了兩種南猿的不同特徵。鋒利的尖門牙（sharp, pointed incisors）被認為是小型食肉物種的特徵。相比之下，教授說大型物種長有大臼齒和一個專門的下顎以便能咀嚼熱帶稀樹草原上的草（large molar teeth and a specialized jaw so that it could chew on the grass in the savannas）。講座沒有告訴我們大型物種或小型物種主要生活在森林區（mainly in forest areas），只說了攻擊性較弱的南猿被迫到熱帶稀樹草原上覓食。教授說大型物種在 100 萬年以前就消失了（large species disappeared a million years ago），因為大型物種無法適應變化的條件。

⑨ 物理科學常考主題 3 聲學和力學詞彙、答案、解析和錄音原文

閱讀模擬試題答案詳解

1. **D** 細節資訊題
   〔**解析**〕作者說合成器有不同的格式和生成聲音的方式。然而，所有合成器在概念上都相似，含有兩個功能部件，其中一個是 control interface（控制介面），因此選項 D 正確。

2. **B** 指代關係題
   〔**解析**〕這題考的關係代名詞 which 前面就是先行詞 performances。從語義上來講，這個句子講得通，因為描繪聲音景觀（sonic landscapes）的就是 sound performances（音效）。

3. **C** 語境詞彙題
   〔**解析**〕本段講聲音合成器的出色之處。此句句意為：它高品質的錄音技術、使它超越了工具的角色。四個選項中，只有 routine（平凡的）符合句意。

4. **B** 細節資訊題
   〔**解析**〕作者說 high quality recording technology has made acoustic sounds much easier for musicians and technicians to mix，因此選項 B 正確。選項中的 mix 不是「混合」的意思，而是意為「混合錄製」。

5. **A** 修辭目的題
   〔**解析**〕作者說 synthesizer（合成器）的定義是生成聲音的電子器具。然而，由於某種原因，單簧管被某些人認為是 natural，而合成器則被認為是 artificial。作者想說服讀者器具的聲音與樂器的聲音並沒有本質區別，單簧管也是一種合成器。因此選項 A 正確。

6. **B** 語境詞彙題
   〔**解析**〕選項 B 的 are eligible for 與片語 qualify for 是同義表達，意為「有……資格」。

7. **D** 語境詞彙題
   〔**解析**〕這道題有點難，fusing 有「熔合」的意思，但在聲學中，fusing 的意思與 blending 相同，意為「聲音的融合」。

8. **A** 細節資訊題
   〔**解析**〕作者說 the general public（公眾）認為合成器顯然是製造 synthetic（合成的）或 artificial（模擬的）聲音的，尤其是廉價樂器。因此，選項 A 為正確答案。

9. **C** 句子簡化題
   〔**解析**〕要回答這道題目，必須先明白 this 是指 CD 製作過程環節中加強某個音色效果。CD 中鼓聲的調音效果讓觀眾的期望值過高，他們希望現場也能聽到那麼好的效果。選項 D 非常混淆視聽，因為有些考生會誤以為現場觀眾對合成器的鼓聲不滿意。但實際上，現場觀眾有時候會不滿意未在 CD 製作「混合流程」中增強的鼓聲。因此，選項 C 為正確答案。

10. **C** 推論題
    〔**解析**〕要瞭解作者的觀點，需要略讀整篇文章。答案可在第二段中提煉出來。作者提到：Used carefully, synthesizers can produce emotional performances which paint sonic landscapes with a rich and huge set of timbres, limited only by the imagination of the creator. 緊接著又說：Without the creative skills of the performer, musician or technician, the music would become mundane. 由此可以斷定選項 C 為正確答案。

11. ■ **1** 插入句子題
    The first synthesizer might have been an early ancestor of Homo sapiens hitting a hollow log or perhaps learning to whistle. ■ 1 **Singing uses a sophisticated synthesizer whose**

capabilities are often forgotten—the human vocal tract. All musical instruments can be thought of as being "synthesizers," although few people would think of them in this way. ■ 2 A clarinet is viewed as being "natural," whereas a synthesizer is seen as "artificial." In recent years the word "synthesizer" has come to mean only an electronic instrument capable of producing a wide range of different sounds. The actual categories of sounds that qualify for the label of synthesizer are also very specific. Purely imitative sounds are frequently regarded as nothing other than recordings of the actual instrument; the synthesizer is seen as little more than a replay device. In other words, the general public seems to expect synthesizers to produce "synthetic" sounds. ■ 3 This can be readily seen in many low-cost keyboard instruments intended for home use, which typically have a number of familiar sounds with names like "piano" and "guitar." But they also have sounds labeled "synth" for sounds which do not fit into the "naturalistic" scheme. As synthesizers become better at fusing elements of real and synthetic sounds, the boundaries are becoming increasingly fuzzy. ■ 4

〔解析〕第三段第一句提到，人類最初的合成器是早期的人類祖先敲打空心木頭或學吹口哨。插入的句子：唱歌利用到了一個複雜的被人們忽略的「合成器」：聲帶。此處的 singing 與 whistle 是一回事，承接了上文，所以應加在第一個標記處。第二個標記處不可能，因為後面句子的主題已從人類轉到了樂器，即單簧管。第三個標記處更不可能，因為前面句子的主題是 imitative sounds（模仿聲音），接著用模仿的「鋼琴」和「吉他」聲音舉例說明。第四個標記處緊跟著一個總結句，這個句子有效地總結了整個段落。在總結之後開始談論歌聲會很奇怪。

12.

Type of Synthesizer	Associated Characteristics
Performance	• 2. Adjustments are possible during real-time sound generation • 6. Signal follows an established conduit • 7. Connections between units are permanent
Modular	• 1. Requires more effort to prepare it for use • 4. Often purchased for university use

資訊歸類題

〔解析〕見本章前文的「托福總監評析」。

● **Answer Key to Exercise 1**

a. Video synthesizers, color synthesizers and sound synthesizers.

b. Reuse existing sounds, generate sounds electronically, generate sounds mechanically / use mathematics, use physics, use biology.

c. Hollow log (beating it), whistling, human voice (singing), keyboard, clarinet, piano, guitar and drum.

聽力模擬試題錄音文本　 *Track 017*

N: Now listen to part of a lecture in a Physics class.

P: Earlier in the term we covered the Physics of Motion, including Newton's laws of motion that talk about the conditions under which there is movement. Today we're going to be applying these principles of motion to flight as we look at some basic Aerodynamics. To do so, I thought I'd tell you the story of how the Wright brothers invented the airplane. Like you, the Wright brothers had to learn Physics, step by step. Wilbur and Orville were both tenacious learners who grappled with the physical properties of Aerodynamics for many years before they built a working airplane. As they became aware of the Physics, they had to invent each of the technologies needed to make their aircraft fly.

All right then. Let's look at some of the problems that they needed to overcome to get their plane to fly.

Now, at the end of the 19th century, the newspapers were filled with accounts of "flying machines". The Wright brothers read about these relatively primitive aircraft and realized none had suitable controls. They hoped that they could learn more about Flight Dynamics by watching birds in flight. The Wrights watched vultures, eagles and hawks maneuver with their wings in unstable air. Wilbur's favorite was the vulture, because it soared more than other birds. In physical terms, a soaring bird is able to achieve a perfect balance of the physical forces of lift, drift and gravity. Wilbur came to the conclusion that birds balance themselves in flight by adjusting the shape of their wings. In order to maintain what we call "lateral control", the Wrights would have first to change the shape of the wing. They learned that a long, narrow wing shape was perfect for flight.

So now they needed to find out how to control the airplane in flight. There were three basic dimensions needed to control an aircraft. Of these three dimensions, the first type of control needed in flight is for pitch. Pitch controls the up-and-down movement of the nose; in other words, pitch is what allows an aircraft to descend or climb.

The second type of control needed is for yaw. Yaw control allows the craft's nose to turn right or left, providing the aircraft's directional control.

And the third type of control is for roll. Roll is the up-and-down movement of the two wing tips; roll control allows for lateral control, which is necessary for turning the aircraft.

Now, to solve the problem of pitch, the Wright brothers built a kind of horizontal movable tail called an elevator, which could control pitch. By moving the elevator up or down, the pilot could produce a change in the fixed horizontal tail's downforce, thereby causing the nose of the aircraft to go up or down.

To address the issue of yaw, the Wrights added at the back of the plane a tail with movable rudders. By moving the rudders left or right, the pilot can create a side force which causes the plane's nose to yaw to the left or right.

For the third problem—that of rolling, the Wright brothers invented a pulley system that used wires to "bend" the shape of one wing or the other. Through this action, they could produce a large lift force pulling on one of the wings, causing the plane to roll to the left or right, for example, in preparation for a turn.

S: It's been over a hundred years now—do airplanes today still have controls for pitch, yaw and roll?

P: Yes, unquestionably. But the aerodynamic structures and systems used to carry out these controls are obviously not the same. For one thing, in modern airliners we rely extensively on computerization. But we also have new parts—for example, aircraft today have a movable part on each wing called an aileron. These moveable wing parts are used by modern pilots to control roll, as opposed to the pulley and cables used by the Wright brothers to "bend" the wings. But both of these methods achieve roll control. Suffice it to say, every aircraft ever built since 1902 and the Wright brothers has had controls to pitch the nose up or down, and yaw the nose from side to side, and roll the wings right or left.

● **Transcripts for Question 2.**

N: Why does the professor say this:

P: Like you, the Wright brothers had to learn Physics, step by step. Wilbur and Orville were both tenacious learners who grappled with the physical properties of Aerodynamics for many years before they built a working airplane.

關鍵語塊

Physics of Motion 運動物理學	Newton's laws of motion 牛頓運動定律
apply these principles to sth. 將這些原理應用於某事物	Aerodynamics 航空動力學
airplane 飛機	grapple with 努力解決
physical property 物理性能	aircraft 飛機，飛行器
Flight Dynamics 飛行動力學	birds in flight 飛行的小鳥
maneuver （敏捷地）飛行	soar 高飛，翱翔
lift （空氣的）升力，浮力	drift 飄移
gravity 重力；吸引力	lateral control 橫向控制
nose 飛機的前部；機頭	directional control 方向控制
elevator 升降舵	downforce 下壓力
rudder 方向舵	pulley system 滑輪系統
for one thing 首先；一則	airliner 客機
rely extensively on sth. 在很大程度上依靠某事物	as opposed to 與……對比，與……截然相反
cable 纜線	suffice it to say 可以肯定地說

聽力模擬試題答案詳解

1. **A** 主旨大意題
   【解析】選項 C 不正確，講座中雖然頻頻提到萊特兄弟，但並沒有提到飛機的動力裝置（引擎）。選項 A 正確，因為教授絕大部分時間都在講述控制飛機的三種方式。

2. **B** 立場觀點題
   【解析】要回答這道題，考生必須瞭解教授談論萊特兄弟學習物理學的原因。他說萊特兄弟一步一步地（step by step）學，是堅持不懈的（tenacious）學習者。言下之意是希望學生不要輕易放棄，要堅持學習物理學。

3. **C** 細節資訊題
   【解析】教授開始說 birds balance themselves in flight by adjusting the shape of their wings。接著他說為了維持 lateral control（橫向控制），萊特兄弟需要改變機翼的形狀。從這點可知，選項 C 正確。contour 意為「外形，輪廓」。

4.

Attributes	Motions		
	Pitch	Yaw	Roll
Motion causing the nose to go left or right		✓	
Upwards or downwards motion of one wing or the other			✓
Motion that makes the aircraft nose move up or down	✓		
Motion that is acted upon by aircraft rudders		✓	

關聯內容題

〔**解析**〕聽音檔的過程中，考生必須把 pitch（俯仰）、yaw（偏航）、roll（橫滾）等內容準確、完整地記下來。教授說 yaw control allows the craft's nose to turn right or left, providing the aircraft's directional control，因此第一項特徵在 Yaw 下方打勾。然後說，為了解決偏航，萊特兄弟添加了 a tail with movable rudders。因此最後一項特徵也應在 Yaw 下方打勾。第二項特徵有點棘手，不過，俯仰是指機頭的運動，而橫滾是指 the up-and-down movement of the two wing tips（兩翼尖的上下運動）。因此，第二項特徵應在 Roll 下方打勾。教授說 Pitch controls the up-anddown movement of the nose; in other words, pitch is what allows an aircraft to descend or climb，因此第三項特徵在 Pitch 下方打勾。

5. **D** 細節資訊題

〔**解析**〕這道題相對較簡單。教授說，1902 年以來的飛行器，包括萊特兄弟設計的飛行器，都有控制裝置，用於控制影響飛行的三種力。因此選項 D 為正確答案。

● **Answer Key to Exercise 2**

a. The Wrights observed hawks use their wings to move around.

b. To turn an airplane, one must have lateral control.

c. They made one wing roll to the left so that they could turn.

⑩ 人文藝術常考主題 3 音樂和音樂史詞彙、答案、解析和錄音原文

● **Answer Key to Exercise 1**

4, 1, 5, 2, 3

Two fallacies underlie most discussions of popular music audiences. The first of these is that studies of youth subcultures are a useful way to understand popular music audiences. Undeniably, more than a few teachers and students believe the study of popular music is the study of music made by and for young people. However, in my view, this assumption is misguided. The popular music experiences of older people should also be taken into consideration.

閱讀模擬試題答案詳解

1. **C** 語境詞彙題

   〔**解析**〕選項 A Exception 有混淆視聽的作用，因為它曲解了 out 的意思。名詞片語 outgrowth of 與片語 development of 近義，意為「自然發展的結果」。

2. **D** 否定事實題

   〔**解析**〕第一段提到：... ragtime drew upon everything that had gone before—spiritual songs and minstrel tunes, European folk melodies, operatic arias and military marches。spiritual songs（聖歌）對應 B 項，operatic arias（歌劇詠歎調）對應 A 項，military marches（軍隊進行曲）對應 C 項。文中沒有說舞蹈音樂是拉格泰姆音樂的源頭，只是說拉格泰姆音樂吸引了年輕舞者的喜愛（caught the fancy of young dancers）。因此選 D。

3. **A** 修辭目的題

   〔**解析**〕在引證中，評論者用苛刻的言辭評價拉格泰姆音樂，說它是頹廢的（decadent）藝術文化中的一種短期現象，還是紮根下來的一種有傳染性的弊病（disease），只有時間才能證明。在引證之前，作者說年輕人熱愛拉格泰姆音樂，但是他們的父母不喜歡。作者想列舉評論者負面言論的實例，因此選項 A 正確。

4. **D** 語境詞彙題

   〔**解析**〕該詞所在句是對拉格泰姆音樂的正面評價，即自信、充滿活力的，所以推測 irresistible 是個褒義詞。四個選項中只有 D 項正確，irresistible 意為「無法抗拒的，吸引人的」。選項 A「reckless」意為「魯莽的」。

5. **C** 細節資訊題

   〔**解析**〕掃讀第二段尋找關鍵字 New Orleans 和 20th century。第二段段末提到，本世紀初，紐奧良的音樂家們（By the turn of the century, New Orleans musicians）在舞廳和大街上用拉格泰姆風格演奏各種音樂。因此選項 C「它影響了很多音樂類型」正確。

6. **B** 指代關係題

   〔**解析**〕指代關係詞 them 前面有很多複數名詞，這就意味著考生不能單靠文法來得出正確答案，還必須利用上下文的邏輯關係。根據 songwriters started to see commercial possibilities in them，可知作詞家希望從「它們」中賺錢，但「它們」不是樂器（instruments），也不是他們自身（songwriters），因此選項 C 和 D 在邏輯上不成立。選項 A「musicians」有混淆視聽的作用，因為歌曲作家可能會從演奏者身上賺錢；但讀到最後一個分句：an agreed-upon form was developed，可推測這是一種音樂形式，而不是人。這樣我們就明白了該句的意思：因為越來越多的演奏者開始演奏藍調，所以作詞家就開始創作越來越多的藍調歌曲，一種令雙方都滿意的「藍

調形式」就此形成。

7. **D** 細節資訊題

〔**解析**〕在第三段，作者提到非洲裔美國人湧入新奧爾良，那些河堤上的辛苦工作者促進了爵士樂的發展，其中就有「藍調」，所以選 D。

8. **B** 語境詞彙題

〔**解析**〕選項 D trimmed 意為「修剪」，如 trimming a tree。但 trimmed with something 的意思同 decorated with something（用某物來裝飾）。語塊 stripped to 與 reduced to 同義，因此答案為 B。

9. **C** 細節資訊題

〔**解析**〕作者說藍調中的和弦模式能演奏很多變奏曲，表達各種各樣的情感（somehow allowed for an infinite number of variations and were capable of expressing an infinite number of emotions），因此選項 C 正確。

10. **A** 推論題

〔**解析**〕這道題有點難，因為每個選項看似都合理。文中提到：The blues were good-time music, which was why, to many churchgoers, they were considered the work of the devil. 由此可推斷，一些經常去做禮拜的人認為藍調是聚會音樂（歡樂音樂），如果人們總是享受歡樂時光和聚會，他們便會不工作。因此選項 A 正確。

11. **A** 推論題

〔**解析**〕第六段提到最早模仿教堂會眾的集體沉吟，最早複製了教會領導人和追隨者們之間呼召與回應模式（call-and-response patterns）的人是紐奧良的音樂家，通過他們的小號音樂來表達無盡的藍調音樂情思。由此可知小號手與到教堂做禮拜的人進行了互動。

12. ■ **2** 插入句子題

〔**解析**〕見本章前文的「托福總監評析」。

13. **3** The syncopated rhythms characteristic of ragtime influenced the full spectrum of music in New Orleans and paved the way for the development of jazz.

4 Fostered by the singers and guitar players coming from Mississippi farms, improvisation and the emotional telling of stories became a fundamental expression of jazz.

6 In New Orleans in the 1890s, both sacred and secular influences came to shape the form and content of jazz expression, in the form of spirituals and the blues.

內容總結題

〔**解析**〕第一個選項不符合事實，因為三弦序列是藍調音樂的一部分。文中未說樂儀隊（marching bands）允許爵士樂手讀曲子，所以第二個選項不正確。第三個選項正確，因為它符合第一段和第二段的內容，文中提到了拉格泰姆音樂是影響爵士樂的三種主要音樂類型之一。第四個選項也正確，因為文中提到從密西西比河遷移來的歌手和吉他手的影響下，即興音樂和深情述說故事的風格成為爵士樂的基本表達方式，該項與本文陳述相符。第五個選項不正確，雖然第一個分句正確（經常去做禮拜的人對藍調心存疑慮），但後半部分說法有誤，因為文章說教堂音樂與藍調的元素有很多共同之處。第六個選項正確，因為它綜合了有關宗教音樂和世俗音樂對爵士樂的影響的觀點。第七個選項不正確，因為本文說年輕人從一開始就伴著拉格泰姆音樂跳舞。

● **Answer Key to Exercise 2**

Professor: Now I want to talk about a remarkable example of a musician who transitioned from Classical music to jazz. This is the story of violinist Regina Carter, who was born in 1966 in Detroit, the home of the Motown Sound and R&B. Her earliest musical training was completely classical; she started piano lessons at age two. But by age four, she'd switched to the violin.

Later on, during high school, she fell in love with jazz after hearing a French violinist play that kind of music. Following that, Carter attended the New England Conservatory, and joined a jazz band, performing and recording records. Ultimately, Regina Carter launched a solo career, creating an album for Atlantic Records. Ever since then, she's proved that the violin has a home in the realm of jazz.

聽力模擬試題錄音文本　 *Track 019*

N: Now listen to part of a lecture in a music history class.

P: Now that we've finished the Classical epoch, we'll turn to Romanticism. I want to make it clear that when we talk about "Romantic music," we could be talking about a historical period. Or we could be talking about an artistic style, a style with certain identifiable characteristics. In today's lecture, I'll be giving you quite a bit of information about both the Romantic period and the Romantic style. So that's a heads-up for you on terminology.

Similarly, before I begin in earnest, I want to clear up another potentially confusing semantic issue involving the word "romantic." Some people, when they hear the word "romantic," think of hearts and Valentine's Day. But in the arts, Romanticism encompasses a whole host of themes—including the notion of romantic love—but the scope goes well beyond that.

Now, when we talk about historical epochs, it's important to remember that there is no clear break between one epoch and another. In this case, there's no obvious split between Classicism and Romanticism. An artistic movement involves gradual change, involving different composers, in different countries. This said, most scholars believe the Romantic Movement in the arts began with Romantic literature in Germany at the end of the 18th century.

What about Romanticism in music, then? There's much discussion among musicologists about when Romanticism in music first began; some historians say the Romantic Epoch runs from 1815 to 1910. But we can point to definite changes occurring around 1800. It's helpful to look at the transition from Classicism to Romanticism by looking at the works of Beethoven, and not only because Beethoven's life runs roughly concurrent with the span of the Romantic period. It's also because many of Beethoven's greatest works epitomize key aspects of the Romantic style. His famous Eroica Symphony—the Third Symphony, first performed in 1805, shows a marked departure from Classical themes and forms. Beethoven's Third Symphony constitutes a turning point in musical history because of its unconventional format—it was much longer than previous symphonies—and because of its ability to evoke emotion. It also shows Romantic characteristics in that it was originally composed to commemorate the achievements of Napoleon. Although Beethoven later changed his mind about dedicating the work to the French leader, it was typical of Romantic composers to create bold statements about great leaders and celebrated national events.

What were the social and economic factors shaping this artistic movement? The changes in society accompanying the Industrial Revolution, including the emergence of a strong middle class, changed the way that musicians and audiences interacted with music. Along with the growing middle class, we see the rise of individualism. Economically, musicians were no longer dependent on a few aristocratic patrons. Composers could reach out to audiences who could now afford to attend public concerts. This meant that musicians could write and express music based on their individual tastes.

Also, as the middle class became educated about music, audiences became increasingly sophisticated. Composers took advantage of their new resources and created large numbers of symphonies and "tone poems." Numerous concerts were given in Paris, London and Italy. One new kind of public performance was the virtuoso concert, which featured one individual—a virtuoso musician—who'd perform technically challenging music for a doting audience. In a way, they were the "superstars" of their day. Concerts featuring violin and piano players became especially popular.

We all take pianos for granted nowadays, but you may not be aware of how pivotal the Industrial Revolution was in the history of the piano. For one thing, improved metal technology allowed the tension of the piano strings to increase quite a bit through steel piano wires, and this increased tension of the strings added resonance and carrying power to piano acoustics. In addition, during this time the price of pianos became very affordable in Europe and America, making it possible for everyday people to own an instrument that used to be owned just by the wealthy.

Of course, when we think of Romantic piano music, we think of Chopin. Chopin did not make more than 30 public appearances in his life, but his virtuoso works for the piano were considered essential fare for his contemporaries—and this continues to this day. His piano compositions took advantage of the technical improvements in the piano, including the extension of the keyboard to more than six octaves. Chopin's music requires that the performer make the piano "sing;" it has expressive textures and colors. Chopin's most important "genre" for the piano is the "character piece," a short composition designed to express a definite mood or idea. You know these short character pieces by different names—for example, you've certainly heard of nocturnes—those dreamy "night songs" —and piano preludes. We'll be listening to a nocturne or two later on in the hour.

● **Transcripts for Question 2.**

N: What does the professor mean when she says this:

P: **Some people, when they hear the word "romantic," think of hearts and Valentine's Day. But in the arts, Romanticism encompasses a whole host of themes—including the notion of romantic love—but the scope goes well beyond that.**

● **Transcripts for Question 5.**

N: Listen again to part of the lecture. Then answer the question.

P: **One new kind of public performance was the virtuoso concert, which featured one individual—a virtuoso musician—who'd perform technically challenging music for a doting audience. In a way, they were the "superstars" of their day.**

N: What does the professor mean when she says this:

P: **In a way, they were the "superstars" of their day.**

關鍵語塊

Classical epoch 古典主義音樂時期	Romanticism 浪漫主義音樂時期
historical period 歷史時期	artistic style 藝術風格
identifiable characteristic 可識別的特徵	that's a heads-up〔口語〕這是個提醒
begin in earnest 正式開始	clear up (an issue) 澄清（一個問題）

semantic issue 語義問題	Valentine's Day 情人節
a whole host of 大量的	break 中斷，分割點
split 劃分	this said 也就是説……
musicologist 音樂學家	run from... to... 從……到……
transition from... to... 從……過渡到……	concurrent with sth. 與某事同時發生
epitomize 代表	symphony 交響樂
marked departure from... 明顯偏離……；與……迥然不同	a turning point in... ……的轉捩點
unconventional format 非傳統的風格	evoke emotion 喚起情感
commemorate the achievements of... 紀念……的成就	dedicate the work to sb. 將作品獻給某人（為表示感情或敬意）
middle class 中產階級	sophisticated 講究的，有品位的
tone poem 詩曲；交響詩	virtuoso concert 名家音樂會
virtuoso musician 大師級音樂家	doting audience 著迷的觀眾
take... for granted 認為……是理所當然的	... is pivotal in... ……是……的關鍵
tension of the piano strings 鋼琴琴弦的張力	resonance 共鳴；共振
carrying power （音波的）力度	piano acoustics 鋼琴的聲音；鋼琴的音效
essential fare 必做的事情；必彈的曲目	extension of the keyboard 琴鍵擴展
octave 八度音；八度音階	expressive textures 扣人心弦的諧和統一感
color 音色	genre 流派
nocturne 夜曲，夢幻曲	prelude 序曲，前奏曲

聽力模擬試題答案詳解

1. **D** 主旨大意題
   〔**解析**〕教授只是附帶提到浪漫主義音樂源於德國文學，但這不是講座的主旨，因此選項 A 不正確。選項 B 也不正確，因為教授介紹了浪漫主義音樂時期的鋼琴和鋼琴音樂，但鋼琴並不是講座的主旨，本文主旨則是浪漫主義音樂的發展歷史和特徵。

2. **B** 語用功能題
   〔**解析**〕教授説浪漫主義包括「浪漫愛情」的概念，但不僅僅限於此範圍（the notion of romantic love—but the scope goes well beyond that）。因此，選項 B 為正確答案。

3. **B、C** 細節資訊題
   〔**解析**〕教授介紹《英雄交響曲》（即《第三交響曲》）時説這是浪漫主義音樂，因此，選項 A「新古典主義音樂的典型代表」不正確。她指出貝多芬最初想將該交響曲獻給拿破崙，以體現拿破崙的英雄氣概，因此，選項 B 正確。教授還説該交響曲喚起情感的能力（its ability to evoke emotion）非凡，因此選項 C 也正確。講座中沒有提到貝多芬的耳聾，因此，選項 D 不正確。

4.

	YES	NO
The middle class preferred popular music to romantic music.		✓
Following the Industrial Revolution, more people acquired the pianos.	✓	
Audiences began to ask for musical compositions about love.		✓
With stronger steel, the pianos produced louder acoustical sounds.	✓	

關聯內容題

〔解析〕在第五至第七段中，教授介紹了 19 世紀社會和經濟方面的背景資訊。教授説聽眾越來越有品味（became increasingly sophisticated），紛紛湧向技藝精湛的音樂會，所以第一句錯誤。教授説在工業革命期間，市井小民（everyday people）都買得起鋼琴了，所以第二句正確。教授沒有提到聽眾對愛情樂曲的需求，因此第三句不正確。第四句正確，因為教授説 increased tension of the strings added resonance and carrying power to piano acoustics。

5. **C** 立場觀點題

〔解析〕教授談到了 19 世紀大師級音樂會和音樂家，然後説這些音樂大師是那個時代的「超級明星」（in a way, they were the "superstars" of their day）。教授將 19 世紀的藝術大師與 21 世紀的超級明星進行了對比，潛在的意思是 19 世紀的觀眾也有當代觀眾的藝術熱情，選項 C 最恰當。

6. **A** 組織結構題

〔解析〕教授定義了 character pieces，即為表達特定的情感或想法而創作的一種短小曲子，教授也説蕭邦是這類鋼琴曲的代表音樂家，然後列舉了這類曲子的三種形式：You know these short character pieces by different names—for example, you've certainly heard of nocturnes... 因此選項 A 正確。

生命科學常考主題 3 細胞生物學詞彙、答案、解析和錄音原文

● **Answer Key to Exercise 1**

a. <u>The resolution of the image was greatly improved by the use of three pairs of matched lenses.</u>

b. <u>In hopes of getting a better glimpse into natural phenomena, scientists were already creating simple microscopes prior to the 18th century.</u>

c. <u>If William Harvey had only known about microscopes, he could have made use of them in his study of the heart and blood circulation.</u>

閱讀模擬試題答案詳解

1. **C 細節資訊題**
　　〔**解析**〕第一段最後一句，作者說每一次細胞方面發現的里程碑都與一種新工具或儀器有關（every milestone about cell discovery bears the name of a new tool or instrument）。因此，正確答案為 C，instrumentation 也有「儀器」的意思。

2. **A 語境詞彙題**
　　〔**解析**〕prying 與 inquisitive 是同義詞，意為「愛打聽的、好奇的」。

3. **D 指代關係題**
　　〔**解析**〕指代關係詞 them 所在句中有多個嵌入式片語和分句。從上下文看，them 指代與之最近的名詞 lenses。

4. **B 否定事實題**
　　〔**解析**〕在第二段找到關鍵字 Robert Hooke。文中說他出版過一個作品集，裡面畫有他觀察到的東西的漂亮畫（among the beautiful drawings of his observations），所以 A 項是作者描述過的內容。雖然他出版過作品，但作品是微小生命體的圖紙，所以 B 項（他出版過有關顯微鏡簡介的書）不符合事實。

5. **B 推論題**
　　〔**解析**〕文章提到了 Leeuwenhoek 利用簡單的顯微鏡看到了被他稱為微生物（animalcules）的東西，包括細菌。根據上下文以及作者講述的科學家如何觀察活細胞的歷史事實，可以推斷答案為 B。microorganism 意為「微生物」。

6. **C 語境詞彙題**
　　〔**解析**〕這道題有點難。在上下文中，動詞 manipulated 與 guided 同義。thread 的意思雖然與「針」（needle）有關聯，但與 manipulated 無關。

7. **A 修辭目的題**
　　〔**解析**〕這道題有點難，因為作者說的是反話。這種能力（this faculty）是指上句提的「想像力」。從上下文可知作者認為那時的顯微鏡作用有限，科學家需要發揮自己的想像力來瞭解細節。一些發揮想像力的科學家作出了準確的解釋，而「過度」發揮想像力的科學家最終得出了荒謬的假設，認為精子細胞中便有成型的嬰兒。選項 A 最符合語義。

8. **D 語境詞彙題**
　　〔**解析**〕從上下文可知，aberrations 與 deviations 同義，optical aberration 意為「光學像差」。cracks 有混淆視聽的作用，因為裂縫（cracks）也可以指材料中的缺陷，但是，裂縫（cracks）是線狀的，與 aberrations 不是同義詞。

9. **A** 細節資訊題

〔**解析**〕從第五段開頭可知，1827 後的幾年內 the generalized theory was formulated that plants and animals are made of one or more similar units—cells。選項 A（similar units = core elements）為正確答案。文中沒有提到 cell systems，因此選項 B 不正確。

10. **B** 句子簡化題

〔**解析**〕分析該句結構：investigators 碰到了難題，其餘內容都是説明該難題。選項 A 中「科學家發現了一個原理」是誤解了 found。選項 C 中「科學家致力於研究物理的新興分支學科（novel branch of physics）」是曲解了 new obstacle 的意思。選項 D 中「他們樂觀地認為這一科學障礙將會被克服」是曲解了 seemingly insurmountable 的意思。

11. **C** 推論題

〔**解析**〕作者並沒有因為 Harvey 缺乏儀器（儀器當時尚未發明出來）暗諷他是一位糟糕的科學家，所以選項 A 不正確。選項 D 不正確，因為事實上 Harvey 發現了血液循環。作者告訴我們 Harvey 的理論接近 Virchow 的理論，雖然他的理論不完全準確。作者進一步提到 Harvey 在第一台顯微鏡發明前不久就去世了，言下之意是：如果他有顯微鏡，可能會進一步發展他的理論。因此選項 C 正確。

12.

Microscope	Features
Leeuwenhoek	• 1. A glass droplet causes the specimen to be enlarged almost 300 times • 4. The specimen to be viewed is manipulated by the means of screws • 6. The microscopes allowed the viewer to see microorganisms, including bacteria
Amici	• 3. The enhanced image resolution led to the theory that plants contain similar cells • 7. The design made use of multiple pairs of matched lenses processed light without color separation

資訊歸類題

〔**解析**〕這道題目並不難，因為圖表中不包括對第一台顯微鏡（Hooke 的顯微鏡）的介紹。可以略讀開頭兩段，然後開始核對第三段中的每項特徵。第一個選項應放入 Leeuwenhoek 對應的資訊欄裡，因為作者説科學家得到了 270 倍於肉眼所見（270 times that of the naked eye）的放大率。第三個選項有點棘手，因為理論本身屬於 Schleiden。但是，文章説 Amici 的顯微鏡大大地改善了圖像，從而得出了植物含有細胞的理論。第四個選項很容易確定，文中提到 Leeuwenhoek 用一個螺絲來控制一根針。第六個選項應放入 Leeuwenhoek 對應的資訊欄裡，因為作者説科學家能看到並準確地畫出細菌。第七個選項應放入 Amici 對應的資訊欄裡，因為作者説 Amici 改進了顯微鏡的圖像（through three pairs of matched lenses that could deflect light without separating it into colors）。

第二個選項不選，因為該項指的是 Hooke 的顯微鏡。文中沒有提到微生物圖紙導致了顯微鏡的普及，因此第五個選項也不選。

聽力模擬試題錄音文本 *Track 021*

N: Now listen to part of a lecture on cell biology.

P: I'd like to continue talking about cells now. The first cells appeared 3.5 billion years ago and quickly evolved into bacteria. For more than one billion years, these bacteria were the only things alive on the face of the Earth. Back then, bacteria were confined to shallow ocean waters, but eventually they moved to inhabit virtually every place on land, sea and air. Now, billions of years later, those simple cells have evolved into complex types of cells and into complex multicellular organisms. And, uh, living creatures continue to create new cells. Each second of our lives, humans make millions of new cells! But remember, even complex forms of life begin life as a single cell.

In evolution, plants and animals diverged at least 700 million years ago and maybe longer. On the surface, we can see these organisms differ. An apple does not look like the cousin of an antelope. But if you look at plant and animal cells under a microscope, you find there are great similarities. Some organisms are large; some are small, but the cellular dimensions do not vary in a significant way. For example, activities occurring in molecules, such as the duplication of DNA, are much the same for plant and animal cells. Plant and animal cells each have a nucleus. Inside the membranes of both plant and animal cells there's watery fluid. And these are just a few of the many similarities.

But there are also some important differences between plants and animals at the cellular level. Oh, before I forget—this topic will be a large part of Friday's quiz.

Right. [pause] Now where plant and animal cells differ most are in their structure and function. In terms of structure, the first difference I'd like to talk about is the cell wall. There is no cell wall in animal cells, and so the animal cell is soft and flabby. The only way an animal cell gets its structure is from a thin outer layer—not the wall, but a layer we call the cell membrane. Plant cells also have a membrane, but their membranes are surrounded by an outer wall, and this wall is what gives it a rigid structure. And—this is pretty interesting—a cell's shape is influenced by whether or not that cell has a wall. So, animal cells tend to have more rounded edges, because they have no walls, whereas plant cells tend to be long and rectangular, because they do have walls. And because plant cells have this fixed structure, most of them look pretty much alike, which is not true of animal cells.

OK. A second important difference is that animal cells can move. In plants, however, the cell cannot move on its own because it's constrained by its rigid wall. See how the structure—the plant's unbending wall—affects its biological functioning?

But it's not all bad; the cell wall benefits the plant, too. The wall surrounding the plant cell makes it possible for plants to keep growing and growing—to a very large size. And this leads to another significant feature of plants—something different from animals—a plant organism has a large surface compared to a relatively small volume.

OK. Now let's talk about the space inside the plant cell. What's inside the cell wall? One thing inside the plant cell is a structure called a vacuole, something animal cells do not have. What's a vacuole? It's essentially a bag filled with water. These vacuoles are very large relative to the size of the cell, and often take up much of the volume of a plant cell. What does the plant vacuole do? It promotes growth without using up too much energy—but there's a catch. It needs to have water to do its work. And in case you don't think vacuoles are important—the reason lettuce is crunchy when we chew it is because vacuoles are filled with water! When there's no water in those lettuce vacuoles, your salad will wilt. Oh, and I should add: Animal cells do not have large vacuoles, but they do have some tiny ones, which are not as important.

OK, we're almost out of time so let me stop for a moment and ask—are there any questions so far?

S: Is every plant cell bigger than every animal cell? Or does it just depend?

P: Good question. The quick answer is that plant cells tend to be bigger because of the large vacuoles filled with water. Of course, within plants, there's a range of cell sizes and within animals, there's also a range. But the variance in cell size is minimal when compared to the huge variance in the size of the organisms themselves.

● **Transcripts for Question 2.**

N: Listen again to part of the lecture. Then answer the question.

P: On the surface, we can see these organisms differ. An apple does not look like the cousin of an antelope.

N: What does the professor mean when he says this:

P: An apple does not look like the cousin of an antelope.

關鍵語塊

... evolved into... ……進化成……	bacteria 細菌
face of the Earth 地球表面	be confined to... 侷限於……中
multicellular organism 多細胞生物	plants and animals diverged 植物和動物出現差異
cellular dimension 細胞大小	duplication of DNA DNA 的複製
nucleus 細胞核	membrane （連接或覆蓋身體某些部位的）膜
in terms of... 關於；說起	flabby 鬆弛的
rounded edge 圓邊	rectangular 矩形的
plant organism 植物有機體	There's a catch. 這裡有一個問題。
crunchy 易碎的	wilt 發蔫；枯萎
a range of 一系列，一連串	variance in... ……的差異

聽力模擬試題答案詳解

1. **C** 主旨大意題

〔**解析**〕講座中沒有介紹植物是如何繁殖（reproduce）的，因此選項 B 不正確。教授主要在比較植物細胞和動物細胞的區別，因此選項 C 正確。

2. **A** 語用功能題

〔**解析**〕教授在此處開了個玩笑，舉出兩種名稱都以字母「A」開頭的物體，以此說明動物和植物看起來差別很大。因此選項 A 為正確答案。

3. **A、D** 細節資訊題

〔**解析**〕第二段教授說：Some organisms are large; some are small, but the cellular dimensions do not vary in a significant way. 因此選項 A 正確。當學生問植物細胞是否大一些時，教授說：The quick answer is that plant cells tend to be bigger because of the large vacuoles filled with water. 因此選項 D 也正確。

4. **B** 組織結構題

〔**解析**〕教授提到生菜是要說明當植物細胞的液泡（vacuole）中含有水分時植物細胞的表現會有怎樣的不同，並說：And in case you don't think vacuoles are important—the reason lettuce is crunchy when we chew it is because vacuoles are filled with water! 因此選項 B 正確。

5.

Feature	Plants	Animals	Both plants and animals
Have cell membranes			✓
Have relatively large surface-to-volume ratio	✓		
Have a long shape	✓		
Have the ability to move		✓	

關聯內容題

〔解析〕教授在介紹了動物的細胞膜後,說植物也有細胞膜（plant cells also have a membrane）。所以第一個特徵在 Both Plants and Animals 欄中打勾。根據 a plant organism has a large surface compared to a relatively small volume 可知第二個特徵應在 Plants 欄中打勾。教授說動物細胞是圓的,但植物細胞往往是細長或矩形的,因為它們有細胞壁（plant cells tend to be long and rectangular, because they do have walls）,因此第三個特徵應在 Plants 欄中打勾。教授說另一個重要區別是動物細胞可以移動（a second important difference is that animal cells can move）,因此第四個特徵應在 Animals 欄中打勾。

● **Answer Key to Exercise 2**

1. earliest cells — When? 3.5 billion years ago
2. bacteria — Where? first just in oceans, then everywhere
3. cell wall — What organism? only plants
4. animal cells are round — Why? no cell wall for structure
5. vacuole — What function? promotes growth in plants

社會科學常考主題 3 法學詞彙、答案、解析和錄音原文

● **Answer Key to Exercise 1**

a. A contract is broadly defined as an exchange of promises associated with a specific action to be taken when those promises aren't kept.

b. Nowadays, contract breaches are addressed as part of the common law legal system.

c. Although many contracts involve written legal agreements between two parties, there are other types of contracts as well.

閱讀模擬試題答案詳解
- -

1. **D** 細節資訊題
　〔**解析**〕文章說丈夫的納稅支出「覆蓋了」（covered）妻子的納稅，婦女根本不用納稅，所以選項 C「交納的稅比男人少」不正確。作者說受丈夫監護指 the inclusion of a woman in the "legal person" of her husband after marriage，即婚後，女性的「法人」是其丈夫，自己沒有法律地位。因此選 D 項。

2. **A** 修辭目的題
　〔**解析**〕作者告訴我們 feme sole 是古代法語詞彙，用於英國法律，指單身女性，feme covert 意思是被監護或已婚的婦女，coverture 的用法源於此。因此選項 A 正確。common law 意為「習慣法」，statutory law 意為「成文法」。

3. **B** 句子簡化題
　〔**解析**〕該句中有 not only..., [but]... 句型。這種句型可改述為 there was..., and there was also...。因此要找到一個有此含義的選項。選項 A 中的 Although 和選項 D 中的 Even if 都曲解了 not only 的意思，也不是對句子的換句話說。選項 C 中的 Only the husband 曲解了 not only would the husband 的意思。只有選項 B 與該句意思相同（"control any property" = "had authority over the property"; "own any wages she earned" = " [had authority over] her future salary"）。

4. **D** 語境詞彙題
　〔**解析**〕從句型看，this shift 指上句的內容，即大部分國家的受丈夫監護法律廢除了，女性擁有自我權利和勞動所得。這是一種「變化」，所以選 D 項 change。

5. **C** 細節資訊題
　〔**解析**〕在第三段，作者指出：The shift in property rights from coverture is a constructive example of how family economics have shaped property rights, and visa-a-versa. 作者的意思是經濟（金錢）改變了法律，而並非與此相反，因此選項 C 正確。

6. **A** 語境詞彙題
　〔**解析**〕動詞 monitor 與片語動詞 check on 同義，意為「監視，檢查」。

7. **C** 細節資訊題
　〔**解析**〕作者說婦女有可能悠閒地度日，因為她們的丈夫不能總是監視她們做家事（to spend their days in leisure because their husbands could not always monitor their household efforts），因此選項 C 正確。

8. **B** 語境詞彙題
　〔**解析**〕片語 exempt from 與 free from 同義，意為「免於」。

9. **B** 語境詞彙題
　〔**解析**〕形容詞 prevalent 與 commonplace 同義，意為「普遍的」。

10. **C** 否定事實題

〔**解析**〕這道題有點難，因為考生必須讀例子，然後確定每個選項是否與之相符。在第七段，作者說：Examples of such additional rights included the access to labor and commercial markets (= D, "working as a teacher"), ownership of market earnings (= A, "having a separate bank account"), ownership of separate property (= B, "personally owning a summer cottage") and greater control of household output. 只有 C 項 filing a law suit 不符合例子。

11. **D** 推論題

〔**解析**〕從句子 under self-ownership, however, women are free to allocate their time across both market and household activities 可推斷出作者的態度：如今女性能夠掌控自己的生活，這是好事。因此選項 D 正確。

12. ■ **3** 插入句子題

Under self-ownership, however, women are free to allocate their time across both market and household activities. This leads to a different economic model of the family. First, the husband and wife jointly own their final market goods. ■ 1 Second, within a marriage, husband and wife each own one-half of the household products and one-half of the property income. ■ 2 Finally, because the wife has access to labor markets, she is not as likely to be tempted into leisure at home. ■ 3 Rather, she is more likely to work more in the market and purchase market goods. This model means that each partner in the marriage can choose his or her optimal allocation of time between market and household work, based on the nature of the marriage contract and the behavior of the other partner. ■ 4

〔**解析**〕插入句中有兩條線索：1）對比信號詞 rather 和 2）女性更能參與勞動力市場。據此可推測前一個句子可能是傳達相反的意思：女性很少參與勞動力市場。顯然，開頭兩個方塊的位置都不合適。此外，它們是使用 First、second 和 finally 系列句子的一部分，不能中斷。然而，第三個黑色方塊前面的句子說：Finally, because the wife has access to labor markets, she is unlikely to be tempted into leisure at home. 這符合邏輯：女性不太可能在家裡輕鬆度日，而是更能參與勞動力市場。因此第三個方塊的位置正確。

13. **2** Stemming from English common law, the doctrine of coverture limited women's rights up until the 1900s.

3 The coverture model consists of property ownership exclusively by husbands, and a system wherein women own their output is a self-ownership model.

6 Economic interests frequently determine how a married couple spend their time, whether on market activities or in the home.

內容總結題

〔**解析**〕見本章前文的「托福總監評析」。

聽力模擬試題錄音文本 *Track 023*

N: Now listen to part of a lecture in a law class.

P: OK, the next area of concentration for us in the sociology of law is the area of social controls. At first glance, the law seems very official, very formal. But as we'll see today, social control is not limited to the use of explicit rules.

I want now to talk about how socialization causes people to conform to social rules. In a society which is small and relatively homogeneous, conformity in behavior happens because social experiences are much the same for all members of society. Social norms tend to be consistent across all sectors of society. There is agreement about these norms, and they are strongly supported by tradition. For example, in a village, rules may be passed down orally from one's parents or from the village elders. Social control in this kind of social context relies on the fact that an individual is sanctioning his or her own actions.

What do we mean by "sanction"? A sanction is an action taken to address and alter behavior. Some people mistakenly think that sanctions are all negative, but sanctions can be positive as well. A positive sanction is offered as an incentive, to encourage a certain behavior. A negative sanction is meant to discourage a behavior. All societies have sanctions, but as I mentioned just now, these don't have to be formal. The social mechanisms can be informal and come from our friends and neighbors. For example, we may choose not to throw litter on our neighbor's sidewalk because we know it will cause them to be disappointed in us.

OK, so in our example of a homogenous society, people most frequently decide for themselves to act acceptably. In other words, these people have internalized social norms. The people who do deviate from social norms may receive what we call "external" sanctions, but these can be formal or informal. An example of an informal external sanction would be that the people who deviate from norms become subject to gossip, ridicule or humiliation.

Now interestingly enough even in complex, heterogeneous societies such as the United Kingdom or the United States, social control typically occurs because people have already internalized social norms. Of course, individuals in heterogeneous societies also feel the tug of a guilty conscience, and they will sanction their own actions. They're also influenced by external pressures; that is to say they care what family, friends and neighbors might say about them. Indeed, these internal or informal factors are usually enough to keep most people from deviating from the norms. In the broader scheme of things, formal punishment such as imprisonment is relatively rare.

But across the various segments in diverse societies, people may not always share the same value systems. Or there may be struggles between groups with different interests who are competing for economic gain. In these situations, there is often a need for more formal mechanisms of social control.

Now a word about formal control in society. Formal control can be broken into three components. First, formal control is characterized by very explicit rules of conduct. In other words, the rules or laws are clearly communicated in an official capacity. An instance of an explicit rule is a red traffic light. Citizens may not cross the road when the traffic light is red; that is an explicit rule.

OK, the second aspect of formal control is the planned use of sanctions to support the rules. Obviously, leaders and legislators would like the members of society to abide by those rules. That means the leaders will think of ways to create incentives—positive or negative—causing citizens to conform.

And the third aspect of formal control is the need to appoint people to interpret and enforce these rules. A legal system carries out many rules of social control. Police arrest burglars, prosecutors prosecute them, juries convict them, judges sentence them, prison guards watch them, and parole boards release them.

Of course, as we shall see, there are other types of formal control mechanisms, such as firing and promoting employees, and providing other types of compensation for work. These control mechanisms can be found in universities, governments and businesses.

Now the framework of formal legal controls provides a means for citizens to resolve disputes.

Increasingly, people go to the courts for matters that used to be handled informally through negotiation or mediation. Still, when we legally resolve a conflict, we do not necessarily remove the hostility between the parties. A legal case, for example, may involve a claim that a company discriminated against an employee because he was an older worker, say, in his fifties. In making the ruling, the court may successfully settle one specific matter of law, and at the same time fail to address the broader, underlying social issues that have produced that conflict.

● **Transcripts for Question 2.**

N: Why does the professor say this:

P: **At first glance, the law seems very official, very formal. But as we'll see today, social control is not limited to the use of explicit rules.**

● **Transcripts for Question 6.**

N: What does the professor imply about the legal system when he says this:

P: **Increasingly, people go to the courts for matters that used to be handled informally through negotiation or mediation. Still, when we legally resolve a conflict, we do not necessarily remove the hostility between the parties.**

關鍵語塊

area of concentration 研究的領域	sociology of law 法律社會學
explicit 明確的	socialization 社會化
conform to social rules 遵守社會規則	homogeneous 單一的
social norm 社會準則	sectors of society 社會階層
passed down orally 口頭流傳下來	village elders 村裡的長輩
sanctioning one's own actions / self-sanctioning 自我約束	sanction 約束；處罰
incentive 激勵	social mechanism 社會機制
throw litter on... 在⋯⋯上丟垃圾	sidewalk 人行道
internalized social norms 使社會規範內在化，將社會規範融為自我意識	deviate from social norms 背離社會規範
external sanction 外部獎懲	become subject to 有⋯⋯傾向的
gossip 流言蜚語	ridicule 愚弄
humiliation 羞辱	heterogeneous societies 多元社會
tug of a guilty conscience 內疚	imprisonment 監禁
value system 價值體系	compete for economic gain 爭取經濟收益
official capacity 法定資格	legislator 立法者
abide by those rules 遵守這些規則	arrest burglars 逮捕竊賊
prosecutor 原告	prosecute sb. 起訴某人
juries convict sb. 陪審團宣告某人有罪	judges sentence 法官宣判
prison guards watch sb. 獄警看守某人	parole boards release sb. 假釋委員會釋放某人
fire sb. 解雇某人	promote sb. 給某人升職

compensation for ……的賠償	resolve dispute 解決爭端
negotiation 談判，協商	mediation 仲裁
claim 宣稱	discriminate against 歧視
make a ruling 作出裁決	matter of law 法律問題
fail to address sth. 沒有提到某事	hostility between the parties 雙方之間的敵意

聽力模擬試題答案詳解

1. **B** 主旨大意題

〔解析〕選項 A 和 C 文中只是提到，並不是主題。全文談論的是社會制約問題，所以選項 B 正確。

2. **A** 立場觀點題

〔解析〕選項 B 是干擾項，因為含有 socially，但教授並沒有主張通過某些法律。這句話的意思是：初看起來，法律似乎非常官方、正式，但從當前的實際面來看，社會制約並不侷限於採用明確的制度。隱含的意思是為了有效性，法律並不一定要非常正式。因此選項 A 符合。

3. **C** 組織結構題

〔解析〕本題展現了聽例子做筆記的重要性。教授說：The social mechanisms can be informal and come from our friends and neighbors. For example, we may choose not to throw litter on our neighbor's sidewalk because we know it will cause them to be disappointed in us. 他想說明社會機制對人的制約作用，因此選 C。

4. **B、D** 細節資訊題

〔解析〕教授說社會規範在社會各界都是一致的，例如，在一個村子裡，規則可能是由父母或長輩口頭傳下來的（consistent across all sectors of society... For example, in a village, rules may be passed down orally from one's parents or from the village elders）。因此選項 B 和 D 均正確。

5.

	YES	NO
Positive sanctions have been proven to be impractical.		✓
Societies count on individuals to self-sanction.	✓	
Disgracing a person who deviates from the norm is an external sanction.	✓	

關聯內容題

〔解析〕講座中，教授給 sanctions 作了定義，並列舉了幾個例子：A positive sanction is offered as an incentive，to encourage a certain behavior. ／ That means the leaders will think of ways to create incentives—positive or negative—causing citizens to conform. 他並沒有說正面懲罰不起作用。因此，第一個觀點在「NO」欄下方打勾。教授說：... in our example of a homogenous society, people most frequently decide for themselves to act acceptably. In other words, these people have internalized social norms. 還說：... and social control typically occurs because people have already internalized social norms. 因此，第二個觀點在「YES」欄下方打勾。最後，教授說：The people who do deviate from social norms may receive what we call "external" sanctions, but these can be formal or informal. 因此，第三個觀點在「YES」欄下方打勾。

6. **D** 推論題

〔解析〕該句意為：如今，人們頻繁地去法院解決過去經常以非正式的方式處理的問題，但法院的解決並不能消除雙方之間的衝突。他是在巧妙地暗示法律可能無法改變人們的態度。因此，選項 D 正確。

物理科學常考主題 4 化學和生物化學詞彙、答案、解析和錄音原文

閱讀模擬試題答案詳解

1. **B** 細節資訊題

   〔**解析**〕作者說 radiation may have helped to keep the atmosphere rich in reactive molecules and far from chemical equilibrium（輻射有助於大氣保持豐富的活性分子，遠離化學平衡）。沒有說輻射會破壞臭氧層，也沒有說輻射會導致閃電。Rich in reactive molecules 和 far from chemical equilibrium 都表示有很多化學反應，因此選項 B「促進化學反應」正確。

2. **D** 指代關係題

   〔**解析**〕這道題有點棘手，因為此處的 its 並不是指代其前面最近的名詞 Sun。by its photochemical action（通過光化作用）是一個副詞片語，修飾以 the radiation may have helped... 開頭的分句。輻射是如何使大氣中富含活性分子的？通過光化作用。因此選項 D 正確。

3. **A** 否定事實題

   〔**解析**〕作者提出了生命的三個必需條件，並說活細胞的集合 1）能利用化學能或電磁能進行化學反應（對應 C 項）；2）能通過控制化學合成增加品質（對應 D 項）；3）擁有一個資訊編碼系統和一個將編碼資訊轉換成分子的系統，分子可以進行自身維護和繁殖（對應 B 項）。只有選項 A 沒有提到。

4. **C** 語境詞彙題

   〔**解析**〕在本文，presumably 有「大概，可能」的意思，只有 apparently（似乎，表面上）與它的意思最接近。

5. **D** 細節資訊題

   〔**解析**〕作者說在 stromatolite（疊層石）中發現的藍綠菌最可能 produced oxygen by splitting water molecules into hydrogen and oxygen。因此，選項 C 為正確答案。

6. **A** 語境詞彙題

   〔**解析**〕儘管選項 B 中 relatives 在意思上與 precursors 接近，但其含義更為籠統。forerunners（先驅，前輩）的意思與 precursors 相同。

7. **B** 細節資訊題

   〔**解析**〕文中說 Miller 通過將水、蒸汽和其他氣體置於一個模擬自然閃電的放電環境中來模擬大氣條件。因此選項 B 為正確答案。

8. **D** 修辭目的題

   〔**解析**〕見本章前文的「托福總監點評」。

9. **C** 關鍵技能 1 語境詞彙題

   〔**解析**〕這道題有點難。選項 B、C 和 D 都有混淆視聽的作用，因為它們都含有年齡增長或品質增加的意思。proliferate 在此處有「激增」的意思，與 multiply 同義。

10. **C** 推論題

    〔**解析**〕作者說實驗室中的微球體是 about the same size and shape as spherical bacteria，而且有的能夠生長和繁殖。與活體細菌的類似之處及其生長能力使我們能推斷出微球體與古細菌的進化有關。

11. ■ **1** 插入句子題

    In May 1953 the graduate student Stanley Miller, at the suggestion of his mentor Harold Urey, used a reflux apparatus to reproduce ancient atmospheric conditions that existed prior to the chemical evolution of biological molecules. ■ 1 **Specifically, he hoped to create certain**

small molecules of life (monomers), such as amino acids. To do this, Miller recirculated water, vapor and other gases (CH4, NH3 and H2) through a chamber where they were exposed to a continuous high-voltage electrical discharge that simulated natural lightning. ■ 2 After a few days, the mixture was analyzed and found to contain sugars, lipids and some of the building blocks for life, nucleic acids. ■ 3 However, nucleic acids (DNA, RNA) themselves were not formed! ■ 4 The experiment also produced compounds which would be toxic to most life forms. But these compounds, which include formaldehyde and cyanide, are necessary for creating important biochemical compounds, including amino acids. Subsequent experiments by Miller and other researchers using different molecule mixtures and energy sources produced a variety of other building blocks of more complex molecules. These molecules may have accumulated and provided a rich environment for chemical evolution. However, the spontaneous formation of complex, long-chain polymers from small, chemically generated monomers is not at all a straightforward process.

〔解析〕從這個插入句可得到兩條線索：1）Specifically 表明這個句子還會繼續重複前一個句子的意思，只是會用到一些更具體的術語；2）he hoped to create certain small molecules of life 表明科學家仍然處於實驗的設計階段。第一個黑色方塊緊跟的句子是說 Miller 用一個裝置來類比化學進化之前的遠古大氣條件。要插入的句子放到這句後面似乎很合適，因為它更加詳細地傳達了 Miller 的意圖。後面的三個黑色方塊處都不正確，因為 Miller 的初始設計不可能在實驗的後續步驟之後再介紹。

12.

	Scientific Theories
Areas on which scientists agree	• 3. The Earth's climate was very destructive • 4. There is evidence of amino acids in meteorites • 5. The earliest instance of fossilized life dates back 3.5 billion years
Areas on which scientists disagree	• 1. Life came into existence from nonliving chemicals • 6. The Earth's atmosphere included methane gas

資訊歸類題。

〔解析〕要回答這道題，考生必須掃讀全文，看看作者是否說了科學家們贊同的觀點。第一段的前幾個觀點應放在 disagree 後面，因為作者在第一句中說某些條件是「有爭議的問題」。以 everyone seems to agree... 開頭的兩個句子所含的觀點應放在 agree 後面。根據這個資訊可知第三個選項應放在 agree 後面，第六個選項應放在 disagree 後面。

在第三段，作者說 the oldest microfossils superficially resembling bacteria have been dated at 3.5 billion years。因此，第五個選項應放在 agree 後面。

在第五段，作者說：There are two major scientific theories regarding how life came to be on Earth. It either evolved on Earth from nonliving chemicals, or it evolved elsewhere in the universe... 因此，第一個選項應置於 disagree 後面。在同一段，作者說 amino acids and other precursors of modern macromolecules have been found in meteorites，因此第四個選項應置於 agree 後面。

第二和第七個選項的表述與文章不符。

● **Answer Key to Exercise 1**

a. <u>To give an example of the violent conditions in early Earth / To show how violent Earth was during its first billion years.</u>

b. To explain one of the theories about how life came to be on the Earth.

c. To illustrate how microspheres are able to "grow."

● **Answer Key to Exercise 2**

a. Cameras must be cool because warm cameras are unable to see the warmth, or infrared radiation, generated by other objects.

b. A decrease in pressure occurs when gas expands, which in turn causes molecules to move more slowly.

c. As a result, the gas is cooled.

聽力模擬試題錄音文本　*Track 025*

- -

N: Now listen to part of a lecture on chemistry.

P: We've talked about the states of matter. And water, like all forms of matter, has states. As we know, water exists in three states: Solid, liquid and gas. Each of these states is stable under certain conditions. When conditions change, the state changes. That's the easy part, but now it gets tricky. Think that scientists know all there is to know about water? Think again! Sure, we rely on water for life, and water covers some 70 percent of the Earth's surface. But in fact there are lots of things we still don't entirely understand. Take ice, for example. The freezing of water and the melting of ice are among the most common and dramatic examples of matter changing states, yet basic aspects of how these transformations take place have puzzled chemists—[pause] and physicists—for years.

Many of the properties of water are due to its strong hydrogen bonding, the bonds formed between a hydrogen atom and other atoms. Each water molecule has two hydrogen atoms and one oxygen atom, allowing the molecule to form many hydrogen bonds with adjacent molecules. Because it is difficult to break these bonds, water can stay liquid at ordinary temperatures.

Now, as you know, liquid water forms a hard solid when the temperature drops below 32 degrees Fahrenheit or zero degrees Centigrade at one atmosphere pressure. Water, unlike most liquids, expands on freezing, so ice is less dense than liquid water. Because of this lower density, ice can float in water. So water is unusual. For most other substances, the solid form has a greater density than the liquid form.

And one of the interesting things about ice's relatively low density is that pressure can decrease ice's melting point. That means that great pressure can force ice back into a liquid state. [pause] Ah, yes?

S: About melting. Um, I read once in the newspaper that scientists keep arguing with each other why it is we're able to glide on ice when we go ice skating.

P: That's true! The slipperiness of ice continues to be a "hot" topic, no pun intended. There isn't total agreement yet, but we know more than we did. Let me go over the three major theories.

Until recently it was widely believed that ice gets slippery because of pressure. According to this first theory, the weight of the skater pressing down on a blade of an ice skate exerts pressure on the ice, causing it to melt the ice crystals on a very thin layer at the surface. The melted layer provided lubrication between the ice and the blade.

But the pressure explanation is no longer accepted by many scientists. OK, yes, some melting does occur from pressure, but the changes are too small to be considered the primary reason that ice gets slippery.

So why, then? The second contending theory is related to friction, as opposed to pressure. In this model, the assumption is that the fast-moving blade of the skate creates friction on the ice, generating heat to melt a thin layer of water under the skate. We know that there is some friction and that melting occurs. But this theory is also problematic since it doesn't fully explain how it is that a person who's standing still on ice will also slip.

So that leads us to the third theory, the hypothesis that ice has an inherently slippery layer at its surface. The scientific basis for this theory is that there are chains of water molecules on the part of the ice closest to the air and these molecule chains are not able to form ice crystals. The reason they can't form crystals is that the molecule chains are vibrating like liquid water molecules, so they can't properly bond with the molecules underneath them, the molecules in the mass of ice. That's why we now think that this wet layer composed of molecule chains is what makes ice slippery for skaters.

We also think that the principle of an inherently slippery layer on ice may help explain how glaciers flow. The film, which is in the state of solid ice, acts sort of like a liquid. So ice has some of the structural characteristics of the solid below it, but has the mobility of a fluid.

● **Transcripts for Question 2.**

N: Listen again to part of the lecture. Then answer the question.

P: Think that scientists know all there is to know about water? Think again! Sure, we rely on water for life, and water covers some 70 percent of the Earth's surface. But in fact there are lots of things we still don't entirely understand.

N: What does the professor imply when she says this:

P: Think again!

● **Transcripts for Question 4.**

N: Listen again to part of the lecture. Then answer the question.

S: About melting. Um, I read once in the newspaper that scientists keep arguing with each other why it is we're able to glide on ice when we go ice skating.

P: That's true! The slipperiness of ice continues to be a "hot" topic, no pun intended.

N: What does the professor mean when she says this:

P: The slipperiness of ice continues to be a "hot" topic, no pun intended.

關鍵語塊

solid 固體	liquid 液體
gas 氣體	get tricky 變得複雜
dramatic example 生動的例證	adjacent molecule 相鄰的分子
atmosphere pressure 大氣壓強	low density 低密度
melting point 熔點	glide 滑行
"hot" topic 「熱門」話題	no pun intended 並不是要說雙關語
blade 刀片	ice skate 溜冰鞋
ice crystal 冰晶	lubrication 潤滑
contending theory 爭辯中的理論	friction 摩擦力

inherently slippery layer 自身就有的滑層	glaciers flow 冰川運動
film 薄層	mobility of a fluid 液體的流動性

聽力模擬試題答案詳解

1. **D** 主旨大意題
   〔**解析**〕教授用了大部分的時間來介紹冰的光滑性的三個理論，因此選項 D 正確。

2. **B** 語用功能題
   〔**解析**〕Think...? Think again! 是一種口語表達，其意思是：Do you think...? If so, you're mistaken; ... is untrue! 因此，選項 B 是正確答案。

3. **C、D** 細節資訊題
   〔**解析**〕教授說：Water, unlike most liquids, expands on freezing, so ice is less dense than liquid water. 因此選項 C 正確。她又說冰相對較低的密度（ice's relatively low density）意味著壓力能降低冰的融點（pressure can decrease ice's melting point），因此選項 D 也正確。

4. **A** 語用功能題
   〔**解析**〕當說話者使用一個具有雙重意思的表達時，口語中往往會幽默地用到 No pun intended。此處，教授在介紹冰和光滑性時，用到了 hot 的雙重含義：熱的氣溫（warm temperature）和爭議大的（often debated）。因為冰本身非常冷，這樣說是為了製造幽默效果。因此選項 A 正確。

5. **B** 組織結構題
   〔**解析**〕教授在總結第三個理論（inherently slippery layer theory）時，提到了分子鏈。她說 there are chains of water molecules on the part of the ice closest to the air and these molecule chains are not able to form ice crystals，因此 B 項正確。選項 C 不正確，因為該層的分子不緊密。

6.

	YES	NO
Ice has a natural, very thin layer of liquid on it.	✓	
Friction on ice causes some melting.	✓	
Pressure from skates is what allows skaters to glide on ice.		✓

   關聯內容題
   〔**解析**〕第一個說法應在「YES」欄中打勾，因為教授說 ice has an inherently slippery layer at its surface。第二個說法也應在「YES」欄中打勾，因為教授說：We know that there is some friction and that melting occurs. 第三個說法應在「NO」欄中打勾，因為教授說 the changes are too small to be considered the primary reason that ice gets slippery，教授還說 inherently slipper layer 是光滑性的主要原因，使溜冰者能在冰上滑行。

⑭ 人文藝術常考主題 4 歷史詞彙、答案、解析和錄音原文

● **Answer Key to Exercise 1**

a. Blue jeans can be traced back to Europe of the 1500s.

b. The coarse cloth called "jean" was named after the Italian city where it was produced—Genoa, and it was worn by Genoan sailors.

c. Jean was also being manufactured in Lancaster, England, by the late 1500s / by the end of the century.

閱讀模擬試題答案詳解

1. **D** 語境詞彙題
　〔**解析**〕選項 A 有混淆視聽的作用，因為片語動詞 to be bound for 的意思與 to be headed for 相同。片語 defined by 與 bounded by 同義，意為「以……為分界，……的界線」。

2. **C** 細節資訊題
　〔**解析**〕由題幹中的關鍵字 17th century 找到第一段的 in 1658。作者説 in1658 this land was still a rolling pastoral landscape（1658 年，這塊土地依然還是綿延的田園風光），因此 C 項「廣袤的緩坡地形」最符合。選項 D 不正確，因為直到很久之後，道路才修建。

3. **A** 語境詞彙題
　〔**解析**〕speculative building 是固定搭配，意為「為出售、出租建房」。

4. **B** 語境詞彙題
　〔**解析**〕flee 有「逃避」的意思，與 escape 同義。

5. **C** 細節資訊題
　〔**解析**〕作者説：The extension of the subway line up Lenox Avenue in 1904 encouraged another wave of speculative building, especially above 130th Street. 因此，選項 C 正確。

6. **B** 句子簡化題
　〔**解析**〕該句談到了西哈萊姆區的三排聯排別墅的豪華名稱。第二個分句修飾 Kingscourt Houses。選項 D 不正確，因為作者沒有説居民住在那裡感到尷尬。只有選項 B 準確地改述了加粗的句子（exclusiveness = quite prestigious；new black residents = new occupants; made every effort to live up to [its exclusiveness] = tried to act as if they too were very elite）。

7. **D** 修辭目的題
　〔**解析**〕第五段介紹了被稱為 Sugar Hill 的區域，作者説 Sugar Hill 比 Strivers Row 要高級。通過描寫住在 Sugar Hill 頂部的人們俯視低處（既有字面意義又含社會意義），作者用 looked down 一語雙關。因此選項 D 為正確答案。

8. **B** 細節資訊題
　〔**解析**〕這道題比較簡單。作者説 sugar 是俚語，意思是「金錢」，所以選 B 項。

9. **C** 否定事實題
　〔**解析**〕在第六段，作者説：Sugar Hill became a black neighborhood some years after Strivers Row did. 因此選項 C 説法不對。

10. **D** 指代關係題
　〔**解析**〕這道題有點難。選項 A 不正確，因為 Harlem 是主詞：Harlem is home to... 同樣，選項 B 也不正確，因為 especially above 125th Street 是一個副詞片語，修飾主詞 Harlem。home to its political institutions and cultural life 與 capital of Afro-America 意思相同，因此選項 D 正確。

11. **A** 細節資訊題

〔**解析**〕在第六段和第七段中，作者說地位高的名人居住在 Sugar Hill，而且那裡有 tremendous outpouring of African American arts and letters, which would become known as the Harlem Renaissance. 因此選項 A 正確。

12. ■ **3** 插入句子題

■ 1 Bounded by the Harlem River to the northeast and Washington Heights to the north; by 110th Street to the south and Morningside Heights to the southwest—Harlem would become the biggest and one of the most important African American communities. But in 1658 this land was still a rolling pastoral landscape, reminding the newly arrived Dutch farmers of the Holland town of Haarlem. ■ 2 Their new settlement, christened "Nieuw Haarlem," was a distant nine miles away from New York City, whose population was still clustered around the southern tip of Manhattan Island. ■ 3 **Only when Dutch rule ceded to British in 1664, was the name Anglicized to the present spelling.**

During the 18th century, elite New Yorkers came to Harlem to establish working farms and country estates. The area remained an agricultural community until after the Civil War. ■ 4 The gentlemen farmers had overworked the land, depleting the soil, so that by the Antebellum Period Harlem was home to mostly poor farmers and Irish squatters.

〔**解析**〕需要注意兩條線索：1）時間 1664 和 2）名稱被英國化這一事實。因此要找的位置必須適合這一事件，並且前面需提到過非英語名稱。第一個黑色方塊選項不可能，因為其時間在 1658 年之前。第二個黑色方塊選項有混淆視聽的作用，因為 1664 年在 1658 年之後，且作者剛剛談到了荷蘭人定居點。但該選項不正確，因為它後面跟著紐約鎮的名稱 Nieuw Haarlem。第三個黑色方塊選項緊跟著這個名稱，因此正確。第四個黑色方塊選項不可能，因為第二段已開始介紹下個世紀的哈萊姆。

13. **1** The first European settlement in what is now Harlem started out as a Dutch farming community and remained a rural area for almost a hundred years.

4 Over the years, Harlem attracted residents from many different backgrounds, including prosperous people who moved into stylish neighborhoods.

6 By the 1920s, Harlem had become an African American community, which hosted rich cultural offerings and produced the Harlem Renaissance.

內容總結題

〔**解析**〕第一個選項總結了哈萊姆的早期歷史發展，因此正確。第二個選項不正確，因為愛爾蘭移民不是主題，他們定居在哈萊姆北部也不正確。第三個選項不正確，因為作者說 Strivers Row 房屋建於 1891 年，是為哈萊姆有錢的白人建造的房屋。第四個選項正確，因為該項綜述了有關猶太家庭、德國家庭和愛爾蘭家庭以及來自加勒比海和南方的黑人家庭的重要資訊。第五個選項不正確，因為貧農並不是被富農驅趕走的。作者說：The gentlemen farmers had overworked the land, depleting the soil, so that by the Antebellum Period Harlem was home to mostly poor farmers and Irish squatters. 第六個選項正確，因為該項強調了哈萊姆作為 20 世紀 20 年代的文化中心在文化上的重要性。

聽力模擬試題錄音文本 **Track 027**
- -

N: Now listen to part of a lecture about a topic related to history.

P: Part of the thrust to economic development in the United States in the 19th century was related to the advances in transportation during that period. We've seen how, before the railroads were built, the settlers moving West often chose to settle near a canal to make it easier to drop off their crops at a canal landing. But from the 1840s on, trains became an increasingly important mode of transportation. The pinnacle achievement in the area of railroad technology was the building of the first transcontinental rail, from Nebraska to California. We'll talk about that milestone later on in the lecture, but now I'd like to provide an overview of the economic growth that accompanied the rollout of the railroad system.

At first, the technology was imported. The earliest locomotives used in North America ran on steam and were of British design. The first American railroad began operations in 1827, out of Baltimore. Just a coincidence? [pause] By 1825, Baltimore had become the second largest city in the US. But its seaport—unlike New York City's—did not have a major river system reaching into the interior of the country. Unlike New York, where shippers could use steamboats to travel up the Hudson River, Baltimore shippers did not have river access to the hinterland. So Baltimore had a lot of incentive to develop the new technologies needed for railroad shipping.

OK. This is probably a good time to say a few words about how transportation in general can promote an economy. Transportation—no matter what form—is important in forging social, political and commercial ties. And on a practical level, transportation makes it possible for goods to reach distant markets. These potential benefits were certainly factors driving the building of railroads in the 19th century.

Earlier in the 19th century, Alexander Hamilton—the very first US Secretary of the Treasury—had said that "internal improvements" were necessary for economic growth. He proposed that the government subsidize manufacturing. Hamilton knew that transportation facilitated communication and commerce. These "internal improvements" included a network of seaports, railroads and roadways, what today we call the "infrastructure" of the economy. In Hamilton's time, the president vetoed his proposal to use government funds to strengthen manufacturing. But farsighted private investors were more than willing to invest in the infrastructure of the railway system.

Business enterprises wanted to operate railroad networks for both technological and organizational reasons. Whereas the companies that owned shipping canals rarely owned the boats that traveled on the canals, the investors in railroads looked at the big picture—they took an ownership stake in both the railways and the trains. The American railroads attracted considerable attention from European investors as well. This capital infusion allowed the railroads to be built quickly, and to be built with high quality iron and steel. Especially in the West and the South, this robust approach led to a strong demand for the steel rails needed to build the new railways. So you can see how, in this way, the building of railroads served as a major impetus in the expansion of the iron and steel industry. It also increased the railroad mileage.

OK. As the technology continued to improve, railroads become the favorite means of overland transportation. Trains not only captured passenger traffic from the canals, they began to compete to carry grain and coal. Indeed, some of the first railroads in the north were built by textile manufacturers and coal mine owners to replace canals they had already constructed. The various railroad companies worked out complicated inter-company arrangements so that the goods placed in the train car by the initial company did not have to be reloaded by other companies and stayed on board until they reached the final destination.

Another outcome closely tied to the development of a national system of transportation was the dramatic growth of regional agriculture. We can see, for example, the relationship between wheat production and the boom in railroad expansion. By 1850, the Northwest exceeded the Northeast in wheat production as areas for wheat-growing moved westward. Growth in meat packing and the production of corn and hogs also moved westwards at lightning speeds.

A related benefit was the increase in population in the western areas. Wherever railroads went, they created stopping points with water tanks, eating places and hotels. These little train stops evolved into farms, villages and eventually cities. Thus the population in western regions grew steadily, broadening the economic base and providing new markets for eastern goods.

It was in this boom climate that the transcontinental railroad project was finally authorized. By 1862, the federal government was finally willing to back railroad infrastructure and provide subsidies to the railroad companies. In 1869, the final rail stake was hammered in place, signifying a new era of consolidation.

● **Transcripts for Question 2.**

N: Listen again to part of the lecture. Then answer the question.

P: The first American railroad began operations in 1827, out of Baltimore. Just a coincidence?

[pause] By 1825, Baltimore had become the second largest city in the US. But its seaport—unlike New York City's—did not have a major river system reaching into the interior of the country.

N: What does the professor mean when she says this:

P: Just a coincidence?

關鍵語塊

thrust to... 推動……	settler 移民
canal 運河	drop off sth. 卸下某物
canal landing 運河碼頭	mode of transportation 運輸方式
pinnacle achievement 最大的成就	transcontinental rail 跨洲鐵路
rollout of... ……的推出，首次展示	locomotive 火車
begin operations 開始營運	seaport 港口城市
steamboat 汽船	reach into the interior 延伸到內地
access to 通向	hinterland 內地，遠離城市的地方
forge... ties 建立……聯繫	factors driving... 迫使……發生的因素
Secretary of the Treasury （美國）財政部長	subsidize manufacturing 資助製造業
infrastructure of... ……的基礎設施	veto his proposal 否決了他的提議
more than willing to... 非常願意……	capital infusion 資本注入
robust approach 強硬的方法	steel rail 鋼軌
major impetus 主要動力	overland transportation 內陸運輸
capture passenger traffic 奪取客運市場份額	inter-company arrangement 公司之間的協議

boom in... ……的興起	meat packing 肉類加工
stopping point 停靠站	evolve into 逐步發展成
broaden the economic base 擴大經濟基礎	back 支持
provide subsidy to 提供補貼	hammer in place 錘擊定位
signify 表示	era of consolidation 整合時期

聽力模擬試題答案詳解

1. **D** 主旨大意題
   〔**解析**〕教授雖然提到了技術、政府支持和私人投資者，但是這些都不是主旨。講座的核心主題是伴隨著鐵路發展的經濟增長，因此選項 D 為正確答案。

2. **A** 語用功能題
   〔**解析**〕教授告訴學生 Baltimore 是美國第一個修建鐵路的城市，然後説 Baltimore 沒有河口，不能利用河流運輸貨物。通過一個反問句：Just a coincidence? 她希望給學生説明因果聯繫：正因為沒有河流，所以 Baltimore 需要鐵路來彌補這一缺陷。

3. **C** 細節資訊題
   〔**解析**〕教授告訴學生美國第一任財政部長 Hamilton 提出用政府資金來修建鐵路和其他運輸通道，因此選項 C 為正確答案。

4. **A**、**B** 細節資訊題
   〔**解析**〕選項 C 有混淆視聽的作用，因為教授將運河所有者與鐵路所有者作了比較，但她沒有説鐵路所有者也投資了運河。她説鐵路所有者取得了鐵路和火車的股份所有權（took an ownership stake in both the railways and the trains），所以 B 項正確。接下來她説美國鐵路吸引了大量歐洲的投資商（American railroads attracted considerable attention from European investors as well），因此，選項 A 正確。

5. **D** 推論題
   〔**解析**〕教授説鐵路向西推進後，西北的小麥產量超過了東北的小麥產量，從這裡可以推斷，東部農民需要種植不同於小麥的其他作物以保證自身的競爭力，因此選項 D 正確。

6. **B** 組織結構題
   〔**解析**〕教授説：Wherever railroads went, they created stopping points with water tanks, eating places and hotels. These little train stops evolved into farms, villages and eventually cities. Thus the population in western regions grew steadily, broadening the economic base and providing new markets for eastern goods. 由此可知 B 項「為了方便中途停留（stopovers）促進了城市發展」正確。選項 C 可能有混淆視聽的作用，但是講座中沒有提到城鎮合作。

● Answer Key to Exercise 2

CHUNK	Paraphrase
1. pinnacle achievement	highest accomplishment / greatest success
2. ownership stake	possession / financial interest
3. favorite means of...	preferred way to...
4. closely tied to...	strongly related to...
5. lightning speed	remarkable speed / remarkable quickness

⑮ 生命科學常考主題 4 解剖學和生理學詞彙、答案、解析和錄音原文

● **Answer Key to Exercise 1**

Paragraph 1:　A general description of blushing. An overview of the physiology of blushing, including what happens when adrenaline is released.

Paragraph 2:　A description of the sympathetic nervous system and how it relates to blushing.

Paragraph 3:　The anatomical features of the face that are related to blushing.

閱讀模擬試題答案詳解

1. **B** 細節資訊題
   〔解析〕第一段作者說人類有兩種光感受器，因為我們生活在白天和黑夜這兩種視覺世界中，因此選項 B 正確。

2. **C** 語境詞彙題
   〔解析〕詞彙所在句修辭 retina（視網膜），意為「眼球後部的一層神經細胞薄膜」，line 有「在某物的內部形成一層」的意思，與 cover 意思相近。

3. **A** 語境詞彙題
   〔解析〕short 有混淆視聽的作用，但其意思與 plump 不同。在該句中，roundish 與 plump 同義，意為「圓圓的」。

4. **D** 修辭目的題
   〔解析〕作者說這兩種光感受器的差別猶如彩色膠捲和黑白膠捲的差別。作者將攝影用的兩種膠捲等同於用來觀看的兩種細胞，因為選項 D 正確。

5. **C** 指代關係題
   〔解析〕指代關係詞 it 前面的名詞是 film（膠捲），但 it 並非指 film，因為名詞片語 camera with two kinds of film in it 的核心詞是 camera，因此正確答案為選項 C。

6. **B** 否定事實題
   〔解析〕在第三段，作者說中央凹（fovea）是在視網膜的中心（與 A 項符合）；那是亮光中視覺最準確的位置（與 C 項符合）；並且只有有限的視野（與 D 項符合）。只有選項 B 說法不對，因為中央凹在弱光中不起作用。

7. **D** 句子簡化題
   〔解析〕該句主詞是 eyeball，因此選項 C 不選。選項 D 正確，the eyeball must move almost continuously to keep the image = the eyeball has to keep moving to focus；this constraint = inherent limitations。

8. **A** 細節資訊題
   〔解析〕作者說，由於視錐細胞在白天對紅色作出反應，但在夜間不能正常工作，且視杆細胞對紅色不敏感，所以紅花在夜間可能會呈現黑色，因此選項 A 正確。

9. **C** 細節資訊題
   〔解析〕紅色在夜間不容易被看出來，因此選項 A 不選。作者說眼睛必須有時間調整（the eyes must have time to adjust）以適應夜視，因此選項 C 正確。

10. **A** 語境詞彙題
    〔解析〕coloring 與 pigment 同義，意為「色素」。

11. ■ **4** 插入句子題
    To record the scene, the photographer must give up the idea of getting a color picture and settle for

one in black-and-white. Black-and-white film is much more sensitive and will respond in dimmer light. ■ 1 In a sense, the human eye viewing an object is like a camera with two kinds of film in it at all times. ■ 2 The cones come into play when the light is strong and give humans color vision. ■ 3 But at night, only the rods will work, and they give only black-and-white responses.   ■ 4 **This explains why colors disappear at night and all things appear to be different shades of gray.**

〔解析〕插入句裡有兩條線索：1）this 和 2）對夜間看不見顏色原因的解釋。在這個插入句前面的句子需要符合這些條件。第一個黑色方塊選項後面的句子談論黑白膠捲，句中沒有提到顏色，因此不正確。第二個黑色方塊選項後面的句子將人眼比作攝像機，但句中沒有提到顏色和夜視。第三個黑色方塊選項後面的句子說：光線較強時視錐細胞開始工作，能使人類產生色覺。插入句講的是顏色消失（disappearing），所以與此處邏輯上不連貫。第四個黑色方塊選項後面的句子說視杆細胞只在夜間工作而且只能產生黑白視覺。插入句是對前面所有句子的最終總結，解釋了光感器的機制以及在夜間看不見顏色的原因，因此最後一個方塊處是正確答案。

12.

Type of Photoreceptor	Associated Characteristics
Rods	• 5. Have a slender profile • 6. Are used in dark conditions
Cones	• 4. Allows humans to see the color red • 7. Are clustered on the fovea
Both rods and cones	• 2. Are located behind the retina

資訊歸類題

〔解析〕作者沒有討論近視或遠視，因此第一個選項不能歸入圖表中。第二個選項應放在 Both rods and cones 欄中，因為作者說兩種類型的細胞 lie tightly packed together on the back of the retina。第三個選項不能歸入圖表中，因為作者沒有說過光感受器使眼睛內部產生暗色。第四個選項應放入 Cones 欄中，因為作者說視錐細胞通常對紅色作出反應（respond to red）。第五個選項應放入 Rods 欄中，因為作者說視杆細胞又直又細（straight and thin）。第六個選項也應放入 Rods 欄中，因為文中說只有視杆細胞在夜間工作。第七個選項應放入 Cones 欄中，因為作者說視網膜的中央凹只含有視錐細胞（contains only cones）。

● **Answer Key to Exercise 2**

a. The professor did not accept the hypothesis that the function of perspiration sweating is to release salt.

b. She thought sunlight was beneficial to human eyes.

c. The professor admired the research Harvey did that led to our understanding of blood circulation.

聽力模擬試題錄音文本　 *Track 029*

N: Now listen to part of a lecture in a physiology class.

P: In your reading for today, you should have read about the various stages of sleep. This is complicated stuff, and scientists are still arguing about what happens in each stage. But one straightforward way to classify the stages of sleep is to distinguish between REM [pronounced *rem*] sleep and non-REM sleep. There are several types of non-REM sleep, but I want to focus on REM sleep for now.

Adult humans devote about one quarter of their sleep time in REM sleep—not a lot in the greater scheme of things. REM sleep typically comes at the end of each sleep cycle, and a complete sleep cycle including all five stages typically lasts from 90 to 120 minutes. On an average night, we usually have about 4 or 5 periods of REM sleep. These periods are short at the beginning but get longer at the end of the night.

We know that REM sleep is physiologically different from the stages in non-REM sleep. Certain neurons in the brain are particularly active during REM sleep. The term REM, of course, is an abbreviation for rapid eye movement, and we know these eye movements take place while we're dreaming. Note as well—the rate of our heart beat and our breathing is irregular during REM sleep. And our body temperature fluctuates.

Keep all of this in mind as I tell you how REM sleep may be related to our ability to consolidate learning while we are sleeping. Research suggests that memory consolidation takes place during sleep because the neural connections in our brains that form memories are strengthened.

Many studies show that REM sleep is important in the consolidation of the type of memory we call "procedural memory"—how we remember the procedure of how to do something. Examples of this would be, say, using our fingers to play the piano or to use a computer keyboard. In one study, the subjects were observed learning to do new jumps on a trampoline, a task which required new, complex motor skills. The best trampoline learners showed increases in REM sleep and no differences in non-REM sleep. But the subjects in the control groups, who weren't able to learn new trampoline skills, showed no difference in either REM or non-REM sleep.

So what is REM sleep doing? We think the explanation is that—after we learn something—the memory of it is not in its final form. The brain still has to get the memory into a form where it will be useful. So during REM, we think that the neurons are strengthening certain connections that constitute the most important memories, and that it's also taking those memories and it's shuffling them around to different parts of the brain, to increase brain efficiency.

S: I've noticed that I need a lot more sleep than my Russian grandmother does. Which set me thinking—do people in different countries have the same sleep processes—I mean, biologically?

P: [laughing] Grandmothers all over the world are going to show different sleep patterns from their granddaughters, because grandmothers are older in age. But to answer your question directly, neuroscientists worldwide are looking at sleep behaviors across cultures, and there are indeed some differences. One very obvious divergence can be found between those societies which use lots of artificial light and those which do not.

If you look at the satellite pictures of Earth at nighttime, you can see the major metropolitan areas all lit up. It's kind of surreal. Take New York, for example, or even better, Los Angeles—it's light all night long—which means a lot of people there aren't sleeping. Before the invention of the light bulb, people weren't able to use artificial light to such an extent, and the data shows that people were sleeping a lot more hours a night then. The people in Los Angeles and these other "lit-up areas" may get up a little later in the morning, but they're still sleeping less than they did before. Which is a scary thing, because chronic fatigue is simply not healthy over the long term.

Also, another difference we see in societies without artificial light is that the people there tend to have sleep patterns which are more broken-up. We call this sleep "segmented sleep," because there are multiple segments of sleeping and waking within a 24-hour period. One example we all know of is the habit of people in remote regions of Africa, for example, or Latin America—where people will sleep for several hours in the afternoon. These folk are used to breaking up their sleep in several segments, so that their bodies process the information they gather during their waking hours in somewhat different "rhythms," if you will.

● **Transcripts for Question 4.**

N: Listen again to part of the lecture. Then answer the question.

S: I've noticed that I need a lot more sleep than my Russian grandmother does. Which set me thinking—do people in different countries have the same sleep processes—I mean, biologically?

N: What does the woman mean when she says this:

S: Which set me thinking—

關鍵語塊

physiology 生理學	stages of sleep 睡眠階段
complicated stuff〔口語〕複雜的東西	straightforward way 簡單明瞭的方法
distinguish between... and... 區別……和……	devote 投入（時間）
in the greater scheme of things 從更廣的角度來考慮	sleep cycle 睡眠週期
neuron 神經細胞	abbreviation for... ……的縮寫
rate of our heart beat 心跳速率	body temperature fluctuates 體溫上下波動
consolidate learning 鞏固所學知識	neural connection 神經元連接
control group 實驗對照組	neuroscientist 神經系統科學家
divergence 差異	artificial light 人造光
satellite picture 衛星照片	metropolitan area 大都市區域
surreal 夢幻般的，離奇的	or even better〔口語〕甚至更好，或者更好
chronic fatigue 慢性疲勞	over the long term 長期

聽力模擬試題答案詳解

1. **D** 主旨大意題
   〔解析〕教授說學生應該讀過與睡眠階段相關的文章（作業），但他沒有在講座中介紹這些階段，選項 A 不正確。教授只是順帶提到了非洲人的睡眠方式，因此選項 B 不正確。教授前後都在談論 REM 睡眠，因此選項 D 正確。

2. **A** 細節資訊題
   〔解析〕教授說 memory consolidation takes place during sleep because the neural connections in our brains that form memories are strengthened，因此選項 A 為正確答案。

3. **C、D** 細節資訊題
   〔解析〕教授提到的程式性記憶的例子有 using our fingers to play the piano or to use a computer keyboard... to do new jumps on a trampoline（跳床），因此選項 C 和 D 正確。

4. **A** 語用功能題
   〔解析〕片語 to set someone thinking 的意思是使某人思考，因此選項 A 正確。

5. **B** 立場觀點題
   〔解析〕見本章前文的「托福總監評析」。

6. **B** 組織結構題
   〔解析〕教授說在沒有人造光的社會，人們 tend to have sleep patterns which are more broken-up，並列舉了非洲和拉丁美洲的例子，因此選項 B 正確。

⑯ 社會科學常考主題 4 大眾傳播學詞彙、答案、解析和錄音原文

● **Answer Key to Exercise 1**

a. <u>With the exception of professional and high-end news publications, news reporting in countries with relatively high standards of living does not provide much coverage of foreign news.</u>

b. <u>During the early Middle Ages, people thought that books were supposed to store knowledge and were not designed to communicate.</u>

c. <u>A person will not care about the media unless he or she relies on the media.</u>

閱讀模擬試題答案詳解

1. **D** 語境詞彙題
   【**解析**】obtain 與 procure 同義，意為「取得，獲得」。

2. **B** 細節資訊題
   【**解析**】文章中並沒有用諸如 because 之類的詞給出兒童缺乏興趣的原因。在談到兒童對教育節目毫無興趣之後，作者說：Educational programming output for children lacked an organizing framework, and the production quality was low. 因此選項 B 正確。

3. **C** 語境詞彙題
   【**解析**】從上下文可知，該節目獲得了大量資金，所以選 generously，意為「充足地」。

4. **A** 否定事實題
   【**解析**】見本章前文的「托福總監評析」。

5. **C** 細節資訊題
   【**解析**】這道題目很簡單，因為第三段第一句提到：Unlike most educational programs, Sesame Street was designed to speak directly to the child, acting as the teacher. 因此選項 C 正確。

6. **D** 句子簡化題
   【**解析**】這個句子的主詞為 investment in research，表語是 key element。因此，需要到選項中找出對這兩個部分的改述。選項 D 有這兩個部分的改述，但位置被顛倒過來（reason for the program's ultimate effectiveness = a key element in the success of the program；large focus on research = heavy investment in research）。

7. **B** 細節資訊題
   【**解析**】作者說 The influence of this formative research on the morale of professionals using television worldwide... is hard to overstate，因此選項 B 為正確答案。

8. **A** 語境詞彙題
   【**解析**】tentative 與這個句子中的 precarious 同義，意為「不確定的」。to lead a tentative existence 為一個語塊。

9. **C** 細節資訊題
   【**解析**】作者在第五段開頭說 Public demand for more and better children's television led to the creation of the Public Broadcasting Service，因此選項 C 為正確答案。

10. **D** 指代關係題
    【**解析**】從該句可以看出一個問題：What emerged in schools? 答案顯然是 television。介系詞片語 at the outset of its emergence in schools in the 1950s and 1960s 修飾 television。

11. **A** 修辭目的題
    【**解析**】某些考生看到文中的 finally，就判斷 C 項正確，但其實意思相差很大。作者說當

technical performance of video recorders (VCRs) rose and prices fell 時，人們找到了使用這些機器的方法。因此選項 A 為正確答案。

12. **B** 推論題

〔解析〕這道題有點難，因為考生必須推斷作者的觀點，而且題目中沒有給出參考段落。因此，考生必須略讀和掃讀全文以尋找表達觀點的詞語。在第五段末尾，作者提到：As national excitement over the educational potential of computers and online resources grew, observers noted that the strengths of educational television were being forgotten...，然後在第六段，作者談到教育節目的價值。因此選項 B 正確。

13. **1** Although the government provided significant funding for educational television early on, educators waited for over fifteen years to take action.

4 The impetus for quality children's television programming was the recognition that many children needed education in literacy, numeracy and other skills.

5 Color monitors and quality content persuaded child viewers and school teachers that television could be put to good use in teaching.

內容總結題

〔解析〕第一個選項正確，因為它對教育節目之前的時期進行了總體描述。第二個選項不正確，因為作者並未説在 20 世紀 70 年代有很多針對學齡前兒童的具有教育意義的商業電視節目。第三個選項不正確，因為文章中並沒有説很難設計出能滿足所有人的節目。第四個選項正確，作者的一個觀點就是在識字和算術方面的教育需求構成了高品質節目的驅動力之一。第五個選項正確，因為它抓住了兒童教育電視節目歷史上的主要轉捩點，彩色顯示器和優質內容的出現改變了兒童和老師的態度。第六個選項明顯不正確，因為它與作者的觀點相矛盾，電腦並未滿足教育電視的需求。

● **Answer Key to Exercise 2**

The communication cycle includes a sender and a receiver. In this example, we see that the sender is sending a message through his computer. After reading his message, the receiver sends back her feedback.

聽力模擬試題錄音文本　　 *Track 031*

N: Now listen to part of a lecture about mass communication.

P: In our discussion of mass media so far, we've looked at the issues related to how we target audiences for broadcast and print media. There are clearly differences in the way we communicate through the various media, including online communications. But there's one type of writing that's common to many communication platforms—news writing, and that's what I'd like to turn to now. I should add—a familiarity with news writing conventions is probably one of the more valuable skills that you'll take away from this class, even if you don't plan on becoming a reporter. Any communicator worth his—or her—salt should understand these strategies.

What I'm about to cover may be old hat to those of you who worked on school newspapers, but for the rest of you, I want to quickly go over some of the key terminology. Then we can cut straight to the meat of our lecture, which will be how to write a hard news story using the inverted pyramid format. OK?

Now the news style is not only determined by the type of words and sentence structures we use, it is also determined by the way in which we present information.

What is "hard news," then? For one thing, hard news focuses on facts in a no-nonsense way. And a hard news story often reports on recent events of significance. It could be the signing of a peace treaty, the passing of a law or the death of a famous person. It doesn't contain a lot of extraneous detail or editorializing. Soft news, in contrast, is often about less serious topics, such as entertainment news, and includes feature pieces that may be written in a chatty tone.

In any news article, hard or soft, the most important part is the lead. What's a "lead"? The lead is the introductory part found in the new story's first paragraph. In many stories, the "lead" may constitute only one sentence, since in newspapers paragraphs are very short.

OK, so much for terminology. You will find that in a hard news story the important information and any background material often form the shape of an inverted pyramid. The small part of the pyramid is at the very top, and the widest part is at the bottom. In this approach, some of the most newsworthy information comes at the beginning, or top, and then the remaining information follows in order of importance, with the least important details at the bottom.

So the lead is at the very top of the inverted pyramid. The rule is that the lead of a hard news story should contain what we call the 5 W's: Who, What, When, Where, and Why. If all the 5 Ws can't be squeezed into the first sentence, they should definitely come soon thereafter.

Did you notice? The inverted pyramid structure does not frame a story around a chronology, but rather around the importance of facts. That's a tricky concept for beginners, because it seems backwards. It runs counter to the storytelling tradition that has a beginning, middle and end. In fact, the inverted pyramid news story contains just two parts: a lead and a body. That means there's no real conclusion. As soon as you've finished stating the facts, you stop! For example, if you just found a new job and were asked to use an inverted pyramid format to write a story about the great news, you would not start out chronologically by saying that first you took a cab to the office at seven a.m., and then you interviewed for a reporting job in the afternoon, and several weeks later you received a great job offer. Rather, you'd start out like this: "Today I heard from the *Wall* Street *Journal* that they want me to work full-time as a reporter, starting in two weeks." Following that lead, you could write more background about the job itself and how you happened to get it.

Now a lot of beginners ask me just how long their hard news articles should be. My answer is that your hard news story should be as long as a piece of string. Why string, you may ask? A piece of string is as long as it is and no longer. And if it needs to be shorter, you can cut it.

What this means is that you as a writer should let each story guide how long your article needs to be. There is no predetermined length. And your editor will cut out words. So remember "string": In hard news, when you're done communicating the key facts, stop writing.

● **Transcripts for Question 3.**

N: Why does the professor say this:

P: Today I heard from the *Wall Street Journal* that they want me to work full-time as a reporter, starting in two weeks.

關鍵語塊

mass media 大眾媒體	target audience 目標觀眾
broadcast media 廣播媒體	print media 印刷媒體

writing convention 寫作規範	skills that you'll take away 你要學的技能
worth one's salt 稱職	old hat 老一套的
cut straight to 直接切入	meat of ……的實質性部分
hard news 重要新聞；硬新聞	news story 新聞報導
no-nonsense way 嚴肅的方式	passing of a law 通過一項法律
extraneous detail 不相干的細節	editorializing 發表社論，作出評論
soft news 軟新聞	feature piece 特別收錄
chatty tone （文章的）語氣很隨意	so much for... 關於……就說這麼多
newsworthy information 有新聞價值的資訊	squeeze into 擠入
frame a story around... 圍繞……組織一個故事框架	chronology 時間順序
tricky concept 複雜的概念	run counter to 違反；與……背道而馳
Wall Street Journal 《華爾街日報》	work full-time 全職工作
string 細繩	predetermined length 預定的長度
when you're done V-ing 當你已經做了……	

聽力模擬試題答案詳解

1. **D** 主旨大意題
   〔解析〕選項 A 太籠統，不正確。教授一直在介紹重要新聞的倒金字塔寫作技巧，因此選項 D 正確。

2. **B、C** 細節資訊題
   〔解析〕教授說 in a hard news story the important information and any background material often form the shape of an inverted pyramid。還說一個倒金字塔形式的新聞包括兩個部分：導言和主體（a lead and a body），因此選項 B 和 D 正確。

3. **A** 語用功能題
   〔解析〕教授利用找工作的例子來說明如何以倒金字塔形式寫一篇文章，因此選項 A 為正確答案。

4. **B** 組織結構題
   〔解析〕教授說很多新聞系學生問他重要新聞應該寫多長。他的答案是 your hard news story should be as long as a piece of string。選項 B 符合句意。

5.

Characteristic or example	Hard news	Soft news	Both hard and soft news
Features		✓	
Leads			✓
Inverted pyramid	✓		
String	✓		

關聯內容題
〔解析〕教授說：Soft news, in contrast, is often about less serious topics, such as entertainment news, and includes feature pieces... 因此，Features（特別收錄）應在 Soft news 欄打勾。教授說：In any news article, hard or soft, the most important part is the lead. 因此，Leads 在 Both hard and soft news 欄打勾。教授說重要新聞故事頻繁使用倒金字塔形式，因此，Inverted pyramid 應在 Hard news 下方打勾。教授說：My answer is that your hard news story should be as long as a piece of string. 因此，String 在 Hard news 欄打勾。

物理科學常考主題 5 電腦和軟體工程詞彙、答案、解析和錄音原文

閱讀模擬試題答案詳解

1. **B** 語境詞彙題
   〔**解析**〕見本章前文的「托福總監評析」。

2. **D** 否定事實題
   〔**解析**〕選項 A「破壞公用事業工廠」對應 intrusion into a nuclear power plant control system。選項 B 對應 defeat of copy protection in a video game。選項 C 對應 accessing customer databases。只有選項 D「電子郵件帳戶」沒有提到。

3. **C** 細節資訊題
   〔**解析**〕作者說和定制的（custom-written）軟體相比，購買的現成軟體（off-the-shelf software）可以大大節省資金，但經常遇到的問題是沒有原始程式碼（source code）或軟體設計資料，因此選項 C 符合。

4. **A** 句子簡化題
   〔**解析**〕主詞 security requirements 後面的動詞是 have，但是後面的句子結構就不好分析了。其文法結構是 have not been the beneficiary of... [that is] so often carried out... 有些考生可能不能識別子句 [that is] so often carried out...。選項 B 曲解了 beneficiary 的意思。選項 C 曲解了 so 的意思，有些考生看到句子中的 so，把該句理解為因果關係。選項 A 正確（security requirements have not been the beneficiary of the type of rigorous analysis = less attention has been paid to security requirements）。

5. **C** 指代關係題
   〔**解析**〕回答這道題的關鍵是單字 deploying（部署）。軟體工程師部署了什麼？答案為 features，即他們選用的功能。

6. **D** 語境詞彙題
   〔**解析**〕見本章前文的「托福總監評析」。

7. **B** 細節資訊題
   〔**解析**〕第三段，作者將安全軟體工程師與系統軟體工程師進行對比，說在設計階段沒有正確分析安全需求和功能。因為安全功能一般是後期添加的（afterthought），所以工程師不得不將就這些功能。選項 B 為正確答案。

8. **A** 細節資訊題
   〔**解析**〕作者說當要求最終被加入時，其後果就是 costly and sometimes impossible design challenges，因此正確答案為選項 A。

9. **B** 語境詞彙題
   〔**解析**〕refine 與 hone 同義，意為「改善」。

10. **D** 修辭目的題
    〔**解析**〕在第五段開頭，作者說：Apart from poor planning, there are other reasons that security fails to be considered in the initial systems design. 作者接著提到舊系統，作為「其他原因」的一個例子。因此選項 D 為正確答案。

11. **C** 推論題
    〔**解析**〕要回答這道作者觀點題，考生需要略讀整篇文章。在第三段，作者說：In mature markets, non-security software engineers have strategically chosen features from a variety of possibilities, deploying those most in demand by customers and most likely to maximize revenue.

作者認為，生產者只關注市場和顧客需求，而軟體安全問題卻被忽視，選項 C 符合。

12. ■ **2** 插入句子題

Changes in software development practices and software architectures have opened up opportunities for applying security engineering. Techniques such as cryptography and tamperresistant hardware can be used to safeguard software tools and processes. ■ 1 Opportunities for enhanced security arise in part because software systems are no longer monolithic, single-vendor creations. ■ 2 **Instead, systems are becoming ever complex configurations pieced together with commercial off-the-shelf elements.** Off-the-shelf software offers significant savings over custom-written software, though this advantage is somewhat offset by the fact that vendors, seeking to protect intellectual property, routinely sell components without source code or design documentation. ■ 3 Faced with the risks of constructing systems out of unknown, black-box components, developers must spend more time on due diligence analyses. ■ 4 In this context, there is even more of a need to become versant with the ever-expanding array of defensive technologies. Tamper-resistant microprocessors, for example, can be used to store and process sensitive information as in electronic transfers using credit or debit cards. The microchips in these cards are designed so that information is accessed through embedded encryption software.

〔解析〕分析插入句得出幾條線索：1）對比信號詞 instead；2）主詞 systems；和 3）軟體的發展趨勢似乎是從一種狀態變為另一種狀態。越來越多的「現成」軟體被購買方打包買入，然後「拼湊」在一起。這些線索告訴我們目標句前面的句子很有可能是講述過去的情況，而且可能包含事情正在變化的某種暗示。

首先看第一個黑色方塊位置，前一句敘述軟體方面的技術進步，如加密（cryptography）。這在邏輯上與 instead, systems are becoming ever complex configurations 不相符，因為加密技術本身就很複雜。然而，下一個黑色方塊位置前面的句子說機會正在出現，因為系統不再是某個生產商單獨能完成的產品（are no longer monolithic, single-vendor creations）。將以 instead 開頭的句子放在這裡似乎很合適：Systems are no longer... Instead, they are... 但是，為了確保無誤，應檢查最後兩個黑色方塊位置。第三個黑色方塊位置不正確，因為它前面的句子是解釋現成軟體的優點，在邏輯上說不通。第四個黑色方塊位置更說不通，因為此處前一個句子講的是另一個問題：關於購買沒有文字檔資料的代碼的問題。再說，要插入的句子需要放在此類討論之前。因此可以確定第二個黑色方塊位置是正確答案。

13. **2** Software developers have traditionally not taken into account security considerations in the early design stages.

4 The current level of threat from cybercriminals necessitates that engineers take active steps to prevent breaches.

5 In addition to analyzing customer preferences, software designers should identify defensive features as part of product development.

內容總結題

〔解析〕這篇文章中最重要的觀點包括過去和現在的成果。第一個選項與文章內容不符，在介紹軟體安全時，作者沒有說用戶所知不多。第二個選項正確，因為將安全問題納入早期設計階段的要求在全文中是被作為主題來強調的。第三個選項不正確，因為它是次要觀點。第四個選項正確，因為它抓住了作者的重要觀點，即軟體安全問題需要由工程師來解決。第五個選項也正確，該句傳達了作者反復警告的資訊：對安全威脅的實際防禦與瞭解客戶的需求一樣重要。最後一個選項不正確，因為網路安全應用程式的開發不是文章要點。

● **Answer Key to Exercise 1**

1. (bad + ware) software that is bad for you; malicious software 惡意軟體
2. (secret/ hidden + picture + noun ending) the science of secret writing; in computer science, the study of analyzing codes 密碼學
3. (one + large block of stone) uniform; in computer science, when all components are manufactured on a single silicon chip 完全統一的；單片的
4. (sell + person who does something) seller 賣主，供應商
5. (put into + secret/ hidden + noun ending) encoding; in computer science, converting data or information into code 編碼；加密

● **Answer Key to Exercise 2**

a. It's so frustrating. I refuse to talk to a computer if I can at all help it. / I hate it when I get a machine. It takes forever.
b. Let me help you with that. / Tell me exactly where you think you're going wrong.
c. I have no idea. Was it in the 20th century? / I think I read somewhere that the first electronic computer that could store its own programs was made in the 1940s.

聽力模擬試題錄音文本 *Track 033*

N: Now listen to part of a lecture in a computer engineering class.

P: In this class I'll provide an overview of what many people call "cloud computing." There are several notions about what cloud computing means, which I'll get to in a minute.

But first let's talk about the word "cloud." Why cloud computing? As you know, a flow diagram for a computer network—one that maps out the data flow—will often show a drawing of a little cloud. This cloud is the "network cloud." It could represent the worldwide Internet, or just a local area network, limited to users in one company. The cloud symbol is put in as a placeholder—as a general representation that indicates we don't really care about the specifics of the network architecture. Similarly, when we say that such-and-such operation is taking place "in the cloud," we mean that it's taking place within some undefined network or networks.

Increasingly, the phrase "computing in the cloud" has come to mean computer services that are run on web-based browsers. What are some examples of popular applications in cloud computing? Well, e-mail services, for one. And map programs that allow you find where you're going. Ever use online auction sites, where you can buy and sell stuff? Or web-based applications where you make new friends or share videos? The list goes on and on. In each of these cloud applications, we see the trend toward network computing. When you use a web-based e-mail application, for example, your laptop functions as a terminal, and the processing is not done where you are. It gets done remotely. And the data isn't on your machine, either.

Why does it matter where computing happens? Location is important for several reasons. For one thing, the location affects efficiency. And another factor influencing where data resides is who will control that data. If, for example, the data is on my computer, I control when it gets deleted. I can copy it and move it around. But in the cloud computing model, the user is distant from the data and from the processing.

Another way of thinking about cloud computing is historically. So indulge me for a moment as I take you on a trip through technology, so we can take a look at computers in terms of centralized versus decentralized models. In the beginning, there were mainframes—large workhorse computers that had many terminals hooked up to them. In this model all the applications resided on a central computer. And all the data was there, too. This was centralized computing, in that all computing was performed by one big brain—a central processing unit in the mainframe. It was not the most efficient arrangement.

S: [interrupting] Sorry to interrupt, but I would think one centralized "brain" would be super efficient, 'cause you'd have one decision-making center that would be reliable.

P: Problem was, everyone who wanted to use a computer had to line up at terminals and share computing time on the mainframe. Users had to wait to access data and request programs. Mainframes were big and expensive! But because the average guy on the street couldn't afford to buy one, centralization was an economic necessity. Time-sharing was cheap, and the user didn't do any maintenance.

Then, about twenty some years ago, personal computers became affordable for the consumer market. In this era, things started to become more decentralized. The software industry created a lot of fancy tools that allowed a user to do things right on the PC. The PC's processor, or brain, and its data resided on the user's hardware. That meant everyday work tasks like wordprocessing, spreadsheets and presentations could be done easily, whether on a desktop model or a laptop.

Now in this cloud computing paradigm, computing essentially moved away from the mainframe to the multitude of personal computers in offices and people's homes. Suddenly, we had lots of little brains all over the place. We moved away from centralization and toward decentralization. We call this a "distributed" model of computing, because the processing function is distributed to many people and locations.

So that's a little history. With networking, we're back full circle to centralization. Almost all the brain's intelligence has been moved to the server. To use our cloud analogy, in this new model, the servers are hiding somewhere out there in the cloud. In the Internet era, the servers are the data centers. And we're using a common interface, a standardized web browser that links our PCs to the servers.

This new model also has weaknesses. Web-based applications like word-processing are limited in what they can do. And slow. So there's a trade-off: In a centralized model, you get economy of scale and low cost. But you don't get the full power of applications that reside on your laptop. Suffice it to say, in cloud computing countless improvements need to be made on the browser interface before the move back to centralization is considered complete.

● **Transcripts for Question 3.**

N: Listen again to part of the lecture. Then answer the question.

P: Another way of thinking about cloud computing is historically. So indulge me for a moment as I take you on a trip through technology, so we can take a look at computers in terms of centralized versus decentralized models.

N: What does the professor mean when he says this:

P: So indulge me for a moment as I take you on a trip through technology

關鍵語塊

| notion about... 關於……的觀點 | flow diagram 流程圖 |
| worldwide Internet 全球互聯網 | local area network 區域網路 |

placeholder 預留位置	network architecture 網路（體系）結構；網絡架構
such-and-such operation 這樣那樣的運算	undefined network 未定義的電腦網路
... run on... ……在……上運行	online auction site 線上拍賣網站
terminal 終端機	remotely 遠程地
reside 位於	get deleted 被刪除
indulge me for a moment 請容我講一下	take you on a trip through technology 帶你進行一次科技旅行
centralized model 集中化模式	decentralized model 分散模式
mainframe 主機；大型機	workhorse computer 重負荷電腦
hook up to 連接到	computing time 計算時間
central processing unit 中央處理器	average guy on the street 街上的普通人
personal computer 個人電腦	fancy tool 奇特的工具
word-processing 文字處理	spreadsheet 電子製表程式（主要用於制定財務計畫）；試算表
presentation 陳述；報告	desktop model 桌上型電腦
laptop 手提電腦；筆記型電腦	paradigm 模式
multitude of... 眾多的……	"distributed" model 「分散式」模型
we're back full circle 我們又回到原點	server 伺服器
common interface 公共介面；通用介面	economy of scale 規模經濟

聽力模擬試題答案詳解

1. **D** 主旨大意題
   〔解析〕教授花了一點時間來談論雲端計算中應用程式的例子，因此選項 A 和 B 都有混淆視聽的作用。教授沒有強調雲端計算的弱點，所以 C 項錯誤。在講座中，教授重點討論用來處理資料的雲端計算模式，因此選 D。

2. **A** 細節資訊題
   〔解析〕說到雲端，教授說 we mean that it's taking place within some undefined network or networks。因此選項 A 為正確答案。

3. **B** 語用功能題
   〔解析〕教授說他想從歷史角度來給學生講講傳統電腦中的集線模式和分散模式。indulge me for a moment 表示教授在向學生表明他將暫時中斷雲端計算這一話題說點別的，因此選項 B 正確。

4. **C、D** 細節資訊題
   〔解析〕教授說在採用集線模式的大型主機中，time-sharing was cheap, and the user didn't do any maintenance，因此選項 C 和 D 為正確答案。

5. **C** 組織結構題
   〔解析〕教授說：This was centralized computing, in that all computing was performed by one big brain—a central processing unit in the mainframe. 因此選項 C 為正確答案。

6. **B** 立場觀點題
   〔解析〕要回答本題，考生需要仔細聽關於雲端計算的評價性語句。在講座的結尾，教授談到一些新模式的弱點時說：Suffice it to say, in cloud computing countless improvements need to be made on the browser interface before the move back to centralization is considered complete. 因此選項 B 為正確答案。

⑱ 人文藝術常考主題 5 藝術和藝術史詞彙、答案、解析和錄音原文

閱讀模擬試題答案詳解

1. **B** 細節資訊題
   〔**解析**〕第一段很短，但是意思很明確。作者說：Picasso was the one to watch. He was also the one to beat. 在上下文中，beat 的意思是 surpass（超過）。因此選項 B 為正確答案。

2. **D** 語境詞彙題
   〔**解析**〕動名詞 decoding 與 deciphering 同義，意為「解讀」。

3. **C** 語境詞彙題
   〔**解析**〕這道題目有點難。單字 absorbed 與片語 came to grips with 同義。

4. **A** 細節資訊題
   〔**解析**〕作者談到 Pollock 千方百計想擺脫畢卡索各個方面對他的影響（tried to blot out the Spaniard's influence—figuratively, but also literally），因此選項 A 為正確答案。

5. **B** 句子簡化題
   〔**解析**〕目標句子的文法結構是 not even（沒有）..., much less（更不用說）...，可以將其換句話說為 ...was not VERB, and... was certainly not VERB。選項 C 曲解了 entered much into American sensibilities 的意思，誤認為某人進入美國。選項 B 正確，因為 entering into American sensibilities 可以換句話說為 influencing American artists。much less 表達了 and so of course 的意思。

6. **A** 細節資訊題
   〔**解析**〕作者說：It was the painter Max Weber, a Russian Jewish emigre, who brought the first Picasso canvas to New York in 1909. 因此選項 A 為正確答案。

7. **C** 語境詞彙題
   〔**解析**〕形容詞 rundown 與 shabby 同義，意為「破敗的」。

8. **B** 修辭目的題
   〔**解析**〕見本章前文的「托福總監評析」。

9. **A** 語境詞彙題
   〔**解析**〕做這道題目，上下文很重要，片語 near idol (almost an idol) 與 virtual icon 同義。

10. **C** 否定事實題
    〔**解析**〕作者提到 Bourgeois 時，說她在參觀了畢卡索的作品回顧展後，一個月都沒有拿起畫筆（did not pick up a paintbrush for a month），因此選項 A 和 D 的說法正確。Bourgeois 將畢卡索的作品描述為收藏珍品（a collection of treasures），因此選項 B 也正確。文中沒有提到 Bourgeois 最初不願意去參觀回顧展，因此選 C 項。

11. **B** 修辭目的題
    〔**解析**〕見本章前文的「托福總監評析」。

12. ■ **4** 插入句子題

    In the Depression years of the thirties, the obscure painters who would one day revolutionize American art, many recent immigrants, talked well into the night in shabby New York cafeterias over nickel cups of coffee. ■ 1 They spoke passionately about the painters of the past, including Michelangelo; they debated about the innovative pioneers, especially Cezanne. ■ 2 They held forth on their near contemporaries, including Miro, Matisse and Mondrian. But the artist they talked about the most was Picasso. ■ 3 Not because he was the biggest or best; others were arguably as important. But the other painters kept to their games, working within boundaries. ■ 4 **They did not possess modernity itself.**

〔解析〕這個句子很短，而且看起來比較簡單，但是將這個句子放入正確的位置則需要考生把握文章的連貫性。插入的句子裡有兩條線索：1）指代關係詞 they 和 2）they 所代表的那些人的藝術表現手法不是現代（modern）的。

第一個黑色方塊位置不可能，因為前句談論後來改變了美國藝術的畫家，由此可推斷作者認為他們的藝術作品是現代的。第二個黑色方塊位置不可能，因為前後兩句邏輯性很強，不可分割。通過這兩個句子，作者實際上指出了 30 年代美國畫家所受的現代主義影響。第三個黑色方塊也不可能，因為接在後面的句子的主詞是 he，而不是 they。第四個黑色方塊位置為正確答案。作為本段的最後一句，這個句子給出了其他畫家（other painters）沒有嘗試探索諸多新的藝術形式的原因。

13. **1** Although the American art scene was late to receive the influence of Picasso, the impact when it did come was immense.

4 An elite group based in New York was captivated with the multifaceted aspects of Picasso's modernism and went on to forge new American art styles.

5 Just as American artists were inspired by Picasso's genius, they were at the same time also crippled by it.

內容總結題

〔解析〕第一個選項正確，因為它綜述了第三段到第七段的內容。第二個選項不正確，因為它沒有抓住 Jackson Pollock 故事的要點，與文章意思不符。第三個選項不正確，因為文章沒有提到美國人到西班牙觀看畢卡索的畫展。第四個選項正確，因為它抓住了重要的觀點：美國藝術家受畢卡索作品的影響，最後美國現代畫派在紐約出現。第五個選項正確，因為它強調了文章的一個要點，即美國藝術家受到畢卡索的啟發，又難以超越他。第六個選項不正確，因為文中提到在大蕭條時期，紐約畫家談論畢卡索，並不是因為 he was the biggest or best; others were arguably as important。

● Answer Key to Exercise 1

a. To illustrate how Picasso influenced other artists and caused them to imitate what he was doing.

b. To emphasize how the modern painters other than Picasso tended to do the same thing and did not explore new media to the extent that Picasso did.

c. To give an example of an artist who was not "energized" by Picasso and who, upon seeing Picasso's works, felt intimidated and did not paint for a month.

聽力模擬試題錄音文本 *Track 035*

N: Now listen to part of a lecture in an art class.

P: This course will introduce you to some of the methods used in creating murals. But before we start our studio project, I thought it might be helpful to go over some of the concepts and history related to murals. Hopefully you'll walk away with ideas for your own work.

People have always painted on walls. But the earliest images on cave walls were not painted for decoration; these paintings were instead an attempt to somehow capture their beliefs for posterity. These artists put paintings on walls deep within caves, we think, because they didn't want anyone else to have access to them. Besides caves, we can find murals all over the world in many environments—in tombs, churches, government buildings, corporations and even in people's homes.

Now a lot of people think that every mural is a fresco painting, but that's not the case. One type of mural is what we call a "true fresco." In a true fresco, pigments are applied to wet plaster that has lime in it. As the plaster dries, the plaster reacts chemically with the air, thus binding the pigments to the plaster. In a true fresco, the painter has only ten hours to work before the plaster dries. "Dry fresco," on the other hand, is a method of mural painting in which pigments are applied to dry plaster. Traditionally, pigments are mixed with egg yolk or egg white or with an adhesive such as vegetable gum, and then painted on the wall. The results of dry fresco will not be as long-lasting as in true fresco. And the colors of true fresco are more brilliant.

Now fresco painting was known to the ancient Egyptians as well as the ancient Greeks and Romans. As artists, we can get a lot of ideas from these old fresco designs, because we are facing the same design challenges as they were.

One of the oldest frescoes we have to look at is a fragment from an ancient Egyptian tomb. This fragment shows several geese and is, if you can believe it, around three thousand years old. The fact that the geese have lasted all these years is amazing because it was painted using powdered pigment mixed into adhesive gum. This dry fresco was found on a coat of plaster in a tomb chapel.

I want to call your attention to one characteristic of these geese, because it is typical of Egyptian frescoes. This design obeys a basic principle of mural painting that is relevant for us today. You can see that the geese are beautifully rendered; each one is slightly different. Yet the style used is simple and somewhat stylized. Notice how the geese are painted in flat colors, with no attempt to create a three-dimensional effect. In many ways, simplification is fundamental to all fresco painting. Murals that are overcrowded and overworked are rarely successful.

The Egyptians did not paint this way just for aesthetic reasons. Their art served a sacred purpose: they wanted to represent the form of people and things simply so that these things would be present in the afterlife. In fact, did you know that in ancient Egyptian, there was no special term for the word "artist?" One word—the word *sekh*—was used to mean writing, drawing and painting! So the purity of line found in Egyptian painting is related to the hieroglyphic shapes used in ancient Egyptian writing.

The Egyptians made no attempt at perspective as we know it today. No doubt, you'll find the Egyptian style of murals simple to imitate; however, it is the concept of simplicity behind the images you should try to take with you.

Now, Greek and Roman mural painters used their talents in different ways and for different purposes. Their ornamental schemes were intended to be backdrops in their homes. Because rooms in Roman houses were windowless and dark, they relied on painted decorations to visually open up their living spaces. With paint, they created the illusion of light and shadow. Designs were supposed to stimulate and amuse. The Romans were capable of creating perspective and multidimensional depth, and they created realistic images which could "fool the eye." So the technical aspects of art that were ignored by the Egyptian scribes were enthusiastically and systematically explored by ancient Greek and Roman painters.

I like to tell you one story: Two famous Greek fresco painters wanted to see who was best and had a contest. The first painter created a still-life painting of fruit that was so realistic that birds flew down from the sky to peck at the painted grapes. That artist then turned to his opponent, demanding that he pull back the curtains to reveal his painting. But it was the second artist who won the contest, because his painting was the curtains themselves!

● **Transcripts for Question 3.**

N: Listen again to part of the lecture. Then answer the question.

P: In fact, did you know that in ancient Egyptian, there was no special term for the word "artist?" One word—the word *sekh*—**was used to mean writing, drawing and painting! So the purity of line found in Egyptian painting is related to the hieroglyphic shapes used in ancient Egyptian writing.**

N: Why does the professor say this:

P: One word—the word *sekh*—**was used to mean writing, drawing and painting!**

關鍵語塊

studio project 工作室專案	capture their beliefs for posterity 記錄他們的信仰,永久留存
true fresco （在濕灰泥上作的）壁畫	pigment 顏料
plaster 灰泥	lime 石灰
binding... to... 將……結合到……上	dry fresco （在乾灰泥上作的）壁畫
egg yolk 蛋黃	egg white 蛋白
adhesive 黏合劑	vegetable gum 植物膠
fragment 片段,不完整部分	powdered pigment 粉狀顏料
coat of plaster 灰泥塗層	tomb chapel 墓室小禮拜堂
obey a basic principle of... 遵循……的基本原則	be beautifully rendered 描繪得很漂亮
flat color 平面色彩	three-dimensional effect 立體效果
overcrowded 過度擁擠的	overworked 做得過於精細的
aesthetic reason 審美原因	serve a sacred purpose 出於宗教的目的
hieroglyphic shape 象形文字的形狀	perspective 景觀;透視法
no doubt 無疑地;肯定地	take with you 從中學到
ornamental scheme 裝飾方案	backdrop 背景
decoration 裝飾品	open up their living spaces 擴展生活空間
still-life painting 靜物畫	peck at 啄

聽力模擬試題答案詳解

1. **B** 主旨大意題

〔解析〕教授將古埃及、古希臘和古羅馬的壁畫作一些比較,但這並不是她的講座目的。教授說:But before we start our studio project, I thought it might be helpful to go over some of the concepts and history related to murals. 她講述壁畫法歷史是為了給學生一些概念,好完成自己的畫作,因此選項 B 正確。

2. **A、D** 細節資訊題

〔解析〕教授說,在濕灰泥壁畫法（true fresco painting）中,pigments are applied to wet plaster that has lime in it. As the plaster dries, the plaster reacts chemically with the air, thus binding the pigments to the plaster. In a true fresco, the painter has only ten hours to work before the plaster dries. 因此選項 A 和 D 都正確。

3. **A** 語用功能題

〔**解析**〕通過舉出一個表示畫、塗和寫的詞，教授希望説明古埃及文字中包含簡單的圖畫，因此選 A。

4. **C** 組織結構題

〔**解析**〕教授講了一個幽默的故事來説明前段的句子：The Romans were capable of creating perspective and multidimensional depth, and they created realistic images which could "fool the eye." 用畫的葡萄和窗簾都被認為是實物（fooled the eye），因此選項 C 正確。

5.

Characteristic	Ancient Egypt	Ancient Greece and Rome
Impression of light and shadows		✓
Flat, two-dimensional surface	✓	
Images that play tricks on the eye		✓
Patterns served a decorative function		✓

關聯內容題

〔**解析**〕第一個特點應在 Ancient Greece and Rome 下面打勾，因為教授説他們 created the illusion of light and shadow。第二個特點應在 Ancient Egypt 下面打勾，因為教授説：Notice how the geese are painted in flat colors, with no attempt to create a three-dimensional effect. 第三個特點應在 Ancient Greece and Rome 下面打勾，因為教授談到了一些可能會讓眼睛產生錯覺的逼真的畫，就像軼聞中所説的那樣。第四個特點也應在 Ancient Greece and Rome 下面打勾，因為教授説：Their ornamental schemes were intended to be backdrops in their homes.

● **Answer Key to Exercise 2**

a. However, the purpose of the first drawings found on cave walls was not to decorate the dwelling.

b. Because we are artists who are facing the same design problems as the earlier mural makers did, we should be able to learn a lot from these old fresco designs.

c. I'm confident you will think it is quite easy to imitate the Egyptian mural style.

⑲ 生命科學常考主題 5 進化學和遺傳學詞彙、答案、解析和錄音原文

● **Answer Key to Exercise 1**

5, 3, 1, 2, 4

Of all the animals to have become adapted to human environments, cats are the only ones which "domesticated" themselves. In contrast, cattle, sheep, goats, horses and dogs were intentionally domesticated by people for milk, meat, wool or labor. It is likely that the cat domestication process began almost 10,000 years ago, when wildcats crept into villages where people were just beginning to plant wheat and barley. Rodents living in the villagers' homes and granaries attracted the wildcats, and they were also eager to escape forest predators such as hyenas. The fact that the wildcats freely chose to come to human habitats might account for the relative independent attitude of cats today.

閱讀模擬試題答案詳解

1. **B** 細節資訊題
   〔解析〕作者在談生態群落的適應性時說，雖然動植物之間相互依存的關係很重要，但群落之間的適應性非常強，超出了傳統觀點的認識（are more resilient than the stereotypical view might suggest），因此選項 B 為正確答案。

2. **C** 語境詞彙題
   〔解析〕這道題目有點難。在上下文中，long accepted 與 deeply ingrained 同義，意為「根深蒂固的」。

3. **A** 語境詞彙題
   〔解析〕選項 B 是干擾項，因為冠軍會有很多成就，但此處並沒有「獲得」的意思。此處 championed 位於 model 之後，ecologists 之前，表示是生態學者「提倡」的一種生態模式，因此選 A。

4. **D** 語境詞彙題
   〔解析〕從上下文推測，該問題「相關」物的滅絕，所以選 D，germane to 意為「與……有關」，片語 pertinent to 也有此意。

5. **A** 否定事實題
   〔解析〕在第三段，作者說琴雞 highly edible, easy to kill and abundant throughout much of the eastern seaboard, from Maine to Virginia。文中沒有提到琴雞在島上是否快樂，因此選 A。

6. **C** 指代關係題
   〔解析〕這道題很簡單。作者說琴雞的滅絕過程分為兩個階段，然後分別對這兩個階段進行了陳述。the first 為 the first stage 的省略形式。

7. **C** 細節資訊題
   〔解析〕幾次意外事件發生之後，諸多因素導致琴雞生活的地理範圍急劇減小。然而，作者說如果物種活動範圍不僅僅侷限於馬撒葡萄園島的話（had the range of the species not been limited to Martha's Vineyard），這些事件都不會導致滅絕，因而選 C。

8. **B** 句子簡化題
   〔解析〕這個複雜的句子含有一個以 whereas（= although）開頭的子句和一個以 it is... 開頭的主句。子句的基本意思是「儘管一些因素影響了群落和生態系統（although some factors affect the community and ecosystem）」。主句的基本意思是「群落規模小導致了這個問題（the

small size caused the problem）」。選 項 B 首 先 對 獨 立 分 句 進 行 了 改 述 （population's smallness = the small size；itself = the key factor；drives it to extinction = causing extinction），然後對子句進行了換句話説（whereas = even though），符合文中意思。

9. **C** 細節資訊題

〔**解析**〕作者説到「滅絕漩渦」時，用定語子句 interacting factors work progressively to make small populations smaller and smaller, drawing them into extinction like a whirlpool 來修辭，根據此意，選項 C 正確。

10. **C** 推論題

〔**解析**〕作者例舉了一系列導致琴雞滅絕的無法預料的自然事件（unanticipated and mostly natural events），其中，有因種群減少和性別比例失調（火災期間，雌性動物不願意離開巢穴）導致的近親交配。由此可推斷不正常的性別比例是繁殖率低的主要原因。因此選 C。

11. **■ 4** 插入句子題

見本章前文的「托福總監評析」。

12.

Extinction Process	Factors
Phase 1	• 1. Targeting of heath hens for food • 5. Commercial land development
Phase 2	• 2. Bitterly cold winter season • 4. Burning of grassland nesting area • 6. Bringing domestic fowl into the habitat

資訊歸類題

〔**解析**〕在第五段，作者總結了琴雞滅絕的兩個階段和滅絕原因。作者説：The first involved the devastation of habitat and the drop in population due to a new and sudden stress—human hunting. These factors led to a drastic reduction in geographic range. the first 指代「第一階段」。第一個選項是對 human hunting 的換句話説，應放在 Phase 1 欄中。第五個選項也應歸入 Phase 1 欄中，在第三段作者提到：Intensive hunting, coupled with habitat destruction by an expanding human population, gradually reduced the heath hens' geographic range.

至於第二個階段，作者説：The next stage involved a series of accidents—some physical and some biological—that led to the final extinction. 第四段列舉了這些事件：1）隨狂風蔓延的自然火災，燒毀了很多草地；2）火災之後出現嚴冬，捕食琴雞的老鷹反常湧入；3）群落規模減小和性別比例失調（火災期間，雌性動物不願意離開巢穴）導致的近親交配；4）家養火雞引發的禽病。第二、第四和第五個選項是對這些事件的換句話説。

第三個選項説法錯誤，文中只是説雌性動物太少。第七個選項文中沒有提及。

● Answer Key to Exercise 2

a. Now I am going to talk about another genetic model which is frequently used, the fruit fly. We often see these insects near over-ripe fruit during the summer.

b. The position of the human larynx, also known as the "voice box," is the factor that enables us to make more sounds than our Neanderthal ancestors. The larynx controls the air flow coming in and out of the lungs.

c. Charles Darwin had no interest in becoming a physician, unlike his father. Because his father thought that being a minister was a prestigious career, Charles ended up studying theology at university.

聽力模擬試題錄音文本　**Track 037**

N: Now listen to part of a lecture in a genetics class.

P: In today's lecture, I'll continue discussing how human cells reproduce and divide. We'll still be talking about the non-sexual division of body cells better known as mitosis. You'll remember, it's non-sexual division that produces most of our cells, cells that allow us to grow from infancy and to replace the older cells.

And you'll remember that in non-sexual cellular division, two identical daughter cells are created from the mother cell. Before cell division, each of the chromosomes duplicates by producing two strands of DNA that are joined at the center. The membrane of the nucleus dissolves, which allows the DNA strands to separate. From these strands, two daughter cells are formed; but they're still inside the mother cell. Then, finally, the membrane of the mother cell divides in two to complete the separation of the daughter cells. So that's the division process for most of the cells in our bodies.

One thing which is very magical is the way cells know when to reproduce and divide and how often to divide. For instance, we know that certain types of human cells are frequently replaced by new ones, like skin and fingernail cells. But other cells are rarely duplicated—the cells in our brains and hearts, for example.

So at the molecular level, there clearly are some other interesting things going on. We know each chromosome is filled with important encoded information—the genetic code of our genes! But there's also a lot of what we call non-coding DNA. Non-coding DNA is important, too. Right now I want to talk about one type of non-coding DNA—the DNA segments called telomeres.

So what's a telomere? Telomeres are found at the ends of chromosomes, and their function is to protect the chromosome ends. A telomere keeps the end of a chromosome from being mistakenly fused together with another chromosome. If it weren't for telomeres, when a chromosome was duplicating itself, it might become damaged and lose vital genetic information. We can liken a strand of DNA to a shoestring—say, the shoestrings of your tennis shoes, where there's a little bit of plastic at the very tip. What's that plastic for? It keeps the shoestring from becoming frayed, so that you can thread the shoelace through the holes in your shoes. The telomere is just like that plastic tip—it stops the end of the chromosome from becoming worn.

But that's not all. Each time a normal body cell divides, its telomeres become a little shorter. This keeps happening until eventually they are so short that no further cell division can occur. Cells with extremely short telomeres don't work properly and eventually die. What's more, we know cells have a finite limit of how many times they can divide. So this shrinkage of telomeres may be like a clock that determines the longevity of a cell. We're not sure how this clock works, but scientists believe the shortening of telomeres is related somehow to the aging process, at least in some cells.

S: What about animals? Do they have telomeres?

P: Most plants and animals do, but bacteria do not. And scientists are doing a whole range of studies on this topic.

S: So is there evidence in animals that short telomeres cause—I mean are linked to—aging?

P: That's a bit of a puzzle. Take mice, for example. Mice have much longer telomeres than humans do, so in theory they should live longer. But they live only two years. And one other study, one that looked at a variety of birds, showed that species with short lives get shorter telomeres more quickly than birds with long life spans.

S: But what about humans? I mean, if I want to live longer, is there some way to make my telomeres stay long longer?

P: I'll answer your question in two parts. First off, we know that a four-year-old child will have telomeres that are longer than her parents. Her grandparents' telomeres will be shorter than her parents. So your age affects the length. [pause] As for the other part of your question: What you can do. There are many factors related to how quickly we age and how long we live. For example, exercise. Let me tell you about one study involving twins. Researchers looked at the length of telomeres in the white blood cells of many pairs of twins and found the telomeres of the twin who exercised the most were longer than the telomeres of the co-twin who exercised the least. I think the frequent exercisers were working out something like three hours a week, while the non-exercisers were doing only fifteen minutes a week. Anyway, the relationship between the level of physical activity and telomere length in white blood cells was found to be significant, even after scientists adjusted for other possible factors.

● **Transcripts for Question 2.**

N: Listen again to part of the lecture. Then answer the question.

S: So is there evidence in animals that short telomeres cause—I mean are linked to— aging?

P: That's a bit of a puzzle. Take mice, for example. Mice have much longer telomeres than humans do, so in theory they should live longer. But they live only two years. And one other study, one that looked at a variety of birds, showed that species with short lives get shorter telomeres more quickly than birds with long life spans.

N: What does the professor mean when he says this:

P: That's a bit of a puzzle.

關鍵語塊

non-sexual division 無性分裂	mitosis 有絲分裂
from infancy 從嬰幼兒期開始	daughter cell 子細胞
mother cell 母細胞	DNA 去氧核糖核酸
duplicate 複製	strand of... ……的鏈（如 DNA 鏈）
encoded information 編碼資訊	genetic code 基因序列；遺傳密碼
gene 基因	non-coding DNA 非編碼 DNA
liken... to... 將……比作……	shoestring 鞋帶
become frayed 受磨損	becoming worn 用壞的；穿破的
what's more 而且；此外	finite limit 有限次數
shrinkage of... ……的縮小	longevity of... ……的壽命
aging process 老化過程	first off 首先
white blood cell 白血球	co-twin 孿生兄弟（姐妹）
work out 鍛煉	adjust for 調整以適應

聽力模擬試題答案詳解

1. **D** 主旨大意題
   〔解析〕講座中附帶提到了 DNA 損壞，因為選項 B 不選。因為講座中沒有詳細介紹細胞有性分裂，所以 C 項也不正確。因為教授回顧了細胞無性分裂的整個過程，並詳細地介紹了染色體端粒：這種分裂的一個重要部分，所以 D 項符合。

2. **D** 語用功能題
   〔解析〕教授引述了老鼠和鳥類研究中的矛盾結果，這就是為什麼教授說情況還是有點令人感到迷惑。選項 D 符合此意。

3. **B** 組織結構題
   〔解析〕這道題有點棘手，因為教授提到的鞋帶，給人留下了深刻的印象，但鞋帶代表的是 DNA 鏈，而塑膠頭代表的是端粒，因此選 B。

4. **A、C** 細節資訊題
   〔解析〕根據教授所說：Each time a normal body cell divides, its telomeres become a little shorter. 和 If it weren't for telomeres, when a chromosome was duplicating itself, it might become damaged and lose vital genetic information. 選項 A 和 C 正確。

5. **C** 立場觀點題
   〔解析〕這道題的每個選項好像都對。教授沒有提到片語 clock theory，但是他的確有說：... we know cells have a finite limit of how many times they can divide. So this shrinkage of telomeres may be like a clock that determines the longevity of a cell. We're not sure how this clock works, but scientists believe the shortening of telomeres is related somehow to the aging process, ... C 項符合此意。最大的干擾項是選項 A，但教授並沒有說不能延緩衰老，所以不正確。事實上，他在後文談到一個有關鍛煉的研究，該研究顯示鍛煉可以延緩衰老。

6.

	YES	NO
More white blood cells were found in people who exercised more.		✓
Telomere length was shorter in people who exercised less.	✓	
Exercisers tend to have children with relatively long telomeres.		✓

關聯內容題
   〔解析〕教授說經常鍛煉的人的白血球細胞中端粒的長度比較長，他並沒有說在他們身上發現了更多的白血球細胞，因此第一項在「NO」下面打勾。第二項文中明確提到了，在「YES」下面打勾。講座中沒有提到鍛煉者中兒童的端粒長度，因此第三項在「NO」下面打勾。

⑳ 社會科學常考主題 5 市場行銷學與商學詞彙、答案、解析和錄音原文

● **Answer Key to Exercise 1**

a. Insurance policies which are purchased by an individual are paid for directly by that individual, unlike the policies purchased by groups.

b. If people don't keep good records when they start new businesses, they may not know how to avoid risk and optimize profits.

c. Advertising for brand names which are well known and have a long history is not as important as it is for brands of new products.

閱讀模擬試題答案詳解

1. **C** 細節資訊題
   〔解析〕選項 D 是干擾項，作者説：Yet systematic fact-finding and analysis can enrich decision-making and make results more likely. 但並未提及編輯資訊核實。因為作者説市場調查在出版業不常見（less common in publishing），所以選項 C 正確。

2. **A** 語境詞彙題
   〔解析〕to have a hunch 這個片語可以換句話説為 to have an intuitive feeling，意為「有一種預感」。選項 A「gut feeling」意為「直覺」。

3. **D** 細節資訊題
   〔解析〕作者説專業出版商通過 contact with selected people in the chosen market sector 來收集市場訊息，因此選項 D 為正確答案。D 項中的 well-versed 意為「熟知的」。

4. **B** 指代關係題
   〔解析〕從上下文可知，此處的 it 指代 Cuba。閱讀能力強的讀者會發現這道題很簡單，而那些閱讀能力不強的讀者則可能會被專有名詞和名詞片語迷惑住了。

5. **C** 修辭目的題
   〔解析〕找到類比的關鍵在於第四段的第一個句子，這個句子説出版業和「新大陸」之間有類似之處。因為哥倫布沒有做調查或者聽取他人的意見，所以他以為古巴是亞洲的一部分。哥倫布與出版業管理者作類比；古巴與銷售目標作類比。因此選項 C 為正確答案。

6. **D** 語境詞彙題
   〔解析〕選項 B 和 C 是干擾項，因為它們都有正面的含義。然而，在此處情境中，它們的意思與 in earnest 都不同。副詞 seriously 與副詞片語 in earnest 同義。

7. **A** 否定事實題
   〔解析〕本題的答案在第五段：Solid market research can serve publishers in many ways. 作者繼續説市場調查 can identify the size, shape and nature of a market（對應 D 項）。so as to truly understand that marketplace; it can investigate the strengths and weaknesses of competitive titles（對應 B 項）。it can test out strategic ideas; and it can define when marketing expenditure, promotions and sales targeting need to be adjusted（對應 C 項）。其中沒有提到廣告代理公司，因此選 A。

8. **C** 句子簡化題
   〔解析〕見本章前文的「托福總監評析」。

9. **A** 細節資訊題
   〔解析〕作者説：Strategic research can help marketing professionals make prudent decisions

about advertising formats, the content for press releases and the product mix, so that titles can be bundled optimally to enable distributors to maximize their merchandising efforts. 其中 titles can be bundled optimally 的意思與 selecting an assortment of suitable books 相同。

10. **B** 語境詞彙題

〔解析〕選項 C 和 D 是干擾項，因為這兩個選項都說明了有利的特徵。片語 in the best way 與副詞 optimally 同義，意為「最佳」。

11. **D** 推論題

〔解析〕作者沒有明確批評哥倫布。哥倫布至死都認為自己建立了一條通往東印度群島的通道，他不允許人們質疑他的想法。作者說出版業管理者也一樣，僅僅根據假設來作出決定。從這些說法可以推斷作者認為哥倫布應該聽取他人的意見。因此選項 D 為正確答案。

12. ■ **3** 插入句子題

Although market research can be expensive, the expenditure is minimal when compared to the cost of failure. A defining characteristic of the book trade is that most books are sold on consignment. ■ 1 In this model, wholesalers and bookstores, as well as most other retail outlets, are generally allowed to return unsold copies of books to the publisher for credit, resulting in significant risk for publishers. ■ 2 The successful selection of titles will fuel strong direction and growth, and a research agenda can certainly help guide acquisitions. And a formal research agenda isn't enough in itself; a publishing house should be just as concerned with having a research-oriented business approach. Too many companies do too much on the basis of hunch. Intuition should not be decried in principle, but rather used in harness with sound information. ■ 3 **It is easy to assume that one knows the market; yet sooner or later market visions become dated or inaccurate—or at worst, wishful thinking.** Research at its simplest level is a genuinely objective view of the marketplace. ■ 4 In some instances this can be achieved without great cost, even by the smallest firm.

〔解析〕插入句的第一個分句中，關鍵字是 the market。插入句的第二部分（以 yet 開頭）是說那些想當然地認為自己瞭解市場的人，必然會發現他們錯了。因此可以斷定該句之前的句子是在說瞭解市場情況似乎很容易，或者是在說很多人誤認為自己瞭解市場。

第一個和第二個黑色方塊位置不適合。因為寄售書與市場無關。第三個黑色方塊位置前面的句子是說太多的公司都依靠直覺，後面接的句子是說調查是一種客觀手段。第三個方塊位置符合插入句的邏輯。為了保險起見，還要檢驗第四個黑色方塊選項，最後一句說 this can be achieved，表示這個句子是討論的正面結果，而非負面結果，所以也不適合。

13. **2** In the past, rigorous market research did not constitute an integral part of the planning process in publishing companies.

3 The benefits of market research include not only formal studies, but also a data-driven business strategy.

4 Research can serve various purposes, including but not limited to, decisions about new projects, tracking of ongoing operations and use of marketing dollars.

內容總結題

〔解析〕要選出正確的選項，必須能挑選出出版史上與市場調查相關的重要發展。過去的發展和現在的發展之間應該有一個平衡。作者沒有說盯住「核心市場」比盯住競爭對手更重要，所以第一個選項不選。第二個選項正確，因為該項總結了過去出版行業的特點：出版商不習慣利用市場調查。第三個選項也正確，因為作者強調市場調查應該用研究性的商業方法（a research-oriented business approach）來完善。第四個選項正確，因為三個方面綜合了第五段的資訊。第五個選項本身的說法沒錯，但並不是本文的要點。第六個選項不正確，因為文中沒有提到行業刊物。

● **Answer Key to Exercise 2**

Now I'd like to talk about a case study involving the Xerox Corporation. In this story, you'll see how technical knowledge was used to improve the repair service of Xerox photocopiers. In the 1980s and early 90s, Xerox invested a lot of money to create technical manuals to help their repair technicians. These manuals were very long and very boring. They documented in total detail how to repair the photocopiers. The problem was, the people in the field didn't want to read them.

But, as it turned out, the repair technicians would talk with each other about the various problems they had in fixing machines. They would use their lunch times and breaks to share stores. And then company managers noticed that the technicians started communicating with each other while they were on the job, calling each other on the phone, sharing even more ways to trouble-shoot and repair the machines. From this phenomenon, experts in knowledge management realized that it was the social interaction between repair technicians that was improving efficiency. This case teaches us that technical knowledge is a socially distributed resource that is disseminated orally.

聽力模擬試題錄音文本　　 *Track 039*

N: Now listen to part of a lecture in a management class.

P: We've talked about financial management, and you're now familiar with some of the financial metrics managers use to gauge how well an organization is performing. But financial management needs to be integrated into overall strategic planning and strategic management. One classic example of how this integration can be accomplished is the story of Lee Lacocca and how he began using the quarterly performance review in a strategic way. None of you will remember—since you weren't even born yet—when the US automobile industry first started to react to government regulations for safer cars and cleaner emissions. Back during the 1960s, the auto industry was going through a lot of changes. That's when Lee Lacocca became an executive at Ford Motor Company. In his role as president, Lacocca had to pull together financial information to create interim financial statements. As we learned last week, interim statements are financial reports that are created periodically during the accounting year. They can be done every month, or every quarter. Company stockholders receive this financial data quarterly, along with a summary that explains the business trends. So stockholders can read this report and understand why they are earning—or oftentimes not earning—money on that stock.

As Lacocca was working to prepare these quarterly reports for stockholders, it occurred to him that it might make sense to hold quarterly reviews with his managers. He began to develop a performance evaluation system that was in sync with the quarterly financial reporting system. The idea was that each manager would meet every three months with his or her boss. The two of them would talk about what the manager accomplished during that past quarter. And then they would talk about whether the manager's objectives needed to be changed, based on the situation in the previous quarter.

Briefly put, there are three main benefits to the quarterly performance review system. First, it makes each manager "own" his or her work objectives, which motivates that manager to excel—to become more invested in the goals.

Another advantage to this performance review system is that it forces all the managers and their bosses to sit down together at least four times a year and communicate. When they have these discussions, even if the two individuals don't get along very well, the result is that big problems and great ideas get surfaced. In other words, a by-product is that problems are identified and can be solved through the help of the executive leadership. And new ideas bubble to the top, which allows innovation to occur.

Now there are also downsides to the quarterly review system. Can you think of any? Well, for one thing, you've got people who are already very busy who now have to spend a lot of time four times a year sitting down and evaluating all the managers who report to them. That means staff is spending time on tasks other than their everyday duties. And if you've ever worked in a corporation, you know that whenever job performance is being discussed, there's a lot of emotion. A lot of effort is devoted to writing stuff down. So a second drawback of a quarterly review is that you get floods of paperwork which you can drown in. Paperwork that will start piling up and may never get acted upon.

We can see there are pros and cons to this system. But let's talk more about how a performance management system, even an imperfect one, can help benefit an organization strategically. I mentioned the interim financial statements that are issued quarterly to stockholders and to key stakeholders. This communication puts everyone on the same page. Quarterly performance reviews serve this same function within the organization itself—at least in theory—because the conversations allow management and employees to be working toward a common set of objectives, which can be adjusted every three months.

One of the things that new MBAs often fail to remember is that spreadsheets and financial reports are not the key to productivity. Rather, the first step to harnessing organizational potential is to build on human capital! And one way to do that is to make sure employees understand how their jobs fit strategically into the big picture.

To help keep employees informed, managers can leverage information systems, which track productivity and financials. Most IT systems are good at accounting and providing numbers of past results. But systems are not as good at providing strategic information about market trends and how competitors are doing. Your next week's reading assignment is Chapter 7, related to the design of decision support systems. As you read, reflect on the type of information you'd like to have available, if you were leading a company.

● **Transcripts for Question 5**

N: Listen again to part of the lecture. Then answer the question.

P: **One of the things that new MBAs often fail to remember is that spreadsheets and financial reports are not the key to productivity. Rather, the first step to harnessing organizational potential is to build on human capital!**

N: What does the professor say about financial knowledge?

● **Transcripts for Question 6**

N: Listen again to part of the lecture. Then answer the question.

P: **But systems are not as good at providing strategic information about market trends and how competitors are doing. Your next week's reading assignment is Chapter 7, related to the design of decision support systems. As you read, reflect on the type of information you'd like to have available, if you were leading a company.**

N: Why does the professor say this:

P: **reflect on the type of information you'd like to have available, if you were leading a company**

關鍵語塊

financial management 財務管理	financial metric 財務指標
gauge 測量，評估	be integrated into 被納入
strategic planning 戰略性規劃	cleaner emission 更清潔的排放
Ford Motor Company 福特汽車公司	pull together 把……串在一起；把……連成一個整體
stockholder 股東	performance evaluation system 績效考核體系
in sync with 與……同步	briefly put 簡單地說
own... 負責……	excel 表現出眾，突出
become more invested in 在……更加投入	by-product 附帶產生的結果；意外收穫
executive leadership 上層管理人員	bubble to the top 和最高層溝通
bedownside 不利的一面；負面效應	floods of paperwork 大量的文書工作
which you can drown in 你可能會被淹沒；會使你負擔過重	key stakeholder 主要利益相關者，大股東
new MBAs 剛畢業的工商管理學碩士	harnessing organization potential 利用機構潛能
human capital 人力資本；技能資本	fit strategically into the big picture 策略上符合總體目標
leverage 利用	decision support system 決策支持體系

聽力模擬試題答案詳解

1. **C** 主旨大意題
   〔**解析**〕財務資訊是講座的重要資訊，但與 A 項「財經期刊」相去甚遠。教授談到了如何將財務報告整合到企業的總體戰略規劃中，因此選項 C 正確。

2. **A** 細節資訊題
   〔**解析**〕選項 D 錯誤，因為 Lacocca 在考慮期中財務報表，但是教授並沒有說 Lacocca 認為需要更多的財務報表。相反，教授說 Lacocca 認為每季度對他的經理們進行考評很有意義（make sense to hold quarterly reviews with his managers），而且每位經理每三個月須與其上司見一次面（meet every three months with his or her boss）。選項 A 為正確答案。

3. **D** 組織結構題
   〔**解析**〕教授在介紹公司如何準備每期的財務報表時，談到了公司股東。沒有特殊的含義，只是講 Lacocca 的故事時提到股東，所以選項 D 正確。

4. **B**、**C** 細節資訊題
   〔**解析**〕儘管教授說老闆們很忙，但她並沒有說老闆們消息不靈通。因此選項 D 不正確。教授說考評不利的一面是原來就忙碌的人要將時間花在這些事務上，而非他們的日常職責上（on tasks other than their everyday duties）。這項工作帶來的大量文書，可能會讓人負擔過重（which you can drown in）。因此選項 B 和 C 正確。

5. **A** 立場觀點題
   〔**解析**〕教授說掌握電子製表程式不會提高生產力。相反，公司應該建立人力資本（build on human capital）。因此選項 A 正確。

6. **D** 語用功能題
   〔**解析**〕教授給學生的建議是：如果學生擔任管理者，要考慮自己想要的資訊（reflect on the type of information），考慮 IT 系統中的哪些資料來 明他們作出決策。因此選項 D 正確。

㉑ 常考校園生活場景 1 詞彙、答案、解析和錄音原文

● **Answer Key to Exercise 1**

1. b   2. c   3. d   4. e   5. a

CONVERSATION 1 錄音文本 *Track 041*

N: Listen to part of a conversation between a graduate student and a professor.

P: Tim, hello! Haven't seen you for a couple of weeks!

S: I've been checking the data analysis for one project and writing up the final report. How's everything in your experimental psychology lab?

P: No complaints here. We just got funded for a new project where we'll be working with children, so that should be interesting. Now Tim, when you called, you said you wanted to talk about some decisions you're facing.

S: It's a bit awkward. As you know, I've been doing graduate work here for a year now, working in Professor Allen's psychology lab.

P: [joking] And I'm sure Dr. Allen has been keeping you busy.

S: And I've learned a lot about research methodology. But to be honest, this lab program has been somewhat limiting. I'm envious of the graduate students who have been able to rotate through several different labs and get exposure to a lot of projects.

P: Have you thought about what you want to do next year?

S: There are a couple of neuroscience labs at other universities that I'd like to work at. I've even sent out some feeler emails, and the principal investigators seem potentially interested. So now I need references.

P: Have you told Dr. Allen your plans? He is your principal investigator.

S: That's just it. I haven't told him outright, but I've hinted that I'd like to gain more diverse experience. He seemed kind of hostile. Plus, the grapevine says that people who leave his lab can't get positive references from him.

P: I see.

S: And well, since you are on the committee for my Master's thesis, I was wondering if you'd be willing to write a recommendation for me. Even though I haven't formally worked in your psych lab.

P: I'd be happy to write a letter of support, although I'll need more information. The final draft of your thesis isn't complete yet, is it?

S: No. I think you all on the committee have got the most recent draft though, and that shows my research design and sample. But I could send you a report I just did for a study on how aging affects language processing.

P: Do that. And send me your most recent CV as well. Also, if you're willing, email me the names of the people and the labs you're talking to.

S: All right. But what about my other references?

P: Tim, you're going to have to sit down with Dr. Allen and be candid with him. Personality aside, he is a giant in the field. And he is your principal investigator.

S: So I can't get around it—I have to ask him?

P: It's sort of protocol and, quite frankly, you don't want to burn any bridges. Besides, you've done good work for him in his lab, so he should have no complaints. In fact, I'd love to have you here—in my psych lab. There's a slot still open for next year...

S: I'm flattered; I know you do top work. But my future calling is in neuroscience, where I can do multidisciplinary research in a big lab. To tell you the truth, I can't wait to start doing brain imaging.

● **Transcripts for Question 5**

N: Listen again to part of the conversation. Then answer the question.

P: It's sort of protocol and, quite frankly, you don't want to burn any bridges. Besides, you've done good work for him in his lab, so he should have no complaints. In fact, I'd love to have you here—in my psych lab. There's a slot still open for next year...

S: I'm flattered; I know you do top work. But my future calling is in neuroscience, where I can do multidisciplinary research in a big lab. To tell you the truth, I can't wait to start doing brain imaging.

N: What does the man imply when he says this:

S: I'm flattered; I know you do top work.

關鍵語塊

check the data analysis 檢測資料分析	experimental psychology 實驗心理學
lab 實驗室	No complaints here. 一切都挺好的。
got funded for... 在……上得到資助	It's a bit awkward. 這事說起來有點尷尬。
research methodology 研究方法論	has been somewhat limiting 有所限制
envious of 羨慕	rotate through 輪流去……
get exposure to 接觸	neuroscience 神經系統科學
feeler email 試探的電子郵件	principal investigator 主要研究者
That's just it. 正是這個問題。	I haven't told him outright 我還沒有坦白地告訴他
I've hinted that... 我已經暗示……	grapevine says that... 有傳言說……
positive reference 褒獎的推薦信	on the committee for... ……委員會的委員
Master's thesis 碩士論文	you'd be willing to... 你會願意……
letter of support 推薦信	final draft 最終稿
research design 研究設計	(research) sample （研究）抽查的樣本或人員
how aging affects language processing 衰老如何影響語言處理能力	Do that. 去做吧。
CV 簡歷	sit down with sb. 和某人坐下來談談
be candid with... 對……坦白	I can't get around it 我迴避不了
protocol 禮儀	burn any bridges 不留退路
slot 位置	I'm flattered 我受寵若驚
do top work 工作做得很好	future calling is... 未來感興趣的職業是……
multidisciplinary research 多學科研究	

聽力模擬試題答案詳解 --

1. **A** 主要目的題

    〔**解析**〕選項 B 與原文不符。選項 C 也不正確，因為儘管學生談到了論文，但他與教授會面的主要目的並不是為了論文。選項 D 不正確，因為神經科學不是教授的領域。儘管學生談到了好幾個話題，但他的主要目的是請求教授給他寫一份推薦信，所以正確答案為 A。

2. **B** 細節資訊題

    〔**解析**〕選項 A 不正確，因為學生沒有抱怨 Dr. Allen 利用他。選項 C 和 D 與原文內容不符。因為學生說 ... this lab program has been somewhat limiting，所以選項 B（too narrow）正確。

3. **C** 細節資訊題

    〔**解析**〕選項 D 不正確，因為雖然教授能得到研究經費，但學生不需要經濟援助。選項 A 和 B 有違事實。學生實際上說明了原因 ... since you are on the committee for my Master's thesis，因此選項 C 正確。

4. **D** 立場觀點題

    〔**解析**〕教授說：... you've done good work for him in his lab, so he should have no complaints. 由此可以推斷她認為 Dr. Allen 會公平處理推薦信的事，因此選項 D 正確。

5. **D** 推論題

    〔**解析**〕I'm flattered 的意思是「我真是受寵若驚（您過獎了）」。在不同情境中，you flatter me 還可以表示 you think I am more qualified than I really am，但是因為學生對這個職位不感興趣，所以從邏輯上來講他不會談到資格問題，因此選項 C 不正確。選項 B 曲解了 I know you do top research 的意思。

CONVERSATION 2 錄音文本 *Track 043*

H= Housing office employee 下同。

N: Listen to part of a conversation at the student housing office.

S: Good morning. I'm here to follow up on a problem in my dorm room.

H: This isn't the usual channel for students to make complaints. You're supposed to contact the maintenance people in your dorm. Which is...?

S: I live in Thomas Hall. On the second floor, in 208. I put in the complaint a week ago. About a leaky ceiling and mold growing all over the place.

H: Oh my goodness! And it's been raining all this week. [pause] So you say you've got mildew in your dorm room?

S: Not just my room; it's the whole second and third floors. The water's seeped through the ceiling, and now the mold is spreading everywhere. We're all getting sick.

H: OK, I do see from the computer record that the Thomas Hall roof needs extensive repairs. So perhaps that's the delay.

S: Actually, they're going to have to tear out all the carpeting, too, because the mold is deep down in the rug fibers. My roommate's allergic to mold, and her father—he's a doctor—he's very concerned.

H: [increasingly worried] What's your resident assistant doing to get you through this?

S: She's helped us fill out all the forms and has tried to push our maintenance guy in Thomas Hall. But she's not a miracle worker, you know?

H: Hmm. It appears from the damage report that there are also loose electrical wires coming out of the phone sockets in your room.

S: Yup. Ever since I moved in, the phone jack was hanging from the wall, and for a while the phone was working. But then it quit all of a sudden.

H: Well, the phone problem should be easier to tackle. [pause] You know, I'm surprised at this delay. Maintenance requests are usually addressed on the day the request is issued.

S: Who knows what's going on! All I know is that I'm getting really tired of this. I pay a lot of money for housing.

H: Well, I'll certainly jump on this. The phone connection and wiring for your room should be up and running by the end of the day.

S: Um, also... Do you think I could move into another room? This whole situation is a health risk. And my roommate's dad—you know, the doctor? I heard he's considering filing a suit against the university.

H: [curtly] Legal action won't be necessary. As I said, I'll certainly get in touch with the building maintenance crews responsible for roofing and try to expedite these repairs.

S: So can you get me—and my roommate—another room in the meanwhile?

H: Let me talk today with your resident assistant to see how many people are being affected by the mold. I'll explore with her the possibility of finding some temporary living space for the most critical cases.

● **Transcripts for Question 2**

N: Listen again to part of the conversation. Then answer the question.

H: [increasingly worried] **What's your resident assistant doing to get you through this**?

S: **She's helped us fill out all the forms and has tried to push our maintenance guy in Thomas Hall. But she's not a miracle worker, you know?**

N: What does the woman mean when she says this:

S: **But she's not a miracle worker, you know?**

● **Transcripts for Question 4**

N: Why does the woman say this:

S: **This whole situation is a health risk. And my roommate's dad—you know the doctor? I heard he's considering filing a suit against the university.**

關鍵語塊

follow up on... 跟進……的情況	usual channel for... ……的通常管道
maintenance people 維修人員	put in the complaint 投訴
leaky ceiling 有漏隙的天花板	mold 黴菌
mildew 黴	water's seeped through the ceiling 水從天花板滲出
tear out 扯去	rug 地毯
be allergic to 對……過敏	resident assistant 宿舍管理員
get you through this 幫你解決這個問題	fill out all the forms 填寫所有表格
she's not a miracle worker 她並非奇蹟創造者	damage report 損壞報告
loose electrical wire 鬆動的電線	phone socket 電話插座

phone jack 電話插孔	phone was working 電話正常
requests are usually addressed 要求通常會得到處理	jump on 立刻關注
up and running 運行正常的	file a suit against 對……提起訴訟
legal action 訴訟	expedite 使加速完成；促進
temporary living space 臨時住處	

聽力模擬試題答案詳解

1. **D** 主要目的題
   〔**解析**〕選項 B 不正確，因為女學生無意責備宿舍管理員，她只是希望其住處能得到修理。因為女學生已經 put in the complaint，由此可知她來住宿辦公室是為了進一步詢問此事，所以選項 D 正確。

2. **C** 語用功能題
   〔**解析**〕女學生沒有抱怨宿舍管理員缺乏解決住房維修問題的能力，因此選項 A 不正確。選項 B 對 miracle worker 的理解不正確，女學生說宿舍管理員已經盡力了，但還是沒法解決問題，因此選項 C 正確。

3. **B** 細節資訊題
   〔**解析**〕儘管女生提到了寢室的屋頂和線路，但她沒有說是這些耽擱問題的解決，因此選項 C 和 D 都不正確。選項 A 中的宿舍管理員也不是耽擱的原因。女學生反覆提到維修人員沒有對解決各種問題的請求作出回應，因此選項 B 正確。

4. **A** 推論題
   〔**解析**〕選項 B 不正確，因為對話中沒有提到該女生的室友要搬走。選項 C 不正確，因為住宿辦公室的人並沒有被告知她的室友生病了。選項 D 是干擾項，因為該女生提到她室友的父親有可能會起訴大學，但沒有說自己要提出法律訴訟。女學生只是在威脅，以便給住宿辦公室施加壓力，從而允許自己換房間。因此選項 A 正確。

5. **C、D** 細節資訊題
   〔**解析**〕住宿辦公室員工說他會與宿舍管理員聯繫，並當天解決電話連接問題，因此選項 C 和 D 正確。

● **Answer Key to Exercise 2**

a. <u>What sort of things is your resident assistant doing to help you?</u>

b. <u>We should have less trouble resolving the problem with the phone.</u>

c. <u>I'll work with her to see what kind of rooms we may find for the most serious cases.</u>

常考校園生活場景 2 詞彙、答案、解析和錄音原文

● **Answer Key to Exercise 1**

a. Yes, I just barely passed the test.

b. But I don't quite understand why you didn't go talk to your teaching assistant about the problem early on.

c. But now I'm scared that I'll do poorly on the final exam.

● **Answer Key to Exercise 2**

1. I'm a sophomore. / I'll be a junior in the fall.

2. That's the kind of thing we like to hear. / Great. It's really a matter of courtesy.

3. So you don't think I should take the parking lot job?

CONVERSATION 1 錄音文本　 *Track 045*

N: Listen to part of a conversation between a student and a professor.

P: Mary, I take it you're here to talk about Organic Chemistry? The semester is quickly coming to an end, so whatever the issue is, we need to address it quickly.

S: [sigh] Here's the deal. Do you remember how, the evening before the midterm exam, there was a big ice storm? Well, I slipped on the steps to the library and broke my wrist.

P: Ouch. That can't have been pleasant.

S: It's healing well—actually, my arm is doing better than my Chemistry. My grade on that midterm was not nearly as high as it could have been.

P: My record indicates you got a 61 on that test.

S: Yeah, just borderline passing.

P: And so?

S: When I was at the university health center that night, I told them I had a test the next day and they mentioned the possibility of exempting the grade. At the time, I had taken a painkiller and I didn't really know what "exempting" meant.

P: When we exempt a grade for a test, we don't count that test. Essentially, we pretend it never existed, and then we average all the other grades.

S: Do you by any chance have my cumulative grade for this semester, counting that one? I'm trying to figure out how to handle this.

P: Including the midterm exam, your average is 69. Which isn't failing. [peeved] But I'm rather curious as to why you didn't go to your Section TA with this problem earlier.

S: The day of the midterm, he saw my arm all bandaged up and mentioned in passing there were special accommodations for medical situations like mine.

P: The problem is that, if we go by strict university policy, students are supposed to make a request to drop a test within seven days of the exam.

S: I didn't bother to pursue it because I figured I wasn't close enough to a B for it to make a difference. But now I'm afraid I'm going to mess up on the final exam.

P: If you're having trouble on the exercises—say, the current stuff on compounds like amines— you should meet with your teaching assistant. You've got a couple of weeks before the final, so there's still time.

S: I'll contact him during his office hours this week. But I'd like to ask you if you'd consider dropping my midterm score now.

P: It's not that you don't have a reasonable reason for missing the midterm, but I wish you had come to me sooner. Can you get me some documentation from the health center?

S: I happen to have the doctor's note right here.

P: If you're certain this is the way you want to go, I'll turn a blind eye to university policy this time, despite my misgivings. Dropping a score before we turn in final grades is as simple as a few clicks on my computer.

S: Don't you think this makes sense?

P: It's your call. A lot will hinge on how well you fare on the upcoming final. And another thought—have you ever visited the university's Chemistry Tutoring Center?

S: As fate would have it, my roommate's a Chemistry major, and she did mention it to me.

P: They've got half-hour sessions where you can talk with a specialized tutor. But to my mind the best thing is to spend real time working through the exercises yourself.

● **Transcripts for Question 2**

N: Listen again to part of the conversation. Then answer the question.

S: Do you remember how, the evening before the midterm exam, there was a big ice storm? Well, I slipped on the steps to the library and broke my wrist.

P: Ouch. That can't have been pleasant.

N: Why does the professor say this:

P: Ouch.

關鍵語塊

Organic Chemistry 有機化學	Here's the deal. 事情是這樣的。
midterm exam 期中考試	ice storm 冰暴
slip on the steps 上下樓梯時滑了一跤	break my wrist 手腕骨折
Ouch. 哎喲！	It's healing well 癒合狀況良好
borderline passing 勉強及格	university health center 大學健康中心，大學診所
exempt the grade 免除成績；允許成績不算數	painkiller 止痛藥
don't count... 不將……納入	pretend it never existed 假裝它不存在；完全忽略它
cumulative grade 累積學分	how to handle this 如何解決這種情況
which isn't failing 而不是不及格	I'm rather curious as to why... 我很好奇為什麼……
Section TA 課程助教	bandaged up 纏滿了繃帶
special accommodation for 給予特殊待遇	drop a test 刪除考試成績
didn't bother to pursue it 無意追訴這件事情	mess up on 〔俚語〕搞砸
compound 化合物	amine 有機胺
documentation 證明資料	doctor's note 醫生記錄
the way you want to go 你想要的解決方法	turn a blind eye (to) （對……）視而不見
despite my misgivings 儘管我有些不安	It's your call. 你自己決定。

hinge on 取決於	fare on... 在……上的表現，進展
another thought 另一個想法	As fate would have it, ... 碰巧的是……
work through the exercises 仔細研究練習題	

聽力模擬試題答案詳解

1. **C 主要目的題**
   〔解析〕這位學生化學期中考試考得不理想，因為在考試前一天她的手腕受傷了。她去見教授是為了看看她的累積學分有多少，當她發現累積學分不高時，就請求教授將她的期中考試成績作不計分處理。選項 C 正確，因為學生找教授是為了找到化學課能通過的對策。

2. **D 語用功能題**
   〔解析〕見本章前文的「托福總監評析」。

3. **A 細節資訊題**
   〔解析〕本題為否定句。女學生只是説止痛藥讓她頭暈，所以選項 B 不正確。她説：I didn't bother to pursue it because I figured I wasn't close enough to a B for it to make a difference. 因此選項 A 為正確答案。

4. **B 立場觀點題**
   〔解析〕要回答這道題目，考生必須注意教授在整個對話中説了什麼。教授好幾次提到 TA（助教）。他説學生應該早點與 TA 聯繫，但並沒有指責 TA，所以選項 C 不正確。選項 A 是一個肯定的觀點，但我們可以從教授的言談中得知他對女學生的行為不是特別高興。如，他説：It's not that you don't have a reasonable reason for missing the midterm, but I wish you had come to me sooner. 因此選項 B 正確。

5.

	YES	NO
Talk with her TA	✓	
Solve problems independently	✓	
Study with her roommate		✓
Arrange for a make-up test		✓

關聯內容題
〔解析〕第一個句子在「YES」下面打勾，因為教授建議學生去找助教。如，他説：If you're having trouble on the exercises—say, the current stuff on compounds like amines—you should meet with your teaching assistant. 第二個句子在「YES」下面打勾，因為教授説：But to my mind the best thing is to spend real time working through the exercises yourself. 學生的室友學的是化學專業，但是教授並沒有叫學生跟她的室友一起學習，而是建議學生去化學輔導中心。教授從未提到補考。因此最後兩個句子在「NO」欄中打勾。

CONVERSATION 2 錄音文本 *Track 047*

E= Employee下同。

N: Listen to part of a conversation at the student employment center.

S: I've been looking at the job list online, but I'm not sure how to handle a situation I've gotten myself into.

E: First things first: Do you have work-study status?

S: Yes. I had a job off campus, working at a bank downtown. But I was just fired, I think.

E: You're not sure?

S: Put it this way, I told them last Friday I had to study for midterms all this week and the manager told me that if I wasn't going to come to work this week, not to come back at all.

E: Well, we need to firm up your status. You'll need to give formal notice, and I'll talk to their HR department. It sounds like a bank teller job might not have been a good fit.

S: It was fine until exam time rolled around. The money was great and there was air-conditioning. But the manager said they don't have a lot of backup tellers who are trained and ready to go.

E: It's a little disturbing when our students don't live up to the expectations of off-campus hiring organizations. I assume you need to find another position?

S: Yeah. Right away, because I need this money for living expenses. I guess I should find something on campus this time round.

E: The university hiring supervisors tend to be more flexible about student schedules, definitely. I saw on the job postings this morning that there's a new opening in the undergraduate admissions office.

S: I saw that one; it's in the Administration Building, right? But they want some one to come in almost every day for a couple hours. That sounds too hard to work around, in terms of my class scheduling.

E: There's a server job working in the Rollins Dining Hall for the evening meal. Helping serve food, with some clean-up tasks. How about that one?

S: I'm a pre-law student, so I have to protect my GPA at all costs. I need at least at 3.7 or I won't get into a good law school. So, I was hoping to work as the parking lot attendant for the Visitor's Parking Lot.

E: That job is going to be a big stretch from a job as a bank teller, and there's a fair number of people who've applied for that post. Are you sure?

S: To tell you the truth, it probably will be kind of monotonous, but I have reasons. I probably shouldn't even be telling you them.

E: Trust me, I've heard everything. I've been in this job for almost ten years.

S: Well, I've heard that the parking lot gatehouse is a good place to study. All you do is sit in the booth and take the parking ticket and the money when people leave.

E: There are definitely peaks and valleys in the work. But the job is actually pretty important, since that gate also functions as a security checkpoint.

S: I know. When I was a bank teller, there were also security issues for us. I like that aspect of the job, actually. It's one reason I want to go to law school. Maybe get involved in some sort of law enforcement.

E: Well, go ahead and give it a shot, then. But you should probably have a backup in mind, since as I mentioned, a number of candidates have responded.

● **Transcripts for Question 3**

N: Listen again to part of the conversation. Then answer the question.

S: **To tell you the truth, it probably will be kind of monotonous, but I have reasons. I probably shouldn't even be telling you them.**

E: **Trust me, I've heard everything. I've been in this job for almost ten years.**

N: What does the employee mean when she says this:

E: **Trust me, I've heard everything.**

● **Transcripts for Question 5**

N: What does the employee imply when she says this:

E: **But you should probably have a backup in mind, since as I mentioned, a number of candidates have responded.**

關鍵語塊

student employment center 學生就業中心	job list （就業）職位列表
a situation I've gotten myself into 自己造成的境況	work-study status 半工半讀的情況
off campus 在校外	Put it this way, ... 這麼説吧，……
not to come back at all 不用再來了（被解雇）	firm up 弄清楚
give formal notice 發佈正式通知	HR department 人力資源部
bank teller 銀行出納員	good fit （工作）合適
live up to the expectations of sb. 不辜負某人的期望	job postings 招聘職位列表
undergraduate admissions office 大學招生辦公室	class scheduling 課程安排
server job 服務員工作	pre-law student 法律預科生
GPA 平均積分點（Grade Point Average）	parking lot attendant 停車場服務員
a big stretch from... 〔口語〕與……有很大的不同	post 職位
monotonous 單調的	Trust me, ... 相信我，……
parking lot gatehouse 停車場警衛室	booth 崗亭，門衛室
parking ticket 停車計時票	peaks and valleys 最繁忙時段和最清閒時段
security checkpoint 安檢關卡	law enforcement 執法
give it a shot 試試	have a backup in mind 心裡有準備

聽力模擬試題答案詳解

1. **B** 主要目的題
   〔**解析**〕學生説了他的處境，自己剛剛被解雇。他沒有抱怨銀行主管，因此選項 A 不正確。選項 B 才是正確答案。

2. **B** 細節資訊題
   〔**解析**〕就業中心的工作人員説：It's a little disturbing when our students don't live up to the expectations of off-campus hiring organizations. 雖然她説得有點輕描淡寫，但很顯然，她擔憂並關心大學的聲譽。因為學生沒有「通知」，所以選項 B 為正確答案。

3. **C** 語用功能題
   〔**解析**〕當工作人員説 trust me, I've heard everything 時，領會其意思的一種方法是聽她的語調。另一種方法是注意她所説的強調性片語 trust me。這個慣用語表明她認為她已經聽過很多學生説過很多事情。此外，I've been in this job for almost ten years 也可以幫助考生理解上下文。因此選項 C 為正確答案。

4. **D** 細節資訊題
   〔**解析**〕這個學生讀書是為了成為一名律師，但是他説他想在停車場工作，以便能有更多讀書時間。因此選項 D 正確。

5. **A** 推論題
   〔**解析**〕本題並不難推理。工作人員説 you should probably have a backup in mind（心裡有備案），很顯然她認為學生獲得停車場工作的機會很小，因此選項 A 正確。

(23) 常考校園生活場景 3 詞彙、答案、解析和錄音原文

● **Answer Key to Exercise 1**

a. He makes me laugh / I think he's really funny.

b. You look totally exhausted / You look stressed out.

c. Wasn't your application for a bank internship successful? / Didn't the bank internship opportunity turn out?

● **Answer Key to Exercise 2**

a. There are oversized books in several parts of the library. It depends on the type of book. / Oversized books are housed on the same floor as their regular-sized counterparts.

b. Here's the kind of thing you may be looking for—a volume about modern architecture. / Is this the kind of book you were looking for?

c. I searched all over Floor A but couldn't locate the volume of Arabic poetry I wanted. / I give up! I looked at all the shelves on the ground floor and everything was in English.

CONVERSATION 1 錄音文本　 *Track 049*

N: Listen to part of a conversation between a student and a professor.

P: You're late to our meeting, Bob. And I asked you to come see me last week. I really wonder what you want out of this class, whether you want to succeed.

S: I've sort of given up. I thought this class would be much easier. It's Astronomy for non-science majors, for goodness sakes!

P: The major distinction between the class for science majors and this astronomy class is that this one requires less math. In terms of basic concepts, though, we cover a lot of material.

S: That's an understatement. The pace zips along so majorly fast that the concepts go right over my head.

P: What's your major, Bob? If you don't mind my asking.

S: Political Science, with a minor in Philosophy. I need your class for my science requirement. Otherwise, I would've withdrawn the second week.

P: If you like philosophy, you should enjoy this class. You know, not all astronomers start out as mathematicians. But all astronomers like to observe things and think about them—as do philosophers.

S: I like thinking about ideas. Hey, I even like looking up at the stars! But that sure didn't help me pass the last quiz about how the Earth's seasons are related to the Sun.

P: How about now? Can you explain to me why it is hotter here in Boston in June than it is in December?

S: What I wrote in my quiz was that it's hotter in Boston in June because the Northern Hemisphere is closer to the Sun than it is in December. Of course I failed that quiz, so that answer must be wrong.

P: OK, let's be simple observers for a moment. If we look at the Earth from somewhere far out in space, we observe the Earth's yearly orbit around the Sun to be almost a perfect circle.

S: A circle? You're not saying that Boston is the same distance from the Sun during all four seasons?

P: There is indeed some fluctuation, but in the greater scheme of things, the difference is not significant. The Earth is an average distance of 93 million miles from the Sun all year long.

S: OK.

P: However, because of the tilt of the Earth, sunlight hits different latitudes at different angles at different times of the year. So in June, Boston and the rest of the Northern Hemisphere is tipped toward the Sun.

S: So we're getting more direct sunlight then. It seems so obvious when you explain it. Wish it were that easy during the quizzes.

P: You may not be putting in enough hours of study. This is a three-credit course. How much do you study every week for this class?

S: Me? About three hours. Maybe four.

P: My rule of thumb for students is to study three hours a week for each credit hour. That means, for this class—

S: [interrupting] I should put in almost nine hours a week in study time. Whoa! That math I can do.

P: And one more tip. Next Friday night we go to the university observatory. Between now and then, go over the star charts. And then try drawing the relative positions of the stars from memory.

S: For another quiz?

P: No, as a learning tool. When you write something down—in this case, by drawing your own charts—you reinforce the learning in many parts of your brain. Try these methods, Bob, and the concepts will come easier.

● **Transcripts for Question 4**

N: Listen again to part of the conversation. Then answer the question.

P: My rule of thumb for students is to study three hours a week for each credit hour. That means, for this class—

S: [interrupting] I should put in almost nine hours a week in study time. Whoa! That math I can do.

N: Why does the man say this:

S: That math I can do.

關鍵語塊

I've sort of given up. 〔口語〕我有點想放棄了。	non-science major 非主修理科的學生
for goodness sakes 〔口語〕看在上帝的份上	major 主修課程;專業
That's an understatement. 完全不是那麼回事。	pace zips along 快速前進
majorly 〔俚語〕非常	go right over my head 令我無法理解
if you don't mind my asking 如果你不介意我問的話	minor 輔修課程
withdraw 退出	Northern Hemisphere 北半球
fail that quiz 沒有通過測驗	yearly orbit 公轉軌道
some fluctuation 一些波動	sunlight hits... 陽光照到……
latitude 緯度	Wish it were... 〔口語〕但願……
put in 投入(時間或精力),花費	three-credit course 三學分的課程
rule of thumb 經驗法則	university observatory 大學天文臺

star chart 星圖	relative positions of the stars 星體的相對位置
from memory 根據記憶	reinforce the learning 鞏固所學的知識

聽力模擬試題答案詳解

1. **C** 主要目的題
   〔解析〕回答本題的關鍵在於注意教授開始說話時的語氣，以及句子：And I asked you to come see me last week.。因此選項 C 正確。

2. **B** 細節資訊題
   〔解析〕學生提到上一次測驗是關於地球上的季節與太陽有何關係。教授要求學生解釋為什麼波士頓的 6 月比 12 月要熱，因此選項 B 為正確答案。

3. **A** 組織結構題
   〔解析〕教授對學生感到失望，因為學生沒有認真學習這門課程。當教授瞭解到學生選修了哲學，她說：But all astronomers like to observe things and think about them—as do philosophers. 她希望學生明白天文學的思維方式和哲學相似。選項 A 為正確答案，因為教授正在鼓勵學生。

4. **D** 語用功能題
   〔解析〕對話之前，學生表示他並不想上科學課。教授說，事實上天文學和哲學的相關程度與其和數學的相關程度一樣。當學生說 that math I can do，他是帶著開玩笑的口吻說自己數學能力沒問題，同時也是在表示他會接受教授的建議每週讀天文學 9 個小時。因此選項 D 為正確答案。

5. **D** 細節資訊題
   〔解析〕教授建議學生畫星圖並說：When you write something down—in this case, by drawing your own charts—you reinforce the learning in many parts of your brain. 學生問是否是為了測驗，教授說是為了鞏固所學的新知識，因此選項 D 為正確答案。

CONVERSATION 2 錄音文本 *Track 051*

L= Library employee 下同。

N: Listen to part of a conversation in a university library.

S: Is this the place to ask about reference books for a paper?

L: This is the reference desk, but, like, I'm just a work-study student. The reference librarian is out today.

S: I'm sure you know more about this main branch than I do. I'm more at home at the university's Fine Arts Library.

L: Oh. You an artist?

S: My major's Photography. But I'm taking a course in Art History and I have to write a monster twenty-page paper. I'm having trouble tracking down what I need.

L: Have you crystallized your ideas at all? I mean, in terms of your focus?

S: I want to talk about the aesthetics of Roman art. Or maybe the style of Roman art.

L: Keep going...

S: Huh? [pause] Oh, yeah—more detail. I thought I'd look at portrait sculpture. Do you know what that is?

L: Not really. But how about I write down "Roman sculpture," 'cause I think that'll cast a wider net. We can search these terms as keywords in just a minute.

S: Portrait sculptures are three-dimensional portraits of people. For an example, an artist might use bronze to create a portrait sculpture of a person instead of painting a picture.

L: Got it. Moving on... Do you have a sense of what period you're interested in? I'm kinda sure the history of Rome spans several thousand years.

S: Yeah, that's a lot of sculpture portraits to choose from. But I think the third century's most fascinating, because Rome was starting to go downhill then. I wanna look at portraits of the "Soldier Emperors" from that period—none of whom stayed in power very long.

L: OK, so let's put down "third century" as another key term to search on. Any emperor in particular?

S: Yeah, try Trebonianus Gallus. Here, let me type it in the computer for you—his name is impossible to spell. Can we run the search now, on those three search terms? [reciting so he can input the search terms] Roman sculpture. Third century. And the name of that one emperor.

L: Sure. Here it is—it looks like we got four reference works that are a pretty relevant to your topic.

S: So now how do I hunt all these down? They seem to be scattered all over the place.

L: That's not unusual for art books. You can see from the search screen that the location is listed next to each reference. The easiest will be this art history book—it's an electronic resource, so you can access that from anywhere.

S: Nice! Now two of these say "oversized," which means they'll weigh a ton but they'll probably have a lot of pictures. Oddly, the computer says they're here in the main branch, in the general collections.

L: Yeah, there are some oversized art books and art folios upstairs in the stacks. I'm gonna show you a map in a minute. And, before you forget, you should jot down the call number for all four of these.

S: OK. And it looks like this last one is housed in the Fine Arts Library, so that'll be simple. Unfortunately, however, the text's written in Italian.

L: Are you surprised, given your topic? Seriously, I think you're in good shape. This is a pretty robust first-pass search, even though you only got four books. It's better to start out with a few, very well-targeted references.

S: Well, I don't doubt that I'll be able to find some other decent sources sitting on the shelf right next to these.

● **Transcripts for Question 3**

N: Listen again to part of the conversation. Then answer the question.

S: Portrait sculptures are three-dimensional portraits of people. For an example, an artist might use bronze to create a portrait sculpture of a person instead of painting a picture.

L: Got it. Moving on… Do you have a sense of what period you're interested in? I'm kinda sure the history of Rome spans several thousand years.

N: Why does the library employee say this:

L: Moving on…

● **Transcripts for Question 5**

N: What does the woman mean when she says this:

S: Well, I don't doubt that I'll be able to find some other decent sources sitting on the shelf right next to these.

關鍵語塊

reference book 參考書	reference desk 諮詢台
work-study student 半工半讀的學生	reference librarian 圖書館諮詢員
main branch 圖書館總館	Fine Arts Library 美術圖書館
monster twenty-page paper 〔俚語〕長達 20 頁的學期論文	track down 查找
crystallize your ideas 把你的想法說得具體點	aesthetics of Roman art 羅馬藝術的美學
keep going 繼續說	portrait sculpture 肖像雕塑
cast a wider net 把網撒得更大	keyword 關鍵字
Got it. 〔口語〕明白了。	Moving on... 繼續下一個話題……
have a sense of 知道	span... years 跨越……年
go downhill 衰退	Soldier Emperors 軍人皇帝
search term 搜索詞	electronic resource 電子資源
access 訪問	general collection 一般書庫區（指社會科學和人文方面的書籍）
oversized (book) 超大尺寸的（書本）	art folio 藝術作品集
in the stacks 在書庫中	jot down 草草記下
call number 圖書編目號碼	be housed in 被存放在……
given 考慮到	in good shape 處於良好狀態（準備充分）
robust 強勁的	first-pass search 首次搜索

聽力模擬試題答案詳解

1. **B** 主要目的題
   〔解析〕學生來到圖書館的諮詢台詢問圖書資訊，說她需要 reference books for a paper。雖然學生是在寫關於藝術歷史的文章，但是選項 A 不正確，因為她沒有提到尋找藝術收藏品。選項 B 為正確答案。

2. **B** 細節資訊題
   〔解析〕學生告訴圖書館管理員，與 main branch 相比，她對美術圖書館更為熟悉，因此選 B。

3. **A** 語用功能題
   〔解析〕moving on... 作為一個過渡性片語，其含義與 moving along... 相同，表明說話者希望轉入一個新話題。此處，圖書館雇員很可能是對三維肖像雕塑的具體介紹不感興趣，他只想盡快地找到資料。因此選項 A「他想叫這位學生快一點」正確。

4. **A、C** 細節資訊題
   〔解析〕對話中，圖書館管理員說他們應該搜索三個關鍵字：Roman sculpture、third century 和那位皇帝的姓名 Trebonianus Gallus。因此選項 A 和 C 均正確。

5. **D** 立場觀點題
   〔解析〕當學生說：And I don't doubt that I'll be able to find some other decent sources sitting on the shelf right next to these. 可以從中知道她確信在已經找出的四本書旁邊還會找到更多參考資料，因此選項 D 為正確答案。

㉔ 常考校園生活場景 4 詞彙、答案、解析和錄音原文

● **Answer Key to Exercise 1**

1. e   2. d   3. a   4. c   5. b

● **Answer Key to Exercise 2**

a. register for   **b.** declared a major   **c.** track   **d.** prerequisites for
e. waiver   **f.** place out of   **g.** requirement

CONVERSATION 1 錄音文本   🎧 **Track 053**

- -

N: Listen to part of a conversation between a student and a professor.

P: It's nice to meet you, David. I'm still getting to know our first-year students. Professor Stone mentioned that you two had met, and that you're somewhat frustrated.

S: Yes, Doctor Stone told me that the undergraduate chair of the International Studies—you—need to approve my special requests. I have to map out my courses for the next three years.

P: I see you've brought the worksheet for class planning—that's helpful. Why don't you tell me a little bit about your academic goals before we look at specific course selections?

S: I guess I'm most interested in transnational social movements. The flow of people and ideas across borders. Economics is not really my thing.

P: You might find you like Economics when you study economic issues related to your special area. Which brings me to my next question—what part of the world are you most interested in?

S: What I'd like is to concentrate on is the Balkan States, which is tricky, since there are so many diverse ethnic and linguistic groups in that region. Anyway, I thought I would focus on Turkey.

P: You're quite right; the ethnic mix in all of Eastern Europe is profoundly complex. So David, what are your languages? You'll need advanced proficiency in at least one foreign language in order to graduate from our department.

S: I took French in high school, and I'm enrolled in beginning Turkish now, which is challenging. And, uh, I'd like to learn some German—since that's where so many Turkish workers go.

P: That's a tall order! Let's turn back to your planning worksheet. Just what is it that bothers you about the International Studies departmental course requirements?

S: A couple of things. OK, first, there's the rule that we can only participate in overseas programs sponsored by this department. And there's no program where I want to go—the closest city to Turkey is Vienna, in Austria!

P: If you want to learn about migrant worker movements in Europe, you could also benefit from in-country experiences in Paris or London.

S: I guess. But it wouldn't be the same. And another thing, there aren't any courses offered in the International Studies Department about the Balkan area.

P: [defensively] Come on, now. We're heavily multidisciplinary, but you have to remember that in an undergraduate program it's not possible to explore every country in the context of globalization.

S: That's what Professor Stone told me. And he went on to say I needed the general foundation courses, to get a handle on the theoretical framework used in International Studies.

P: He's right. [pause] But I can see your dilemma. I do have a couple thoughts, though. You could get a double major—one with us and one with the Department of Near Eastern Studies.

S: Wouldn't that take longer to finish? If I have to cram in another thirteen courses, it might take me an extra year.

P: It might. And you'd have to decide what to do with your senior thesis, because unless your topic is chosen carefully, you'd have to write two senior theses—one for each major.

S: Whoa! That sounds like a lot of work.

P: Or you could change majors and transfer from our department over to the Near Eastern Studies Department. That way, you'd spend your undergraduate years learning about the Balkan region—and then you could get a Master's degree in International Studies later on.

S: Near Eastern Studies. Hmmm. [pause] I don't look forward to taking all those ancient civilization courses, but I definitely need to learn that history some time. Gee, I'm sure going to miss everyone in this department!

● **Transcripts for Question 3**

N: Listen again to part of the conversation. Then answer the question.

P: **If you want to learn about migrant worker movements in Europe, you could also benefit from in-country experiences in Paris or London.**

S: **I guess. But it wouldn't be the same.**

N: What does the man mean when he says this:

S: **I guess.**

● **Transcripts for Question 5**

N: What can we infer about the man when he says this:

S: **I don't look forward to taking all those ancient civilization courses, but I definitely need to learn that history some time. Gee, I'm sure going to miss everyone in this department!**

關鍵語塊

frustrated 沮喪	undergraduate chair 系裡負責大學生事務的人
map out 籌畫	worksheet （初步記錄考慮的問題、想法等的）備忘單
Why don't you tell me... 請告訴我……	academic goal 學習目標
transnational social movement 跨國社會運動	... is not really my thing... 〔口語〕……不是我真正喜歡的
Turkey 土耳其	That's a tall order! 那可是一件難事！
what is it that bothers you about... ……的哪方面讓你煩惱	Vienna 維也納（奧地利首都）
migrant worker 外來勞工	in-country experience 在國內的經歷
multidisciplinary 多學科的	globalization 全球化
foundation course 基礎課程	get a handle on 掌握
theoretical framework 理論框架	dilemma 進退兩難的困境
cram in 勉強塞入	senior thesis 畢業論文
change majors 換主修科系	transfer from... over to 從……轉到

聽力模擬試題答案詳解

1. **A** 主要目的題
   〔**解析**〕考生必須聽完很多對話內容後才能找到本題的答案。一開始，教授說她理解學生的煩惱。接著，學生說他瞭解到自己的特殊要求必須由負責大學生事務的負責人（即這位教授）批准。當教授問學生哪些國際關係課程的要求給他帶來麻煩時，學生列舉了自己不喜歡的幾個方面。選項 A 正確。

2. **B** 細節資訊題
   〔**解析**〕學生說他對 transnational social movements 和 flow of people and ideas across borders 感興趣。他還說想專門研究巴爾幹半島諸國，所以選項 B 正確。

3. **C** 語用功能題
   〔**解析**〕I guess 有很多含義，其中包括 I suppose that it is true。在該情境中，男生承認他可能會 benefit from in-country experiences in Paris or London，因此選項 C 正確。

4.

	YES	NO
Select special courses to create his own major		✓
Travel to Vienna this summer to learn German		✓
Join the Near Eastern Studies Department	✓	
Enroll in the university's double major program	✓	

   關聯內容題
   〔**解析**〕在對話過程中，教授給出了幾條建議。第一個句子在「NO」欄中打勾，因為對話中沒有提到學生選擇特殊課程來給自己設立主修。第二個句子在「NO」欄中打勾，因為教授建議 in-country experiences in Paris or London。第三個句子在「YES」欄中打勾，因為教授說：Or you could change majors and transfer from our department over to the Near Eastern Studies Department. 第四個句子也正確，因為教授說：You could get a double major—one with us and one with the Department of Near Eastern Studies.

5. **D** 推論題
   〔**解析**〕這道題目有些考生可能會根據 I don't look forward to taking all those ancient civilization courses 認定選項 C 為正確答案。但正確答案應該是選項 D，因為學生說他會想念本系的同學，這說明他最終會選擇轉系。

CONVERSATION 2 錄音文本　 *Track 055*

C=Center employee　下同。

N: Listen to part of a conversation at the university's technology center.

S: I've brought my laptop for a diagnosis. I can't get it to work.

C: Before I do anything, there's one thing I need to get straight—did you purchase this machine through us?

S: Yup. I bought it at the university bookstore, back when I was an incoming freshman. Here's the receipt and my student ID.

C: Very good. That means we can go ahead and try and solve your problems. All my labor will be covered by the university, per the standard maintenance agreement. [pause] OK, so what's with this thing?

S: [hesitating] I'm not sure. I was working over in a friend's dorm last night and my laptop just crashed.

C: Um, if you could just pop it up on the table while we talk. I'll run some diagnostics in a minute, but first I'd like you to walk me through what you saw and what you heard, if anything.

S: As I said, I was hanging out with a friend, over at Norton Hall, and I took out my laptop so we could listen to some music. I wanted to use the wireless interface, so I tried to connect there, at her dorm. But my screen went blue.

C: Ahhhh. The famous "blue screen of death."

S: Oh, no! [frantic] Did I lose all my data? All my music files and pictures! The notes for all my classes. And a fifteen-page draft for my Economics term paper.

C: It may not be as grim as you think. But I should probably ask you if you've been backing up your data religiously. On a backup drive or on the university's backup system?

S: [thinking and asking herself out loud] When did I last do a full backup? Maybe two weeks ago. I have a little bit of stuff on this little backup drive. But none of my pictures and music is here...

C: [interrupting gently] Well, there's no use shutting the barn door after the cows have got out. I hate to preach, but it's critical that you back up every night. You don't know how many horror stories I see every day.

S: [not really listening to his advice] So do you think it's a hardware or software problem? It's already six o'clock, and I've got a lot of work yet tonight.

C: I hope to tell you in just a second. But don't worry too much about the hardware—if you need to borrow a laptop for work, we can give you a loaner machine to take home with you overnight.

S: That's a relief. So yeah, I guess my biggest concern is my data. There are three of us working on a case study for a business class, and we said we'd pull the report together tomorrow evening.

C: We have some tools here to salvage data, but it may not come to that. Now, you said you got a blue screen when trying to connect to the university wireless network?

S: Yeah. And then my laptop just sat there and would not respond to anything I did.

C: That blue screen could be the result of a wireless device driver that's gone bad. It can happen if you install bad software or because of some other weird things in your computer.

S: If that is the problem with my laptop, can you fix it tonight?

C: There's a chance. Why don't you get a coffee over at the snack shop and come back in half an hour? If I'm right about my diagnosis, all I have to do is reinstall some software.

S: OK. I'll go grab a cup of herbal tea and settle into my Economics book. Text me when you're done? Meanwhile, I'll be thinking happy thoughts and crossing my fingers!

● **Transcripts for Question 3**

N: What does the employee mean when he says this:

C: **Well, there's no use shutting the barn door after the cows have got out. I hate to preach, but it's critical that you back up every night. You don't know how many horror stories I see every day.**

● **Transcripts for Question 5**

N: Listen again to part of the conversation. Then answer the question.

C: **If I'm right about my diagnosis, all I have to do is reinstall some software.**

S: **OK. I'll go grab a cup of herbal tea and settle into my Economics book. Text me when you're done? Meanwhile, I'll be thinking happy thoughts and crossing my fingers!**

N: What does the woman mean when she says this:

S: **Meanwhile, I'll be thinking happy thoughts and crossing my fingers!**

關鍵語塊

technology center 技術中心	diagnosis 診斷
one thing I need to get straight 我需要瞭解的一件事情	incoming freshman 下屆新生
student ID 學生證	labor will be covered by... 將由……支付勞務費用
per 按照	maintenance agreement 維修協議
laptop just crashed 筆電剛才當機了	pop... up on the table 〔口語〕將……放在桌子上面
run some diagnostics 進行檢查	walk me through... 將……從頭到尾告訴我
be hanging out with... 〔俚語〕與……在一起	wireless interface 無線介面
blue screen of death 當機，螢幕變藍	grim 糟糕的
back up your data 將資料備份	religiously 嚴謹地，認真地
do a full backup 做完整的備份	shut the barn door after the cows have got out 〔諺語〕賊走關門，為時已晚
I hate to preach 我不想說教	horror stories 慘痛的經歷
hardware 硬體	software 軟體
loaner machine 借用機器	overnight 一整夜
case study 案例研究	pull the report together 整合報告
salvage data 挽救數據	it may not come to that 事情可能不會到那個程度
device driver 設備驅動程式	gone bad 損壞
snack shop 小吃店	reinstall some software 重裝一些軟體
herbal tea 花草茶	think happy thoughts 〔口語〕保持樂觀的想法
cross my fingers 祈禱好運	

聽力模擬試題答案詳解

1. **C** 主要目的題

   〔**解析**〕這道題相當容易。即使你沒有理解單字 diagnosis 的意思，至少也能明白 I can't get it to work 的意思。

2. **C** 細節資訊題

   〔**解析**〕工作人員問學生她的電腦是從哪裡買的，因為他只維修從大學購買的機器。他說：All my labor will be covered by the university, per the standard maintenance agreement. 因此選 C。

3. **A** 立場觀點題

   〔**解析**〕工作人員引用了諺語 shutting the barn door...，　　　　　然後說學生每天晚上備份檔案（back up every night）非常重要。選項 A 正確，因為工作人員告訴學生要備份資料以防資料丟失。

4. **B** 細節資訊題

   〔**解析**〕要正確回答本題，考生必須熟悉技術情境中的語塊。工作人員說出現藍色螢幕可能是因為無線設備驅動程式壞了（blue screen could be the result of a wireless device driver that's gone bad），因此選項 B 正確。

5. **D** 語用功能題

   〔**解析**〕crossing one's fingers 表示「某人祈禱好運」，即使考生不知道這個用法，也可根據 I'll be thinking happy thoughts 來確定。

25 常考校園生活場景 5 詞彙、答案、解析和錄音原文

● **Answer Key to Exercise 1**

a. documentation   **b.** standing   **c.** full-time

d. paid up   **e.** an outstanding balance   **f.** enroll in

● **Answer Key to Exercise 2**

a. Although your draft essay is very long, it needs a lot more work before you can hand it in.

b. Mark, it is very important that you not simply relate the storyline of the movies.

c. Yes, now you understand!

CONVERSATION 1 錄音文本 *Track 057*

N: Listen to part of a conversation between a student and a professor.

P: Mark, I spent a fair amount of time going over your thesis on Hong Kong cinema, and there are several issues that require your attention.

S: I've spent hours on this project! And I must have included over thirty sources in my bibliography.

P: Your draft has a lot of bulk, but this is nowhere near ready for submission to the Department of Film Studies. I've marked the draft with comments, but I thought we could chat a bit about the major problems.

S: I'm kind of shocked; I thought I was really thorough. You know? I did the history of the Hong Kong film industry. And current trends, like how Hong Kong martial arts movies have influenced Hollywood action movies.

P: There's no question that you've done a lot of work. Touched on many aspects, such as the influence of Hong Kong films on mainstream action films—but that's part of the problem. A thesis needs focus and in-depth analysis.

S: But I talked specifically about some Hong Kong directors—like John Woo and Wong Kar-wai. And I described their most important movies.

P: First of all, your section on the history of Hong Kong cinema runs seven pages. That part should be shortened to a page or two. And in terms of the directors, well, I'd prefer you choose just one filmmaker and then go into meaningful detail.

S: If that's the case, then I'll choose Wong Kar-Wai. His movies move so quickly and are filled with atmosphere. They feel so nostalgic.

P: You can certainly talk about the stylistic moods evoked in Wong's movies. Remember, Mark, you can't just retell the plot. I'm expecting a rigorous film analysis that illuminates Wong's style of filmmaking.

S: You mean you want me to do an analysis that talks about each camera shot, frame by frame?

P: Yes. In fact, in a paper this size, I think you should do analyses of film sequences in several of Wong's films. For example, you could take Wong's earliest movie—*As Tears Go By* and, well, maybe two others.

S: So I should analyze three movies, frame by frame?

P: You won't be able to analyze the whole movie. Select a sequence in each movie—a portion which best illustrates how the director uses unconventional camera techniques to achieve his style.

S: OK. So talk about the details of the camera position—like the angle. And how close the camera is to what's being filmed.

P: Yes, what we call a "close analysis." I'd say each film sequence should be two or three minutes long. Oh, and another thing, Mark—I think you should eliminate Chapter Three, the one on globalization and cultural alienation.

S: That was my favorite chapter! I think the themes of cultural identity in Hong Kong movies are really important.

P: Mind you, I'm not telling you not to write about cultural identity; rather, I'm suggesting you not frame your discussion thematically. This paper is for the Film Studies Department, not the English Department.

S: So what should I do?

P: Again, I recommend you organize your discussion around your analyses. For example, you could choose the opening sequence in Wong Kar-wai's *Chungking Express*. For each frame you analyze, you could tell us how Wong's choices help the viewers get to know the movie's characters.

S: I see. Maybe I'll change my thesis so that there's one chapter for each of the three movies. And for at least one of those chapters, I'll show how the film's technical choices convey the loneliness of the characters.

P: You got it! Oh, and one last piece of advice—when you're carrying out each analysis, watch the movie sequence several times. Take notes and then keep expanding on those with each additional viewing. That will make your analysis even stronger.

● **Transcripts for Question 5**

N: Listen again to part of the conversation. Then answer the question.

S: I think the themes of cultural identity in Hong Kong movies are really important.

P: Mind you, I'm not telling you not to write about cultural identity; rather, I'm suggesting you not frame your discussion thematically. This paper is for the Film Studies Department, not the English Department.

N: Why does the professor say this:

P: This paper is for the Film Studies Department, not the English Department.

關鍵語塊

a fair amount of time 大量時間	go over 對……進行潤色，改進
bibliography 參考書目	bulk 大（容量）
nowhere near ready for 遠遠不能達到標準	submission 提交
film industry 電影業	martial arts movie 武術片，功夫片
action movie 動作片	There's no question that you... 毫無疑問，你……
in-depth analysis 深入分析	John Woo 吳宇森
Wong Kar-wai 王家衛	filmmaker 電影製作人
go into meaningful detail 研究有意義的細節	nostalgic 懷舊的
stylistic moods 藝術氛圍，藝術風格	evoked in... 由……中喚起

retell the plot 重述情節	illuminate 闡釋
camera shot 鏡頭（單個電影畫面）	frame 畫面，鏡頭
film sequence 畫面順序	*As Tears Go By* 《旺角卡門》
camera position 攝影機的位置	angle （攝影機的）角度
close analysis 詳細分析	alienation 疏遠
cultural identity 文化認同；文化特徵	frame your discussion thematically 圍繞主題展開討論
Chungking Express 《重慶森林》	technical choice 技術選擇
convey 傳達	You got it! 你懂了！
one last piece of advice 最後一條建議	keep expanding on those 在那些方面進行擴展

聽力模擬試題答案詳解

1. **A** 主要目的題
   〔解析〕教授沒有說 I asked you to come today because... 這樣的話。教授說：Mark, I spent a fair amount of time going over your thesis on Hong Kong cinema, and there are several issues that require your attention. 從這裡可知選項 A 正確。
2. **D** 細節資訊題
   〔解析〕學生說他寫這篇論文的目的是為了展示當前電影業的趨勢，如 how Hong Kong martial arts movies have influenced Hollywood action movies。因此選項 D 為正確答案。
3. **C** 立場觀點題
   〔解析〕當教授要求該生選擇一位電影製作人進行研究時，學生說他選擇王家衛，因為他的電影 move so quickly and are filled with atmosphere。選項 C 為正確答案。
4. **B** 細節資訊題
   〔解析〕這道題目有點難，因為教授要求學生從幾個方面修改論文。其中之一是要求學生刪掉第三章 the one on globalization and cultural alienation 部分。
5. **C** 語用功能題
   〔解析〕考生做這道題時需要弄清楚教授說話的潛在意思，即學生不應圍繞主題（thematically）展開討論。因此，當教授說：This paper is for the Film Studies Department, not the English Department. 她是在告訴學生，論文一定要圍繞電影拍攝技術分析，而非圍繞電影主題或故事。因此選項 C 正確。

CONVERSATION 2 錄音文本 Track 059

R=Registrar employee　　　　下同。

N: Listen to part of a conversation between a student and an employee in the Office of the Registrar.

S: I was just over in the gymnasium trying to register for the spring semester, but they wouldn't let me sign up for my courses. There must be some misunderstanding—can you check?

R: According to our files, there's a hold on your account. We can't release the hold until you have cleared your current debt to the university.

S: They froze my account? That's got to be a computer error or something. I paid all of last semester's fees at the beginning of the term, including housing and tuition.

R: What I'm seeing here on the computer screen is a charge for three hundred dollars for lab tests at the university Health Center, in late November. Does that ring a bell?

S: I had some blood work done last fall when I was feeling tired all the time. But I'm covered by the university insurance, so they should have paid all those lab costs.

R: Did you get an order for lab services from a doctor on the health service staff? That's the customary procedure.

S: The student handbook says that lab tests done are free of charge for anyone who is enrolled full time.

R: They are, but only when the lab gets a signed order from the university physician. Otherwise, you get billed. You've also been assessed with a fifty dollar late fee.

S: This is ridiculous. For one thing, no one at the lab ever told me that I needed a doctor's order. And how come I never got a copy of the bill?

R: Were you on campus during December and over the winter holiday?

S: For most of the time. I live in a big house off campus with a bunch of other people.

R: By now you should have received at least one overdue notice from the Health Center. In any event, I won't be able to release the hold on your account until the balance is paid. Do you want to talk to the people at the Health Center Office or at the lab—to dispute the bill?

S: I'd like to. But since classes start in two days, I doubt there's time to go back and forth with them now. This is so annoying. I wonder what other important mail I didn't get.

R: [wanting to clarify situation] I'm sorry—are you saying you're going to go ahead and pay the fee to the Health Center?

S: I'm not crazy about the idea, but I can't register. Um, can I write you out a check?

R: You'll need to pay the full amount in person at the Cashier's Office, which is up on the second floor. But—and you're not gonna wanna hear this—it takes five to seven days for them to process a check.

S: Well, then hopefully they'll accept a credit card. I'd vastly prefer not to pay for the lab tests myself, but if I don't get all my courses lined up by tomorrow, I'm in trouble.

R: They take a couple of credit cards, or you can always give them cash. Oh, and by the way, for the future, you might want to go online and apply for electronic billing.

S: That's probably not a bad idea. And while I'm at it, I should also talk to my housemates to see if they've been throwing away my mail!

R: For real? You think they'd do it on purpose? Nowadays we all get so much junk mail in the mail—sometimes it's hard to keep track of the important pieces.

● **Transcripts for Question 4**

N: Listen again to part of the conversation. Then answer the question.

S: **I'd like to. But since classes start in two days, I doubt there's time to go back and forth with them now. This is so annoying. I wonder what other important mail I didn't get.**

R: **[wanting to clarify situation] I'm sorry—are you saying you're going to go ahead and pay the fee to the Health Center?**

N: Why does this employee say this:

R: **I'm sorry**

關鍵語塊

gymnasium 體育館	sign up for my courses 選課程；報名參加課程
there's a hold on... ……有限制，……暫停	release the hold 解除限制

cleared your current debt 結清你的欠款	froze my account 凍結我的帳戶
charge for... ……的收費	lab test （醫院）實驗室體檢
Does that ring a bell? 〔口語〕想起什麼了沒有？	blood work 驗血
customary procedure 標準流程	anyone who is enrolled full time 全日制在校生
get billed 收到帳單	assessed with a... late fee 交……滯納金
overdue notice 催還通知	balance is paid 付清餘款
go back and forth with them 與他們對話	pay... in person 親自去繳付……
Cashier's Office 收款辦公室	electronic billing 電子付款
For real? 〔俚語〕是真的嗎？	on purpose 故意地
junk mail 垃圾郵件	

聽力模擬試題答案詳解

1. **D** 主要目的題
   〔**解析**〕當學生進行春季學期的註冊時，被告知不能選課程，因此她到教務處要求工作人員為她核查原因。選項 D 為正確答案。

2. **A**、**B** 細節資訊題
   〔**解析**〕學生說自己從未收到過醫院的帳單，最後，她說要問問室友在寒假期間是否扔掉了她的一些郵件。她還說自己以為醫院實驗室體檢費用是在大學的醫保範圍之內（covered by the university insurance）。因此選項 A 和 B 正確。

3. **C** 細節資訊題
   〔**解析**〕工作人員說學生需要在帳戶限制解除之前支付全數金額。學生不能開支票，因為支票需要花時間來處理；工作人員表示學生可以用信用卡或現金支付。選項 C 為正確答案。

4. **D** 語用功能題
   〔**解析**〕I'm sorry 有很多含義，包括「我很抱歉」、「我很難過」、「對不起」等等。在這種情形下，工作人員試圖理解學生的思路，但不太清楚學生打算如何解決問題。選項 D 為正確答案。

5. **B** 立場觀點題
   〔**解析**〕當學生提到室友可能扔掉了她的郵件時她有點憤怒，工作人員說她的室友可能不是故意的，並說：Nowadays we all get so much junk mail in the mail—sometimes it's hard to keep track of the important pieces. 由此可知工作人員對他們寬容的態度，選項 B 正確。

㉖ 常考校園生活場景 6 詞彙、答案、解析和錄音原文

● **Answer Key to Exercise 1**

a. lost property   **b.** stolen   **c.** personal asset   **d.** only gone

e. deter theft   **f.** retrieving   **g.** filed a report

● **Answer Key to Exercise 2**

a. <u>My records say that you were supposed to be here at 10:00.</u>

b. <u>Someone told me that this manufacturing approach was being attempted.</u>

c. <u>Even so, I am obliged to take points away. / No matter what I find, I will need to lower your score.</u>

CONVERSATION 1 錄音文本   🎧 *Track 061*

- -

N: Listen to part of a conversation between a student and a professor.

P: Jackie, weren't you supposed to be here this morning? I had you down for ten o'clock.

S: Yeah. I set my alarm but I must have slept through it. I was up most of the night, trying to finish up my final paper for your Design Class.

P: You understand that all papers were due yesterday, by midnight.

S: Yeah, the paper's a few hours late. That's what I wanted to explain. I found some more information that was really important.

P: You were still doing research the day the paper's due?

S: I hadn't planned to. My topic is on how wallpaper design has been influenced by technology, and I had been focusing on the nineteenth century. But then I found this new information, which I just had to include.

P: My policy is clear: I take ten points off any paper I receive after the deadline. Unless there was a family crisis or some other circumstance beyond your control...

S: [interrupting] No, nothing like that. I was—um—creating a better paper! I came across important material on wallpaper design techniques, so I postponed my writing. Actually, I think you'll be interested in what I found.

P: I'm not so sure it'll affect my opinion about the timeliness of your work, but go ahead.

S: Well, I found out about a new patent for a wallpaper manufacturing method. It's software that allows a computer to function as a wallpaper manufacturing apparatus. In other words, the images of the design are stored in a company database, but the customer can order the design off the Internet.

P: So how did you plan on incorporating this into your paper?

S: I did already; the paper's finished! What I did was to draw comparisons about the varieties of wallpaper designs now available to people, due to this new web-based technology. People can get almost any color or design printed off the server.

P: I'd heard that this kind of manufacturing technique was in the works. It's a sort of "mass customization" approach, isn't it? Being applied to producing wallpaper designs for consumers.

S: Exactly. Wallpaper customers get a "custom-made" design. And there's no limit to the number of people who can order wallpaper in this way, so it's definitely a form of mass production.

P: So what was your thesis?

S: My thesis. Uh, during the late nineteenth century, when wallpaper printing began to be done by using metal cylinders, instead of by hand, prices went down and quality designs increased. And now in the twenty-first century, the same thing is happening, only through web-based technology.

P: Sounds like you're looking at economics and technology, in addition to the ultimate designs provided to consumers.

S: I am. And you'll see I've got a whole section with graphics that shows many of the different types of patterns.

P: Well, it sounds like a fine paper, Jackie, and I look forward to seeing your ideas. But the fact remains that I'll have to deduct points.

● **Transcripts for Question 2**

N: Listen again to part of the conversation. Then answer the question.

S: **I came across important material on wallpaper design techniques, so I postponed my writing. Actually, I think you'll be interested in what I found.**

P: **I'm not so sure it'll affect my opinion about the timeliness of your work, but go ahead.**

N: What does the man mean when he says this:

P: **but go ahead**

● **Transcripts for Question 5**

N: What does the professor mean when he says this:

P: **Well, it sounds like a fine paper, Jackie, and I look forward to seeing your ideas. But the fact remains that I'll have to deduct points.**

關鍵語塊

I had you down for ten o'clock. 我的記錄上顯示你 10 點應該來這裡。	sleep through... 在……中沉睡不醒
wallpaper 壁紙、（電腦）桌布	go ahead 繼續說下去
patent 專利	manufacturing apparatus 生產設備
web-based technology 基於網路的技術	get... printed off the server 從伺服器上下載列印……
in the works 在進行中	mass customization 大規模訂製
consumer 消費者	"custom-made" design「訂製」的設計
metal cylinder 金屬圓筒	deduct points 扣分

聽力模擬試題答案詳解

1. **D** 主要目的題

   〔**解析**〕學生與教授約了當天上午見面，但學生遲到了。學生出現在教授的辦公室，當面遞交論文，並解釋為什麼遲到和晚交論文。因此選項 D 正確。

2. **A** 語用功能題

   〔**解析**〕go ahead 有多種含義，如「往前走」、「去吧」、「開始吧」等。在這段對話的情境中，是「去吧」的意思。教授表示什麼也改變不了他扣學生論文分數的決定，但他願意聽學生把話講完。他説 ..., but go ahead 時，是表示允許學生講新技術。因此選項 A 正確。

3. **C** 組織結構題

〔**解析**〕見本章前文的「托福總監評析」。

4. **B** 細節資訊題

〔**解析**〕學生説自己的課題是關於技術如何影響壁紙設計。她列舉了實例，説明隨著技術的進步，不同時代的人如何設計和生產壁紙。選項 A 不正確，因為她關注的不是製造企業，而是消費者。選項 C 不正確，因為範圍太窄，不僅僅是價格，還有新設計的種類也對消費者的偏好有影響。選項 B 為正確答案。

5. **A** 立場觀點題

〔**解析**〕這裡需要注意聽兩句話。教授的第一句話已明確他會接受學生的解釋和論文。第二句話表示學生交論文時間延遲了，他還是要扣減她的分數。因此選項 A 為正確答案。

CONVERSATION 2 錄音文本 *Track 063*

O= Officer 下同。

N: Listen to part of a conversation between a student and an officer at the Office of Campus Security.

S: Hi, my name's Mark Johnson. I'm here about a bike.

O: If you could just step up and fill out this form. [pause] OK, "bike"—this is a motorcycle or a bicycle?

S: A regular bike. I had it parked in the racks outside the Student Center Sunday night.

O: Oh, so you believe it was taken. Was it secured to the racks with a lock?

S: [embarrassed] Uh—I was just popping into the Student Center to get a cup of coffee. I came right out, but, well... [awkward pause]

O: All right, let me have the serial number for the bike and I'll check the campus bicycle registration database.

S: I don't think I have the serial number. Not even back at the dorm. I bought the bike last week from my cousin, and we never exchanged any paperwork. So I don't know what number is on the bike—if there is one at all.

O: That's going to make it tough to track down. Do you think you could get in touch with your relative? Lots of times, stolen bikes will show up in other parts of town, and we share our campus database with the municipal police force.

S: He—my cousin's—studying overseas this year, but I can try and get a hold of him. But what if the serial number's not on the bike?

O: Well, before I answer that, what do you think the value of the bike is?

S: I got a special price—so I only paid about fifty dollars for it. It's not a super fancy racing bike, but hey, it's not garbage either.

O: A lot of times, insurance companies won't cover the loss of a bike if the owner doesn't give them the serial number. So that's another place you might check.

S: Right! If need be, my cousin can contact his old insurance company. Oh, and I just thought of another thing—I carved the face of a tiger on the front wheel. I thought it would be cool because that's our university mascot.

O: OK, I'll write that down as an identifying mark. Your bike may or may not turn up. The majority of our bike thefts are done by young people from off campus, kids who are just fooling around. A lot of time they'll ride it for a while and then leave it somewhere in town, like—near the shopping district.

S: You think? I've been borrowing a bike that belongs to my roommate, since I don't have the money to buy a new one.

O: If you can phone in that serial number when you get back to the dorm, the chances will be a lot greater. A lot of these turn up at pawn shops downtown. The owners of those shops routinely send us the numbers of the bikes they get in, so that's another channel we have.

S: OK. So how long do you think it'll take? I mean, how soon do they usually show up?

O: If we can pin down a serial number, it might show up right away. It might even be in a police warehouse already. Without a number, you'll have to check back with us every so often. We hold valuable items for five months—then it becomes ours and we donate them to charity.

S: All right. Maybe I'll pedal over to the shopping district now, to see if I can spot it lying around.

O: You never know.

● **Transcripts for Question 2**

N: Listen again to part of the conversation. Then answer the question.

O: Oh, so you believe it was taken. Was it secured to the racks with a lock?

S: [embarrassed] Uh—I was just popping into the Student Center to get a cup of coffee. I came right out, but, well… [awkward pause]

N: What does the man imply when he says this:

S: I came right out, but, well… [awkward pause]

關鍵語塊

Office of Campus Security 校園保全辦公室	fill out this form 填寫表格
rack 架子	be secured to... 被固定在……上
pop into 跑進	serial number 編號
bicycle registration database 自行車登記資料庫	exchanged any paperwork 交換任何書面材料
track down 追蹤	show up 出現
municipal police force 市員警機關	try and get a hold of sb. 試圖聯繫上某人
fancy 昂貴的	insurance company 保險公司
face of a tiger 虎臉	university mascot 大學吉祥物
identifying mark 識別標記	turn up 出現
bike thefts 自行車盜竊	fool around 閒蕩，遊手好閒
shopping district 商業區	pawn shop 當鋪
another channel 另一個管道	pin down 確定
police warehouse 警方庫房	check back with us 回頭再聯繫我們
pedal over to 騎腳踏車去	spot it 發現它
You never know. 很難預料。	

聽力模擬試題答案詳解

1. **B** 主要目的題

　　〔解析〕學生説：I'm here about a bike. 校園保全人員便知道他的自行車被偷。選項 B 正確。

2. **A** 推論題

   〔**解析**〕保全人員問學生自行車被偷之前是否上鎖了，學生説自己只是進活動中心喝了一杯咖啡，很快就出來了。説到一半他停下來了，由此可斷定他感到自己的失誤之處。因此推測他顯然忘了鎖腳踏車了。

3. **A** 細節資訊題

   〔**解析**〕學生是從他表哥那裡買到腳踏車的。腳踏車被偷後，學生從他的室友那裡借了一輛腳踏車。丟失的腳踏車是屬於學生自己的。

4.

	YES	NO
In the municipal police database		✓
In the old insurance records	✓	
In the pawn shops		✓

關聯內容題

   〔**解析**〕當學生表示他不知道自己的腳踏車編號時，保全人員給了他幾條找到編號的建議。她建議學生問他表哥，看看他表哥的保險公司是否存有編號，所以第二項在「YES」欄中打勾。警方和當鋪均沒有該自行車的編號，因此第一句和第三句在「NO」欄中打勾。

5. **D** 細節資訊題

   〔**解析**〕對話結束時，學生説：Maybe I'll pedal over to the shopping district now, to see if I can spot it lying around. 因此正確答案為選項 D。

㉗ 常考校園生活場景 7 詞彙、答案、解析和錄音原文

● **Answer Key to Exercise 1**

a. fill out   **b.** club   **c.** not formally

d. recognized by   **e.** do the paperwork   **f.** make a good case

CONVERSATION 1 錄音文本 *Track 065*

N: Listen to part of a conversation between a student and a professor.

S: I wasn't sure if you'd be here the day before spring break.

P: I've got a couple more meetings this afternoon, and then some papers waiting for me to grade. [pause] Now then, you mentioned you're applying for a teaching job?

S: Maybe. I was thinking of going to Asia to teach English; but more and more I'm thinking I'd enjoy teaching high school students here in the US.

P: Remind me, what track are you on?

S: I'm an English major, with a concentration in British literature. Oh—do you mean, am I taking education courses?

P: Yes. Will you have teaching credentials by this summer?

S: No, I haven't taken any classes in the School of Education. So I guess that means I'd have to apply to teach at a private high school, because I don't have the certificate for public school.

P: Well, you could try some of the private schools. But there are a couple of other options. One path that's—in my mind—really worthwhile is going to public schools with high need.

S: High-need schools? How does one find those?

P: Take a look at the public schools in some of the urban school districts. Schools in Los Angeles or New York, for instance, are always looking for motivated college graduates. You wouldn't have to have a lot of experience.

S: I don't really picture myself teaching in a big city. Or being such a long way from my family.

P: OK. Well then, if you want to stay closer to home, you could try to get a provisional certificate over the summer so you could start working in a public school in the fall.

S: Um, what's a provisional certificate?

P: Essentially, it's a document that certifies you temporarily, to get you going. But in the fall they expect you to take additional education classes on nights or weekends, so that you can get full certification later on.

S: That would be incredible. [pause] Somebody will actually give me a job! I'll be fresh out of school—do you think I have a shot?

P: If you've done some tutoring before, you could put that down as experience.

S: I helped some high school kids getting ready for the college entrance exam one summer. Does that count?

P: That's a start. Over the break, why don't you try re-working your resume so that it's tailored to the high school level?

S: OK. Right now my resume's only half a page, so I'm gonna have to be pretty creative if I want to pass myself off as a prospective teacher.

P: When you're done with your draft, email it to me, and after the break we'll see how we can beef it up even more.

● **Transcripts for Question 2**

N: What can we infer about the professor when he says this:

P: Well, you could try some of the private schools. But there are a couple of other options. One path that's—in my mind—really worthwhile is going to public schools with high need.

● **Transcripts for Question 4**

N: Listen again to part of the conversation. Then answer the question.

S: I helped some high school kids getting ready for the college entrance exam one summer. Does that count?

P: That's a start. Over the break, why don't you try re-working your resume so that it's tailored to the high school level?

N: Why does the professor say this:

P: why don't you try re-working your resume so that it's tailored to the high school level?

關鍵語塊

spring break 春假	concentration in... 專攻……
teaching credential 教學證書	School of Education 教育學院
private high school 私立中學	certificate 證書
public school 公立學校	college graduate 大學畢業生
provisional certificate 臨時證書	be fresh out of school 剛從學校畢業
have a shot 有機會	tutoring 家教
college entrance exam 大學入學考試	Does that count? 那個算嗎？
That's a start. 那是一個開始。	re-work 修改
be tailored to 調整使適應	beef it up 使之更充實

聽力模擬試題答案詳解

1. **D** 主要目的題
   〔**解析**〕當教授說 you mentioned you're applying for a teaching job 後，學生說她想成為一名教師。選項 A 不正確，因為學生沒有問及具體的教育課程。她的目的只是想探討利用她現有的文憑成為教師的途徑。

2. **B** 推論題
   〔**解析**〕本題要求推測教授對學生的看法。教授說：One path that's—in my mind—really worthwhile is going to public schools with high need. 由此推測他希望學生在「高需求」學校任教。因此選項 B 為正確答案。

3. **C** 細節資訊題
   〔**解析**〕當教授建議學生在紐約或洛杉磯任教時，學生說 I don't really picture myself teaching in a big city，因此選項 C 為正確答案。

4. **A** 語用功能題
   〔**解析**〕如果考生掌握了用否定方式來表達禮貌請求的用法，如：... why don't you try re-

working your resume so that it's tailored to the high school level? 這道題目就相對容易了。選項 A 為正確答案。

5.

	YES	NO
Enroll in his spring course		✓
Modify her resume	✓	
Register for the teaching test		✓
Tutor a high school student		✓

關聯內容題。

〔解析〕教授沒有叫學生選他的課程，因此第一項在「NO」欄中打勾。教授讓學生修改簡歷，因此第二項在「YES」欄中打勾。對話中提到了教師證書，但是沒有談到教學測試，所以第三項在「NO」欄中打勾。學生說她曾教過一些高中生，而教授沒有讓學生去教任何人，所以第四項在「NO」欄中打勾。

CONVERSATION 2 錄音文本 *Track 067*

E=Employee 下同。

N: Listen to part of a conversation between a student and an employee at the Office of Student Affairs.

E: I understand you're here about the Aquatic Club—you're the president, if I'm not mistaken.

S: Right. I called you earlier about changing the focus of the club, and I wanted to follow up in person. What we've seen is that the students are really passionate about diving, so we want to create a Scuba Club.

E: Whoa—you're way ahead of me. Now according to my records the Aquatic Club is all about swimming—students swim in the university pool and in the ocean. And I have down that your faculty advisor is Professor Morgan.

S: Dr. Morgan's still working with us. For this club—which would replace the Aquatic Club—what we envision is that we'd still be using an Olympic-sized pool in the University Athletic Center. And we'd continue to go over to Sunset Beach. But we'd be doing scuba diving, not just swimming.

E: [not happy with this idea] You might not know this, but some students tried to get a scuba club going once before. I have to tell you, the university had real problems with it.

S: Professor Morgan mentioned something about that. He personally wasn't involved with the group back then. I gather that you all were kind of nervous somebody might get hurt.

E: We have to put safety concerns before all else. For legal reasons, among others. Fortunately no one was ever seriously hurt, but it was clear that that faculty advisor did not have—how shall I put this—the time or the experience.

S: You mean to oversee things like equipment and training of new divers?

E: That's exactly what I mean.

S: But wasn't that advisor a professor in the Department of Physical Education? He probably saw diving as, well, sort of an elective class, as an extension of the other water sports. But he wasn't really a professional-level diver.

E: Look, I sympathize with your wanting to go to the beach. We're so close to the water here; it makes total sense. But why don't you keep the Aquatic Club and organize several ocean races for swimmers? You could compete with neighboring universities.

S: You can't compare ocean racing to diving. If you've ever done an open water dive out in the ocean, you know it's incredible. The rocks, the coral, the aquatic life. Diving raises awareness about the environment!

E: So environmental education would be part of your club mission?

S: Yes. The details are all in our proposal here, but to give you a quick example, once divers were up to snuff, we'd let them do some open water dives, to show them how elevated water temperature is harming certain types of algae and the coral reefs. You may know, Professor Morgan is a marine biologist.

E: Let me look at your application now. [reading out loud from the application form] "The Scuba Club proposes to conduct weekly meetings, host guest speakers and plan activities that aid in the certification of new divers. The club will also help divers improve their skills through trips."

S: The training will be open to all students, and diver certification is based on training in our university pool and out in the ocean.

E: How can you possibly assure the safety of all these students? Or maintain all the equipment? I'm sorry; this just doesn't seem workable—and I mean no disrespect to Dr. Morgan. He's very responsible.

S: Let me explain. We've spoken with a local Dive Shop—you know, Smith's Dive Shop, on the pier? They're willing to help the Scuba Club with training and certification. That'll facilitate safe diving practices. And they'll inspect equipment as part of the rental fee.

E: I'm a little skeptical. Students don't have a lot of money, and our office can't provide a lot of funding. So why would a private company like the Smith's Dive Shop want to donate all those hours of training?

S: For a couple reasons. They see this as a community service and a way to get some good public exposure. But another reason is they want to attract as many people as possible to the sport of scuba diving.

E: OK. You say all of the details are in this application form, right? I'll read through this, but I have to warn you, I still need to be convinced that there are solid mechanisms in place to safeguard club members.

S: There's a whole section in there on safety and how certification for new divers takes place. After you read it, if you have any questions, you can call me—or Professor Morgan—or the Master Trainer over at Smith's.

● **Transcripts for Question 3**

N: Listen again to part of the conversation. Then answer the question.

E: We have to put safety concerns before all else. For legal reasons, among others. Fortunately no one was ever seriously hurt, but it was clear that that faculty advisor did not have—how shall I put this—the time or the experience.

N: What can we infer about the employee when she says this:

E: how shall I put this—

關鍵語塊

Office of Student Affairs 學生事務處	Aquatic Club 水上運動俱樂部
focus of the club 社團的主旨	be passionate about 熱衷於
Whoa〔口語〕哇	you're way ahead of me 你說得太快了
what we envision 我們所設想的	Olympic-sized pool 奧林匹克規格的游泳池
University Athletic Center 大學運動中心	scuba diving 佩戴水肺的潛水
get... going 使……運作	I gather... 我猜想……
put... before all else 把……放第一位	how shall I put this 我應該怎麼說呢
Department of Physical Education 體育系	elective class 選修課
extension of... ……的延伸	sympathize with... 同情……
it makes total sense 似乎很有道理	coral 珊瑚
club mission 俱樂部的使命	up to snuff 達標
open water 海洋中	algae 海藻
marine biologist 海洋生物學家	conduct weekly meetings 每週召開會議
host guest speakers 邀請外部人員來演講	certification of new divers 新潛水夫的證書
assure the safety of... 確保……的安全	workable 切實可行的
I mean no disrespect to... 我沒有不尊敬……的意思	pier 碼頭
rental fee 租賃費	skeptical 懷疑的
community service 社區服務，公共服務	public exposure 宣傳
safeguard 保護	

聽力模擬試題答案詳解

1. **C** 主要目的題
   〔**解析**〕工作人員說：I understand you're here about the Aquatic Club...，接著學生說：I called you earlier about changing the focus of the club...，因此選項 C 為正確答案。

2. **B、D** 細節資訊題
   〔**解析**〕學生說了：... what we envision is that we'd still be using an Olympic-sized pool... 和 The Scuba Club proposes to... plan activities that aid in the certification of new divers. 因此選項 B 和 D 為正確答案。

3. **A** 推論題
   〔**解析**〕how shall I put this 可以用在幾種不同情景中，如當你想不起來要說什麼時，或者當你知道你要說什麼，但怕說得太難聽或冒犯了別人時。在這裡，工作人員是在儘量避免直接評論先前擔任指導老師的那個人，因此選項 A 為正確答案。

4. **C** 細節資訊題
   〔**解析**〕學生說 Smith 潛水商店的合作夥伴願意幫助潛水俱樂部進行訓練和提供資格認證（willing to help the Scuba Club with training and certification），這將為潛水活動提供安全保障。因此選項 C 為正確答案。

5. **B** 立場觀點題
   〔**解析**〕考生要注意整段對話中工作人員的意見。能夠表現工作人員態度的兩個句子是：We have to put safety concerns before all else. 和 I'm a little skeptical. 這說明該工作人員對設立潛水俱樂部這件事有疑義。

● **Answer Key to Exercise 2**

	YES	NO
Work with Dr. Morgan		✓
Sponsor ocean races	✓	
Hold environmental awareness activities		✓
Practice diving in the university swimming pool		✓

28 常考校園生活場景 8 詞彙、答案、解析和錄音原文

● **Answer Key to Exercise 1**

a. applications for   **b.** transcript   **c.** a resume builder

d. of advice   **e.** be interviewed   **f.** are assigned

CONVERSATION 1 錄音文本 *Track 069*

N: Listen to a conversation between a student and a professor of Plant Genetics.

P: Tim, I'm glad you're here. I wanted to go over this week's lab results for the research on genetically modified corn.

S: No problem—I'll get the lab notebook in just a minute. Actually, I stopped by to ask about a concern I have with the lab environment for that study.

P: Have a seat.

S: Well, I've noticed that some of the mice seem to be sneezing more than usual. And what I'm wondering is if they might be developing allergies. They may be allergic to the wood chips that we use as bedding in their cages, to keep them clean and comfortable.

P: Sneezing, eh? That's something we'll want to monitor. You know, we've used wood chips in our lab cages for years, but, coincidentally, just this week I read a journal article saying bedding made of paper may be preferable to wood chips.

S: I'm glad I brought this to your attention, then.

P: Wait, I'm not finished. It's not just allergies—these researchers also found that the mice with wood chips tended to gain more weight than the ones with paper bedding.

S: Hmm, that's interesting. I wonder if they're eating some of the bedding material. Or if there's some other factor at play.

P: Regardless, it's a potential concern, since we're observing the rate of growth of the animals as one way of determining whether genetically modified corn is different from regular corn. If the mice are gaining weight due to the bedding materials, well then...

S: Do you think our findings are going to be biased?

P: Tim, biological research can never be perfectly controlled. And of course, when we write this up, we'll want to talk about the issue of cage bedding material in our discussion. At the very least, because the mice were all in cages with wood chips, there's no difference across the groups.

S: You know, from what I've seen, the animal caretakers do a really great job of cleaning the cages and spraying disinfectant. The mice seem to appreciate clean homes.

P: Sure, we've had a few glitches in the past, but all in all our lab conditions for animal care have been pretty good. Yeah, and we're supposed to be plant specialists! [joking]

S: Hey, corn, mice—it's all biology! But, if you don't mind me asking, what about all the other research projects that are going on?

P: As I mentioned, it's premature to take any actions now, and not really feasible to stop our experiments midstream. But you should continue to keep meticulous records. Write down everything in your lab book, and we'll make sense of it later.

S: OK.

P: On my part, as director of the lab I think I'll do a couple of things. First, I'm going to contact a friend of mine at the National Research Council and see if he's aware of any other research on lab animal cage environments—research that hasn't been published yet.

S: Oh, one thought—do you want me to start looking at possible sources of paper bedding for the future? Just in case? I could call some supply companies and get some quotes for the lab.

P: Tim, it's not urgent, but some information wouldn't hurt. And I'll bring up the topic at our next Research Committee meeting here in the School of Agriculture. Depending on what we decide, we may well want to make a recommendation to the rest of the university.

S: It'll be interesting to hear what comes out of all of this. In the meantime, I'll go grab my lab notebook and we can talk about the corn study data from this past week.

● **Transcripts for Question 3**

N: Listen again to part of the conversation. Then answer the question.

S: Do you think our findings are going to be biased?

P: Tim, biological research can never be perfectly controlled. And of course, when we write this up, we'll want to talk about the issue of cage bedding material in our discussion.

N: What does the professor say about the research findings?

● **Transcripts for Question 4**

N: Listen again to part of the conversation. Then answer the question.

P: Sure, we've had a few glitches in the past, but all in all our lab conditions for animal care have been pretty good. Yeah, and we're supposed to be plant specialists! [joking]

N: What is the professor's attitude when she says this:

P: Yeah, and we're supposed to be plant specialists! [joking]

關鍵語塊

Plant Genetics 植物遺傳學	genetically modified corn 基因改良玉米
lab notebook 實驗記錄本	stop by 順便拜訪
lab environment 實驗室環境	Have a seat. 請坐。
developing allergies 患過敏症	wood chip 木屑
bedding 墊子	cage 籠子
journal article 期刊文章	paper bedding 紙質墊子
other factor at play 其他影響因素	difference across the groups 實驗組間的差異
animal caretaker （實驗室的）動物管理員	spray disinfectant 噴灑消毒劑
glitch 小問題	it's premature to ……為時過早
not really feasible to... ……不太可行	stop... midstream 中途中斷……
keep meticulous record 詳細地記錄	we'll make sense of it 我們會搞清楚它的意思
National Research Council 國家研究委員會	get some quotes 獲取報價

聽力模擬試題答案詳解

1. **C** 主要目的題

   〔解析〕教授見學生是為了討論實驗結果，但學生卻是由於另一個原因想見教授。學生說：Actually, I stopped by to ask about a concern I have with the lab environment for that study. 接著他又說：They may be allergic to the wood chips that we use as bedding in their cages to keep them clean and comfortable. 因此選項 C 為正確答案。

2. **B** 細節資訊題

   〔解析〕學生懷疑老鼠對鼠籠中使用的木屑過敏。選項 B 為正確答案。

3. **C** 語用功能題

   〔解析〕教授說：Tim, biological research can never be perfectly controlled. 教授表示研究中會經常遇到意想不到的因素，因此選項 C 為正確答案。

4. **D** 立場觀點題

   〔解析〕教授介紹了實驗室中實驗用動物的生存條件，認為目前的條件已經很好了。然後她戲謔地開玩笑說：Yeah, and we're supposed to be plant specialists! 那是因為他們研究的主題是基因改良玉米，而有些老鼠正在吃。因此選項 D 為正確答案。

5. **A、B** 細節資訊題

   〔解析〕教授說了幾個後續步驟來處理木屑問題。她說：Write down everything in your lab book, and we'll make sense of it later. 稍後她說：I'm going to contact a friend of mine at the National Research Council... 和 I'll bring up the topic at our next Research Committee meeting... 因此選項 A 和 B 為正確答案。

● **Answer Key to Exercise 2**

a. He did not expect to be chatting about the research study on genetically modified corn. / He's happy to be flexible.

b. She's somewhat surprised that the mice would be sneezing. / She finds it very interesting that mice would be sneezing.

c. She doesn't want to deal with the mice issue right now, but she definitely wants to have the data to make a good decision later. / She wants to encourage the student to keep on taking good records, so that they can do good research.

CONVERSATION 2 錄音文本 **Track 071**

N: Listen to part of a conversation between a student and an employee in the housing office.

S: Um, I received a fire code violation in my dorm room, and I don't think I should have.

E: You need to give me your name and violation number.

S: My last name is Wilson. John Wilson. And the violation number is—uh—25.

E: Yes, I've got the record here. Now this indicates you had some sort of a heating device in your room that produced an open flame.

S: It was a couple of candles on a little coffee table. But I want to make clear I didn't break this rule. My two roommates were the ones burning them.

E: You share a room with two other students and...

S: [interrupting] Yes, with two first-year students. Did I ask to be put with younger students? No, I'm a senior! I know better than to light a fire. And I wasn't there that evening!

E: Our regulations stipulate that we apply punishment equally to all residents of the room. The housing inspectors just follow the rules.

S: [sarcastically] This stuff would have to happen when I was working at the chemistry lab!

E: [apologetically] It's always awkward when there are multiple roommates.

S: You don't even give a first warning? There was no damage.

E: The regulations relating to fire safety are somewhat strict; the inspectors typically take disciplinary action on the first offense.

S: The slip here says there's a one-hundred dollar fine for this violation. You're surely not expecting each of us to pay this much?

E: That's the way it works. You can try to appeal, if you want. But in this case, the only way you'll succeed is to get your two roommates to talk to the inspector—and explain to him you weren't involved.

S: And then I won't have to pay the one-hundred dollar fine?

E: There's no guarantee. But listen, take this appeals form back and fill it out. You can write down all the nitty-gritty details in the comments section.

S: [gets a new idea] I know! What if I talk to my resident assistant and ask him to vouch for me? He can testify to my good character.

E: I seriously doubt that the inspector will care what your resident assistant thinks. But if you want to give it a shot, just note down his name and number on the form.

S: I'll do that. And to tell you the truth, I'm also going to ask my resident assistant if I can change rooms, so I don't have to be with these two individuals any more.

E: That's between you and him. He'll probably want to sit down with the three of you and work things out. Maybe you can take this form to that meeting and fill it out all together.

S: Yeah, that's not a bad idea. But I'm still going to try and find a way to get new roommates. I don't feel like paying for a second offense a few weeks from now.

● **Transcripts for Question 3**

N: Listen again to part of the conversation. Then answer the question.

E: Our regulations stipulate that we apply punishment equally to all residents of the room. The housing inspectors just follow the rules.

S: [sarcastically] This stuff would have to happen when I was working at the chemistry lab!

N: What does the man mean when he says this:

S: [sarcastically] This stuff would have to happen when I was working at the chemistry lab!

● **Transcripts for Question 5**

N: Listen again to part of the conversation. Then answer the question.

S: Yeah, that's not a bad idea. But I'm still going to try and find a way to get new roommates. I don't feel like paying for a second offense a few weeks from now.

N: What does the man imply when he says this:

S: I don't feel like paying for a second offense a few weeks from now.

關鍵語塊

fire code 消防規範	violation 違反（行為）
heating device 加熱設備；加熱器	open flame 明火

break this rule 違反這項規定	regulations stipulate that... 規定指出……
apply punishment to... 對……施以懲罰	give a first warning 給出第一次警告
take disciplinary action 給予紀律懲罰，給予紀律處分	first offense 初犯
slip 紙片	you weren't involved 你沒有牽涉其中，與你無關
There's no guarantee. 不能保證。	nitty-gritty detail 具體細節
comments section 評論欄	vouch for... 為……擔保
testify to... 證實……	give it a shot 試試

聽力模擬試題答案詳解

1. **B** 主要目的題
   〔**解析**〕一開始，學生說他收到了違反消防規範的通告，但他本人並沒有違反消防規範，不應受罰款。因此選項 B 正確。

2. **A、C** 細節資訊題
   〔**解析**〕工作人員建議該男生去找宿舍檢查員申訴（You can try to appeal, if you want.），然後說該宿舍的每名成員都必須因這次違紀而支付 100 美元的罰款。因此選項 A 和 C 都正確。

3. **D** 語用功能題
   〔**解析**〕當學生說：This stuff would have to happen when I was working at the chemistry lab! 他是在發洩憤怒，後悔他當時沒在寢室阻止火災。因此選項 D 為正確答案。

4. **B** 細節資訊題
   〔**解析**〕工作人員說宿舍管理員可能會與這三位室友坐下來解決問題。選項 B 為正確答案。

5. **D** 推論題
   〔**解析**〕學生說這句話，其實是暗示他認為室友還會給自己帶來麻煩。因此選項 D 為正確答案。

Note

你想要出書嗎？
對創作有著無限的熱忱嗎？
覺得有什麼非得透過出書
來傳達給大家的理念嗎？

捷徑文化誠徵
百萬大作家！

不管你是想要傳播知識的熱情教師、
還是滿載醫學新知的專業醫生、
或是天馬行空、充滿想像力的小說家，
無論任何類型的書籍 ─
醫療、語言、理財、小說、旅遊、美食、親子……
只要你想得到、寫得好，
就有機會成為捷徑專聘的火紅作家！
有著強烈出書渴望的你，
是不是開始手癢了呢？

原來如此 系列 **E107**

托福命題總監教你征服新托福閱讀聽力

托福總監親自出馬！真的不是權威不出書！

作　　者	秦蘇珊
顧　　問	曾文旭
總 編 輯	王毓芳
編輯統籌	耿文國、黃璽宇
主　　編	吳靜宜
執行主編	姜怡安
執行編輯	李念茨、林妍珺
美術編輯	王桂芳、張嘉容
封面設計	阿作
特約編輯	費長琳
法律顧問	北辰著作權事務所　蕭雄淋律師、幸秋妙律師

初　　版	2014年12月初版一刷 2019年再版六刷
出　　版	捷徑文化出版事業有限公司
電　　話	（02）2752-5618
傳　　真	（02）2752-5619
地　　址	106 台北市大安區忠孝東路四段250號11樓之1

定　　價	新台幣480元／港幣160元
產品內容	1書

總 經 銷	采舍國際有限公司
地　　址	235 新北市中和區中山路二段366巷10號3樓
電　　話	（02）8245-8786
傳　　真	（02）8245-8718

港澳地區總經銷	和平圖書有限公司
地　　址	香港柴灣嘉業街12號百樂門大廈17樓
電　　話	（852）2804-6687
傳　　真	（852）2804-6409

捷徑 Book站

現在就上臉書（FACEBOOK）「捷徑BOOK站」並按讚加入粉絲團，
就可享每月不定期新書資訊和粉絲專享小禮物喔！
http://www.facebook.com/royalroadbooks
讀者來函：royalroadbooks@gmail.com

國家圖書館出版品預行編目資料

托福命題總監教你征服新托福閱讀聽力 / 秦蘇珊著. -- 初版. -- 臺北市：捷徑文化, 2014.12
面；　公分（原來如此：E107）
ISBN 978-986-5698-27-0(平裝)
1. 托福考試　2. 考試指南
805.1894　　　　　　　　　　　103021300

TOEFL
iBT READING &
LISTENING

不是權威不出書！練托福，
當然就讓最專業的托福總監帶你練！

捷徑文化
Royal Road Publishing Group